PENGUIN BOOKS

THIS CHARMING MAN

Praise for *This Charming Man*:

'Another great novel . . . touching and funny' *Woman*

'Packed full of her usual sincerity and charm' *Heat*

'Her writing is of the highest order.
Someone should give this woman a Booker'
Sunday Tribune

Praise for Marian Keyes:

'Yet another corker from the undisputed queen of chick-lit' *Company*

'Another beautifully written triumph' *Heat*

'Keyes writes brilliantly, as always, about love, grief,
jealousy and friendship' *Daily Mail*

'Emotional and entertaining' *Closer*

'High-quality entertainment' *Marie Claire*

'A rare blend of genres, a richly enjoyable satire and an inspirational
tale of one woman's triumph over despair' *Telegraph*

'Both hilarious and heartbreaking' *Daily Express*

'It takes real talent to make a reader laugh and cry, but Marian's a
genius at tapping into the two emotions' *Heat*

This Charming Man

MARIAN KEYES

PENGUIN BOOKS

PENGUIN BOOKS

Published by the Penguin Group
Penguin Books Ltd, 80 Strand, London WC2R ORL, England
Penguin Group (USA) Inc., 375 Hudson Street, New York, New York 10014, USA
Penguin Group (Canada), 90 Eglinton Avenue East, Suite 700, Toronto, Ontario, Canada M4P 2Y3
(a division of Pearson Penguin Canada Inc.)
Penguin Ireland, 25 St Stephen's Green, Dublin 2, Ireland (a division of Penguin Books Ltd)
Penguin Group (Australia), 250 Camberwell Road, Camberwell, Victoria 3124, Australia
(a division of Pearson Australia Group Pty Ltd)
Penguin Books India Pvt Ltd, 11 Community Centre, Panchsheel Park, New Delhi – 110 017, India
Penguin Group (NZ), 67 Apollo Drive, Rosedale, North Shore 0632, New Zealand
(a division of Pearson New Zealand Ltd)
Penguin Books (South Africa) (Pty) Ltd, 24 Sturdee Avenue, Rosebank, Johannesburg 2196, South Africa

Penguin Books Ltd, Registered Offices: 80 Strand, London WC2R ORL, England

www.penguin.com

First published by Michael Joseph 2008
Published in Penguin Books 2009

1

Typeset by Rowland Phototypesetting Ltd, Bury St Edmunds, Suffolk
Printed in England by Clays Ltd, St Ives plc

A CIP catalogue record for this book is available from the British Library

ISBN: 978-0-141-02675-6

www.greenpenguin.co.uk

Penguin Books is committed to a sustainable future
for our business, our readers and our planet.
The book in your hands is made from paper
certified by the Forest Stewardship Council.

For Caitríona Keyes, the funniest person I've ever met

Acknowledgements

This book took an embarrassingly long time to write, also my short-term memory isn't what it was – apparently this is what happens when you're perimenopausal (not menopausal, I should stress; that's still decades away, and by the time it happens I'll be grand again and back winning *Mastermind*) – so there's a very good chance that someone may have given me invaluable help at an early stage in the book and that I've now completely forgotten. If you are that person, I am truly sorry.

Thank you to my extraordinary, visionary editor, Louise Moore, and everyone on the team at Michael Joseph for their friendship, enthusiasm and phenomenal hard work on behalf of my books. Blessed am I, among authors.

Likewise, thank you to the legendary Jonathan Lloyd and all at Curtis Brown for their unstinting support. We have all – Louise, Jonathan and I – worked together for over eleven years and it's been a blast.

Thank you to Bob Holt, who, along with his sons, Bobby, Billy and Jamie Holt, paid a weighty sum of money to the Bobby Moore Fund for Cancer Research UK for his wife, Marilyn Holt, to appear as a character in this book.

Likewise thank you to Angus Sprott, who handed over a similarly hefty wedge to Breast Cancer Campaign in order to have his name appear as a character.

As with all my other books, several people have acted as guinea pigs, reading the book as I wrote it, suggesting changes and improvements. Yes, many improvements. Although I may have cried at the time, I would like to stress that I am in fact very grateful for this service. Thank you Chris Baines, Suzanne Benson, Jenny Boland, Ailish Connolly, Debbie Deegan, Susan Dillon, Caron Freeborn, Gai Griffin, Gwen Hollingsworth, Cathy Kelly, Mammy Keyes, Ljiljana Keyes, Rita-Anne Keyes, Eileen Prendergast, Kate Thompson and Louise Voss.

Special thanks to AnneMarie Scanlon, who helped with my research and baldly demanded answers to the questions I was too morto to ask. And extra-special thanks to my sister Caitríona Keyes, who has given me so many funny stories and sayings over the years and which I have nicked shamelessly. In a belated attempt to give her credit for all her contributions, this book is dedicated to her.

As always, thank you to my beloved Tony, without whom none of this would be possible.

A quick explanatory note: part of this book is set in the unattractive, broken-veined world of Irish politics and I've taken the liberty of changing the names of Ireland's two main political parties from Fianna Fáil and Fine Gael to the Nationalist Party of Ireland and the Christian Progressives. This wasn't an attempt to avoid a libel suit – I really do think Irish politicians are as hideous as they appear in these pages, *worse*, if anything – it was just an attempt to make pronunciation, etc., a bit easier for non-Irish readers. Also, the acronym TD (short for Teachta Dála) indicates a member of the Irish parliament (called the Dáil). (Which is located in Leinster House.) (Finally, most Irish governments are coalitions.) (This is probably all the explanation you'll need.)

While writing this book I had to do tons of research, which I absolutely hate, but people were incredibly generous with their time and patience. Any mistakes are mine. Thank you to Martina Devlin, Mary O'Sullivan, Madeleine Keane, Barry Andrews TD (see, TD, you know what that means now!); all at LHW Property Finance (especially Niall Coughlan); Ben Power, 'Amanda', 'Chloe', Natalie and all the girls.

Thank you to Andrew Fitzsimons for the word 'fabulize'.

Thank you to everyone at Women's Aid, at both the Irish and British offices. And finally, thank you to all the survivors of domestic violence who – anonymously – told me what had happened to them. When writing this book, it was my humble intention to honour their stories.

What! You too? I thought I was the only one.

C. S. Lewis

'Everyone remembers where they were the day they heard that Paddy de Courcy was getting married. I was one of the first to know, what with working in a newspaper when word came in from David Thornberry, political correspondent (and tallest man in Dublin), that de Courcy was calling it a day. I was surprised. I mean, we all were. But I was extra surprised and that was even before I heard who the lucky woman was. But I couldn't act upset. Not that anybody would have noticed. I could fall down dead in the street and people would still ask me to drive them to the station. That's what life is like when you're the healthy one of a pair of twins. Anyway, Jacinta Kinsella (boss) needed a quick piece on the engagement so I had to put my personal feelings to one side and be a professional.'
Grace Gildee

'It would have been nice if you had asked me first.'
Alicia Thornton

'I was on the net, checking e-bid for owl handbag (by Stella McCartney, not just any 'oul' handbag) for a client to wear to a wildlife charity thing when I saw the headline. **De Courcy to Wed**. Thought it was a hoax. The media are always making stuff up and faking cellulite on girls who don't have it and taking it off girls who do. When I discovered that it was true, I went into shock. Actually thought I was having heart attack. Would have called an ambulance but couldn't remember 999. Kept thinking 666. Number of the beast.'
Fionnola 'Lola' Daly

*

3

'Don't you dare be happy, you bastard. That's what I thought when I heard. Don't you dare be happy.'
Marnie Hunter

De Courcy to Wed

Women throughout the land will be donning black armbands with the news that Ireland's most eligible politician, Paddy 'Quicksilver' de Courcy, is to hang up his gloves and settle down. Over the last decade, de Courcy, a popular figure in the VIP rooms of Dublin's hot nightspots, and often said to physically resemble JohnJohn Kennedy, has been linked with a number of glamorous women, including the model-turned-actress Zara Kaletsky and Everest mountaineer Selma Teeley, but, until now, showed no signs of making a permanent commitment.

Not much is known of the woman who has won his notoriously wayward heart, one Alicia Thornton, but she's certainly no model or mountaineer – the only climbing she seems interested in, is social. Ms Thornton (35), allegedly a widow, has been working for a well-known property agency but plans to give up her job once married, in order to 'devote herself' to her husband's burgeoning political career. As the wife of the famously ambitious 'Quicksilver', she'll have her work cut out for her.

De Courcy (37) is the deputy leader of New-Ireland, the party founded three years ago by Dee Rossini and other TDs disaffected with the culture of corruption and croneyism prevailing in Ireland's main political parties. Contrary to popular opinion, de Courcy is not one of NewIreland's founding members, but joined eight months after the party's inception, when it became clear that it was a viable prospect.

Lola

Day Zero. Monday, 25 August 14.25

The worst day of my life. When the first wave of shock released me from its fiendish grip, I couldn't help but notice that Paddy hadn't called me. Ominous. I was his girlfriend, the media was going wild that he was getting married to another woman, and he hadn't called me. Bad sign.

Called his private mobile. Not his ordinary private one, but the *private* private one that only I and his personal trainer have. It rang four times, then went to message, then I knew it was true.

End of world.

Called his office, called his home, kept ringing his mobile, left fifty-one messages for him – counted.

18.01

Phone rang – it was him!

He said, 'You've seen the evening papers?'

'Online,' I said. 'I never read the papers.' (Not relevant, but people say the oddest things when in shock.)

'Sorry you had to find out in such a brutal way. Wanted to tell you myself but some journalist –'

'What? So it's true?' I cried.

'I'm sorry, Lola. I didn't think you'd take us so seriously. We were just a bit of fun.'

'Fun?' *Fun?*

'Yes, only a few months.'

7

'Few? Sixteen of them. Sixteen months, Paddy. That's a long time. Are you really marrying this woman?'

'Yes.'

'Why? Do you love her?'

'Of course. Wouldn't be marrying her if I didn't.'

'But I thought you loved me.'

In a sad voice, he said, 'Never made you any promises, Lola. But you are a great, great girl. One in a million. Be good to yourself.'

'Wait, don't go! I have to see you, Paddy, please, just for five minutes.' (No dignity, but couldn't help myself. Was badly distraught.)

'Try not to think badly of me,' he said. 'I'll always think fondly of you and our time together. And remember . . .'

'Yes?' I gasped, desperate to hear something to take edge off the terrible, unbearable pain.

'Don't talk to the press.'

18.05 to midnight

Rang everyone. Including him. Lost count of number of times, but many. Can be certain of that. Double, possibly triple figures.

Phone was also red-hot with incoming calls. Bridie, Treese and Jem – genuine friends – offered much comfort even though they didn't like Paddy. (Never admitted it to me, but I knew.) Also many fake friends – rubberneckers! – ringing to gloat. General gist: 'Is it true that Paddy de Courcy is getting married and not to you? Poor you. Is terrible. Is really, really terrible for you. Is so humILiating. Is so MORTifying. Is so SHAMEing! Is so –'

Kept my dignity. Said, 'Thank you for kind wishes. Must go now.'

8

Bridie came to see me in person. 'You were never cut out to be a politician's wife,' she said. 'Your clothes are too cool and you have purple highlights.'

'Molichino, please!' I cried. 'Purple makes me sound like a . . . a teenager.'

'He was too controlling,' she said. 'We never got to see you. Especially in the last few months.'

'We were in love! You know what it's like to be in love.'

Bridie had got married last year, but Bridie unsentimental. 'Love, yes, very nice, but no need to live in each other's pockets. You were always cancelling on us.'

'Paddy's time is precious! He's a busy man! I had to take what I could get!'

'Also,' Bridie said, 'you never read the papers, you know nothing of current affairs.'

'I could have learnt,' I said. 'I could have changed!'

Tuesday, 26 August
Feel the whole country is looking at me, pointing and laughing. Had boasted to all friends and many clients about Paddy and now they know he is marrying someone else.

My equilibrium destroyed. On a photo-shoot in the Wicklow Hills for Harvey Nichols Christmas catalogue, I ironed oyster-coloured silk bias-cut Chloé evening dress (you know the one I mean?) at too high a heat and burnt it! Scorch mark in the shape of the iron on the crotch of iconic dress worth 2,035 euro (retail). Destroyed. Dress was intended to be the pivot of the shoot. Was lucky they didn't charge me (i.e. bill me, not have me arrested, but could be either, actually, now that I think about it).

Nkechi insisted on taking control — she is an excellent assistant, so excellent that everyone thinks she is my boss

9

– because my hands were trembling, my concentration was in ribbons and I kept having to go to portaloo to vomit.

And worse. Bowels like jelly. Will spare you the details.

20.30–0.34
Bridie and Treese visited me at home and physically restrained me from driving round to Paddy's apartment and demanding audience with him.

3.00
I woke up and thought, Now, will go! Then noticed Treese was in bed beside me. Worse, was awake and prepared to wrestle.

Wednesday, 27 August 11.05
Constant loop in my head: He is marrying another woman, He is marrying another woman, He is marrying another woman. Then every few hours I think, What? What do you mean, he is marrying another woman? As if discovering it for the first time, and SIMPLY CANNOT BELIEVE IT. Then am compelled to ring him, to try to change his mind, but he never picks up.

Then the loop starts again, then the surprise, then I have to ring him, then I get no answer – again and again and again.

Saw picture of this so-called Alicia Thornton. (In the newsagent buying a Crunchie when I saw it on the front page of the *Independent*.) Snapper had caught her coming out of her Ballsbridge offices. Hard to be certain but looked like she was wearing Louise Kennedy. Said it all. Safe. Elegant but safe.

Realized I recognized Alicia Thornton – she had been photographed four times with Paddy in glossy society pages over last few months. Caption had always read, 'Paddy de Courcy and companion'. When photo number three appeared, I had felt emboldened enough to question him about her. He accused me of not trusting him and said she was a family friend. I believed him. But what family? He has no family!

12.11

Call from Bridie. 'We are going out tonight.'

'No!' I cried. 'Cannot face world!'

'Yes, you can! Hold your head up high!'

Bridie is very bossy. Known as Sergeant-Major to her nearest and dearest.

'Bridie, I'm in shreds. Shaking and everything. Cannot go anywhere. I'm begging you.'

She said, 'Is for your good. We will take care of you.'

'Can you not come over to my flat?'

'No.'

Big long pause. Pointless putting up a fight. Bridie is the strongest-willed person I've ever met.

I sighed. Said, 'Who is going?'

'The four of us. You, me, Treese, Jem –'

'Even Jem? He got a pass from Claudia?'

Claudia is Jem's fiancée. Very possessive of him, even though she's good-looking and thin.

'Yes, he got pass from Claudia,' Bridie said. 'I fixed her.'

Bridie and Claudia shared much mutual antipathy.

Jem was great friends with me, Bridie and Treese, but oddly he wasn't gay. Not even metrosexual. (Once he actually bought a pair of jeans in Marks & Spencer. Saw nothing wrong with it, until I gently pointed out the error of his ways.) We lived on the same road when teenagers, him and me. Bonded at cold bus stops, on rainy mornings, in duffel coats, on our way to college. Him to be brainy engineer, me to get diploma in fashion. (Just for the record, my duffel coat was electric-blue vinyl.)

20.35
Café Albatross
Shaky legs. Nearly fell down the stairs into the restaurant. Stumbled on the bottom three steps and almost made my entrance skidding across the floor on my knees like Chuck Berry. Worse, didn't care. Couldn't possibly be more of a laughing stock than I currently am. Bridie and Treese were waiting.

Bridie – like always – was working a most peculiar look. Her straight blondey-red hair was gathered into a low granny-style bun and she was sporting an astonishing green jumper – shrunken, lopsided and embroidered with tiny jockeys. The oddest taste, she always had – right from her first day at school, aged four, when she insisted on wearing tights the colour of dried blood. But she couldn't care less.

Treese, a fund-raiser for a big charity, was much more chic. Flaxen hair in screen-goddess-of-the-forties waves and wearing an impressive dress-and-jacket combo. (From Whistles but on Treese you might mistake it for Prada.) You would think if you worked for a charity you could come to work in beige cords and a hoodie but you'd be wrong. Treese's is a big charity working in the developing world (not third world, cannot say that any more, not PC). Sometimes she has to meet government ministers and ask for money, sometimes she even has to go to The Hague and ask EU for cash.

I asked, 'Where's Jem?'

Was sure he had cancelled because it was a very rare occasion when all four of us managed to get together, even when the arrangement was made several weeks in advance, never mind a mere matter of hours, as in this case. (Had to admit that in recent months I'd been the worst offender.)

'Here he is now!' Bridie said.

Jem, rushing, briefcase, raincoat, pleasant roundy face.

Wine ordered. Drink flowed. Tongues loosened. As I said, I'd always suspected that my friends didn't like Paddy. But now that he had publicly shamed me, they could speak freely.

'Never trusted him,' Jem said. 'He was too charming.'

'Too charming?' I said. 'How can you say he was too charming? Charming is a wonderful thing. Like ice-cream. No such thing as too much!'

'There is,' Jem said. 'You can eat a litre carton of Chunky Monkey, then a litre carton of Cherry Garcia, then get sick.'

'Not me,' I said. 'Anyway I remember that night and it was the doobie, not the ice-cream, that made you sick.'

'He was too good-looking,' Bridie said.

Again I expressed incredulity. 'Too good-looking? How can such a thing be? It's impossible. Goes against laws of physics. Or laws of something. Laws of land, maybe.'

And had I been insulted? 'Are you saying he was too good-looking for me?'

'No!' they exclaim. 'Not!'

'You are as cute as a button,' Jem said. 'Button! Easily as good-looking as him!'

'Better!' Treese said.

'Yes, better!' Bridie said. 'Just different. He's too obvious. You look at him and think, There is a tall, dark, handsome man. Too perfect! But with you, you think, There is a very pretty, medium-height, girlish woman with a well-cut bob, lovely brown colour with bits of purple –'

'Molichino, please!'

'– and a very neat figure considering you're a non-smoker. A twinkle in your eye – both eyes, in point of fact – and a small symmetrical nose.' (Bridie was convinced her nose pointed to the left. Was envious of all those with noses poking out of their fizzogs with straight-ahead precision.) 'The more you look at you, Lola, the more attractive you get. The more you look at Paddy de Courcy, the less attractive he gets. Have I left anything out?' she asked Treese and Jem.

'Her smile lights up her face,' Jem said.

'Yes,' Bridie said. 'Your smile lights up your face. Not like him.'

'Paddy de Courcy's a fake smiler. Like the Joker in *Batman*,' Jem said.

'Yes! Like the Joker in *Batman*!'

I protested, 'He's not like the Joker in *Batman*!'

'Yes, he IS like the Joker in *Batman*.' Bridie was adamant.

21.55

Bridie's mobile rang. She looked at the number and said, 'Must take this call.'

She got up to leave, but we indicated, Stay! Stay!

We wanted to hear. It was her boss (important banker). Sounded like he wanted to go to Milan and for Bridie to organize flights and a hotel. Bridie got a big diary out of bag. (Very nice bag. Mulberry. Why a nice bag but peculiar clothes? Makes no sense.)

'No,' she said to the boss. 'You cannot go to Milan. Is your wife's birthday tomorrow. No, not booking flights for you. Yes, refusing. You will thank me for this. Am keeping you out of the divorce courts.'

She listened a bit more, then gave very scornful laugh.

'Sack me? Don't be so silly!' Then she hung up. 'Right,' she said. 'Where were we?'

'Bridie.' Treese sounded anxious. 'It's not right to refuse to book flights to Milan for your boss. It might be important.'

'Not!' Bridie dismissed it with a flourish of her hand. 'I know all that goes on. Situation in Milan doesn't require his presence. I suspect he has his eye on an Italian lady. Will not facilitate his philandering.'

22.43

Desserts. I ordered Banoffee pie. Bananas tasted slimy, like wet leaves in November. I threw down my spoon and spat the bananas into my napkin. Bridie tried my pie. Said it wasn't slimy. Nothing like wet leaves in November. Treese tried it. Said it wasn't slimy. Jem tried it. Said it wasn't slimy. He finished it. As compensation, he offered me his cold chocolate slab. But it tasted like chocolate-flavoured lard. Bridie tried it. Said it didn't taste like chocolate-flavoured lard. Chocolate, yes, but lard, no. Treese concurred. So did Jem.

Bridie offered me her apple tart, but the pastry tasted of damp cardboard and the apple pieces like dead things. Others did not concur.

Treese didn't offer me her dessert because she had no dessert to offer — once upon a time, she'd been a tubster and now tried to stay away from sugar. It was okay to eat other people's desserts but not to order one for herself.

Her overeating was mostly under control now but she could still have bad days. Example, if stressed at work because she'd been turned down by the EU for a grant for latrines in Addis Ababa, she could eat up to twenty Mars bars in one go. (Could possibly manage more but the woman in the shop beside her office won't sell them to her. She says to Treese, 'You've had enough, love.' Like a kindly publican. She says, 'You worked hard to lose all that weight, Treese, love, you don't want be a porker again. Think of that nice husband of yours. He didn't know you when you were stout, did he?')

I decided to give up on desserts and ordered a glass of port instead.

'What's it taste of?' Bridie asked. 'Rotting ankle boots? Maggots' eyeballs?'

'Alcohol,' I said. 'It tastes of alcohol.'

After the port, had an amaretto. After the amaretto had a Cointreau.

23.30

I braced myself to be forced to attend a nightclub, so I could 'hold my head up high' there also.

But no! No mention of nightclub. Talk of taxis and work in the morning. Everyone returning to their loved ones – Bridie got married last year, Treese got married this year, Jem was living with possessive Claudia. Why go out for steak when you've hamburger at home?

Jem dropped me off in a taxi and insisted that any time I wanted to hang out with him and Claudia, I was welcome. He is lovely, Jem. A kind, kind person.

But lying, of course. Claudia doesn't like me. Not as much as she doesn't like Bridie, but still.

(Quick aside. You know how they told me Paddy was far too good-looking for me? Well, the same could be said for Claudia and Jem. Claudia is 'leggy' – marvellous word, so sixties – tanned, blonde and has breast enlargements. She is the only person I know who's actually had them done. To be fair, they aren't grotesquely large but, nonetheless, you can't miss them. Also I suspect her of hair extensions – one week I met her and she had shoulder-length hair, the following week it was twenty inches longer. But perhaps she had simply been taking lots of selenium.

She looks like a model. In fact, she used to be a model. Sort of. She sat on car bonnets in bikinis. She also tried to be a singer – auditioned for You're A Star (reality TV talent thing). She also tried to be a dancer. (On another reality TV show.) She also tried to be an actress. (Spent small fortune on headshots, but was told to piss off for being crap.) Also a rumour circulated that she had been sighted in a queue for Big Brother auditions but she denies that.

But am not judging. Good lord, I only came by my own career by trial and error, failing at everything else, etc. Fair play to Claudia for her have-a-go spirit.

The only reason I don't like Claudia is because she is not pleasant. She barely bothers to speak to me, Treese and especially Bridie. Her body language always says, Can't ABIDE being with you dullards. Would prefer to be in a nightclub snorting cocaine off a newsreader's thigh.

She behaves as though we would all steal Jem from under her nose, given half a chance. But she has nothing to worry about. None of us has designs on Jem. We all got off with him when we were teenagers. His face was not as round and trustworthy back then. Had slight rakish edge.

If you want my honest opinion, sometimes I worry that Claudia doesn't even like Jem. Feel she treats him like an idiotic, repeat-offender dog, who would chew good shoes and tear open goosedown pillows if he wasn't watched with a basilisk eye.

Jem is a lovely, lovely person. He deserves a lovely, lovely girlfriend.

Final piece of information. Jem is very well paid. Am not implying anything. Just making an observation.)

23.48
Let myself into my tiny flat. I looked around at a life that amounted to nothing and thought, I am all alone. And will be for the rest of my days.

Not self-pity. Simply facing facts.

Thursday, 28 August 9.00
Phone rang. Very friendly female voice said, 'Lola, hi!'

Cautiously I said, 'Hi.'

Because it could be a client. I have to pretend I always know who they are and must never say, 'Who's that?' They like to think they are the only one. (Don't we all?)

'Lola, hi!' the female voice goes on, very friendly. 'My name is Grace. Grace Gildee. I wonder if we could have a chat.'

'Certainly,' I said. (Because thought it was woman looking to be styled.)

'About a good friend of mine,' she said. 'Believe you know him too. Paddy de Courcy?'

'Yes,' I replied, wondering what this was all about. Suddenly I got it! Oh no! 'Are you . . . a journalist?'

'Yes!' she said, like it was all okay. 'I'd love to have a chat about your relationship with Paddy.'

But Paddy had said, No talking to the press.

'Obviously we will compensate you well,' the woman says. 'Believe you've lost a couple of clients recently. Money might come in handy.'

What? Had I lost a couple of clients? News to me.

She said, 'It'll be your chance to give your side of the story. I know you feel badly betrayed by him.'

'No, I . . .'

I was afraid. Really quite afraid. Didn't want a story about Paddy and me in the paper. I shouldn't even have admitted I knew him.

'I don't want to talk about it!'

She said, 'But you *did* have a relationship with Paddy?'

'No, I, er . . . No comment.'

Never thought I'd have a conversation where I said the words, No comment.

'I'll take that as a yes,' the Grace woman said. She laughed.

'Don't!' I said. 'Don't take it as a yes. I must go now.'

'If you change your mind,' she said, 'give me a shout. Grace Gildee. Features writer for the *Spokesman*. We'd do a lovely job.'

9.23

Call from Marcia Fitzgibbons, captain of industry and important client. 'Lola,' she said, 'I heard you were jonesing at the Harvey Nichols shoot.'

'Jonesing?' I said, high-pitched.

'Having withdrawals,' she said.

'What are you talking about?'

'I heard you were a shaking mess,' she said. 'Sweating, vomiting, unable to do a simple task like press a dress without destroying it.'

'No, no,' I insisted. 'Marcia, I mean Ms Fitzgibbons, I wasn't jonesing. All that is wrong is that my heart is broken. Paddy de Courcy is my boyfriend but he's getting married to someone else.'

'So you keep telling people, I hear. But Paddy de Courcy your boyfriend? Don't be ridiculous! You have purple hair!'

'Molichino,' I cry. 'Molichino!'

'Cannot work with you any longer,' she said. 'I have strict zero-tolerance policy on druggies. You are an excellent stylist but rules are rules.'

That is why she is a captain of industry, I suppose.

Further attempts to defend myself proved futile, as she hung up on me. Time, after all, is money.

9.26

Missed my mammy very much. Could really have done with her now. I remembered when she was dying – although I didn't really know that was what was happening, no one said as such, I just thought she needed lots of bed-rest. In the afternoons when I came home from school, I'd get into bed beside her, still in my uniform, and we'd hold hands and watch *EastEnders* repeats. I'd love to do that now, to get into bed beside her and hold hands and go to sleep for ever.

Or if only I had a big extended family who would cosset me and surround me and say, 'Well, we love you. Even if you do know nothing about current affairs.'

But I was all alone in the world. Lola, the little orphan girl. Which was a terrible thing to say, as Dad was still alive. I could have gone and visited him in Birmingham. But I knew that would be unendurable. It would be like after Mum died and we were living side by side in a silent house, neither of us with half a clue how to operate a washing machine or roast a chicken and both of us on anti-depressants.

Even though I knew it was a pointless exercise, I rang him.

'Hello, Dad, my boyfriend is marrying another woman.'

'The blackguard!'

Then he gave big, long, heavy sigh and said, 'I just want

you to be happy, Lola. If only you could be happy, I would be happy.'

I was sorry I'd rung. I'd upset him, he takes everything so hard. And just listening to him, so obviously *depressed* . . . I mean, I suffered from depression too but didn't *go on* about it.

Also he was a liar. He wouldn't be happy if I was happy. The only thing that would make him happy would be if Mum came back.

'So how's Birmingham?' I asked.

At least I got on with my life after Mum died. At least I didn't move to Birmingham, not even Birmingham proper, which has good shops, including Harvey Nichols, but a Birmingham suburb, where nothing ever happened. He was in such a hurry to move. The minute I turned twenty-one, he was off like a shot, saying his older brother needed him; but I suspected he moved because we found it so hard being with each other. (In fairness, I must admit I was considering moving to New York myself but he saved me the bother.)

'Birmingham's grand,' he said.

'Right.'

Big, long pause.

'Well, I'll be off so,' I said. 'I love you, Dad.'

'Good girl,' he said. 'That's right.'

'And you love me too, Dad.'

18.01

I go against every one of my instincts and watch the news, hoping to see coverage from the Dail and possibly catch a glimpse of Paddy. Have to sit through terrible, terrible stuff about seventeen Nigerian men being deported even though they have Irish children; and European nations dumping their rubbish mountains in third world countries (and yes, they said 'third world', not 'developing world').

Kept waiting for Dail report, for pictures of fat, red-faced, corrupt-looking men standing in a room with a blue carpet, shouting Rawlrawlrawl! at each other. But it never came.

Too late I remembered it was the summer holidays and they wouldn't be back in session (or whatever they call it) until two weeks before Christmas. When they would have to break for Christmas. Lazies.

Before I turned the telly off, my attention was caught by an item about the Cavan to Dublin road being closed because a lorry carrying six thousand hens had overturned and all the hens had got loose. The screen was full of hens. I wondered if my grief was inducing hallucinations. Hens are funny things to hallucinate about, though. I looked away, squeezed my eyes tightly shut, then opened them and looked at the telly again and the screen was *still* full of hens. Marauding gangs making for the open road, a great swathe of them disappearing over a hill to freedom, locals stealing them, carrying them away by their legs, a man with a microphone trying to talk to the camera but up to his knees in moving sea of rust-coloured feathers.

18.55

I can't stop ringing Paddy. It's like OCD. Like washing hands constantly. Or eating cashew nuts. Once I start, I can't stop.

He never answered and he never rang back. Was aware I was debasing myself but couldn't stop. I longed for him. *Yearned* for him.

If I could just speak to him! Maybe I wouldn't get him to change his mind, but I could get answers to questions. Like, why did he make me feel so special? Why was he so possessive of me? When there was another woman all along.

There was a horrible niggling feeling that this was my own fault. How could I have believed that a man as handsome and charismatic as Paddy would take a person like me seriously?

I felt so very, very stupid. And the thing was, I wasn't stupid. Shallow, yes, but not stupid. There was a big difference. Just because I loved clothes and fashion didn't mean I was a thicko. May not have known who the president of Bolivia was but I had emotional intelligence. Or at least, had thought I had. I always gave great advice on other people's lives. (Only on request. Not uninvited. That would be rude.) But clearly I'd had no right to. Cobblers' children, etc., etc.

Friday, 29 August
The worst week of my life continues with no respite.

At a photo-shoot for author Petra McGillis, I'd staggered along to the studio with three massive suitcases of clothes I'd called in according to Petra's specifications, but when I opened them up she said, outraged, 'I said no colours! I said neutrals, camels, toffees, that sort of thing!' She turned on a woman whom I later discovered was her editor and said, 'Gwendoline, what are you trying to turn me into? Pistachio green? I am NOT a pistachio-green author!'

The poor editor insisted she was not trying to turn the author into anything, certainly not a pistachio-green person. She said that Petra had talked to the stylist (me) and told her her requirements and that no one had interfered.

Petra insisted, 'But I said, "No colours!" I was quite specific. I never wear colours! I am a serious writer.'

Suddenly everyone was looking at me – the photographer,

23

the make-up artist, the art director, the caterer, a post-man delivering a parcel. It's her fault, they all accused me with their eyes. That stylist. She thinks Petra McGillis is a pistachio-green person.

And they were right to accuse me. No way could I blame Nkechi. It was me who had taken the call, and when Petra had said, 'No colours!' my scrambled brain must have heard, 'I love colours!'

It had never happened to me before. I was usually so good at channelling the clients' requirements that they tried to steal the garments from the shoot and got me into trouble with press office.

'I'll wear my own bloody clothes,' Petra said, tightly and tetchily.

Resourceful Nkechi made many calls, seeking an emer-gency care package of neutral-coloured garments, but none was available.

At least she tried, all the accusing faces said silently. That Nkechi is mere assistant but she showed more gump-tion than the stylist herself.

I should have left there and then, as I was no use to anyone. But for the rest of shoot (three hours), I stood by, smiling gamely, trying to bring the twitch in my lip under control. Now and then, I'd nip forward to adjust Petra's collar, to pretend I had a reason for existing, but it was a disaster, a horrible, horrible disaster.

I'd spent a long time building up my career. Was it all to be destroyed in a matter of days, because of Paddy de Courcy?

Hard to care, though. All I was interested in was how to get him back. Or failing that, how to endure the rest of my life without him. Yes, I sounded like overblown Gothic-type

24

person, but really, if you'd met him . . . In person he was so much more good-looking and charismatic than on telly. He made you feel like you were the only person in the world, and he smelt so nice that after I first met him I bought his aftershave (Baldessini) and although he brought an extra-special additional de Courcy ingredient to the mix, one whiff was enough to make me feel tunnel-visiony, like I was about to faint.

15.15
Another call from this Grace Gildee journalist. Pushy. How did she get my number in the first place? And how did she know Marcia Fitzgibbons was going to sack me? In fact, I thought about asking her who else was going to sack me, but desisted.

After a certain amount of pussy-footing (on my part) she offered five grand for my story. A lot of money. Styling was an uncertain business. You could have twelve jobs one week and none at all for the rest of month. But I was not tempted.

However – I was not complete fool, despite feeling like one – I rang Paddy and left a message. 'A journalist called Grace Gildee offered me lots of money to talk about our relationship. What should I do?'

He rang back so fast I had barely hung up.

'Don't even think about it,' he said. 'I'm a public figure. I've a career.'

Always about him and his career.

'I've a career too, you know,' I reminded him. 'And it's going down the Swanee due to my broken heart.'

'Don't let it,' he said, in a kindly manner. 'I'm not worth it.'

'She offered me five grand.'

'Lola.' His voice was persuasive. 'Don't sell your soul for money, you're not that kind of girl. You and I, we had good times together. Let's preserve the memory. And you know that if you're ever stuck for a few quid, I'll help out.'

I didn't know what to say. Although he was behaving like a supportive friend, was he, in fact, offering to pay me to keep shtum?

'There's plenty I could tell Grace Gildee,' I said bravely.

A different voice from him this time. Low, cold. 'Like fucking what?'

Less confidently I said, '. . . The . . . things you bought me. The games we played . . .'

'Let's make one thing clear, Lola.' Arctic tones. 'You talk to no one, especially not her.' Then he said, 'Must go. I'm in the middle of something. Take care of yourself.'

Gone!

20.30

A night in with Bridie and Treese in Treese's big house in Howth. Treese's new husband Vincent was away. I was secretly glad. I never feel welcome when he's there. Always feel he's thinking, What are these strangers doing in my house?

He never joins in. He'll come into the room and nod hello, but only because he wants to ask Treese where his dry-cleaning is; then he goes off to do something more important than spend time with his wife's friends.

He calls Treese by her proper name, Teresa, like it wasn't our friend he married but a different woman altogether.

He is quite elderly. Thirteen years older than Treese. On his second marriage. His first wife and three young children are stashed somewhere. He is a big cheese in the Irish rugby organization. In fact, used to play for Ireland and he knows everything about everything. No room for discussion with Vincent. He says one sentence and the entire conversation shuts down.

He has a rugby-player physique — muscles, wideness, thighs so enormous he has to walk in a strange side-to-side, just-got-off-a-horse motion. Many women — indeed Treese obviously does; she married him, after all — might find this comely. But not me. He is too butty and . . . wide. He eats phenomenal quantities and weighs about forty stone, but — I want to be fair — he isn't fat. Just . . . compacted. Very dense, like he's spent time living in a black hole. His neck is the circumference of a rain barrel and he has a stunningly enormous head. Also big hair. Gak.

21.15
Food was delicious. Treese had done a course in classical French cuisine so she could cook the type of food Vincent's rugby cronies expected. I ate two mouthfuls, then my stomach contracted into a tiny walnut and I had the taste of sick in my mouth.

Bridie was wearing her peculiar green jumper again. Even though I was obsessed with myself and my pain, I couldn't stop looking at it. As before, it was lopsided, shrunken and embroidered with jockeys. What was that all about?

I wondered if I should say something? But she liked it. She must. Otherwise why would she wear it? So why burst her bubble?

23.59

Many bottles of wine later, although not ones from the bottom shelf, as they are Vincent's special ones and he would be annoyed if we drank them.

'Stay the night,' Treese said to me.

Treese had four spare rooms.

'You have a dream life,' Bridie said. 'Rich husband, fabulous house, lovely clothes . . .'

'And the first wife always asking for money! And bratty stepchildren giving me the evils. And terrible worry . . .'

'About what?'

'That my eating disorder will kick in again and I'll balloon to eighteen stone and have to be cut out of the house and taken away on a flatbed truck and Vincent won't love me any more.'

'Of course he will love you! No matter what!'

But, in a secret little chamber in my heart, where I thought my darkest thoughts, I wasn't so sure. Vincent did not jettison his first wife and children in order to shack up with Jabba the Hutt.

0.27

Tucked up in Number One Spare Room. Softest pillow I'd ever laid my head on; magnificent, carved, antique French bed; brocade chairs with bandy legs; mirrors of Murano glass; weighty, lined curtains in luxurious fabric; and the sort of wallpaper you only get in hotels.

'Look, Treese,' I said. 'The carpet is the exact same colour as your hair! It's beautiful, beautiful, everything's beautiful . . .'

I was quite drunk, in retrospect.

'Sleep tight,' Treese said. 'Don't let bugs bite and don't wake at four thirty-six a.m. and decide to sneak out and drive over to Paddy's flat to throw stones at his windows and shout abuse about Alicia Thornton.'

4.36

I awake. I decide to sneak out and drive over to Paddy's flat to throw stones at his windows and shout abuse about Alicia Thornton ('Alicia Thornton's mother blows the parish priest!' 'Alicia Thornton doesn't wash her lady-bits!' 'Alicia Thornton's father is cruel to the family Labrador!'). But when I opened Treese's front door, alarm siren started screeching, searchlights snapped on, and there was the distant sound of dogs barking. Was half expecting a helicopter to appear overhead when Treese came floating down the stairs in a silky, shell-pink negligee (nightdress) and matching peignoir (dressing gown), searchlights glinting silver on her shiny pale coiffeur (hair).

Calmly she chastised me. 'You promised you wouldn't. Now you are snared. Return to bed!'

Red-faced.

Treese reset alarm, then glided back up the stairs.

Saturday, 30 August 12.10
At home
Bridie rang. After an enquiry about my well-being, a strange little silence ensued. Expectant almost.

Then she asked, 'Did you like green jumper I was wearing Wednesday night and last night?'

I could hardly reply, No, it was the strangest thing I've seen in a long, long time.

I said, 'Lovely!' Then, 'Er . . . new?'

'Yes.' Bridie sounded almost shy. Then she blurted out, like someone with a big, thrilling secret, 'Moschino!'

Moschino!

I had thought perhaps she had purchased it at a sale-of-work at her local lunatic asylum! Good job I didn't say so.

Although I wouldn't. Not my way. Mum always told me that if I couldn't say something nice, to say nothing at all.

'Where did you buy it, Bridie?' I was wondering how, with my encyclopaedic knowledge of clothing, I'd never before come across this item.

'On eBay.'

Cripes! Perhaps fake!

'It cost me a fortune, Lola. But worth it. Worth it, yes?'

'Oh yes, yes, worth it! Jockeys very . . . um . . . fashion-forward.'

'I noticed you looking at it, Lola.'

Oh yes, I was looking all right.

Sunday, 31 August

Articles about Paddy in all the newspapers. I bought several. (Was surprised by how cheap newspapers are compared to magazines. Good value. Funny the things you notice even when your life has fallen apart.) But the articles said nothing really. Just that he was a hunky ride, the poster boy for Irish politics.

There was no mention of me in any article. I should have felt relieved – at least Paddy wouldn't be annoyed – but instead I felt bereft, like I didn't exist.

Monday, 1 September 10.07

A call from *Irish Tatler* cancelling a job next week. The message was clear: no one likes a stylist who destroys the collections. Word gets round.

10.22

Mobile rang. Thought I recognized number, wasn't sure, then realized it was that Grace Gildee journalist woman again. Hounding me! I didn't pick up, but listened to the message. She was pushing for a face-to-face meeting and offering more money. Seven grand. She laughed and accused me of playing hardball. But I wasn't playing any kind of ball! Just wanted to be left in peace!

Tuesday, 2 September

Worst blow to date. Alicia Thornton was on the front cover of *VIP*, with the headline, 'How I won Quicksilver's heart'.

The nice man in the newsagent's gave me a glass of water and let me sit on his stool for a little while, until the dizziness passed.

Twelve pages of photos. Paddy was wearing make-up in them. Silicon-based foundation, with silicon-based primer, so that he looked plastic, like a Ken-doll.

I didn't know who had styled the shoot, but they'd had a very definite brief. Alicia (tall, thin, blonde bob, quite horsey-looking, but not in nice way, not like Sarah Jessica Parker, more like Celine Dion. Neigh!) in a cream tweed Chanel dress and jacket. Paddy in a statesman-like suit (Zegna? Ford? Couldn't be sure) sitting at a mahogany desk, holding a silver pen like he was about to sign an important treaty, Alicia standing behind him, her hand on his shoulder, in a supportive-wife pose. Then, Paddy and Alicia in evening wear.

Paddy in black tie and Alicia in a long, red, off-the-shoulder MaxMara. Red not her colour. Also a small glimpse of stubble under her right arm.

Worst of all, Paddy and Alicia in matching chambray jeans, polo-shirts with collars turned up, cable-knit jumpers slung around their necks and HOLDING TENNIS RACKETS! Like a cheap mail-order catalogue.

These photos managed, despite Paddy being the most handsome man alive, to make him look like a male model down on his luck.

The interview said they had known each other since they were teenagers, but had been seeing each other romantically, 'in a low-key' fashion, for the past seven months. Past seven months! I had been seeing him 'in a low-key' fashion for the past sixteen months! And no wonder he said we should be 'low-key'. He said life (mine) would be a living hell if I appeared at his side at official shindigs and red-carpet events. The press would torment me and I'd be obliged to wear a full face of make-up at all times, even when asleep, to avoid photos captioned with, 'Paddy's girl is spotty minger'. (During the summer there had been two mentions of me in gossip columns but Paddy's press office said I was helping him with clothing, and everyone seemed to believe that.) I had honestly thought he was thinking of my best interests. Instead he was keeping Alicia, his 'soul friend' (that's what he said in the interview), from finding out about me. How thick am I?

Later Tuesday
VIP photo-shoot was the final blow. I spent the day analysing the photos and brooding. What had this Alicia Thornton got that I hadn't? I was flicking through the pages, studying the

pictures of him and her, searching for clues. Again and again. Trying to believe this was real. But I ended up staring at them too much so that it didn't look like him any more, the way if you stare at your own face in the mirror for too long, it goes weird, almost scary.

Even later Tuesday

Angry. Thinking dark, bitter thoughts. Full of bad, burny feeling. Breathless. Suddenly I dashed VIP magazine to the floor and thought, I deserve answers!

Drove to Paddy's apartment and rang bell. Rang it and rang it and rang it and rang it and rang it. Nothing happened but I decided, To hell with it, I'll stay! I'll wait until he comes back. Even if I have to wait a number of days. A couple of weeks, even. He'll have to come home eventually.

Bad, burny feeling made me strong and I felt I could wait for ever. If necessary.

I made plans. I rang Bridie and asked her to bring a sleeping bag and sandwiches. Also a flask of soup. 'But not minestrone,' I said. 'Nothing with lumps.'

'What?' she asked, incredulous. 'You are camped outside de Courcy's flat?'

'Must you dramatize everything?' I said. 'I'm just waiting for him to come home. But it may take a few days. So, like I said, a sleeping bag, sandwiches and soup. And remember: nothing with lumps.'

She was squawking about being worried about me and I had to hang up. Short of patience.

Time passed. Bad, burny feelings keeping me focused. I was unaware of discomfort, cold and need for loo. Like a Buddhist monk.

Intermittently I rang Paddy's bell, as much for something

33

to do as anything else. Then I realized bad, burny feelings must have abated slightly as I was finding this quite boring. I rang Bridie again. Asked, 'Could you also bring the new *InStyle*, a sudoku book and my biography of Diana Vreeland?'

'No!' she said. 'Lola, please! Please come away from there. You have lost your reason.'

'On the contrary,' I said. 'I've never been so sane in my life!'

'Lola, you are *stalking* him. He's a public figure, you could get into trouble! You could –'

Had to hang up again. I didn't savour being rude but I had no choice.

Entertained myself by ringing Paddy's doorbell a few more times, then my mobile rang. It was Bridie! She was at the gate! She couldn't get in because she didn't know the code!

'Have you a sleeping bag?' I asked her. 'And soup in a flask?'

'No.'

'Is Barry with you?' (Barry was her husband.)

'Yes, Barry's here beside me. You like Barry, don't you?'

Yes, but I had visions of her and Barry manhandling me into their car and driving me away. Not having it.

'Lola, please let us in.'

'No,' I said. 'Sorry.'

Then I switched my mobile off.

I continued to ring Paddy's bell, not expecting any result, when, all of sudden, the outline of a man appeared behind the textured glass door.

It was him! It was him! He'd been there all along! I was relieved, excited – then darker thoughts occurred: Why didn't he come down before now? Why must he further humiliate me?

But it wasn't him at all! Instead it was Spanish John, his driver. Knew him well because he sometimes collected and delivered me to Paddy. Although he had never been less than cordial to me, was quite frightened of him. A big, bulky type, who looked as if he could snap your neck in two as if it were a chicken wing in barbecue sauce.

'Spanish John,' I beseeched, 'I need to see Paddy. Let me in, I'm begging you.'

He shook head and rumbled, 'Go home, Lola.'

'Is she up there with him?' I asked.

Spanish John was a master of discretion (and not Spanish). All he said was, 'Come on, Lola, I'll drop you home.'

'She *is* up there!'

Gently, almost kindly, he steered me away from the door and towards Paddy's Saab.

'It's okay,' I said huffily. 'I've my own car, I can drive myself.'

'Good luck, Lola,' he said. With finality.

Such finality emboldened me to ask the question which I'd always wanted to know the answer to.

'By the way,' I said, 'I've always wondered. Why do they call you Spanish John when you're not Spanish?'

For a moment I thought he would step forward and do a very painful karate chop on me, then he seemed to relent. 'Just look at me.' He pointed to his red hair, white fizzog and many freckles. 'Did you ever see anyone who looks less Spanish?'

'Ah.' I understood. 'Irony?'

'Or possibly sarcasm. Never sure of distinction.'

Tuesday night, later still

That was it, had been turned away from Paddy's door, like a smelly beggar.

Sanity returned like a bucket of cold water thrown in my face and I was scandalized by my behaviour. I'd been like a mentally ill person. *Deranged.* Stalking Paddy. Yes, Bridie was right. *Stalking* him.

And I was appalled at the way I'd treated Bridie. Asking for a flask of soup. Where would Bridie get soup? Then refusing to tell her the gate code and hanging up on her. Bridie was a concerned friend!

I saw how mad I'd been, and the worst thing of all – while in the grip of my lunacy, I'd been convinced that I was perfectly sane. The final blow.

Couldn't go on like this, not eating, not sleeping, making a shambles of work, treating friends like servants and driving around the city without due care and attention . . .

I drove to Bridie's house. She was in her pyjamas and glad to see me.

I apologized profusely for the sleeping-bag business, then the gate-code business.

'Accepted,' Bridie said. 'Accepted. So what's up?'

'I've made a decision,' I said. 'Have decided to pack up my life and move to the end of the earth. To a place with no reminders of Paddy. You have a globe, haven't you?'

'Er, yes . . .'

(From studying geography when she was at school. She never throws anything away.)

On Bridie's globe the end of the earth (from Ireland) was New Zealand. Fine. That would do. I believed they had lovely scenery. I could go on a *Lord of the Rings* tour.

But Bridie was the voice of reason. 'New Zealand is costly to get to,' she said. 'Also very far away.'

'But that is the very point,' I said. 'I have to get far away from here, so I don't see Alicia's picture every time I go to buy a bar of chocolate, or hear about Paddy on evening news, not that I watch evening news – God, it's so depressing, apart from that thing about the hens, did you see it?'

'What about Uncle Tom's cabin?' Barry suggested. Barry was also in his pyjamas.

Uncle Tom's cabin was a holiday home that Bridie's uncle Tom had in County Clare. Had been there for Treese's hen weekend. Broke many things. (Not me personally, just between the lot of us.)

'That's remote,' Barry said.

'It doesn't even have telly!' Bridie agreed. 'But if you go mental all on your own, you can be home in three hours, since they've opened the Kildare bypass.'

(The Kildare bypass is the best thing to ever happen to Bridie's extended family, as many of them live in Dublin but love Uncle Tom's cabin. It knocks forty-five minutes off the drive, Bridie's dad says. But what do I care? I am thirty-one and, if I don't kill myself, am likely to live another forty years. I can spend all that time sitting in a traffic jam outside Kildare and it will make no difference to anything.)

'Thank you for kindly offer,' I said. 'But I can't stay in Uncle Tom's cabin for ever. Some of your family might want to use it.'

'They won't, it's the end of the summer. Look,' she said. 'Your heart is broken and you feel like you'll never get over it. But you will and then you'll be sorry you moved to New Zealand and threw away your business here. Why not go to

Clare for a couple of weeks to recuperate? Get Nkechi to keep things ticking over at work. How's your schedule at the moment? Busy?'

'No.' Not just because jobs kept being cancelled, but because of the time of year. I'd finished all the autumn/winter wardrobes for private clients – busy, rich women, who had no time to shop but needed to look stylish, businesslike, pulled-together. The next demanding time would be the Christmas party season, which kicked off the minute Hallowe'en was out of the way. There was no need to start on it for a couple of weeks. I mean, there was always work which could be done. I could be taking buyers from Brown Thomas and Costume and other good shops to lunch so they would earmark their best dresses for me and not for other stylists. Cut-throat business, styling. Really vicious. Only so many good clothes to go around and the competition is fierce. People don't realize. They think it's all great girly fun, wafting around with expensive frocks, making everyone look fabulous. Far from it.

Bridie said, 'And when you come back, if things are as bad as ever, then you can go to New Zealand.'

'I know when I am being humoured, Bridie. The laugh will be on other side of your fizzog when I am living in a nice little house in Rotorua. However, I will accept your kindly offer.'

Even later still
Driving home
Suddenly realized that Bridie's pyjamas were not in fact pyjamas but strange 'leisure' pants for lounging in at home. Mail-order. Would swear to it. Under normal circumstances the shock would have swerved me off the road and straight

38

into a pole. Even as things were, I was pretty disturbed. Next she'll be wearing them out in public. She needed to be taken in hand. Barry should have a word but, now that I remembered, he was also wearing a pair. He was her enabler. She would never get help as long as he was encouraging her.

Wednesday, 3 September 10.00

Went to my 'office' (Martine's Patisserie). I would have worked from home but my home was too small. That was the price you paid for living in the city centre. (Another price was drunken men having grunty wrestling matches outside your bedroom window at 4 a.m.)

I ordered hot chocolate and an apricot Danish. Normally I loved apricot Danishes so much, I had to ration myself. I could eat ten in a row, no bother. But today the jammy glaze looked revolting and the apricot stared up at me like a baleful eye. Had to push it away. I took a sip of my hot chocolate and immediately wanted to vomit.

Bell tinged. The arrival of Nkechi. Everyone looked. Plenty to look at. Nigerian, excellent posture, braids hanging all the way down her back, very long legs, then a really quite large bottom perched on top of them. But Nkechi never tried to hide her bottom. She was proud of it. Fascinating to me. Irish girls' lives were a constant quest for bottom-disguising or bottom-reducing clothing tactics. We can learn much from other cultures.

Nkechi, although young (twenty-three), is a genius. Like the time Rosalind Croft (wife of dodgy rich bloke Maxwell Croft) was going to a benefit dinner at the Mansion House. The neckline on her dress was so fashion-forward that none of the jewellery was working with it. We tried everything. A nightmare! Mrs Croft was about to ring up and cancel, when

Nkechi said, 'I have it!' And whipped off her scarf, her own scarf (that she bought in a charity shop for 3 euro), draped it around Mrs Croft's neck and saved the day.

'Nkechi,' I said. 'I am going to take a couple of weeks off and go down to Uncle Tom's cabin.'

Nkechi familiar with same. She was there for Treese's hen night. Now that I thought of it, she broke the toaster, trying to fit in an entire bagel. Quite spectacular carnage. Black smoke started spewing from the side of toaster, followed by a big whoosh of flame. Also she broke a ceramic dolphin which had been in Bridie's family for thirty-eight years. She'd been dancing drunkenly and did a big high kick which sent the dolphin flying, like a rugby ball over the bar, into a wall, where it smashed into smithereens. But it was a hen night, these things happen. At least no one ended up in hospital. Not like at Bridie's hen night.

I said, 'I know it sounds dramatic, packing up my life, but really, Nkechi, the state of me. I can't work, can't sleep, my digestive system's in flitters.'

She said, 'I think it's good idea. Take yourself out of circulation for while, before you damage our reputation even further.'

An awkward little silence ensued.

Just one slight quibble about Nkechi – she's an excellent stylist, really really excellent, but slightly lacking in TLC. Part of a stylist's job is to prevent the client going out looking like a total tit. It's our job to protect them from the gossip columnists' harsh comments. If the client has a wrinkly décolletage, we steer them away from plunging neck-lines. If they have knees like a bloodhound's jowls, we suggest floor-length gowns. But subtly. Kindly.

However, Nkechi wasn't always as diplomatic as I would

have preferred. For example, the time she was dressing SarahJane Hutchinson. Poor woman. Her husband had left her for a young Asian boy. Public humiliation. This was the first charity event she was attending as a deserted wife so it was important that she looked and felt good. She tried on a very pretty strapless Matthew Williamson, but it was obvious it wasn't working. Everything going south. I was just about to tactfully suggest a Roland Mouret (gave much more support, had built-in but hidden corset) when Nkechi exclaimed, 'You can't go out with those bingo wings! You need sleeves, girlfriend!'

I said, 'Nkechi, I would appreciate it if you could take over the reins for the short time I'll be away.'

'Sure,' she says. 'Take over. Will do.'

I tried to swallow away my anxiety. Everything was under control. Nkechi would do it well.

Possibly too well.

I didn't like the way she said, 'Take over.'

'Nkechi,' I say, 'you are a genius. You will go on to be a brilliant stylist, possibly the greatest of us all. But for the moment, just keep things ticking over. Please do not do a putsch on me while I'm gone. Please do not set up on your own. Please do not poach my richest clients. Be my friend. Remember: your name means "loyal" in Igbo.'

10.47

Trailing dispiritedly home to pack when I see someone waiting outside my building. A woman. Tall, jeans, boots, hoodie, short spiky blonde hair. Leaning against railings, smoking. Two men passed her and said something. Her response was carried to me on the air. Go fuck yourselves.

Who was she? What fresh hell? Then I knew! It was that

journalist, Grace Gildee! I was being door-stepped, like . . . like a drug baron or . . . or . . . a paedophile!

I paused in my tracks. Where should I go? Flee, flee! But flee where? I had a perfect right to go to my flat. After all, I lived there.

Too late! She'd seen me!

'Lola?' Smiling, smiling, speedily stubbing out her cigarette with a nifty swivel of her ankle.

'Hi!'

Extending her hand. 'Grace Gildee. Lovely to meet you.'

Her warm, smooth hand was in mine before I could stop it.

'No,' I said, jerking my hand away. 'Leave me alone. I'm not talking to you.'

'Why?' she asked.

I ignored her and fumbled in my bag for my keys. Fully intended not to make eye contact but, against my will, found myself looking straight into her face.

Up close, I could see she wasn't wearing make-up. Unusual. But she had no need to. Very attractive in a tomboy sort of way. Hazel-coloured eyes and a scatter of freckles across nose. The kind of woman who could run out of shampoo and have no problem washing hair with washing-up liquid. Good in an emergency, I suspected.

'Lola,' she says, 'you can trust me.'

'You can trust me!' I exclaimed. 'You're a cliché!'

Nonetheless, something about her. Persuasive.

In a soft voice, she said, 'You really can trust me. I'm not like other journalists. I know what he's like.'

I stopped twirling my hand around the hidden depths of my bag, seeking my keys. I was mesmerized. Like being hypnotized by a snake.

42

'I've known him half his life,' she said.

All of sudden, I wanted to put my head on the shoulder of her hoodie and sob and let her stroke my hair.

But that was what she would have wanted. That's what they all do, journalists. Pretend they're your friends. Like the time SarahJane Hutchinson was interviewed at the Children at Risk Ball. The journalist woman was all lovely, asking where SarahJane got her gorgeous dress. And her delicious jewellery. And who did her hair? *Trust me, trust me, trust me.* Then the headline was:

Mutton Dressed As Pig

What forty-something, recently deserted wife has lost the run of herself? Running around town dressed in her teenage daughter's clothes. A bid to recapture lost youth? Or a bid to recapture lost husband? Forget it, babes. Either way, it ain't working.

My hand closed over my keys. Thank God. I had to get into my flat. I had to get away from this *Grace Gildee.*

17.07

Arrive in Knockavoy! Uncle Tom's cabin is in a field, a short way outside town.

I drove down the bumpy boreen and parked in the gravel patch outside the front door.

Lime-washed cottage. Thick lumpy walls. Small windows. Red-painted latched door. Deep window ledges. Charming.

I got out of the car and was nearly blown away. Had a vision of being picked up and twirled high into the sky and out over the bay, then dashed to a watery grave in the

Atlantic waves. Paddy would be sorry then. Would rue the day he ever heard of Alicia Thornton.

Go on, wind, I begged. Take me!

I stood with my eyes scrunched shut and my arms out-stretched invitingly, but nothing happened. Annoying.

Leaning into the wind, I battled towards the front door. The air was *riddled* with sea salt. My hair would be destroyed. Although was very proud of my Molichino highlights, had to admit they made hair prone to dullness and breaking. Hoped they had deep-conditioning treatment in the local chemist. Cripes! Hoped there was a local chemist. All I remembered from every other visit was pubs, many pubs, and a nightclub so extraordinarily bad it was hilarious.

I unlocked the adorable red door and the force of the wind made it fly back against the wall with an almighty bang. Dragged bags in across the flagstones. Was I imagining it or did the house still smell of smoke from the broken toaster even though several months had elapsed since the hen night?

There was one big living room, with sofas and rugs and a big open fire with rocking chairs in the alcove. The back windows looked out over fields, then the Atlantic, maybe a hundred yards away. Actually I'm just making that bit up, I had no idea how far away the sea was. Only men could do things like that. 'Half a mile.' 'Fifty yards.' Giving directions, that sort of thing. I could look at a woman and say, '36C.' Or, 'Let's try it in next size up.' But I had no idea how far away Uncle Tom's sea was except that I wouldn't want to walk to it in high heels.

In the kitchen there were scorch marks on the wall be-hind the (new) toaster, a table with a cherry-patterned oil-cloth cover, six hard wooden chairs, yellow free-standing cupboards, like from a kitchen of the 1950s, and old, mismatched delph, many with faded floral patterns. The kitchen windows also looked towards the sea. I shut my left eye and squinted out at it. Still had no idea how far away it was.

My mobile rang. Bridie. 'How was the drive?'

'Good, fine,' I said. Hard to be enthusiastic.

'How long did it take?'

I couldn't remember. I hadn't been paying attention. But she had told me to time the journey. So I said, just off the top of my head, 'Two hours, forty minutes.'

She whistled and said, 'That's the fastest yet. I have to go, have to tell Dad. He managed two hours fifty in July but that was at half five in the morning. He'll be upset to have been bested. Especially by a girl.'

'Don't tell him, then,' I said. 'Why upset him? There's enough upset in the world.'

17.30

Upstairs there were three bedrooms. I chose the middle-sized one. Wasn't so up myself that I had to pick the biggest but self-esteem was not so low that I automatically gravitated to the smallest. (Good sign.) A double bed, but very narrow. How did people cope in the olden days? Was not exactly a fatso (although would have liked a much, much smaller bottom) but there was really only room for me in it. The frame of the bed was iron and at first glance the quilt looked like patchwork and I was charmed. Then I took a closer look. Not patchwork at all. Fake patchwork business that cost a tenner in Penneys. All the same, looked good from a distance.

The same white lumpy walls as downstairs and two small

45

windows with red-painted frames. Cheery. With flowery curtains. Cosy.

I opened my suitcase. Shock. The clothing I'd packed was evidence of my unsettled mental state. Nothing practical. No jeans. No boots. Foolish! Was living in a field! Needed mucker-style clothing! Instead had brought dresses, spangles, ostrich feather boa! Where did I think I'd be going? The only thing that might be useful was a pair of wellingtons. Did it matter that they were pink? Did it make them any less practical?

I hung my impractical clothing in the mahogany wardrobe. Carved. Curved. Solid. Flyblown mirror on the front. Looked antique. You'd pay a fortune for that in Dublin.

18.23

Back downstairs I noticed a telly in the corner! Quite annoyed with Bridie! Rang her.

'There's a telly here! You said there was no telly!'

'It's not a telly,' she said.

'It looks like a telly!'

But, worried, I had to go closer and crouch down and check. Was I so distraught that I'd mistaken something else for telly? A microwave, perhaps?

'Yes,' she said. 'It's *physically* a telly. But it's not connected.'

'So what's the point, then?'

'You can watch DVDs on it.'

'Where will I get DVDs?'

'In the DVD shop.'

'I am a long way from a DVD shop.'

'You're not. The supermarket on main street has a good choice. Up to date.'

'Okay. So . . . ah . . . any news?'

I meant, any news about Paddy?

'You've only been gone a couple of hours,' she said.

But had detected hesitation in her delivery. 'There *is* news,' I cried. 'Please tell me!'

'No,' she said. 'You've gone down there to escape from news!'

'Please tell me! Now that I know there is news, I must know. I will die if I don't know. I won't ask again, but I need to know now.'

She sighed. Said, 'Okay. In the evening paper. Date set. Wedding to be held in March. Reception in the K Club.'

Two thoughts. First one: March a long, long way away. He might change his mind. And second thought: 'The K Club? Only horsey types have their wedding reception in the K Club. He's not a horsey type. Is she?'

Bridie said, 'Well, she *looks* like one. A horse, I mean.'

Bridie, loyal friend.

'But don't think she is a horsey *type*,' she said.

I said, 'Everyone knows it's not on to hold your wedding reception in the K Club if you're not a horsey Kildare type.'

'Is tacky,' Bridie said.

'Yes, is tacky.'

18.37

Nice little town. Plenty of people about. A lot going on. More than I'd remembered. Hotel, one (small). Pubs, many. Supermarket, one. Boutiques, one. (Awful — Aran ganzies, tweed capes, crocheted bobble hats. Aimed at tourists.) Chipper, one. Surf shops, two! Internet café, one. (Yes, I *know*. Unexpected.) Huxtery, all-purpose, seaside-town shop, selling Jackie Collins novels, souvenirs and ashtrays shaped like toilets, with writing, 'Rest Your Weary Ash' (criminal!), one.

Decision. Would have my evening meal in a pub. I had no one to talk to, but I had a magazine to hide behind. All pubs advertised food so decided to choose one at random and take a chance it wasn't the place we got barred from on Treese's hen night.

(Hen nights should be banned. You're honour-bound to behave atrociously, then feel terribly ashamed afterwards. Didn't remember much of Treese's, except that the ten of us — only eight actually, as Treese had passed out in the cottage and never made it to town and Jill was in the pub toilet, collapsed on the floor — draped ourselves all over the barman, pulling at him and saying, 'Oh baby! You drive me wild!' And stuff like that. Had a vague memory of the barman begging, 'Come on now, girls. Cut it out. Is a family pub! Am asking nicely.' Remember he had seemed on the verge of tears.)

Opened the door of a place called the Dungeon and a knot of hostile male fizzogs glared up like creatures disturbed under a rock. An impression of red eyes, pointy chins and smell of sulphur. Like the video of 'Bohemian Rhapsody'. Recoiled.

Next pub, the Oak, bright lighting, upholstered seating, family groups eating chicken nuggets. Safer. No one glared.

Took a seat and a barman came over and asked, 'Have you decided?'

Realized perhaps he wasn't Irish — non-Irish accent, toffee-coloured skin, black hair and eyes like raisins (actually that makes them sound small and shrivelled, which was not the case at all. Big dark eyes. If looking for comparison to dried fruit, the best description was, eyes like prunes. But could not say that as prunes had unfortunate connotations, putting everyone in mind of old folk in homes, getting stewed prunes and custard to keep them 'regular'. However, once I had thought it, couldn't stop thinking of him as Prune Eyes. Ol' Prune Eyes, even.)

Asked him, 'What's soup of the day?'

'Mushroom.'

'Is it lumpy?'

'No.'

'Okay. And a glass of red wine.'

'Merlot?'

'Grand.'

20.25

Finished my dinner. (After the soup of the day, had had the cheesecake of the day – strawberry.) I was standing outside the Oak, wondering what to do next.

I could go for walk. It was a beautiful bright evening and there was a lovely beach down there. I could blow away the cobwebs, as people might say. (Actually don't like that saying. Makes me think of spiders. Will not say it again.) Or I could get a DVD. Yes, I decided. Would get a DVD.

20.29

Supermarket

Wide choice of DVDs. Boy and girl behind the counter (name badges: Kelly and Brandon) tried to help me.

'Wedding Crashers is good,' Kelly said. Quite a stout girl. Looked like she enjoyed chips. (Indeed, who doesn't?) Poker-straight, stripey blonde hair. Pink trackie bottoms pulled very low. Two inches of belly rolling over waistband.

49

Gold bar through belly button, acrylic French manicure. Tacky, yet admired her confidence.

'Not *Wedding Crashers*,' I said.

'Like your highlights.'

'Thank –'

'Did you *do* them yourself?'

'No. Er . . . no. In hairdresse –'

'Like your jacket. Where d'you get it? Topshop?'

'. . . No . . . Got it in work.'

'Where d'you work?'

'. . . Work for self.'

'How much was it?'

'. . . Well, got it on discount . . .'

'How much would it be before the discount?'

'. . . Not really sure.'

Was plenty sure, but it was expensive. I was too ashamed to say the price.

'Shut up,' Brandon said. Like Kelly, he obviously took an interest in his appearance. Neck-chains, rings, blond hair in Tintin quiff, yellowish tinge to it, probably the result of a home-bleach job, but applauded his efforts.

'How about *Lord of the Rings*?' he asked. 'We have special extended versions.'

'No. Good film, am not saying it's not, but . . .'

'What you in the mood for?'

'Need cheering up.'

'Why?' Kelly asked.

Cripes, so nosy!

'Wee . . . lll,' I said, suddenly mad keen to talk about Paddy. 'My boyfriend is getting married to someone else.'

'Okay,' Kelly said, contrarily refusing to take the bait. 'What about *Sleepless in Seattle*? That's sappy.'

Frustrated! Hadn't wanted to discuss cost of jacket but wanted to splurge info about Paddy.

'Or *One Fine Day*. Also sappy. You could have a good cry.'

'No!' Brandon said. 'Get revenge film! *Kill Bill*. *Dirty Harry*.'

'*Dirty Harry*,' I cried. 'Perfect!'

23.08

Dirty Harry is a marvellous film! Was exactly what I'd wanted. There's a great bit when he gets revenge.

At one stage I looked up from Clint Eastwood and out through the back window of Uncle Tom's cabin and for a moment thought there was great big Berocca tablet in the sky. Bright orange and looked like it was fizzing, infusing the sky with health-giving vitamin B. The sunset! Suddenly glad I had come to this place. Had learnt to appreciate the beauty of nature.

Quite nice evening. Thought about Paddy non-stop, but only picked up the phone to ring him four times.

23.31

Bedtime. Afraid I wouldn't sleep, so took two NatraCalms and turned off the light.

23.32

Turned on the light. Took half a Zimovane (a real sleeping tablet jam-packed with chemicals, not some namby-pamby herbal malarkey). Would be terrible if I couldn't sleep. No point risking it. Turned off the light.

23.33

Turned on the light. Took the other half of the Zimovane. Couldn't take a chance on not sleeping. Turned off the light. Pulled the fake patchwork quilt up to my chin and snuggled into the pillow. Now that I was doped up to the gills, I was looking forward to a lovely night's sleep.

23.34

Very quiet in the country. Nice. Soothing.

23.35

Comforting. Not sinister.

23.36

Calming. Not a bit sinister.

23.37

Is sinister! Too quiet out there. Menacing. Like the fields are planning to ambush me while I'm asleep! Turn the light back on. My heart was pounding. Needed something to read but was too afraid to go downstairs for my *InStyle*. Bookshelf in room with ancient paperback books. Thrillers by someone called Margery Allingham. Picked *The Fashion for Shrouds*, because about fashion designer in 1930s. Although book gone a bit damp, enjoyed it very much. Everyone in story wore hats. No one wears hats any more. Tragic. March of modernity.

Thursday, 4 September 9.07

Woken up by silence. Is very disruptive. Never thought would miss drunken men grunting and wrestling outside window. Life full of surprises.

Mattress feels filled with tennis balls. How *did* people cope in olden days? Different value systems. Community and wearing hats and children being able to walk to school by themselves. No value put on high-grade mattress, nice sheets, nice pillows.

Lean over the side of the bed and grab copy of VIP and stare, for millionth time, at Paddy, with his grin and his tennis racket, and am astonished by how wholesome he looks. Cripes, if only they knew . . .

Trip down memory lane

Last year, Sunday in April, blustery and cold. I was visiting Mum's grave. Perched on little kerb, talking to her, telling how job was going, how Dad was – just a general catch-up, really. Funnily enough was in middle of telling her that still hadn't a boyfriend, not since gave Malachy the elbow for wanting me to be thinner (photographer, spent too much time hanging around with models), when noticed someone a few rows over, looking at me. A man. Not my type. Too grown-up. Tall. Sober, single-breasted, navy overcoat, cashmere/wool mix (at quick glance), holding armload of technicolour-yellow daffodils. Dark hair, a bit bouffed (although that could have been by-product of windy day).

Instantly felt touchy. I mean, was graveyard. If you couldn't talk to your dead mother there, where could you talk to her?

'Mum,' I said, 'there's some bloke over there watching me talking to you. Rude!'

In my head her voice said, 'Maybe he isn't looking at you. Maybe he's staring into space. Give people a chance.'

I looked again. He was definitely watching me and I got

sudden flash of his hair slick and flat with sweat, as result of having sex with me.

Sacrilegious! In graveyard. But suppose it makes sense – sex and death.

'Well?' Mum asked.

'Er . . . is fine . . .'

Eventually said goodbye to Mum and walked towards exit. Had to pass Overcoat Man to get to main path and although not normally the type who challenges people, was defensive over dead mother. When I reached him, I stopped and said, 'I'm only talking to a marble headstone because I have no choice. I'd prefer it if she was alive, you know.'

'Your mother?'

'Yes.'

'Me too.'

Suddenly didn't feel touchy any longer, but sad. Sad for both of us.

'Didn't mean to make you uncomfortable,' he said.

'Well you did.'

He had strewn his mother's grave with daffodils and don't know why, but it touched me. Man like him could have (judging from quality of overcoat) bought big exotic bouquet, orchids and lilies and similar, but daffodils humble flower.

He said, 'I thought it was . . . good . . . you could talk so freely . . .' He paused, looked down, then looked up again, causing maximum impact with blue eyes. He said, 'I envied you.'

11.08
I opened front door and took deep inhale of fresh country air. Smelt of cow-shite. Five red and white cows in nearby field lazily flicking tails at me. Culprits.

Walked round to back of house and there was wild Atlantic. Waves and swelling and white bits and sun glinting. Smell of ozone and salt and all that. Gazed upon nature and beauty and everything and thought, I miss shops.

Was no good. Mistake coming here. Had no one to talk to, no telly to watch. Too much time on my hands to think about Paddy.

Should have done bunk to exciting, lively place, like New York, with its many distractions. But New York hotels expensive. Uncle Tom's cabin is free.

Texted Bridie:

Lonely. Mght cum hme.

Reply:

Frst day alwys hrdest. Stik wth it!

11.40

Ringing clients all morning, explaining 'out of circulation' for couple of weeks. Leaving them 'in capable hands' of Nkechi. Some happy enough with it. But others not. Afraid of Nkechi. SarahJane Hutchinson point-blank refuses to have any dealings with her.

Made self walk into town. Could have driven, but only five minutes' walk. Shameful to drive. Also remember what shrink used to say after Mum died. Best way to keep depression at bay is to get out and about and take short walk. Quite funny really when you think about it. Because when you're depressed, the last thing you want to do is get out and about and take short walk. Tablets far better.

11.42

Strangest thing. Beautiful really. Tramping into town in pastel wellingtons, nearing next-door-neighbour's cottage, when through small window in the side of house, high up under the roof, caught a glimpse of sparkles and shine.

Stopped. Twisted head. Something about the direction of the window — it faced almost towards the sea — meant it was unlikely passers-by would see in. (Hard to describe. Not good at things like that. A man-type 200-yards-style description.) I had been at peculiarly angled bend in road and just got lucky.

Next thing, I saw woman in a wedding dress twirling around and around! Smooth, shiny, white satin, tight bodice, wide skirt, not risible meringue, but like exaggerated A-line, if you can imagine. Like upside-down cone. Almost certain was a Vera Wang. Arresting image. Despite self's tragic circumstances, couldn't help but be happy for her beauty and evident happiness.

White elbow gloves. Elaborate diamanté choker — might have been Swarovski, but couldn't be certain at this distance. Stunning dark hair, thick and long and smooth, swinging as she twirled, perfect little tiara perched on crown of head.

She came right up to window, mouthing words — probably practising vows — chatting away to herself, good old chinwag, then she did that thing people do in films when they suddenly realize they are standing on a crocodile. She froze, slid eyes downwards very, very slooooowly until got to my level, when she forced herself to look at me, standing in road, gazing up at her, like supplicant. Even though still too far away to be able to say if choker was Swarovski, no denying the shock, horror even, on her face. She backed away from the window as if on castors. Why? What is big secret?

I remained rooted in place, wondering if she would reappear, until farmer chugging along in tractor emitting evil-smelling black smoke, shouted, 'Out of the way, Jackeen!' and tried to run me off the road.

11.49
Internet café

Have BlackBerry, no real need to go to internet café but, honest admission, wanted reason to talk to someone.

Inside was a girl, smoking a cigarette, sitting on a stool, legs crossed elegantly. Very short dark hair, like Jean Seberg in *À Bout de Souffle*. Few faces can take haircut that severe. Beautiful pointy eyebrows. Dark red lipstick. Matte. Interesting choice in these glossy times.

I said, 'Er . . . hello.'

''Ello.'

She had to be French. That or cockney.

Clothes simple but beautiful. Black polo-neck, black and white skirt, almost puffball, but pulling back just at vital moment. Wide belt tight around waist. Black ballet slippers. Understated but chic. French women simply have knack. Like Irish people are skilled at being great craic and getting green freckles instead of tan.

Said, 'Can I use internet?'

'*Certainement,*' she said. 'Work away.'

Asked her, 'You local girl?' (Knew she wasn't. A conversational pretext.)

'*Non. De France.*'

Can understand now why girl in DVD shop was so forward

last night. Only way to get kicks around here is to poke nose into other people's lives.

Said, 'I love France! In fact, *j'aime* France!'

Hoped we could talk about shops in Paris. But she wasn't from Paris. From somewhere called Beaune. Never heard of it but she seemed proud. That is French people for you. They are proud of being French, smoke Gauloises and are excellent at going on strike. Sometimes whole country does it.

Introduced myself. Hoped not coming across as too desperate.

She said, '*Bonjour, Lola. Je m'appelle Cecile.*'

Asked, 'Why you live here, Cecile?'

Reason? A man.

'Am crazy in love,' she said. 'He is surfer.'

'What is name?'

'Zoran.'

'Irish?' Thinking, Can't be.

'No. Serbian. Lives here now.'

Only one email of interest. From Nkechi. She has per-suaded woman who imports Roberto Cavalli to Ireland to sell to 'us' exclusively. Is good news. Excellent news, really. All Irish women hot for Cavalli will have to be styled by me — or 'us' as Nkechi so ominously put it. Cripes. Have only been gone a day and already she is taking over the world.

12.16

The Oak

Same barman as last night. Ol' Prune Eyes. Asked him, 'What is soup of day?'

'Mushroom.'

'Okay. And cup coffee.'

'Latte? Cappuccino? Espresso?'

'Er . . . latte.'

'Soy milk? Skinny?'

'Er . . . skinny.'

Not expecting so much choice.

Found self asking, 'So, where you from?'

Cripes! Have become irritating person who instigates conversation with everyone she meets, which I so am not. In Dublin, make point of principle to talk to as few people as possible. Especially when buying things. Have you noticed lately how shop assistants have been told to say validating bon mot about purchase when wrapping it? They say, 'Gorgeous colour!' Or, 'Beautiful, isn't it?'

Always find self wanting to say, 'Actually no, dislike colour very much. One of least favourites.'

I mean, would hardly buy it if didn't like it!

But they are just doing their job. Not their fault.

'From Egypt,' Ol' Prune Eyes said.

Egypt! Multinational! Is like cast of *Lost* here in Knockavoy!

'You are long way from home!' Thinking, What a stupid thing to say. Sound like wolf in *Little Red Riding Hood*.

Then I say, 'You must miss warm weather.' Thinking, That is also stupid thing to say, and bet everyone says it.

'Yes,' he says. 'That is what everyone says. But more to life than weather.'

'Like what?' Suddenly curious.

He laughed. 'Like three meals a day. Like freedom from political persecution. Like opportunity to provide for family.'

'Right,' I say. 'I see your point.'

Feel bit better. Have connected with another human being.

Warmish glow interrupted by man at the end of the bar –

slumped, unkempt creature – calling, 'Osama! Enough of chat! Where's my pint?'

I asked, 'Is your name really Osama?'

Thinking, Cripes! That would be hard cross to bear. Even worse than Ol' Prune Eyes. No wonder he got political persecution!

'No. Is Ibrahim. Osama nickname from locals.'

Late afternoon

Walked home by seafront. Passed funny old house. Houses on either side had been modernized – PVC windows, fresh paint – but this one was weather-beaten and sort of slumped-looking. Faded blue paint on front door was coming off in handfuls. Reminded me of time I'd had chemical peel. On window sill, sea anemones, pebbles, sand, periwinkles. No curtains, so could see right into front room. Fishing nets hanging from ceiling, starfish shells, conches, driftwood pieces like sculpture. Name of house, 'The Reef'.

Magical place. Wanted to go in there.

18.03

Mobile rang. Recognized number: Grace Gildee, charismatic journalist woman. Was stalking me! Threw mobile into handbag as if red-hot. Get away, get away, get away! Ten seconds later, double beep of message. Get away, get away, get away!

Deleted message without listening. Afraid. Obviously no one can make self talk if self doesn't want to talk. But still afraid. Grace Gildee pushy, persuasive, determined. Also – possibly – nice.

20.08

Grocery-cum-newsagent-cum-DVD-shop

Brandon and Kelly on duty again. On Brandon's recommen-
dation, got *The Godfather*. Kelly tried to steer self in direction of *Starsky & Hutch*. She said, 'Two hunks like them,
they'll take your mind off your fella getting married to someone else. So did he tell you to your face?'

She was agog to hear and I was agog to tell. As soon as
I said, 'Paddy de Courcy,' she exclaimed, 'I know that name!
Politician man, yes? I've seen him! In *VIP*! Get it!' She directed
Brandon to the magazine rack. 'Go on, get it, get it!'

She *devoured* pictures. Made many comments. Said
Paddy was 'way lush' 'for older man' and Alicia was 'minger'.
Brandon said Alicia was 'bowler', word I hadn't come across
before. Learnt it means same thing as minger. Increase
your wordpower. Both of them very impressed that my ex-
boyfriend was in a celebrity magazine, even if it was only an
Irish one.

'Anything about him in *Heat*?' Kelly asked. 'Or *Grazia*?'

'No.'

'Well, sure, never mind. And you knew nothing about the
other woman? Nothing AT ALL?'

I shook head.

'I'd have killed him,' she marvelled. 'Killed him with my bare
hands.'

'You could just sit on him,' Brandon said, with unexpected
venom. 'That'd do the trick. Not many men would survive
being sat on by your arse.'

She responded with gusto. 'All you'd have to do is breathe
on someone!'

Revised original assessment that Brandon and Kelly were
boyfriend and girlfriend. Brother and sister, more likely.

'And now you're down here in Tom Twoomey's house nursing a broken heart.'

'We get a fair bit of that,' Brandon said. 'Women. Arriving here. With broken hearts. Don't know why. Maybe they think the waves will fix them. Walking the beach twenty times a day. Often they go exploring up on sand dunes. Don't realize they're owned by golf club. Suddenly find themselves in middle of the eleventh hole, balls whizzing past their heads. Escorted off in buggy. Usually very upset.'

'Very upset,' Kelly said.

Strange pause ensued. Then both of them convulsing with laughter.

'Sorry,' Brandon said, shaking with mirth. 'Is just ... is just –'

'– they think they're being all soulful,' Kelly said, face contorted from laughing. 'Communing with nature ... and then ... and then ... they nearly get brained by golf ball ...'

'Have no intention of walking on any beach or up any sand dunes,' I said coldly.

Is not nice to laugh at heartbroken women.

Abruptly they stopped laughing. Cleared their throats. Kelly said, 'You might start painting. Getting all that heartbreak out of your system.'

'Really?'

'Oh yes, happens a lot. Painting.'

'Or poetry,' Brandon interjected.

'Or pottery.'

'But mostly painting. Let's face it, better than cutting off your man's lad with a bread knife.' Brandon gave Kelly meaningful look.

'What?' She turned and yelled into his face, 'That was an ACCIDENT!'

Then to me, 'We have crayons and copybooks, but if you need proper paints and all, there's shop in Ennistymon.' (Ennistymon nearest proper town.)

No intention of starting painting.

Or poetry.

Or pottery.

Things bad enough.

23.59

Godfather marvellous film. Simply chock full of revenge. And quite fancy Al Pacino. Hopeful sign. All evening only picked up the phone to ring Paddy three times. Or thrice, if you prefer. Like that word. Got it in Margery Allingham book.

0.37

'Turned in' as they say in Margery Allingham. Strange saying. But so are many sayings when think about it. Example, 'Don't go there!' That is very odd saying, unless you are talking about Afghanistan, or Topshop on Saturday afternoon, two weeks before Christmas.

2.01

Jerked awake, in the absolute horrors. Gripped by terrible compulsion to get into car and drive straight across country to Dublin, to find Paddy and beg him to be with me. Began flinging things into bag. Heart pounding. Mouth dry. Waking nightmare. He was getting married to someone else? But that couldn't be!

Should I have shower? No. Should I get dressed? No. No, yes. What if I actually found him? Couldn't be like an asylum escapee in my pyjamas. What should I wear? Couldn't decide.

Couldn't decide. Muzzy from sleeping tablet but thoughts going too fast. Whizzing past before could snag one.

Bumped first bag down stairs. Must go to bathroom to collect things. No. Leave them. Who cares? It's just stuff. Opened front door, cool night air, flung bag into car boot, back into house for other bag.

But by the time I was lugging second bag down stairs, my heartbeat had slowed. Thoughts more ordered. Saw my lunacy. Pointless driving to Dublin. He wouldn't see me. That had been his plan all along and was hardly likely to change his mind now.

I sat on front step in my pyjamas, staring out at darkness. Fields out there, couldn't see them.

Trip down memory lane

Funny thing is, when first met Paddy de Courcy in graveyard, didn't think would end up falling for him. So not my type. Previous boyfriend, Malachy the photographer, very different. Small, neat, sparkly-eyed charmer. Loved women, women loved him back. Charmed models like Zara Kaletsky into doing mad poses for him. (In fact, that was how I met Malachy. I was Zara's stylist until she left Ireland so abruptly. She fixed us up.)

Malachy not very hairy. But, as I was buffeted by icy winds that day in the cemetery, I could tell simply by looking at Paddy de Courcy's overcoat that he would have hairy chest. Picking up on subliminal signs. Dark raspy stubble on jaw. Backs of hands scattered with dark hairs. (Not like woolly mammoth King Kong paws – nice coverage.) Smooth hair-free chest simply wouldn't fit.

He asked, 'Do you come here often?'

I said, 'Do I come here often?' I surveyed marble slabs of

death stretching out in all directions. Just goes to show, you can meet a man *anywhere*. 'About once a month.'

'This is slightly unorthodox . . .' he said. 'Graveyard and all that . . . Could come back in a month's time hoping to bump into you, or . . . would you like to come for hot chocolate now?'

Clever. Hot chocolate the one thing — the *only* thing — I would have accepted. Safe. Totally different if he'd invited me for alcoholic drink. Or, indeed, cup of tea. Alcoholic drink — lecherous sleaze. Cup of tea — dullard with mother fixation.

Went to pub across road (Gravediggers Arms) where drank hot chocolate with marshmallows and reminisced about dead mothers.

He said, 'Every time something good happens to me, I want to tell her, and every time something bad happens, I want her help.'

Knew *exactly* how he felt. We were both fifteen when our mums died. Was nice — glorious relief, actually — to meet someone who had lost their mum the same age I had. Talked openly, compared feelings, was drawn to him but didn't fancy him. Actually felt I was almost doing him a favour, spending time with him, so he could talk about his mother.

He said, 'Probably in bad taste, considering where we met, but any chance I could see you again? Promise I won't talk about my mother the next time.'

I retreated against upholstery. Assailed by image of him looming over me, him naked, hairy-chested, hard-on in hand. My stomach did unpleasant squeeze. Excitement? Possibly not. Maybe nausea. He wasn't my type. I thought he looked too old, also (shallow, shallow! Yes, I know) I didn't like his clothes. Too buttoned-up, too safe. But why not give it a try?

65

Wrote my phone number on ancient cinema stub.

He looked at it. Said, 'Mission Impossible? Any good?'

'You didn't see it?'

'Never get time to go to pictures.'

'Why not?'

'Am politician. Deputy leader of NewIreland. Full-on job.'

Felt had better ask him his name – is what you have to do when people say they are writer or actor or – yes – politician. Almost as if they are angling to be asked.

'Paddy de Courcy.'

Nodded and said, 'Mmmm,' to disguise fact had never heard of him.

He watched me shoot past in my red Mini, admiration in his eyes. I looked at him in rear-view. Even from distance could see blueness of his eyes. Coloured contact lenses? No. Coloured contact lenses make eyes strangely starey and dead-looking. Wearers look like aliens. Sometimes clients take a notion to wear them for big night out. ('I fancy being a green-eyed temptress tonight.') I always talk them out of it. Tacky. Very . . . Mariah Carey.

Wondered if Paddy de Courcy would call. Wasn't sure he would. Suspected he might be married. Also we weren't, on the face of it, a likely match. I had red Mini Cooper, he had navy Saab. I had sharp-cut, wide-lapelled, teal jacket, he had sober navy overcoat. I had angular Louise Brooks bob and Chiarascuro highlights (colour before Molichino), he had bouffy hair.

Didn't Google him. That's how interested I wasn't.

Early next morning my mobile rang. I didn't recognize number but answered because could be new client. Some woman said, 'I'm calling from Paddy de Courcy's office.

Mr de Courcy was wondering if you are free this evening. He will pick you up at seven p.m. I need your address please.'

I was startled into silence. Then laughed. Said, 'No.'

'No, what?'

'No, not giving address. Who's he think he is?'

Her turn to be startled. Said, 'Is Paddy de Courcy!'

'If Mr de Courcy wants to make arrangement with me, Mr de Courcy can pick up phone and call me himself.'

'. . . Yes . . . but Ms Daly, Mr de Courcy very busy man . . .'

Understand busyness. Most of my clients very busy people and usually clients' assistant, rather than clients themselves, call to set up styling appointment. But that was *work*. This was *not* work.

'Must go now,' I said. 'Thank you. Nice talking to you. Goodbye.' (Costs nothing to be polite. Also she might want to be styled at some time in the future.)

I wasn't even indignant. Simply realized had been right to think he wasn't my type. Maybe that is how some people live their lives, getting their assistants to set up romantic assignations. Perhaps it is considered perfectly fine in certain circles.

I didn't expect him to ring back and I really didn't care. When think now of the risk I ran, I go hot and cold all over. Could have blithely thrown it all away. Over before it ever started. Then realize it's all over anyway, and maybe would have been better off being spared the pain. But couldn't imagine not having had him in my life. Was the most intense experience. The most intense man. Most beautiful, most sexy.

Anyway, a few minutes later, he *did* call. Laughing. Apologizing for being arrogant asshole.

I said, 'You politicians have totally lost touch with reality.' (Light-hearted tone. Banter.)

'No, haven't.'

'Oh really? If so, tell me price of litre of milk?' (Once, by accident, saw programme where minister of something was shamed for not knowing that. Actually felt quite sorry for him. Not so sure of price myself. But could tell you to the nearest euro, exact cost of entire Chloé collection. Wholesale, discounted and full retail. We all have our gifts.)

Paddy de Courcy said, 'Don't know. Don't drink milk.'

'Why so? Too busy?'

He laughed. Banter going well.

I said, 'No milk on your cereal?'

'Don't eat cereal.'

'What you have for breakfast?'

Pause. Then he said, 'Would you like to find out?'

Cheesy. Remembered his bouffy hair. Didn't want to banter any longer.

'Sorry,' he said. Sounded humbled, then he asked, 'You free this evening?'

'No.' (Was, but really . . .)

'How about tomorrow . . . uh, no, can't do tomorrow. Or Wednesday. Just a minute,' he said, then called to someone, 'Stephanie, can you get me out of that thing with Brazilians on Thursday?' Then he was back. 'Thursday?'

'Let me look at appointments.' I checked, then said, 'Yes, okay for Thursday evening.'

'Thursday it is,' he said. 'I'll pick you up. Seven?'

What was this thing with seven? Why so early?

'I'll book couple of tables for dinner and you can choose.'

Bridled at way he was calling all the shots, then . . . don't know . . . stopped bridling, is best way to put it.

'Just one thing,' I said. 'You married?'

'Why? You offering?'

Further cheesiness. I said, 'Yes or no? Married or not?'

'Not.'

'Fine.'

'Really looking forward to seeing you,' he said.

'. . . Yes, me too.'

But wasn't sure I was. And when I climbed into the back of his car and he was Mr Grown-up in his suit and briefcase, I thought, Oh no, terrible mistake. Stomach did that rolling, tilty nausea thing again. And, of course, things got worse in the shop. But then . . . undressing for him . . . everything changed. Started to really fancy him. Never looked back.

Friday, 5 September 12.19

Woke up. Had gone back to bed around 6 a.m., when sun was rising.

No longer felt crazed desperation for Paddy. Simply felt of no value. Wasn't good enough for him. Not good enough for anyone.

13.53

Walked into town. Sea mist hanging in air, playing merry hell with hair.

When I reached special spot on bend of road, stopped and gazed up at next-door's window, hoping to see woman in wedding dress. Intrigued. In fact, maddened with curiosity. But no sign of her.

14.01

The Oak

Soup of day, mushroom. Beginning to wonder if any other kind. Cheesecake of day, strawberry. Ditto.

15.05

Internet café

Thought would visit couple of nice sites. Net-a-porter. LaRedoute. Gazing upon beautiful things might bring sparkle back into world. But café closed! Crooked handwritten sign said, 'Gone to lunch.' Annoyed. These French people with their lunch hours! Stomped off towards home. Decided on seafront route, to get little infusion of magic house, and who did I see, outside magic house, only Cecile! Hooked by her knees, she was hanging upside down on the railings overlooking the waves, giggling with three surf boys in wetsuits.

Her skirt was up around her shoulders, as result of gravity. Her knickers on show. Cute. Cotton. White with red poppies and red trim. Nice for her to be so uninhibited. Actually no . . . not really a good thing. Was uncomfortable with her exhibitionism . . . we're not on Côte d'Azur now.

Semi-circle of surf boys. General impression of wet sand, large bare male feet, tangled salty hair, surfboards, wetsuits unzipped, smooth bare chests, eyes bright from salt water, thin chains around tanned throats, tiny gold rings through male eyebrows. Couldn't tell any of them apart, just generic cluster of young male yumminess.

'Cecile?' I asked.

'*Oui?*'

'Are you on your lunch break?'

'*Oui.*'

'When will it finish?'

Even hanging upside down, she managed Gallic shrug. 'I cannot say.' She giggled, giving one of surf boys a minxy glance.

Front door of magic house slightly ajar. Glimpse of bare, faded floorboards, old-fashioned banisters, white paint flaking, leading up the stairway to a magic bedroom.

Cecile would be going into magic house to have sex with one of surf boys. Terrible pang. Jealousy. Loneliness. For things lost and things never had. Wished I was young. Wished I was beautiful. Wished I was French.

19.57

Trying alternative bars to Oak. Cannot face another bowl of mushroom soup. Also didn't want to get too dependent on the Oak. It might burn down or something and where would that leave me? Look what happened the last time I depended on someone (Paddy).

Stuck my head into golfing bar, called Hole in One, or some such dreadful golfing pun. Couldn't go in. Packed to gills with men (and one or two women who should have known better) exchanging posh insults about how badly the other man played. (You know how men are. Can only bond by being horrible.) Noisy. Shouty. Rawlrawlrawl. Like politicians in Dail. And such bad clothing! Yellow sweaters. Spats. Visors! I ask you. Not even useful, not in Ireland, not enough sun. Is . . . is . . . *wilful bad taste.*

Tried Butterly's. Very small place. Size of a front room. Flagstoned floors, bare wooden counter, three high stools at it. Small television on overhead shelf. Smiley old woman behind bar, looking keen as mustard. (Margery Allingham phrase.) Otherwise place empty. Wanted to back out, saying, 'Sorry, looking for chemist! My mistake!' But was too polite.

71

Did running jump, like pole vaulter, to seat self on high stool. (Can't abide high stools, so uncomfortable. Too high, to begin with, and nothing to hold on to, nothing to support your back, nothing for your feet. You are quite adrift. Breakfast bars, there they are again! Why would I choose to start my day wobbling atop a high stool when could sit on a normal-height chair? And why only for *breakfast*?)

Butterly's was the oddest-looking bar had ever seen, offering most peculiar selection of drinks – all seemed to be sweet sticky liqueurs. Also sundry other items for sale, to wit: cans of marrowfat peas, boxes of matches, packets of instant custard. Like when playing shop when small. (All same, might be handy to know. Some night, might be halfway through glass of red wine and get sudden unbearable craving for custard, which needed immediate gratification.) (Sarcastic.)

The old woman was Mrs Butterly herself. Nice to be in proprietor-run establishment. Extremely chatty. Said the bar was her parlour and she only opened it when she felt like company and closed it again when she didn't.

Though my hopes weren't high, I asked, 'Do you do food?'

She pointed at strange collection behind bar.

'I meant . . . something . . . could eat now.'

Had horrible fear she would offer to heat up can of marrowfat peas. Even *look* of marrowfat peas makes me want to take my own life.

'Could make you little sandwich. Will see what's in fridge.'

She disappeared into other room, presume it was kitchen. Returned with processed ham piece between two slices of woolly white bread. In strange, retro way, quite satisfying. When I finished, she made us both a cup of tea and produced a packet of Hobnobs.

I tried purchase a glass of red wine but she said, 'Don't carry wine. How about Tia Maria? Or what's this here? Cointreau?'

Closest thing to a normal drink was Southern Comfort. No ice available so had it with a dash of the flattest Sprite have ever had. From a 2-litre bottle that had been on shelf for oh, about sixty years. Not a bubble left in entire bottle.

Cajoled Mrs Butterly to join me in a drink. Invitation accepted.

Revised original impression. Mrs Butterly had woven web of charm around me. Liked it. Liked it all. Best bit of entire bar was neon green poster, saying, 'No Stag Parties!'

Stag party wouldn't fit! They would have to be refused in instalments. Would have to send delegation of two or three in to be barred, then leave and let next tranche in to be turned down.

When I was leaving, Mrs Butterly refused to take money for the food. She said, 'Only couple of Hobnobs, for the love of God.'

'But Mrs Butterly, the sandwich . . .'

'Only couple of slices of bread, for the love of God.'

Kindly. Very kindly.

But no way to run a business.

21.59
DVD shop

Wanted to ask about Kelly and the bread knife, but shop thronged. Many people visiting. Tourists for weekend, their baskets filled with frozen pizzas and six-packs of lager. I resented their presence, as if I live here.

Brandon distracted but recommended *Goodfellas*.

0.57

Enjoyed *Goodfellas*, not saying I didn't. Don't mean to be picky. Much violence, but no actual *revenge* as such.

1.01

Realization. Why I felt so comforted in Mrs Butterly's. It was the flat Sprite. Flat Sprite is a convalescent's drink. Mum used to give it to me when I was sick. She used to heat it up to cleanse it of all bubbles, so it wouldn't hurt my sore throat. Flat Sprite makes me feel loved. As no one is handy to administer it to me, will do it myself.

Saturday, 6 September 8.01

Woken by slam of next-door-neighbour's front door. I hopped from bed, into other bedroom to look out front window, hoping to see Wedding Dress girl in her civvies. But no girl, just her boyfriend – fiancé, I suppose – alone. Studied him. Interested to see what kind of man had bagged the Vera Wanged beauty. At quick glance, not exactly kempt. He would need haircut before wedding. Out-doorsy-loving-style clothing: jeans and big, thick navy fleece suitable for North Pole. Footwear, however, cause for interest: trainers in anthracite colour – in fashionista circles anthracite known as 'Black for risk-takers'. He got into car – couldn't be sure what kind it was – banged door shut, drove away.

I returned to bed.

13.10

Town busy. Day-trippers. Blue skies, sunshine, heat, weather very nice for September, apart from never-ceasing, hair-destroying wind.

My attention caught by woman on beach, walking alone. Had half-noticed her over previous few days and just knew she was one of the heartbroken painters or potters or poets. Even from distance, her face was stiff, the way heartbroken faces are. What is it about being rejected by loved ones that locks face muscles into inactivity? Special enzyme? (Possible scientific discovery. You know how dumpees don't smile? Everyone puts it down to them having nothing to smile about. But perhaps it is as result of special enzyme which means they *cannot* smile. This is the sort of discovery that wins prizes.)

20.10
DVD shop
Brandon recommended *Kill Bill*, vol. 1. Excellent. Revenge – 10 out of 10.

Sunday, 7 September
Ol' Prune Eyes is Muslim! Don't know why I'm so surprised. He is from Egypt, which believe has large Muslim population. Suppose I didn't think devout Muslim would work in pub. Den of alcohol.

He made casual reference to praying towards Mecca and I asked, 'You Muslim?'

And he said, 'Yes.'

No big deal but am suddenly uncomfortable ordering glass of wine from him. Feel he is thinking, Stinking Whore. Whore of the Infidel.

Also ashamed of my beloved Molichino highlights. Not only have I my hair on display but am drawing attention to it with lovely highlights. He is very friendly – seems like lovely man, really — but fear he is faker and in his head he is thinking terrible things about me. Maybe even muttering under his breath. Like this . . .

'Hi, Ibrahim.'

'Ah, hello there, Lola. Stinking whore of the Infidel. How are you today?'

'Good. You?'

'Excellent. Considering I'll be going to Paradise and you haven't a hope. What can I get you?'

'Glass of Merlot please, Ibrahim.'

(Big, big smile.) 'Glass of Merlot, Lola. Filthy Western whore. You will burn in hell, you alcohol-drinking, pork-eating, bare-haired unbeliever. Coming right up!'

Am I racist? Or am I only saying what everyone is thinking? The way everyone used to think all Irish people were IRA bombers. 'Hello, yes, Paddy, come in, sit down, have a cup of Earl Grey. Tell me, were you good at chemistry at school?'

Don't want to be racist. But undeniable clash in value system. I like Merlot. Muslims disapprove of Merlot. Would not refuse person a job because they didn't like Merlot. Would not refuse person citizenship. But want to enjoy Merlot. Don't want to feel afraid that I will burn in hell if have glass with my lunch.

Is it better to acknowledge how uncomfortable Ibrahim makes me? Or just pretend all is fine, no difference between me and him? What is best way to handle multicultural society? Nkechi's big bottom, Ibrahim's Armageddon. Such lofty worries. Cripes, don't know. Exhausting, whole bloody thing.

14.38

Cecile has taken over running boutique as well as internet café! Apparently now that season is officially over, owner of boutique (who is also owner internet café, which, don't mean to be picky, is not actually café at all, as you cannot buy anything to eat or drink) has gone off to Puerto Banus for a month and Cecile is running both all on her own. Or not running. I wanted to surf net but sign on café door saying, 'In Monique's.' And sign on Monique's door saying, 'At lunch.'

Between Cecile's double-jobbing and European-style lunch breaks, is a wonder anyone in Knockavoy gets to send any emails at all.

Trip down memory lane

Remembering my first date with Paddy. Got picked up at flat in car driven by Spanish John. Paddy sitting in the back, wearing a suit. Open briefcase on lap.

'What you like to do?' he asked. 'You hungry?'

'No, not really. Is a bit early.' (Was only 7 p.m. Unusually early for date.)

'Okay,' he said, 'let's go shopping.'

'For what?'

'Clothes.'

'For me or for you?'

I was wondering if he was trying to get styling from me on the cheap. On the free, in fact.

'For you.'

Didn't know what to say. Funny sort of date. Cannot usually make man come shopping with me for love nor money. Also had strange suspicion that this wouldn't be normal shopping.

Next thing, Spanish John opening car door, Paddy's arm

on my back, ushering me up steps, discreet dark-glass door, soft carpeting, friendly woman's voice welcoming us, feel free to browse. Thought I knew every shop in Dublin. I was wrong. Pools of light highlighting dark shiny items. Closer look. Vibrator. Black satin blindfold. Spanky device. Small onyx things thought were cufflinks, then realized were nipple clamps.

Knickers, bras, suspender belts, satin, silk, lace, leather, spandex, black, red, pink, white, blue, nude, patterned . . .

Trying to behave like woman of the world – had been in this sort of emporium before; after all, had organized two hen nights, admittedly not in place of this high quality – but had to confess, felt rather uncomfortable. Anxious. Very. Hardly what had expected from first date.

Drifted over to underwear. Expected to receive mild electric shock from shoddy man-made fibres, but quality good. Real silk, satin, lace. Actually some lovely 'pieces', as we in fashion world say (when I say that, I sound light-hearted, but believe me, was not feeling light-hearted at the time). Dark blue set embroidered with butterflies, appliquéd with feathers and diamantés. Silky mulberry and black polka-dot knickers with ribbon ties at sides. Demure pink set festooned with pink roses – not embroidered but actual little roses – on bra cups and crotch. Would look terrible under clothes. All lumpy.

Surprised to see nice plain black knickers. Completely unremarkable. Then realized they were crotchless, and jumped back as if burnt. Same with low-cut balconette bra. Seemed very low-cut, so low-cut would hardly cover nipples! Then realized – cripes! – that was the whole point.

Beside me, Paddy's voice said, 'Would you like to try any of them on?'

Froze. Stomach curdled. He was dirty pervert. Dirty pervert weirdo. Treating me as sex object. What was I doing here?

But what should I expect when I pick up man in graveyard? Hardly going to take me for pizza and Ben Stiller movie.

'Lola, are you okay? Is this okay?' He skewered me with blue gaze. Expression sympathetic, well, sympatheticish. Hint of challenge there also.

Held his look. This is the moment, I thought, where I decide to trust him, or to leave. Teetered on high wire. Looked at door. Could just go. No harm done. Would never see him again. I mean, in sex shop! On first date! I was horrified . . .

. . . but a bit excited. If left now what would I miss . . . ?

Looked back into blue gaze, may even have tilted chin upwards in attitude of slight defiance and said, 'Okay . . .'

Assistant came to help. Sort of mumsy. She looked at chest. '34B?'

'. . . Yes . . .'

'What ones you like?'

'These,' I said, pointing out pretty, most demure set could see. (Pale blue, generously cut, robust-looking crotch.)

'And maybe these,' Paddy suggested, indicating saucier stuff.

'And maybe not,' I said.

'Sure, why not try?' mumsy woman said, ferrying armload of underwear off to changing room. 'What's to be lost?'

Big changing room. Almost same size as my bedroom. Rose-coloured lighting, curly-legged brocade chair, Chinese-style wallpaper patterned with winter flowering cherry — and wire grille in wall, like in a confessional . . . What was that for?

'Would you like your friend to wait in the anteroom?' mumsy woman asked.

'An . . . teroom . . . ?'

'Yes, just here.'

She indicated a smaller room next to the changing room, with a chair in it and a grille in wall. Same grille as in my room.

'Where he can watch you,' mumsy woman said.

Cripes! Where Paddy de Courcy could sit and watch me try on underwear. Where he could observe me take off current clothes and see me naked, like in tacky peep show! Aghast. Frozen indecision seemed to last for decades, then I crumbled. In for a penny, in for a pound.

Reasons:

1) Had been waxed to kingdom come. Only hair on body below waist was small square on pubic bone reminiscent of Adolf Hitler's moustache.

2) Pink lighting flattering.

3) Didn't want to seem like prude.

4) Was undeniably excited. Conflicted but excited.

While taking off ordinary clothes I flattened self against wall, out of view of peephole. Not sure what to do. Too self-conscious to dance, also no music. Considered walking to and fro, but held back by fear I would look like animal in zoo — lion, maybe — with cabin fever. Might start wobbling head and moaning.

However, once I stepped into teetery-high pair of white fluffy mules and very flattering black silk knickers and bra, felt like a different person. Pretended Paddy de Courcy wasn't sitting in next room watching me through mesh hatch. Pretended I was on my own. (But if on own, would never lean forward and shimmy in order to shake breasts into bra. Would never lick finger then rub it against nipples so they stood out like rubber stoppers on water wings, then admire self in mirror. Ordinarily when trying on knickers, wouldn't bother running hand up and down along pubic bone, checking fit just right.)

Leisurely I changed into next set, unhooking bra and slowly removing it, sliding straps down arms, as if I had all the time in world. Next was fifties-style garter and bra, in stiff pink satin. Bra made breasts high and jutty – when leant forward could see nipples. Garter went from waist to top of legs, giving extreme hourglass curve. Rosy glow from fabric made thighs look creamy and smooth and I sat on brocade chair, liking rough feel of fabric against naked bottom. Slowly rolled silk stockings up legs and attached them to rubber suspenders on garter.

Heightened awareness of him behind grille, watching me.

Sexy. Oh so sexy.

Now and then mumsy woman popped head round door, displaying hangers. 'This lovely crotchless corset,' she said wistfully. 'Be gorgeous with thigh boots.'

Or, 'Would you like to try rubber catsuit? Red one in your size. Be gorgeous with thigh boots.'

Wanted her to go away. She was disturbing mood.

Very turned on. But turned on by self? Mad?

Tried excellent little bra made with overlapping layers of sheer fabric, like petals of flower. Opened little pearl button on cup and unpeeled petal after petal until nipple exposed. Didn't know when I'd get to final layer. As much a revelation to me as to him. When it finally appeared, I said, 'Ooh!' and looked straight at him. Saw gleam of his eyes in dark room looking back at me and that was it. I was overtaken by unendurable desire and brought matters to an abrupt close. I got dressed, my fingers shaking, wondering how soon I could have sex with him.

When I bolted out of changing room, Paddy asked, 'Which ones you like?'

Quickly I shook head. Prices out of my league.

'Let me,' he said.

'No!' Felt like kept woman, mistress, prostitute, all those things.

'I insist,' he said.

'You insist?'

'Please,' he said. 'Let me. I'm one who'll benefit.'

'You're taking a lot for granted!'

He was mortified. Caught out. Apologized profusely. Sounded sincere. Offered again to buy them. 'For you,' he said. 'Not for me. How about it?'

Still uncomfortable. Felt wrong. Didn't like it. But, in strange, messy mix, also liked it.

So I let him.

Later (in bed, as happened) said to him, 'You took a big risk. What if I'd been offended?'

'Then you wouldn't have been the girl I'd thought you were.'

'What kind is that?'

'Dirty little girl.'

Wasn't sure that I was, had always suspected I was bit of a prude, but nice of him to say so.

Monday, 8 September

Serendipity! Happenstance! At 7.25 p.m. popped into Mrs Butterly's for some healing flat Sprite and she said, 'Do you mind if I put on telly?'

Next thing, she put on *Coronation Street*! My favourite! When it finished at 8 p.m. she switched over to *EastEnders* – my other favourite! Then at 8.30 put on *Holby City*. Hospital soap. Never seen it before but prepared to love it.

Veritable orgy of soaps, washed down with Southern Comfort and flat Sprite. Enjoyed it hugely. You'd swear I hadn't seen proper telly for months!

Mrs Butterly said she had developed a fondness for me and issued an open soap invitation for any night. Then asked me to leave, she wanted to go to bed.

'Anything else I can get for you, Lola, before I shut up?'

In rush of goodwill, I said, 'Ah sure, I'll take a packet of custard.'

21.03

Wandered slightly aimlessly round town, carrying my custard, then sat on a wall, facing towards sea. Had been in Knockavoy nearly a week and hadn't put foot on beach. Took pride in this. Had retained sense of self.

Man walking dog passed me and said, 'Evening. That's what I call a sunset.'

I replied, 'Evening, yes indeed.'

Hadn't been paying attention but now that I looked, the sun was doing its impression of a great, big, fizzy vitamin B tablet. Sky all orange. Supporting immune system.

Cripes! Just noticed. Heading in my direction was the woman I'd seen walking alone on the beach. Grey-skinned, sunken-eyed, sweats flapping against emaciated body. Been here in Knockavoy for some time judging by condition of her hair.

Instinct was to run away. But she was too near. We'd locked eyes. She was bearing down on self. Homing device.

She stopped and tried to engage me in chat about sunset. 'Beautiful, isn't it?'

'... Yes ...'

Not entirely sure what to say. I don't have those kinds of conversations — sunsets, nature, etc. Now, if it was *white Stella trouser suit* she was talking about ...

She sighed heavily. 'The sun still sets every evening. Still rises every morning. Hard to believe, isn't it?'

'... Yes ... Must be off now.'

Suspected Kelly and Brandon had told her my story and suspected she was sounding me out for membership of Heartbroken Women's gang. Didn't want to sign up. All very well for them doing painting and poetry and pottery. But not for me.

Although will never love anyone again, don't want to become bitter. Or creative.

Middle of night

Woken by ... something. What was it? Became aware of red glow beyond window. Sunrise? Instinctively knew it was too early. For moment wondered if sun had decided to pop its head back up over horizon so could do encore sunset, seeing as people so pleased with it first time round.

Looked out window. Behind house and also sort of behind next-door was semi-circle of red. Flames. A fire!

Should have rung fire brigade but instead decided to investigate. Such nosiness. Proof of danger of being without distraction of telly! Would never 'investigate' anything in Dublin.

Wellingtons, big mohair jumper over pyjamas. Torch. Out into chilly night.

Ducked under wire fence thing and tramped through field.

Moon spreading reflection across vast area of sea, lighting up whole area. Grass smelt nice at night. Cows in bed.

Not out-of-control fire. Simply bonfire. But unattended. How very strange. Got closer. Sudden shock. Fire being fuelled by clothes! Black tulle, blue taffeta, all melting. Then horrors! White satin! The wedding dress! Not the wedding dress! Tried to pull it from flames but shower of sparks jumped out at me and heat too great.

Distressed. It pains self to see clothes being abused. (Yes! Also pains self to see children and animals abused! Of course! Am not total shallow fashion type. Care VERY MUCH about children and animals, so much so have to change channel when sad ads come on.)

Had burny thought. If beautiful painting gets knife stuck in it by madman, everyone appalled. Experts come on telly to talk about it. But if perfect frock – which is also work of art – is destroyed, no one comes on telly to protest. Is discrimination. Is because perfect frock is girly concern, whereas paintings are serious, manly stuff, even when done by women.

Sound of approaching feet. Frightened. Who was coming? Outline gradually appeared through flickering gloom. It was the unkempt fiancé carrying an armload of clothes. Was it light from flames causing his eyes to shine or was he – horrors – crying?

Alerted him to my presence by saying, 'Ahem! Hello.'

'Jesus Christ!' He nearly dropped his bundle. 'Where the hell did you come from?'

'Sorry,' I said. 'But saw flames. Worried was a fire.'

He stared at me. Attitude brooding. Stamped on his fizzog was weary question: If a man can't burn a load of lovely clothes in middle of night, when can he burn them?

'I'm staying in Tom Twoomey's for while. Am Lola Daly.'

Unfriendly pause. 'Rossa Considine. Didn't mean to cause scare. Should have warned you but was spur-of-moment thing . . .'

Mealy-mouthed apology.

'What's going on?' I asked. 'There was a woman . . . in a wedding dre –'

'She's gone.' Abrupt.

'Will she be . . . coming back?' (Stupid question, not very likely when her wedding dress was being torched.)

He shook head. Mood dark. 'Nope. Not coming back.'

Awkward pause. He gave bundle in arms a little shake. Clearly he was itching to get on with his burning.

'Well, I'll get back to bed, then.'

'Okay. 'Night.'

I tramped back through the fields. Other people have tragedies also. This poor man.

Wouldn't kill him to be civil, though.

Tuesday, 9 September 8.00

Woken by slamming of front door (not mine). Hopped out of bed and into front bedroom. Stared out window. There was Firestarter in his anthracite trainers, going to work. No scorch marks or black stains on fizzog to indicate he had caused conflagration only hours previously.

Still cannot identify the make of his car.

18.47

Kelly and Brandon ARE girlfriend and boyfriend! Could have sworn they hated each other! Plucked up courage to ask what had happened with the bread knife.

They'd had sex, Kelly said, then a fight. Brandon was lying on the couch with his willy out in post-coital repose.

I asked, 'Whose couch?'

'My parents',' Kelly said.

'And where were they?'

'In armchairs beside the couch, watching *Winning Streak.*'

'Were they?'

'Got you there! No! They were upstairs asleep in bed, where else? Would hardly be doing it with them in the room. If I got caught, my dad would KILL Brandon. Anyway, for a joke I got bread knife from kitchen to pretend was going to chop off Brandon's willy.'

As you do.

'But I tripped coming back into sitting room and accidentally got tiny, tiny cut on his lad. *Tiny* cut. He went MENTALIST, said was bleeding to death, would get gangrene and lose lad, wanted to ring for ambulance. I couldn't stop laughing. Put a Barbie plaster on it. God, was hilarious.'

'Suppose it was really, looking back on it.' Brandon gave little chuckle.

Young love. I envy them their uncomplicated happiness.

Wednesday, 10 September 13.28
The Oak

'Hi, Ibrahim.'

'Hello there, Lola.' Stinking whore of the Infidel.

Can't shake it! Thing is, Ol' Prune Eyes is so nice. Handsome, twinkly-eyed, pleasant man. Obliging, cheerful, chatty but not pushy. But surely he must disapprove of me. I am many of the things Muslims don't like. I am independent(ish) woman. With face, hair and sometimes legs on display. Who

87

drinks alcohol. And enjoys smoky bacon-flavoured crisps. It is his *duty* to disapprove of me.

20.15

Three women came into Mrs Butterly's while we were watching *EastEnders*. Without missing a beat, Mrs B says, 'We're closed.'

'. . . But . . .'

'Yes, closed. Goodbye.'

'. . . Oh, well, right . . .'

'What is the point,' she says, 'of having your own pub if you do not exercise small amount of power every now and then?'

21.08

Sun setting. Walking home after soap orgy at Mrs Butterly's. Firestarter's car parked outside his house. Tiptoed up rough-hewn boreen to take closer look. Unfamiliar car. Prius. What did I know about it? Aha, yes! Eco-swot car. Could run on electricity.

What worthy person he is.

Thursday, 11 September 13.01
Internet café

Someone already in there talking to Cecile. A man. I came to involuntary halt at door. Internationally good-looking — long, salt-tangled blond hair, deep smooth tan, one of those special mouths also owned by Steve Tyler (when young), Mick Jagger (also when young).

He was lounging across two chairs. Relaxed. The kind of man who stops people in their tracks. Like a god.

Felt slightly uncomfortable, like I might be interrupting something.

'Hi, Cecile. How are you?'

'*Bien*, Lola. Pulling ze divil be the tail.' Whatever that means. 'Lola, this is my friend, Jake.'

He looked at me with silvery eyes — and I blushed! Was simply too much. So sexy, he was almost feral creature. As if had been brought up by good-looking wolves.

He nodded and said, 'Lola.'

'Jake,' I replied.

Question. When people call their boy-children names like Jake, how do they know they're going to grow up sexy? Nature or nurture? If someone is called bog-standard name like Brian or Nigel, will they grow up to be bog-standard person? If they are given sexy-hero name like Lance or — as in this case — Jake, do they feel they have a duty to live up to it?

He muttered in low, deep voice, 'I'll be off, Cecile.'

Then he nodded at me again. 'Nice meeting you, Lola.'

'. . . You too . . . Jake.' And I blushed for second time! Blood had barely departed face from first time and almost met itself coming back.

I let a few minutes pass after his departure. Didn't want to seem too avid.

'. . . So, ah . . . Cecile, was that your boyfriend? The one you're crazy in love with?'

'Jake? No! My little turtle dove is Zoran. Jake is Zoran's friend.'

'Where is Jake from? Serbia also?'

'Jake? No, Cork.'

'You mean he's Irish?'

'As Irish as Guinness.'

Unexpected.

Friday, 12 September 13.45

New soup of the day at the Oak! Mixed vegetable. Lots of lumps, so cannot stomach it. Nevertheless, mild thrill.

16.33

Grace Gildee rang again! Thought she'd lost interest in me. Didn't answer, of course, and took every ounce of courage simply to listen to her message.

'Hi, Lola, me again, Grace Gildee. Just wondering if you'd made up your mind about doing the interview. You can trust me, I've known Paddy long time.' (Laughs.) 'I know where all his bodies are buried!'

If that is the case, then she can do interview with herself!

18.04

Fall into emotional slump. Why was I not good enough for Paddy? Was it because I didn't show enough interest in his job?

He used to come in and throw himself on couch, in bad mood, and complain bitterly about minister for something or other doing something he shouldn't have. He would rant and rant and eventually would say, 'You haven't a clue, have you?'

'No.'

I thought that's what he liked about me!

I thought I was his escape from all that.

And, after all, how much did he know about Roland Mouret frocks?

But it was obvious, in retrospect, that I should have

massaged his temples and plotted with him to overthrow minister for health or inveigle Taoiseach into compromising sexual situation with a herd of goats.

Funny thing is that always, all my life, my worst fear is of being abandoned, and it keeps happening. When I was a child, I used to say to Mum and Dad, 'Can we all die at same time?' Mum promised yes, we could. But she was liar. Went ahead and died all by herself when I was fifteen. But, to be fair, she couldn't help herself. About a week before she died, she blurted out, 'It's breaking my heart to have to leave you, Lola. I hate not being there for when you grow up. I hate not being able to mind you and I hate not knowing what's going to happen to you.'

Realized then that she might be on the way out. No one had told me.

19.12
Looking for comfort, rang Dad.

He asked, 'Are you still shook up over that scut?'
'Yes.'
'Let that be a lesson to you, Lola. Never trust a politician.'
'Thanks, Dad. Bye.'

Monday, 15 September 12.12
Internet café
'Hi, Cecile. How are you?'
'*Bien*, Lola. On the pig's back.'
'. . . Yes . . .'

She keeps saying all these bizarre rural Irish greetings – like, 'Sucking diesel, please God.' And, 'Mighty, mighty!'
Even I do not know what they mean and I am Irish!
'Oh Lola, you 'ave a hadmire-air.'

'A hadmire-air?'

'Yes. A man hadmires you.'

'Oh! An admirer! No! Really?'

'My friend Jake. 'E says you har cute.'

Jake? The Love-God? No! He couldn't. He could have any-one! Said as much.

Cecile shrugged. 'You are holder woman. 'E likes holder women.'

'How much holder? I'm only thirty-one.'

''E is twenty-five. Also 'e 'as slept with every other woman in Knockavoy. You har "fresh blood".'

Cripes! You ever have something to sell? Don't let Cecile do it.

Deflated, got on with my business of checking emails. But Cecile wasn't finished.

'Lola,' she said, 'what will I tell him?'

What will you tell him? Are we back at school? My friend fancies your friend?

As fast as it had arrived, ire of indignation snuffed out.

'Nothing to tell,' I said. 'Anyway, going back to Dublin on Wednesday.'

20.16

Two men tried to have drink in Mrs Butterly's.

She said, 'We're closed.'

'But you're not.'

Pushy types.

She said, 'Are you stag party?'

'No.'

'Dutch?'

'No.'

'Golfers?'

'. . . Er, yes . . .'

'Cannot serve you. Golfers barred. Have had trouble with your type before.'

'You're refusing to serve us?'

'Yes.'

'. . . but that's . . .'

'By order of the management. Unless you would like take-away? Can of marrowfat peas? Box of matches?'

Tuesday, 16 September

Ready to go back to Dublin. Was like being on holidays here – first day or so, ants in pants. Then calming down, then enjoying it. Establishing regular routine, then days speeding up, until circle completed, back to start, ants in pants.

Agony about Paddy had levelled out. No longer felt curiosity or desperation to see him or even (rare) indignation that he discarded me so easily.

Not cured, of course. In a way, worse. When I was all tangled up in hope and shock and bad, burny feeling, couldn't see full picture.

Overwhelming feeling now is that I am worthless. All my confidence gone.

Also feeling bad loneliness. Paddy was my one big love and I will never meet anyone else. I know everyone says that when their heart is broken and people roll their eyes at display of naked self-pity and say, 'Don't be so silly!' But he was a unique man. A one-off. Never met anyone like him before. Never will again.

This is my burden. I accept it. My work will be the saving of me. Intend to devote rest of my life to doing missionary work – making women of Ireland look spectacular for very reasonable cost.

Wednesday, 17 September 10.13–11.53
Leavetaking
Visited all my Knockavoy friends – Ol' Prune Eyes, Mrs Butterly, Kelly and Brandon, Cecile.

'Yes, *oui*, goodbye, leaving Knockavoy, returning to metropolis, lovely, yes, thank you, you too, pleasure, if ever in Dublin. No, no plans to return.'

11.55
Drove up the hill, watching Knockavoy get smaller and smaller in rear-view mirror, wondering when – if ever – I'd be back.

18.30
Home
Could hardly get into my flat. Full of suitcases, suit-carriers and clothes. None of them mine. Nkechi had been busy. Calling in lots of stuff. Storing it in my flat.

Phone rang. Bridie. 'How long did journey take you?'

Said, 'Three hours twenty.' (But had no real idea.)

'I seeeee,' she said. 'Three hours twenty? Slap bang in middle of table. Mean journey time three hours twenty-seven.'

Heard clicking of keys, like she was inputting something.

'Bridie, are you keeping *record*?'

'Yes. Graphs. Pie-chart. Spreadsheets. Lovely software. Such variety of different ways to present things.'

Thursday, 18 September 9.00
Martine's Patisserie
Bright and early. Fresh start. Meeting in 'office' with Nkechi. As usual, Nkechi late.

9.14

Nkechi swans in, braids piled high on top of her head. Long, shapely neck. Very elegant. Walks like queen. Lazily swings her bottom into seat. Asks, 'Nice break?'

'Yes, yes,' I said breezily. Implying, That beastly (Margery Allingham) business all behind me now. I am restored to old efficient self.

'So!' I say, trying to sound dynamic. Even clap hands together in attitude of zeal. 'What's happening?'

Nkechi reads from her BlackBerry. 'Tonight Rosalind Croft. Gala dinner at her house. Conference in Ireland at moment, world debt, Africa . . .' waved her hand vaguely '. . . that sort of thing. Lots of famous people here. Kofi Annan, President South Africa . . .' another wave of hand '. . . those types. All main players invited to Crofts'. She's been insane. Rang me in middle of night, wanted Versace dress she saw in American *Vogue*. Couldn't get fucking thing, was special creation for catwalk. She told me to fly to Miami to find it. Talked her down, dress selection narrowed to three. Balenciaga, Chanel, Prorsum Burberry. All flown in from London. Matching shoes, jewellery, etc., packed in your flat, ready to go.'

'Okay.'

'Tomorrow, ski chic shoot for *Woman's World*. Usual winter wonderland bollocks. Furry boots, earmuffs, minging knit-wear. Following day, evening dress fittings for Tess Bickers.'

'Who?'

'New client. Corporate wife. Tons of jingle. Wants kitting out for party season. Called in eighteen frocks. Reckon she'll take most of them.'

'You've been very busy, Nkechi. I'll take over, do Mrs Croft this evening.'

'But —'

'You've been working very hard, Nkechi. Take the night off.'

Time to assume control. Show her who's boss.

She didn't want to give in. She has fostered 'special relationship' with Rosalind Croft since the time she saved her bacon with scarf from charity shop. Mrs Croft very powerful. Knows what's hot and what's shot. Handy person to have on your side.

Repeated, 'Really, Nkechi, I'll do it.'

'. . . Well, okay. She wants you at the house at six-thirty. Well, she actually wants *me* at the house at six-thirty, but if you insist . . .'

Nkechi radiating resentment. Giving me 'tude, as she would say. As a rule, do not savour unpleasantness, but imperative to regain upper hand.

17.08

Finishing informal meeting with Brown Thomas buyer
Better get skates on. Had to pick up clothes for Mrs Croft and get out to Killiney for 6.30. Lagging behind all day. Still on Knockavoy speed. 'Speed' wrong word. 'Slowth' would be more apt.

17.15

Nipping along South William Street, weaving through people. Car double-parked. Holding up traffic. Knew before I knew, if you know what I mean. Maybe subconsciously I recognized car, or something, because had bad, burny feeling before I knew exactly why.

It was Paddy. Helping a woman — the horse, who else? — into back seat of double-parked car. Solicitous.

I stood and stared. Appalled by scene. I used to be the

woman in the back seat of his car. But I had been cast aside, like cheap red dress with cigarette burn on nipple.

Living proof of my insignificance.

Knew I was going to vomit. Beseeched God, *All I ask is don't let me do it in the street.*

17.18

Hogan's Public House

I lurched towards Ladies like a sailor on dry land, black dots swimming before my eyes. Nick of time. Threw up into handbasin. Sank to knees. Whispered, 'Sorry,' to two disgusted girls applying lipgloss in mirror. Who, once they realized I wasn't stotious drunk, were kindness itself. Gave me a tissue, stick of Orbit and said, 'All men are bastards.'

They stuck with me while I waited for legs to stop trembling and could take weight of body, then escorted me to street to hail taxi. Kindness of strangers. Just before I drove away, I whispered to them about secret sample sale in Lainey Keogh's atelier.

17.47

My flat

Rushed in. Brushed teeth. Speedily loaded self like packhorse and staggered out to car.

Taxi driver looked at luggage and asked, 'You doing moonlight flit?'

'Excuse me?'

'My wife left me. I came home one day and found all her stuff gone. Cannot be party to woman doing secret runner.'

'Oh, no, no, just work.' Then added, 'Sorry for your trouble.'

18.05

Traffic terrible. Rush-hour gridlock. Wedged between man in Nissan Sunny (in front), man in Toyota Corolla (behind), man in Opel Corsa (beside) and man in Skoda Skoda (don't think they have different types) (facing, going in opposite direction).

18.13

Haven't moved in ten minutes. Am going to be late. Possibly very late. I am never late.

Considering rolling down window and striking up conversation with man in Opel Corsa. Might take mind off my anxiety.

Made the mistake of sharing my pain with taxi driver. He despises Paddy. Says he is 'ruthless'. Although driver is bitter man — he has never forgiven his wife and swears he wouldn't trust a woman to give him the right change from a euro — I suppose I agree.

18.28

Traffic still terrible. Officially almost late. Should have left town no later than 5.30. Sighting of Paddy and the horse threw me right off schedule. If I hadn't needed to duck into pub to puke and recover aplomb, would have been fine. Can't BEAR being late.

18.35

Officially late and nowhere near Killiney. Gnawing hand with anxiety.

18.48

Toothmarks on hand.

19.03

Hand bleeding.

19.14

Arrive! Through electronic gates, up long drive lit with flaming torches. Front door open, framing frantic housekeeper. 'Quick, quick. Mrs Croft going mad!'

Hive of activity, canapés, uniformed staff, light glinting on champagne glasses.

Race up the stairs, dragging one suitcase, the housekeeper and unidentified male employee hot on my heels carrying the rest of the stuff. Mrs Croft in silky robe, sitting at mirror in her dressing room, a picture of fretfulness. Hairdresser pacing room, rapping curling tongs against his palm. Sees me. Exclaims, 'Thanks be to Christ! What the hell kept you?'

I gasp, 'So sorry, Mrs Croft. So sorry. Traffic terrible.'

'Where's Nkechi?'

'Not coming. Night off. Me instead.'

'Oh . . .'

I clunked open suitcases, unwhizzed zips on carriers, while housekeeper and unidentified man begin unpacking things onto hangers.

'What's this?' Mrs Croft picked up a little white angora sweater.

'. . . I . . . ah . . .'

'And this?' Red jumper patterned with snowflakes.

'And this?' Stripey knitted hat.

Self baffled. Snowflakes? Then hideous understanding dawned. Hideous, hideous, unbearably hideous. Prickly heat flushed down my body and vomit rose in my throat for second time that evening. This couldn't be happening. Really couldn't be happening.

I'd brought wrong clothes.

I hadn't noticed until now, but Nkechi had labelled them. Clearly said 'Ski Shoot'.

'Where're my dresses?' Mrs Croft was pawing through the carriers and emerging with padded anoraks with cute furry trims on hood.

'It's all anoraks,' the hairdresser said.

Frisson ran through other staff. Anoraks! But where're Mrs Croft's couture dresses? The ones she had flown in specially from London?

Mrs Croft caught me by the shoulders, looking like a soul in hell. 'Where are my dresses?' she beseeched me.

'It's all okay,' I said, my voice thin and high and shaking. 'It's all okay. Just have to make quick phone call.'

'You mean they're not here?'

'Not just yet.'

'Oh Jesus! Oh sweet Jesus! What happened? You brought wrong ones?'

'Mishap, Mrs Croft. So very sorry. All will be well.'

Trying to stay calm because, of the two of us, she was more likely to descend into hysterics requiring slap to face and Pull Yourself Together.

'Where are my dresses?'

'In my apartment.'

'And where's that?'

'In town.'

'IN TOWN? But that's ten miles away!'

Someone said, 'Bumper-to-bumper traffic. Three hours to get here.'

Could hardly hold phone, my hand was so sweaty with fear.

'Nkechi?' My voice was shaking. 'Nkechi. Something terrible has happened. I brought wrong clothes to Mrs Croft.'

Long, long judgemental silence.

Out of corner of my ear, I heard housekeeper say, 'Maybe could borrow Bono's helicopter.'

Nkechi finally spoke. 'I'm on my way.'

I snapped phone shut. In tone of hysterical joy, I said, 'Nkechi's coming! Correct clothes will be here in no time.'

'So will my guests!' Mrs Croft stood up and began gasping. 'Bono is coming! Bill Clinton is coming! To my house! Here! To my house! And I have nothing to wear!'

Struggling for breath. Began hitting her chest with her fist.

'Paper bag!' someone shouted. 'Bring a paper bag! Mrs Croft is hyperventilating!'

Paper bag appeared and Mrs Croft put it to her face, like a nosebag, and heaved in and out of it.

'That's it,' the housekeeper said. 'That's it. In and out, nice and easy.'

Mrs Croft sat down, stood up, took bag from her face, sat down, put head between knees, took it up again, stood up, turned and screeched at us all, 'Oh God, oh my God! Oh God, Maxwell will kill me!'

19.32

A man's voice intruded into dressing room. 'Where the hell's my wife?'

Oh no! Not Maxwell Croft!

Yes. In dinner jacket and dicky-bow. Short man. Enormous chest. Always seemed in bad mood.

He looked at Mrs Croft. Fizzog like thunder. 'What the hell's going on? Why you not dressed?'

He took her wrist and pulled her out of the dressing room and into main bedroom.

Me, hairdresser, housekeeper and unidentified male employee looked at the floor, trying to pretend horribleness wasn't happening.

Maxwell Croft demanding in low menacing voice, 'What hell's going on? What you mean dresses not here yet? Why can't you use reliable stylist? You fucking useless –'

Mrs Croft tried apologizing, 'Sorry, Maxie, so so so sorry.'

But Mr Croft not listening, speaking over her. 'You know who's downstairs? Bill Clinton. Bill fucking Clinton. Alpha male of all alpha males. And you are making fucking holy show of me. You should be down THERE, you are fucking hostess!'

'Will wear other dress,' Mrs Croft said nervously.

'No, you fucking won't. Wear an old dress for Bill Clinton? What you want people to think of me? Think I can't afford to buy wife new season couture? Oh thank you, Rosalind. Nice one.'

Then it all went quiet and hairdresser mouthed, 'Is he gone?' Gave me shove in the back and whispered, 'You take a look.'

Stuck my head around wall for little peek, but surprised to find them both still there, locked in odd embrace. Then saw. Horrors! Mr Croft holding Mrs Croft's wrist between both his hands and giving her Chinese burn! (Quick aside – in these PC times are we allowed to say 'Chinese' burn?)

Stretching and twisting poor Mrs Croft's skin. Long mew of pain from her. Then Mr Croft let go, gave her rough push and barrelled from the room.

19.43
Waiting for Nkechi. Mrs Croft trying discreetly to rub her smarting wrist, us pretending not to notice. Bad 'burn'. Perfect bracelet of little red dots, burst blood vessels. Conspiracy of silence. Although others hadn't seen what had happened, it was as if they knew. Regular occurrence?

Mrs Croft began to cry softly.

19.51
Waiting unendurable.

I rang Nkechi. 'Where are you?'

'Two minutes away.'

'Two minutes away? HOW?'

Two minutes later
Arrival of Nkechi like the Rapture. People almost fell to their knees and began blessing themselves. She strode into house and straight up stairs, accompanied by another Nigerian girl, her cousin Abibi.

I asked, 'But how you get here so quickly?'

'Public transport,' she said. 'Luas, then Dart. Abibi picked me up from Killiney station.'

This caused astonishment. PubLIC transport! How clever of her! *Public* transport. As if she'd said, 'Angel descended from heaven and gave me piggy-back over the gridlock.'

Immediately Nkechi took control. Like a paramedic, all short, efficent gestures and snappy orders. (BP 60 over 90 and ... CLEAR!)

She took one look at Mrs Croft's hair and said, 'The Balenciaga.'

Clicked fingers at Abibi and said, 'The Balenciaga.'

I said, 'But the Chanel –'

'There's no time!' Nkechi bit out the words. 'Mrs Croft would need change of hairstyle if wearing Chanel.'

Of course she was right.

'You!' Nkechi rapped knuckles on suitcase and clicked fingers at me – me! 'Underwear,' she said. 'Sort it.'

'You!' She clicked fingers at Abibi. 'You're on jewellery. I'll do shoes.'

Like a heist.

'Quickly!' Nkechi said to me. 'Can't do anything else until underwear on!'

My fingers trembling, I sorted through cornucopia of 'smalls'. Old-fashioned, I know, but good underwear is the key to looking fabulous in couture. Sturdy foundation garments, your only man. Knickers which go from under bust to tops of knees. Yes, really. In tough, barely stretchy fabric. Exhausting to wrestle with when going to the loo, but worth it.

Also slips. Special laughter reserved for slips. Fuddy-duddy joke, but they hide a multitude.

I threw robust knickers to Nkechi, who caught them like a professional catcher, then manhandled Mrs Croft into them. Gown slipped over Mrs Croft's head and slithered down her body. Magnificent piece. Ivory crêpe silk, inspired by toga. Off one shoulder, falling in soft pleats from brooch on other shoulder. Very thin belt at waist and slight flare when it reached floor. Queenly.

At its beauty, everyone breathed, 'Oh!'

Like little elves, we scurried around Mrs Croft, Nkechi

slipping her shoes onto her feet, Abibi fitting pendant around her neck, hairdresser winding renegade curl on tongs, me nimbly adjusting tit tape so not visible. Then ready.

'Go! Go, go, go!'

20.18
Taxi back into town. Mood deeply subdued. Mrs Croft would never use me again.

But she might use Nkechi.

Friday, 19 September 8.30
Mobile rang. Nkechi. Asking for a meeting before today's shoot.

9.30
Martine's Patisserie
Nkechi already there. Slumped self into chair. Said, 'Sorry about last night.'

'Last night? That could have caused international incident. What if my mobile was switched off? What if no way of getting dress there in time? And Mrs Croft couldn't host dinner? Kofi Annan and all those types could have thought slur! Snub! Insult on behalf of Irish people. Deal brokered could have fallen apart.'

'Really think you're overreacting.'

'Point is, Lola, you in no fit state to be back.' She spread hands on table. 'Look, Lola, have . . . proposition.'

Bad sinking feeling.

'You, Lola, have been good to me. Decent pay. Responsibility. Learnt a lot while your assistant. But while you going through your broken-heart stuff, you are out of control.'

'It was only because actually saw Paddy yesterday!'

'Dublin small town,' she said. 'Danger you could see him at any time. Then will mess up whatever you're working on. If continue like this, Lola, you will have no clients left at all.'

'Not true! One mistake!'

'One *terrible* mistake. Anyway, more than one. Lots.'

She became a little shamefaced. Said, 'Look, Lola, I always planned to set up on own, you know that.'

Hadn't. Suspected. Knew she was ambitious. But never actually articulated. However, nodded wearily.

'What I propose is to cover your clients until end of year.'

Excuse me?

'Will keep your business strong. At end of year, I will set up on my own. Whatever clients want to come with me will be mine. Whatever ones want to stay with you will be yours. Client list growing all the time. Will be enough for both of us. Win—win.'

I was staggered. Speechless. I found voice. Croaked, 'And in meantime what will I do?'

'Take yourself out of circulation. Go away. Back to Uncle Tom's cabin, if you like. But —' Nkechi held up index finger — 'do not tell people you are gone to rural place, they will think you loser. Say you're going to New York for work. Research. Scouting out new designers. Okay?'

I nodded.

'Now, ching ching!' She rubbed fingers together in international 'money' gesture. 'Obviously am doing work of senior stylist AND saving your business. Also need to pay Abibi. Need more jingle in my pocket. Have scribbled some figures.'

Spreadsheet shoved across table. All laid out for me. Nkechi very clever girl.

Shoved it back at her. Said, 'Okay.'

'Okay?' Sounded like she expected more of a fight.

But was beaten. Broken.

'Okay, okay. Okay to everything. Right, we'd better get going.'

'For what?'

'Ski chic shoot.'

'You're not going, Lola. Remember?'

Oh yes, remember.

9.50
Walking home

Only twenty minutes had elapsed since I'd met Nkechi. A short time for a life to be completely filleted.

Reminding me of other terrible time in life when younger. Twenty-one. Mum dead, Dad in Birmingham, boyfriend I'd had for two years in college had kicked self to kerb and gone to New York, full of talk of taking on Wall Street. (As happened, he developed severe cocaine habit and came back to Ireland several years later in disgrace and penury, which, if had known, would have been balm to pain, but at time, all I knew was had been abandoned.) Only thing had going for me back then was my job. Working with Freddie A, top designer. However, after only three weeks, he gave it to me straight: 'Lola, you are good, but not good enough.'

Confirmed what had begun to suspect myself. Had been afraid of going into work in case would make unfixable mistake. Having recurring dream that catwalk show about to start and none of the clothes made. Me frantically sewing in massive warehouse filled with bales of fabric and models in their bras and knickers clamouring for outfits.

'Mr A, will work harder! I promise!'

'Not a question of hard work, Lola. Is question of talent. And you haven't got enough of it.'

He did his best to be kindly, but devastating blow. Had always loved, loved clothes. Would cut out patterns for dolls and sew own stuff, even as twelve-year-old. Friends Bridie, Treese, Sybil O'Sullivan (not friends with her any more, had terrible falling out, can no longer remember about what, but rule is must hate her, and whenever any of us catch glimpse of her, must say, 'She has really let herself go. Gone very fat and hair in terrible condition') would ask me to shorten skirts and suchlike. Ambition from very young age to be a designer.

Now admitted, not talented enough.

Last rope anchoring self had gone. Felt like utter failure.

(All worked out in the end, I suppose. Went back on anti-depressants and went to counselling. While wondering what to do with life, accidentally fell into being stylist. Because knew so much about clothes, got odd freelance gig being assistant on shoot. Worked very hard. Maximized every opportunity given. Spent long hours concentrating, concentrating, concentrating. In what way can I make this outfit more original? More beautiful? Slow climb. Bad money. Uncertainty. No job security. But people began talk about me. Odd mention. 'Lola Daly is good.' Like way people say it about Nkechi now.)

19.01

'Best thing if you go back to Knockavoy, just for a while,' Treese said.

'Yes, best thing to go back to Knockavoy,' said Jem.

'But how will she manage for money?' (Bridie, keen grasp of practicalities.)

I said, 'I've worked in pubs. Can pull pints, collect glasses. Or am not above cleaning in hotel.'

'How long you think you'll stay there?' Treese asked.

'For ever,' I replied. Then, 'Don't really know, let's play it by ear.'

22.56

Parting words from Treese. 'Forget Paddy de Courcy,' she said. 'He's not worth wrecking your life over. Even Vincent doesn't like him.'

I closed door, then thought, What she mean, *even* Vincent? As if Vincent is kindly man like Nelson Mandela who sees good in everyone!

Paddy and Vincent met only once and it was indescribably appalling evening.

Treese held dinner party for me, her, Bridie and Jem and our partners. Like grown-ups. Soon as we arrived, Vincent took immediate interest in Paddy. Thought he was being kind because Paddy was new to gang, but should have known.

Without asking what he would like to drink, Vincent gave Paddy glass with inch of red wine in bottom. 'What you think of that?'

With his meaty frame, big hair and neck as big as my waist, Vincent looked like malevolent ox. Especially compared with Paddy's sexy, good looks.

Paddy sniffed, swirled wine, took sip, other sip, squirted it noisily round in mouth, like mouthwash, then swallowed.

'Excellent,' he says. 'Yes, excellent.'

Jem and Bridie's Barry watched with expectant little expressions, like puppies hoping for kindly word from master, but they were not offered any of this special red wine. (Nor were Bridie, Treese, Claudia or I, but it was joke to even consider it. Vincent a 'man's man'.)

'What is it?' Vincent asks Paddy. Challenge.

'Wine?' Paddy says, with laugh. Hoping to charm his way out of not having clue.

'What kind of wine?' Vincent asks impatiently.

'Red?'

'You're showing your ignorance, my friend,' Vincent said loudly, so we all could hear.

Jem and Barry suddenly very relieved not to have been offered any.

'Is Côtes de Something or other,' Vincent boasted, '1902, from cellar of Counte Some Frenchbloke. Paid —' (he mentioned extortionate sum of money) 'for it at auction. Beat Bono. Only box of its kind in Ireland.'

Vincent happy. He had got one over on Paddy and the night had hardly begun.

All night he chipped away. Soon as starter was cleared, he said belligerently, 'You so-called NewIreland will never win election while woman is leading party.'

'Never stopped Tories under Margaret Thatcher,' Paddy said politely.

'That was in Britain, my friend. I think you'll find Ireland's a bit more conservative.'

'Not any more —'

'— yes any more! Irish women will never vote for a woman. If they vote at all — and they don't — it's for a man.'

Vincent was leaning across the table at Paddy. Paddy also leant forward, so they were almost forehead to forehead.

Paddy said, 'We've had two female presidents.'

'Presidents!' Vincent did fake chortle. 'Shaking hands with trade delegates from China. But real power? Not to a woman.'

It was awful. The rest of us sweating with tension. Paddy

having to be pleasant because a) was politician and had to be pleasant to everyone so they would vote for him, b) was guest in Vincent's home.

Treese wasn't there to rein Vincent back in. She was in the kitchen, taking tinfoil off catered food (this was before she'd done her cookery course), and secretly cramming chocolate after chocolate into her mouth from 500 g box of Butler's which Jem brought. She returned, all flustered and guilty-looking, with gin and tonic sorbets in eggcups. Asked, 'Vincent, can you change CD?'

'Certainly, love.' Then 'In the Air Tonight' filling the room.

Vincent came back to table and Paddy was laughing energetically. But fake mirth. He said to Vincent, 'Phil Collins? You're showing your age, my friend. Why not Cliff Richard, while you're about it?'

'What's wrong with Phil Collins?'

'He's shit.'

But Vincent not to be deterred. Ranted, 'Phil Collins consummate artiste.' (Pronounced it 'arteeste'.) 'Has had more number one records . . . highest-selling artist in thirty-two countries . . . How can you argue with that?'

'All it means is a lot of people are prepared to buy shit.'

'Well, you'd know all about that.'

Atmosphere terrible. I was desperate to leave. But long wait. Many courses. Treese had gone for de luxe, most expensive version. Amuse-bouches. Palate-cleansing sorbets. Mini-desserts before the real ones.

At one stage I thought to self, Ah! I understand now – I have died and am in hell. I will be trapped here for ever, my boyfriend being insulted, air toxic with hostility.

Once I knew it was hell and not real life, I cheered up.

And then . . . Blue Mountain coffee. Petits fours. End in sight!

Relaxed too soon. Tricky, tricky moment. Vincent said to Treese, 'Let's have some of chocolates Jim brought.' (Vincent always called Jem 'Jim'. Knew what his name was, just did it to be unpleasant.)

'No!' Bridie, Treese, Jem and I said together. Even Claudia joined in, for once allied with us instead of standing against us. 'Full!' we exclaimed. 'No need for chocolates!'

'Would puke if saw one,' Bridie said.

'Yes, would puke!'

We knew Treese had eaten most of them.

'Get them,' Vincent said to Treese.

'I'll get them,' I said. Then simply went and got my jacket and Paddy's coat. Could take no more.

'Was wonderful evening,' I said, sounding hysterical even to self. 'But late. Must go now. Come on, Paddy!'

Paddy, all smiles, until final goodbyes said and front door had closed behind us. Then sudden change. Stiff-backed, he strode ahead of me to car. Got in, and slam of door closing was like thunderclap. I got in beside him. Anxious. We revved away in shower of gravel. (Spanish John on rare night off.) Drove in silence, Paddy looking straight ahead.

'Sorr –' I started.

But he cut across me. Bit out the words, voice low and full of fury. 'Don't ever do that to me again.'

Sunday, 21 September
Back in Knockavoy. Greeting old friends. 'Hello, yes, *oui*, back. Unexpected. Hahaha, yes, life full of surprises.'

Mortified.

Monday, 22 September 15.17

Asking in local hostelries for work. Started with hotel. But they were closing end of month. Invited me to come back next April when they reopened. No good to me, but appreciated their positive attitude: 7 out of 10 for courtesy.

15.30

The Hole in One. Golfers' pub. Manager quite mean. 'It's September,' he pointed out. 'End of season. We're laying people off, not taking them on.' Scornful: 2 out of 10 for pleasantness.

15.37

The Oak. Ol' Prune Eyes, blunt but sympathetic. Just enough work for him. However, 9 out of 10 for kindness.

15.43

Mrs McGrory's pantry. Peopled with young surfy men eating all-day breakfasts. (Did quick scan, no sign of the Love-God.) Dopey youth said he thought they might have a job. Made me wait fifteen minutes while he went to ask someone called Mika, but Mika sent word back that there were no jobs until next May. Nevertheless, 7 out of 10 for effort.

16.03

The Dungeon. Dark, charmless place, peopled with day-long drinkers. All men, who laughed cruelly when I enquired about work, then offered to buy me drink. About to refuse, wavered, then accepted. Why not? Sat on high stool, with a trio of men I later discovered were collectively known as Alco's Corner.

Immediately they began bombarding me with personal questions. What was my name? Why was I in Knockavoy?

Played coy for a few minutes, but when spilled story about Paddy, they admitted they already knew. No secrets in a town this small. Chief questioner, a lively man called Boss, with many, many broken veins, and mad head of springy grey curls, like Art Garfunkel gone to the bad, was father of Kelly in DVD shop. Kelly had told him everything.

'Dying to meet you, so I was,' he said. 'Sorry for your trouble, but poor judgement. What you expect from Christian Progressive?'

'Paddy de Courcy not Christian Progressive. Member of NewIreland actually.'

'He was Chrisp before NewIreland. Will always be Chrisp. Not something you can wash off.'

'Oh no, not something you can wash off,' agreed man next to Boss. Fat, shaved head, 98fm T-shirt, name of Moss.

'The soap that could wash away stench of Christian Progressives not invented yet,' said third man, a small, intense, stale-smelling individual in black suit shiny with age.

'Will be stinking Christian Progressive person until end of his days.'

'Will go to his grave as filthy Chrisp.'

Boss said, 'Would have been different if Paddy de Courcy had been from Nationalist Party of Ireland.'

Chorus of agreement: 'He wouldn't have let you down if he was Nationalist. Nationalist Party of Ireland, your only man.'

Suspect they are supporters of the NPI. ('Nappies' for short.)

'But Nationalist Party very corrupt, no?' Repeating what little I had learnt from Paddy.

'Oh yes! Corrupt! Yes, good. You get nothing done in this country without little corruption. Keeps the wheels turning.'

I had another little titbit of information for them. 'I heard Teddy Taft — leader of the Nappies and Taoiseach of this country — doesn't change his underwear every day. Paddy says he turns them inside out to get second day's wear out of them.'

'Don't call them "Nappies",' Boss admonished, climbing down from his stool. 'Disrespectful.'

All three had climbed down from their stools.

'Up de Valera!' they yelled and raised their glasses. 'Up de Valera!'

(De Valera, former president of Ireland, dead at least thirty years. Irish people have long memories.)

Later discovered they did this little de Valera-praising ritual every day around 4.30.

Small ruckus ensued. A man at far end of the bar got off stool and slowly approached us. My three new friends nudged each other. Sniggered, 'Look what's coming.'

Newcomer extended shaking finger. In strange, quavery voice, he announced, 'De Valera illegitimate son of stinking Spanish whore-master!'

Was he? Spanish? Hadn't known. Mind you, name a bit of a giveaway.

Further insult-calling ensued.

'You dirty turncoat!'

'You filthy free-stater!'

Much antipathy. Reason? Their grandfathers had fought on opposite sides in the civil war.

A few more insults were flung, then newcomer returned to his place and Boss said to barman, 'Give him a drink on us.'

Meanwhile another drink had appeared in front of me. Hadn't planned to stay, but as drink was there . . .

'Tell us more,' Boss ordered, his eyes very bright due to drunkenness and redness of face.

And actually great relief to talk, to get it all off chest. Another drink appeared. Explained my financial position. They didn't like the sound of Nkechi.

'What's yours is mine and what's mine is my own,' the small, dark, smelly man said, in attitude of great wisdom.

'Never a truer word! Never a truer word!'

(They were calling small, dark, smelly man the Master. Not because good at Eastern mysticism or martial arts but because he used to be headmaster in boys' school.)

Boss exclaimed, 'But why you looking for work? You can claim dole!'

Idea a novel one. Yes, had been on dole for brief spell ten years ago, after got sacked from fashion house for not making the grade and before started work as stylist. But had been earning own living for long time now. Had forgotten there was such a thing as welfare state.

'You've looked for work,' Boss said. 'There isn't any. Why shouldn't you get dole?'

Awash with drink, 'Yes!' I agreed. 'Why shouldn't I get dole?'

'You've worked hard, yes? Paid your taxes?'

'Ah no,' said Moss. 'Let her alone.'

'Actually have paid taxes.'

'You have?' They were astonished, then scandalized. Insisted on buying me other drink because of novelty.

General consensus, 'You deserve the dole.'

'We're going to sign on tomorrow morning. We'll collect you in van.'

Right! Good! Excellent! Great idea!

Tuesday, 23 September 8.30

Awoke! A noise! What was it? Lay in bed, rigid with listening. Something moving around downstairs. Person. No, people! Voices talking.

Was being burgled!

Frightened. Couldn't believe it was happening. More noises. Sounded . . . actually . . . like kettle boiling. Burglars making tea? Unusual. Murmur of voices again, followed by tinkle of sugar being stirred and stirred and stirred in mug. Then slurp. Actually heard it! Slurping of tea worst sound in world. Makes me want to go on *Falling Down*-style rampage.

I pulled on jumper over pyjamas. Found Boss and Moss sitting at kitchen table drinking – nay, *slurping* – tea. Boss said, 'Ah there she is.'

'There's tea in the pot,' Moss said. 'Pour you cup?'

All came rushing back. New friends. Trip to Ennistymon to sign on.

They looked even more washed-up in unforgiving light of day. Art Garfunkel hair, hadn't seen comb since 2003; 98fm T-shirt on Moss less than pristine. But they were happy to see me. Smiles.

I asked, 'Where's the other one? The small one? The Master?'

'Doesn't come. Bad back. Disability allowance.'

Hadn't noticed anything wrong with his back yesterday. Uncertain about moral calibre of my new friends.

'. . . Will get dressed.'

9.51

Not proper van. Like car with two seats in front but van bit in back, where back seats would usually be. Ushered into front seat beside Boss. Moss crouched in back, hugging his knees. Van remarkably filthy. And smelly. Tobacco. Animals. Cinnamon air-freshener. Had to roll down window in case I vomited.

10.17
Ennistymon

Not much bigger than Knockavoy but real town, not tourist place. Shop selling animal feed and innoculations, another one which seemed to sell only ropes. Surprisingly large number of chemists. People of Ennistymon prone to illness? (*Love* chemists, maybe I could have quick browse.)

In shower of dirt from van wheels, we parked in Disabled space right outside Welfare Office. Boss rooted around on filthy floor, produced Disabled sticker and threw it on dashboard.

I didn't want go into Welfare Office. Had all made perfect sense last night, when drunk. But was sober now.

Not that I thought myself above claiming welfare. Oh no. Simply wearied by futility of what lay ahead.

Claiming welfare, like twelve labours of Hercules. Should be simple — had paid contributions, had lost job, had tried without success to get another one, was skint. But obstacle course. Fill in this form. Fill in that form. Produce last year's accounts, this year's accounts, utilities bill, proof of Irish citizenship, letter from last employer . . .

If, by monumental effort, produced everything, it still wouldn't be enough. More requests, progressively more challenging. Photo of my first pet. Three white truffles. Tom Cruise's autograph. First pressing of 'Lily the Pink'. Bottle of limited-edition Vanilla Tango (trick task, as Vanilla Tango only ever came in cans). Charcoal illustration Zinedine Zidane's bottom. Brass rubbing of Holy Grail. If I did them all, would then get letter saying, 'We have found other query. You are not entitled to any dole, you will never be entitled to any dole, but bring us 10 grams of powdered unicorn horn in a nice box and we will see if can make discretionary payment.'

If people ever get payment from Welfare Office, it is not because they're entitled to it. It is a reward for tenacity, for sheer bloody-mindedness, for enduring Kafkaesque pettiness of their requests and not blowing up and shrieking, SHOVE YOUR SHITTY LITTLE PAYMENTS! I'D RATHER STARVE!

10.45

As expected, given short shrift (what *is* that exactly?).

'You are new claimant?'

'Yes.'

'You need assessment!'

'Okay, can I have assessment?'

'You cannot just waltz in expecting assessment. You need appointment.'

'Okay, may I book appointment?'

(Wouldn't have bothered if hadn't been for Boss and Moss crowding around me, saying, 'Go ON, Lola! It's your RIGHT, Lola.')

'Actually have appointment free this morning.'

'What time?'

'. . . Now.'

10.46

Grim back room, with assessor man. Don't mean to be unkind, but could see why he wasn't front-of-house person. Looked all . . . pointy. Like fox. Sharp, inquisitive features, nose, chin. Fox-like colouring, reddish hair in ponytail at nape of neck. Wearing the special glasses that all interrogators seem to wear. Ones with narrow silver frames, which light glints off in manner intended to unsettle. The Silver Frames of Suspicion.

'A stylist?' he asked, full of contempt. 'What kind of job is that?'

'I source clothes for people.'

'Source?' he asked, making fun of the word. 'What does that mean?'

'I . . . find . . . clothes for people. If someone has to go to a fancy red-carpet do, I get designers to send over a selection of dresses. Or if someone is very busy, I call in stuff and they try it all on without having to traipse around shops.'

He gave me strange look.

'Look,' I said defensively, 'I know it's not a very worthwhile job. Not like being a nurse or . . . or . . . aid worker in Bangladesh. But there is a demand for it and someone has to do it and I like it and it might as well be me.'

'Not much call for it round here,' doleman said.

'I know. That's why I'm here. I looked for jobs in all the bars in Knockavoy, but end of season, nothing doing.'

He asked, 'Why have you come to live in Knockavoy?'

'Personal reasons,' I replied, trying to keep voice steady. Lip started its mad twitch, like it was trying to send a message in Morse code.

'You'll have to do better than that! No secrets here.'

'Okay,' I said, blurting it all out. 'My boyfriend is getting married to someone else. The shock has had bad effect. Have messed up every job I've done. Have been sort of sent into exile to get over it before I destroy my business completely. Having to pay my assistant and her cousin while I'm away. No jingle left for me.'

'Okay,' he said, writing it all down. 'We'll be in touch.'

Wondered which way they'd block my claim. Almost curious. Would it be because I was self-employed? Or should I be claiming in Dublin? Or was this ill-health, rather than unemployment per se, so should I be claiming disability benefit? Oh I knew all their tricks.

19.22

On my way to Mrs Butterly's for soap-watching, passed the Dungeon. Heard, 'Hey, Lola!' Three eager fizzogs were beaming out: Moss, Boss and the Master. They'd been watching for me.

Called from street, 'Going to watch *Coronation Street* with Mrs Butterly.'

'Come in for one!'

'One quick one!'

'Will come on the way back, when all the soaps are over.'

They seemed quite disappointed.

19.57

While waiting for *EastEnders* to start, I said, 'Mrs Butterly, you know the house next door to me?'

'Rossa Considine's? Nice lad. What about him?'

'You know how he was supposed to be getting married?'

'To who?'

'He's not any more, but he was going to . . .'

'No, he wasn't!' Mrs Butterly quite categorical. 'He's been footloose and fancy-free this last eight months since he broke the heart of Gillian Kilbert. Nice girl but terrible ferrety look about her.'

'. . . Yes . . . but . . .'

Vacillated. Should I ask her about the woman in the wedding dress? Vacillated small bit longer, then got bored vacillating. Limited enjoyment potential, vacillating. (Don't think I could ever take it up as hobby, vacillation. Imagine putting it on speed-dating form. Or job application. 'List interests.' 'Fashion. Billy Wilder movies. Yoga. Vacillating.')

Anyway I digress (and actually that is something I *do* enjoy). *EastEnders* was starting and Mrs Butterly was elderly lady. Possibly senile. I let Rossa Considine's mystery woman go.

21.40

The Dungeon

I was greeted like homecoming queen. A high stool was found and brushed clean, drinks were set in front of me, also KitKat. Turned out the Dungeon housed not one but two Alco's Corners. Bitter enemies. The other Alco's Corner had a dog. Boss's one had me.

I said, 'Tell me about the couple living next door to me.'

'No couple,' Boss said. 'Just a man. Rossa Considine. Single gentleman.'

'Nothing suspect about that, though,' the Master chimed in. 'Not like in times past, when if man didn't take a wife, everyone would say was a woofter. Sociological shift.'

'But Rossa Considine had a girlfriend?' I asked. 'Until a couple of weeks ago? They were getting married.'

Chortles of laughter, indicating I couldn't be more wrong if I tried.

'But,' I protested, 'I've seen a woman in his house.'

'A man is entitled to some R and R!'

'What kind of woman?' the Master asked. 'Small, blondey,

has the look of a ferret about her? Gillian Kilbert. All the Kilberts have the same ferrety cast. They get it from their father's side.'

I considered. 'No,' I said, 'nothing ferrety about her. And she was wearing a wedding dress. Standing at an upstairs window, staring down at me.'

The three men shot each other alarmed looks and Boss went quite white, no mean feat with the vast network of red veins littering the landscape of his face. Then they turned their startled gazes on me.

'Why . . . why . . . you staring at me like that?'

They said nothing. Just kept on looking.

'You have the Sight,' Boss said.

'. . . What? You mean, you think . . . the woman I saw was . . . a ghost?'

Involuntarily I shuddered. I remembered her white dress and her dark hair. Then, just as quickly, I got a grip. That was no ghost dress Firestarter had been burning on his bonfire. But for some reason I didn't want to tell Alco's Corner about that. Just felt it was . . . I don't know . . . Firestarter's business.

Boss furrowed brow. 'Did this woman look anything like Our Lady?'

What lady? 'Who?'

'The MOTHER OF GOD. You are a crowd of pagans above in Dublin.'

'No, nothing like the mother of God,' I said.

'Think hard,' he said. 'Blue frock? Halo? Small child?'

'No, I'm sure.' I could see where Boss's make-a-quick-buck brain was going with this. Trying to talk me into having had a vision of the mother of God, so he could set up Knockavoy as a new site for Catholic pilgrims.

123

'Leave it,' the Master advised. 'There were no witnesses. Rome would never buy it.'

'Bloody sticklers,' Boss muttered. 'Anyway, yes, Rossa Consi-dine, nice fellow apart from forever climbing up the side of a mountain or swinging on ropes into potholes. Works for Department of Environment. Something to do with think tank on recycling. A proper job. I remember when people had proper jobs. In the bank. Or civil service. Now it's all web designers and . . . and . . . cognitive behavioural therapists and your thing. Stylists. Useless, fecky, meaningless jobs.'

I said nothing. But was affronted. Felt like saying, At least have a job. Unlike you trio of drunken layabouts.

Then remembered actually *didn't* have job.

Sudden change of mood. One of the men from competing Alco's Corner called, 'Give us a recitation, Master!'

Transpired the Master knew vast reams of terrible poetry. Without further encouragement, he cleared his throat, rolled eyes back into his head and gave 'recitation' of something called 'The Green Eye of the Little Yellow God'.

It went on for fearsomely long time.

Wednesday, 24 September 8.01

Woken by slamming of front door (not mine). Hopped out of bed and into front bedroom to stare down on Firestarter Considine leaving for work.

Whole thing very odd. Firestarter Considine having a woman in his house, fine. But woman in wedding dress? And no one in town knowing he was getting married? Then him burning the dress on big bonfire?

Wild thought — had he kidnapped and killed her? But that was absurd. If she'd been kidnapped, she wouldn't have been twirling around in a Vera Wang dress. When she saw me in road, she'd have banged window and mouthed, 'Help me! Being held against will by environmental man!'

Mystery. Undeniable mystery.

Thursday, 25 September 11.27

Mobile went. Local number. It was the foxy dole-bloke. (Not foxy as in attractive, foxy as in fox-like. Vulpine, if you will.) He wanted to see me.

'Which obscure bit of paperwork you want me to bring?' I asked.

'No, want to see you outside work,' he said.

Foxy doleman fancied me! Cripes! I'd have to sleep with him if I wanted any dole!

Once I thought about it, didn't really care. So long as could just lie there.

'Look, Mr Doleman —'

'— Noel, call me Noel.'

Noel from the dole. Okay, should be easy to remember.

'Noel,' I said, 'I'm just out of relationship, I'm in no fit state —'

'That's not why want to see you.'

Oh?

'Will explain when we meet. In meantime, watchword is discretion. We cannot meet in Ennistymon. Walls have ears.'

'Come to Knockavoy.'

'No —'

'Walls have ears here too?'

Was being sarcastic, but he just said, 'Copy.'

Copy? God's sake!

He asked, 'You know Miltown Malbay?'

Miltown Malbay, town further along the coast from Knockavoy.

'Meet me tomorrow night, ten p.m., Lenihan's, Miltown Malbay. Don't ring this number.'

He hung up.

Friday, 26 September 8.08

Woken by 'bip' of car horn. Propelled self from bed, into other bedroom, to look out front window. Some manner of filthy four-wheel-drive vehicle gunning engine outside next door. Men within. Hard to see because of mud-flecked windows, but impression of roistering machismo.

Sound of front door slamming. Rossa Considine appeared in stampy boots, rucksack and black North Face fleece. Coils of rope were slung over his shoulder, small metal things dangling from them.

He strode towards the soiled charabanc and called some early morning manly greeting. (Something along the lines of 'Didn't expect any of you girls to be able to get out of bed this morning after great feed of pints we had last night.' Didn't catch exact wording but divined message from tone.)

Suddenly, as if intuited he was being spied on, his head turned to look back over his befleeced shoulder at Uncle Tom's cabin. Jerkily I withdrew from sight. But too late. Had been spotted. Rossa Considine did lopsided *Caught you, you spying oddball* smile, gave sarcastic-style wave, wrenched open the door of the vehicle, vaulted in and screeched away in shower of mud.

22.12

Lenihan's, Miltown Malbay

Noel from Dole was sitting in alcove, pointy knee crossed over other pointy knee, pointy elbows resting on table. He looked around and gave me full 180 of his pointy foxy features. If toppled on top of him, could sustain quite nasty puncture wound.

He leapt up, summoned me into alcove and whispered, 'Did anyone see you come in?'

'I don't know. You didn't tell me to sneak in.'

'Yes, I know, but this is highly confidential.'

I waited.

'It's about your job,' he said. 'Being a stylist. You ever help people track down clothes in difficult-to-find sizes?'

That was it?

'Certainly,' I said. 'Actually my speciality. Worked for wife of investment banker who had to go to unmerciful number of gala dinners, but, unusually for wife of investment banker, was a size fourteen. Rarely come in such a large size.'

'What about accessories?'

'I do everything. Shoes, handbags, jewellery, underwear.'

'I have this friend, you see,' he said. He sounded nervous. Suddenly he declared, almost in anguish, 'Look, I'm married! And I have a friend.'

'A lady-friend?'

He nodded.

Married and with a girlfriend? Just goes to show, looks aren't everything. Perhaps he is very good at telling jokes.

'My girlfriend. I like to buy her nice things. But she has trouble getting nice shoes in her size. Can you help?'

'I'm sure I can. What size feet has she?'

After perplexingly long pause, he said, 'Eleven.'

Eleven! Eleven is HUGE. Most men aren't even size eleven.

'. . . Is quite large size, but will see what can do . . .'

'How about some clothes for her?'

'What size is she?'

He stared. Stared and stared and stared.

'Wha – at?' I asked. He was beginning to scare me.

He exhaled with abnormal heaviness, as if he'd made decision, then said, 'Lookit.' Expression of intense distress. 'Can you keep a secret?'

'Oh God,' he groaned into his hands. 'Oh God.'

He looked up at her and to her surprise his face was wet with tears. 'I'm so sorry, I'm so fucking sorry. You're the best thing in my life, the only thing of any goodness. Forgive me, for the love of Jesus say you'll forgive me. It'll never happen again. I don't know what happened. Stress at work, been building for ages, but to take it out on you, of all people –'

He broke down into proper shoulder-jerking crying. 'What kind of animal am I?' he moaned.

'It's okay.' She touched him with tentative fingers. She couldn't bear to see him so prostrate.

'Thank you! Thank God.' He grasped her to him and kissed her hard, and although her split lip was raw to the touch, she let him.

Grace

Dad opened his front door and asked, 'What happened to your face?' Then he looked over my shoulder, an automatic reflex to make sure I hadn't stolen his parking spot. 'What have you done with your car? I can't see it.'

'That's because it's not here.' I followed him down the stairs to the kitchen. 'As we speak, my car is on the Tallaght bypass, burnt to a crisp.'

'Stolen?'

'No, did it myself last night. Nothing good on telly. Of course stolen!'

'Ahhh dear, dear. ''When sorrows come, they come not single spies, but in battalions.''' That's what Dad always says. That's because Dad's an intellectual. '*Hamlet*. Act four, scene five,' he informed me.

'Where's Ma?'

'With Bid.' Bid is my mother's sister and has lived with my parents since before I was born. 'Collecting her from her chemo.'

I flinched. Bid had been diagnosed with lung cancer ten days ago. It was taking some getting used to.

'God, it's perishing in here.' Even when it's the height of summer, it's always stone-cold in that house. It's big and old and has no central heating.

Down in the kitchen I clung to the Aga. I would have sat

up on it if it wasn't for the danger that I'd fry myself. (An Aga! I ask you. In a city.)

'Do you want to hear what other sorrows are going on?' Dad asked.

'You mean there's more?'

'Ma says we have to give up the fags. All of us.' He glared to emphasize his point. 'Not just Bid. All of us. And I'm very fond of my fags,' he added wistfully.

I knew how he felt. I couldn't imagine a life without nicotine.

I stared out of the window, lost in a cigarette reverie. In the back garden, Bingo was chasing a late-season bee. Eagerly leaping and lolloping and tripping over his legs, his russet ears swinging, he looked mentally ill.

Dad caught me looking. 'I know he's a handful, but we love him.'

'I love him too. And he hasn't run away in a while.' Or if he had, they hadn't involved me in tracking him down.

'Well, that's a fine injury you have there,' Dad said. 'Fighting again outside pubs, were you?'

I clicked my tongue. The bruise was nearly gone and I was sick of talking about it. 'It's such a silly story –'

'Wait a –' He seemed to suddenly notice something. 'Grace! Have you been growing again?'

'What? No!' I'm only five foot nine, but they make me feel like a freak.

'You must have been! Look at us, we're the same height, you and I! And we never were before. Look!' He gestured for me to stand beside him and measured a line with his hand from the top of his head to the top of mine. 'Look!'

He was right.

'Dad, I'm the same height I've always been.' I gestured hopelessly. 'I don't know what to say. You must be shrinking.'

'Gaah! Old age. It's so undignified. Sorrows etc., etc.'

Dad was a small-boned man with soulful eyes and a big nose. Between the nose and the cigarettes, he could have passed for French. On holidays, once in Italy and another time in Bulgaria, people thought he actually *was* French and he couldn't hide his pleasure. He thinks the French are the most civilized nation on earth. He loves, loves, loves J-P Sartre. Also, hearteningly, Thierry Henri.

There was the sound of the front door opening and closing. Ma and Auntie Bid were home.

'We're in the kitchen,' Dad called.

They fluttered down the stairs, taking off gloves and unbuttoning raincoats and complaining about the smallness of ten-cent coins (obviously continuing some conversation they'd been having in the car). They looked very alike, both tiny little creatures, except that Auntie Bid was half bald and the colour of urine.

'Bid . . . ?' I asked helplessly.

'I'm grand, grand.' Feebly she waved away my concern. 'Don't try hugging me, I'll puke.'

'Grace!' Ma was pleased to see me. 'I didn't see your car outside.' She furrowed her forehead. 'What's up with your face?'

'Her car got stolen and burnt out on the Tallaght bypass,' Dad said. 'And I'm shrinking.'

'Oh! Oh Grace!' Ma was saddened. '"When sorrows

come, they come not single spies, but in battalions.'' *Hamlet*, act four, scene five.' (Ma is also an intellectual.) She put gentle fingers on my cheekbone. 'What happened here? Surely it wasn't Damien!'

I had to laugh.

'Damien's a handsome man,' Auntie Bid croaked.

'What's that got to do with anything?'

'Nothing. Just saying. Don't mind me, I'm not myself. I think I'll sit down.' We all leapt to usher her into a chair, from where she continued her unexpected speech. 'I always liked a man with a powerful build. I'd say when he's naked, Damien has a fine pair of thighs? Does he?' she asked, when I didn't answer. Too startled to. Naked thighs! Could the cancer have spread to her brain?

'Um, yes, I suppose he does.'

'And moody, of course; nothing as alluring as a moody man.' She sighed wistfully. 'His intelligence, his sensitivity, his essential unknowability.'

Now there she was wrong. The thighs I could go along with, but not the allure of moodiness. Not that Damien was exactly Heathcliff.

'If Damien ever hit me,' I tried to wrest control of the conversation, 'I'd clobber him right back, and he knows it.'

'Lovie, if he ever touched you, there's always a bed for you here.' Ma just lives for a good cause.

'Thanks, Ma, but the cold would kill me.'

Ma and Bid had inherited the house when their great-uncle Padraig – the only member of their family to have 'done well for himself' – shuffled off his mortal coil. Thirty-nine Yeoman Road was a Georgian Preservation Society's delight: high-ceilinged rooms, all the better for frozen air to circulate mistily in; original multi-paned windows which courteously permitted all draughts ingress and rattled like a box of cutlery whenever a lorry passed.

Every other resident on Yeoman Road – well-upholstered gynaecologists and estate agents – had bought their house with their own money. And indeed, had plenty more to pay for underfloor heating and ergonomic German kitchens, and to freshly lacquer their front door so it shone as sparkly and confident as a politician's smile.

Defiant in shabby, chilly gentility, Ma and Dad were never invited to the Yeoman Road Residents Association, mostly because the meetings were about them and the fact that they hadn't repainted their facade in fourteen years.

'Bid, cup of tea?' Dad was poised with the kettle.

Bid shook her patchy little head. 'I think I'll go upstairs for a while and do some vomiting.'

'Good woman.'

As soon as poor Bid had headed off, I rounded on Ma. 'What's she *on*? That stuff about Damien?'

Ma shook her head sadly. 'She's been reading Mills and Boons. Too sick to concentrate on anything else. They're poison, those things. Refined sugar for the brain.'

'Dad says you're giving up smoking?'

'That's right. We must provide a supportive environment for Bid. In fact, Grace, if she knew *you* were giving up too, she'd appreciate it.'

'. . . Er . . .'

'Ask Damien as well.'

'God, I don't know about that . . .'

'Solidarity! Go on, he's scared witless of you.'

'Ma, he's not.'

'Everyone's scared witless of you.'

'Ah Ma . . .'

'Tell me what happened to your car.'

I sighed. 'Nothing much to tell. It was outside the house when I went to bed last night, it wasn't there this morning. I rang the rozzers and they found it, a charred husk, on the Tallaght bypass. It happens. It's just a great big pain in the arse.'

'Were you insured?' Ma asked, triggering a rant from Dad.

'Insured?' he cried. 'As if it would make a difference. You check the small print on your policy, Grace, and it wouldn't surprise me to discover you're covered for absolutely everything, *except* burn-outs on the Tallaght bypass on a Thursday at the end of September. A crowd of amoral crooks, insurers. Big business holding the ordinary man to ransom, putting the fear of penury in him, leaching billions a year from his meagre pay packet, with no intention of honouring their side of the bargain –'

Dad looked set to run for some time, so I answered Ma. 'I was insured but, like Dad says, they're bound to pull some stunt so I won't get enough money to replace it.' A pang of loss pierced me. I'd loved that car – zippy, sexy, all mine. The first new car I'd ever owned and I'd only had it four months. 'I'll have to get a loan or something.'

This brought Dad's rant to an abrupt end. Both he and Ma said quite quickly, anxiously even, ' ''Neither a borrower nor a lender be! For loan oft loses both itself and friend.'''

I shook my head. 'I won't be looking for anything from you.'

'Just as well. We haven't a pot to piss in,' Dad said.

'I'd better go.'

'Where?'

'Hairdresser's. Getting my colour done.'

Ma disapproved. Her own hair was a short grey pudding bowl that she cut herself with the nail scissors. Even Dad took more pride in his appearance. Aged sixty-nine, he still had a thick sweep of silvery hair and attended Champs Barbers on a monthly basis to maintain his favoured style of Left Bank Thinker, circa 1953.

Into the quiet came the sounds of Auntie Bid puking her guts out in the upstairs (only) toilet.

Ma asked, 'Do you know how much Irish women spend annually on haircare? Money that could be better spent on –'

'Please, Ma, it's just some highlights!' I did a quick sweep of my appearance, from my black trouser suit to my flat boots. 'I'm hardly Barbie!'

In the hairdresser's, my bruised cheekbone caused a stir.

'You must have really riled him,' Carol said. 'What d'you do? Burn his dinner? Forget to wash his jocks?'

I started channelling Ma and wanted to say something po-faced like, 'Domestic violence is no joke.' But I kept my mouth shut. No one with sense locks horns with their hairdresser.

'I'm a journalist,' I said. 'It goes with the territory.'

'You? You write about breast-feeding and drunk teen-agers. Like, you're not a crime reporter.'

137

Carol knew me well. I'd gone to her for years. She had no imagination and neither had I. All I had ever wanted was for her to make my mousey roots blonde. I didn't want lowlights or stripes or anything fancy and, as luck would have it, she didn't know how to do them. It was an arrangement that suited us both.

'Tell me what happened,' she said.

'You won't believe me.'

'Tell me anyway.'

'I fell over in the street. I tripped on a loose paving stone outside Trinity and landed flat on my face. Everyone waiting for the 16A saw me. Lots of people laughed.'

Carol thought I was holding out, so she left the stuff on for too long and burnt my scalp. Out at the rainy bus stop it was rush hour and I had to jostle with what seemed like hundreds of teenage schoolboys to get on the bus, and when I was turned away because the bus was full my mood took a downward turn. I was sad about Auntie Bid, even though she was a contrary old boot, and sad about my car and full of dread that I might have to give up smoking.

Also quite annoyed because, in the melée as we'd tried to board the bus, one of the schoolboys had pinched my arse and I wasn't able to identify the culprit in order to 'discuss' it with him.

Despite swathes of them having swarmed onto the bus – *my* bus, taking *my* seat – there were still an unholy number left at the bus stop. Sourly I eyed them swinging their satchels at each other and passing around a single cigarette. I hated teenage boys, I decided. I absolutely hated them.

I hated their spots and their randiness and I hated the way they were different sizes. I mean, look at them! Some were miniature four-foot squirts and others were six-foot lummoxes with overextended, gangling arms that scraped off the ground, and they all hung around together in one ridiculous mismatched gang.

My disconsolate gaze landed on a cluster of schoolgirls covertly watching the boys from beneath sparkly eyelashes, and I decided I hated them too. Their exaggerated giggles and stench of fake strawberry and inch-thick layers of sticky lipgloss literally dripping off their pouty mouths. Also the way they tended to despise me for being ancient (thirty-five) and not wearing high heels or enough make-up. *If I ever turn into her, just shoot me.* I once heard one of them actually say that! (Which was very unfair as I'd just spent forty-nine hours in a freezing, muddy field, without bathroom or coffee-making facilities, trying to get a story. That's why I don't work hard news any more. Too much time standing in a ditch in the pelting rain, day in, day out.)

Nursing my grievances, I sent Damien a text.

R u cooking 2nite?

No. R u?

I sighed. Put my phone back in my pocket. We'd go to the Indian.

Another bus rounded the corner and the crowd surged forward. God, this was so stressful. I clenched my jaw with grim determination. I was getting on this bus, as God was my witness. (Actually he probably wasn't. Not according to letters sent from readers, telling me I would burn in hell.) And if any of those spotty oiks tried pawing me, they were getting an elbow in the spleen. Pinch my arse once and get away with it, shame on you. Pinch my arse twice and get away with it, shame on me.

This time I got on, I even got a seat, and I tried to lose myself in my Dennis Lehane, but the journey took for ever, letting the entire population of Ireland on and off at each stop, and every now and again I'd have to put my book down and sigh heavily to demonstrate how pissed off I was.

On the up side, at least I'd have something to write about for next week's column. But all the same. It's not every day your car is stolen and burnt out, and even though it was nothing personal – at least I hoped it wasn't . . . I've offended one or two people over the years, but surely I couldn't have riled them to that extent? – I still felt slightly paranoid, like the world wasn't a very nice place, which of course it wasn't, but most of the time I didn't mind.

I was hungry. I didn't know how I'd let that happen. I feared long stretches without food and believed in pre-ventative eating, eating even when I wasn't hungry, just to avoid it.

My pocket started vibrating, and when I got my phone out I nearly elbowed the woman beside me onto the floor.

'You're not going to like this.' It was one of the subs, Hannah 'Dreary' Leary. 'Big Daddy won't go with your column. Not controversial enough. Look, I'm only the messenger. Can you file another?'

'When?' I knew when. I was just being awkward.

'Next half-hour.'

I snapped my phone shut and my hand lit up with pain. I kept forgetting about it, then being reminded in the most unpleasant way possible. Proceeding with more caution, I gingerly extracted my laptop from my satchel, apologized to the unfortunate woman next to me for once again invading her space with my elbows, and started typing.

Controversial? I'd give him controversial.

It was ten to eight before I got home. Home was a red-brick terrace in 'the upmarket suburb of Donnybrook'. (Quote from estate agent.) A pretty house, very charming with original features. *Extremely* small.

Of course it wasn't exactly in the heart of Donnybrook, because if it was it would have cost us an awful lot more and wouldn't have been such a long walk from the bus stop outside the Donnybrook Pharmacy. In fact, none of the shops near us was called the 'Donnybrook' anything. Not a good sign. Perhaps we didn't live in Donnybrook at all. Perhaps we'd been had by the estate agent and actually lived in Ranelagh, which wasn't half as nice.

Damien – he of the powerful build and fine naked thighs – was standing at the kitchen counter, the paper open in front of him, colouring black teeth into a picture of Bono. He looked knackered.

'Finally!' he declared. He baulked, the way he did every time he saw my bruised face. 'I was just going to text you. What kept you?'

'Fecking bus.' I threw down my bag and started unbuttoning my jacket. 'Ten minutes at each stop.'

'Sorry I didn't get to talk to you all day,' he said. 'Small scandalette emerged in the Dail session and it was all hands to the pumps.'

I waved away his apologies. Damien was also a journalist, the political correspondent on the *Press*. I knew about deadlines.

'What did the insurance company have to say for themselves?' he asked.

'Ha! You'll love this. If my car had been just damaged, I'd be entitled to a loaner until it was fixed. But because it's a write-off, no loaner. Can you believe it? I spent the whole morning on the blower to them, I did no work. Jacinta wasn't happy –'

'– Jacinta's never happy.'

'*Then* I disappeared early to get my hair done.'

'It's very nice,' he said quickly.

I laughed.

'How long before the money comes through for another car?' he asked.

'Your guess is as good as mine. And whatever they give me, it won't be enough to buy a new one.' Gloomily I unzipped my boots.

'Don't take them off,' he said. 'Stick your jacket back on, let's go down to the Indian and get a takeaway.' He wrapped his arms around me. 'Grace, we'll do the sums, see if we can get a bank loan to buy you new wheels right now. And until then I can bring you to work on the bike.'

Damien was too impatient to drive a car. Instead he wove in and out of the ranks of Dublin gridlock on a black and silver Kawasaki. (Ma calls it a Kamikaze. She worries.)

'But you'll have to go miles out of your way.'

The *Press* were based in some wretched industrial estate on the M50, where you can buy eight thousand scanners but you can't buy a single sandwich, while the *Spokesman*'s offices were in the city centre.

'It's okay. You're worth it. So how's Bid?'

'Bad. Out of the blue she said she reckoned you have a fine pair of thighs when you're naked.'

'Jesus! What brought that on?'

'Nothing.'

He went quiet, locked inside himself for a few moments. Then gave a little laugh. 'God. Anyway, how's the chemo going?'

'She looked awful. The colour of butter.'

'Butter? But that's a nice colour.' He thought about it. 'Maybe not in a human being.'

Almost eight months ago Bid had gone to the doctor because her persistent cough was driving Dad round the bend. The doc had told her to have a bronchoscopy, but an appointment didn't come free for seven months. When it finally did, cancer was diagnosed immediately. Surgery followed, when a ten-centimetre primary tumour was removed from her left lung, but her lymph nodes showed 'positive for metastatic disease'. Translation: it had spread to her lymph nodes. (I was fooled briefly by the word 'positive', thinking it meant something good.) To treat the lymph nodes, she was to get six rounds of 'aggressive' chemo, at four-week intervals. It would be next February before we knew whether or not she'd be okay. If she'd been given the bronchoscopy when she'd first gone to the doctor, the cancer wouldn't have had time to metastasize to her lymph nodes and she'd be better already.

'Poor Bid,' Damien said.

'. . . Ah . . . listen.' I decided to go for it. 'I'm glad you're sympathetic because I've something to tell you and you're not going to like it. Ma and Dad are giving up smoking. And so are you and I.'

He stared at me.

'In solidarity,' I urged.

'Solidarity,' he muttered. 'With Bid, it's like having a second mother-in-law. I'm the most misfortunate man alive.'

Now and again Damien and I discussed giving up cigarettes. Usually when we were skint and one of us added up how much we spent on them. We always agreed that the right thing would be to give up, but rarely did anything about it.

'I'm worried about Bid,' he said. 'I *need* to smoke.'

'Nice try. Go again.'

'Grace, if we stop smoking, we'll put on four stone each.'

'We could start jogging again. We were going great guns there for a while.'

'Easy in the summer.'

We'd been so good. All through May and June, we had gone running in the early morning, in our matching sweats, like a couple from a mortgage ad. I used to watch us from the outside and marvel at how convincing we looked. Sometimes I'd smile at people coming home from getting their paper. Once or twice I even waved at a milkman. He never waved back, just stared after us suspiciously, wondering if we were somehow taking the piss out of him. Over the weeks, we'd built up the distance covered, making measurable progress. Then we'd gone on holiday in July and ate and drank our heads off and just never got back into it.

'Even talking about giving up is making me want to smoke more.' Damien reached for his pack, the way devout Catholic women reach for their rosary beads. 'Let's have one for the road.'

We sat outside on the back step, savouring cigarettes that seemed even more delicious than usual.

Blowing out a long plume of smoke, his eyes narrowed, Damien said, 'Are you serious?'

'Ma has put the guilts on me,' I said. She's a master at that. Always for a good cause, though. 'If Bid doesn't get better and I haven't stopped smoking, it'll be my fault. And yours too, Damien Stapleton,' I added. 'Murderer.'

'Take a look at this.' Damien picked up the remote.

'What is it?'

'You'll see.'

The screen went blue, then jumped into life. A man, a young man was emerging from the front door of a suburban-looking house. Longish, mid-brown hair and oozing sex, he walked with a hint of a swagger, very sure of himself. 'Oh my God!' I yelped. 'What age were you?'

'Twenty, as far as I can figure out.'

On the screen, Damien stopped and leant against a car, then gave a slow smile straight at the lens. 'What?' his voice asked. 'You filming me?'

'Yes,' a girl's voice said. 'Say something.'

'Like what?' Damien laughed, a little bit awkward, a little bit shy, more than a little bit sexy.

God, I thought. Sixteen years ago. Half a lifetime.

'Say something profound,' the girl's voice urged.

The twenty-year-old Damien shrugged. 'Don't eat yellow snow.'

'That's your message to the world?'

'Work is the curse of the drinking classes!' He gave a clenched-fist salute. 'Power to the people.'

'Thank you, Damien Stapleton.'

The screen went blue again. It was over.

'Where did you get this?' I asked.

'Juno.'

'...*Juno*?'

His ex-wife.

To be fair, it's probably not as dramatic as it sounds. They'd only been married for three years, from the ages of twenty-two to twenty-five. (Yes, both of them; they were the same age, they'd been at school together.) It was just the usual twenty-something relationship that everyone has, the only difference was that they'd made the mistake of actually getting married.

All the same, though ... We could have done without another blast from the past; we were still getting back on our feet after the last one.

'Juno?' I prompted Damien. 'What's the story?'

'She's putting all her old family videos on DVD and came across this. Sent it to Mum, who sent it on to me.' He added, 'She told Mum there was more to come.'

*

It was ten years since I'd met Damien, on a press trip to Phuket, when I was a features writer on the *Times*. Damien shouldn't have been there; he was a serious political correspondent who had no place covering trips to Thailand, but he was skint and desperate for a holiday and his features editor had taken pity on him.

I noticed him at the airport check-in queue. He was standing in a cluster of other journos but somehow on the margins, and I swear to God, I felt like I'd had a blow to the head.

There was just something about him, a self-containment, an independence, that made me throb with fascination.

Right away I knew he'd be choosy. Tricky even. I knew he'd put up a fight. Up until then I'd never understood those women who thought so little of themselves that they fell in love only with emotionally unavailable men. Now look at me.

But I couldn't help it. I just gazed at this man – whoever he was – and I thought, I want *you*. The whole thing gave me quite a fright.

I cornered my friend Triona (features writer at the *Independent*) and asked, 'Your man over there . . . ?'

'Damien Stapleton from the *Tribune*?'

'Yes. You know him?'

'Yes, what about him . . . wha –? Oh no, Grace, no.'

I was surprised. I thought everyone else would lust after him too and I'd have a fierce battle on my hands.

'He's not your type at all.' Triona sounded alarmed. 'He's too . . . you'd never know where you were with him.'

I hardly heard her. I was noticing ancillary details, a secondary layer of attractiveness. He had a great body.

Powerful-looking. And although he wasn't what you might call lanky, he was tall *enough* – i.e. as tall as me. (Maybe even an inch or two more.)

'He has no sense of humour,' Triona warned, the very worst thing that could be said about an Irish man.

But I made him laugh.

On every bus trip and tourist-board dinner in Phuket, I engineered it so that I was sitting next to Damien Stapleton. Even when we had days 'at leisure' he'd find himself cheek by jowl with me at the poolside. But if he was bemused by me popping up wherever he was, he didn't say.

That was the whole problem – he said almost nothing. I was the one who did all the talking, wheeling out my best anecdotes and entertaining stories. Often he looked confused – at times even pained – but his eyes never left my face, and now and again, if I said something he agreed with, he'd give a slow nodding smile or even laugh softly. I took this as sufficient encouragement to keep going.

All the other journos begged me, 'Grace, would you leave that poor fella alone? You've the life scared out of him.'

Even Dickie McGuinness from crime on the *Times* – who'd spent so much time hanging around with criminals that he'd developed a menacing persona himself – muttered an intimidating warning out of the side of his mouth. 'A word to the wise, Grace. Men like to do the chasing.'

'No,' I said belligerently. 'Men are lazy and will take the path of least resistance. And stop looking at me like you're going to staple me to the wall. You shouldn't even be on this trip, you work in crime.'

'I needed a . . . holiday.' He invested the word with heavy meaning.

'I appreciate your advice, Dickie – actually no, that's a lie, I don't. And don't give me any more because I'm not going to take it.'

The truth was I couldn't stay away from Damien – it shocked me, to be honest – and now and then he dropped a little nugget of information that convinced me we were perfect for each other. For example, he didn't like radishes (neither did I) or boating trips on the Shannon (neither did I). He liked thrillers (so did I) and staying up late, watching reruns of bad eighties' shows like *Magnum PI* and *Knight Rider* (so did I). He thought fruit-picking holidays were a swizz. (Again, so did I and no one else did. Everyone else enjoyed them.)

Looking for advice, I rang my twin sister, Marnie. She was always reading books about relationships. Full of wisdom, so she was. Also she wouldn't laugh at me.

'Describe *everything*,' she asked. 'What he looked like the first time you saw him, what you were wearing . . .'

It was a pleasure simply talking about him and I went on and on. I finished up with, 'Tell me what to do.'

'Me?' Marnie said. 'I'm hardly the poster girl for how to get a man.'

'You get plenty.'

'And never manage to hang on to them. I'm too mental.'

Sad but true. Marnie was deeply intuitive, but it only seemed to work on others; she was unable to use her razor-sharp analysis to sort out her own life. Her relationships usually ended in some sort of disaster. But unlike me, who fell for a man about once a decade, Marnie threw herself into grand passions every second week. In fact, our attitude to romance was similar to our health: Marnie got every bug that was going, but recovered quickly; I, on the other hand, hardly ever got sick but, when I did, I'd parlay a nondescript cold into bronchitis, tonsillitis and, one memorable December, foot and mouth (not as funny as it sounds).

'Just how serious is this?' Marnie asked.

'Pneumonia. Both lungs. Pleurisy . . . and possibly TB.'

'That's bad . . . But, at the risk of sounding like Ma, Grace, the best advice I can give is to just be yourself. No one is better than you.'

'Aw come on . . .'

'You are! You know exactly who you are, you don't take crap from anyone, you can do long division in your head, you tell a good story, you don't mind getting caught in the rain without an umbrella –'

'But shouldn't I be playing games? Pretending I don't like him? Oh Marnie, it's all such bollocks! If a man likes a woman, he sends her flowers –'

'You wouldn't want flowers. You'd laugh.'

She was *exactly* right. That was precisely what I would do.

' – or he simply picks up the phone and asks her out. Why can't women do that? Why do we have to pretend we feel the opposite to how we actually feel? It's just yet another way that women get shafted –'

'Are you trying out a column on me?'

'No. No. No.' Perhaps, actually. I meandered to a dispirited halt. 'He's divorced.'

'So what? Everyone has baggage.'

Usually press trips were debauched affairs but I behaved impeccably. If I couldn't have Damien, I didn't want anyone else.

At the airport taxi rank, it was no surprise that he didn't ask for my number. And I didn't ask for his because after ten days of getting nowhere, I'd got the message.

I knew how hard it was to decide that you didn't care about someone simply because they didn't care about you. You can't just unplug your heart at the mains. But I was a practical person and did my best. So Damien wasn't interested, but there were others who were. (Not loads, I'm not saying that, but one or two possibles.) So I gave it a go with Scott Holmes, a fast-living Kiwi who worked for the *Sunday Globe*. But, despite my best efforts – and I'd tried really hard to like him – at most he amounted only to a ticklish cough.

Occasional Damien-rumours reached me – that he was getting back with his wife, that he'd been seen getting into a taxi late at night with Marcella Kennedy from the *Sunday Independent* . . .

Now and again I even bumped into him (despite my determination to put my unrequited love behind me, I'd befriended people at the *Tribune* and even occasionally snuck along to the launch of a political manifesto) and he always seemed pleased to see me. Well, not exactly pleased – not like a cocker spaniel when his master comes home – but he answered my questions without evident reluctance.

The night of Lucinda Breen's thirtieth-birthday party appeared to be no different. It was late in the evening and

I was feeling a bit drunk, a bit dangerous and a bit angry, even though it wasn't his fault that he didn't fancy me.

'How are you, Grace?'

Even the way he said my name hurt.

'Annoyed. Why is everything so much easier for men?'

'Is it?'

'They can pee standing up.' Then, segueing from the general to the particular, 'And when they fancy someone they can just throw them a cheesy chat-up line.'

'Like what?'

'Like . . . if I said you had a beautiful body would you hold it against me?'

'Yes,' he said.

'Yes, what?'

'Yes, I would hold it against you.'

I was dumbstruck for a good ten seconds. 'You would?'

'Yes. I thought you'd never ask.'

Again I was dumbstruck.

'Why should I have to ask? You're the man.'

'Grace Gildee, I never knew you were such an old romantic.'

'I'm not.'

'That's what I thought.'

'But if you were . . . interested . . . you *are* interested, aren't you? I'm not making a big fool of myself here, am I?'

'No.'

'No?'

'No, you're not making a fool of yourself. Yes, I am interested.'

Was this really happening?

'So why didn't you let me know?'

'. . . I wasn't sure. You were friendly, but you're friendly to everyone . . . I've been out of the game a long time.'

I couldn't believe he was saying these things. It was as if my real life and my fantasy life had merged. Every word I'd ever wished for was coming from his mouth.

'You're so full of life,' he said. 'I thought I'd never be enough for you. Dazzler.'

'What?'

'That's my name for you. Dazzler Gildee. Because you dazzle me.'

He had a name for me?

Extract from the *Spokesman* **Grace Gildee, She's Sugar-free** column, Saturday, 27 September

I hate teenage boys. I hate their spots and their randiness and, above all, the way they see a woman's bum as something to be pinched. Every arse is an *opportunity*.

And frankly they're an eyesore. As soon as puberty kicks in, all teenage boys should be rounded up and incarcerated in a compound until the age of eighteen. That'll clean up our streets.

While they're in there, they can forget about reading *Nuts* and *Loaded* and *Maxim*. Feed them a strict diet of feminist literature, everything from Germaine Greer to Julie Burchill. So, when we let them out, they're fully grown, spot-free and informed about women. Maybe even with a little respect for us?

*

Harsh, I know, but they pay me to be controversial.

'Squeeze your mumble in mumble!' Damien called over his shoulder.

'What?'

'Your legs!' He lifted the visor on his lid. 'Squeeze them tight to the bike!'

I saw why. He was about to take us through a slender channel between a dark blue van and a people-carrier. 'Breathe in!' he yelled.

The journey to work on the back of his bike was thrilling. In a very bad way. Damien saw everything as a challenge, almost like a personal test. No space was too tight, no light too amber, no gridlock too dense that it couldn't be negotiated with a series of cunning zigs and zags. If he'd been given the chance to fly over eighteen buses, to gain a couple of seconds, he'd have jumped at it.

Maybe he didn't have enough excitement in his life?

He pulled up outside the *Spokesman* and took off his lid to kiss me. His biker leathers, the throb of the machine between my legs, well, it was all quite sexy . . .

'Be strong,' I said.

I wasn't talking about the remainder of his journey. I was talking about something far more daunting – our decision to stop smoking. Ma had caught Bid having a sneaky fag in the bathroom and blowing the smoke out of the window, 'Like a teenager!' as Ma had said in her call. 'The last straw.' Then she'd put Bid on the line and I found myself telling her that if I could knock cigarettes on the head, so could she.

'And Damien,' Ma had called.

'And Damien,' I'd said reluctantly, while Damien buried his head in his hands and groaned, 'No!'

'Strong,' he repeated sardonically.

'Damien, you're not so much losing a –'

' – friend,' he said.

' – habit. As gaining a healthy new body.'

He didn't answer. Just shoved his lid back on and roared away, like a cat showing me its bum.

This wasn't going to come off, him taking me to work on the bike. To do my job properly I had to have a car. Not just for getting around, but as a wardrobe. In the boot of my old car, I'd had outfits for all situations. To persuade a nice, middle-class woman to talk about the death of her baby, I had a neat, pretty suit, low-heeled courts, even a string of pearls. For standing by a freezing dockside, waiting to discover if fishermen from an overturned trawler had lived or died, I had gloves, boots and a thermal vest (my secret weapon). For a feature on drugs I had skanger-chic sportswear.

Yusuf leapt forward to open the glass door. Not something he normally did, but he had a question. Already he was laughing, his teeth very white in his dark face. 'Was that you on the bike?'

I nodded. No point lying, much as I wanted to, because I was carrying a helmet. He shot an excited look at Mrs Farrell, the receptionist and most powerful person in the *Spokesman*. Woe betide anyone who fell foul of her. You might as well resign. She could withhold phone calls from your dying mother, 'accidentally' give your home address to maniacs, or 'forget' to let you know that the fresh kidney for your kidney transplant had arrived. Even Big Daddy (Coleman Brien, the editor) took care around her.

'What happened to your car?' she asked.

'Stolen. Burnt out.' Again there was no point lying. Dickie McGuinness in crime would get it from the police database in two seconds. (Dickie and I seemed to always end up working in the same place. We'd been in the *Times* together; when I left for the *Independent*, he showed up after a month; then he moved to the *Spokesman* and six months later they offered me a job.)

'God, that's terrible.' Then Yusuf and Mrs Farrell exploded with laughter.

When Yusuf had first arrived, he'd been a sweet, gentle Somalian man. Then he'd got infected by Mrs Farrell and the *Spokesman* ethos. He was horrible now, horrible like the rest of us.

Mrs Farrell hit the phones. It was like a rerun of the Friday before last when my bruised, cut face had caused a similar stir. She was gleefully telling everyone my sorry story. It had been idiocy to think my stolen car could remain a secret and now I was facing a day of major mockery, with all kinds of presents left on my desk: boxes of matches; small scorched red cars; a bus timetable . . .

'Morning, Sugarfree.'

I'm called Sugarfree because I have a reputation for being acerbic. (If I was a man, however, I'd simply have a reputation for being straight-talking.) Also Sugarfree rhymes with Gildee. Everyone in the *Spokesman* has a descriptive nickname that rhymes with their surname. For example, Hannah Leary is always complaining about late delivery of copy and never comes for a drink on Friday night. So hers is, 'Hannah Leary, she's very dreary.' (Hannah knows about this. Everyone knows their rhyme. A newspaper office is a harsh, honest environment.)

In Features, phones were ringing and nearly everyone was already in. Apart from Casey Kaplan, of course. He kept his own hours. Monday morning at 9 a.m.? Casey was probably drinking Jack and Coke in some early house with Bono. I said hello to Lorraine, Joanne, Tara and Clare – Features was staffed almost entirely with women; the hours were more regular than news, which made life easier if you had kids. Because I was the only features writer who didn't have any, I got sent on all the unpredictable jobs, which couldn't guarantee to end at five-thirty on the dot.

At the desk next to mine, TC Scanlan was typing at speed. Being that rare creature, a male features writer, he was the butt of many a sexist comment, the favourite being, 'He sits down to pee.' (Like I said, a newspaper office is a cruel place.)

'Sorry to hear about your car,' he said. 'You know, I was *wondering* what you were up to on Friday, all those hush-hush phone calls!' A great big smile, now that he knew. He stood up and rummaged around in his trouser pocket, then counted out some change. 'There you go. One euro twenty. Your bus fare home.'

The phone rang and went straight to voicemail – we never answered. 'Irate readers out in force this morning,' he said. 'That piece about the teenage boys. It's nearly as bad as when you wrote about not wanting children.'

Yes. I'd realized I'd overstepped the mark when I got a message from Ma on Saturday morning. The *Spokesman* isn't her usual reading material, she's a *Guardian* woman through and through, but she likes to keep an eye on what I'm writing.

'Grace,' she'd said. 'Your column, that's going too far! Yes, I can't abide teenage boys either. They're so . . . well . . . *greasy*. Not just their skin, they genuinely can't help that, you know, it's their hormones. But they put stuff in their hair which makes it . . . well . . . *greasy* is the only word I can think of, or perhaps they simply don't wash it for weeks on end. But you can't make jokes about internment, not even about teenage boys.'

She added, 'I liked the notion of the feminist literature, though.'

'Any death threats?' I asked TC.

'Just the usual.'

'Grand, grand.'

They say you always remember your first time: your first love, your first car, your first death threat. About three years ago, when I'd just started at the *Spokesman*, to lay out my stall, I did a controversial piece on the tyranny of breast-feeding. The following morning, a message was waiting on my voicemail. 'I'm going to kill you, Grace Gildee, you feminist slut. I know what you look like and I know where you live.' Although his lines were a little unoriginal, I was trembling like a child. I'd never before had a death threat. Not even, at the start of my career, when I'd been working crime at the *Times*.

I'd always thought of myself as a bit of a crusader but

I couldn't believe how frightened I was. And it made me wonder how I'd have coped in a place like Algeria, where if you write that the president's new haircut makes him look like Elton John, you could look forward to your car going up like a fireball the next time you turned the key in your ignition.

I'd told TC about the message, who'd told Jacinta Kinsella, who'd listened to the first two seconds of it then said with exasperation, 'Oh that fool. Mr I Know Where You Live. I thought we'd got rid of him.' She'd deleted it with a sharp jab. ' "I know what you look like"'? All he has to do is look at your photo, for God's sake!'

'So there's nothing to worry about?'

'Nothing, nothing.' Said impatiently. She'd been on her way out to lunch (at 10.35 a.m.).

Now I get death threats on a fairly regular basis. (All you have to do is ring the switchboard and say to Mrs Farrell, 'I want to leave Grace Gildee a death threat,' and you'll be put through.) I have five or six regulars who seem to have a rota. But none of them has followed up on their promises, so I've sort of relaxed and accepted that they're just all talk.

'What've you got for me, Grace?'

'And hello to you too,' I said.

It was Jacinta Kinsella, carrying one of her five Birkin bags. Her husband had bought her one every time she gave birth, and to be honest I'd rather carry my stuff in a plastic bag that smelt of curry, if that was the price. Today's bag was black, to match her mood. Whenever she showed up with her yellow one, there was rejoicing all round. It meant she would probably buy us ice-cream out of petty cash.

Very glam, was Jacinta. She got her raven's-wing hair blow-dried every single morning of her life and she was always dressed as if she was going to the races. Whenever a funeral needed to be covered, Jacinta got sent, because she had the best coat.

'Let me get my notes,' I said.

Jacinta is Head of Features and I'm Chief Features Writer and we have a good relationship. Well, good*ish* – if she wasn't so rattly about me wanting her job, and, of course, if I wasn't praying for her to take early retirement or to be head-hunted by another paper . . .

Now and again something blows up in her face and Big Daddy tries to sack her but she calls in the union and flings around blame like Jackson Pollock with a can of paint. Basically there's no getting rid of her. (Her little rhyme goes, 'Jacinta Kinsella, she's invincible.')

'Jacinta,' TC called to her. 'Message from Casey. He's chasing up a story so big, quote ''it'll rock our world'' unquote.'

'Did he actually say that?' I exclaimed. 'That it'll rock our world?'

'What time will he be in?' Jacinta asked sharply.

TC shook his head sadly. 'Why ask me? I'm nobody.'

Jacinta was in way over her head with Casey. No control at all. Big Daddy had lured him from the *Sunday Globe* to 'sex us up', then foisted him on Jacinta. 'Another man for Features.'

Big Daddy was as pleased as punch with his acquisition:

Casey had made such a name for himself doing big inter-views that he was sort of a celebrity in his own right. His profiles had become water-cooler material and fell roughly into two types. Version one, a savage (admittedly amusing) deconstruction of the celebrity, their vapid stupidity, the bizarre requests they made of their staff and how unattractive they were up close without the benefit of air-brushing.

Version two, a stream-of-consciousness, present-tense account of eighteen-hour marathon drinking sessions with rock bands or movie stars as they ricocheted around the city from club to club, finally coming to rest in a hotel suite strewn with baggies of coke and half-eaten club sandwiches.

I hated his work. It was self-serving and egotistical. But I couldn't say that because everyone would think I was jealous. Which I was.

'Sugarfree? Cigarette break? It'll rock your world.'

'Can you credit that idiot?' I produced a packet of Nicorette gum. I believed in arming myself with as much protection as possible. 'Anyway bad news, TC, I'm giving up.'

'Again? Good luck,' he said. 'Nothing to it. I've given up loads of times.'

Wistfully I stroked my packet of gum and watched him and the others heading off to the fire escape. It wasn't just the nicotine I wanted, it was the human contact. The best conversations I've ever had have been over cigarettes. Smokers were like a secret society and even – as happened in pubs – when we were corralled into smokers' paddocks, like untouchables, cigarettes provided camaraderie and intimacy. I'd given up before so this feeling – a deep sadness, like a very good friend has moved to Australia – was familiar, but that wasn't making it any easier.

Nineteen new emails since the last time I'd checked – less than an hour ago. Press release after press release from PR firms, all looking for coverage: indoor barbecue sets; the benefits of tea-tree oil; a report on incontinence; a cookbook from a celebrity chef; a newsletter from Women's Aid . . .

Anything at all I could work with? As I scanned down, a report on penile enhancement caught my eye. That might be fun.

Then I saw something that made my heart beat faster: Madonna was coming to Ireland to do three concerts. But every media outlet in the land would be begging for her – what made me any different? I just knew I could do a good job. Better than anyone else.

I abandoned everything to compose an agonizingly perfect pitch to Madonna's publicist – trying to sound simultaneously craven, intelligent and fun – thus beginning the complex process of wooing a big star.

I was coming back from buying a bag of wine gums, a cheese roll and two packets of crisps – I'd eaten a bar of fruit and nut coming up the stairs, anything to cushion the fall from Mount Nicotine – when I got enmeshed in the rush for the morning editorial meeting. All the heads of department were moving, as a single body, towards the editor's office. ('Coleman Brien. We're too scared of him to do a rhyme.')

Jacinta came clipping over. 'Grace, where did you get to?'

I indicated my haul.

'Look, I can't do this meeting.'

There was always something. She had to bring a child to the dentist, or to the nutritionist, or to EuroDisney . . .

'Okay. Which of these will I pitch?'

She scanned my notes. 'Go for lunchtime eye-lifts. Breast cancer. Fat brats.'

I tore open the wine gums and crammed a handful of dark-coloured ones into my mouth. I couldn't bring the bag to the meeting because Big Daddy went berserk at the sound of rustling.

I slid into his office, the meeting had already started; Jonno Fido from the newsdesk was going through today's big stories. I leant against a filing cabinet, half listening while sucking quietly. Lovely sweets. Then . . . no! A sour taste. I'd got a yellow one! How had that happened? It must have been lying in wait, camouflaging itself among the reds and blacks.

I couldn't spit it out and shout, like I would have at home, 'Yellow one, yellow one! Mission abort!' I had to keep sucking until it dissolved.

Jonno finished up; foreign went next, then sport and then crime, of which there was tons.

'Political?'

David Thornberry sat up straighter. 'The Dee Rossini story won't go away. On Friday the news broke about her getting her house painted for free.' I knew about this. It was the mini-scandalette which had kept Damien late at work.

163

I stopped my mental grousing about yellow wine gums and their inherent treachery and started paying real attention. Dee Rossini was the Minister for Education and leader of NewIreland, Paddy's party.

'Over the weekend, it's been explained away – Rossini sent the decorating firm a cheque last November but they never cashed it – but I've been leaked another story. An exclusive. She was supposed to pay for her daughter's wedding, but the hotel haven't been paid. I did a bit of digging – the hotel is owned by the Mannix Group.' He paused for impact. 'The same group which owns R&D Decorators, the crowd who painted her house for free. Obviously she's got some in with them.' The implication was that, as Minister for Education, Dee Rossini had the power to issue contracts for building schools and the Mannix Group were giving her freebies in exchange for future commissions. If it was true, it would do long-term damage to NewIreland.

'Or maybe she's being set up?' Big Daddy said. He was a fan of NewIreland. 'Go soft on it.'

'What if she's on the take and it looks like we've condoned it?' David was flushed with anger. He was watching his big exciting exclusive disappear. 'If we don't splash on this, someone else will. My source will take this elsewhere.'

'I'm telling you, go soft on it,' Big Daddy repeated. He had a deep rumbly voice, which made windows vibrate.

'If we go soft, everyone else will pick it up tomorrow and we'll look like saps for downplaying a dirty story. And how does it make the Nappies look, in coalition with crooks?'

'Dee Rossini is no crook. And if the Nationalist Party of

Ireland objected to crooks being in power, they'd all have to resign.'

'For fuck's –'

'Right,' Big Daddy said. 'Features?'

He looked around for Jacinta and I put my hand up. 'She sends her apologies.'

'What've you got?'

'Lunchtime eye-lifts?'

'Jacinta Kinsella is not getting her eyes done on my time. Next!'

'Breast cancer. Report just in. Ireland has a high percentage of false negatives, much higher than the EU average.'

'Anything else?'

'Obesity in schoolchildren. New figures, it's getting worse.'

'No. No, no. Sick to my craw with that. PlayStations, convenience food, trans fat. Stick to the breast cancer.'

Good. That was the one I wanted to do.

My mobile rang. 'Sorry.' Unlike in the rest of the world, it wasn't a heinous sin to have your mobile on in a newspaper meeting because the heads of news and crime needed to be constantly accessible to their staff out in the field.

I looked at the number and thought I was seeing things. What did he want?

Quickly I switched it off.

Moving on. 'Saturday Supplement?'

That was Desmond Hume, a small, pernickety man with an astonishingly tedious line in conversation. ('Desmond Hume, can empty a room.') He shook his head. It was too early in the week.

'Social Diary?'

Declan O'Dowd said, 'Here.' He wasn't the actual social diarist. The real one – 'Roger McEliss, he's always on the piss' – was at home, probably bent over his toilet bowl puking his guts up. (An oft-debated chicken-and-egg-style conundrum: which comes first, the social diarist or the drink problem?)

'Declan O'Dowd, he never gets out' was a poor sap who had to labour at his desk trying to patch together a page from whatever scraps he could decipher from McEliss between his dry heaves. He only got to be a real social diarist, going to the premieres and parties, when McEliss was incarcerated on his twice-yearly drying-out sessions.

'Paddy de Courcy's wife-to-be was seen trying on wedding dresses.'

'Pics?'

'Yeah.'

I bet. Being nicotine-free made me more impatient than usual. 'From an anonymous source?' I asked. 'And I bet they weren't looking for money?'

It was obvious that the pictures had come from New-Ireland's press office. At a time when mini-scandals were surrounding Dee Rossini, photos of Paddy's radiant wife-to-be, in a white lace extravaganza, could have a somewhat neutralizing effect.

We were all filing back out to our desks, when Big Daddy called, 'Oh Sugarfree?'

Christ alive, what did he want? A puff-piece on his daughter-in-law's kebab shop? A two-thousand-word spread on his grandson's new haircut?

166

'Here.' He passed me a coin. 'For your bus fare. I heard about your car. Only four months old? The first new car you ever owned?' His face was creased with mirth.

'Hahaha,' I said. I mean, I had to. Then, *'Fifty cents?'*

'Isn't it enough?'

'No. One euro twenty.'

'That much?' He began jingling around in his trouser pocket while I backed away. 'No, Mr Brien. I don't actually need it.'

He handed me a euro. 'Keep the change. In fact –' he paused to enjoy a chuckle – 'put it towards tomorrow's fare!'

David Thornberry was venting in a terrible fury. I could hear him from twenty desks away. 'Can you fucking believe the dopey old fool? You can't withhold stories just because you like the person they implicate. It's no fucking way to run a newspaper.'

But he was wrong. Newspapers have always supported their friends and shafted their enemies. Journalists have taken to their graves stories which would have brought down governments if they'd ever been revealed, and perfectly innocent people have been hounded out of job and country, just because the media decided a witch-hunt was in order.

'Anyone got Paddy de Courcy's mobile number?' David called.

'On the database.'

'I mean his real one.'

I dipped my head. I should give it up – what difference would it make? I was never going to talk to him again – but . . .

Jacinta still wasn't back. I tried to commandeer TC but he was working on something else, so I bagged Lorraine. 'Lovely report here,' I said. 'Lots of figures. Translate it into English, would you? And could you do a quick four hundred words on how breast cancer metastasizes? Timescales, response to treatment, etc.'

Then I hit the phones trying to track down women who'd been told they didn't have breast cancer, when in fact they did. I tried the Irish Cancer Society, St Luke's Cancer Hospital and four hospices – all very pleasant – who took my number and said they'd see if they could find a patient who'd be prepared to talk.

'Today,' I emphasized. 'It's for tomorrow's paper.'

I tried internet support groups but no luck there either. Then I gave Bid a ring, in the hope that a breast cancer sufferer might have been in the next bed during her chemo, but no. Bowel cancer, she could do me. Prostate, ovarian and of course lung, but no breast.

'Christ, here he comes,' TC muttered. 'Lock up your cowboy accessories.'

The molecular structure of the air had changed: at twelve thirty-seven, Casey Kaplan had finally shown up for work. In he swaggered in black leather trousers, tight enough to let the world know that he dressed to the left, a black shirt with white ranch-style piping, a brown leather waistcoat, a leather neck-string and scuffed hand-tooled shit-kickers.

He pointed at me. 'Message from Dan Spancil.' A musician I'd profiled. It had been so bloody difficult to get that interview, I'd had to do the back-and-forth with the publicist for weeks, and here was Casey Kaplan behaving as though he'd just spent the weekend with him. 'He says you rock.'

'How nice,' I said briskly. 'So does he.'

'Is Jacinta around?' He lounged in front of my desk.

I made a big show of looking up from my notes. 'No.'

'Where is she?'

'Out.'

'You busy?'

'Yes.'

He laughed. Mocking my diligence? 'Good woman.'

In leisurely fashion he went off and I refocused, trying to remember people I had spoken to at parties, met at functions. Had anyone mentioned they were an oncology nurse, or that their sister had breast cancer? But, despite having contacts in the oddest of places, I drew a blank in the breast cancer world. Bitterly I blamed the absence of nicotine in my system. I bet if I had a smoke I'd gear up enough to remember something.

As a last-ditch resort I could use the testimonials on the internet site, but it wouldn't really work. I needed 'colour' – descriptions of stuff like the sufferer's home ('pretty floral curtains, the mantelpiece crammed with family photographs taken in happier times').

I bounced a pen up and down against my desk. I wanted to do this well. I wanted to do all my stories well, but the slapdash, penny-pinching approach to women's health sometimes made me want to cry with frustration. If such a high number of false negatives had happened with testicular cancer – man cancer – there would be pandemonium.

'Stop clicking that pen!' TC yelped.

I could simply show up at a hospice, and prowl the corridors, asking among the dying until I found a woman to interview, but I had some scruples.

The only thing to do, I decided, was to go into the belly of the beast and contact one of the specialist hospital units which had been the subject of the report. There was little point ringing them, they were bound to be on the defensive. I'd keep my powder dry and go in person.

I switched my mobile back on and tensed for the double beep. But it didn't happen. He hadn't left a message.

'I'm out on a story.' Very quickly I clicked my pen nine or ten times into TC's ear, then swung out of the office.

'Biopsies?' I murmured to the receptionist.

'Left, left again at the double doors, right at the crucifix.'

I emerged into a waiting area, took a seat and flicked through surprisingly up-to-date magazines. I wondered how to play this. I needed access to the patients' computerized records, which I couldn't do without the help of someone who worked here. Preferably someone who hated their job.

The girl behind the Welcome desk was clicking away at a keyboard in a swotty fashion. A jobsworth. No use to me.

A good journalist is a blend of patience and pushiness. Right now, I just needed to be patient. I watched and waited and watched and waited, drumming my fingers on my knee.

It was a busy place. People arrived and gave their details to the swotty girl and sat down and eventually got called by nurses. On the pretext of going to the loo, I took a little wander and discreetly stuck my head around several doors but apart from startling a man having an anal examination,

I saw nothing of interest. I came back and sat down. My stomach started to hurt as the truth trickled through me. This wasn't going to happen, I'd have to go back empty-handed.

I hated to fail, it made me feel so shit about myself, and there was no creature so pitiful as the journalist who came back without the story. A wild thought struck me. I could make it up! I could base it on Auntie Bid! And the internet stuff!

As quickly as it arrived, the idea dissolved. They'd find out and I'd get sacked and no one would employ me ever again.

I'd have to suck it up. It wasn't often that I didn't get my story. Then I remembered – the sand in my oyster, the stone in my shoe – that bloody Lola Daly. How everyone had laughed at me. A sappy fashion stylist with purple hair and I hadn't been able to get her to talk about her ex-boyfriend.

But unlike Lola Daly, this story *mattered.* All those poor women who'd been told they were in the clear and were sent away to let their disease march unimpeded throughout their body, they deserved to have their say. Not to mention the small possibility of shaming the Department of Health into ensuring it didn't happen again.

I was so sunk into gloom that I almost missed the woman huffing and puffing past me. She was talking to herself like the White Rabbit and she radiated resentment.

She barged into the office beside the desk and banged the door, but not before I heard her voice raised querulously. 'How many times . . .'

Thank you, God!

She emerged some minutes later and huffed and puffed

back down the corridor, me following her. When she stopped outside a door and opened it, I made my move. I'd been patient long enough; time to be pushy.

'Excuse me,' I said.

She turned around, her face hostile. 'What?'

Definitely not a people-person.

I smiled as wide as I could. 'Hi! My name is Grace Gildee. Could we have a quick chat about biopsy results?'

'I'm nothing to do with biopsies. Go down that corridor. Ask at the desk.' She'd turned away and was halfway into the room when I said, 'Actually, it's probably better that you've nothing to do with biopsies.'

'Why?' She turned around. Now she was interested.

'Because I'm wondering if you can help me.' I smiled my head off.

Emotions moved behind her eyes. Confusion. Curiosity. Cunning. Understanding. It was like a slide show. 'Are you a journalist? Is it about the report?'

'Exactly!' Another enormous smile. I've discovered that when you're trying to persuade people to do something underhand, if you keep smiling, it confuses them into thinking that they're not doing anything wrong.

This was the moment. She'd either call security or agree to help me. She seemed frozen with indecision.

'I just need a couple of names and addresses,' I cajoled. 'No one will ever know it's you.'

Still she hesitated. She'd like her employers to be shafted, but clearly it just wasn't in her nature to help anyone.

'Will the unit get into trouble?' she asked.

'Yes,' I said pleasantly. 'They will. All I need is a couple of names and addresses from you. Three at the most. Definitely no more than four. And if they could live in Dublin.'

'You're not asking for much.'

I ignored the surge of irritation and fag-longing that rushed up through me and forced another beam. 'Just the names and addresses of five women in Dublin who were given false negatives. You'd be doing me a massive favour.'

She bit her lip and thought about it. 'It's not my area, but I'll try. Wait in the car park. There's a big white statue. Jesus on the cross with his grieving mother. If I get anything I'll meet you there.'

I wanted to ask how long she'd be, but sensed it would be a bad idea. This one could turn quicker than a very quick thing.

I sat myself down on the other side of the grieving mother, then I waited. And waited. And waited. And wished I could have a cigarette. A journalist really needs to smoke. There's so much hanging around, how else are you meant to pass the time? And once you've got your story, there's the mad rush to write it up against the clock; you need cigarettes to aid that also.

But in a perverse way the self-denial appealed: atonement.

More time elapsed and the burning pain in my stomach started up again. Had the White Rabbit lost her nerve? Had she been toying with me all along? You never know with her type. I hunted in my handbag for a Zotan (tablets for stomachs that are thinking about getting an ulcer) and swallowed one down.

I started thinking again about having to go back without

my story. I was visualizing it in some detail – the scornful laughter, Jacinta's fury, Big Daddy's outrage at the great big hole in the paper – when the woman darted in front of me. She shoved a page into my hand, said, 'You didn't get this from me,' and disappeared.

'Thanks a million!' Six names and addresses. Fair play to her. I figured out the nearest one, hailed a taxi and rang the picture desk, looking for a photographer.

I pulled up outside the house. ('A neat semi with an obviously well-loved garden.') A teenage girl answered the door. ('Fresh paintwork, gleaming brass.') I cranked up my smile muscles. This is where the respectable suit and string of pearls would have come in handy. 'Hello. Can I speak to your mother?'

'She's in bed.'

'My name is Grace. I'm from the *Spokesman*. I know your mum is very sick, but I was wondering if I could have a quick word with her. I'll only keep her a few minutes.'

Her face didn't alter. 'I'll ask her.' She pounded up the stairs, then back down again. 'She says, what's it about?'

Gently I said, 'About her biopsy results. The ones that said she was okay.'

The girl's face spasmed, a movement so small you'd hardly have noticed it. She pounded up the stairs again and when she reappeared she said, 'She says come in.'

Up the narrow stairs ('beige carpet, Jack Vettriano prints') into a back bedroom. The curtains were drawn and there was a horrible smell of sickness. The creature in the bed looked exhausted and jaundiced. This woman was dying.

'Mrs Singer.' I advanced slowly towards her. 'I'm so sorry to descend on you like this.' I explained about the report. 'I was wondering if you would like to tell your story?'

She didn't react, then wheezed, 'Okay.'

Christ alive, it was tragic. She'd found a lump in her breast – a bombshell for any woman – and when the biopsy came back negative for cancer, they were so relieved that the whole family had gone on holiday. But about six weeks later she was laid low by bone-tired exhaustion and began having night sweats that drenched the bed. She went for a multitude of tests, but breast cancer had been ruled out because of her biopsy results. She asked for another biopsy, because she suspected, with the intuition that people have about their own bodies, that that was where the trouble lay, but she was overruled. By the time she found a second lump, it had invaded her lymph nodes. They blasted her with chemo – like they were doing with Bid at the moment – but it was too late. Game over. The tips of my fingers tingled with fear. What if it was too late for Bid too?

Mrs Singer's voice was so wheezy from the chemo that the tape recorder couldn't pick it up. I was scribbling into my notebook, trying to get everything down, when there was a thundering up the stairs. The girl who'd opened the door to me burst into the room and complained, 'Mu-um, Susan won't peel the potatoes.'

'Would you mind doing them, then, Nicola, love?'

'But I've to stick my hand up the chicken's bum. That's worse!'

Nicola stomped back down the stairs and raised voices reached us from the room below.

'I worry about the girls,' Mrs Singer said. 'They're only fourteen and fifteen. It's a bad age to leave them.'

I nodded. I never cried on a job, over the years I'd trained myself not to. But sometimes I got a forward-pushing sensation in my sinuses, a crowding and gathering beneath the bridge of my nose, accompanied by a wash of extreme sadness. I got that now.

Nicola was back. 'There's a man at the door. He says he's a photographer.'

'Mrs Singer –' Christ, this was pushing it – 'I should have mentioned he'd be coming.'

'I look too awful to have my picture taken.'

Alas, that was the whole point.

'Susan and I could put some make-up on you!' Nicola said. 'And could we be in it too?'

We waited twenty minutes while Nicola and Susan piled on bronzer and bucketloads of sticky pink lipgloss and the picture – two young, healthy girls, one on either side of their dying mother – would have broken your heart.

Keith Christie, the snapper, had his car. He drove us to the next nearest address on the list, where the woman's husband told us to piss off. 'Fucking vultures,' he yelled after us as Keith reversed out of the cul-de-sac.

'Where now?' Keith asked.

'Booterstown.'

My mobile rang. Dad, in a terrible fluster. 'Bingo's got free. Postman. Front door open. Saw his opportunity. Made a break for it. Indomitable spirit. He's been spotted in Killiney. We need you to come.'

'Dad, I'm on a story.'

'But Ma doesn't know how to focus the binoculars.'

'Then let her drive.'

'Her responses are too slow. If I say "left", I mean "left, *right now*!" Not "left in ten minutes' time".'

'Dad, I'm at *work*.' I couldn't spend the rest of the afternoon driving around the countryside, binoculars clamped to my face, scouring the landscape for Bingo. 'Good luck, I hope you find him.'

I snapped my phone closed.

'Is it the dog?' Keith asked. 'He's at large again?'

I nodded.

'If he wants to escape that badly,' Keith said, 'maybe they should just let him go.'

'Maybe.' I sighed.

'Okay, we're here. You go and do the talking, I'll keep the engine running in case they turn nasty.'

This time, we were let in and although the woman was in her fifties, about ten years older than Mrs Singer, her story was just as grim.

In silence, Keith and I returned to the office, me to write up my story and him to develop the photos. Even though I'd been hardened by years of exposure to the most heartbreaking stories you can imagine, being in such close proximity to death had brought my mood low. I was thinking of Bid. She'd better not die.

Christ, I'd love a cigarette.

Coming up the stairs to the newsroom, I heard bellows of laughter, then one or two shrieks. I pushed open the door. Loads of people were gathered around reading from a sheet of paper. Someone would read out a sentence then another roar of laughter would rise towards the rafters.

'Grace, Grace, c'mere, take a look at this,' a mirthful voice said.

'What is it?' I came closer, bursting with curiosity. Then I stopped. I'd guessed what it was. 'Hahaha,' I said.

It was a copy of the police report of my stolen car. Dickie McGuinness had hacked into the police database and emailed it to the entire staff. For extra enjoyment, certain sentences had been highlighted. '. . . car four months old . . .' '. . . doused in petrol and set alight . . .' '. . . nothing remaining but the metal framework . . .'

Just tell me this, *why* do dithery swimmers go in the middle lane when there's a nice, slow lane for them to dawdle around in like Sunday drivers? And *why* do aggressive, choppy, water-slapping types come into the middle lane and intimidate us all when they can be among their own in the fast lane?

It's hard enough to gear myself up to go near the pool, it'd be nice to feel afterwards that it was worth it.

I'd finished up late at work. Most days I didn't get the chance to make the world a better place and the breast cancer story needed the right balance. It had to be crusading but not ranty, and moving but not so maudlin that people wouldn't read it. It was a challenge, and as soon as I'd filed it I wanted alcohol, but because it was Monday no one was going to Dinnegans. Instead – bloody reluctantly, I can tell you – I went for a health-giving, stress-busting swim, but there were so many people in the lane, swimming at all the wrong speeds, that I was far narkier after I got out than before I went in.

And I don't know what it is about swimming-pool changing rooms but I can never get myself properly dry afterwards. The backs of my thighs stay defiantly damp and if I'm wearing tights (to be fair, almost never) it's a real struggle to tug them up as far as my waist.

Outside, with the wind blowing through my trousers and chilling my damp legs, the thought of the bus was too much. All that stopping and starting, too reminiscent of my disappointing swim. So I walked, formulating an ambitious plan to do it every day until my car was sorted out. It might combat the inevitable weight gain from giving up the fags.

On the way I listened to my messages. There was one from Dad. Bingo had been run to ground and returned to custody. 'No thanks to you,' he added snippily.

'Fuck *off*,' I said to the message. 'I was at *work*.'

Then I rang Damien and told him about Mrs Singer. 'I felt so sad.'

'That's good,' Damien said. 'You're not so jaded that you don't care.'

'Thanks for that. Enjoy your me-time.'

Monday night was Damien's night with 'the boys'. He drank whiskey and played poker and generally indulged his oft-repeated need for his 'own space'.

'I'll be late,' he said.

'Be as late as you like.'

'Sarcasm, Grace? Why do you begrudge me this one night?'

He liked to behave as if I resented every second he spent

with his pals, and I was happy to indulge him. A man needs his struggles.

I let myself into the empty house – I liked having it to myself – and rummaged around in the kitchen looking for food. I'd been eating all day, I should stop now, but I knew I wouldn't. Out of habit, I put the news on in the living room and when I heard '. . . Paddy de Courcy . . .' I darted from the kitchen and stood in the doorway, watching the television. Paddy was striding through a corridor wearing an expensive-looking, dark blue suit. An efficient-type woman carrying a clipboard scurried along in his wake, and a reporter lolloped alongside him in an undignified crouching lope, holding a microphone to his beautiful mouth, to catch whatever gem of wisdom he was about to impart. Paddy was smiling. Paddy was always smiling. Except when some tragedy had happened, when he was appropriately grim.

He was being asked about Dee Rossini. 'Dee is as honest as the day is long,' he said. 'She has my full support and the backing of the entire party.'

The phone rang and I jumped guiltily.

It might be Damien. Sometimes, between his fourth and fifth drinks, he came over all sentimental.

'Grace?'

'Marnie!'

'Quick!' she said. 'Turn on Sky.'

I grabbed the remote and found myself watching a segment about a man who'd taught his pet monkey to knit. It was amazing really. The monkey – whose name was Ginger – held the needles in his paws and awkwardly added a couple of stitches to a little red monkey-sized scarf. The man said that when the scarf was finished, the plan was for Ginger to knit bootees. I watched in Dublin and Marnie watched in London, both of us howling with laughter.

'Oh God, that's fantastic,' Marnie said. 'I needed that.'

My heart clenched. I'd always worried about her and recently more than ever.

More than anything I wanted her to be happy and she never seemed it. Not fully. Even on the most joyous days of her life – the births of Daisy and Verity – she seemed to be holding on to a little pocket of melancholia.

'What's up?' I asked.

'I can't stop thinking about Bid,' she said. 'I was talking to her yesterday, she sounded okay, but how do you think she's doing?'

'Hard to say. We won't know until she's done the six goes of chemo.'

'Well, I can see for myself in three days' time.' As soon as Bid had got her diagnosis, Marnie booked time off from work. She was coming from London on Thursday with the girls and her husband, Nick.

'I'll be straight out to Ma's as soon as I finish work,' I said.

'How *is* work?' I'd kept her abreast of my insecurities about Kaplan. She was the only person, apart from Damien, in whom I felt I could confide.

Of the two of us, Marnie was far more clever, but somehow she had ended up punching in the hours in some mind-numbing mortgage brokers' office, while I sometimes got to profile celebrities.

But she never made me feel like I'd got her share of the luck.

'Let me guess,' she said. 'You got sent to cover the ploughing championships while your man Casey Kaplan interviewed the Pope, Johnny Depp . . . say one more.'

'JD Salinger, he hasn't done an interview in a hundred years.'

'I thought he was dead.'

'God, maybe he is.'

'Well, if he is, that'd be a great coup. Wait, I've got a better one. Marilyn Monroe's made contact from the other side and she's only doing one interview and she insists it's with Kaplan.'

I was about to go to bed with my Michael Connolly when the phone rang again.

'Hello, Grace, this is Manus Gildee, your father, calling.'

'Hello, Dad.' He was about to apologize – a formal introduction always preceded his eating humble pie, as if to distance himself from the shame of it.

'I believe I owe you an apology. Ma said I was hard on you earlier, about Bingo. It's the cigarettes, Grace. I'm finding it next to impossible to do without them. Am I forgiven?'

'You're forgiven.'

'Also, Ma wants to know what time you're fetching Marnie and co. from the airport on Thursday?'

'Me?'

'Who else?'

'Ahhh . . . you?'

'I don't want to fetch them,' he stuttered. 'Verity puked in the car the last time. The floor mat is still smelly. It upsets Bingo.'

'Dad, I don't even have a car at the moment.'

Mutterings of 'What fresh hell' reached me. 'Still burnt out, is it?'

'Yes, Dad, still burnt out.'

'Let me tell you what my life is like at the moment. People say to me, Any plans for this evening, Manus? Theatre, perhaps? A concert? A meal with friends? And I reply, Not smoking. Yes, all evening, from the moment I finish dinner to when I retire, I'll be Not Smoking. It's an activity in itself.'

Christ, it had only been a day. What would he be like after a week of nicotine-deprivation?

'So you'll do the airport run, Dad?'

'Without cigarettes, I feel, how can I put it . . . *unfinished*?'

'You'll fetch them from the airport?'

'What's the line from that asinine film that Marnie made me watch?' I heard him click his fingers. 'Yes, I believe I have it. ''They complete me.'' '

'Am I to understand –'

'Yes, yes,' he interrupted irritably, 'I'll go to the feck-bollocky airport.'

I was just drifting off to sleep when I heard the front door open, followed by the sound of a briefcase being kicked under the hall table. Damien was home from his me-time.

'Grace –' he came up the stairs – 'are you awake?'

'I am now. What's up? And make it quick, I've got to get up in about four hours to fly to London.'

'Okay. Should we have a baby?'

'Right now?' I eyed him speculatively.

He laughed and sat on the bed to pull off his boots.

'What's brought this on?' I asked. He usually raised this subject when he was dissatisfied with his life. And when it wasn't babies, it was that we give up our jobs and rent out our house and go travelling. 'Someone at the poker game's just had a baby?'

'Yeah, Sean. And everyone at work's got one.'

'. . . Christ, Damien . . . a baby's not like a company car.'

'Ah I know, I know . . . but you should hear them – all men – boasting about having to get up three times in the night to feed the baby.'

'Really?' I yawned. Just the thought of middle-of-the-night feeds was enough to set me off.

'Four of them have new babies and every morning they come in with stories, Grace. Competitive sleeplessness. Angus Sprott hasn't been to bed since July – now *I'm* yawning – they make me feel . . . left out, like I've got no balls . . . for getting my full seven hours.'

'The grass is always greener.'

'Say something else.'

'You'd be a terrible father, you're too moody.'

He seemed to brighten at that. 'I would, wouldn't I?'

'Christ, yes. And if we had a baby we'd have to sell this house. It's too small. We'd have to move very far away and buy a starter home in an estate with twenty thousand identical ones.'

'Maybe we shouldn't have a baby,' Damien said. 'Moment of madness there. I'm over it now.'

'Maybe we shouldn't.'

I didn't want children. And of all the shameful things a woman could admit to – breast enhancement, sex with her boyfriend's father – this was the most taboo.

I'd read enough magazines to expect that in my late twenties my hormones would seize the controls and I'd find myself in the grip of a powerful baby-hunger. I was quite excited about it – but it simply never happened. Marnie, on the other hand, had always *adored* children and couldn't wait to have her own. Sometimes I wondered if there had been a mix-up in the womb and she'd got my share of baby-longing as well as her own.

Oddly – or maybe not, I didn't know – I had heartfelt sympathy for women who couldn't get pregnant, because I knew what it was like to be unable to control my own body. I wanted *to want* to get pregnant and never got it.

Damien was more vague than I was. If pressed, he'd mumble something about there already being far too many people in the world and it would be wrong to bring yet another one into it. But I suspected that the real issue was Damien's family. This is hard to understand if you haven't spent time with them, because they're lovely people. They really are, I'm not just being polite. They're warm, fun, kind, clever. Clever. Especially clever. And that's really where the trouble lies. Damien has two brothers and two sisters: a brother and sister older than him; a brother and sister younger. He's the middle child. And of his four siblings, three of them – Brian, Hugh and Christine – are surgeons.

In fact, Damien's dad, Brian Senior, was also a surgeon. (Further information that you might find interesting: Damien's mother is called Christine. In other words, Mr and Mrs Stapleton called their two eldest children after themselves, which says plenty, really, if you think about it.)

The only Stapleton sibling to not be a surgeon – other than Damien – was Deirdre. And that was because she successfully ran her own business, 'creating' children's bedrooms. It had started as a hobby with her own kids, but she'd conjured up such magical, thrilling kingdoms that everyone started asking her to do it for their children, and before she knew it she had a wildly successful enterprise on her hands. Not that she would ever boast about it. None of them ever boasts. (Further information: despite their graciousness, Bid hates the Stapletons. She says, 'They'd sicken you.')

*Any*way, in any other family, Damien would be regarded as the Mensa candidate. But not in the Stapletons'. Damien once told me that he feels like he's only an associate member of his family, not a full member with all the accruing rights and privileges, and I think that the real reason he doesn't want to have children is nothing to do with the overcrowded planet but is because he doesn't want anyone else to feel left out, the way he does.

(Further information: I would never say any of this to Damien. He doesn't believe in pop psychology analysis stuff. In fact, neither do I . . .)

Occasionally I tried to write columns crusading for women like me, but judgement always rained down like bricks and I got tons of letters telling me I was 'unnatural', I was 'a freak', I was 'feminism gone mad'.

I was warned (often by men, like how the hell would *they* know?) that the day I started the menopause, I'd be crippled by loss and it would be too late to undo my 'selfish' choice.

Which was unfair because I didn't judge those who'd had babies, even though they became – on behalf of their child – the most selfish creatures on earth.

Did I care that their baby liked puréed aubergine but not puréed parsnip? No. But I've stuck on my interested face and moved the conversation beyond the point of no return with leading questions about puréed carrots, puréed potatoes and – a controversial one, this – puréed chicken.

Did I mind if they opened the window so that 'the baby' (warm as Thailand beneath a pile of technologically adapted blankets) got some air, even though the room was already freezing?

Did I mind that even though a plan had been fashioned to go to the park and we were all standing by the front door with our coats and hats on, 'the baby' suddenly fell asleep and all activity was suspended for an unquantifiable length of time?

The strange thing was that I was 'good' with babies. I loved their milky, powdery smell and their warm, soft weight in my arms. I'd never objected to changing a nappy and I didn't care if they puked their bottle back up on me. And, for some reason that really pissed off those who disapproved of my childless-by-choice state, I could always stop them crying.

I loved babies. I just didn't want one of my own.

Dazzler. Dazzler! Even now I can remember the exact mix of giddy joy and hope when Damien told me at Lucinda

Breen's thirtieth-birthday party that he had a name for me – and such a brilliant name! I was so tingly that for a short while I lost the feeling in my feet and it took weeks to come down from the high. (I've always had a soft spot for Lucinda Breen since that night.)

However, as soon as the first loved-up flush had passed, I needed to get to the bottom of this ex-wife business. All men have ex-girlfriends, but Damien had married this woman.

'Go easy,' Marnie had counselled anxiously. 'This is one sure way to make him scarper.'

'But I have to find out!'

'If you must do it, do it subtly!'

But when had I ever been subtle?

I waited until after a bout of particularly passionate sex, and when our breathing had finally returned to normal, I said, 'Damien, you're a man and you're not going to want to answer these questions, but tell me about your ex-wife. Juno, that's her name?'

He lay back on the pillow and whispered, 'Oh no.'

'I need to know,' I said. 'What if you're still hung up on her –'

' – I'm not. She's my ex-wife. Ex.'

'Yes, but what happened? You got married? Why? And why didn't you stay together? And why –'

Eventually, after he simply couldn't continue deflecting me, he broke down and burst out, 'There were three reasons it didn't work out.' He listed them on his fingers. 'One. We got married too young. Two. I was working long hours so we never saw each other. And three. She started shagging her boss.'

He thought the discussion was over – whereas I thought his three-point breakdown was simply an interesting opening gambit.

I rolled over on top of him and stared into his eyes. 'Just tell me everything,' I said. 'Make it easy on yourself.'

'No.'

I continued to hold eye contact. 'You are strong-willed,' I said. 'But I am stronger.'

We stared and stared and stared, the muscles around our eyes rigid – then he blinked.

'You blinked! I win.'

He closed his eyes, opened them again and said, almost laughing, 'Okay. What do you want to know?'

'Where did you meet?'

'At school. Marfleet's.'

Marfleet's was a fee-paying establishment for privileged children, which offered an 'all-round' education. What this meant in practice was that even if pupils were as thick as a plank, their potato cut-out shapes would be so celebrated that the fact that they were almost unable to write their own name would pass them by entirely. Having said that, Marfleet's turned out a higher than average quota of diplomats, triathlon winners, surgeons and hedge-fund managers.

Although Juno and Damien had been in the same class, it wasn't until they'd left school and were both doing degrees in Trinity that they fell in love.

'But why did you get *married*?' I asked. Couldn't they just have been in love like normal people?

'It sort of started as a joke,' Damien said, as if he could hardly believe it himself.

Reading between the lines, I guessed that Juno was bored and thought getting married would be a great excuse for a party. But what really gave the thing impetus was that both sets of parents opposed the idea. The pair of them were far too young, they said.

Now, the thing about Damien, which I was learning fast, is that he's stubborn. You can't tell him not to do something. The more he was told he was too young to get married, the more determined he became that the wedding would go ahead.

'You know yourself, the more they said we were too immature, the more we decided that we were far more clued-in than them.'

' "They say we're young and we don't know, we won't find out until we grow," ' I said.

'*What?*'

' "I Got You Babe". Sonny and Cher.'

'Right, yes, exactly.'

Eventually he and Juno got their way. So the summer they graduated, they got married.

'So there you were, twenty-two and married,' I prompted.

'Utter lunacy.' He shook his head. 'Working sixty hours a week as a cub reporter for the *Times* and studying at night for an MA in Political Science. And we were skint.'

Sympathetically I said, ' "They say our love won't pay the rent, before it's earned our money's all been spent." '

'Exactly.'

'And Juno?' I asked. 'Hanging around the house making cupcakes?'

'No, she had a job too. In PR.'

'Which firm?'

'Browning and Eagle.'

This told me everything I needed to know about Juno. Contrary to popular opinion, not all PR girls are despicable leeches – I came across an above-average number of them in my job, so I knew what I was talking about.

But there are a certain breed who combine pushiness with a soul-destroying absence of belief in their product. They couldn't sell a can of 12 per cent cider to an alcoholic, and you get the feeling that they're only in the job so they can get their hair blow-dried and stand in a function room in the Four Seasons, patronizing people.

Juno was one of these.

Of course I knew all of this without ever having met her.

'And what happened next?' I asked.

'Oh God.' He ran his hands through his hair. 'I was working all the time. You know what it's like when you're starting out.'

I certainly did. You're at the mercy of your editor. You could be sent to Antwerp at a moment's notice and you have to suck it up because you're getting experience and earning your stripes.

'And when I wasn't working, I was studying. But her job was very sociable. And *she* was very sociable. There were always launches and parties and weekends away and I couldn't keep up. I needed the MA to get a decent job. So we sort of got into a routine – she did her stuff and I did mine, and maybe she wasn't that bored for the first couple of years. But by the third year . . .'

He trailed into silence and I waited.

'There was this Saturday night,' he said. 'She was gone to Ballynahinch Castle for a weekend, for some launch of something or other. I'd worked an eighty-hour week and the only time I'd seen her was for fifteen minutes while she packed. Then off she went and I started writing a five-thousand-word paper on Marxism and globalism. I worked on it all Friday night, then all day Saturday, and I finished it around ten o'clock on Saturday night . . .'

'Yes . . .'

'And suddenly I had nothing to do. It was a hot night. There must have been a match on, because every now and then I'd hear this big roar. I suppose someone must have scored or nearly scored. The whole world was out having a good time. I felt like the loneliest man in Ireland. And then . . . then I remembered Juno packing. I just had this picture of her getting this black shiny thing out of a drawer.'

'A black shiny thing?'

'Yeah. A basque thing. And I wondered, Why's she bringing a basque away on a working weekend?' He looked at me. 'Then I remembered the number of times she'd been mentioning Oliver Browning. Her boss.'

I knew him. He was a creepy creep who dyed his hair; it was meant to be brown but it had a terrible orangey hue.

'It felt like every conversation I'd had with her over the past God knows how many months had been about him and how great he was.' He shrugged. 'Suddenly it was just obvious. And there you have it, Grace.'

'Oh,' I said. What a sad story. 'And did you have a showdown with her?'

'Showdown's probably too dramatic a word. When she

came home I asked her what was going on. She told me. She said we'd grown apart.'

'Grown apart . . . ?'

'Yeah, like a crappy made-for-TV thing. But we *had* grown apart; we'd grown up and in different directions. The whole bloody thing was riddled with clichés from start to finish.' He laughed. 'But I loved her. It hurt.'

'You're laughing.'

'I'm laughing now. I wasn't laughing then.'

After a respectful pause I got the narrative under way once more. 'So you got divorced?'

'We got divorced. And she got married again.'

'Not to Oliver Browning?' I was sure I'd have heard.

'No, to someone else. But he's the same type. Rich and corporate. A great man for the jollies. Forever at Ascot and Wimbledon and Glyndebourne. He could give her what she wanted. They're made for each other.'

'Are you bitter? Underneath this dour, uncommunicative facade are you nursing a wellspring of bitterness?'

'No.'

'Words are cheap.'

'I went to her wedding!'

'Did you really?' *Fascinating*. 'What was that like?'

'Oh Grace.' He groaned into his hands.

'Happy? Sad? Neither?'

With a heavy sigh he gave in. 'Not happy. I felt like I'd failed. I'd meant my vows. When I'd said ''for ever'', or whatever the phrase is – '

' – ''as long as we both shall live''.'

'Actually I think it was ''until death do us part''.'

'I don't think they say that any more.'

'So you were there, at my wedding, were you?'

'No, but –'

'Anyway, whatever the wording was, I'd meant it at the time. I know, I know, I was a clueless twenty-two-year-old. I knew nothing about anything and I thought I knew everything. Anyone could have predicted it wasn't going to work. But, watching my ex-wife getting married again, I felt surprised. In a bad way.'

'Who did you bring as your plus-one?'

'No one.'

'You went on your *own*? To your ex-wife's wedding?'

'I didn't have a girlfriend,' he protested. 'And I'm hardly going to say to some stranger, "Hi, there. Doing anything on Saturday? Fancy coming along to watch my ex-wife getting married again?"'

'Why go at all?'

'Come on, Grace, I had to.'

'Your pride?'

'And Juno would have been upset –'

'Tough!'

'I had to go,' he said simply.

I understood. 'But to show up on your own . . . talk about a spectre at the feast. Did you wear a black suit?'

'Of course.' He flat-eyed me. 'A long frock coat –'

' – with black leggings –'

' – and a stovepipe hat. I looked like an undertaker –'

' – a *Victorian* undertaker –'

It was Damien who began to laugh first, then it was safe for me. It was the image of him in the stovepipe hat that I found unbearably funny and tragic. We laughed and laughed and Damien stopped for just long enough to say, 'And when the priest asked if anyone knew any reason why the marriage couldn't go ahead, I played two bars of the death march –'

'– on a tin whistle –'

'– no, a one-man-band machine –'

'– which you played with your elbow.'

The mirth seized me again and held me in its grip until I thought I was going to choke. But even while I was in fits, I still thought it was sort of sad. Poor Damien. Having to go – alone – to witness his ex-wife in a ten-thousand-euro dress (I'm guessing, but I bet I'm right), twirl her way into her new life; being saddled with enough of a sense of duty that he felt compelled to attend, but being slightly too much of a loner to get comfort from the company of another human being.

'Just one more question, Mr Stapleton.'

'No! No more.'

'Do you ever see Juno now?'

'No.'

'What if you bumped into her?'

'It would be . . . fine.'

God, I was dying for a wee.

Frantically I jiggled my leg and wondered if I could ask one of the others to guard my place while I bolted to the Ladies. I was in a corridor outside a hotel room in central London, with a dozen other journalists. We were all there to interview Antonia Allen, a glossy young Hollywood actress. Everyone's call time had been 9 a.m., it was now lunchtime and there was no recognizable sequence in which we were summoned to the inner sanctum.

I slid a glance at the girl next to me. Could I trust her to keep my spot? No, I decided. She was all hard edges; I could practically smell her killer instinct. As soon as I'd run down the corridor she'd tell the scary woman with the clipboard that the journalist from the *Spokesman* had gone home.

The chair was so hard that all sensation had left my buttocks. I could stick pins into them, turning my arse into a pincushion, and I wouldn't feel a thing. Maybe I should do it for the entertainment of the other journos? ('Go on, no, go on, harder, I can take it.') It might help to pass the time.

But they didn't look like a fun lot and I abandoned the idea. I wanted a bathroom, a cigarette and eight slices of toast.

I closed my eyes. Oh toast, toast, how I love you, toast. I'd have one slice with butter, one with peanut butter, one with Philadelphia, one with strawberry jam and four with Nutella. I'd have a Nutella one first, then the peanut butter, then another Nutella, then the jam, then twenty cigarettes, seeing as this was a fantasy. I'd have six empty toilet cubicles to choose from, a feather cushion for my bum, then more toast and more cigarettes . . .

And to think that my job was sometimes considered glamorous. Because the stars couldn't be bothered coming to Dublin to be interviewed, I went to London fairly regularly and, because of that, people (non-journalist ones) were always saying, 'You lucky bitch.'

If only they knew. This morning I'd had to get up at

4.45 a.m. to catch a 6.45 Ryanair cattle-truck in order to be in London for 9 a.m. I hadn't eaten anything on the plane because it was so early I was afraid I'd puke. Now I was starving and hadn't done any preventative eating.

'I bet they've handmade biscuits in the room,' I said to no one in particular. 'They always have them in hotels like this, but I'd be just as happy with a Jaffa Cake.'

A couple of people looked up from their hardware (laptops, BlackBerries, mobiles) but were too tense to answer. Normally the likes of Antonia Allen wouldn't cause undue distress – she was just another skinny blonde with a central casting wheat allergy, starring in a formulaic movie with a sickmakingly large budget. But four days earlier her boyfriend had been busted having sex with a (male) undercover reporter and suddenly she was white-hot. I was dispatched to London. 'Come back with the gay-boyfriend story,' Big Daddy had ordered me, coming over all tabloid, 'or don't come back at all.'

I had a Val McDermid book with me, but I couldn't concentrate on it because anxiety was burning a hole in my stomach lining. Antonia's people had said that if the word 'gay' was even mentioned the interview would be terminated. How was I going to get her to open up?

I'd done a bit of digging on the internet and all I'd discovered was that she was utterly unremarkable. Hanging over me, making everything extra-pressured, was the knowledge that Casey Kaplan would pull it off. In the three weeks since he'd started at the *Spokesman*, he'd dazzled us with the celebrity kill he dragged back from his hunting sessions. Even though we had different titles and different briefs

(I was 'Chief Features Writer', he was 'Celebrity Features Writer'), I was being measured against him.

I rang TC. 'Any news?'

'Casey Kaplan's finally made us privy to the story that's going to rock our world.'

'What?' *Don't let it be something good.*

'Wayne Diffney's wife is pregnant.' Wayne Diffney was once in the atrocious boy-band Laddz (he was the 'wacky' one with the hair that looked like the Sydney Opera House). Now he was desperately trying to make it as a rocker. He'd grown a wispy beard, boasted that he never wore anti-perspirant and tentatively said 'fuck' on national radio.

'That's it? A Wayne Diffney story? Right. How's your world?'

'Unrocked. Yours?'

'Steady. Quite steady.'

More waiting. More leg-jiggling.

My phone beeped. A text from Damien.

loan approved! nu car 4 u!

We'd been horse trading with financial institutions since the weekend; this was welcome news.

A journalist emerged from the hotel room and we all looked up. How was Antonia? Chatty? But his poker face gave nothing away. Either Antonia spoke and he was guarding his exclusive. Or she didn't and he was masking his failure.

My phone rang. 'TC?'

'You're not going to like it.'

'Hit me.'

'Wayne Diffney isn't the father. It's Shocko O'Shaughnessy.'

A fireball roared in my stomach. Harry 'Shocko' O'Shaughnessy was the real thing, a bona fide rocker. World-revered, rich as Croesus, he occupied a security-bound mansion in Killiney from which he occasionally emerged, smiling and unkempt, to present prizes at high-profile charity events and to pleasure visiting supermodels.

'Hailey has left –'

'Who?'

'Mrs Diffney – Hailey's her name. She has left Wayne and moved in with Shocko. Kaplan was actually there *in Shocko's billiards room, playing billiards with Bono* when she arrived in a taxi. He and Bono walked down to the local chemist and actually *bought* the *actual* pregnancy test. Or so he says. Would they not have lackeys to do that? An hour later Diffney arrives with a hurley – he had to come on the Dart, the poor bastard, Hailey had taken him for his last twenty – to sort out O'Shaughnessy, and of course couldn't get past the gate. But Kaplan – Kofi fecking Annan – persuaded Shocko to let him in so he could have his say. Once he's in, Diffney goes on a spree with the hurley. He broke four platinum discs, landed Bono ''an unmerciful clatter'' on the left knee and said, ''That's for *Zooropa*,'' then hit Shocko ''on the hair''. It's the hottest story in the world and Kaplan was at it.'

Antonia was smaller in the flesh. They always are. Weary and shrunken – for some reason reminding me of a dried mushroom – she was nothing like the radiant princess who appeared in couture frocks on red carpets. ('The pain of her recent betrayal is taking its toll, rendering her oddly fungus-like . . .')

'Are you enjoying London?' I asked. 'Or is this hotel room all that you get to see?' (Once upon a time, an over-interviewed Bruce Willis told me shrilly that he didn't get to see anything of any place he visited, that actors on publicity tours never did. I seized this piece of information and I use it when I need people to think I'm insightful.)

Antonia nodded. 'Just these four walls.'

'My twin sister lives in London.' It never hurt to give a subject a little personal information. 'But I never get to see her when I come here for work.'

'That sucks,' Antonia said, not terribly interested.

'Yes,' I said, trying to look wistful. 'It does.'

The clipboard harridan took her place on a nearby sofa and watched our exchange with hard eyes. The empty space between my first two fingers twitched. I always wanted a cigarette when I was anxious and right now I was very anxious. This precious half-hour window was my one shot at the gay-boyfriend story and all the odds were stacked against me.

Antonia was drinking herbal tea. I hadn't genuinely expected that she might be hitting the sauce – mind you, you'd be surprised; she had suffered a terrible shock, after all – but it was another avenue closed; not much chance of her tongue being loosened by a few dried raspberry leaves.

I started off with a couple of warm-up, lick-arsey questions about her 'craft'. Actors love nothing more than to talk about their craft. However, it makes for staggeringly tedious reading, which is why it never appears in the actual article.

I nodded earnestly as she crumbled shortbread biscuits (yes, the handmade ones I'd predicted) onto her plate and explained how she'd felt her way into the role of Owen Wilson's hard-working girlfriend.

'I spent time working in a lawyer's office, answering the phones.'

'For how long?'

'Just for, like, a morning, but I'm a quick study.'

I choked down a large shard of biscuit, almost puncturing my oesophagus. She'd answered too quickly, hadn't given me enough time to chew it. As soon as I could speak, I mentioned some crappy art-house film she'd been in, a couple of years back. 'That was an important piece of work,' I said, to show that I 'got' her: she wasn't just another 6-stone, wind-up doll, she was a serious actor. 'Any plans for similar work in the future?'

She shook her head. Feck. I'd been hoping to lead the conversation round to the handiness of personal pain in her craft. It was time to jolt her off auto-pilot.

'Antonia, what's the last lie you told?'

She flashed a frightened look at Mrs Clipboard and I said quickly, trying to recover lost ground, 'Only kidding. Tell me your best points.'

'I'm ... ah ... I'm a team-player. A great sense of humour. I see the best in people. I'm thoughtful, sensitive, caring –'

Yes, yes.

'And – not so easy this one – your worst points?'

She pretended to think about it. 'I guess . . . I'm a perfectionist. A workaholic.' Yes, yes. They always said the perfectionist thing.

'What makes you angry?'

'Injustice. Poverty. World hunger.' The usual. How about your boyfriend taking it up the bum from another bloke? Christ, Antonia, that'd be enough to annoy a saint!

But I felt something change. A tiny little flicker of a shift in her mood. She began to break a new biscuit onto her plate and I took a risk. 'Antonia, why don't you eat that?'

'*Eat* it?'

Mrs Clipboard watched suspiciously.

'It's only a biscuit,' I said. 'It's comforting. And without getting into things –' meaningful pause, compassionate look – 'you could probably do with some comforting right now . . .'

Still staring at me, she ate the biscuit in three quick chomps.

'Nice?' I asked.

She nodded.

I closed my notebook. My tape recorder was still running but shutting the notebook gave the impression that it was all over.

'Are we done?' She was surprised.

Finishing up early is a good move. The fear that someone's interest is waning panics them.

'I don't want to take up too much of your time. Especially considering what you've gone through recently. The press . . .' I shook my head. 'The way they've hounded you . . .'

Trust me, trust me, I'm the kindly, insightful journalist with the twin sister she doesn't get to see very often. And you're probably dying to give your side of the story . . .

'My own editor told me not to come back without asking about you and Jain.' I shrugged helplessly. 'But . . .' I put my notebook in my satchel.

'Oh. Will you get in trouble?'

I made a gesture that I hoped would convey that I'd be sacked. 'But who cares?' I brushed crumbs off my trousers, about to stand up.

'Look,' she said urgently. 'It's not such a big deal. It was over anyway. I didn't love him any more. And whatever anyone says, I'm not dumb, I knew he was cheating. I just didn't know it was with a guy.'

Mrs Clipboard looked up sharply. 'Antonia! Miss, um –' She reached for her clipboard. Who was I? 'Ms Gildee!'

'I'm glad to see you've got good people who care about you,' I said quickly. 'Did Jain give any indications that he might be gay?' *Keep talking, Antonia, keep talking.*

'He worked out a lot, he took care of his skin, but what guy doesn't?'

'Judy Garland records?'

'Miss Gildee!'

'You know what? No. But he did go to Vegas to see Celine Dion.'

'How about sex?'

'Miss Gildee, I am ordering you to stop right n –'

'The sex was great!'

'But was it straightforward?' I was going for broke, a race to the finish between me and Mrs Clipboard.

'This interview is over as of right now –'

'What I mean is – I can't think of a less crude way to put it . . .' There's a time to be ingratiating and a time to be obnoxious. 'Was it through the front door or the tradesman's entrance?'

'The wha –? Oh! Is that what everyone is saying?' Antonia was flushed with outrage. 'That we had only anal sex?'

'Antonia, no! Don't say any –'

'For the record, it wasn't always anal sex! It varied!'

'For the record?' I picked up my tape recorder and switched it off. 'Thank you, Ms Allen, Mrs Clipboard.'

As I tore down the corridor to the Ladies, I felt ashamed. I'd conned Antonia into breaking her cover. Then I thought, Oh come on. She was a twenty-one-year-old beauty who got free clothes from Gucci and who picked up five million dollars a movie. I was an underpaid journalist who was just doing her job.

'My throat is bruised from swallowing spiky bits of biscuits.' I dodged a shoal of people just in on a flight from Zakynthos, and kept walking, my mobile clamped to my ear. 'My bladder is stretched out of shape, it'll never go back to the way it was before –'

'Like a jumper washed on the wrong setting.'

'If you want a jumper washed on the right setting, do it yourself.' I continued my litany of woe. 'I'll be blacklisted by the studio. They'll never let me interview any of their people ever again. I didn't have to go that far, Damien. Big Daddy is never going to publish anything as crude as

"Antonia Allen confirms anal sex." It just suddenly got to me. The dance between the stars and the media is always on their terms. And – ' this was hard to admit – 'the spectre of Casey Kaplan was breathing down my neck. But I don't like dirty tricks. I've broken my own rules and it feels wrong . . .'

'Have we had anal sex?' Damien asked.

'Oh for God's sake! Sort of.'

'Sort of?'

'A drunken experiment. It didn't really work out. And we're not trying again.'

'I don't remember.'

'Well, I do and we're not trying it again.'

I twitched as I walked past the duty-free cigarettes. Even though they're not duty-free any more. And I no longer smoke.

'Are we going to buy you a car this evening?' he asked.

'But it's the last day of the month. Date night.' Because our hours are so long, Damien had decided we should try for one romantic (read 'sex') night a month.

'Oh Christ!'

'Thanks a million! It was your idea.' I'd been quite opposed to something so contrived.

'Not the idea, it's the word. "Date",' he said. 'When did it become part of our vocabulary? Like "cheating". When did we achieve consensus as a nation to change over from "two-timing"? And "there for you". That's another one. "I'm there for you." "She's there for me." "We're all there for each other." Cultural imperialism. We're all Americans now.'

'Is it happening or isn't it?' I was in the mood for sex.

'Do you want to?'

'Do you?'

'Yes.'

'Then yes.'

Bizarrely my flight wasn't delayed and I got home before Damien. I put on music, turned off lights and lit candles. There was ice-cream in the freezer, blueberries in the fridge (they'd have to stand in as strawberries) and a bottle of red wine on the coffee table. (No proper food. I'd had a disgusting panini on the plane and he said he'd get something at work.)

I was impatient now. I undressed to my bra and knickers and put on a robe and, unexpectedly, noticed my underwear. Black cotton pants, plain black bra. (Two different blacks.) Nothing wrong with it, but it wasn't much . . . fun. Would it have killed me to buy nice stuff? Technically, no. But I suppose I didn't really approve. I was a real woman so why should I dress up like a male fantasy?

Damien said he didn't care about tricky knickers. But what if he was lying? What if he left me for some silken-skinned girly with a drawer full of red suspender belts and diamanté thongs . . . ?

For a few moments I indulged myself in the bleak fantasy. Then I stopped. If he was that stupid, I decided, she was welcome to him. They were welcome to each other.

I sipped my wine and stretched out on the couch. I was dying for it now. It had been ages.

*

He was home!

I bolted to the hall and presented him with a glass of wine. Like a 1950s wife, I was keen to wipe away the stresses and strains of the outside world – so that he'd quickly get in the mood for sex.

'How was your day? Drink this.'

Pleasantries had to be observed, although Damien was never not in the mood. Which I appreciated – it must be horrendous to be rebuffed when you were desperate for it. Sometimes I felt sorry for men. (But most of the time I didn't.)

His hair was sticking up in tufts from the lid. With a whizz, he unzipped his bike jacket and revealed his suit; it was like watching Superman in reverse.

I pulled him by his tie into the living room.

'Jesus, give me a minute,' he said, trying to drink his wine, then bumping his knee against the bookshelf that I'd accidentally steered him into.

On the couch, I straddled him and slid my hand under his shirt and up to his chest; I've always liked his chest.

But I was too impatient. I climbed off him and worked my hand under his waistband, then began moving my finger-tips in circular, teasing, downward motions, my nails gently scraping his skin.

'Whatever happened to foreplay?' he asked.

'No time. Too horny.'

There were instant stirrings, like a speeded-up video on the life-cycle of a plant – a tiny, harmless-looking sleeping bud, beginning to uncurl, unfold, straighten up, thicken, strengthen, harden, flipping up from the final fold, to stand upright and proud. I loved the feel of it, rock hard, resting in the palm of my hand.

'Lift,' I said, shifting his hips, so I could pull off his trousers. Already he was unbuttoning his shirt and with a rustle of starched cotton had discarded it.

He unhooked my bra and I leant forward until it fell away. Instantly he reached for my boobs, weighing them in his palms and pinching my nipples between his index and middle fingers. His eyes had become glazed and I had a sudden unwelcome insight: how strange that sex was meant to be about intimacy; sometimes it could feel like the opposite, as if we became inhabited by different people.

'Tell me your fantasies,' I whispered, trying to retrieve the closeness. His fantasies usually involved me getting it on with another woman. A little repetitive, but harmless. I wasn't sure how happy I'd have been if they'd involved dressing up in adult nappies or weasel outfits.

'Grace,' he whispered.

'Yes?'

'Let's move to the bedroom.'

'No. We're being spontaneous.'

We were on the living-room floor, me on top, moving up and down onto him. I shut my eyes to get back into the feelings.

'Grace.'

'What?'

'It's killing my shoulder blades. Let's go upstairs.'

'Okay.'

My knees were starting to hurt.

*

'This is when I miss them the most,' Damien said, punching his pillow like it had called his mother a whore. 'Post-coital bliss isn't half as good without cigarettes.'

'Be a hero,' I said.

'Some people are just born smokers,' he said. 'It's a fundamental part of their personality.'

'Have a blueberry.'

'Have a blueberry, she says.' He stared up at the ceiling. 'A million blueberries wouldn't fill the hole. I dreamt about them last night.'

'Blueberries?'

'Cigarettes.'

'You should really try the gum.'

'Ah no,' he said. 'It doesn't work.'

I kept my mouth shut, but it was hard. He had this macho self-reliant thing, where he believed nothing could help him. When he had a headache (often) he wouldn't take painkillers. ('What good would they do?') When he had a chest infection (every January) he wouldn't go to the doctor. ('He'd only write me a prescription for antibiotics.') It's maddening.

'Don't forget,' I said. 'On Thursday night Marnie, Nick and the kids are coming from London. Ma is doing dinner.'

'I hadn't forgotten. Don't leave me alone with Nick.'

Nick was Marnie's husband, a handsome little devil who'd transcended his working-class origins to become a commodities trader awash with cash. (Ma and Dad, the old socialists, tried to disapprove of him and his Thatcherite economics but he was irresistible.)

They lived in a big house on Wandsworth Common and

they were very 'lifestyle' – Marnie's car was a Porsche SUV.

'No room for gloom in Nick's world,' Damien said. 'I'll have to listen to him going on about the merits of the new Jag versus the new Aston Martin and which one he should get.'

'Maybe he won't. It looks like he won't get his bonus again this year. Second year in a row. World hemp prices aren't what they were.'

I knew all about their finances. Marnie told me everything.

'Nothing gets him down. And don't *you* forget that on Friday night we've been summoned to Christine's for dinner.'

Christine was Damien's elder sister and we suspected that this wasn't just a routine catch-up visit. It wasn't very often that we had intimate dinners with his siblings, there were just too many to get round to them all. Mostly we met Damien's family en masse (and I mean en masse: there are ten nieces and nephews aged between twelve and zero – we actually have a spreadsheet of their birthdays) at big, overwhelming shindigs: fortieth birthdays and golden weddings and first communions.

But we'd deduced that the reason we'd been invited over to Christine and Richard's, just the two of us, was because they'd recently had their fourth child and they were going to ask us to be godparents. It made sense. All three of Damien's other siblings – Brian, Hugh and Deirdre – were already godparents to Christine's eldest three children. Now that a fourth child had arrived, it was obvious that Damien, and probably I, would fill the vacant slot.

'What exactly does a godparent have to do?' Damien asked.

'Nothing,' I said. I was Daisy's godmother. 'Just give them money at Christmas and on their birthdays.'

'Don't you have to take care of their spiritual welfare?'

'Only if the parents die.'

'But Christine and Richard won't die.' No, they'd never do anything so crass.

'Hey, Bomber Command,' Damien suddenly exclaimed. 'I'm not doing anything the Friday after next, am I?'

'I'm not your keeper.'

'Hah! Now that's funny. Have you anything lined up for me?'

'Why?'

'It's my twenty-year school reunion.'

'School reunion? *You?*'

Damien was one of the most unsociable people I'd ever met. It was hard to get him to go anywhere. Frequently he said that he hated everyone, that he wanted to live on top of a lonely mountain and that the only person he could stomach for any length of time was me.

Suddenly I knew what this was about. My stomach sank. 'Will Juno be there?'

'Yeah, I suppose.'

'You suppose?'

'She's the one organizing it, so yes, I suppose.'

Since Juno had sent that bloody DVD, I'd been waiting for something like this.

'What's going on?'

'Nothing!'

'She rang you? You rang her? What?'

'She rang Mum. Mum rang me. I rang Juno.'

'When?'

'I dunno. When was Monday?'

'Yesterday.'

'Yesterday, then.'

I stared at him long and steadily. 'What's going on?'

'Don't you trust me?'

'Yes. No. I don't know.'

'One careful owner . . . and a few careless ones too. Only messing. Hahaha.' Terry, the second-hand car salesman (another chicken-and-egg-style conundrum: which comes first, the job selling second-hand cars or the sleazy, over-familiar persona?), looked Damien dead in the eye. 'Seriously. One lady owner, never went above forty.'

I was bobbing up and down, trying to break the eye-lock between Damien and Terry.

'. . . full service history . . .'

I just needed to get the laser beam of Terry's gaze redirected onto my face instead of Damien's.

'. . . new set of tyres . . .'

Damien was gesturing in my direction. 'Tell Grace,' he said, but Terry had him in an ocular death-grip.

'Terry!' I called.

He pretended not to hear me. '. . . fully taxed . . .'

'Terry.' I stood four inches away from him and said, very loudly, into his face, 'The. Car. Is. For. Me.'

'Oh sorry, love.' He winked at Damien.

'That's not okay, love. But I don't blame you for winking at Damien. Gorgeous, isn't he?'

'It was like being hypnotized,' Damien apologized, as we drove away. 'I just couldn't make my eyes stop looking at him.'

'No problem!' It was great having a car again! Another Mazda, not as nice, not as new, but I wasn't complaining. 'Let's go for a drive!'

'Out to Dun Laoghaire? Look at the sea?'

'Then we can drop into Yeoman Road? See if Bid is better and if we can start smoking again?'

He barely hesitated, which just goes to show what a fantastic mood he was in. (He always hesitated whenever a visit to my family – or indeed his family, but you could expect that – was proposed. He insisted he was very fond of my parents – and quite fond of Bid, which is the most she deserved, the way she sometimes carried on – but that families *per se* gave him the heebie-jeebies.)

We were greeted by deafening Shostakovich. Dad was in his chair, his eyes closed, conducting the music. Bingo was delicately stepping forwards and backwards, dancing like someone in a Jane Austen adaptation. All he was missing was the bonnet. Ma was at the kitchen table, reading *Islamophobia: How the West Reconfigured Muslim Ideology*. Bid was wearing a yellow-and-white-striped knitted hat on her bald head – it looked like an egg cosy – and flicking through something called *Sugar for Susie*. Everyone –

including Bingo – was drinking Dad's disgusting dandelion wine.

Ma saw us first. 'What are you doing here?'

'I got a new car!'

Dad's eyes flew open and he sat bolt upright. 'Did those extorting crooks actually pay up?'

'Yes!' Damien lied. It would be months before we saw a penny but none of us could take a Dad-rant. 'How're you feeling, Bid?' Damien asked.

She laid down her book. 'Dying for a fag, thank you for asking.'

'I meant your general health . . .'

'Oh that,' she said sadly. 'Only five more goes of chemo, then we can all start smoking again.' A tear rolled down her yellowish cheek.

'Please don't cry,' I said in alarm.

'I can't help it. I miss . . . I miss . . . I miss cigarettes so much,' she choked out.

'Oh so do I, Bid, love, so do I.' Ma closed her book then she began to cry too – then Dad!

'It's exhausting,' he said, his voice hoarse and desperate, his shoulders shaking. Bingo rushed to him, his nails clicking on the lino, and laid his head on Dad's lap. 'It's utter bloody torment.' Dad rubbed Bingo's head a bit manically. 'It's all I think about and it's a full-time job just staying away from them.'

'I don't mind having cancer.' Bid looked up, her face wet. 'It's the not smoking that's killing me.'

'I dream about them,' Ma admitted.

'Me too!'

'Me too,' Damien said.

'And me,' Dad said wetly. 'I've never eaten so much cake. I can't see what benefit there is in giving up nicotine only for trans fat to kill us.'

'How's your Mills and Boon?' I nodded at Bid's book.

'It's not, it's erotica. About this girl called Susie who keeps going to bed with people. Silly, very silly, but the sex bits are good.'

'Right! Lovely!'

Jesus, Marnie had got so *thin*. Through one of Ma's woolly cardigans, I could feel her ribs. She'd always been skinny but she seemed thinner than ever. Aren't we supposed to plump out a bit as we get older? Even if you haven't given up cigarettes? (It had only been four days and already I was having trouble getting my waistbands to close.)

'I'm frozen,' she said. 'This house. Where's Damien?'

'On his way.' He'd bloody better be. 'You're very thin.'

'Am I? Good.'

Oh God, I thought, I hope on top of everything else that she hasn't gone and caught anorexia. I'd recently done a piece on it being a growing trend among women in their forties, and although Marnie was only thirty-five she liked to be ahead of the curve.

Down in the kitchen, there was shouting and chaos. Daisy and Verity were galloping around the table being ponies, Ma was stirring a pot and doing the crossword and Dad had his face buried in a biography of Henry Miller.

It looked like a pink bomb had exploded: pink rucksacks, pink anoraks, dolls dressed in pink . . .

'Hello, Sweets.' Nick stretched over (actually he stretched *up*, if I'm to be honest) to kiss me hello. 'You look gorgeous!'

So did he. He was only about five foot eight, but had mischievous good looks. His haircut was noticeably cool and his jeans and long-sleeved T-shirt looked new and (as Ma said later) 'maginey'.

'Say hello to Auntie Grace!' Marnie ordered the girls.

'We can't,' Daisy said. 'We're ponies. Ponies can't talk.'

She thundered past and I grabbed her and kissed her petal-like face. She twisted away, yelling, 'You kissed a horse, Grace kissed a horse.'

'She's kissed worse in her time.' Damien had arrived.

'Glad you could make it,' I said quietly.

'I'm not.'

I shouldn't laugh, it only encouraged him. I pinched his thigh, hard enough to hurt. 'You're very bold. Who let you in?'

'Bid. She's gone back to bed. Why's Bingo outside?'

Bingo's face was pressed up against the glass, mournfully watching all the fun in the kitchen.

'Verity's suddenly afraid of dogs.'

'Uncle Damien!' Daisy launched herself at him and tried to clamber up his leg, like a monkey up a tree. He held her upside down by her ankles and carried her around while she shrieked in terror and delight. He put her down, then held out his arms to Verity. But she'd taken a defensive position behind the kitchen table.

'Say hello to Damien,' Marnie said. But Verity retreated

further and stood with her back against the wall, staring fearfully at Damien.

'Don't worry, Verity,' he said kindly. 'Not the first time I've been rejected by a woman.'

Poor Verity cut an unattractive little picture. She was small and oddly shrunken-looking but had an old face. There was something wrong with her eyes – nothing serious – but it meant she had to wear glasses, which made her look adult and knowing.

It must be hard being Daisy's little sister. Daisy was so cheery and confident, tall for her age and as clear-eyed and velvet-skinned as an angel.

'Beer, Damien?' Nick asked.

'Yeah, Nick, beer, great!' Damien always went extra-blokey around Nick, to compensate for the fact that he had nothing to talk to him about. 'So! How's work?'

'Great! You?'

'Yeah! Great!'

'Is there wine?' I found a bottle of red and poured four glasses.

'None for me,' Marnie said sorrowfully. 'I'm on anti-biotics.'

Dad looked up from his book, his face alert, about to launch into his anti-drug companies tirade.

'Somebody stop him,' Damien said.

'Shut up,' Ma said to Dad. 'You stupid old man. No one wants to hear.'

'What's wrong with you?' I asked Marnie.

'Kidney infection.'

God Almighty, it was always something. She was the sickest person I'd ever met.

'It's your fault, you know.' She grinned. 'Hogging all the nutrition in the womb. Leaving me with nothing.'

A familiar refrain, and to look at us, you'd agree. She was tiny, fine-boned and barely five foot. With her thin little face, big blue eyes and long chestnut hair, she was a beauty. I felt like a lumbering carthorse beside her.

The galloping began again, the ponies bashing into chairs (particularly Dad's), shrieking, laughing and thundering.

'You two!' Dad suddenly screeched, when they'd knocked his book from his hand for the fifth time. 'Stop it, stop it! In the name of all that's holy, stop it! Go and watch telly in the other room.'

'There's nothing to watch,' Daisy said. 'You don't have cable.'

'Read a book,' Ma suggested. Everyone ignored her.

'Tell us to watch a DVD,' Daisy ordered me.

'Watch a DVD,' I said.

'We can't.' Daisy gripped my wrist and said, her limpid eyes alight with genuine astonishment, 'Because there's no DVD player!'

We stared at each other in mock amazement.

Dad got to his feet. 'I'm going to walk Bingo.'

'You've walked him already,' Ma said. 'Sit back down. Marnie! How did you get those bruises?'

'What bruises?' Marnie's cardigan sleeves had slipped up to her elbows, revealing livid, purple blooms on both forearms. She took a look at them. 'Oh those. Acupuncture.'

'What do you have that for?'

218

'Cravings.'

I cast an involuntary glance at Nick. His eyes slid away from mine.

'What cravings?' Ma asked.

'Oh you know. To be five foot six. To be a natural optimist. To win the lottery.'

'Is acupuncture supposed to give you bruises like that?'

'Probably not, but you know me.'

'A slight problem.' Nick came down the stairs into the kitchen. 'Verity won't go to bed. She says the house is haunted.'

Ma seemed dumbfounded. '. . . But it's not. It's about the one thing that isn't wrong with it.'

'If it was, we could start charging,' Dad said.

'She wants to go home to London.'

Verity was standing on the landing, her little pink rucksack packed, sullenly refusing eye contact.

'There are no ghosts in this house,' I told her.

'They all moved next door when they got cable.' Damien came up the stairs behind me.

'Not a man!' Verity screamed, suddenly animated. 'I want Mum!'

'Fine, grand, sorry.' Damien retreated.

Marnie took control. She crouched beside Verity, talking quietly with her, trying to quell her fears without once sounding patronizing. She was endlessly patient. So patient that I was afraid we'd be there all night but Verity abruptly capitulated. 'Sorry, Mum. I love you, Mum.'

'I love you too, sweetheart.'

She got into bed and Marnie lay next to her. 'Just for a little while, until she's asleep. I won't be long.'

As I came back downstairs, Damien collared me. 'She asleep? Can we go? Please, Bomber Command.'

'I want to have a proper chat with Marnie.'

'Can *I* go? I've an early meeting. And I'm losing the will to live. I've been talking to Nick for the past nine life-times. Seasons have changed. The trees have blossomed, withered, then bloomed again. Maybe if I was smoking, but my tolerance isn't what it was . . .'

No point in forcing him. 'Oh all right.' I laughed. 'I'm going to stay, though.'

Dad noticed Damien gathering up his stuff and became instantly alert. 'Are you going for a pint?'

'No, ah . . . just going home.'

'Oh are you?' Cries of disappointment all round. 'Why? Why are you going? Why?'

'Early start.' He grinned uncomfortably.

'Bye, Damien.' Ma patted his face. ' "I love the majesty of human suffering." Vigny. *La Maison du Berger*.'

'Bye,' he said, and skedaddled.

Dad looked at the door that Damien had disappeared through and remarked thoughtfully, 'The interesting thing is that, underneath all of it, *all* of it, he's a decent man. He'd give you the shirt off his back.'

'Even though he'd complain that it was his favourite shirt and that he was going to miss it terribly,' Ma said, then she and Dad dissolved into sudden hard laughter.

'Leave him alone!' I protested.

Marnie reappeared. 'Where's Damien gone?'

'He needs his space.'

Marnie shook her head. 'I don't know how you do it. I'm far too insecure to be with someone like Damien. Whenever he was in a bad mood, I'd think it was my fault.'

'But he's always in a bad mood!' Dad cried, as if he'd just said something tremendously witty, then he and Ma laughed again for a very long time.

I tried to sneak in without waking him but Damien sat up and turned on the light.

Blearily he asked, 'What's up with Verity?'

'I don't know.'

'Those glasses? They make her look like an economist.'

'Or an accountant. I know.'

'She's freaky.'

'She's only a little girl.'

'She's like Carrie. I bet she could start fires.'

I said nothing. I knew what he meant.

'Come in, Grace, come in.'

Dee Rossini. Early forties. Olive skin. Red lipstick. Snapping brown eyes. Black corkscrew curls caught up in a twisty bun. Wide-cut Katharine Hepburn trousers. A hip-length cardigan, tied tight around a slender waist.

She led me down the short hall. 'Tea? Coffee? Macaroon? They're just out of the oven.'

'What? You made macaroons? Yourself?'

'One of my army of aides bought them in M&S and stuck them in the oven ten minutes before you were due.' She smiled for the first time. 'Yes, home-made.'

She had one of those kitchens, you know the type – basil plants lined the window sill, and shelves overflowed with jars and retro tins full of arborio rice and peculiar-looking misshapen pasta (like off-ends that you'd think they'd give away at the end of the day to the local peasants but, strangely, was more expensive than the normal unpeculiar stuff). It was cosy, welcoming and fragrant with warm chocolate air and you could tell that if Dee was challenged to make *anything* in the whole world, she'd have the ingredients to hand. (Mongolian yak stew? 'I'll just thaw out a couple of yak steaks.' Fresh truffle soup? 'I've a small truffle patch in the garden, I'll just go and snuffle them.') It was some comfort to notice that the ceiling above the cupboards could do with a good dust.

Big Daddy had decreed that we were profiling Dee, but Jacinta refused to do it. Something to do with an Hermès scarf – she claimed Dee Rossini had whipped the last one in Ireland from right under her nose – so I'd asked if I could go.

Ma was pleased; she loved Dee Rossini – who was one of seven children from an Irish mother and an Italian father, a survivor of domestic violence, a single mother and the first woman in Irish politics to have set up a mainstream political party. Starting your own political party usually ended in tears, especially in Ireland where politics were run by a tight club of men. But against all expectations, NewIreland had survived, not as a joke fringe party, but as a partner in a successful coalition government with the Nappies (Nationalist Party of Ireland). Despite having to sing from the same hymn sheet as the Nappies, Dee Rossini was nevertheless vocal about anything to do with women –

Ireland's comedy child-care provisions, the dearth of funds for women's refuges, the absence of regulation for plastic surgery.

'Sit down, sit down.' She pulled out a kitchen chair for me.

It was rare to get an interview at a politician's home. Even rarer for the politician to make coffee and to produce a mountain of warm macaroons on her granny's willow-pattern plate.

'Did you get parking okay?' she asked.

'Grand. I came from the office, but would you believe I live only five minutes away from you? In Ledbury Road.'

'Small world.'

'Is this okay . . . ?' I indicated my tape recorder.

Impatiently she waved away any concerns. 'Fine. I'd rather you quoted me correctly. Do you mind me painting my nails while we're talking?'

'The many roles of women.'

'That's not the half of it. I'm doing my pelvic-floor exercises as well. And thinking about what I'll make for tonight's dinner. And worrying about third-world debt.'

'Okay, Dee.' I opened my notebook. 'The "scandals".' No point pussyfooting. The purpose of this piece was to let Dee defend herself. 'Who'd want to stitch you up?'

'All kinds of people. The opposition, obviously. Plenty of mileage for them if the Nappies' coalition partners are damaged. Even within the Nationalists there are plenty of people who think I'm a pain in the arse.'

Good point. She was always highlighting unpalatable treatment of women, even when the Nappies were to blame.

Only last week she'd objected to the appointment (by the Nappies) of a male judge, who'd stood against a female candidate, pointing out that rapists and wife-batterers rarely got anything but joke sentences from a sympathetic, almost entirely male judiciary.

'But do you have any specific theories? Specific individuals?'

She laughed. 'And have a writ for slander slapped on me before you can say knife?'

'Let's go through what happened. You got your house painted. How did you choose the firm? Did they approach you?'

'God, no. Like I'd be that stupid – "Hello, Minister for Education, can we paint your house for free?" Someone recommended them.'

'Okay. So they arrived, painted your house, made your life a misery for a couple of weeks, then sent an invoice?'

'No invoice. I rang four times, eventually got a verbal total and sent a cheque.'

'So, no invoice. And no proof that you paid. How much was the job?'

'Two grand.'

'Most of us would notice if a cheque for two grand hadn't cleared our account.'

'Tell me about it. Show me the handbags. But it was from an account that I pay something into every month, for big jobs, like replacing the boiler and getting the roof retiled. There isn't much activity in it, so I don't check it often. I work eighteen-hour days. Seven days a week. Not everything gets done.'

While she was speaking, she was painting her fingernails with the skill of an expert. Three perfect strokes – middle, left side, right side – on each nail, then she'd move on to the next. It was very soothing to watch. And the colour – a pale, pale brown, like very milky coffee, that most women (i.e. me) wouldn't even notice on the display yoke – looked so off-beat and beautiful on, that I bet people were always asking her where she got it. She was astonishingly stylish. (That would be her Italian side.)

'Okay. Your daughter's wedding? Why didn't you pay for it?' (Despite Big Daddy's attempts to downplay the story, every other paper had gone huge on it.)

'Most of it had been paid for before the actual wedding. I paid an 80 per cent deposit way back in May and yes, the cheque cleared. Admittedly the balance hasn't been paid because, God – ' she sagged – 'they got so much wrong on the day. No vegetarian meals, they ran out of the main meal, seven people didn't get fed. They lost the wedding cake, we still don't know what they did with it. The Ladies was out of order and the dancefloor was like an ice rink. Everyone was slipping and sliding and Toria's new father-in-law had to go to casualty with a dislocated knee. I know I'm a government minister and I have standards to uphold, but this was my only daughter's wedding.'

I nodded with sympathy.

'It was only a couple of months ago – in August – and we're still in dispute, but of course I'll pay them when we've agreed on a figure.' She looked forlorn.

'Doesn't it scare you that someone would set you up? To follow your life in such detail that they'd know you hadn't paid the balance on the wedding? Then use it to discredit you?'

'It's part and parcel of being a politician.' She smiled wryly. 'I've faced worse.'

I was reminded of her past. She'd been hospitalized eight times by her ex-husband, before she eventually left him – and was ostracized by her devout Catholic family for doing so.

With sudden, genuine curiosity, I asked, 'Do you ever make risotto just for yourself?'

Risotto is such a pain, all those lovingly added spoonfuls of stock, who'd be bothered?

'It's not a trick question,' I added.

She thought about it. 'Sometimes.'

I knew it. I was in awe of those types who, even when they're starving, would prefer to take time to prepare something wonderful. When I was hungry, I'd eat anything, so long as it was immediately available: stale bread, black bananas or handfuls of cornflakes, crammed into my mouth, straight from the packet.

'So what about men?' I asked.

'What about them?' A gleaming smile.

'Anyone special?'

'No, no time. And the only men I meet are politicians and, really, you'd have to be in a bad way . . .'

But she was sexy. And, of course, hot-blooded. Well, half of her anyway. I could imagine her having lengthy sex and eating poached peaches with all kinds of men – laughably handsome actors, arrogant racehorse-owning millionaires . . .

'Okay, Dee, I think I've got all I need. Thanks for the macaroons. I'm sorry I didn't eat any.'

'It's all right. Paddy's coming over later for a working supper, I'll make him eat them.'

'What's it like working with Paddy?' I shouldn't ask.

'Paddy?' She tipped her head and stared up at a corner of the ceiling, a little smile on her lips. 'Would you look at the size of that cobweb. Normally I don't wear my contact lenses at home. When the place looks dirty I just take my glasses off. Instant soft-focus.' She turned back to look at me. 'You know,' she said, 'Paddy's great.'

'Well, we all know that. Can I use your loo before I go?'

For a split second she looked anxious. 'It's upstairs. Come up, I'll show you.'

I closed the bathroom door behind me. Dee was hovering on the landing, looking edgy. I understood her anxiety. Journalists were always writing terrible things about the personal stuff they found in subjects' bathrooms. Not that I was planning a stitch-up. Just as well, the bathroom was clean and there wasn't even a mildewed shower curtain, or a home Botox kit. A poor haul.

When I re-emerged, Dee was gone. Three shut doors faced me. Bedrooms, and it was like they were whispering, Open me, go on, Grace, open me. And I just couldn't resist. I pretended it was my journalist's dogged instinct in the quest of a little extra colour; but to be honest, I was just being nosy.

I turned the knob of a door and pushed it open and, although the room was dark, I was surprised to feel the heat of another human being within. A thrill of fear zipped through me. I'd gone too far. What if it was some muscly brickie that Dee had picked up for rampant, anonymous sex?

I was already backing out when I saw that it was a woman – a girl, really – who was lying on the bed. She sat up when the door opened and as the light from the landing window travelled across the room, I was stunned with shock. Her nose was spread halfway across her face and her eyes were so swollen and purple she couldn't possibly be able to see. She opened her mouth. Two of her front teeth were missing.

'Sorry!' I retreated.

'Dee!' the girl called, panic in her voice. 'DEEEEE!'

'No, shush, please, it's okay, shush.' Dee would kill me.

Dee was out of the kitchen and up the stairs. 'What's going on?'

'It's my fault! I was having a sneaky look. I shouldn't have.'

Dee sighed. 'If you wanted to see my underwear drawer, all you had to do was ask.'

She moved past me and took the girl in her arms, and I wished that I'd resisted the siren call of the shut door and had just gone back downstairs like a normal person.

'I didn't mean to scare you,' I called at the girl from across the threshold. 'I'm very sorry.'

'Elena, *pulako*, *pulako*,' Dee crooned, making soothing noises in some foreign language. Eventually, giving me an anxious look, the injured girl was persuaded to lie down again.

Dee shut the bedroom door firmly and said to me, 'You didn't see this.'

'I'll say nothing. I swear.' I was tripping over my words

in my desire to reassure her. I understood now why Dee had been so uncomfortable about letting me upstairs. Nothing to do with me reporting nasty things about her bathroom.

'I mean it, Grace, you can't tell anyone. For her safety. She's only fifteen.' For a moment Dee looked like she was going to break down into tears.

'Dee, I promise on all I hold dear.' (I wasn't entirely certain what that was, but I wanted to convey my sincerity.) 'But what happened to her? Elena, is that her name?'

'Her boyfriend, pimp, whatever you want to call him, happened to her. He doesn't know where she is. If he does, he'll come after her. She was brought here just a couple of hours ago. It was too late to change our interview to another location and if you hadn't needed to use the loo –'

' – and poked my nose in where I shouldn't have. I swear to God, Dee, I won't say a word.'

'Not even to your partner. He's a journalist, isn't he? Can you keep a secret from him?'

'Yes.'

'She makes her own macaroons. She can paint nails with her left hand.' *She harbours women on the run. She speaks some sort of Slavic-sounding language.*

I'd developed a bit of a crush on Dee Rossini . . .

'And she's sexy,' Damien said. 'Very good-looking party, NewIreland. Aren't they?'

. . . but she also made me feel slightly inadequate.

He pressed when I didn't answer. 'Paddy de Courcy? Half man, half press release? Good-looking, isn't he?'

'I should be doing more,' I muttered.

'More what?' Damien asked.

'Just . . . more.'

'It's Uncle Damien! Damien, Damien, Damien!'

On the far side of a heavy, oak front door, Damien's four-year-old nephew, Alex, was going wild. 'Julius, Julius, man!' Alex called to his seven-year-old brother. 'Open the door, man. Damien's here.'

The door swung open and Alex rushed at Damien and me. He was wearing Superman underpants, blue patent zip-up boots (I was guessing they belonged to his nine-year-old sister, Augustina) and a colander on his head.

'Bike! Motorbike!' In a way he reminded me of Bingo, he had the same joyous sort of energy. 'Nnnnnnearrrrrrrrnnnn!'

He tried to dodge past Damien, heading for the outside world, so he could sit on the Kamikaze and pretend to drive it, but Damien used his knees to block the way. 'There's no bike tonight, Alex.'

Taxi instead. So we could get drunk.

'No bike?' The energy went from Alex as though a plug had been pulled. 'Why not, man?'

'Just one of those things, man.' Damien crouched down to Alex's level. 'Next time I come, I'll bring the bike.'

'Promise, man? They got a new baby here. But don't let him on the bike, just me?'

'Just you. Promise.'

Christine, tall and elegant and astonishingly svelte for a woman who had given birth only five weeks ago, came to welcome us. 'Come in, come in. Sorry, I'm just in myself, it's all a bit . . .' She swiped the colander from Alex's head. 'I've been looking for that.'

Alex gave a little howl of protest. 'That's my lid, man.'

'Richard should be home soon.' Richard was Christine's husband. He had one of those mysterious jobs where he spent fourteen hours a day on the phone, making money. Damien and I joked privately that every day he was locked into his office and wasn't allowed to leave until he'd made another hundred million euro. ('Ninety-eight . . . ninety-nine . . . still ninety-nine . . . ninety-nine – and a hundred! Well done, off you go home, Richard.')

We followed Christine into the enormous Colefax and Fowler kitchen, where a nervous-looking Polish girl was doing something at the microwave.

'This is Marta,' Christine said. 'Our new nanny.'

Marta nodded hello and promptly scarpered.

'And this . . .' Christine gazed fondly into a bassinet, in which a tiny pink-skinned baby was asleep. '. . . is Maximillian.'

(Yes, Christine and Richard had named their four children after emperors. I know it makes them sound like grandiose nutters, but they're not.)

Damien and I stared politely at the sleeping child.

'Okay, you can stop admiring him now.' Christine reached for a corkscrew. 'Wine?'

'Yes. Can I do anything to help?'

It was a fake question. No one could ever help Christine. She did everything so much better and faster than everyone else that there was no point. Anyway I didn't want to help.

I was at someone else's house for my dinner, why would I want to do stuff I'd have to do at home?

'All done,' Christine said. 'Did most of it last night. Just a few last-minute fiddly bits.'

'What's with your trouser suit?' I asked her. 'How come you're looking so clean? You're not back at work already?'

'God, no. I'm just popping in for a couple of hours a day, just to keep an eye on things.'

Christine was so clever and accomplished that she no longer did much actual scrubbed-up, green-gowned, hands-on surgery stuff. Instead she was Head of Surgery at Dublin's most expensive hospital, the first woman to have ever held that post. (Or perhaps she was the youngest ever Head. It was hard to keep track because the Stapletons seemed to be always winning accolades. If, every time one of them got a promotion or won an award, we gave them the celebration they deserved, we'd all end up in the Priory.)

'So where's Augustina?' I looked around.

'At her Sanskrit lesson?' Damien asked.

'Haha. Mandarin, actually.'

It took me a moment to realize that Christine was serious.

'We don't make her go,' Christine said, as I tried to hide my astonishment – well, actually distress, if I'm to be honest. 'She *asked* to go to lessons.'

Too weird. What nine-year-old would *ask* to learn Mandarin?

'And we keep an eye on her,' Christine said.

'On her work–life balance?' Damien suggested.

'If your tongue could get any further into your cheek . . .'

232

Christine said. 'Anyway, cheers.' She held up her glass. 'It's lovely to see you both.'

An expectant little moment followed and Damien and I assumed our 'Yes, we'd be honoured to be Maximillian's spiritual guardians should you and Richard die, which of course you won't' faces, but Augustina scuppered the moment by walking into the kitchen and saying coolly, 'Hello, Uncle Damien, hello, Auntie Grace.'

With no great show of enthusiasm, she kissed us both. She was tall for nine and very pretty. She sniffed the air with her dainty nose and sighed. 'Moroccan for dinner again.'

'How was today's lesson?' Christine asked. 'What did you learn?'

'May I check something?' Augustina asked Christine. 'You can't speak Mandarin, can you? So what's to be gained by my telling you what I learnt? You wouldn't understand a word of it.'

Little bitch, I thought. No wonder I don't want children. You give them everything and they thank you by growing up to despise you.

Augustina turned her attention back to me. 'I've a surprise for you two.'

'Oh? What is it?'

She furrowed her brow as if she couldn't quite comprehend our idiocy. 'A s-u-r-p-r-i-s-e,' she spelt out. 'You're not supposed to know what it is. You'll find out later.'

'Hello,' a voice said quietly. It was Richard, home from making his daily hundred million euro. Grey-suited, grey-haired and grey with exhaustion.

He managed a few moments of perfunctory conversation

with Damien. 'That was a good piece you did on Belarus,' he said. 'So how's everyone at the *Press*? Mick Brennan still editor?'

All the Stapleton menfolk – brothers, brothers-in-law and Mr Stapleton senior – seem to do this whenever they meet Damien. They praise one of his recent articles, then they ask if Mick Brennan is still the editor of the *Press*.

Maybe I'm oversensitive on Damien's behalf but I always feel they're implying that Damien had failed in some sort of way by not ousting Mick Brennan from his editorship, and assuming power himself.

Damien is only thirty-six and I've no doubt that he will edit a national newspaper some day, but in this family of overachieving clever-clogs, expectations are abnormally high.

'Dinner,' Christine declared. 'Everyone sit at the table.'

She produced a shank of lamb, fragrant with cumin, and a platter of steaming couscous.

'Not couscous,' Julius wailed. 'I hate couscous.' He stabbed the back of his hand with his fork.

'Just eat it, man.' Alex was now wearing a sieve, the handle to the back of his head, so it looked like a baseball hat. 'Make it easy on yourself.'

The food was delicious but I almost forgot to compliment Christine on it because it was just sort of accepted that everything she did, she did with excellence. The conversation, however, did not match the quality of the food.

Richard ate quickly and silently, then muttered something about the Hawaiian stockmarket and left the room.

'Dessert?' Christine stood up and began clearing plates.

'Yes.'

'Augustina has made chocolate brownies for you.'

'Don't tell them!' Augustina exploded. 'That's the surprise. I want to tell them!'

'So tell them.'

'Damien and Grace, I've made chocolate brownies in your honour. But you may not like them.'

'I'm sure we'll love them,' I said.

'Grace.' She closed her eyes in a gesture she'd obviously learnt from Christine. 'There's no need to humour me. If you would let me finish . . .'

Jesus Christ! I waved my hand in a please-go-on gesture.

'What I'm trying to tell you,' Augustina sounded like she was trying very hard to be patient, 'is that you may not like them because the chocolate I've used is 85 per cent cocoa solids. It's not to everyone's taste.'

'I like dark chocolate.'

'But you probably think 70 per cent cocoa solids is a big deal. This is Fairtrade 85 per cent.'

'Sounds great,' Damien said. 'Ethical *and* delicious.'

Augustina flicked her eyes back and forth from Damien to me, as if trying to decide if we were worthy. Finally she said, 'Very well.'

Christine had finished clearing the dinner debris and was clattering out dessert bowls. 'Richard,' she called. 'Richard! Come back in here.'

'He's on the phone. He's shouting,' Julius said.

'Tell him to get in here. I need him here for this.'

Julius thundered off and reappeared shortly. 'I don't think he's coming. Someone in Waikiki has fucked up.'

'Oh man.' Alex shook his head sorrowfully and his sieve fell off. 'Someone will have to sit on the fucked-up step.'

Christine couldn't decide whether to chastise Alex or insist that Richard get in here pronto. 'Oh never mind!' she exclaimed. 'I'll do it myself.'

She took a deep breath and I found myself sitting up straighter and already preparing my gracious smile of acceptance.

'Grace and Damien, as you know I've had a new baby.' She nodded at the bassinet. 'And he'll need godparents. And we thought Brian and Sybilla would be the best people. They're already Augustina's godparents, and you don't know this yet but Sybilla is expecting again, so Maximillian will be close in age to his new cousin.'

My gracious acceptance smile had frozen. Events had veered off in an unexpected direction. Damien and I weren't going to be asked. It was to be Brian and Sybilla. Again.

My 85 per cent cocoa-solids brownie had appeared in front of me and automatically – the way I do whenever I see any kind of food – I put a piece in my mouth.

'I'm sure you don't mind,' Christine was saying. 'I'm sure it's a relief. It's just not your thing, is it? The church, renouncing Satan and all his works. And you don't want kids of your own. But I just wanted to have a quiet word with you both before you heard that we'd asked Brian and Sybilla. It just seemed polite.'

The lump of brownie sat on my tongue, I couldn't get any further with it. It's not that I'd wanted to be Maximillian's godmother, it made no difference whatsoever to me. But, unexpectedly, I had a huge upsurge of rage on behalf of

Damien. Four children, four siblings, there should be four godparents.

Damien was great with children and far better with these kids than Richard, their own bloody father.

Augustina was watching me. 'You're not eating your brownie.'

'. . . No.'

She was pleased. 'Too bitter?'

'Too bitter.'

Monday morning and it was a red-handbag day: impatience.

'Get back.' Jacinta waved her arms at us. 'You're flocking me.'

It was our weekly meeting to discuss upcoming ideas. All of Features – with the exception of Casey Kaplan, whose whereabouts were unknown – were clustered around Jacinta's desk.

'Back,' she repeated. 'I can't breathe. Grace. Ideas. And I want good ones.'

'. . . Right.' Without nicotine I was slower, sleepier and the synapses in my head fired with less of a snap. Even after a full week I hadn't bounced back. 'How about domestic violence?'

'*What?*' Her screech was so shrill that heads turned as far away as Sport. 'You needn't think that just because you got Antonia Allen to admit she takes it up the bum that you can write your own remit!' (Over the weekend, my story on Antonia Allen got syndicated around the world, bringing in much-appreciated revenue for the *Spokesman*. It was the only interview where Antonia referenced 'My Gay Jain

Pain'. (Not my words.) Big Daddy was very pleased. He'd vacillated between lowering the tone and going for the splash and in the end had followed the money.

No one made any comment on my breast cancer story. Because it hadn't been published. A surprise avalanche in an Argentinian ski resort meant my story got killed. Mrs Singer and her tragedy would never see the light of day because the report was no longer current. That's how it is with journalism, it moves fast, too fast to let yourself get attached. One of the first things you learn is to get used to it. But I'd never learnt.)

'I was thinking,' I continued speaking as though Jacinta hadn't just shrieked at me, 'that over six weeks we could profile six different women from diverse backgrounds. We could do a campaign.'

'What in the name of fuck has brought this on?'

'It's a real proble –'

'Is there a report?'

'No.'

'Not even a report to hang it on! No one cares about domestic violence! It's Dee Rossini, isn't it? You've fallen under her spell.'

'I have not.'

Actually I might have. My profile on her, which I'd spent all of Friday afternoon lovingly crafting, had been luminescent; and on Saturday, when I'd been in Boots, I'd looked for the funny light-brown nail varnish but hadn't found it. Yesterday, I'd even rung to enquire about Elena. (Dee had said tersely that she was 'safe'.)

'One in five Irish women will experience domestic

violence at some stage in their lives,' I said. So Dee had told me.

'I don't care,' Jacinta said. 'I don't care if every single one of them experiences it – '

' – us,' I interrupted.

'What?'

'Every single one of *us*, not them. It's *us*, Jacinta.'

'It's not fucking *us*! I don't experience it, you don't experience it, Joanne doesn't experience it, do you Joanne? Lorraine, Tara and Clare, none of them experiences it! You ARE under Dee Rossini's spell. But we're not doing it!'

'Grand,' I muttered, dying, oh dying for a cigarette. A whole pack of twenty, one after the other after the other. The longing was so great that I got the I-wish-I-could-cry pain in my sinuses, a tight band of contained tears pushing out against my facebones. I didn't listen to the others presenting their ideas and my hearing only returned when I heard Jacinta say, 'We're profiling Alicia Thornton.'

'*Who?*' Maybe there were two Alicia Thorntons.

'Paddy de Courcy's fiancée.'

'But . . . *why*?'

'Because Big Daddy says so.'

'But who is she?' I asked. 'What's interesting about her?'

'She's the woman "who won Quicksilver's heart",' Jacinta said.

'But she's dull and . . . she's just an obedient political spouse. How're you going to get two thousand words out of that?'

'You'd better change your attitude pretty quick because you're doing the interview.'

'No!' I took a moment to compose myself. 'No way.'

'What do you mean, no?'

'I mean no, I don't want to do it.' I pointed to TC. 'Send him. Or Lorraine. Send Casey.'

'You're doing it.'

'I can't.'

'What do you mean, can't?'

'Jacinta.' I'd no choice but to come clean. 'I know . . . knew . . . Paddy de Courcy. In another life. My integrity is compromised. I'm the wrong person.'

She shook her head. 'You're doing it.'

'Why?'

'Because she asked for you. Specifically for you. If you won't do it, she's taking it to another paper. You have to do it.'

She tried to twist away from under his grasp but he was so much stronger.

'I don't want to do this.' Her pyjama bottoms were yanked down to her knees, her thighs goosepimpling at the air, and he was shoving his way up into her despite her dry resistance. It hurt. Short brutal thrusts, each one accompanied by a grunt.

'Please –'

'Shut. Up.' Ground out between clenched teeth.

Instantly she stopped struggling and let him batter his way in, the rim of the sink digging painfully into her back.

The grunts got louder, the thrusts became more like stabs, then he was shuddering and groaning. He went slack, draping his body over hers, so that her face was buried in his chest. She could barely breathe. But she didn't complain. She waited for him to do whatever he needed. After some time had passed, he pulled himself out and smiled tenderly at her. 'Let's get you back to bed,' he said.

Marnie

On the in breath, 'I'm.' On the out breath, 'Dying.'
  On the in breath, 'I'm.' On the out breath, 'Dying.'
  On the in breath, 'I'm.' On the out breath, 'Dying.'
  On the in breath, 'I'm.' On the out breath, 'Dying.'
  On the in breath, 'I'm.' On the out breath, 'Dying.'
  On the in breath, 'I'm.' On the out breath, 'Dying.'
  On the in breath, 'I'm.' On the out breath, 'Dying.'
  On the in breath, 'I'm.' On the out breath, 'Dying.'
  I'm dying. I'm dying. I'm dying. I'm dying. I'm dying. I'm
dying. I'm dying. I'm dying. I'm dying. I'm dying. I'm dying.
I'm dying. I'm dying. I'm dying. I'm dying. I'm dying. I'm
dying. I'm dying. I'm dying. I'm dying.
  On the in breath, 'I'm.' On the out breath, 'Dying.'
  That was the wrong mantra. It should be: On the in breath,
'All.' On the out breath, 'Is well.' All is well. All is well. All is
well. All is well. All is well. I'm dying. I'm dying. I'm dying.
I'm dying. I'm dyingI'm dyingI'm dyingI'mdyingI'mdyingI'm
dyingI'mdying.
  But she wasn't dying. She just wished she was.
  The light chime of bells. Poppy's voice saying, 'Come back
to the room.'
  She opened her eyes. Eight other people, mostly women,
were sitting in a circle, in the flickering candlelight.
  'Did you feel it?' Poppy had told them to focus on their
soul. 'Did you feel a connection?'
  Yes, the voices murmured, yes, yes.

'Let's go round the circle and share our experience.'

'My soul is silver light.'

'My soul is a golden ball.'

'My soul is white and shimmery.'

'Marnie?'

Her soul? It felt like a tomato which had been left at the bottom of the fridge for four months. Black, reeking, rotting. One touch and it would collapse. It sat at her centre, infecting her entire being with filth.

She spoke. 'My soul . . .'

'Yes?'

'. . . is like the sun.'

'Beautiful imagery,' murmured Poppy.

She tiptoed to the mosaic bowl and put in a carefully folded ten-pound note. She always left more than the others.

'See you next week,' Poppy whispered, cross-legged and long-limbed on the floor.

Yes, yes, and remember to smile.

She clicked quickly down the path, keen to reach her car. She got in and slammed the door. Possibly harder than was needed.

She'd had it with meditation.

Medi*cation*, though. That was a different matter.

'No improvement?' Dr Kay asked.

'No. Worse if anything.' She shouldn't have gone to Dublin. Over the weekend, putting on a cheery show in front of her family had depleted her, leaving her lower than ever.

'In that case, let's increase your dose.' Dr Kay consulted Marnie's file. 'You could go up another 75 mgs.'

'I'd prefer . . . can I change brands?' It was time to try a better one. 'Can I have Prozac?'

'Prozac?' Dr Kay was surprised. 'Prozac is a bit of a dinosaur. No one really prescribes it any more. Your current medication is from the same family but newer, more sophisticated. Fewer side-effects, more effective.' She reached for her drug encyclopaedia. 'I can show you.'

No, no, no. 'Please, no, it's okay.' There was no way of enduring it while Dr Kay found Prozac in the book, showed her the contraindications, then found the other drug. It would probably take less than a minute, but she didn't have a minute in her. 'Please. I'd like to try Prozac. I have a good feeling about it.'

'But . . . how about . . . have you considered therapy?'

'I've done therapy. Years of it.' On and off. 'I've learnt things but . . . I still feel terrible. Please, Dr Kay . . .' She knew only one thing: she could not leave until she'd got a prescription for Prozac.

She flicked a glance at the shut door, to remind Dr Kay of her waiting room, crowded with sick people, clamouring for entry. It was cruel but she was desperate. She couldn't go on as she was. Please give me Prozac.

Dr Kay was staring doubtfully at her.

Please give me Prozac.

Then Dr Kay dropped her eyes. It was over. Marnie had locked herself so tight into waiting mode, she was surprised. Like when a tyrannical regime crumbles in one's lifetime; the way she'd felt when the Taliban had been ousted from Afghanistan.

'Okay. We'll try you for a couple of months, see how you do on it.' Dr Kay reached for her prescription pad. 'Is there anything else, Marnie? Anything else you're . . . concerned about?'

'No. Thank you, thank you, thank you.'

She left, gratefully holding the prescription.

Everyone knew. Prozac worked.

When she pushed open her front door, Nick zipped from the kitchen into the hall. He looked distraught. What was it?

Then she knew. 'No bonus again?'

'What?'

'No bonus? You found out?'

'No, not that.' He gripped her arms. 'Where the hell have you been?'

'I told you. The doctor.'

'But it's eight o'clock.'

'I didn't have an appointment. I had to wait. Where are the girls?'

'In the playroom.'

They were watching *Beauty and the Beast*. Again. Daisy was sprawled the length of the sofa, her legs slung over the armrest; Verity was curled in a ball, sucking her thumb.

'Hello, babies.'

'Hi, Mum.'

'How was school?'

Neither answered her. They were in a trance. She'd read that when children were watching television, their metabolic rate was lower than when they were asleep.

'How long have they been watching that?'

'About an hour.'

'Oh Nick. Couldn't you have played with them? Instead of sticking them in front of a DVD?'

'Couldn't you have come home earlier?'

He followed her into the kitchen, one step behind her, her shadow. She opened the fridge and wondered about food.

She felt him staring and turned to look.

'What?' she asked.

'What, what?'

'What are you staring at me for?'

'What time did you leave work?'

'What did you feed them?'

'Lasagne. What time did you leave work?'

'How much did Verity eat?'

'Enough. What time did you leave work?'

'Six.'

'Six exactly?'

'Nick, I don't know.' She sighed. 'Close enough. Maybe three minutes past, maybe five past.'

'And you went straight to the doctor?'

'I went straight to the doctor.'

'And you've been there all that time?'

'I've been there all that time.'

'What did you do while you were waiting?'

'Read magazines.'

'Which ones?'

'Let me see . . . *Good Housekeeping*. *Red*. And another one, I think it was *Eve*.'

'Then you came straight home?'

'I came straight home.'

He stared hard at her and she dropped her eyes.

There was probably something in the freezer that she could defrost. She opened and shut a couple of drawers; Marks and Spencer moussaka, that would do. And frozen peas. Protein; if you didn't get enough, it made things worse. She closed the freezer door with her hip and when she turned around, he was right behind her, so near she bumped against him. 'Jesus!'

He didn't move.

'You're in my way.'

247

His body had blocked her into the corner between the freezer and wall, close enough so she could smell his breath.

'Nick.' Her voice was reasonable. 'You're in my way.'

'Am I?'

He studied her face, seeming to catalogue all that he saw. She couldn't read his expression, but it made her nervous. The moment went on for a very long time, then he moved aside to let her pass.

There was something a little shameful about having a short drive to work. Twenty-minute commutes were for losers. Real people endured a macho hour and a quarter; it was important to have something to complain about.

While she was stopped at the traffic lights on Wimbledon High Street, a bus passed in front of her, the huge letters on its side – an ad for a DVD – streaming down the street like a banner. FEARLESS. It hit like a stamp to her heart. It was a message.

Fearless. Today I will be fearless. Today I will be fearless. Today I will be fearless.

But even after repeating it several times, she remained doubtful. It didn't feel right. No, this wasn't meant to be her message. The ad on the next bus would be the one.

But what if a bus didn't come by the time the lights changed? Then she would have to do without a message today.

She was anxious. She wanted her instructions.

Don't change, don't change, don't change, she pleaded with her traffic lights.

Between the trees to her right, a large patch of red flickered. A bus was coming. She watched expectantly. What would it say? One by one, the words appeared. Put. Everything. On. Ice. Put Everything On Ice.

248

What could that mean? Keep everything steady? Don't make any big decisions? Or was it more practical advice? *Literally* put everything on ice? Yes, that too could work.

Then she remembered that it was only an ad on the side of a bus and that, in terms of her life, it probably meant nothing at all.

As she waited for the barrier to the underground car park to lift, she noticed that she was ten minutes late. She couldn't understand it. She'd had spare time this morning. But time played tricks on her: it jumped, stretched, swallowed itself. It wanted her to know that she couldn't control it and this frightened her.

She parked between Rico's Aston Martin and Henry's LandRover. Craig's Jag, Wen-Yi's Saab, Lindka's TransAm – the garage was like a luxury-car salesroom. Mortgage brokers were well paid, at least this lot were. Her four-wheel-drive Porsche looked just the part, except, unlike everyone else, she hadn't paid for her own car.

She looked around, hoping not to see it: a Lotus. But there it was; Guy was already in.

It was time for her to open her car door and join the world; instead she slumped back against her headrest. Eight hours. Of other people. Of having to talk. Of having to make decisions.

Get out get out get out.

She was as powerless to move as a butterfly pinned to a card, but her paralysis mixed unpleasantly with the knowledge that she was late again and getting later with every second.

Get out get out get out.

She was moving. She was outside the car and on her feet. The lump of lead in place of her stomach was so dense, she could hardly stand for the weight of it. She felt as if she was staggering as she walked towards the lift, as if her knees couldn't support the burden of herself.

Kill me kill me kill me.

She looked at the lift call button. Her hand was supposed to press it. Nothing happened.

Press it press it press it.

Rico was the first person she saw when she opened the door. He'd been watching for her. His dark eyes kindled with warmth. 'How are you?'

I'm dead I'm dead I'm dead. 'Fine. You?'

At the sound of her voice, Guy looked up, his haughty face cold. He tapped his watch. 'Twelve minutes, Marnie.'

'I'm really sorry.' She hurried to her desk.

'Sorry?' he called after her. 'That's it? No explanation?'

'Roadworks.'

'Roadworks? Roadworks affect us all. No one else is late.'

Henry hung up his phone. 'New case! Director of Coutt's. Serious up-trading. Lots of wonga.' Some of it coming Henry's way. Brokers got 1 per cent of the price of every house sale they brought in.

'Where did you find him?' Craig asked jealously. A new mark for one broker meant one fewer for the others. Competition was fierce.

'At my cousin's wife's father's funeral,' he boomed.

'You gave someone your business card at a funeral?' Lindka asked.

Henry shrugged good-naturedly. 'Nice guys finish last.'

Lindka reached for Guy's *Telegraph* and rustled through to the obituaries. 'Shedloads of them here. Let's share them out. "So sorry for your loss. Need a mortgage?"'

Everyone laughed.

Marnie managed a wobbly smile. Once upon a time she'd been one of them: sharks. At weddings and birthday parties, she'd moved among the guests, smiling, chatting, asking general-sounding questions ('Where are you living?'), and moving as tactfully as possible to the specific ('Have you thought about moving?'), trying to ignore the voices in her head telling her it was horribly inappropriate to tout for business at a family celebration. All that had mattered, she'd told herself, were the follow-up phone calls. When she was getting paid 1 per cent of the purchase price, it was worth enduring myriad looks of distaste.

However, even at her most productive, she'd never been one of the high-generators, like Guy, the owner of the company, or Wen-Yi, who seemed to conjure up a never-ending stream of house-buyers out of thin air. She hadn't got what it took to pursue people to the bitter end. If she'd intuited that they were irritated or uncomfortable, she'd backed down. Paradoxically this had at times worked in her favour. People had liked that she was gracious – well, some of them had; others had thought she was a no-mark who wouldn't have the grit to get them a good deal, and they'd gone instead to a swaggery wide-boy like Craig or an overconfident posho like Henry.

When she got pregnant with Daisy, she'd given it up. There was no reason not to: Nick earned enough for both of them and she wanted to be a full-time mother. But the truth was, she'd been rescued by pregnancy. Her luck had been on the turn, she'd felt it slipping away from her. She'd got out before everyone else knew too.

She had never planned to return, but a year ago Nick hadn't got his annual bonus and there was a sudden, terrifying hole in their finances. A huge block of money for mortgage payments and school fees simply wasn't there.

After the shock wore off and the readjustment began, the thought of returning to work after a six-year break began to seem exhilarating. Suddenly she understood that the reason she was so unhappy was because she wasn't suited to being a stay-at-home mum. She loved Daisy and Verity to the point of pain but perhaps outside stimulation was vital for her.

Guy had welcomed her back and as she showed up on her first day, in her new trouser suit and high-heeled shoes, she was buoyant with pride: a useful member of her family. She mattered. But – literally within days – it became obvious that she could no longer do the job.

She brought in no new business. The analysis she brought to bear on her life showed that she didn't go out as often as she used to before the kids, so there were fewer opportunities to make contacts. However, Nick had plenty of well-paid colleagues, she could have put the moves on them if she'd been committed enough. But it was impossible. She just couldn't talk to people any more. She certainly couldn't hustle for business and she couldn't articulate precisely why. The only explanation she could find was that it shamed her. She didn't want to bother people; she didn't want to draw attention to herself; she didn't want to ask for anything, because she couldn't endure the rejection.

Because she had no other choice, she forced herself to try. But she couldn't strike the right note of breezy fun (usually with men) or trustworthy calm (women). Her true voice was buried beneath a mountain of rocks, her treacherous mouth wouldn't say the right words, and when she tried to smile, she found that she twitched instead. She came across as pushy, strange and desperate; she was embarrassing people.

She'd thought returning to work would fix her but it had made everything worse.

After four months, she hadn't brought in a single new client, which was bad news for the company but worse news for her, because she had earned no commission.

Guy was patient, long past the point where any other boss would have told her to go, but she knew his forbearance couldn't go on indefinitely.

Then Bea, the office manager, had left and Guy had suggested that Marnie step into the breach. It was both a relief – at least now she had a regular salary – and a humiliation. She was a failure. Again.

Her demotion meant that she was now a lowly administrator, so there were no more long boozy lunches and no more clocking off at midday on Fridays.

As a nine-to-sixer, she was obliged to be in the office, even if everyone else had skived off, to answer the phones, sign for deliveries, calm down hysterical house-buyers . . . It was like being cast out of paradise; once she'd been on a level with the others, now she had to do their photocopying. And yet she was desperately grateful to have a job. Guy paid her more than she was worth. He could have got someone else for less money.

A file was waiting – like an accusation – on her desk. One of Wen-Yi's. It was the Mr Lee sale. Her heart dropped like a rock off a cliff.

This file was cursed. So many things had gone wrong. She had mailed the original documents to the wrong address, to one of Mr Lee's many rental properties, where they had gathered dust on an unoccupied mat for two and a half weeks. She had sent photocopies rather than originals to the building society: a heinous offence. She had lost – no other explanation – the direct-debit form authorizing the building society to recoup their monthly payments; it should have been in Mr Lee's file and it simply wasn't and she had no idea, no idea at all, where it could have got to. Worse, she remembered having seen it, so it wasn't as though she could blame Mr Lee by saying he had never filled it in.

Her glitches and omissions had slowed down this sale by several weeks; she couldn't bear to let herself know exactly how many, but sometimes her brain broke free of her control and ran off, taunting her by totting up the different delays, while she desperately tried to recapture and silence it.

'Proof of his residency in the UK,' Wen-Yi said. He sounded calm, but she knew he was trying to restrain his anger. 'Where is the form?'

She stared at him blankly. 'I didn't know ... he needed one.'

'So you haven't got it?'

'I didn't know he needed it.'

'UK Homeloans require proof of residency for foreign nationals. It's standard.'

The brokers did business with twenty-six different banks and mortgage companies, all of which had their own set of requirements. This was the first time she'd dealt with the combination of a foreign national and UK Homeloans, but it was no excuse. She should have known.

'I'll send one to him right now, Wen-Yi. I'm sorry, I'm really sorry.'

'The money's in place,' Wen-Yi said. 'We could close today but this is holding everything up. The vendors have been very patient but they're talking about putting the property back on the market. That better not happen.'

He turned his back to her and walked away. The rest of the office pretended they hadn't been listening and flicked their gaze to their screens, except for Rico, who semaphored sympathy with his eyes.

She went to the cupboard behind her and, with trembling fingers, sought the right form. There were literally hundreds of different ones, but Bea had set up a good system, and when she located it, she made herself read it several times. Yes, it was from UK Homeloans. Not UK Houseloans. Not British Homeloans. And it was 'Proof of Residency for Foreign Nationals'. Not 'Proof of Citizenship'. Not 'Proof of Non-Criminal Status'.

Satisfied that she really had the correct piece of paper, she began to fill it in, paying such attention to the details that she began to sweat. What had happened to her? When had she bruised her confidence so badly that she couldn't trust herself to do this simple task?

'Post,' Guy said, dumping a large, messy pile of envelopes on her desk and making her jump. 'Sorry. Did I scare you?'

'It's okay.' She laughed shakily.

'You're a wreck,' he said thoughtfully. To the uninitiated, his pale blue eyes looked cold, but when you knew him well you could locate kindness in there.

'Can you open it quickly, please.' Guy's requests were always delivered politely. 'The signed forms from the Findlaters should be in there. I need to get them off straight away.'

Guy trumped Wen-Yi; she had to do the post. She moved Mr Lee's form to the safety of her in-tray and began tearing at the envelopes with her nails.

Guy frowned at her. 'Use your letter knife.'

'Of course.' She couldn't even open the post properly. She reached for her desk-tidy and drew out a letter knife, and had a sudden flash of plunging it into her heart.

Instead she mechanically opened envelopes and arranged their contents into tidy piles.

'Guy, they're here.' She held up the Findlaters' forms for him to see.

'Excellent. Photocopy them and get the originals off to the bank.'

While she was at the photocopier, she decided to copy all the other signed documents which had come in the post. She forced herself to concentrate hard – on not mixing up the forms and on ensuring that it was the photocopies which went into the files and the originals which were put aside to be sent to the banks. It wasn't rocket science, she was well aware of that, but so much of the time she seemed unable to get it right.

She grabbed a bunch of A4 envelopes and returned to her desk to mail the originals to the appropriate bank. It was soothing work and when she discovered that she was using the last envelope in her pile for her last document, it lightened her heart.

A coincidence, a happy one, she hadn't counted out how many envelopes she'd need, she had just happened to accidentally select the exact number.

I feel better, she thought. It must be the Prozac.

Even though she hadn't started actually taking it yet. Simply carrying the prescription in her handbag seemed to be having a positive effect.

Then her gaze fell on Mr Lee's form – still waiting patiently in her in-tray, to be enveloped and mailed – and all the light went out. She didn't have an envelope for him. The stationery cupboard was no more than four or five yards away, but she was unable to get her legs to stand up and walk. She couldn't understand it. It wasn't physical exhaustion, as if her legs were tired. It was like there was a force field around her, pressing down on her with irresistible weight. She could have jokingly asked one of the others to help – Rico would do it – but it was an odd thing to request. And by now, she couldn't even speak. She'd used herself all up.

It's urgent it's urgent it's urgent.

But that was why she couldn't do it: it was too frightening.

I'll do it soon I'll do it soon I'll do it soon.

But whenever she caught a glimpse of the form out of the corner of her eye, she felt as though she were being flayed alive, so she took it from the in-tray and shoved it in her drawer, beneath a jar of vitamin B5 – 'the happy vitamin' – and a packet of St John's Wort.

'Marnie!' Ma cried. 'How funny you should call. I was *literally* just reading Bid's nasty tabloid – well, I say *reading*, not much literacy required, of course – and there was a picture of Paddy de Courcy and his "lovely bride-to-be".'

It was like stumbling: Marnie had only to hear his name. Automatically she reached her middle finger into the centre of the palm of her right hand; any mention of Paddy and it began to itch.

Back in August, as soon as word of his engagement had got out, Grace had phoned. 'I've news. It's Paddy. He's getting married.'

Don't you dare be happy, you bastard.

'You okay?' Grace had been terse; she couldn't bear to visit pain on Marnie.

Instantly Marnie's unexpected spike of anger had died a death and it became more important to reassure Grace. 'I'm fine. But I'm glad you told me. It mightn't have been . . . good, to find out another way.'

'Ma and Dad might bring it up. I wanted you to be prepared.'

There had been every chance that Ma and Dad might have referred to it; they didn't approve entirely of Paddy's politics but they had been unable to shake their interest in him.

Ma was wittering on. 'It says here that Sheridan is going to be the best man at the wedding. Heartening, isn't it, in these disposable times that their friendship has lasted all these years? I must say I look at Paddy now in those suits, and I think back to him sitting at my kitchen table, without an arse to his pants and those big hungry eyes, and none of us knew he'd grow up to become this . . . well, statesman is the only word. A bit thin on concrete policies, but the irritating thing is that with his kind of charisma, people don't seem to care. Of course your father insists he never liked him, but he's simply being awkward.'

'Mmm.' She was okay now, she usually managed to right herself quickly.

'In some ways Paddy reminds me of a young Bill Clinton,' Ma said. 'I wonder if he has the same problem keeping his cock in his pants.'

'Ma, you musn't say cock.' Luckily all the others were out at lunch, there was no one in the office to hear her.

'Thank you, lovie, you were always such a kind girl. What should I say instead? Penis? Johnson? Dick?'

'Dick is probably best.'

'To repeat my earlier question, I wonder if he has the same problem as Bill Clinton over keeping his dick in his pants? Is it okay for me to say pants?'

'It depends. Do you mean trousers or jocks?'

'Trousers, I suppose.'

'Then say trousers. Pants is American for trousers.'

The one thing Ma didn't want to be accused of was being American. 'I wonder if he has a problem keeping his dick in his trousers?'

'I would imagine so.'

'So would I. Of course I have no reason for saying that except that he's often "linked" to beautiful accomplished women. If you've got a taste for it, it must be difficult to give up. "Men need four things: food, shelter, pussy and strange pussy." Jay McInerney, I can't remember which novel. Of course I'm being ironic, I can't abide unfaithful men using the biological imperative as an excuse, nevertheless Alicia Thornton has her work cut out.'

'She knows what she's getting into.'

'What's this about her being a widow? What did her husband die of?'

'He probably killed himself because he couldn't take being married to her.'

Ma was astonished. 'Now why would you say that? And what age is she?'

'You know what age she is, she's thirty-five, same as me.'

'How would I know that?'

'. . . Ma . . . because you know her.'

'I assure you I don't.'

'. . . Ma, I can't believe . . . I thought you knew . . .'

'Knew what, lovie?'

'Take a look at her picture, Ma. Imagine her without the blonde highlights.'

There were rustling noises as Ma picked up the paper.

'And without the make-up. And with longer hair. And a lot younger.'

Ma took a sharp intake of breath. 'Christ on a bike, it's not . . .'

'It is.'

She hadn't taken any vitamin B5 all day – no wonder she felt so wretched – but when she opened her drawer she saw, lurking beneath the vitamin jar, Mr Lee's form. Still there. Still unsent. The floor tilted beneath her. How could she not have done this? When it was so important?

And it was too late now, she had missed today's post.

She vowed, with fierce promise, that she would mail it first thing the following morning. But what if Wen-Yi found it? What if he decided to check up on her and look through her stuff when she had left for the day?

Seized with terror, she slid the piece of paper from the drawer and shoved it into her handbag in a quick, jerky movement.

As if Wen-Yi had sensed something, he lifted his head and asked her, 'Did you send Mr Lee his residency form?'

'Yes.'

'Marnie? Quick drink?' Rico asked. 'Help me celebrate my biggest-ever commission?'

She considered it. Only briefly, but long enough to trigger a powerful yearning. The possibility of escape . . . But she couldn't. The kids were expecting her home at a quarter past six. Melodie, her nanny, would be in the starting blocks, ready to run to her next job. And remember what had happened the last time she'd gone for a drink with Rico.

'No, I –' Suddenly she was aware of being watched. She twisted her head: Guy was following the exchange. Immediately he looked away and she turned back to Rico.

She shook her head. 'No, Rico, I can't.'

'That's a pity.' He seemed genuinely sorrowful.

But he'd find someone else, a good-looking man like him.

Five a.m. Too early to get up, too late to go back to sleep. She should do something useful with the time. She could go downstairs and do yoga, but it didn't work. Not for her. It was supposed to be calming. Or uplifting. Or life-changing, if you were really lucky. Jennifer Aniston had said that it had got her through her divorce from Brad Pitt.

So why did it grip her with such a frantic, panicky boredom that the only way she could attempt it was by doing a sudoku at the same time?

Mr Lee's form. Why couldn't she have posted it? It was a small, small job. It would have taken her all of twenty seconds. But she hadn't done it and now she was suffering for her laziness, lying awake in the early hours, worried and afraid.

The only comfort available was to promise herself – again – that she would do it the moment she got into work. She wouldn't even take her jacket off. Until then, she was powerless: I can do nothing I can do nothing I can do nothing. She let her mind drift, seeking something soothing to latch on to. Words spoke in her head: In some place in the world, right now, someone is being tortured. Make it stop. Make it stop. Make it stop. Make it stop. Make it stop. Make it stop. Make it stop.

Whoever they are, wherever they are, give them some relief.

This was her own fault. There had been an item on last night's news about two teenage girls who'd been kidnapped by four men. The men had inflicted a variety of unspeakable acts on them in revenge for a soured drug deal involving, not the girls, but their fathers.

She'd known that she shouldn't stay in the room. She'd known that, at some stage, she'd pay the price. But a hideous fascination kept her immobile before the screen, desperate not to hear and yet appallingly curious about the range of terrible things human beings do to each other.

She thought about it happening to the girls. To Grace. She felt like vomiting.

Torturers were so much more imaginative than she could have known and she had to wonder what kind of people they were. Were they forced to do it? Some had to, in order to avoid it being done to them. But others must enjoy it.

And why did no one else seem to obsess as she did? When, as a teenager, she'd taken her horrors to Grace, Grace had responded with cheery practicality: if it ever happens to you, she'd advised, just tell them everything they want to know.

That was before Marnie had discovered that some people torture just for fun.

She stretched her arm to the floor and picked up her book. She was reading *The Bell Jar*. Again. No wonder she felt depressed, Nick said. But she'd tried reading cheery stuff – novels which promised she would 'laugh out loud' – and had had to stop because it was all so silly. At least with Sylvia Plath she had the comfort of knowing that someone else had been through it. Mind you, look at how she'd ended up.

She held the book close to her face, trying to decipher the words in the grey, early morning light. Nick shifted in the bed: she'd woken him by turning the pages.

'What time is it?' he mumbled.

'Twenty past five.'

'Oh for God's sake.'

He bunched into an angry ball under the duvet, and flung

himself against the mattress, trying to get back to sleep. There was a tap at the door. Light fairy feet. Verity.

Poor Verity. Or 'Variety' as the other kids called her. Or 'Freak'. She never slept through the night.

'Can I come in, Mum?'

Marnie nodded, put her finger to her lips – don't wake Daddy – and threw back the duvet in invitation. Verity's small warm body squirmed into the bed and she gathered her tight.

'Mum?' Verity whispered.

'Sssh, don't wake Daddy.'

'Daddy's awake.' His voice was thick and petulant.

'Mum, what will happen if you die?'

'I won't die.'

'What if you get ill and have to go to hospital?'

'Whisper it, sweetheart. I won't get ill.'

'What will happen if Daddy loses his job?'

'Daddy won't lose his job.'

But he mightn't get this year's bonus. Again.

She stroked Verity's hair and tried to soothe her back to sleep. Where was she getting all this anxiety from? She couldn't conjure it up just from thin air.

She was Verity's mother, it had to be her fault.

'Mum, will you do my hair in a plait? Not a flat one, a high one.'

'Mum! I can't find my pink notebook.'

Marnie, frantically threading laces into Verity's mud-covered trainers, cast a look around the kitchen. 'There it is.'

'Not that pink one, my pink sparkly one!'

'Look in your schoolbag.'

'It's not in my schoolbag.'

'Look again.'

'Oh will you look, Mum?'

'Mu-um,' Daisy said in frustration. '*Please* can you do my hair? I never ask for anything.'

'Okay, okay. Let me finish this, then I have to pack your lunchboxes, then I'll do your hair. Verity! Where are your glasses?'

'Lost.'

'Find them.'

'No. I hate them.'

Marnie's heart twisted. 'I know, sweetheart. But you won't have to wear them for ever. Here, catch.' She threw Verity her trainers. 'Put them in your sports bag. Okay, Daisy, let's do your hair.'

'But you said you'd find my notebook!' Verity said, aggrieved.

'And you have to do our lunchboxes first,' Daisy said. 'You don't want to forget them again.'

Jesus Christ. She'd forgotten them once. One day out of how many? But there was no such thing as absolution when you were a mother. Every transgression repeated on you, like onions.

'I won't forget, now give me the hairbrush.' With fumbling fingers, she plaited Daisy's hair incorrectly – doing a flat plait instead of a high one. 'But what the hell's a high one?'

'Don't say hell.'

Marnie was getting panicky now. Time was running away. She couldn't be late for work again, she was pushing Guy too far. She didn't know where his breaking point was, but she intuitively knew she was nearing it.

'In a ponytail first, then a plait!'

'Okay, quick.' She undid Daisy's hair and did it again, too

quickly, so that it stuck up and out at a peculiar angle, like it was made of wire.

'There you go, you're beautiful.'

'I look ridiculous.'

'You're too young to say ridiculous.'

'I'm a child, I absorb what I hear like a sponge. How can I know what I'm too young to say?'

'Either way, you're beautiful. Come on, let's go.'

'Lunchboxes!'

While Marnie flung grapes and sugar-free cereal bars into Angelina Ballerina lunchboxes, Daisy oversaw the operation with the gravity of a United Nations weapons inspector.

The tin of mini-bags of organic vegetable chips was empty – how had that happened?

'Dad ate them,' Daisy said. 'I told him they were for our lunch but he said you'd find something else.'

Bloody Nick. So what was she going to give them instead?

What was in the fridge? Beetroot? For a wild moment, she wondered if she could get away with giving them each a beetroot? There was a small chance Verity might accidentally eat it, duped by its pretty colour, but Daisy had too keen an appreciation of what was and wasn't acceptable lunchbox fare among their peers.

In the cupboard was a box of Green and Black's chocolate wafers, brought along by someone who'd come for dinner. That would do.

'Biscuits?' Daisy asked sharply. If they were being permitted refined sugar, it meant that the barbarians were at the gates. 'We're not allowed to have biscuits. As well you know,' she added with a world-weary sigh.

The biscuits were returned to the cupboard.

'More grapes,' Daisy suggested.

More grapes it was. There was no other choice. Marnie clicked the boxes closed and handed them over. But she couldn't let Daisy out as she was – her plait was sticking up so much it looked as though it could pick up signals from outer space. 'Wait, Daisy, let me do something with your hair.'

While she fiddled about with the root of the plait, she said, 'Have a good day at school and take care of Verity.'

Daisy was aware of the natural advantages she had over Verity. She was pretty, popular, clever and good at sports, and she knew that with power came responsibility.

But instead of her usual solemn promise that she would look out for her sister, Daisy said quietly, 'Mum, I won't always be there for Verity. She's got to learn to do it for herself.'

Marnie was speechless. She looked at Daisy and thought, You are six years of age. Whatever happened to the innocence of childhood? The conviction that the world was safe? But she understood how it was for Daisy. Trying to prevent Verity's pain by feeling it for her was too much of a responsibility.

It was her and Grace all over again.

Daisy sighed again, a big, grown-up sigh. 'I'll do what I can, Mum, but I can't always be there.'

'It's okay, sweetheart, it's okay. Don't worry.'

She pulled Daisy close to her. Now she was carrying not just Verity's perpetual anxiety, but Daisy's guilt and resentment.

How can I protect them from the pain of being alive?

'Mum, you're hurting me.'

'Am I? Sorry. Sorry, sorry, sorry.'

She looked into Daisy's clear brown eyes and thought, I love you so much I crumple with agony. I love you so much I wish I'd never had you. Either of you. You'd be better off dead.

It took a moment for her to ask herself, not nearly surprised enough: Am I thinking of killing my children?

She dropped them at the school gates. Most parents walked right into the classroom and delivered the children, like batons in a relay race, relinquishing control of their charges only when they were sure the teachers had a firm grip of them. But she hadn't time today. In her rear-view mirror she watched the two girls trooping across the yard, in their school uniforms, knee socks and straw hats, weighed down and strewn with lunchboxes, sports kits, backpacks and instruments – a violin for Daisy, the more humble recorder for Verity. Still feeling guilty, she pulled out into the traffic.

Wen-Yi was watching her. Because of how the light glinted on his glasses, she couldn't always see his eyes, but she felt him catalogue her every move. It was impossible to remove the form from her handbag and slip it into an envelope: he'd see. At lunchtime she went out, planning to buy an envelope and stamps and post it in an anonymous letter box. But there was a long queue in Rymans. Only one till was operational. A man was buying a huge quantity of items, it looked like he was setting up an office from scratch, and a long time was spent packing his box files and in-trays and lever-arches. First single bags, then double bags. When he eventually tried to pay, it was discovered that the phone line was down. No credit card payments were possible, so he went to the cash-point. When he returned a till roll had to be changed. Other customers were dumping their piles of goods on the counter and walking out, muttering angrily about fuckwits. Marnie was tearful with frustration and rage, but she refused to buckle.

Finally the new-office-man left and everyone moved up a place but the next customer had an armload of index cards, none of which had bar codes. The boy on the till had to leave his post and accompany the customer onto the shop floor to where the cards had been displayed, because there was no record of them on the system. The pair were gone for an endless amount of time.

I am being tested I am being tested I am being tested.

She wouldn't look at her watch. She couldn't. Watching time being eaten up drove her insane. Then the man ahead of her said, 'For fuck's sake, it's five past two!' And she knew she had to get back because, despite abandoning the girls at the school gates, she'd been late again this morning.

Briefly she considered flinging a tenner on the counter and leaving with the envelopes. But she still hadn't got stamps – they were kept in the till – and knowing her luck, she would get arrested for shoplifting; it was too much of a risk. In despair, she surrendered her items and the day ended as it began, with Mr Lee's form still in her handbag.

'Why are you here?'

'. . . I want to be happy.' Such a shameful admission.

'And you're not?'

'No.'

'Why not?'

'I don't know. I have everything . . . a husband, two perfect children, a house . . .'

'That's okay. No judgements.'

Cognitive Coaching. She'd read about it in a Sunday Supplement. In ten short sessions, it had changed the journalist's life, dispersing her lifelong feeling of futility and filling her with a warm hum of satisfaction. Immediately Marnie had phoned the number at the bottom of the page, but couldn't get an appointment with the therapist in the piece – thanks to the positive publicity she was fully booked for the next year. However, a website search had unearthed Amanda Cook in Wimbledon who claimed to offer 'Cognitive Counselling'.

'Is that the same as Cognitive Coaching?' Marnie had asked, over the phone.

'What's Cognitive Coaching?'

'Oh.' Marnie had assumed that someone in the therapy game would be well up in all the different disciplines. 'Well, there was a thing in the paper . . .'

'A word of warning,' Amanda had said sternly. 'There are many fly-by-night types in this business. They give themselves a fancy title and –'

To her alarm, Marnie's hope had begun to ebb away; she couldn't allow that, she needed to believe that someone could help her. This woman's title included the buzzword 'cognitive'; that was good enough.

'Okay, that's fine, that's fine! Can I make an appointment?'

'How about tomorrow?' Amanda had said. 'I'm free all day. Or Wednesday?'

Again, Marnie's hope had dipped: she would have been reassured to know that this counsellor, therapist, whatever she was exactly, was more in demand.

For a moment she'd wondered if she should simply go to a normal non-cognitive therapist . . . But she'd tried them, several of them over the years, and they hadn't worked. And perhaps this 'cognitive' thing was just taking off, perhaps she'd be at the crest of a wave and in three months' time you wouldn't be able to get a slot with Amanda for love nor money. So she'd agreed upon an appointment time of 6.15 on Thursday evening.

'I'm just off the High Street,' Amanda Cook had said. 'There's a parade of shops, I'm over the chemist –'

'And you think you'll be able to help me?'

'Yes, but don't park outside. It's permits only. Try Ridley Road – often there are spaces there; well, at six-fifteen there should be, I wouldn't give much for your chances any time after seven.'

'Okay. And, can I ask . . .' She'd wanted to establish Amanda Cook's exact qualifications, the piece in the paper had advised that – but she lost her nerve. She hadn't wanted to cause offence. 'No, nothing, it's fine. So . . . um . . . yes, see you then.'

As Marnie climbed the narrow dusty stairs to the first-floor office, she wondered about this woman who was going to save her. Like a hairdresser or a yoga teacher, a therapist should be their own best advertisement. If they can't work their magic on themselves, how is anyone else meant to believe in them?

Happily, first impressions weren't discouraging. Probably in her late thirties – although it was hard to tell with the rounder face – Amanda was a cheery woman in a skirt-and-flowing-top combo. She had brown hair, which was neither straight nor curly. Instantly Marnie felt thin and nervy-neurotic in her professional suit and tidy ponytail.

'Come in, my dear.' A trace of West Country could be heard in Amanda's voice. Pleasant and warm, and Marnie tried to forget that that accent always put her in mind of halfwits.

'Where did you park?' Amanda asked.

'Ridley Road.'

'Not outside? Because it's permits only. If you park outside, they'll buzz up and interrupt the session.'

'Yes. You told me on the phone.'

'Please. Sit down.' She pointed Marnie to an orange upholstered armchair. On the opposite chair was a half-eaten bag of crisps (prawn cocktail). Amanda swept them to one side and tumbled into the chair.

Marnie's positive first impressions were dimming fast and she was in the grip of shameful fat-ist anxiety. It was entirely wrong to judge anyone on their appearance. But she needed Amanda Cook to be a miracle worker and if Amanda Cook really was a miracle worker, would she be so . . . bulky?

Don't think this way. Heart surgeons don't operate on themselves. Racehorse trainers don't jump over Beecher's Brook.

Indeed, Marnie reassured herself, perhaps it was because Amanda Cook was so very delighted with herself that she was blithely unaware of being – it was difficult to be precise because of the floatiness of the garments – what, maybe three stone overweight?

'I use a combination of cognitive behavioural therapy and life-coaching to help you to achieve your ideal life,' Amanda said. 'Unlike traditional psychotherapy, where the subject can spend years reliving past hurts, Cognitive Counselling is all about the now. Using a combination of visualization and practical changes, I get very quick results.'

Such confidence! Even with that hair. 'Always?' Marnie asked. 'Very quick results always?'

'Yes.'

'I fail at everything.'

'That's just a perception, my dear.'

Marnie didn't mean to be picky, but it wasn't. It was hard fact, proved over and over. 'You've helped people like me?'

'What are people like you?'

'. . . Hopeless . . . without hope . . . that anything can change or get better.'

'Without breaking client confidentiality, I recently diverted a man from suicide.'

Well, that was impressive.

'You simply need to change your thinking, my dear. Let me take a few details. You live . . . ?'

'Wandsworth Common.'

'Nice. In one of those big houses?'

'Ye –'

'What does your husband do?'

'He's a commodities trader, but –'

'Just getting a feel for you.' Amanda made a mark in her notebook. 'And you've two children. Girls?'

'Girls, six and five.'

'Now, Marnie, I'd like you to close your eyes, let the world disappear, then please describe for me your ideal life.'

This was startling. 'My ideal life?'

Amanda smiled. 'Until you know what it is, how can you make it happen?'

That was a good point. 'But . . . I don't know what my ideal life is.' And if she was to be totally honest, she suspected that the problem wasn't her life; the problem was herself.

'You need to get in touch with your dreams,' Amanda clucked. 'Be ambitious for yourself!'

'Yes, but . . .'

'Remember, the only limit to our happiness is our imagination.'

Again, Marnie didn't want to be pedantic but that statement didn't actually withstand analysis. This was all so unexpected. She'd anticipated a practical focus on the hard facts of her life as it stood, not this airy-fairy, wishful stuff.

'Unlock your dreams,' Amanda urged. 'Surrender to the energy and the right words will come.'

But would they? She doubted it, oh how she doubted it, but still she longed to be proved wrong.

'Come on, Marnie, don't be frightened. You're in a safe place and this is your time.'

For most of her waking hours Marnie ached with yearning but, strangely, now that she had to articulate it, she couldn't formulate a single desire. Panic building, she hunted through her thoughts, seeking anything at all. She couldn't fail at this, surely it wasn't humanly possible.

'Start small, if you must,' Amanda said. 'Just something to get the ball rolling.'

'Okay.' The ball rolling. She took a deep, deep breath. 'This is a bit rubbish but I'd like to be able to . . . fix things. Like make a temporary fanbelt with my tights.'

'Car maintenance?'

'Not exactly.' She quailed before Amanda's confusion. 'I was thinking sort of sexy, good in a crisis . . . but wait, wait! I've got something.' An idea had appeared in her head and she latched on to it with breathless gratitude. 'I'd quite like to be one of those fabulous women . . .'

'Fabulous women?'

'. . . One of those white Africans, from *White Mischief*, even though I haven't seen it. Who can fly a plane and ride and track animals.'

Amanda made another mark in the notebook. 'Describe for me, please, your day-to-day life as one of these "fabulous women".'

'Aaah . . .' For God's sake, how could she do that? She hadn't even seen the bloody film. 'I . . . ah . . . I . . . never have to cook, wash or iron.'

Amanda looked disdainful. 'That's your ideal life. Come on, Marnie, unleash the dream! You have servants, yes?'

'I suppose.'

'Describe an encounter with one of them. Visualize it.'

'Aaaah . . .' This was ridiculous. 'I march into the house. I'm wearing jodhpurs tucked into black leather riding boots . . . I fling myself onto a divan covered with a zebra-skin and say, "Bring me a huge gin and tonic, Mwaba."' After a moment's thought, she added, '"Chop chop, Mwaba."'

'Excellent. Go on.'

'Oh. Well, he gets it for me and . . . and . . . I don't thank him. I never thank anyone for anything. When I arrive at places, I fling the key of my LandRover at the first person I see and say, "Park it, yah."'

This depressed Marnie. Thanking people was the least that one human being could do for another and she had refused to thank poor mythical Mwaba just to get Amanda's approval.

'What do you look like?' Amanda asked.

'God, I don't know.' This was so difficult. 'Tall, I suppose. Thin. But I don't care about my appearance.' She liked the sound of that. 'I never condition my hair or wear face-cream, and I make those sleeveless, khaki, long jacket things look good.'

'But you're beautiful?'

'Oh why not?'

'Are you married? In this ideal life of yours?'

A blank. 'Yes. No. Yes. When I was twenty-one my first husband shot himself, then I divorced the second when I was twenty-seven.' Suddenly ideas were firing in her head. Maybe she was finally starting to do this thing right. 'I'm thirty-five now in my ideal life – I mean, I am in my real life too, but I'm still talking about my ideal life – and in the process of divorcing my third husband. I'm having a torrid affair with a much younger man.' A pause. 'And a much older man.' Why the hell not? 'Not that much older, just a few years. Five. Seven. Yes, seven.'

Another mark in Amanda's notebook. 'Tell me more.'

'The weather is always sweltering hot. I get the odd bout of malaria, but it's just an excuse to drink more gin, because of the quinine in tonic. I say, "Can't stomach the damn tonic undiluted. Would only sick it up." My friends are called Bitsy and Monty and Fenella, and it's the same people everywhere I go. Now and again I fly my own plane to Jo'burg but I'm soon itching to get back to the bush.' She was on a roll now, finally in the zone. 'In the bush, we drink our heads off and dinner isn't ready until eleven at night, at which point everyone is too drunk to eat. We're not interested in food, but we're terrified of running out of gin. We watch the skies, wondering when the supply plane will be in with more gin.'

Amanda had stopped making notes. She simply sat and listened.

'My husband slurs things like, "My beautiful wife." He's trying to be ironic, but he's so obviously in love with me that he simply seems pathetic. I say, "Shut up, Johnny, you're drunk." He used to be handsome but now he's puffy and jowly from the drink. "Cold as ice," he slurs. "Cold as fucking ice." No one, except my younger man, can keep up with my drinking.' Marnie took another breath to continue, she was enjoying herself now – and just as quickly she wasn't.

Amanda was looking at her with a strange expression, part concern, part something else. Contempt perhaps?

'Well!' Amanda sat up straight and said, with a pretence at cheer, 'That's a tall order, Marnie. Let's work with what we have. Have you ever lived on the continent of Africa?'

'. . . No.'

'Can you fly a plane?'

'. . . No.'

'Or shoot a gun?'

'. . . No.' Marnie was whispering now. 'But I do own a sleeveless khaki jacket.' From her short-lived riding lessons. 'And I've got a four-wheel drive.'

'A four-wheel drive? I bet you do.' Amanda stared down at her notebook and Marnie realized the look was going on for too long.

Eventually Amanda raised her head and said, 'I can't help you.'

Marnie froze. Shock muted her.

She thinks I'm just a spoilt, bored housewife.

I'm not a housewife. I have a job. But the words remained unsaid.

'I could take your money, but that wouldn't be ethical. I won't charge you for today's session.'

Marnie's face was hot.

I don't want to live in Africa. I don't want to be rude to people. I only said it to please you.

Her head dipped, Marnie was gathering her bag and putting on her jacket, stunned by whatever had taken place. Could it be that Amanda Cook had judged her by her house in Wandsworth and her – false – soul-destroying aspirations? Could it be that Amanda Cook had simply decided that she didn't like her?

Nothing, nothing, I will feel nothing.

Marnie nodded goodbye to Amanda who was still sitting imperiously in her chair, then she was leaving the room and stopping herself from running down the stairs in case her shaking legs sent her tumbling to the bottom.

As she re-entered the outside world, the cold night air

slapping her flaming cheeks, she realized that she hadn't noticed any framed diplomas on the walls. Was it possible that Amanda Cook didn't have any professional qualifications? But instead of making her feel better – at least it hadn't been a real therapist who had judged her and found her so lacking – it made her feel worse. She had surrendered herself and her mental health to a woman who was perhaps one of the very fly-by-night operators that she had warned Marnie against.

What kind of idiot was she? How could she think so little of herself that she couldn't even check that someone had the right credentials?

Somewhere inside her was a world of shame, but walking fast kept it contained. Listening to the click-click-click of her heels on the pavement was comforting. It meant her legs were moving, even though her knees were watery.

Nick was waiting in the hall. He was very obviously agitated.

She wasn't late. She'd done nothing wrong. It had to be the . . .

'. . . Bonus?' she mouthed.

The look on his face told her everything. It was finally official: no bonus again this year.

Fuuuuuck.

The kids had picked up on the atmosphere of catastrophe and had slunk off to the playroom.

'Bad year in the markets,' he apologized.

'No one's blaming you.'

He was devastated; earning money was how he validated himself.

'We'll sort something out,' she said.

*

Later, when she'd put the girls to bed, she found Nick in his office, surrounded by lever-arch files of bank statements and credit card bills.

'Where the fuck does it all go?' he asked helplessly. 'Everything costs so much.'

Their mortgage, most of all. They'd bought the five-bedroomed house three years ago, just before Nick stopped having the Midas touch. Nick had insisted on buying such a big house. He'd said it was what she deserved. She had liked where they'd been living, but because he'd been so insistent, she went along with it. And she'd believed him when he assured her that they could afford it. Then interest rates had crept up a couple of points, which wouldn't have impacted too much on a normal-sized mortgage, but on a massive one like theirs . . .

'Let's write down everything we spend money on and see what can go,' she suggested. 'School fees,' she started with. 'We could move the girls to a cheaper school.'

'No.' He groaned, like he was actually in pain. He was so proud that his children were in a private school. 'They need stability and Verity wouldn't survive in a state school.' Their current school had small classes with individual attention. 'She'd be bullied to death. What about Melodie? Could we manage without her?'

Melodie was their nanny, a capable Kiwi who had about twenty other jobs on the go.

'She's working the bare minimum as it is.' Marnie got the girls to school and Melodie worked from 2.30 to 6.15. 'If she goes, I can't work.'

'Could you go part-time? Just work mornings?'

'No.' She had already asked Guy about it. 'It's a full-time position.'

Nick scribbled some calculations to see if Marnie's salary was more than Melodie's wages and decided that it was, barely.

'Mrs Stevenson?' he asked. Their cleaning woman.

'I'm a full-time working mother. She's absolutely fantastic. And she costs fifty quid a week.'

'All right, okay,' he grumbled. He tapped his pen nib against his notebook. 'But something has to give somewhere.' He swept a look over her. 'You spend a fortune on your hair.'

Mutely, she stared at him. She needed her hair even more than she needed Mrs Stevenson. The expensive cut she was prepared to forgo, but not the colour. A picture of herself with two inches of grey roots flashed in her head. She could never leave the house again. It was proving a big enough challenge at the moment, even with perfect highlights.

'And all those . . . healing things you do. Meditation and acupuncture and . . . what's that thing you were at tonight? Cognitive something?'

'Counselling. But I won't be going back. And I don't do any of the others any longer.' Because none of them worked.

'How about your gym membership?' she suggested. 'Perhaps you could jog around the common instead?'

Aggrieved, he said, 'I *need* to go to the gym. I'm up to my eyeballs in stress. Anyway I've paid for the rest of the year.'

'Okay.' She braced herself to address a truly painful subject. 'Your car . . .'

'My . . . ? Are you barking? If I show up for work in a Ford Fiesta, it's the same as having "Loser" stamped on my forehead. I need the Jag to keep the respect.'

'I'm not suggesting a Ford Fiesta. But . . .'

'What about yours? A Porsche? Why don't *you* get a Ford Fiesta?'

'Fine. I don't care.' The Porsche SUV was too big, guzzled an appalling quantity of petrol and was far too much of a yummy-mummy cliché.

But that seemed to make Nick angrier. She *should* care.

'Holidays,' she said. 'We spend lots on them.'

'But we need a holiday. It's the one thing we really need.'

'We don't *need* any of it.'

He'd got used to dropping a grand on a suit; buying three of them in one go. She'd got used to it too. Handing over seven hundred pounds for a handbag – merely something to carry her stuff in – when she could just as easily pick up a bag in Next for thirty quid.

But Nick had celebrated her extravagance: if his wife could afford to spend a hundred and fifty pounds on a haircut, it signified that he was a success.

It was humiliating for him to ask for constraints on their lifestyle.

'At least we have each other,' he said. 'We'll get through this.'

It was such a dishonest statement that she couldn't reply. He opened his mouth to press his point home, then abandoned the plan.

Sitting among the files which detailed their extravagant attempts to spend their way to happiness, he looked entirely beaten; the intensity of her sorrow left her breathless.

'I'm sorry, Nick,' she whispered. 'I'm so, so sorry.'

'I want to be a trophy wife.'

It was Marnie's sixteenth birthday – Grace's also, of course – and the conversation over the celebratory dinner had meandered into considering what their futures held.

Grace had declared her ambition to be a journalist; Leechy,

who was always present on family occasions, had said she wanted to work in a 'caring profession'.

'As a nurse, maybe,' she'd said.

'A doctor,' Ma had said quickly. 'Forget about being a nurse in this country. You get paid a pittance and have to work all the hours.'

Then they'd all looked at her. Marnie, what do you want to be when you grow up?

She'd had no idea. She already felt grown-up – in some ways utterly jaded – and had no particular enthusiasm for anything. The one thing she was sure of was that she'd like to have children, but round here that wouldn't count as a career.

'Come on, Marnie, what do you want to be when you grow up?'

'Happy.'

'But what job do you want?' Bid had asked.

Embarrassed at once again being out of step with everyone else, she'd considered saying that she'd like to be an air hostess, then realized that aspiring to be a trophy wife would upset them even more. Not that she had any chance of being a trophy wife; she wasn't tall enough. It was like being a policewoman or a catwalk model, there was a minimum height requirement.

'A wife!' Ma was scandalized. 'Marnie Gildee, I brought you up to think differently.'

'Not just any wife,' Marnie said flippantly. 'A full-on trophy job.'

She'd said it to shock because she'd been so uncomfortable with Grace and Leechy's certainty. 'You got married,' she accused Ma. 'You're a wife.'

'But it wasn't my sole ambition.' Ma had worked in the trade union movement all her life. It was where she'd met her husband.

'You're not even blonde,' Bid turned on Marnie with sudden venom. 'Trophy wives are always blonde.'

'I can be blonde if I really need to be.'

Mind you, she wasn't entirely sure that was true. She'd tried bleaching a handful of her hair and it had gone green. But she wasn't backing down.

'What's the point in me having career plans?' Marnie asked. 'I'm hopeless at everything.'

'You? You're so gifted.' Ma's voice rose. 'You could do anything you wanted. You're far brighter than Grace and Leechy – sorry, girls, just calling a spade a spade. It's a crime to squander such gifts.'

'Me?' Now Marnie was almost angry. 'Who are you confusing me with?'

She and Ma glared at each other, then Ma looked away; she didn't believe in mothers and teenage daughters being at loggerheads, she said it was a myth put about by soap operas.

'Confidence,' Ma said. 'That's all you lack, confidence.'

'I'm hopeless at everything,' Marnie repeated firmly.

And she proved herself right.

By the time Grace was covering mutilated bodies for the *Times*, Marnie had done a degree in economics, graduated with a lacklustre 2:2 and fulfilled her own prophecies by being unable to get a job: she was granted several interviews on the basis of her resumé but couldn't convince anyone to employ her.

It was then that she discovered she hadn't been lying when she'd said she wanted to be a wife.

Without a husband she felt small and raw. A boyfriend wouldn't do, not even a long-term one. She wanted a ring on her finger and a different surname, because, on her own, she wasn't enough.

Her shame was almost as corrosive as her longing – she was

Olwen Gildee's daughter; she'd been hardwired with a certain amount of independent-woman thinking and it sat uneasily with her wish to surrender.

But getting married wasn't as easy as she'd anticipated.

There were two kinds of men: those who fell so far short of Paddy's glittering charisma that she couldn't bear to let them touch her, and the Good Ones. And with them, it was like the job situation all over again. They were initially enthusiastic, but once they reached a certain point in the interview process, something changed: they saw her for who she really was and they started to back away.

It was her fault. She'd get drunk and tell them the contents of her head: her horror of the world and of the human condition. She woke up one morning, hung-over and shaky, and remembered the night before, saying to Duncan, a happy-go-lucky lawyer, 'Don't you ever wonder why we were made with a finite capacity for pleasure but an infinite capacity for pain? Our ceiling for pleasure is low but the floor for pain is bottomless.'

He'd tried putting forward different arguments – after all he was a lawyer – but her misery proved too much for him. Eventually he'd said, close to panic, 'You need help. I hope you sort yourself out.' He'd paid for the dinner, he'd seen her home, but she knew he'd never get in touch again.

By her mid-twenties, she was living in London and a pattern had established itself: she scared away all the Good Ones. And she scared herself, by being unable to stop.

The thing about London was that there was a constant supply of new men. She didn't have trouble with the initial attraction – she had a type of melancholic beauty that men responded to; she didn't see it herself but knew it existed – but she always managed to self-destruct.

In sympathy and exasperation, Grace called her the suicide bomber.

By the age of twenty-seven, Marnie had become accustomed to waking too early in the morning, in the horrors. Slipping further and further into isolation, she had become the sum of her rejections. She was starting to give up.

Then she met Nick. Handsome (if a bit short) in a rough-diamond sort of way, he had a swaggery bantam-cock confidence which made her smile. His job required nerves of steel; he loved children; he had an optimism that was contagious. He was definitely a Good One. From the moment he saw her, he wanted her. She recognized the look, she'd seen it enough times on enough faces, but it didn't make her hopeful. She knew what always happened next. Despite promising herself that she wouldn't, she got drunk and got weird. But the strange thing was that Nick wasn't scared off.

When she told him the terrible things in her head he laughed but with tenderness. 'Tell me why you would think like that, Sweets.'

He didn't entirely get her, but he was willing. His intentions were clear: her happiness was his project. He had never failed at anything and he didn't intend to start now.

For her part, she found him extraordinary. He'd had little education but could survey any situation – human, political – then fillet it with efficient speed and emerge with the salient facts. An energy surrounded him, a type of forward-moving buoyancy and he was always slightly ahead of the zeitgeist in his choice of wine, holiday destinations, haircuts . . .

More reassuring than his coolness was his sentimentality: Nick cried at anything to do with children and animals, and although she teased him for being an over-emotional cockney, she was relieved. Coldness would have been a deal-breaker.

'Why do you love me?' she asked him. 'It's not because I'm middle class, is it? Please don't tell me you think you're trading up?'

'Fuck off!' he declared. 'Who cares about any of that? I love you because you're a shortarse.' Nick was five foot eight. 'We're the perfect height for each other.'

'He calls us Short and Shorter,' she told Grace, in one of her monitoring phone calls.

'Nicknames,' Grace said. 'Things are going well.'

'Yes,' Marnie said, but doubtfully.

'Never mind why he loves you,' Grace advised. 'Why do you love him?'

'I don't know if I do. I fancy him, like I really . . . the sex, you know, it's gorgeous, but I don't know if I love him.'

That changed late one night when they were walking back from a restaurant to where Nick had parked his car. There was the sound of tinkling glass and the whoop of a car alarm, then Nick exclaimed, 'That's my motor.' (He'd once claimed that he could always recognize his own car alarm, it was like a mother hearing her baby cry.) He did a speedy once-over of the street, to establish it was safe. 'Got your phone, Marnie? Wait here.'

Then he began to run towards the three blokes who were breaking into his car. They saw him coming and scarpered but, to Marnie's amazement, Nick ran after them. The three men split from each other and went in different directions but Nick kept running behind one of them – the biggest. Nick had a tight, wiry body and he was fast. They both disappeared into an alleyway which led to a local housing estate and some minutes later Nick returned, panting and disappointed.

'Lost him.'

'Nick, that could have been dangerous . . . you could have been . . .'

'I know,' he gasped. 'Sorry, Sweets. Shouldn't have left you here alone.'

It was the turning point for her: his courage in the pursuit of what was right was what made her fall in love with him.

She believed in him.

She wanted to be his.

It was time, she decided, to take him to Dublin to run him by her family – and it was a success.

Even though they had opposing economic ideologies, he charmed Ma and Dad. Grumpy Bid (who couldn't give a damn about socialism) and Big Jim Larkin (the dog before Bingo) adored him. 'How could you not like him?' Grace said. Even Damien let himself be coaxed into admitting Nick was 'a decent bloke'.

Nick talked incessantly, bought drinks for everyone and declared himself delighted with Ireland.

'It's over,' Grace said to Marnie. 'Your time in the wilderness.'

And so it appeared. A man had seen beyond her misleadingly pretty little exterior to the murkiness within and hadn't run for the hills – but she kept having to check.

'Why do you love me?' she asked Nick again and again.

'You're the salt of the earth.'

'I am?'

'Yeah! Kindest heart of any person I know. See the way you're always crying about people you've never even met.'

'That's not kindness, that's . . . neurosis.'

'Kindness,' he insisted. 'Brainy too. Plus, you've a great pair of pins, you cook a proper hot curry and when you're not

286

boo-hooing about the state of the world, you can be a bit of a laugh. That's why I love you.'

'I won't ask again,' she apologized.

'Ask as many times as you like, Sweets, answer'll be the same. Happy now?'

'Yes.' No. Almost.

Marnie tried to accept that she'd finally got what she wanted. But she couldn't shake the fear that there was a catch.

There was always a catch.

Friday. Wen-Yi was on the prowl. 'Marnie,' he hissed, as soon as he saw her. 'Mr Lee? He should have got that form yesterday. All he had to do was sign it and send it back.'

'The post hasn't come yet. As soon as it does, I'll alert you.'

'Mr Lee is a powerful man,' Wen-Yi said. 'He would be unhappy to lose this sale.'

She hated when he said things like that. It made her feel ill with fear.

'Post has just arrived,' Guy said. 'Let's find out.'

Striving to fake an expression of keen expectation that every envelope might contain Mr Lee's returned form, she opened the post. About halfway through the task, she began to believe that it might actually appear.

So profound was her conviction that, when everything was opened, she was genuinely perplexed.

'That's weird,' she said. 'Not in today's post.'

'What? Why not?' Wen-Yi slammed his stapler against his desk. 'Where *is* it?'

She couldn't stop herself glancing at her handbag. She half expected it to start pulsing and glowing.

'It must be lost in the post,' she said.

She'd tried that before but Guy had told her that that

happens only once every ten million letters. It was as convincing an excuse as saying that the dog had eaten your homework.

Agitated and frustrated, Wen-Yi ordered, 'Ring him. Find out what's happening.'

'Okay.'

But what would be the point? Instead she rang her own phone number and left an efficient-sounding message asking Mr Lee to call her asap.

Then she scribbled his address on a Post-it and announced to the office, 'Just popping out.' She tried to sound cheerful. 'I need to go to the chemist.'

Guy watched her go, saying nothing, but taking it all in.

She ran to Rymans and this time managed to purchase an envelope and a stamp. Mr Lee would get the form on Monday, would sign it immediately and it would be back to Wen-Yi by Tuesday. That should be enough time.

Oh what a tangled web.

'Lunch?' Rico asked. 'Help me celebrate?'

She froze, overtaken by terror and longing.

'It's a nice day,' he said. 'We could go to the park?'

Her body relaxed and she began to breathe again. Yes, she could go with him to the park.

'I'd have to skip my Pilates,' she said.

She'd paid in advance for ten classes but hadn't gone for the past three weeks. She'd hoped, as she did with everything she tried, that Pilates would fix her, but the only effect it had was that – oddly – it made her want to smoke. Unlike the rest of her family, she'd only ever been a tourist smoker, but something about Pilates and its almost-nothingness made her want to rip the cellophane off a packet of twenty and smoke one cigarette after another until the terrifying boredom left her.

'If you'd prefer to go . . .' He looked disappointed.

'No. Pilates, the watching-paint-dry approach to fitness. I'm glad to have an excuse. What are we celebrating this time?'

'Sale of an office block.'

'Only a small one,' Craig yelled.

But still. Rico, charm monster, the youngest and best-looking of Guy's brokers, was having an astonishing year, racking up commission after commission.

It was a bright sunny day, warm for the tenth of October. They sat on a bench, their feet kicking at the drifts of crunchy leaves, in russets and purples, which carpeted the ground.

'Autumn's my favourite season.' Rico gave her her sandwich.

'Mmmm.' She hated autumn.

Autumn rotted. It was death and putrefaction. Beneath those leaves, God-knows-what was lurking.

But she also hated summer. It was too screamy-happy and hysterical.

'What's your favourite season?' he asked.

'Spring,' she lied. She hated spring too. It got on her nerves. All that freshness and hope that ultimately amounted to nothing. If spring was a person, it would be Pollyanna.

Winter was the only season that made any sense to her. But she kept that to herself. If you go public that your favourite season is winter, you're obliged to wax lyrical about snowmen and egg-nog so that no one discovers how weird you are.

'Champagne, madam?' Rico produced a bottle and two flutes, as if from thin air.

She was horror-struck. She hadn't been prepared for this. It took moments to find her voice. 'No, Rico, no. Put it away. I've scads of work. I can't.'

'I thought you liked champagne.' Already he was undoing the foil.

'I do, of course, but don't, Rico, please. Stop. Don't open it.'

'You don't want to help me celebrate?' His voice was over-innocent.

'Of course, but not at lunchtime.'

'After work?'

'Not today.'

'Not today. Okay. I'll keep it for some other time.' Without obvious rancour he returned the bottle and glasses to their carrier bag.

'Are you angry with me?' she asked.

'I could never be angry with you.'

Too quick, too slick a reply, but she hadn't the equilibrium to start delving. Now she wished she'd let him open it.

'Any plans for the weekend?' Rico turned sideways to give her his full attention.

'The usual. Ferrying the girls to their different extramural activities. We'll probably go to a movie on Sunday.'

'What are you going to see?'

'Some Pixar thing. You know, I literally can't remember the last time I went to a film that wasn't PG. How about you?'

'Few drinks after work tonight. Dinner tomorrow night.'

'With a girl?'

He nodded and stared across the park, not meeting her eyes.

An arrow of something painful pricked her – jealousy? – not badly enough to lodge in her flesh but it felt good. A normal response gave her hope.

'Jealous?' he asked.

'A little bit.'

'Don't be. She's not as good as you. No one is.'

Don't make me feel even more guilty.

'But until you're available . . .'

He picked up her hand and played with her fingers. She let him for a moment, then wrenched them away.

In the multiplex, crowds of kids milling everywhere, the smell of rancid butter in the air, Marnie thought, I am the only person alive. Everyone else here is dead but they don't know it. I am alive and alone and trapped. For a moment she believed it and was overtaken by horror that was almost delicious.

Daisy and her friend Genevieve hurtled into her, using her legs as a crash barrier.

'We got sweets!'

Verity and Nick brought up the rear. Nick had bought them way too much at the pick'n'mix but she couldn't be bothered to berate him. Let their teeth rot. One day they were all going to be dead and it wouldn't matter then if every tooth in their head was a black stump.

Then Marnie saw the woman: tall, slender and smiley, her brown hair in a swingy ponytail. At first she didn't know where she knew her from. When she remembered, fear closed around her heart like a fist.

Don't see me don't see me don't see me.

The woman – what was her name again? Jules, that was it – had noticed her and was walking in her direction. She was about to say hello, even stop perhaps, when she saw Nick at Marnie's side. She dropped her eyes and passed by with a bland smile.

Nick, of course, noticed. He noticed everything. He was always watching.

'Do you know her?'

'No . . .'

It was building. She felt it. He felt it. They both knew it was going to happen.

'That's enough!' Wen-Yi said, when Monday's post didn't reveal Mr Lee's signed form. 'Send another one *right* now! Bike it. Get the bike to wait while he signs it, then courier it directly to the bank.' He'd been talking to the vendors over the weekend. 'If we don't close today we've lost the sale.'

Which meant that Wen-Yi would lose his 1 per cent – a lot of money – but far worse, from hints that Wen-Yi had been dropping, Mr Lee would be 'displeased'.

Heart pounding, she picked up the phone. It would all be okay. To find out where she should dispatch the bike, she rang Mr Lee's mobile; a woman answered.

In a Chinese accent she said, 'Mr Lee not here. He in China. Be back next month.'

God, no.

Panic rushed into her mouth, making it tacky and sour.

'When did he go?'

'Last week.'

'I'll . . . I'll call you back.'

She went to Wen-Yi's desk and said quietly, 'Mr Lee is in China. He won't be back until next month.'

Wen-Yi wasn't a shouter. He conveyed rage in a quiet, terrifying way. Speaking barely above a whisper, he bit out the words, 'Why didn't he say he was going to China when you spoke to him?'

'I don't know.'

'Did you speak to him?'

'Yes.' The word had left her mouth without her involvement.

He stared at her; he knew she was lying.

'You didn't speak to him. You didn't ring him.'

'I did.' But her voice was weak and unconvincing.

He looked at her in disgust.

'If we lose this property, Mr Lee . . .' He wiped his hand over his face and thought for a moment. 'Courier the form to China.'

'Will do,' she said, in a travesty of efficiency, earning herself another look of contempt.

Almost unable to breathe, she rang the mobile again and asked the woman, 'Can you give me Mr Lee's address in China?'

'In Shanghai. No address. Phone number.'

'If you could give me the number, then.'

With a shaking hand, she wrote it down, then reached for the phone book, searching for the code for China. What time was it in Shanghai?

'I don't care how late or early it is there.' Wen-Yi read her mind. 'Ring him.'

Her fingers were trembling so badly, it took five attempts before she managed to hit the numbers correctly. After many clicks and hissing, a phone began to ring on a faraway continent.

Answer it answer it answer it.

A woman speaking, a foreign language, her own voice shrill and wobbly, her tongue clicking against her dry palate, as she tried to explain.

'I need to send something to Mr Lee. You know Mr Lee?'

Please know him please know him please know him.

'Yes, I know Mr Lee.' The woman's words bounced like rubber bands. 'I give you address.'

Thank you God thank you God thank you God.

But the woman's accent was difficult to understand and something got lost in translation because UPS had no knowledge of the Shanghai suburb that Mr Lee was allegedly staying in.

'No such place,' the cheery Australian booker said. 'Can't do anything without an address.'

'Does it sound similar to another suburb?'

'Not even close.'

Ring her back ring her back ring her back.

I can't I can't I can't.

She fought a compulsion to get up from her desk and abandon the office and go out into the street and walk and walk and walk, until she'd left London far behind, until she was out on the hard shoulder of the motorway, cars and lorries roaring past, walking and walking and walking for ever. The heels of her shoes would crumble to nothing, her trouser suit would become filthy rags, her feet would resemble steak tartare and still she would keep walking.

'Ring her again,' Wen-Yi said, flashing hatred across the room.

'Okay,' she whispered.

This time the woman's spelling coincided with a suburb. She watched herself prepare the envelope and waited with herself by the office door until the UPS man came and she personally placed the envelope into his hands.

Her self-hatred was so enormous that she'd vacated herself. At some stage she'd have to return to face the music but, right now, she was nowhere.

*

'Marnie? Drink?'

Rico stood before her, so handsome, so kind, so persuasive. Her only ally. There were so many reasons to say no, she knew them all, but, to her surprise, a decisive part of her brain intervened and informed her that she was going to say yes.

After the terrible day, after the succession of terrible days, all fear and restraint fell away and the decision was made. She'd endured weeks of clenched-jawed forbearance, and to let go – so unexpectedly – was giddyingly pleasurable. Suddenly she was gloriously, joyously light and free.

She was Marnie Hunter and she was answerable to nobody.

'Let me ring my nanny,' she told Rico. 'If she can stay with the girls it's a go.'

Even if Melodie couldn't stay, she was still going for that drink. She didn't know how but she knew it would happen.

'Melodie, Marnie here. So sorry, but I'm going to be a little late this evening. A crisis at work.' She saw Rico smile.

Melodie sounded worried. 'Mrs H, I gotta be outa here by six-fifteen.'

'I'll pay you extra.'

Then she noticed Guy. From the other side of the office, he was listening and radiating disapproval.

Well, fuck him. She was going for a drink with a colleague. Everyone did it. It was normal. She felt like putting her hand over the mouthpiece and yelling at him: It's NORMAL.

'Mrs H, it's not the money,' Melodie said. 'I've gotta get to my other job.'

'I'll be home by six-fifteen. For God's sake.' She couldn't hide her impatience. 'It's just a quick drink.'

'A quick drink? You said it was a crisis at work. Does Mr H know?'

Fuck Mr H. She disconnected and smiled at Rico. 'Come on, let's go!'

*

.... *no* ....
.... *weight lifting* ....
.... *no* ....
.... *getting lighter* ....
.... *and rising steadily to pop the surface.*

Suddenly she was there. She hadn't been and now she was. She'd moved from non-existence to existence, from nothing to something. Like being born.

Where? Where had she been born this time?

An impression of ceiling, walls. Sealed. She was indoors. Probably in a house. Softness beneath her. She was on a bed. But she didn't know the room.

Curtains at a window. She tried to focus, but double vision turned them into two sets. They lifted, floated, crossed over and blurred. Try again in a while.

Teeth ached, jaw ached, eye sockets throbbed. Nausea lay in wait, primed to activate on movement.

Now she knew the bed. This was her own bed. Better than a stranger's bed? A hospital bed? Maybe not.

She was dressed, but in what? Her fingertips touched her stomach. She consulted the skin on her back. Cool, smooth cotton. A nightdress.

Checking now to see how bad things were. Face first. But her arm wasn't under her control, it moved too fast and landed on her cheek with a heavy, useless slap. Pain. Shock. Vomit in her throat.

Bones in face bad but lip not split. Carefully she ran her tongue around the inside of her mouth and when a tooth wobbled, she felt the first wave of black horror. Other things can be fixed, but if you lose a tooth, you never get it back. *Permanent damage.*

Checking further down. Ribs bad. Pelvis bad. Vertebrae okay. All frontal damage this time. She tested her legs, using the sole of her foot to feel the opposite leg. Along their length, on both legs, were painful points that would bloom into round, black blossoms.

Finally she rubbed her feet together. Even her feet were bruised. From my head to my toes . . . Another wave of black horror. More would come, the gaps getting shorter until eventually there were none and she was suspended in unending terror, wishing for annihilation.

The living will envy the dead. That was a line from the Bible, the only one that had ever really grabbed her.

How had it happened this time? She couldn't remember. Not yet. Maybe never. *Where are the kids?* Panic. *Where are the kids?*

'Nick.' Her feeble voice surprised her. It didn't fit with her urgency.

'Nick.' The last person she wanted, but there was no choice.

A shadow at the doorway. Nick. He stood and stared in silence.

'Where are the kids?' she asked. 'Are they okay?'

'They're with my mum. I didn't want them to see you like this.'

'Sorry,' she whispered.

'If you ever tell anyone,' he said, 'I'll kill you. Okay? Okay?' he said, louder this time.

She was mopping the blood off her face, astonished at its quantity and redness. 'Okay.'

Alicia

She leant closer to the mirror, inspecting for imperfections. Ah no. She'd just spent the past half-hour doing her make-up more carefully than she'd ever done it in her life and now look: flakes of skin had started to curl up in the hollows around her nose, like cracked earth in a drought area. Grace Gildee would definitely notice. Delicately, with her fingernail, Alicia lifted the flakes off. Gone. But now there were raw, red circles around each nostril. She reached for her foundation sponge and dabbed colour on the afflicted area. Flaky again.

Fuck.

Just fuck.

She was a wreck. She'd done several interviews since the news broke about her and Paddy but she'd never felt as nervous as this.

Not that she had reason to be. This was her time of triumph, her own personal *Pretty Woman*, 'Big mistake, big huge mistake' moment, when she got to say, 'Ha!' to everyone who'd ever been mean to her.

She was the woman who'd waited long enough and finally got everything she'd ever wanted: Grace Gildee was having to interview her because she, yes, *she,* Alicia Thornton, was getting married to Paddy de Courcy.

So there was no need to be nervous, Grace Gildee was the one who should be quaking in her Doc Martens (or whatever brand of strident clumpy boots she wore these days).

She applied one more layer of lipstick then put her finger in her mouth and sucked hard. A handy trick to avoid getting lipstick on her teeth.

But she cast an anxious look in the mirror: had she sucked off too much? The balance was tricky – lipstick too obvious, you look desperate; lipstick too discreet, you look pitifully self-effacing.

She decided to add one more coat because the last thing she wanted to look was pitifully self-effacing. Not in front of Grace. She wanted to look . . . what? Sophisticated, confident, elegant. She'd never be beautiful, she'd accepted that a long time ago. And good job she had because for every fawning mention in the press of her 'elan' there was another sniggery reference to her long features. The first and most wounding had been, 'Giddy up the aisle!' She'd been devastated – and deeply confused – by the hostility with which some newspaper articles had greeted her engagement. One had even implied that the only reason she was with Paddy was because she was a social climber. Which was insane, she thought. Paddy was *beautiful*. Even if he'd been a puppeteer or the person who sat at a conveyor belt and checked for mutant-shaped M&Ms, she'd have loved him.

'Can we sue?' she'd asked, in tears.

'No, we can't.' Paddy had been exasperated. 'Get used to it.'

'You mean there might be more?'

'Yeah.'

'But why?'

She'd had a starry-eyed expectation that the media would shower her with affection because it was Paddy she was marrying. Surely everyone adored him as much as she did?

'They do,' Paddy had said bluntly. 'They're jealous of you.'

Jealous! Once she realized that, it changed everything. She didn't think anyone had ever before been jealous of her; she didn't usually generate that kind of reaction. But now . . . well . . . *jealous* . . .

Sometimes, when she got dressed in the morning, she looked at herself in the full-length mirror and whispered, 'I am jealous of me, you are jealous of me, he-stroke-she is jealous of me. We are jealous of me, you plural are jealous of me, they are jealous of me.'

She blotted her lipstick and glanced at her watch. What time was it?

Five past eleven. Six past, actually. Grace was six minutes late.

Alicia went into the kitchen, opened the fridge and checked that the wine was still there. Yes. She looked out of the kitchen window; yes, the ground was still down there, one storey below. But no sign of Grace.

Another glance at her watch. Eight minutes late now.

What should she do? She'd asked that Sidney Brolly, NewIreland's press officer, absent himself; she wanted privacy for this interview. But if he'd been here, he'd have been ringing Grace's mobile, running her to ground, finding out what the delay was.

Could there be a chance that Grace wasn't coming? After all, you never could tell with Grace –

Christ Almighty! The doorbell! Alicia's nerve endings flared. The bell had never before sounded so harsh. What in the name of God had Grace done to it?

Alicia buzzed open the downstairs entrance and, a few moments later, she heard someone outside in the communal hallway.

Another check in the mirror – still there, bastard flakes – then she opened the front door.

Oh my God. Grace looked exactly the same. Short hair, defiant eyes; wearing jeans and a khaki anorak, one of the ugliest things she'd ever seen.

'Grace! Lovely to see you.' She leant forward for a welcome kiss but Grace turned her head and managed to elude her. 'Come in, please! Let me take your coat.'

'Hello, Mrs Thornton.'

Mrs Thornton? 'Mrs Thornton? Grace! It's me! Call me Alicia!'

'Alicia.'

A sliver of doubt cut in. 'Grace, you do know who I am, don't you?'

'Alicia Thornton.'

'But you remember me, right?'

Grace simply said, 'Let's get started. Where do you want to do this?'

'In here . . .' Considerably deflated, Alicia led the way into the living room. It was obvious that Grace remembered her: she'd be a lot bloody nicer if she didn't.

'Nice flat,' Grace remarked.

'Well, I can't really take any of the credit –'

'– because it's Paddy's, right? When did you move in?'

'I haven't,' she said quickly. 'I still have my own place.' In actual fact, it had been months since she'd spent a single night in her own house, but Paddy said they had to pretend. The Irish electorate was an unpredictable beast, he said: one minute as liberal as you please, the next breathing ire and indignation about people 'living in sin'. In fact, Paddy had tried to insist that they *genuinely* live in their separate homes until after the wedding, but this was one issue that

Alicia stood her ground on. She'd waited too long for him, she loved him so much, she couldn't *not* be with him.

'So why aren't we doing the interview at your place?' Grace asked.

'Because ... ah ...' The truth was that she was showing off to Grace: look, see me, engaged to Paddy de Courcy, actually *living with him*. But who in their right mind would admit to that? For a short crazed moment, the words *Burst pipes* flashed into her head. Yes. *Burst pipes, flooded flat, carpets ruined, two feet of water, wellingtons, ceiling being replastered* ... No. She choked back the lies; no good would come from going down that path – Grace would find out.

All she could do was to ignore the question. 'Can I get you a cup of tea, Grace? Coffee? A glass of wine?'

'Nothing, thanks.'

'Not even a glass of wine?' Boldly she added, 'After all, this is sort of a reunion.'

'I'm good, thanks.'

'An ashtray? Do you still smoke?'

'I'm a non-smoker. Let's get started.' Grace switched on her recorder. 'Where did you grow up?'

'... Dun Laoghaire.'

'Where did you go to school?'

'... But Grace, you know all of this.'

'I need to get all the details square. I'd appreciate it if you'd just answer the questions.'

'I'm not up on a murder charge.' Alicia tried to sound light-hearted. 'I mean, this is all so formal.'

'This is how I work. You requested me specifically. If it doesn't suit you, the *Spokesman* has lots of other journalists.'

'But I thought ... because we knew each other, it would

305

cut out a lot of the formality.' Of course that wasn't the reason she'd insisted on Grace, but what the hell.

'We don't know each other.' Grace was blunt.

'But we do –'

Grace said, 'We might have known each other once but it was a long, long time ago and it has no relevance now.'

Alicia was shocked by the short speech. There it was, all of the hostility Grace had, thus far, hinted at, out in the open. It wasn't what she'd hoped for from today.

She'd had faith that Grace would be friendly, conciliatory, perhaps even *humble*, bound by circumstances to treat her as an equal. She'd actually entertained a tentative fantasy that she and Grace might share a laugh at how things had turned out.

But she'd misjudged the situation entirely.

The giddy anxiety that had buoyed Alicia all morning, drained away. She was dejected, disappointed and – to her great alarm – touched by a flicker of fear.

'So let's just get on with it,' Grace said. She checked her notes. 'So you're a . . . a widow?' she asked, almost as if she doubted it.

'. . . Yes.'

'How did your husband die?' The question was asked baldly, with none of the sympathy that the other journalists had employed.

'A heart attack.'

'Was he old?'

'No. Fifty-eight.'

'Fifty-eight. That's old. Compared to you. What did he do for a living?'

'It wasn't old.'

'What did he do for a living?'

306

'Barrister.'

'Just like Paddy. He must have been worth a couple of bob. Left you nicely off –'

'Look, he wasn't old and I always had my own job, I never depended on him for money.' She wasn't going to stand for Grace Gildee implying that she was Anna Nicole Smith. It genuinely wasn't the case. Mind you, the real situation probably wasn't any more savoury ...

'You'd been married for how long?'

'Eight years.'

'Eight years? Long time. When he died, it must have been rough.'

'Yes, it was ... rough.' Alicia stared off into the middle distance, assuming the wistful look that Sidney had told her to wear any time her dead husband came up in interviews.

'And ten months later you're engaged to Paddy de Courcy. Christ, Alicia, you must have been devastated.'

'It wasn't like that! I've known Paddy for years and years – you know that, Grace – and he comforted me after the death of my husband. That friendship flowered into love.'

'Flowered into love,' Grace repeated, a smirk – an *actual* smirk – on her lips. 'Right. So you're the woman who's finally got the elusive Paddy by the short and curlies? What is it about you that's so special?'

Alicia wondered if she should object to 'short and curlies', but instead settled for, 'I suppose you'd have to ask Paddy that.'

'I'm asking you.'

'I can't speak on behalf of him.'

'Come on, Alicia Thornton, you're a grown woman. Answer the question: What makes you different?'

'I'm very ... loyal.'

'Are you now?' Grace asked with a grim cheerfulness. 'And his other girlfriends weren't?'

'I'm not saying that, not at all!' Christ, Paddy would go mad. He'd told her to never slag off anyone else in interviews. It looked very bad in print, much worse than it sounded in conversation. 'But I'm extremely steadfast.'

'How do you think steadfastness plays out in the modern marriage?'

'What do you mean?'

'It's no secret that Paddy is very popular with the ladies. If there was an adultery scandal, would you stand by him? Would you show up for the family shot at the garden gate? Or would you leave him?'

The questions were coming too fast. She didn't know the right answer. She was bitterly sorry she had banished Sidney; he would have stepped in and put a firm stop to this line of questioning.

'Stay or go?' Grace pushed.

Alicia was rigid with indecision. She didn't know the right answer. She thought of Paddy; what would he want her to say?

'I'd stand by him.'

Grace Gildee's eyes narrowed scornfully. 'You can't think very much of yourself if you've decided in advance that you'll excuse any adultery. Doesn't that give your future husband carte blanche to misbehave?'

'No!'

'No need to shout.'

'I wasn't. And I'm not excusing anything. I'm saying that marriage is a sacred vow.'

'A sacred vow?' Grace repeated. 'Just because one

308

person breaks the vow, it's no reason for the other to do so?'

'Yes.' That sounded good.

After less than fifteen minutes, Grace clicked off her recorder and said, 'Okay, I have all I need.' Somehow it sounded like a threat.

Grace stood up and Alicia remained seated, unable to understand that the interview was over. It was too soon. She'd expected so much but nothing had happened the way she'd planned it.

'My jacket,' Grace prompted, as Alicia remained glued to the couch.

'Oh yes . . .' Alicia finally emerged from her stunned state and retrieved the hideous khaki anorak from the hall cupboard.

'I love your coat,' she said, handing it over to Grace. 'Gorgeous colour.' Fuck it, a woman had to take her pleasures where she could.

Grace gave her a hard stare. Clearly she recognized sarcasm when she heard it. She could never get one over on Grace. Not even now.

Making a last-ditch attempt to rescue things, Alicia said warmly, 'Tell me, how's Marnie?'

'Fantastic. Living in London, married to a fantastic man, two gorgeous kids.'

'Great. Send her my love.'

Grace stared at her. Stared until she quailed.

Alicia listened to Grace pounding down the communal stairs and bursting out into the world. A few moments later a car engine started and tyres screeched away. Grace was gone.

Obviously hurrying back to her office to bash out a hatchet job. For a moment Alicia felt faint with fear.

She had to ring Paddy. He'd told her to call the moment it was over. But she felt too bruised and humiliated to summon the wherewithal.

In the days and weeks before this interview, she'd been confident she was the firm favourite. Instead she'd been soundly trounced. And it was her own fault: she'd specifically requested Grace. Paddy had counselled against it, but she'd wanted it so badly, she told Paddy it could be his wedding present to her.

'And what will your wedding present to me be?' he'd asked.

'What would you like?'

'I don't know the exact details yet,' he'd said obliquely. 'But a time may come when I might ask you to do a little job and I'd like you to remember this and do what I ask.'

She hadn't had a clue what he was getting at but she'd agreed anyway.

Reluctantly she dialled Paddy's office number.

'How d'it go with Grace Gildee?' he asked.

'Well . . . okay.'

'Okay?' All his antennae were up.

'Oh Paddy, she's such a bitch.'

'Why? What? I fucking warned you about this! I'm getting Sidney on to her.'

'No, Paddy, no, no. She said nothing bad, she just wasn't very nice.'

'Well, what did you expect?'

When she married Jeremy, even as she was gliding up the aisle on her father's arm, she'd known that she didn't love him the way she loved Paddy.

But she *had* loved him. Jeremy was a wonderful man.

They'd met through her job – he asked her to agent the sale of his flat – and their connection was instant.

He was a confident, intelligent, kind man who treated life as a great adventure. He had a wide circle of friends and they moved in a pack, hoovering up truffle-tasting menus and jazz festivals and helicopter trips over the North Pole.

Compared to Jeremy, Alicia had seen nothing and done nothing and knew nothing, but her gaucheness was what appealed to him. He took her to opera festivals. He took her shopping in Milan. He took her to a restaurant in Barcelona that had a six-year waiting list. 'You keep everything fresh for me,' he told her.

Life was fast and busy. So busy in fact that she sort of forgot to notice that the sex wasn't up to much.

She fancied him, yes, she definitely fancied him, even if he was twenty-three years older than her – two years younger than her dad. But Jeremy was nothing like her dad; for an older man, he was very handsome. Dark hair (dyed, but then again so was hers), dark eyes always twinkling, truffle-gut kept at bay with regular games of tennis.

With his rampaging appetites, she'd expected him to be demanding in bed, probably a bit kinky (she was quite worried, if she was to be honest), but to her surprise he didn't seem that bothered. Even before they got married it didn't happen often, and when it did, it was a quick, lack-lustre event. It alarmed and disappointed her. If it was this tame at the start of the relationship, when they were meant to be at their wildest about each other, it could only get worse.

She faced the uncomfortable truth: a life with Jeremy would be a life without passion. But that was the price you paid for marrying an older man, and she was meant to be with an older man, that much was clear to her. She was always more sensible than her years – her mother used to say she was 'seven, going on thirty-seven' – and things never worked out with men of her own age. She wasn't pretty enough, or cool enough, or something enough. But whatever it was that she was missing, Jeremy was prepared to overlook it; it took someone with Jeremy's life experience to see her true worth.

She knew something wasn't right when three of his male friends came on honeymoon with them to Lisbon. The full story was revealed in all its bitterness when, one night, they 'just happened' to find themselves in a gay bar. Alicia sat in horror, riveted to a bar stool, while her new husband and his friends, and the young boys they were flirting with, treated her like a tame fag-hag.

She was appalled at Jeremy's cruelty.

So he was gay. But he hadn't had the guts to tell her, so instead he was demonstrating it.

As soon as she was able to move, she slid off the bar stool and headed for the door.

'Where are you going?' Jeremy asked.

'Back to the hotel.'

'I'll come with you.'

Once in the hotel room, Alicia began flinging shoes and clothes into a suitcase.

'What are you doing?' Jeremy asked.

'What does it look like? I'm leaving you.'

'Why?'

'Why? You might have mentioned you're gay.'

'Bi, actually. Alicia, I thought you knew. I didn't think you minded.'

'What kind of woman do you think I am? That I would marry a gay man and not mind?'

The look in his eyes told the whole story. Guilty, shifty. He hadn't truly thought that she knew. But he had thought that when she discovered it, she would put up with it.

Everyone disappoints you in the end, she thought.

'You conned me,' she said. 'Why did you marry me?'

'About time I settled down. I'm fifty.'

'Yes, you're fifty. Why bother?'

'Ouch, Mrs Thornton, you really know how to twist that knife.'

'Can't you ever be serious?'

'Why? When we can have fun instead?'

'Jeremy, I need to know. Why did you marry me?'

He didn't answer.

'Why, Jeremy?'

'You know why.'

'I don't.'

'You wanted it.'

She had. And now that he'd said it, she admitted that all the impetus had come from her. She'd wanted to get married, she always had, it was what you did, it was normal behaviour. And it had been such a joyous change to meet a man who would do what she wanted; before Jeremy, she hadn't been able to get a man to commit to even ringing her. But with Jeremy, she'd been able to come right out and say jokey things like, 'How much are you spending on my engagement ring?' and 'Where are we going on our honeymoon?'

'Well, thanks a bunch,' she said. 'Very decent of you. But seeing as you're gay and all, you needn't have bothered.'

'Alicia, why did you marry me?'

'Because I love you.'

313

'And?'

'And nothing.'

'Right,' he said, looking her dead in the eye.

He knew, she realized. Maybe he didn't know that the man was Paddy, but he knew there was someone. Complicity flashed between them, a moment when their respective dishonesties were highlighted and bare.

They'd both been liars, she as much as Jeremy. They'd both gone into this marriage for the wrong reasons – she'd married Jeremy because if she couldn't have Paddy, Jeremy would do – and the extent of her cynicism left her more ashamed and depressed than she had ever felt in her life.

'Don't go tonight,' Jeremy said. 'Sleep on it, wait until morning. Come on,' and he held out his arms, offering comfort. She let him hold her because, in her way, she loved him.

In the morning, he persuaded her to stay for the rest of the honeymoon. And when they returned to Dublin and moved into their marital home, she was too embarrassed to leave immediately. The mortification of splitting up with her husband on their honeymoon was just too much. She decided to give it a year, just to save face. And somewhere in that year, she forgave him.

They never slept together again – in fact, their marriage was never consummated – but they'd been friends, great friends.

'Why not just be openly gay?' she sometimes asked him. 'Ireland has changed. It's okay now.'

'I'm from a different generation to you.'

'Please,' she said, 'stop reminding me you're ancient.'

'Do you want everyone to know that your husband takes it up the arse from nineteen-year-old rent boys?'

'Do you?' She was fascinated.

314

'Yes.'

No, she didn't want anyone knowing that.

But she wondered if Paddy knew.

She met him from time to time – not properly, not by appointment, but at big social events, like charity balls, where conversation was brief and jokey. The first time he met Jeremy and Alicia after they'd got engaged, he X-rayed them with an impolite gaze that made her uncomfortable with its intensity. She remembered watching him, watching them – scanning, assimilating, filing – and wondering what it was that he saw.

Her sister Camilla knew too – because she told her. She had to tell someone, but then she was sorry because Camilla said the worst possible thing. 'Why are you selling yourself so short? Why don't you leave him and hold out for true love?'

'Because I've met the only one I'll ever love. I know who he is.'

Such certainty was a type of comfort. It wasn't her fault she was hopelessly in love with a man she couldn't have. In olden times she'd have entered a nunnery and that would have been the end of everything. At least with Jeremy she was living a fullish life, going skiing, shopping, having fun.

I have a lizard-skin Kelly bag, she reminded herself.

I have met Tiger Woods.

I have flown in a private plane.

But sometimes in the bleak predawn hours, the truth woke her and she couldn't avoid wondering what was wrong with her. Why did she think so little of herself, that she remained married to a gay man? Why had she settled for a skewed half-life?

But it's fine, she told herself. We're happy.

She had read a feature in *Marie Claire* about relationships where the couples no longer had sex. Apparently they were much more widespread than anyone knew, or admitted to. I am actually normal, she whispered to herself in the pearly grey light. It's the ones who have lots of sex who are abnormal.

She knew it all came back to Paddy. He'd ruined her for anyone else.

'Maybe you should see someone,' her sister suggested. 'A shrink of some sort.'

'A shrink won't help me find a man as good as Paddy.'

Her sister didn't push the point. She fancied Paddy too.

Despite the absence of sex, Alicia's life with Jeremy was a good one. He used humour, money, drink, food and travel to keep things from ever becoming too glum or serious. He loved her, she knew he did. He always treated her with great tenderness and affection.

And when he died, her grief was genuine.

At about ten-thirty most nights, Sidney dropped the following morning's papers over to Paddy. Normally it was no big deal – Sidney handed him the bundle, then legged it and Paddy leafed through the pages at his leisure – but this particular night, Paddy brought such a wash of black energy with him when he returned to the living room that Alicia knew immediately that something was up.

'It's in,' Paddy said. 'The interview with Grace Gildee.'

Alicia's stomach almost flipped out of her mouth. They hadn't been expecting it for another week.

Paddy went straight to the article and was so intent on it that she had to read over his shoulder. It was a big piece, a double-page spread, the headline in big, bold, black print.

STAND BY YOUR MAN

It is a truth universally acknowledged that a single man in possession of naked political ambition must be in want of a wife.

God. Alicia flicked a terrified glance at Paddy. He read on for a few sentences, then made an outraged squeak. 'Why the hell did you offer her a glass of wine at eleven o'clock in the fucking morning?'

'I thought...' What had she thought? That she and Grace might get mildly drunk together and end up giggling over the old days?

Paddy read on avidly: boring details of her upbringing, schooling, work history. So far so safe – then disaster.

Thornton's values are reminiscent of those of the 1950s, when women stuck by adulterous men, because 'marriage is a sacred vow. Just because one person breaks the vow, it's no reason for the other to do so.'

'Did you say that?' Paddy demanded.

'... Some of it ...'

'And she said the rest and you agreed?'

'... Yes ...' Too late she'd remembered that if you agree with any statement that a journalist makes, they can quote you on it.

'I'm meant to represent modern fucking Ireland!'

'Sorry, Paddy.'

'Not some fucking Catholic throwback banana republic!

317

Why the hell did we send you to media training if you can't remember the fucking basics?'

'Sorry, Paddy.'

'Why wouldn't you let Sidney sit in on it?'

But he knew why, they both did.

On she read.

Thornton reckons the reason she caught the field-playing de Courcy is down to her 'loyalty and steadfastness'. This will come as a surprise to mountaineer Selma Teeley who – very *loyally*, it must be said – used some of her substantial sponsorship earnings to fund de Courcy's election campaign six years ago.

Had she? Alicia hadn't known that. She looked in surprise at Paddy, then looked away quickly. Now was not the time for eye contact.

Possibly the worst thing about the piece, Alicia realized, was that Grace was reporting it straight. There were no spiteful interpretations; instead she let Alicia's quotes damn her all by themselves.

Alicia sounded like a submissive doormat and it was all her own fault.

When Paddy finished reading, he threw the paper aside with a sharp rustle and sat brooding in his chair. 'Stupid bitch,' he said.

Lola

Friday, 17 October 11.07

Wake up. Look at alarm clock. Pleased. 11.07 – good time. Less of day to waste. Best waking-up time to date since arriving at Uncle Tom's cabin was 12.47 but had been up very late night before watching *Apocalypse Now*. Intense emotional experience. Also very long. Make coffee and bowl Crunchy Nut Cornflakes, pull kitchen chair round to back of house and break my fast in full view of Atlantic Ocean. Has become my habit because every day, despite it being October, weather is beautiful.

Ireland strange, strange country. July – summer by my reckoning – weather can be embarrassingly cold and wet. All those poor American tourists doing Ring of Kerry in fogged-up coaches and the weather making show of us. But now look! Middle of October! Every day sunny and blustery, huge blue skies, overexcited sea, young men surfing. Massive sweep of beach, deserted during weekdays, apart from heartbroken women traipsing up and down, hoping to – I don't know – walk right back to happiness? Still haven't joined them. Will never join them. Matter of pride.

In leisurely fashion, pour milk over Crunchy Nut Cornflakes. Breakfast in Knockavoy takes average of forty-three minutes – astonishing length of time. In Dublin, would spend nine seconds cramming slice of toast into mouth while simultaneously applying concealer, watching *Ireland AM* and looking for lost things.

Six or seven surfers out there this morning, sleek as seals in their wetsuits. Would love to surf. No, that is wrong. Would love to *be able to* surf. Different thing. Suspect would not enjoy surfing at all. Water up nose and in ears, and think of hair. But if told people – men, let's be honest, men – that I was surfer, they would think I was sexy. All-over tan (despite wetsuit), ankle rope, body confidence. Yes, hair would be in absolute flitters, but people don't seem hold it against you if you explain that you are surf girl. Suddenly tangled, broken hair ceases being tangled, broken hair and becomes sexy, surfy hair. Is this right, I ask you?

Ocean temporarily gone flat. Surfers lying stomach-down on boards, waiting. Surfing requires patience; lots of hanging around and could not pass time sending texts.

Ate slowly. Have taken to chewing every mouthful of food twenty times because of article I read. Alert! In Western world, we do not chew food enough. We are swallowing food almost whole. Bad business because intestines have no teeth. Chewing every mouthful twenty times good for digestion.

Also helps to pass the time.

Chewed and chewed and chewed and chewed and surveyed the surfers. Was I imagining it or was one of them looking in my direction? Jake the Love-God? Sudden flash of silver light – small but intense – seemed to leap from his direction and break over my head. Not mini-bolt of lightning but blink of his silvery eyes.

Was it just sunlight glinting on water? Surely not possible to see colour of his eyes, even if they are abnormally bright? He is some distance away (12 yards? Half a mile?). Narrowed eyes in attempt to see better (strange thing – why would you make eyes *smaller* when trying to see more?). Next thing, the surfer waved.

Must be Jake!

I — slightly self-consciously — waved back. Very faintly, heard call from him. 'Hi, Loh-lah!' Words floated on sea air, carried to me by many, many molecules of salt.

Called back, 'Hi, Jake.' But voice sounded thin and weak. Knew, for sure, salt molecules had not helped out, only person who heard me was me. Feel foolish.

Whenever bumped into Jake in Knockavoy, he gave me sexy smiles and long, meaningful eye-locks, then lounged away without issuing concrete invitation.

''E fancies you,' Cecile says, whenever we meet, which is most days.

'So you keep saying,' I reply. 'But he does nothing about it.'

''E is not used to making the running,' Cecile said. 'The girls always do it for 'im.'

'This girl doesn't,' I said, as if I was full of self-esteem, dignity, self-worth. Not the case. Truth of matter, Jake and his Love-God antics were mild diversion, but too destroyed by Paddy.

Wind quite blustery. Lifted a Crunchy Nut Cornflake from bowl and bounced it across fields to sea. Neck cold. Went inside to find scarf or something. Pink feather boa thrown on couch. That would do. Or would it . . . ? Suddenly noticed was wearing pyjamas, wellingtons and pink feather boa. Danger of living alone. Must take care not to turn into eccentric. If sharp eye not kept on things, might end up asking Bridie to loan me her jockey jumper.

12.03
Did washing-up, bowl, cup, spoons. Daily routine. Wiped down sink, hung up tea towel and had tiny, tiny moment when wasn't entirely sure what next move would be — mistake! It

was enough for terror to barge in and squeeze me so tight I could hardly breathe. *What the hell am I doing here?*

Could set clock by arrival of terror. Every single day, as soon as hung up tea towel, got the twitch. Wanted to ring Nkechi, Bridie, anyone, and beg, 'Please can I come back to Dublin? Can I come home yet?'

Had stopped actually making the calls because was pointless. No one would let me return to Dublin. But oh my job, my job, my lovely job . . .

Because have no husband, no children, no family, no great talent – e.g. ability to carve carrots into flower shapes, foxgloves, rhododendrons – without my job I am nothing.

Couldn't stop thinking of Nkechi plotting and planning to steal business from under my nose, but then remembered appalling shambles had made of it last time had tried to work and acknowledged probably just as well was in Knockavoy. Self could destroy business faster than Nkechi.

Didn't help that phone rang constantly. 'Nkechi doing fabulous job!' 'Nkechi fabulized me for Chicken Pox Gala!' 'Thanks to Nkechi I dazzled them all at the Dysentery benefit!' Message: Nkechi is brilliant, brilliant, brilliant. You are worthless, worthless, worthless.

Bridie takes different view. 'They are being nice –'

'Nice? Those women don't know how to be nice.'

'– and Nkechi is keeping your business up and running while you're away.'

'They'll all want to be her clients when she sets up on her own.'

'They won't. Law of averages, if nothing else.'

Only comfort: Abibi not popular.

12.46

'Lola?' Man's voice calling from outside house. Surprising. 'Lola?'

Paddy coming to claim me! To tell me it had all been terrible mistake!

Not. Of course not. But it just doesn't go away. Even when not thinking specific thoughts, am operating in mesh of free-floating dread and only takes something very, very small – e.g. mention of Louise Kennedy in magazine – to trip off high-speed chain of painful thoughts. Like this:

'Louise Kennedy's latest collection . . .' = Alicia Thornton wearing Louise Kennedy suit in photo in paper = newspaper crowing that she was woman who 'won Quicksilver's heart' = Paddy is getting married to other woman = Excuse me? Paddy is getting married to other woman? = unbearable sorrow.

All happens in less than second. Red-hot skewer of agony has pierced me before my brain has had time to figure out why. Every other cell in body in on the news; poor brain is last to know.

Being without Paddy is defining fact of my life. Whenever had split up with other boyfriends had been sad, yes, not denying it. But always had hope that a future still awaited me. But I'd met Paddy, I'd met my Real One. He'd been and gone and my future was empty.

12.47

Opened door. Heavy-set man. Out on road, DHL van parked.
Heavy-set man said, 'Lola Daly?'
'That's me.'
'Parcel for you. Sign here.'

Wondered what it was. Who was sending me stuff?

Under 'Contents' it said 'Shoes'. Now knew what it was.

DHL man turned box upside down to read it. 'Shoes, is it?'

In Dublin would stare at him coldly for his nosiness. But in Knockavoy can do no such thing. Am obliged to lean shoulder against door-jamb in attitude indicating have all time in world for in-depth chinwag. 'Yes, shoes.'

'For a wedding, is it?'

'. . . Er, no, not for a wedding.' Shoes not even for me, as it happens, but cannot tell him that, no matter how talkative I'm obliged to be. Am bound by bonds of secrecy. Dilemma. Am pulled in two different directions, ruled by two masters.

'Just felt like buying new shoes, was it?'

'That's it. Just . . . you know . . . felt like it.'

'Down here on your holidays, is it?'

'Er, no, longer.'

'How long?'

'No . . . er . . . plans.' Ashamed by my life. Couldn't say, Am stuck here until my friends and colleagues decide I am sane enough to be allowed back to Dublin. 'Just . . . ah . . . playing it by ear . . . you know?'

'So I might see you again?'

'You might.'

'Niall,' he said, sticking out his hand for me to shake.

'Lola,' I said.

'Oh I know.'

12.57

Waited until he was well and truly gone, then opened box to check it was what thought it was. It was. Rang Noel from Dole.

Said to him, 'Your package has arrived.'

'Finally? About time. Mint.' ('Mint' — word he favours, meaning 'great', 'excellent', etc.) 'Will call this evening after work. When suits you?'

Tricky. Evenings my busiest times. Had to sit on sea wall and exchange pleasantries with strangers about beauty of sunset. Had to have non-lumpy soup of day in the Oak. Had to watch soaps with Mrs Butterly. Had to have long, in-depth chat with Brandon and Kelly over DVD selection. Had to spend time in the Dungeon with Boss, Moss and the Master, listening to the Master recite unfeasibly long poems. Packed schedule.

But today there was far bigger spanner in the works.

'I'm sorry, Noel from Dole, I have friends coming for the weekend.'

Startled-sounding pause. Then he said, 'Oh fine! Be like that. From Dublin, I suppose, these friends of yours?' Said sneerily, as if Dublin pretentious hellhole.

Just minute . . . 'You are the one who insisted on absolute secrecy,' I said. 'Don't mind if you come to collect parcel while others are here.'

Noel quite tricky character, prone to volatile outbursts, but my welfare payments had been expedited with unprecedented speed — without me having to produce powdered unicorn horn or brass rubbing of Holy Grail. Most irregular. Still expecting to receive terrifying letter saying it was all a mistake and had to pay back every penny, plus interest.

Under circumstances, probably better not to rub Noel up wrong way.

After surly silence he said, 'Is okay, will wait. But you are not to tell your Dublin friends about me.'

'Of course not.' Was lie. Was going tell them, but —
obviously — swear them to secrecy.

'How about Monday?' Noel asked.

Monday long way away. Might have been pronounced fully
restored to mental health and on way back to Dublin. But
not very likely.

'Monday fine. Come after work.'

13.06

Late. Hurried to town. Like it mattered. Conducted business
briskly — buying food, wine and much, much chocolate for
arrival of Bridie, Treese and Jem — then hurried home again.
Changed back into pyjamas, wellingtons and feather boa.
Pulled couch round to back of house and spent afternoon
lying on it, reading Margery Allingham thriller.

Funny thing. If people were asked to describe perfect life,
they might describe mine: living in beautiful, beautiful place
— sea, nature, all that; not having get up crack of dawn,
sleeping half the day, none of stresses of work, having time
to watch DVDs on revenge, read damp thrillers and chew
each mouthful of food twenty times. But cannot enjoy it.
Anxious, antsy. Feel life passing me by. Feel everything have
worked hard for slipping away.

Ashamed of my ingratitude. Now have other unpleasant
emotion to feel. Variety is nice, I suppose. Makes change
from terror and heartbreak.

Gave self pep talk (silent one, not yet at stage where
talking out loud to self): One day life would be different and
stressy and busy again and I would love to disappear to
small beautiful place and do nothing. So really must try
to enjoy my time here. This is not for ever!

16.27

Put down book, closed eyes and thought about Paddy. Sometimes I thought had made peace with it. But other times, I am seized by frenzy of missing him, of needing him. From time to time, still think: There was such a bond between us, all that feeling can't simply have gone away, just because he's getting married to someone else.

Haven't rung him since return to Knockavoy. Well, only once. Drunk, of course. Only time could convince self to be hopeful. (Had got drunk by accident. Had been bought drinks by everyone from Ol' Prune Eyes to Mrs Butterly to Boss to rival Alco's Corner. Impolite to refuse native hospitality. Could cause terrible insult.)

Had been walking home, happy and hopeful and – let's say it like it was – pissed, and decided ring him. Would convince him to break it off with this so-called Alicia Thornton. Beautiful evening. Balmy. Moon smiling on 'wine-dark' sea (quoting the Master). Everything seemed possible.

Sadly not. Simply drunken misapprehension.

Made call all right. But went to voicemail. Should have hung up, but in grip of unstoppable force.

'Paddy, Lola here. Just ringing say hello. Er . . . that's all. Um, don't marry that other woman. Right . . . ah . . . goodbye.'

All set to ring his landline, but was overtaken with sudden queasiness. Too much emotion, probably. Or perhaps mixture of red wine, Southern Comfort and Guinness, sweetened with blackcurrant.

Next morning, thought I'd dreamt it. Hoped I'd dreamt it. But forced self to check phone. No. Had definitely rung him.

Shame. Bad shame.

Which counted as progress. In immediate aftermath of news, shame conspicuous by absence.

17.30

Not spying. Not this time. Dragging couch back inside when glanced towards Firestarter Considine's house and saw him in his kitchen. First thought, a nosy-neighbour one: He's home early from work. Second thought: Is that ACTUALLY Firestarter Considine, and if so, what on earth is he WEARING?

Stared. Stared hard. Was he really wearing swimming goggles and a shower cap? Yes. Undeniably yes.

Strange goings-on in that house.

18.57

Arrival of Bridie and Barry

Listening for car, like lonely rural person. Hear it long before it arrives. Not because it is only car on road – indeed not, road is main Knockavoy to Miltown Malbay highway, quite busy – but because of music Bridie has on, on car stereo. Oasis, if not mistaken. Bridie's taste in music almost as bad as taste in clothing, but she is unrepentant.

Car pulls up beside me, music abruptly shut off and Barry emerges from driver's side. Barry permitted to come for weekend, because does everything he is told to, does not express opinions of his own, causes no waves. Unlike other people's husbands.

'Three hours, forty-nine minutes,' was first thing Bridie said to me. 'Excellent time for Friday rush hour. Hold on, just have to write it down.'

19.35

Treese and Jem arrive

Treese driving adorable little blue Audi TT – gift from Vincent! Perhaps to apologize for having abnormally large head? Jem in passenger seat looking uncomfortable. Too low to ground and slightly too chubby for car. Also embarrassed to be in such girly vehicle? (Claudia on hen weekend which is reason Jem allowed to visit.)

Treese v. glam-looking, in heels and sleek tailoring.

'You are fabulous,' I say.

People used to say about Treese, 'lovely-looking, for fat girl'. Patronizing. And to her face, 'Treese, you really should knock off the sweets. Worked for my sister-in-law, she lost four stone. If you stopped being porker, you could be quite attractive.'

Once she lost the weight, she suddenly clicked into being soignée woman. All other parts had already been in place, just waiting. People who had urged her to be thin had to swallow hard. Taken aback. Wrong-footed. Unhappy. Kept her away from their boyfriends.

'How is Vincent?' I asked. 'Keeping well?' Had to ask. Polite. He was invited for weekend – obviously he had to be if Barry was – but nothing ever said. Not even, 'Vincent says thanks for invite, but he is busy this weekend trying to get his head reduced in size.' Simply, we all – Treese included – in silent conspiracy that it would be better if he didn't come.

19.38–19.45
Newcomers taking deep breaths of salty air. Standing facing sea, hands on hips, filling lungs with ozone, saying, 'God, that's fantastic!' Took seven to eight minutes. Then Jem clapped hands together and said, 'Right! Which pub?'

20.07
The Oak, for preprandial libations (Margery Allingham)
Ol' Prune Eyes took time out to sit down with us. Very smiley, twinkly-eyed, pleasant. Told others that he had heard lots

about them. Delightful. I felt proud, almost as if he was my invention.

He told them how I came in every lunchtime (it's not every lunchtime, but never mind, no need to contradict, much goodwill floating around) for soup of the day. 'She always says, "Ibrahim, is it lumpy?"' He laughed hard and hit thigh and repeated, '"Ibrahim, is it lumpy?" Every day.'

Everyone joined in with laughter, not quite sure what laughing at, but charmed that he found it so funny. (Different cultures, different senses of humour.)

'Ibrahim, can I buy you drink?' Bridie offered.

'No, thank you. Don't drink.'

'Why not? You an alcoholic?' Bridie so nosy!

'Don't drink alcohol for religious reasons.'

Bridie stared, clearly wondering what kind of peculiar religion forbade alcohol. To be Catholic, is practically obligatory to have drink problem.

'What religion is that? Christian Science?'

'Muslim,' he said.

'Oh yes, didn't think of that one. Well . . . er . . . fair play.'

Subsequent conversation stilted. Then two golfers, seeking respite from rawlrawlrawl of the Hole in One, came in and Ibrahim had to resume his bar duties.

As soon as he was gone, Bridie leant close to rest of us and hissed, in splurge of admission, 'Is terrible, but when I hear people are Muslims, my first thought is that they are secret suicide bombers.'

'Yes!' Jem agreed, in enthusiastic whisper. 'And that they despise me.'

'Yes!'

'When I was in Morocco with Claudia, the men used to look at her like she was a whore.'

That's because she is a whore. Bridie and I had moment of strong, steady eye contact while this message flashed between us.

'They have no respect for women,' Jem said. 'Beating their wives when they don't cover their hair!'

Treese was getting agitated and trying to interject. 'That is outrag —'

'And I bet they are all mad pissheads in private,' Bridie said. 'Getting lamped out of their skulls and pretending to be —'

'That is outrag —'

'— teetotallers and saying everyone else is unclean swine for having glass of wine and ham sandwich once in while.'

'That is *outrageous* way to think!' Finally Treese had the floor. 'You should be ashamed of yourselves! Over two billion Muslims in world — they cannot ALL be suicide bombers! Is nothing but racism!'

Worst fear confirmed. Don't want to be racist.

'Vast, VAST majority of Muslims are moderate.'

'Of course, of course,' Jem said soothingly. But too late. We are treated to lecture, the gist of which is that everyone in world, regardless of race or religion, is entitled to respect and fully functioning latrines.

Two hours later

Back in the Oak after having bite to eat in Mrs McGrory's pantry.

Place far busier. Ol' Prune Eyes rushed off his feet.

Jem went to bar to buy round and returned, flushed and happy. 'We're invited to a party tomorrow night!' He had made new friends while purchasing drinks. Not first time such a thing had ever happened to someone. Don't mean to be cynical, but . . .

'What party?' Bridie asked.

'Those lads at the bar.'

Surf boys. Five or six of them. Barely dressed, flip-flops, cut-offs, tans, earrings, salt. And there was Jake, in washed-out T-shirt, low-slung jeans and shark's-tooth neck ornament, lounging against bar, drink in hand, watching me. He mouthed, 'Lola,' and smiled.

Bridie rounded on me. 'YOU KNOW HIM?'

'Jake? . . . Um . . . yes.' Quite proud, to be honest. Is like buying fabulous new Chloé coat, but not telling anyone, just arriving along in it and seeing everyone's faces.

'He fancies you!' Bridie elbowed Barry. 'Doesn't he?'

'Certainly seems like it.' (Careful to express no opinions of his own.)

'The way he was looking at you!' Bridie snuck another glance at Jake. 'He's still doing it! He fancies you, I could swear it!'

'Actually.' I cleared throat, readying self to enjoy moment. 'He does.'

That stymied her. 'He does? How do you know?'

'Cecile told me.'

'WHO IS CECILE?' Bridie likes know everything. Right now, she knows next to nothing.

'French girl. In fact, there she is.'

Cecile was in thick of surf boys, giggling and shrugging. Wearing capri pants, ballet slippers and scarf knotted jaun-tily at neck, in fashion Irish woman would never achieve even if practised for a month. (Not even Treese could pull it off.)

'Call her over,' Bridie ordered. 'Hey, Cecile, Cecile! Over here!'

Surprised, Cecile pursed red lips and raised perfect eye-brows, but responded to Bridie's summons.

'Cecile?' Bridie demanded. 'You're Cecile?' High-speed introductions. 'Bridie, Barry, Treese, Jem, and Lola you know. Okay, tell me, that blond-haired man at bar – Jake? – is it true? Does he fancy Lola?'

Cecile giggled. 'Oh yes, 'e wants to ride 'er into middle of next week.'

Treese flinched. But not Cecile's fault. She is not really crude, simply French. Does not understand all that she says, merely repeating what she has heard, like small child.

''E wants to ride 'er so she cannot walk straight for a month.'

'Thank you. You've been very helpful.'

Cecile dismissed.

'Right!' Bridie decreed. 'Here's what I think. Best thing that could happen to Lola right now would be a fling with this Jake. Agreed?' Bridie consulted others. Yes, agreed.

'But you must not expect anything long term,' Bridie cautioned. 'He is far too good-looking.'

'What is this thing where you keep telling me all men are far too good-looking for me?'

'No offence, Lola, you are nice-looking too. But just look at this Jake person. He is ABNORMALLY good-looking. He is freak of nature. The mouth on him! Is so sexy! Everyone must fancy him. Even I fancy him!'

'Sorry,' she said to Barry.

'Is okay,' he said. 'I fancy him too.'

'Do you?'

'We could have threesome with him,' Barry said, then they leant into each other and laughed some private laugh, while rest of us watched, slightly uncomfortable.

1.30

Back in house

Drunk as I was, was highly alarmed when Bridie and Barry changed into strange leisure pants had seen them in before. Baggy but gathered at ankle, somewhat like trousers MC Hammer used to wear. Barry's had illustrations of kites and balloons, while Bridie's had blue and red zebra-skin pattern.

Heinous.

Something must be said.

Saturday, 18 October Noon

Everyone up.

Plan for the day: walks, breathing air, being wholesome before going on 'unmerciful batter this evening', to quote Jem. First: short trip to town because we had run out of milk.

'I will go,' I said. 'Because am hostess. My responsibility.'

'No, I will go,' Jem said. 'Because drank it all at five o'clock this morning.'

'No, I will go,' Bridie said. Because she is control freak.

'Why don't we all go?' Treese suggested.

'Okay!'

'You better get dressed.' I looked meaningfully at Bridie and Barry's MC Hammer pants.

'What you talking about? We *are* dressed!'

Oh cripes. Bad enough to wear those terrible things in privacy of own home, but out in public? Gruesome business.

12.18

Walking to town

Bridie starts talking about Jake. Again.

'Good for you to sleep with him. Good for your ego, good for your confidence. What you know about him?'

'Nothing. Is twenty-five, from Cork, has had sex with every other woman in Knockavoy and apparently wants to ride me so I can't walk straight for a month.'

'But has he job?' Treese pressed. 'How does he support himself?'

'Don't know and don't care. Don't want to know that his mother is teacher and his father a guard, that he has older sister and two younger brothers, that at school he was good at hurling but not so good at football. Don't want to know that he shared bedroom with brother and had photos of Roy Keane Blu-tacked to wall. Don't want to know that photos exist of him as cheeky six-year-old with gappy teeth or grinning ten-year-old with awful haircut. Don't want him to be ordinary and don't want any evidence that he wasn't always beautiful.'

'But you are not treating him as human being,' Treese said.

'I know. Don't want to know his hopes and dreams.'

'Is no basis for relationship,' Treese said.

'But she won't get relationship off him!' Bridie said. 'I am sick saying it, but he is just too good-looking.'

'Just minute! What about what I want? You are all acting as if I am luckiest woman on earth that he fancies me – and he only fancies me because I am novelty – but what about what I want? Maybe don't fancy him at all!'

'Well, do you fancy him?' Bridie asked.

Thought about it. 'Not really.'

Clamour of aghast disbelief, even from Jem.

'All right, calm down! He is nice to look at!'

'You are only playing hard to get,' Bridie decided. 'Don't bother. He still won't do relationship with you.'

'Not playing hard to get. Still in love with Paddy.'

'You would turn down hot sex with Love-God just because you are still hung up on slimy politician with smile like Joker from *Batman*!' Bridie indignant. 'Politician who, incidentally, is getting married to a horse.'

12.49

On way back from buying milk, got lured in the Dungeon. Passing open door – rare, rare occasion when Dungeon had its door wedged open. Usually it eschewed daylight as though it were radioactive. Suspected Alco's Corner were on lookout for me. Sure enough, Boss spotted me and yelled out into the street, 'Ho, Lola Daly! Not good enough for you any more, are we?'

Not true, but keen that Dublin friends should not cross paths with Boss, etc. They would worry at dodginess of company I was keeping. So I said, 'Hahaha,' and continued walking, but Bridie said, 'Who is that man? How come you know so many people?'

She insisted on meeting Boss. I tried resisting. Extreme futility. Found self plunging into gloomy interior and making introductions all round. 'Bridie, Barry, Treese, Jem, meet Boss, Moss and the Master.'

Boss beside himself with excitement. His round, red fizzog was lit up and extra red. 'Have heard ALL about ye! Let me see if I have it right.' He pointed at Treese. 'You're the know-all?'

'. . . Ah . . .'

Cripes!

'No, *I'm* the know-all,' Bridie said.

'So you must be the one who used to be fat?' he said to Treese.

She inclined perfect head in assent.

'By gor!' Boss clearly impressed. 'You'd never know it, you're like a whippet now. Isn't she, boys?'

As Boss, Moss and the Master scrutinized Treese and expressed incredulity that she had once tipped the scales at fourteen stone, my temperature rocketed. Experiencing bitter regret at having spoken so freely about my friends to the clientele in the Dungeon.

'And you're the know-all's hen-pecked husband?' Boss said to Barry.

Barry shot nervous glance at Bridie. Was he? 'Yes,' he said, reading signal. 'I am.'

'You're obviously not the ex-rugby player with the ginorm-ous head,' Boss said to Jem. 'So you must be the fellow Lola is Just Good Friends with.'

Invested words 'Just Good Friends' with sleazy meaning.

'... Er ... yes ...'

'And where is your dolly-bird fiancée?'

'On hen night.'

'Not here? I'm disappointed, so I am. Heard she has fake bosoms. Wanted to see a pair before I die.'

Cease and desist, I think. Cease and desist!

Awkward, all terribly awkward. Desirous of moving the party out of the Dungeon and back to Uncle Tom's cabin at fast clip, but Boss insisted – INSISTED – on buying round. Once a man like Boss is insisting on buying a round, there is no choice, no choice at all.

And as for having soft drink? Not a hope.

Jem made mistake of asking for Coke and entire pub seemed to stop talking. Faintly heard voices say, 'Am I hearing things or did your man in the pyjamas just ask for Coke?' 'Twasn't your man in the pyjamas, 'twas the other fellow.'

'COKE?' Boss demanded. 'Are you man or mouse?' Then

337

looked scornfully at Barry. 'I know all about you. You are mouse. But today you can be mouse that roared. Pint? Five pints,' he called to barman.

Accepted Guinness with bad grace. Drank quickly. Wanted to vamoose. (Strange word.) But before we had finished drinks, Moss got another round in. And halfway through second drink, suddenly relaxed. Boss had ceased and desisted with the mortifying revelations and seemed so patently thrilled to meet friends that – against better judgement – I was touched. 'Was great day Lola Daly graced Knockavoy with her presence,' he said, with sincere warmth, to Bridie. 'She has brought us good luck. Since she arrived, the Master won three hundred and fifty euro on scratch card and I won de luxe fruit cake in raffle in aid of new DVD player for parish priest. To cap it all, mortal enemy has been diagnosed with prostate cancer. Inoperable. Lola is lovely girl, we are fierce fond of her.' He dropped his voice, although I could still hear everything. 'Of course, is crying shame the way she was let down by that Chrispy louser.'

'Paddy de Courcy? But he's NewIreland.'

'Was Christian Progressive before he was NewIreland. Once filthy Chrisp, always filthy Chrisp. Doesn't matter what fancy title he assumes these days. Christian Progressive! Pah!'

Please, I think, please do not spit.

More drinks were bought – this time by Barry – and energetic discussions ensued. Mostly, I regret to report, about me.

I heard '. . . too good-looking for her . . .'

'. . . fake smile . . . like Joker in *Batman* . . .'

'. . . wrong suitcase of clothes . . . nearly sparked inter-national incident . . .'

338

Great bonding ensued. In total we had five drinks each before Bridie called a halt. 'We will miss party tonight if don't stop now.'

Bridie made Barry go for stagger along the beach. 'Sea air will sober us up.'

Rest of us went home and fell asleep and woke two hours later covered in drool.

19.25

The Oak

Light dinner. Toasted sandwiches and soup of day (mushroom).

'Say it,' Ol' Prune Eyes begged me. 'Say it.'

'But I know it's not.'

'Say it anyway.'

'Okay. Is it lumpy?'

I never saw anyone laugh so much.

'You might have future as comedian in Egypt,' Jem said quietly to me.

20.39

Mrs Butterly's

Nasty surprise. Two people already in there. Have never before had to share Mrs Butterly – Honour (she doesn't know I know her first name; Boss told it to me; it is like learning name of your teacher when you are in junior infants) – with any other customer.

Then noticed one of customers was Firestarter! Rossa Considine. He was with woman. Reunited with fiancée? But speedy scrutiny revealed that woman he was with was definitely not wedding-dress woman. In fact, she had slight ferrety cast to her features. Could she be the girlfriend

Alco's Corner had told me about? Despite undeniable ferretyness – something to do with her teeth – she was not minger. Or bowler. In fact, cute-looking.

But what was story there? Rossa Considine dumped ferret-girl when he met wedding-dress girl? But now wedding-dress girl had done runner, he was trying to mend fences with Ferret-Face?

Mrs Butterly in a flap. 'Don't know where I will fit everyone. Sorry, Lola, know these are your friends, but can't take them all. Not enough glasses. Will take you –' she pointed at Treese, like this was hot nightclub with savagely cruel door policy – 'and you.' Jem had also made the cut.

But not Bridie and Barry. Bridie looked stunned. Actually very upset. 'Why you pick them and not us?'

'Nothing personal, but cannot serve people in their pyjamas. By order of management. Anyway no room.'

'Is okay,' Rossa Considine said. 'We are finishing up. They can have our seats.'

'All right. Will make exception seeing as you are friends of Lola.'

Rossa Considine squeezed past and said, 'Hello, Lola.'

'Hello, Rossa,' I replied.

To the uninitiated this might seem like benign greeting. But lots unspoken stuff going on. By sarcastic expression in his eyes, Rossa Considine was really saying, *I see you many mornings spying on me like nosy oddball.*

And with my eyes I was saying, *Is that fact? Well, I caught you burning your ex-fiancée's dresses in middle of night. And dancing around your kitchen wearing swimming goggles and a shower cap. You are fine one to be calling me an oddball.*

'Who's he?' Treese asked, when they'd squeezed out.

'Next-door neighbour.'

'Seems nice.'

Shows what little you know, I think.

Mildly wounded. What had I ever done to Rossa Considine? Apart from spy on him some mornings? And what is so wrong with that?

'You have certainly made friends here!' Bridie clearly impressed that I knew so many people. Is hard for Bridie and them. Because I have no family to speak of, they are burdened with me.

Bridie had crow to pluck with Mrs Butterly. 'Is not pyjamas. Is leisure pants.'

'I am old woman. I have lived long time. I know pyjamas when I see them.'

0.12

Party at surf boys' house

Loud music. Rammed. Where did all these people come from? Didn't know were so many young, good-looking types in Knockavoy.

Through throng in hallway saw Jake, talking to girl with long, dark hair. Despite multitudes milling about, he held my gaze for unfeasibly long time and smiled; slow, white, meaningful.

I gave brusque nod of head, face aflame.

Into main room. Treese and I sat primly on futon while Bridie doled out beers like a mother on a picnic. Barry and Jem in top form.

'Knockavoy is great bloody place!' Jem declared, reeling slightly. 'This is great song!'

'Who is it?'

'Haven't clue!' Jem said happily. 'But it is great bloody song! Come on, everyone up dancing!'

Although feeling slightly old and well-dressed, drunk enough to get to feet. Bridie and Barry also took to floor but Treese stayed seated, smiling enigmatically. You would think Treese not dancing because too sophisticated but those closest to her know she doesn't dance because never learnt to enjoy it when fat.

Dancing quite happily when unexpectedly received sharp poke in lower back. Quite painful, if you want honest opinion. Think it got me in the kidney. Turned around. It was long-haired girl Jake had been talking to. Young, surfy, many tattoos. (I have tattoo, but is only discreet one of butterfly on ankle. Way outclassed by this girl with Celtic knot circling her upper arm, sunburst around her belly button and Om symbol on her wrist.)

'You are Lola?' she said.

Am used to everyone in Knockavoy knowing all about me, but this was different.

'. . . Er . . . yes.'

She gave me scorching head-to-toe once-over with her eyes. 'I am Jaz. Remember my name.' Before could laugh at such cheesy line, she stalked away, bumping into Jem, who went staggering into Bridie, who clouted him roughly and said, 'Mind where you're dancing.'

Life sad, no? Tattoo girl clearly besotted with Jake, but he is making play for me. But I am not interested in Jake because in love with Paddy. But Paddy getting married to Alicia and actually, that is where chain ends because Alicia bound to be in love with Paddy because how could she not be?

1.01

'Come upstairs for minute,' Bridie whispered.

'Why?'

'Just come on.'

Pushed way through people snogging on stairs. Then another flight of stairs, no one snogging on this one. Followed Bridie, who was doing exaggerated tiptoe walk, up bare, wooden steps. At top of house, she pushed open a door with tips of her fingers, but didn't cross the threshold.

'This is Love-God's bedroom,' she confided.

'How you know?'

'Asked around.'

We stood at door and peeped in. Like magic-land in there. Light flickering from three fat white candles stuck in Gothic trident candelabra. Bleached floorboards. Sand. Wooden four-poster bed, top draped with fishing nets (but not smelly). Lopsided locker. Paint peeling but not depressing. Somehow beautiful.

Windows open, muslin curtains billowing in breeze, sound of waves rushing and sucking.

'The things that must happen in this room . . .' Bridie sighed. She seized my arm in sudden painful grip. 'Look in drawer beside his bed,' she urged. 'Go on, see if he's got condoms in it. I bet he has. Go on, Lola.'

'No.' Didn't want illusion spoilt simply to satisfy Bridie's sick curiosity.

Didn't want to see matches, broken watch, hair bobble, Anadins, Rizlas, leaking pens, fluff and other bedside-drawer detritus.

'The candles . . .' Bridie breathed. 'So romantic.'

'Probably because he is too lazy to change broken light bulb,' I said.

And what kind of irresponsible fool leaves naked flame unattended?

With three sharp, no-nonsense puffs, I extinguished the candles. Bridie annoyed.

1.12

Back downstairs, Jake in dancing room. He saw me come in, turned quickly to hi-fi, did something and suddenly music changed from Arctic Monkeys (I think) to slow song. Dancers startled. Cut off in their prime. Distinctly heard someone ask, 'What's this shite?' Jake cut swathe through them, stood before me and in low voice asked a question.

'Hmmm?'

Knew what he was asking, but wanted to watch his mouth say it again.

Louder he said, 'Would you like to dance?'

'. . . Okay . . .'

He took my hand in courtly gesture and led me two feet into centre of room.

'Go on, Lola!' Jem called, as if encouraging horse in Grand National. He was really quite fluthered.

Heard Bridie hissing, 'Shut up, Jem, you imbecile!'

Jake opened his arms – beautifully sinewy; biceps bulgy but not obscene, not like Mr Universe – and I stepped into them. Hit by the heat of his body.

Hard to describe how I felt. Not lustful or giddy with romance. But not reluctant either. Not repelled by fact that he wasn't Paddy. I suppose I was . . . I was . . . interested.

He placed one hand between my shoulder blades, other on small of my back. Nice. At moment have so little physical contact in life. (Mrs Butterly very fond of me, but she is rural Irish woman: would kill her to do hug.)

I slid arms around his neck, hands getting tangled in hair at nape of his neck. Nice space under his collarbone, just to the right of the shark's-tooth necklace, to rest head. Experimentally tried it. Yes, pleasant. Nice fit. Relaxed into it. Closed eyes.

His T-shirt warm and soft, chest underneath warm and hard. Pleasant, pleasant, oh undeniably pleasant.

Felt like eight thousand years since had slow-danced with a man. Just doesn't happen past the age of fifteen, does it?

His skin smelt salty. Suspected if I stuck tongue out and touched his neck, would taste salt.

In fact, as took a breath, noticed he smelt slightly of sweat. Unusual. People behave as if to smell of human being is obscene. Him not smelling of sharp citrus scent seemed gauche . . . but perhaps it is me who is gauche? Maybe that is the way of the younger people: not washing so frequently, not clogging up sweat glands with white stuff which then goes all over clothes, not drenching themselves with pungent chemicals (i.e. aftershave). Perhaps I and my attachment to magnolia blossom fabric conditioner seem risible to them.

Jake tightened his hold on me, sliding one hand round from small of back to waist and pressing harder between shoulder blades with other hand. Fine, all fine. But kept my focus above the waterline. If any stirrings below it – in either of us – just didn't want to know.

Song ended. New song started, also slow. But had had enough. Can't describe it any better than that. Had liked the feel of him and smell of him, but no more for tonight.

'Thank you.' I pulled away from him.

He seemed surprised. 'That's it, Lola?'

'That's it, Jake.'

He smiled.

Look in his eyes: admiration? Respect? Maybe not. Who knows?

I went back to others.

'Why you stop?' Bridie demanded.

'Because wanted to.'

'I see, you are playing long game –'

'I'm not.'

'– but it will do you no good. You might as well go up those stairs and get into bed with him right now!'

Said nothing. Bridie doing transference. She fancies him.

Sunday, 19 October 13.17

Awoke feeling peculiar. Hung-over, of course. Jem only person up. In kitchen, reading newspaper.

'Going to ring my dad,' I said. 'Ring him every Sunday around this time.'

Went outside, sat on front step and rang number in faraway Birmingham.

Dad answered by saying their phone number. Is quaint, no? Time-warp stuff. (They do it in Margery Allingham books. 'Whitehall 90210', etc.)

'Dad?'

'. . . Oh . . . Lola.'

'This a bad time?'

'No.'

'You sure? You sound . . .'

'I sound what?'

'. . . Like it's bad time. Like you don't want talk to me.'

'Why wouldn't I want talk to you?'

'. . . Um . . . ah . . .' Sudden courage. 'Dad, why don't you ever ring me?'

'Because you ring me every Sunday.'

But couldn't help wondering: What if I didn't ring? How long would it take before he rang me? Sometimes felt like testing him, but couldn't run the risk that he might simply never call me – ever – and then I would have no father.

Desultory conversation ensued. Most of talking done by me.

Then Dad asked, 'What you want for Christmas?'

'It's only October.'

'It'll be upon us before we know it. So what you want?'

'Bottle of perfume.' Is sort of present he thinks fathers should give to daughters.

'What kind perfume?'

'Any kind. A surprise.'

'You buy it, I will send you postal order.'

Postal order! Why not cheque? He has bank account! No need for postal order!

Whenever I think of life lived by Dad and his brother – Uncle Francis, also a widower, also prone to depression – I always imagine depressing play about rural Ireland in the fifties. Picture in my head has them living in small cheerless cottage where kitchen is full of steam from enormous pot of potatoes constantly on boil. From early morning to sunset, days are spent in back-breaking work, tilling fields and milking cows, while wearing ancient white dress shirts and shiny-bummed suit trousers. Conversation non-existent. Every evening they each eat thirteen floury potatoes, and drink pint bottle of stout, while listening to sea-area forecast on wireless. Then they get on their knees on hard-flagged kitchen floor and, leaning elbows on bokety wooden chair, say fifteen decades of the rosary, before undressing to their vests and long johns and sleeping together in narrow iron bed. For many years, day in, day out, life continues in this vein, until eventually one of them hangs himself in cowhouse.

I know reality is not like that. Uncle Francis's house, in Birmingham suburb, small but modern. Has electricity and running water, unlike house in my head. Also each man has own bedroom and know for a fact that Dad has pyjamas and tartan dressing gown and doesn't need to sleep in long johns. Fair amount of religious iconography, mind you. Pride of place a picture of Sacred Heart: picture of Jesus, revealing red heart – i.e. internal organ – in his chest. Many Catholic homes sport one, but Uncle Francis has de luxe version – red flashing lights inset into heart. Terrifying. Had to get up one night to get glass of water and when saw red heart floating in darkness of hall, own heart nearly seized up in chest from fright. They go to Mass every Sunday but other than that, have no idea what they do with their time. I know they went to grand reopening of Bullring. (FYI, Bullring is shopping centre in centre of Birmingham, not actual bullring.) Another big outing – cinema to see *The Da Vinci Code*. (Were quite defensive about it, poor things. 'Is better to be informed about attacks on Catholic church. Was terrible the way Opus Dei was portrayed. Is fine organization, full of fine people, and you don't have to wear that thing on your leg if you really don't want to.')

Eventually conversation meandered to complete halt. My patience expired, said huffy goodbye, snapped phone closed and marched back in to Jem.

'How's your dad?' he asked.

'Emotionally unavailable to me.' (Had learnt this in therapy.) 'You know what, Jem!' Sudden burst of frustration. 'Is no wonder am a bit fucked-up. I mean, look at family I

348

come from – dead mother, depressed father, depressed uncle. All things considered, am actually pretty normal!'

'Yes!' Jem agreed. 'Yes, indeed!'

Jem, loyal friend.

14.12

Bridie made us go for walk on beach – first time since arrived in Knockavoy that I had put foot on beach. Noted with quiet satisfaction Bridie and Barry wearing normal clothing. Then she made us go to pub and drink several drinks to 'make most of weekend'. (Barry forbidden to drink, as driving home.)

Didn't want any alcohol – felt hung-over, quite sick, actually, from quantities consumed the night before – but Bridie shamed me into it. 'Not every weekend your friends visiting from Dublin!'

17.38

Waved off Bridie, Barry, Treese and Jem. Really quite drunk.

'Feel bad leaving you here on your own,' Jem said.

'Will be fine! Glad you're going back. Am destroyed. Do not have constitution for all this drinking and debauchery. Very fond of you all but do not come again for a while.'

Monday, 20 October 10.07

Woke far too early. Felt mildly wretched. Circadian rhythm knocked way off course by weekend of drinking and late nights.

Rang Bridie for chat.

'Why you ringing?' she asked.

'Chat.'

'Chat? Have spent whole bloody weekend with you. Must go now.'

349

She hung up and I stared at phone. 'Feck you, then,' I said.

When stinging feeling had passed, rang Treese. Someone – not Treese – answered, 'Treese Noonan's office.'

'I speak to Treese, please?' Hard to get to talk to her directly. She is important woman.

'Who's calling, please?'

'Lola Daly.'

'What's it in connection with?'

'Latrines.'

Got put straight through. Knew I would. Latrines, magic word.

'Everything okay, Lola?'

'Oh yes, just ringing for chat.'

But Treese also unable to chat.

'Lola, sorry. Crisis here.'

Lots of anguished shouting and howling in background. Every second word seemed to be 'latrines'.

'By the way,' she said, 'you should sleep with that surf boy.'

Then she was gone.

Deflated. Undeniably deflated. Stared gloomily at phone. Considered ringing Jem, but couldn't take another rejection. Then phone rang! Was Jem!

'Hear you are looking for a chat.'

'Ah,' I said. 'Is okay. Urge has gone off me now.'

Kindly, though, very kindly.

14.08

Didn't go to town. Loitering around house, half-heartedly looking for kicks. Jem had brought my post from Dublin: many, many look-books from designers but too painful to study them. At moment too sad to be reminded of non-working status. In desperation, made terrible error of looking through newspapers Jem had left behind. Shouldn't have. Sure enough, on society page, was picture of Paddy and Alicia the horse at opening of some art exhibition.

Terribly upset. Shaking, all of me – the obvious parts like fingers and knees and lips, but also the hidden bits – stomach lining and bladder and lungs. Ferocious pang of longing for my mother. Missed her with frightful hungry force. Wanted to visit her grave and have chat. But couldn't drive to Dublin. Hands shaking too much. Besides was barred.

Had idea. Would go to Knockavoy graveyard, would visit someone else's grave, some woman of similar age to my mother, and talk to her.

15.04

Walking to graveyard in hope that physical activity might help – endorphins, serotonin et al. – but only on road few minutes when car pulled up beside me, lots of glassy clinking noises. Rossa Considine in his eco-mobile. Bad, burny feeling. What did he want?

'Lift into town?' he said. 'Save you walking eighty yards?'

'Not going to town.'

'Where you going?'

'Graveyard.' Didn't go into details. Why should I?

'Can drop you there. Get in.'

Bad, burny feeling. Didn't want to get in. Didn't want to talk other human being (not live one, anyway). Wanted be left with own bad, burny thoughts. But feared if snubbed him, he would know I suspected him of being kidnapper and goggles-wearing oddball, so got in.

Nothing to say to him. Drove in bad, burny silence.

'Why you going to graveyard?' he asked.

'To talk to my mother.'

'She buried here?'

'No. Is buried in Dublin.' Didn't feel like explaining.

'Is that joke?'

'No.'

More silence.

'Why you not at work?' I asked, feeling obliged to be polite because had been offered lift even though didn't want one.

'Day off.'

More silence.

'Chatty,' I said.

He shrugged, as if to say, Kettle calling pot black.

'Where you off to?' I asked without warmth. 'Or is that top-secret too?'

'Recycling place. Bottle bank. Want come?' Sarky smile. 'Breaking bottles might help your mood.'

'What mood? Am in no mood.'

We approached fork in road and slowed down. 'Decision time,' he said. 'What's it to be? Graveyard or bottle bank?'

'Graveyard or bottle bank? No wonder you're such big hit with the girls.'

His fizzog darkened — annoyance? — and quickly I said, 'Bottle bank.'

I mean, why not? What else was I doing? Could save visit to graveyard for tomorrow.

'Spontaneity spice of life,' I said.

'Variety.'

'Excuse me?'

'Variety spice of life. Not spontaneity.'

Cripes above, what a smartarse.

Sat with my back ramrod straight. Wouldn't actually let

352

it touch seat. Felt would be giving in to him if I did. Also keen to find fault with his car. But had to admit that car driven by electricity seemed to function just as efficiently as car fuelled by petrol.

Countryside we drove through all wild and . . . yes, wild. To our left, frenzied Atlantic bashed living daylights out of coast; to our right, barren fields coughed up rocks and the occasional stunted tree.

After while, without comment, Considine put on radio. Programme about Colin Farrell; apparently he used to be a 'travelling line-dancer'.

'Is absurd!' Rossa Considine suddenly broke silence. 'Colin Farrell is hell-raiser. Hell-raisers don't line-dance.'

For once was in agreement.

'And what exactly is travelling line-dancer?' I asked.

'I wonder.' He sounded genuinely interested. 'Does it mean he travelled across the dancefloor or travelled around the country?'

15.24

Bottle bank in place of extreme natural beauty. Can that be right?

'Here.' Rossa Considine handed me box of jingling bottles. 'Start breaking.'

Can tell lot about person from their rubbish. Rossa Considine drank beer, also red wine, but not worrying amount unless this was just weekend's worth of stuff. He cooked with olive oil and soy sauce, took vitamin C supplements and wore aftershave (Cool Water). Mind you, saw nothing that gave any clue as to why he had mystery bride stashed in his bedroom or wore swimming goggles in his kitchen.

Recycling surprisingly gratifying. Obviously is uplifting to help environment, but should never underestimate how enjoy-able it is to break things. Flinging bottles into skips and hearing them shatter into smithereens on impact was exhilarating. Managed to smash away all the bad burriness.

'Should have brought own bottles,' I said. 'Tons after weekend. Friends visiting.'

'Will let you know next time am coming here.'

'Thank you.' Wanted to add something unpleasant like, 'Big of you,' but didn't. No matter what way you looked at it, him offering to bring me to bottle bank didn't count as sarky remark.

18.33

Car parked outside front door, practically *beside* front door. Almost no room for Noel from Dole to open car door without banging into house door. He emerged. Did furtive running-crouch from car to house. Keen not to be seen. Once in house, straightened up and handed over bottle of wine. Unexpected. Nice thought, even if it is rosé.

'Lola, is beautiful boa you are wearing. What is it ... ostrich feather? Oh is gorgeous.' Taken aback. Not used to him being pleasant. 'So where are they? Where are my babies?'

'Here.' Indicated box.

He alighted upon it and reverently unwrapped pair of leopard-skin stilettos in size eleven. Cradled them to him, like newborn lambs. Rubbed them against his foxy face.

I watched anxiously. Had almost irresistible urge to cover eyes. Feared he was going to do some sex act, like wank into them.

As if he read my mind, he said – angrily – 'Am not pervert. All I want to do is wear them.'

He whipped off trainers and socks and rolled trouser legs up to knees. Removed tie and wrapped it around hairline, like scarf thespian lady would wear.

'And for record,' he added. 'Am not gay. Am straight as Colin Farrell.' Second mention of Colin Farrell in one day. What can it mean? 'I have fine-looking wife, who has no complaints, if you get me.'

Gak! Do not like to think of foxy Noel in that way.

Slowly, respectfully, he placed shoes on floor. Sensuously slid one foot into them, then the other. 'They fit! They fit!' Cinderella moment.

Paraded back and forth across slate floor. 'Love the sound the heels make,' he said happily. Further clattering ensued.

'Oh there's my bus! Wait! Don't go without me!' he squealed, breaking into ludicrous 'run', kicking up heels behind him, as high as his bum. 'Oh thank you, Mr Driver, for waiting for me.' Hand placed at throat in coquettish fashion. 'You've made this lady very happy.'

Cripes.

'Where can I change?' he demanded, back to his man's voice.

Change?

'Change into my dress.'

Dress?

'Yes, my dress!' Tapped his briefcase in exasperated fashion.

Oh God. 'You have trannie clothes in briefcase?'

'Cross-dressing, cross-dressing, I am sick telling you.'

Didn't want him to change into dress. Wanted him to leave. But couldn't say that because feared he would think was judging him. But not judging him for being trannie. Simply didn't like him.

355

'Change in kitchen.' Didn't want him going upstairs. Boundaries already shot to hell.

19.07

He disappeared into kitchen, coyly shutting door. I sat on couch and waited. Quite miserable. Had got self into tight spot. Not sure how it happened.

Had all started when he said to me that night in pub in Miltown Malbay, 'Can you keep a secret?'

I had answered, 'No. Cannot keep mouth shut. Am famous for lack of discretion.'

Not true. Simply didn't want to keep *his* secret. Whatever it was, it would bind me to him in some heinous fashion.

But he didn't care. He needed confessor. 'I like wear ladies' clothes.'

Hadn't known quite what to say. Settled for, 'I like wear ladies' clothes too.'

'Yes, but you are lady.'

'So you are trannie?'

'Cross-dresser.'

Trannie, cross-dresser, is all the one, no?

'You don't really have girlfriend?' I asked.

'No.'

'Those size eleven shoes for you?'

'Yes.'

(Had *known* he couldn't have both wife and girlfriend. Lucky to have even one woman.)

Over course of next hour, got his life story. Had lusted after women's clothes since late teens. When he had house to himself – only happened rarely – he tried on wife's make-up and underwear. But not her clothing – 'too dowdy'.

Over the years he had assembled one outfit of his own –

dress, accessories, wig, make-up but no shoes – was making do with open-toed slingbacks in size 8, biggest he could get, but toes and heels stuck out over edges and were painful to walk in. He kept outfit in bag in boot of his car. Lived in terror of wife finding it.

Then watershed: went to Amsterdam for stag weekend. Slipped away from companions. Found trannie shop. Had time of life trying on shoes that fitted him, wide choice underwear, negligees, frocks. 'Never knew it could feel so wonderful!' Bought large quantity of merchandise, but after leaving shop, lost his nerve. Feared airport customs man might do random search on his bag – in front of all his pals. Shame would kill him. Decided dispose of stuff. Walked around Amsterdam for hours. Eventually threw purchases into canal – littering. When got back to hotel, mates demanded know where he'd been. He had to lie and say he had gone with prostitute. Mates scandalized. Atmosphere strained for remainder of weekend.

Back home, Noel couldn't settle. Friends giving him wide berth for prostitute offence. But far worse, couldn't shake memory of how he had felt while twirling before mirror in trannie shop. 'For that short time I was my true self. Awoke something in me. Tried bury it, but couldn't. And then you walk into office and say you are stylist!'

'. . . Er . . . yes . . . but you don't need me. I'm sure you can get trannie clothing on internet.'

'Can't get it on internet. Can't look at sites at work. They could check. Even if erase, it stays on hard drive. And even if could look at sites in anonymous internet café far from Ennistymon hinterland, cannot have stuff delivered to home. Wife would see. Would open parcels.'

'Even though addressed to you?' His wife has nerve.

'Well, maybe she wouldn't open, but she would drive me up

wall, asking what was in parcel, who was it for, could she see
it . . . She would break me down.'

I had sudden thought. 'Would it be so bad if she knew?'

'Jesus!' He buried fizzog in hands. 'Don't even want to
think about it! No one must know! I have three young children.
I am respected in community. I am taking massive risk telling
you all this.'

'All right, keep pants on.'

Then thought, Pants. Wonder what kind he's wearing right
now. Gak! Gakgakgak!

Somehow ended up agreeing to order trannie catalogues
for him. When first one arrived – for specialist shoes – he
got me to order pair leopard-skin stilettos. 'Cannot put it
on my credit card. Dervla will notice.'

Dervla (wife) sounded like absolute harridan.

Had to pay with my credit card – frankly, lucky it didn't
get declined, considering state of finances – and delivery
address was Uncle Tom's cabin. In fairness to Noel from
Dole, he reimbursed me in cash on the spot.

(Hard thing to admit, but not keen on transvestism. Don't
want to stop them doing it, not at all, but find it a bit . . .
Put it this way, wouldn't have liked if Paddy did it. The
thought of him in women's underwear and lipstick, trying to
be alluring . . . He'd look . . . Actually feel sick thinking about
it . . . Oh no. Now am trannie-hater as well as racist. Am
learning all kinds of unpleasant things about self since came
to Knockavoy.)

19.22

'Da-dah!' Proudly and shyly Noel emerged from kitchen, wearing short, stretchy, orange and black leopard-skin dress,
elbow-length leopard-skin evening gloves and – of course –

the leopard-skin shoes. By look of things, he likes leopard skin. (Have often found that redheads do.) Fishnet tights, Tina Turner wig, badly applied make-up. His look quite trashy. All a little *obvious*. Less is more, often find. But say nothing. He has his look, is working it.

Also do not want to engage with him and prolong his presence here.

'I'm Natasha,' he said, in 'lady' voice. 'Do you have my new catalogues?'

'. . . Er . . . yes . . . here.'

'Let's have little drinky. Little tipple.'

Stared at him. Did not want to have little drinky. Apart from being poisoned after weekend, this was veering further and further into realm of nightmare.

'The wine I brought,' he said impatiently. 'Open the wine.'

Oh. Was not gift for me. Was for him. Well, for *Natasha*.

Opened bottle. Poured him glass. He sipped at wine and perused new catalogues in leisurely fashion, legs crossed, as if at hairdresser's. Shapely pins. Long, slender, not very hairy and what hairs there were, were pale ginger-coloured. Many a woman would be proud.

I watched. Anxious. How much longer was he going stay? I had plans for evening. (Sea wall, Mrs Butterly, etc.)

He looked up. 'Have you any snacks?'

'Snacks? Like what?'

'Cheese straws.'

'Cheese straws? Where would get cheese straws in Knockavoy?'

'Okay. Any crisps? Peanuts?'

'Probably not.'

'Check.'

Grumpily went to kitchen. Located half-bag of greasy peanuts in back of press.

'Found peanuts, but God knows how long they've been —'

'Put them in bowl — nice bowl — and offer them to me.'

Muttering to self, 'What your last slave die of?' returned to kitchen and tipped them into dish, but not very nice one, just out of spite.

'Peanut, Noel?'

'Natasha.'

'Peanut, Natasha?'

'Oh cannot! Watching figure!'

'But you just asked for them!'

Then understood. Was fiction. Obliged to join in. 'But you have gorgeous figure, Natasha. You did not have dessert all week and you did Bums, Tums and Thighs class this morning.' Getting carried away. Feeling mildly hysterical. 'Be naughty girl. Have peanut. And another little drinky!'

Sloshed more rosé into his glass.

'Oh! You are very bold! Will have another drink if you will join me.' Wicked twinkle in his eye — so much blue eye shadow! 'Go on, Lola, one little drinky won't kill you.'

Is this way girls behave? Is this what he sees?

Accepted little drinky. Quite grateful for it at this stage.

'Okay, Lola, can you order me these two sexy frocks — I have ticked them. Also baby-doll negligee, in black and in pink.'

Heart sank. Relationship not at an end. Also, he has such terrible taste.

'Can leave my new shoes here?' he asked. 'Too good to throw into boot of car.'

'But what is use of them if they live here?' Anxiety ratcheting up!

'I can visit them. We could arrange regular time. Like every Friday evening. Wife thinks I go out for few jars after work. Could come here instead.'

Officially in grip of paralysing fear. Do not want regular arrangement with Noel from Dole! 'But this is not my house! And I could return to Dublin at any moment!'

He frowned. Not happy with that. 'You will have to report change of address immediately. As soon as leave jurisdiction, no more payments from County Clare.'

'Yes, know all that.' Had been explained to me until was blue in face.

'Anyway you don't look sane enough to return Dublin yet. Look at cut of you.'

Yes. Favourite outfit. Pyjamas, wellingtons, feather boa.

Regretted feather boa. Feather boa gives people wrong idea. Feather boa is badge of true eccentric.

'From now on, Friday night is girly night!' he decreed. 'Okay, Lola?'

'Will have to square it with Tom Twoomey, owner of this house.'

'Square what? You are simply having friend over for drink.'

'Yes, but . . .'

'Simply having friend over for drink,' he repeated. 'Okay, Lola? We agreed about that?'

Miserably nodded head. No choice. Looks like relationship with Noel from Dole set to run for some time. Unhappy. Really don't like him.

But – as already observed – he has expedited welfare payments with unprecedented speed. He owns me.

20.58

As soon as sound of Noel's car had died away, I decided I didn't care if he owned me. I rang Bridie and explained trannie situation. 'Uncle Tom needs to be told,' I said. 'Is violation of his home. Is likely he'll put foot down and insist on immediate cessation of trannie activities on these premises.'

'Uncle Tom very easy-going.'

'Is likely he will be scandalized,' I said. *'Scandalized!'*

'Isn't,' Bridie replied. 'You sleep with surf boy yet?'

Tuesday, 21 October 10.38

Message on phone. SarahJane Hutchinson. Sounded hysterical. Has had 'disagreement' with Nkechi. SarahJane had given in, and tried Nkechi, but now worst fears realized.

'Is just not working!' she screeched. 'Nkechi not nice, not nice like you. As for that Abibi . . .'

Couldn't help warm glow.

'I can't cope! Going to four charity balls. Can't do it on my own! Those charity-circuit bitches will be looking and laughing at me!'

Sadly, is true. SarahJane not paranoid or with over-inflated sense of self-importance. True, true, true.

'Lola, I need you. Am flying to New York to see you. Where you staying? The Pierre? The Carlyle?'

These rich people! Even nice ones like SarahJane! They haven't clue.

Could not afford single night at either those establishments, never mind open-ended stay.

Rang SarahJane. Knew shouldn't. Part of bargain with Nkechi. But common decency dictated that should.

'Lola, oh Lola, you are lifesaver!' Pitifully grateful to hear from me. 'Cannot work with that Nkechi! And cannot get other stylist to take me on at such short notice. Am coming to see you.'

'Am not in New York.'

'Wherever you are, will come. Will come to Outer Mongolia.'

'Is further. Am in County Clare.'

'In Ireland? But that is no problem. Will drive to you.'

'But it's on west coast, you live on east.'

'With Kildare bypass it takes no length of time.'

Another Kildare bypass person! Should put her in touch with Bridie. They could set up a club.

Talked through SarahJane's needs. Promised would call in gowns, shoes, jewellery, evening bags. Would have to blow my cover, but what the hell? What is so bad about being in County Clare as opposed to New York?

Nkechi, paranoid.

12.05

Rang Marilyn Holt, lovely buyer in Frock (best shop in Ireland, in my opinion).

She exclaimed, 'Is that Lola?'

'Yes, yes.' Briskly explained my situation – to wit: living temporarily in Knockavoy.

'Thought you were in New York.'

'Yes, well, am in County Clare now.'

'Of course,' she said discreetly, 'of course. No need for details.'

Marilyn Holt, very kind woman. Very kind.

Obvious that everyone knows my tragic story. No secrets in this small country. Brief bad, burny feeling.

However, when ended call, with Marilyn promising to send tons stuff, felt quietly pleased. Just goes to show, can still pull rabbit out of hat. Am still force to be reckoned with.

13.12

Knockavoy graveyard

After much searching and tripping over slabs obscured by rampaging weeds, and reading of headstones, found perfect one. Katie Cullinan, died 1897 at age of thirty-nine, same age Mum had been. Would do nicely for while I was in Knockavoy. Pulled up couple of weeds – grave overgrown and mossy, and headstone patchy with discoloration – and had lovely little chat with Mum. Lovely little chat in my head, not out loud, I should add. No one there to see me, but not taking chances.

15.01

Walking home from graveyard
Phone rang. It was Bridie.

'I spoke to Uncle Tom about your trannie,' she said.

'What he say?' Was agog. 'Was he scandalized?'

'He says so long as no one breaks the toaster again, he doesn't care what you do.'

'But did you tell him Noel is wearing women's clothing and make-up and . . . and . . . underwear and everything?'

'Yes, yes! He doesn't mind! He says let he who is without sin cast the first stone. He says trannies are miserable poor divils and what harm are they doing.'

'. . . I see, I see, I seeeeeee . . . Uncle Tom very kindly man . . .'

Unwelcome news.

Wednesday, 22 October 4.18 (estimated time)

Had strangest dream. Was line-dancing with Rossa Considine and Colin Farrell. We were in front row, many, many other line-dancers behind us. We were demonstrating because we were the best. Heel, toe, heel, toe, skip to other foot, heel, toe, heel, toe, thumbs stuck through belt loops. Could even hear song in dream: 'Achy Breaky Heart'. Wearing red stetsons, embroidered shirts and cowboy boots. In dream I was *brilliant* line-dancer, knew all the moves and traversed floor on winged feet. Then it became competition. (Dreams no respecter of believable plot-lines. Like soaps in that respect.) Rossa Considine won first prize. Colin Farrell poor loser: accused him of cheating. Accused him of doing wrong kind of 'travelling'.

14.13

Internet café

Miracle! Place open. Cecile within with Zoran, her 'little turtle dove', and Jake the Love-God.

Cecile leapt up when saw me. "Allo, Lola, by gor but you're thriving. Zoran, come wiz me. We 'ave to see man about a dog.'

She whisked Zoran – dark-haired, dark-eyed, good-looking boy – from premises, leaving me alone with Jake.

He watched them leave, then said, 'Lovely girl but has subtlety of elephant.'

His voice so low that had to study his delicious mouth as he spoke, almost like lip-reading. But charmed by his observation.

Realization: had decided that, as result of extreme good looks coupled with surf-boy lifestyle, he might be bit stupid. Perhaps had judged too hastily?

Question for him. 'Jake, why you called Jake?'

'Short for Jacob.'

'Jacob? You Jewish?'

'No.'

'From strange religious family where you all named after biblical characters?'

'You mean like Dingles in *Emmerdale*?' (Dingles, family in soap opera where all members named Shadrack, Cain, Charity and similar.) 'No. My mum ate lots Jacob's cream crackers when pregnant with me. For months couldn't keep anything else down. Out of gratitude, called me Jacob. Says I wouldn't be here if wasn't for them.'

You see? Too much information. Already Love-God myth dissolving. He watches soaps and his lovely sexy name has been inspired by cream cracker!

Thursday, 23 October 11.08
Took delivery of big box of beautiful clothes from Niall, the heavy-set, chatty DHL man. Thought would never get rid of him.

Gazed at box. Excited. Full of anticipation. Old juices flowing.

Tore open box. Sudden rush of bad, burny feeling. What were these rubbish dresses? Marilyn Holt sending me dregs! Am not a force to be reckoned with at all! I am joke of stylist, fit only to receive non-couture, man-made-fibre rubbish!

Devastated. Frankly devastated.

Took second look. Not lovely dresses from Frock, but tacky trannie things for Noel. Phew!

18.38
Walking into town for evening's activities
Passing Rossa Considine's gate. He was putting something in his eco-swot car. Gave him curt nod. Received curt nod in reply.

Then remembered my dream. 'Hey,' I said, word out of mouth of its own volition.

Considine looked up. Approached me at gate.

'Just remembered,' I said. 'Had mad dream the other night. Dreamt you and I were line-dancing with Colin Farrell.'

'Oh? Oh! Must have been after thing on car radio!'

'Yes. And we were brilliant.'

'Were we?' Looked very taken with this.

'You won first prize and Colin Farrell very sore. Accused you of cheating. Said you did wrong kind of travelling.'

'What is right kind of travelling?'

'Don't know. It was only dream. Not mystic line-dancing lesson. But, all same, very real dream. Could even hear the song: "Achy Breaky Heart".'

He winced. 'Will hear that song in head for next week. Thanks, Lola.'

So cranky.

Next time I dream about him, will not let him win any prizes.

Friday, 24 October 11.09

Niall from DHL – again. This time delivering real dresses. Cripes, the beauty, the beauty, the unbearable beauty. The fabrics, the cut, the detailing. Billowing yards of ivory silk, as lustrous as water; layered skirts in crunchy taffeta; black satin bodices, winking light.

Could have wept for their beauty.

Have missed work more than realized.

16.35

Phone rang. Noel from Dole. Why was he calling? Could only be to cancel!

'Will be over around seven,' he said. Not cancelling! 'Don't forget snacks. Set up mirror in kitchen and put my new clothes in there. And I have little surprise. Am bringing friend.'

'Friend?'

'Yes, found him in internet chat room. He lives only nine miles away. Told him about you and the safe house —'

Safe house!

'Noel, you cannot bring other trannie!'

'Why not?'

Spluttered, 'Why not? This isn't even my house.'

'Is your address for welfare purposes. Anyway doing nothing wrong. Just friends calling round for little drinky. See you at seven.'

Paced. Actually paced. Very distressed. Would have wrung hands if I knew how. Wondered if this was actually illegal? Do you need licence to have gathering of trannies?

19.03

Noel whipped past me, pulling other man into the kitchen. Brief impression of rough-hewn mortification, then the door slammed shut. Much chat and giggling from behind the door.

19.19

Noel emerged looking pretty slinky in his new finery — black spandex tube dress — but other bloke — Blanche — could never pass for woman: a big, solid lump with mile-wide face; mouth a red gash; thick swipes of foundation; visible stubble; Margaret Thatcher wig; old-fashioned mauve tweed suit (at front of skirt, his man-bump clearly visible) and pale pink blouse — exact colour of band-aid — with pussy-bow tied crookedly, just underneath super-sized Adam's apple.

Shook hands with me — his paws enormous and rough as sandpaper. Some sort of manual worker?

'Am grateful to be welcomed into your home,' he muttered, with shy smile and thick, thick culchie accent.

'Not actually my home,' I said quickly.

'Is for moment,' Noel threw over his spandex-covered shoulder, lady-walking back to kitchen to open wine. 'Is where dole money sent.'

Rubbing nose in it constantly!

'Take seat, please.' Indicated couch to Blanche. 'Snack?'

'No,' he whispered to the floor. He sat with legs wide apart, shovel-sized hands hanging over his knees.

Felt uncomfortable. Blurted out, 'Where you get your suit?'

'Me mother's, God be good to her.'

'Is gorgeous ... um ... colour.' I mean, had to say something.

'Time for little drinky!' Noel dispensed glasses of rosé. Couldn't help but notice mine had far less than theirs. Was not worthy of full drink because was not trannie.

'Cheers, m'dear,' Noel said, clinking glasses with Blanche. 'Bottoms up, girls.'

Bad, burny feeling. Felt like telling Natasha that no woman I know would ever say, 'Bottoms up.'

'That's a mighty frock you're wearing, Lola,' Blanche said shyly. '... Is it Dior?'

Actually was! Vintage, of course, could never afford first-hand price, but impressed. 'Is Dior!'

''Tis a work of art,' he muttered. 'A work of art.'

'Mint dress,' Natasha agreed, trying to muscle in.

'How you know it's Dior?' I asked.

'Just knew,' Natasha said.

'Not you!' Couldn't hide irritation. 'Blanche.'

'Read a lot of books about style. In secret, of course.'

'Really? And have you been ... dressing ... in ladies' clothes ... for long?'

'All me life, Lola, all me life. Since I was a gorsoon.' ('Gorsoon' culchie word, means 'little boy'.)

Fascinating. 'And did your parents know?'

'Oh yes. Every time they caught me, my father'd belt me black and blue.' Curiously upbeat delivery. 'But couldn't help meself, Lola. Tried a million and one times to stop. Have suffered desperate shame.'

Chattier than he'd originally seemed.

'And what are your current circumstances ... er ... Blanche? Married?'

'I am indeed.'

'And does your wife know?'

Heavy pause. 'I tried telling her. She thought I was trying to tell her I was homosexual. She reared up on me. 'Twas easier to leave it be ... But it's been hard. I've been living a lie, Lola, living a lie. Then Natasha told me I could come here. 'Twas a lifeline, nothing less than a lifeline. I was thinking I couldn't go on. I was thinking of putting a rope around me neck.'

'You mean ... you were going to kill yourself?'

He shrugged. 'I'm terrible lonely.'

Oh cripes! Feared I might cry.

'I love beautiful things,' he said. 'Sometimes I want to wear them. Does that make me a beast?' (Pronounced 'bayshte'.)

'No. No, not at all!'

'I'm not a ... pervert, a ... a ... deviant. It's nothing at all to do with sex. I'd be happy enough just watching telly in my outfits.'

'Of course!'

'Natasha says you'll help me order clothes and shoes from catalogues?'

Cripes. Swallowed spasm of terror. But I felt for this poor man. I wanted to help. I *could* help.

19.37–20.18
Noel modelled his new clothes, including pink baby-doll nightie and matching knickers.

Difficult to endure.

20.19–20.40
Enthusiastic discussion of gorgeous frocks on *Strictly Come Dancing*. Had not seen it due to lack of telly so could not join in.

20.41–22.10
Noel noisily flicked through *Vogue* and criticized all the models, calling them 'fat bitches'.

Blanche scoured trannie catalogues. Dismissed most dresses as 'too racy' but stabbed a horny finger at navy shift dress and dignified lambswool cardigan. 'Classic.'

'Yes,' I agreed. 'Streamlined. Would be nice on you.' Had sudden idea! 'Could I perhaps make suggestion ... ? You won't be offended? If you wore pearl choker around neck would cover Adam's apple.'

'Not offended in slightest.'

'And maybe navy pumps with little bit of heel?'

'Yes.'

'And . . . again, hope you won't be offended . . . but special underwear to preserve your modesty?' Meant, To tuck in your man-bits so they won't be poking out through your navy dress. He understood. No offence taken. Pleased, in fact.

When selection finalized, he produced pencil, licked it, totted up cost, shoved pencil behind ear, opened ante-diluvian handbag, took out huge dirty-looking wedge of fifty-euro notes, peeled off several and slapped them into my hand as if he had just bought prize bullock from me.

'You've given me too much money,' I said.

'For your trouble.'

Noel looked up, flint-eyed, from magazine. 'You have to declare all income,' he said sharply.

'Isn't income,' Blanche said. 'Is present.'

Felt uncomfortable. Many worries. Was Blanche bribing me to be nice to him? Was I running business from Uncle Tom's cabin? Where would it all end?

22.15

Evening drew to a close. Blanche had to leave. Is dairy farmer. Has sixty head of cattle and has to get up at 5 a.m. to milk them. Blanche is man of means.

'Can I come again next Friday?' he asked.

'Yes, and every Friday,' Noel replied.

'You are decent woman,' Blanche said to me. 'I've felt so alone.'

22.30

Walking into town

Chilly night but warm glow. Fashioned plan. (Pun.) If Uncle Tom agreeable to let not just one but two trannies into his home, then I would help them. Well, actually didn't want to help Noel, didn't like Noel at all, would do bare minimum for him. But this poor Blanche creature. Would give make-up lesson — appalling the way he just slapped it on, like he was whitewashing a wall. Would teach him how to accessorize. Would give lessons in deportment. Had spent my life trying to make women beautiful. No different now just because women were men.

Sudden charming idea — would get nice film for us to watch next Friday. Nice, clothes-based film. Would be doubly wonderful if it could also be revenge film. Would put it to Brandon. A challenge.

0.12

Hmmm. Walking home. Decided cut down to sea route instead of up main street. Justification? None. Just wanted to ... see ... surf boys' house but, as approached, it was in darkness. Deflated.

Stood outside for moment, staring up at top window, watching for flickering of candles. Was he up there?

Nothing. Below me, sea sucking and crashing. Turned to carry on my way when heard someone say in low pitch, voice undercutting rush of waves, 'Lola.'

Startled. It was Jake, sitting on window sill, his legs crossed. Could hardly see him, just occasional glint of silver as light from sea caught his eyes.

'What you doing sitting here in the dark?' I asked.

'Listening to the sea.' Beat. 'Thinking about you.' Beat. 'And here you are.'

All senses leapt to full alert, like animal in danger. Didn't matter that he had been named after cream cracker — fingertips tingled, nipples jumped to attention, suddenly aware of my cotton knickers.

'What you doing?' he asked. His voice . . . so affecting.

'Going home.'

'Not any more. Come here.'

Considered it. What would happen if did?

'Only one way to find out,' he said, reading my mind.

Took three steps towards him and when was close enough he unwrapped his legs and used them to quickly pull me to him. Suddenly close enough to smell the salt, the sweat. Mildly shocked at his nearness. Hadn't been prepared for it. Our faces on a level, his silvery eyes locked on to mine, his legendary mouth six inches away.

He squeezed his legs even tighter so my feet had to shuffle closer to him. Went with it. His hands resting on my shoulders, pulling me nearer still. Slight smile twitching his lips up at corners. Challenge? Admiration?

Didn't know what to do with my arms. Then decided, What the hell? Am grown woman. Slid them around his neck.

'That's more like it.' Staring at his mouth. 'Listen to the sea,' he whispered. 'Close your eyes and listen.'

Shut eyes. Suck and hiss of sea instantly louder. Sound of Jake's breathing. Then, shock! Shock of his touch, as felt tip of his tongue on my mouth. Slowly, achingly slowly, he ran it along my bottom lip. God, was nice. God, was really nice. With agonizing pleasure, tip of his tongue eventually reached corner of my mouth and along top lip in dizzying circle of swollen nerve endings. Then proper hot-monkey kissing.

'Come inside,' he said, low and warm, into my ear.

Thought of the magic bedroom. Thought of all that could happen if I stepped over the threshold.

A rush of panic. He was too near. Too much man-ness that wasn't Paddy.

374

Tore self from embrace, like attention-seeking type in melodrama. 'No, cannot.'

'Oh Lola!' Sounded annoyed, but as I hurried up road, he didn't follow.

Was glad. Shouldn't have gone there. Shouldn't have kissed him. Distressed. Love-God offering me sex. On a plate! And lost nerve at final hurdle. Is all fault of Paddy de Courcy. Has ruined me for normal sex with other men!

Unpleasant thought. In addition to being racist and trannie-disliker, am now also prick-tease.

Trip down memory lane

Paddy so different from all others. Large man. Naked, he looked even larger. Hairy chest. When it came to sex, very focused. Eyes gleaming. Game-player. Inventive imagination. Liked props.

After first date, wanted another. Had gone from being doubtful about his cheesiness to being utterly in thrall. All wanted to do was sleep with him again. Every time closed eyes, saw him leaning over me, slick with sweat, just the way had imagined in graveyard.

Tried to ask Mum about it, but got no answering voice in my head. So called for summit meeting in restaurant with Bridie, Treese and Jem. Told them the whole story: the car, the shop, the underwear, the further underwear, the lust and the rush to my flat to have frenzied sex. At start of story, they oohed and aahed in surprise and appreciation, but as story unfolded, they became quieter. By time finished narration, table silent. Three pairs of eyes slid from my gaze. No one spoke. Sudden regret at having told them.

'. . . Um . . .' I spread fingers and studied butter knife.

Bridie spoke out. 'I have lived too sheltered a life!' she

declared with unexpected bitterness. 'Am jealous of you, Lola, yes, admit it, jealous.'

'God,' Jem muttered. 'Am really horny. Think I might have to go home. Sorry.'

'If that's what happens on a first date with Paddy de Courcy,' Treese said, 'what will the rest be like?'

Jem's eyes lit up. 'Be sure to tell us, Lola.'

Treese wasn't amused. 'Lola, don't do anything you don't want to.'

(And did I ever? Well, maybe hadn't wanted to in the first instance, but sooner or later always changed mind.)

Second date with Paddy began mundanely enough: Spanish John collected me from flat and after time spent in Dublin gridlock, drew up outside some unremarkable Georgian house. He made quiet call saying we were outside, then nondescript door opened and murmury gent escorted me to inner sanctum. Many red-plush booths. Realized was in private club, not ordinary restaurant. Suspected game would feature heavily on menu.

Staff – all men – dropped their eyes carpetward in elaborate show of discretion as I approached.

Paddy already waiting in high-backed booth, marking up some document with red pen. Felt teeniest wobble at his bouffy hair, then skewered by his blue, blue eyes, like human kebab, and was lost.

'This place! What a production!' I was laughing as sat down. 'Bet if waiters saw something they shouldn't, they would happily gouge their eyes out if you asked them.'

'Is somewhat over the top,' Paddy admitted.

'Aged demographic,' I said, looking around.

'Yes. Fear might get gout if spend too long here, but at least can relax. No danger of getting photo in paper.'

Personally would have no problem getting photo in paper, but refrained from saying so. Didn't want him to think was with him for fame and fortune.

Menu much as expected. 'Venison! Roast woodcock! Look at these things! Gammon and pineapple! Blast from the past! My mother used to make this when was little girl. Think will have it for old times' sake.'

Paddy ordered for me – how objectionable! But he said the waiters couldn't hear women, they were like aural eunuchs.

'Tell me about your day,' he said.

Began account of magazine shoot, feeling – ever so slightly – like child recounting day's activities at school.

'Is that what you always wanted to do? Styling?'

'Cripes, no. Had far loftier ambitions to be designer but didn't work out.'

He fell silent, seemingly lost in thought. Suddenly he refocused, fixing me once more with those blue headlamps. 'You think it changed direction of your life, your mother dying so young?'

'Don't know. Suppose can never know. Don't know if I ever had talent to be designer. Maybe with her encouragement, could have done better . . . Who knows? Perhaps I might be better at being happy. How about you?'

Stared into middle distance. Spoke slowly. 'Yes, might be better, like you say, at being happy. When parent dies when you're still young, you know the worst can happen. You lose that innocence, that faith in happy endings. See world in far bleaker way than others. You know what really gets me?' he said. 'The way people always complaining about their mothers!'

'Yes! People going on that mother is naggy nag, forever

asking why you're not married yet to nice man with good pension plan.'

'Or laughing at her for cooking old-fashioned dinners like stew and chops. They would want to do without mother for a while, then they would be damn glad of chop!'

Also discovered we had absent fathers. In way, we were both orphans!

'Mine lives in Birmingham,' I said.

'Mine might as well live in Birmingham.'

'Why?'

'He is waste of space!' Said dismissively. Then slight edge of bitterness. 'Never see him.' Paddy, sensitive man. You would never guess he was such perv.

Meal lengthy. A never-ending saga of cheese trolleys and port and Armagnac. Kept being offered more and more things. Getting slightly desperate by time bill finally appeared in fat, red, leather folder. Man who delivered it so obsequious, almost crawling on his stomach.

'I will get this,' I said.

Paddy indicated no. Whispered into ear, 'If woman tried pay here, shock would kill them. They still think women not allowed rent telly in own name. Will you come back to mine?'

Startled by sudden change of subject and mood. Rallied gamely. 'My place nearer.' But was curious to get a look at where he lived.

Not that got much of chance. As soon as arrived, I went to bathroom and when emerged, heard Paddy calling from another room, 'Lola. In here.'

Followed his voice. Pushed open door. Not living room, as expected, but bedroom.

Paddy lying across his bed, entirely naked, reading some-thing. A magazine. Photographs. I got closer. Suddenly

378

stopped. Aghast. It was porn. Then saw his erection, enormous and purple, springing up from dense, dark pubic hair.

Recoiled. Insulted. Immediately wanted to leave.

'Don't go.' He laughed. Actually laughed. 'You'll enjoy this.'

'No, I won't,' I said.

But although wounded, was curious. Even a little ... aroused.

He patted the bed. 'Come and look.'

I didn't move. My legs couldn't decide what to do.

'Come on,' he urged. 'You'll love this.'

Some part of me couldn't help but believe him. Gingerly approached the bed and sat primly on the edge.

'Look,' he said. 'Look at her.'

The pages were open on picture of Asian girl with long black hair and large breasts. 'Isn't she beautiful?'

I hesitated. Then, 'Yes.'

He was lying on his side, his hand on himself. Realized he was masturbating slowly. Aghast again.

Asked me, 'Would you like to fuck her?'

'No!'

'No? I would.'

His hand moving faster. Faster and faster. He was sweating now, his eyes open, watching me.

'I'd love to see you and her in bed together,' he said.

I felt jealous and sullied and queasy and, against better judgement, oh-so-turned-on.

'I'm going to come,' he told me, his voice thick. 'I'm going to come.'

'Don't!' I said sharply.

I slapped his hand away from himself, picked up the magazine and tossed it across the room.

'Don't come until I say so! Where are the condoms?'

'In there,' he said, with wild eyes.

Wrenched open drawer, found condom, got it on, fastest had ever got one on anyone, grabbed his erection like gear lever and slid down onto him, the first waves of pleasure already starting to break.

Saturday, 25 October 13.25

Rang Bridie. Told her to tell Uncle Tom that trannies in his home had doubled in number.

'Will inform him. Doubt if he'll mind. You sleep with surf boy yet?'

14.01

Knockavoy graveyard

'Mum, what should I do about the surf boy?'

Damn Bridie for putting thoughts into my head!

Sometimes when I asked Mum a question didn't get an answer right away but this time heard her voice immediately, 'Have bit of fun, Lola. Don't take it too seriously.'

'Why I not take it too seriously? You another one who thinks he too good-looking for me?'

'I do not!' Spluttering. 'You beautiful-looking girl. Can take your pick of the men.'

'Thanks, Mum, but you are my mum, you not exactly impartial.'

'Have bit of fun, Lola,' her voice repeated.

'Can ask you something, Mum?' The worry that sometimes plagued me. 'This isn't just me sitting in graveyard talking to self like a nutter? You are there?'

'Of course am here! Am your mum. Always here, watching out for you.'

15.30

Supermarket

'Challenge for you, Brandon. I need a revenge film featuring very nice clothes.'

15.33

Call from Bridie.

'Uncle Tom says so long as no one breaks the toaster again, he doesn't care what you do.'

So be it.

15.39

Internet café

Located wonderful site which does cosmetics specially formulated for men. Placed generous order. Can afford to because of acute overpayment by Blanche. They promised forty-eight-hour delivery, even to Knockavoy! Exhilarated at thought of turning Blanche from sow's ear into silk purse, if truth be known!

Monday, 27 October 9.45

Arrival of SarahJane Hutchinson from Dublin.

'You are now bi-coastal,' she exclaimed, jumping from car (enormously long Jaguar).

Challenging day trying on gowns, shoes, accessories, trying to assemble four outfits that worked for her. Eventually, despite obstacles (e.g. SarahJane's bloodhound knees; SarahJane's unhealthy attachment to the colour coral), fulfilled brief. Suggested hairstyles and make-up colours to accompany each outfit. Wrote it all down and assured her of phone consultations on the night.

Enjoyed self hugely. Miss work very much.

She gave me massive cheque – to cover costs of outfits – then massive bundle of cash for me. 'Our little secret. What tax man doesn't know needn't worry him.'

Am riddled with cash!

19.07
Mrs Butterly's
Rossa Considine and Ferret-Face sitting at counter enjoying libation. They are 'back on' according to Boss, Moss and the Master. Wished they would leave.

Considine said, 'That song still in my head, Lola.'

'What song?' Then remembered. 'Don't say it!'

Too late. '"Achy Breaky Heart".'

'Thanks,' said gloomily. 'Will now be in my head for next week.'

Tuesday, 28 October 11.39
Niall from DHL arrives to return leftover garments to lovely Marilyn Holt in Dublin.

Wednesday, 29 October 11.15
Male cosmetics arrive by DHL!

Thursday, 30 October 11.22
Blanche's lady-clothing arrives by DHL!

13.15
Noel's new negligees arrive by DHL! Niall the DHL man forgot them on first visit today. Had to make second trip. No longer engaging me in lengthy chats. Quite grumpy, in fact. Excellent!

22.35

Lying on couch, reading damp thriller, when heard strange rattles. Clattering, like very short fall of hailstones. But not hailing outside.

When noise happened again, got off couch, opened front door and peered out into the gloom. There was person out there! A man. Jake. Eyes adjusted to darkness just in time to see him pick up handful of gravel and throw it against upstairs window.

'Why you throwing stones against my window?'

Startled him. 'So you'd let me in.' Said in his characteristic low murmur, couldn't hear actual words, but gathered from rhythm of sentence that was what he said.

'You could simply knock on door.'

He lounged over into the light. Grinned at me. 'More romantic this way.'

Type like him who has affairs with married women must be used to proceeding with subterfuge. Nipping out back windows, hiding in wardrobes, dispensing with doorbells, etc.

Walked towards me in careless sort of way. Stood too close, our bodies almost touching. 'Can I come in?'

Moved aside to let him in. I stood in middle of room and, again, he placed himself right up against me, as though we were trapped together in iron maiden. Smiling, he said, 'I waited lots of nights. You didn't come back to see me.'

'No.'

'Why not?'

'Don't know.' Not being coy. Didn't, in fact, know.

'Are you glad I'm here?'

Thought about it. 'Yes.'

'Can we take up where we left off?'

Thought about it again. 'Yes.'

The kissing, the kissing, the giddying kissing. Slow ascent to bedroom, removing clothing in disorganized tangle, on floor, on stairs, finally in bed.

Couldn't help but compare. Very different body to Paddy's. More tanned, more lithe, less hairy. Unlike Paddy, who always smelt crisp and fresh, Jake slightly smelly. Not unpleasant. Musky in a way that actually smelt of sex.

Great man for different positions; doing it with me lying on my stomach, lying on my side, sitting on top of him, facing towards him, sitting on top of him, facing away from him. With his arm clamped around my waist, me still sitting on him, he cautiously sat up, taking care to ensure he didn't slip out. Both of us sitting on edge of bed, him staring over my shoulder, watching us in the mirror. His hands tight on my hips, he slowly moved up and down in me.

'You're gorgeous,' he muttered to my reflection.

I twisted away. Sick of that sort of stuff. Mirrors and kinkiness. How hard is it to just get a normal shag?

Off we went again, this way, that way, and when he somehow ended up on top of me in missionary position, he seemed surprised. In a big hurry to hoist me up and rearrange me into other pose, but I refused. 'Stay where you are.'

Wanted the weight of a man on me. Grabbed his buttocks so he couldn't go away. Said, 'I like it like this.'

0.12
Lying in each other's arms in the afterglow, Jake asked, 'D'you ever think about the universe?'

'No.'

'About all the people in it and all the things that must have happened before our paths crossed?'

'No.' I yawned.

How sweet. He was trying to do afterplay.

'Is okay,' I said. 'Full marks for not rolling over and going straight to sleep. You are excellent. But no need to talk to me.'

Friday, 31 October 7.38
Another afterglow.

'Golly,' I said. 'Talk about six impossible positions before breakfast.'

Jake hopped out of bed. 'Rampant sex and it's not even eight o'clock.' He gazed out low little bedroom window. 'Tide's in. Gotta go.'

'Bye,' I said sleepily.

He left. Lay in bed and considered. So, had had my first post-Paddy shag. Tip-top mood? No, deep sorrow — if I was having sex with surf boys it really was over. Shed a storm of tears into my pillow.

However, a relief to note that everything still in full working order, emotionally speaking. And otherwise speaking.

10.20
Rang Bridie. 'Had sex with Jake.'

Silence. Then whimpering sound. 'I'm so jealous,' she mewed. 'I'm so jealous. What was it like?'

'He is demon for different positions.'

'Oh!' she howled. 'Now you are just taunting me!'

Throughout day
Good wishes continue to pour in from everyone who has heard about me and Jake.

16.12

Supermarket

Buying treats for trannies for tonight. Mini-rolls and suchlike.

Had question for Kelly and Brandon. Hadn't seen the heartbroken woman traipsing the beach in a while.

'Where is she?' I asked.

'Jennifer? Better,' Kelly said. 'Gone back home. Left all her lopsided pottery behind.'

'She got the ride from Frankie Kiloorie,' Brandon said. 'Put the smile back on her face.'

'Who's he?'

'Lives out the Miltown Malbay road. Carpenter. Good with his hands.' Vulgar snigger.

'Jennifer'd never look at him in Dublin because he hasn't bought new clothes since 2001, but he did the trick all right!'

Ribald laughter from both Brandon and Kelly, but I was uplifted. A victory for one is a victory for all.

'Everyone goes through same thing here,' Brandon said airily. 'Crying, walking the beach, artistic leanings. On home stretch when they get the ride from some horny-handed man of the soil.'

'Or the sea,' Kelly chipped in, waggling her over-plucked eyebrows at me.

'Or the surf!' Brandon actually elbowed me!

Kept face haughty while they descended into snorty laughter. No secrets in this town, no secrets at all.

I cleared throat. Abrupt change of subject. 'Have you got my clothing revenge DVD?'

Brandon pulled himself together and placed a DVD box on counter.

'*Funny Face?*' I asked. 'Since when is *Funny Face* a revenge film? Is Audrey *Hepburn!*'

Brandon didn't speak. Simply placed another DVD on counter. *Unforgiven.*

'Double bill,' he said. '*Funny Face* and *Unforgiven*. Best I can do for you, Lola. No such thing as revenge film about clothing.'

18.59

And here they come. Punctual creatures, trannies.

They dived straight into kitchen where new purchases were laid out.

'Blanche,' I called through shut door, 'if you need help getting into your new underwear, please call me.'

Did not relish thought of having to wrestle Blanche's manhood into submission, but am a professional.

'Also do not apply make-up. Have special stuff for you both.'

Have to say, had unexpectedly pleasant evening. Blanche amenable to my suggestions. Permitted me to dress her in beautiful new clothes, paint her fingernails, demonstrate how to apply a discreet maquillage and give lesson in deportment.

'I'm feeling Jackie Kennedy, in the White House,' I said. 'I'm feeling Jack in the Oval Office, Jackie at his shoulder, wearing simple classic shift dress and single string of unfarmed pearls. I'm feeling perfect hair, low-key lips, super-soft cashmere cardigan.' (Sort of thing you have to say as stylist. Is expected of you.)

Blanche thrilled with my monologue. Quite a different woman by time I finished my work. In fact, she might actually get away with being large-boned, mannish woman. (In light shed by 30-watt bulb.)

We shared bottle of wine, ate one mini-roll between us and waxed lyrical about Audrey Hepburn.

Now and again Noel jumped to his feet and danced around in his trashy party-girl outfit, peevishly saying he wished he could go to a disco. But each to their own.

22.20

Trannies depart. Buoyed up by own goodness decided go to the Oak for quick drink. Walked in. Brandon serving behind the bar. Moment of severe dislocation. Had I entered super-market by accident?

'You're all right,' Brandon called. 'You really are in the pub.'

'Where's . . . ?' Cripes, what was Ol' Prune Eyes' real name? 'Ibrahim.'

'Osama? Night off. Has worked ninety-two days straight without a break.'

'Ninety-two days! And he is always so cheerful.'

'So why begrudge him a few hours in Ennis at the pictures?'

'Am not begrudging, Brandon. Simply surprised.'

23.37

Home

Knock at door. Jake. Quite surprised to see him. Genuinely hadn't expected to again. Him very, very, very sexy. The eyes, the hair, the mouth, the body.

'What you doing here?' I said. 'Another booty call, is it?'

Him offended. 'Is not booty call. I am fucking crazy about you.'

'You talk good game, mister.'

388

Offended again. 'Is no game. Let me show you how serious am.'

Immediate kissing. Joined at lips, backed into house, already removing clothes. Aflame with lust. Thrilling.

Sex, however, frustrating. Would be just starting to get into rhythm and enjoy self when would be picked up, twirled about like majorette's baton and entirely repositioned.

Eventually asked, 'Jake, you on mission to do every position in *Kama Sutra* over two-day period?'

Offended again. 'Just want you to have good time.' Look of sincerity in devastating silvery eyes. Touched. Paddy had been so different, especially towards end. Had forgotten what it felt like for a man to be nice to me.

Finally hit on compromise: no more than four different positions per shag. Everyone happy.

Saturday, 1 November 7.32
Early morning sex, then Jake left to 'catch some waves'.

8.14
Call from Bridie. 'Has he been in touch?'

'Yes, called here again last night, looking for sex.'

She wailed so loudly, my ear tingled.

'Have you been in magic bedroom yet?' she asked.

'No. But might tonight. He is cooking dinner for me.'

13.15
The Oak
Congratulated Ol' Prune Eyes on his first night off in ninety-two days.

'Went to Ennis to movies. Wim Wenders double bill. Immensely enjoyable.'

'Good for you!'

Sudden change in his demeanour. Cleared his throat. Looked down at bar counter, then up again, fizzog set in quite formal expression. 'Ah! Ahem! Lola, perhaps you would accompany me next Friday night? Ingmar Bergman season starting.'

'Friday night? Oh Ibrahim, cannot. Any other night of week, no problem, but not Friday.'

'But Friday night only night off I get. How about following Friday?'

'All Fridays bad, Ibrahim.' Terrible pause. Felt I had to say something. Picking up his loneliness, the fact that he was Egyptian far, far, far from home, in non-Muslim country with peculiar weather systems and ingrained drinking culture.

But what could I say? Cannot come because am hosting trannie party?

Suggestion: 'What if you swapped your night off to a Thursday? Or a Saturday? Or any day other than Friday?'

He shook his head, his pruney eyes mournful. 'Has to be Friday. Only night Brandon can manage the pub. Because only night Kelly's mother can help out in supermarket.'

15.15

Into supermarket to return DVDs. As soon as through door, Brandon fronted me up. 'Hear you wouldn't go to pictures with poor Osama. Is it because you are racist?'

Swallowed hard. 'Am not racist. Am very fond of Osama, but busy Friday nights.'

'Busy with what? Watching DVDs about clothes and revenge?'

Can have no privacy in this town, no privacy at all!

'Why don't you let Osama watch DVD with you? He loves films.'

'Sorry, but cannot be done.'

'Why not?'

Cripes.

16.03
The Dungeon

Not even in it. Just passing it, when Boss yelled out at me, 'Heard you turned down poor Osama. Didn't have you pegged as racist, Lola.'

19.48

Clutching bottle of wine, show up at surf boys' house. Jake opens door but does not permit me to enter. Instead leads me down steps to beach where table and two chairs set up on sand, white cloth snapping in breeze. Candelabra, flowers, small bonfire, wine cooling in bucket, night sky pricked with stars. Standing at discreet distance noticed Cecile and her little turtle dove.

Asked, 'What they doing?'

'Our waiters for evening.'

Couldn't stop laughing. Said, 'This is too much. You are hysterical. You are like fantasy man.'

Evening very chilly but kept warm by bonfire, cashmere blanket wrapped around shoulders and warm glow from within.

'Food delicious,' I said.

'Cecile helped. Well –' slightly shame-faced look – 'Cecile did it all. Cannot cook to save life.'

'Thank God. So you are not entirely perfect.' Then uncontrollable laughter began again.

Eventually repair to magic bedroom – every bit as magical and breathtaking as imagined – where enjoy much four-positions-per-shag sex.

Sunday, 2 November
In magic bed all day.

Monday, 3 November
Ditto.

Tuesday, 4 November
Ditto.

Wednesday, 5 November 16.17
Had to get up and go home. Had responsibilities, to wit: deliveries of trannie clothing. Over last couple of days hadn't cared, not a jot, that Niall the DHL man might be calling with boxes of chicken-fillet bra fillers and glittery sandals in size eleven. Wild and carefree and having such a wonderful time, hadn't given a damn.

Jake wrapped his arms and legs around me and refused to let me go. Was pleasing to push against him and feel his muscles locked hard and tight.

'Have to go,' I said. 'Really. Must. But we could see each other tonight.'

Slight hesitation. Loosening of arms and legs. 'Lola, let's take couple days' breathing space.'

Looked hard at him. Was he dumping me? His silvery eyes gave nothing away, just staring blandly into mine. Cold lurch in pit of stomach. Abruptly, it went; just disappeared. Realized wonderful thing about having been destroyed by Paddy: cannot be hurt by other men.

'Breathing space?' I said. 'Yes, let's.'

Hurried home. Was not going to think about Jake. Other anxieties. Head full of disaster scenarios. What if Niall had left packages of trannie clothing outside front door and they had been half-eaten by cows?

No boxes stacked up against house, but note from Rossa Considine: he was holding three days' worth of deliveries for me.

Looked. His eco-swot car in his driveway. At home.

17.29

Considine uncharacteristically gracious. Helped carry boxes of trannie clothing to my house. (Naturally did not tell him what was in boxes and he did not ask.)

'Owe you drink,' I said.

19.29

Mrs Butterly's

Opportunity to buy Considine drink arrived sooner than expected. Him sitting at Mrs Butterly's counter drinking pint. No sign of Ferret-Face.

Mrs Butterly made me ham sandwich, beckoned me closer and in loud whisper asked, 'Is it true you agreed to marry Osama in the Oak, then reneged on bargain because he is Muslim?'

'What?' Cripes above, was this story still doing the rounds? 'No! No! He asked me to go to cinema – as friends! – but have another standing engagement on Friday nights. That is all!'

'Knew it! Didn't think it could be true! You are nice girl, Lola, that is what I told them.'

'Who?'

'Oh nobody. Just nosy parkers, poking noses into other people's business.'

I cut eyes to Rossa Considine. He was staring into his pint.

He looked up, all injured innocence. 'What?'

'Did you tell Mrs Butterly about me and Osama?'

He shrugged. 'Course not.' Then added – quite unnecessarily, I felt – 'What you get up to is your own business.'

Confused. Just what was he getting at? Jake? Narrowed eyes at him.

'In fairness,' Mrs Butterly murmured, 'it wasn't him.'

Rossa Considine finished his pint in big swallow and swung himself off stool. 'I'm away.'

'Ah stay,' Mrs Butterly urged. 'Don't leave in a temper.'

'Not in temper. Meeting Gillian.'

'Oh well, have enjoyable evening, so.'

1.01
No word from Jake.

Thursday, 6 November 11.15
Bridie rang. 'Has Love-God dumped you yet?'

'Yes.'

'What?'

'He's dumped me.'

'Was only joking. But, sorry, Lola, was bound to happen. He was –'

'Yes, I know. Too good-looking for me.'

'Are you upset?'

I sighed. 'What is life but fleeting moments of happiness strung together on necklace of despair?'

'But are you upset?'

394

'... Is hard to describe. Am sorry I had anything to do with him. Didn't even fancy him to begin with. Now feel ... dunno ... shit. But had been feeling atrocious anyway. Put it this way, don't feel any worse.'

12.11
Frenzied phone call from SarahJane Hutchinson. 'Lola, have met new man –'

'Congratulations.'

'– we are going Sandy Lane for Christmas and New Year and have nothing to wear. Shops full of sparkly red dresses!'

'Relax, relax. Resort-wear.'

'Resort-wear?'

'Yes. Any designer worth their salt does special collection at this time of year for this very purpose. Called resort-wear. Or sometimes Cruise Collection. But don't worry, don't have to be going on cruise in order to wear it.'

Got on blower. Phoned Dublin, London, even contact in Milan.

17.57
The Dungeon
Boss and his crew had just discovered Baby Guinnesses (shot glasses of Kahlua topped with Baileys) and were charmed by them. Bought me unfeasible number. Sickly but potent.

Almost walked by Jake's house on way home. Persuaded self not to.

Despite sweetness of drinks, was quite bitter.

Friday, 7 November 10.23

Weather reflecting mood. Blue skies have finally gone. Grey, misty, drizzly, cold. Uncle Tom's cabin has central heating. Thank God. Couldn't be dealing with coal. Am not a coal person.

14.22

Supermarket

Brandon in state of high excitement. 'Have revenge film about clothing! *Legally Blonde*. Lots of clothes in it and she gets her own back on people.'

Had seen *Legally Blonde* and knew it to be more of a comeuppance film than a pure revenge one, but lavished praise on Brandon. Is good to encourage those who have made effort.

'No, wasn't my discovery,' Brandon admitted. 'Was Osama!'

'Well . . . er . . . will thank him.'

'Why won't you let him come tonight? He is lonely and lives for the movies. Is what you get up to on Friday nights so depraved that he cannot come?'

Couldn't say anything. All twisted up with conflict. Dreadful guilt about Osama but fear of giving away Blanche's secret and Noel stopping my dole . . .

14.44

On way home

Woman I didn't even know shouted across the street, 'Why you not let Osama watch DVDs with you? He is refugee, you know. Have you no Christian charity?'

Called weakly, 'He is not refugee, he has work permit and everything.'

Woman not convinced.

In despair. Everyone hates me.

19.02

Arrival of trannies. I let them get into their glad rags before outlining Osama situation for them.

'Could we change from Friday to another evening?' I suggested. 'Any evening?'

Grim shakes of head. Noel has to do homework with kids and Blanche muttered something about having to get up very early every other day except Saturday. Didn't really understand – maybe cows get lie-in on Saturdays? Life of a farmer alien to me.

'In that case will have to permit Osama to join our little group.'

'No way.' Noel was tight-lipped.

'All of Knockavoy thinks I am a racist! No one can understand my reluctance. Safer to give in. Drawing attention to situation by holding out.'

'I will stop your dole.'

'Do it, then,' I said wearily. At that moment suddenly felt full disappointment of Jake's disappearance. 'Maybe it's time I went back to Dublin. Am sick of all this.'

Blanche scandalized. Started to cry.

Noel also pretty scandalized-looking as he saw his 'safe house' disappear. I experienced – indeed savoured – moment of satisfaction.

Silence all round. Only sound that of Blanche's sobbing. Noel spoke up. 'Can he keep his mouth shut? This Osama chap?'

'Don't honestly know. He seems decent type but it's a chance we have to take.'

Noel and Blanche had lengthy, muttered, head-to-head talk.

'. . . certain could get him deported if he tells on us . . .'

'. . . cannot go back to old life. Need this outlet . . .'

'. . . need never see us in our civvies . . .'

'. . . all day long looking at cows' backsides . . .'

Some sort of resolution finally reached. 'Okay,' Noel said to me. 'Invite him. So long as he doesn't come until after we are changed. We need to keep our identities secret.'

22.56
No word from Jake.

Saturday, 8 November 12.30
The Oak

'Ibrahim, we need to have private chat.'

He looked nervous. 'Never said you were racist, Lola.'

'Never thought you did. As you probably know, from Brandon, I hold . . . club . . . on Friday nights in my house.'

'The revenge film club!'

'Er, yes.' In a way. 'You are welcome to join us. Only condition of membership — and you must tell NO ONE, not now, not ever — is that you have to dress up like a lady.'

Long pause. Eventually Ibrahim spoke. 'In order to join your film club, I would have to dress up in women's clothing?'

'And keep it secret.'

He thought about it. 'Very well.'

'Very well?'

'Very well.'

Very well . . .

0.16
No word from Jake.

Sunday, 9 November All day
No word from Jake.

Monday, 10 November 11.17
Arrival of SarahJane's resort-wear. Swimsuits, beach-wraps, filmy kaftans, palazzo pants, towering wedges, whimsical sunhats, massive sunglasses and many, many DVFs. (Diane Von Furstenberg wrap-dresses. Can't go wrong.)

So many adorable pieces. Prada beach bag, adorned with seahorses. Best bit – matching seahorse-encrusted sandals! Turquoise Lisa Bruce swimsuit with coordinating wrap-around. Raspberry-coloured Gucci sunglasses and vertiginous wooden-soled mules in same colour. Blindingly bright hues, wonderful antidote to dismal grey grip of winter.

Niall from DHL officially hates me. Says he is doing Ennistymon to Knockavoy drive so often, he is actually dreaming about it. After I signed for parcels he stared out at waves and said, 'If never see that fecking view again, it'll be too soon.'

Still no word from Jake.

Tuesday, 11 November 19.07
Frenzied knocking on front door. Jake!

No. Considine.

'Quick, quick!' He was frantic. 'Turn on your telly!'

'No telly.'

He pointed at telly behind me. 'That looks like telly.'

'No, is microwave.' Too complicated to explain true situation.

'Come to my house, so. Quick. Put on shoes!'

'Why?'

'Colin Farrell on telly. Footage of him doing travelling line-dancing.'

Magic words, 'travelling line-dancing'.

Shoved feet into Chinese satin slippers. Unsuitable for rough terrain, but didn't care. Ran across field, ducked under wire fence, ran across other field and into Rossa Considine's house. Sat on edge of couch glued to Colin Farrell programme but there was nothing about him doing line-dancing. Just lots and lots about all the girls he slept with. Went on fearsomely long time.

When show ended, Rossa Considine defensive. 'There was stuff about line-dancing.'

'Oh sure.' Jocular. 'You just wanted to lure me over here.' Then remembered girl in wedding dress who was perhaps kept prisoner in bedroom. Brief but genuine moment of fear. Jocular no more. 'I'll be off.'

'How you manage without telly?' he asked.

'Oh reading, other things. Don't miss it at all.' Airy. Smug. 'If emergency, need to see documentary or something, can call upon friend.'

'That's right. Remember Mrs Butterly mentioning you watch soaps with her every evening.'

Wednesday, 12 November 9.45
SarahJane Hutchinson arrived.

Wonderful day. Uplifting being with magnificent clothing. Both of us in top form. Everything worked.

'SarahJane, am feeling candy stripes, deckchairs, salty air, screech of seagulls . . .'

'So am I, Lola, oh so am I!'

400

Wrote out detailed list of what SarahJane was to wear every day: for breakfast; at poolside; to dinner; for New Year's Eve gala knees-up.

She tried to reject list. 'On holiday. Relaxing. Surely can mix and match?'

'No! Not! Please do not make that mistake! Remember, SarahJane, you may wear the Missoni swimsuit with the Missoni sarong, but NEVER with the Missoni sandals or sunhat.'

'Why not?' Quite mutinous.

'Unwritten fashion rule. Cannot fully explain. All I know is you will be laughing stock if you do.'

This carried weight. SarahJane does not want to be laughing stock. Has had quite enough of that, what with husbands running off with Filipino houseboys, thank you very much.

Thursday, 13 November
No word from Jake. But forgot to notice.

Friday, 14 November 10.14
Into Ennistymon with Boss and Moss to sign on. Didn't want to. Getting plenty of money 'under the counter' from Blanche and SarahJane, but Boss wouldn't hear of it. 'Is your right, Lola,' he kept insisting. 'Is your right.'

Mart Day. Place overrun with filthy lorries; mooing, slow-moving cattle doing poos in middle of street; farmers in antediluvian three-piece suits and pork-pie hats spitting on their hands and doing deals. Disgusting. Very swaggery farmer-type swaggered towards me in swaggery fashion. Our eyes met, normal eyes to swaggery eyes. Why would my eyes meet with swaggery eyes of swaggery farmer-type? Then knew! It was Blanche. Swaggery farmer was Blanche!

12.23

Boss and Moss dropped me home in filthy van.

'You have company,' Boss said.

Looked. Stunningly handsome man was sitting on my front step.

Jake.

Just when I had decided I no longer cared about him. Effing typical.

I emerged from van, which immediately screeched away, Moss and Boss yelping, 'Yee-haw!' like ribald country and western types.

Jake clambered to his feet. Asked, 'Can I come in?'

'No.'

'Oh . . . Can I talk to you out here?'

'Make it quick. Is cold.'

'Oh . . . Where've you been?' he asked. 'You didn't call round, you didn't ask Cecile about me . . .'

'You wanted breathing space.'

'Yes! But thought you would . . .' Big, frustrated sigh.

Suddenly I understood. Jake was used to 'breathing space' women stalking him and lurking outside his house in floods of tears, the way I did to Paddy.

'Have been waiting to hear from you,' he said.

'You could have got in touch with *me*.'

Extreme bad, burny feeling. Jake is spoilt brat, too sexy for his own good.

'Let's get back together,' he said.

'Why?'

'Why?' Manifestly unsettled by my question. I experienced strong sense of satisfaction. 'Because am crazy about you. Have had many girlfriends, but you are different.'

'Am only different because I didn't stalk you.'

'No! Nothing like that. Is because you are sweet. Cute. You are like kitten. Little quirky kitten. Knew from first time I met you, you were different. Asked for breathing space because was afraid of feelings for you. Too strong, too quickly.'

Either he had read manual on winning women over or was sincere.

'Please give me second chance,' he asked.

'No.' But was weakening. Was flattering, him being so tortured.

'Please.'

'No.'

'Could you even say you'll think about it?'

Made him wait long time for answer. 'Okay. Will think about it.'

19.01
Noel and Blanche arrive. Disappear into kitchen to change.

19.47
Knock on door.

'Probably Osama,' I say.

But wasn't Osama. Was a woman, swaddled from head to toe in black cloth. Even her face wasn't visible.

'Hello,' I said, thinking, What now? Hallowe'en was a couple of weeks ago!

'Lola! Is me!' woman said. 'Ibrahim!'

'Ibrahim! What you wearing? Oh! I get it, you are in burka!'

'Is only ladies' clothing I have. Not exactly clothing but drop cloth left over from painting pub.'

'Come in, come in.'

In he came, acres of black cloth flapping. He nodded

at trannies in all their finery, refused Noel's offer of 'little drinky', and eyed television, clearly keen for movie to start.

19.54

Noel tried to persuade Ibrahim to try a little black eyeliner. 'Is kohl. Is Egyptian, part of your culture.'

Ibrahim eschewed it firmly.

I started film.

20.13

Knock on door.

We froze. Air electric with fear. If we were animals, our fur would have stood on end.

'Upstairs, upstairs,' I hissed at the three men. 'Quietly.'

When they had vamoosed (that strange word again) I composed self. Cleared throat. Opened door. Beautiful woman standing there.

'Is this party invite-only?' she asked in sexy, husky voice. 'Or can any girl join in?'

I was struck dumb. Like automaton, I opened door wide in invitation to join us. This creature was dazzling. Tall, elegant, glossy dark hair, black satin cocktail dress, elbow gloves, taffeta wrap and Swarovski-like choker.

Not exactly sure when I realized she was a man. Perhaps slight ungainliness in narrow, high heels gave game away. But that realization was simply subsumed in all the other dazzlement.

'I'm Chloe,' she said, smiling winning smile, navy-blue eyes sparkling. Her eyeliner perfect! Better than when I do own! She flicked quick glance at television. 'I *knew* that wasn't a microwave!'

404

Excuse me . . ?

'I hope you don't mind me arriving like this.'

'No, no, more the merrier.' Didn't mean it. Noel had gone too far this time. 'I'll just get the others for you. Girls, you can come down now!'

Chloe put the others to shame. Beside her groomed beauty, they looked like brickies in lopsided wigs.

'I'm Chloe.' Chloe extended elegant arm.

'Natasha,' Noel grunted shyly.

'Blanche.' Poor Blanche couldn't even make eye contact.

Osama pulled her burka tighter and hung back on fringes of little group.

'Lola, a word.' Noel grabbed my arm, moved me short distance and in small, angry voice said, without moving his jaw, 'You didn't say other lady would be joining us tonight.'

'Wha –? What you mean? I didn't invite her. You mean, you don't know each other?'

Much shaking of heads. Sudden and extreme fear in me. How did this Chloe get here? Where did she come from? Is Uncle Tom's cabin on trannie ley line? Will more and more trannies start making their way here every Friday night, impelled by forces greater than themselves? Where will they all fit?

'Please! Let me explain,' Chloe said.

'Yes, would be obliged if you would!'

'Saw the girls getting changed in the kitchen. Have seen it for past few weeks. Wanted to be sure before showing up.'

'But how did you see?' The kitchen is at back of the house. Chosen for its hiddenness.

'From over there.' She tipped elegant head towards Rossa Considine's house.

'You know Rossa Considine?'

Long pause.

'Lola,' said very, very gently, 'I *am* Rossa Considine.'

20.27

Extreme shock. Had to repeat words to self a few times before I understood.

Peered at beautiful woman and once I knew what was looking for, could definitely see Rossa Considine under there somewhere.

'Oh my God! You are girl in Vera Wang wedding dress!'

'Only a copy, not actual Vera Wang, but yes! I thought you knew all along I was cross-dresser!'

'Why? How would I know?'

'Whenever meet you, you are sarcastic.'

Am I? No, am not. Am not sarcastic person at all. Except, actually, had to admit something about Rossa Considine did trigger sarcastic impulse . . .

'And you caught me burning clothes.'

'What was that all about?' I asked.

'The purge.'

Noel and Blanche nodded and repeated, 'The purge.' Rueful laughs.

'What on earth is the purge?' I asked.

'When we decide we are giving up cross-dressing for good and burn all lady belongings.'

'A regular thing?'

'Oh yes!' Laughter all round. 'Always regret it!' Further group laughter. 'But can't help it. Self-hate. Resolution to never lapse again. Always do.'

'Then I saw the girls getting ready in the kitchen every Friday and was like all my dreams had come true.' Sudden look of mortification crossed her face. 'Apologies! Should

406

have waited for official invitation before landing on top of you. Got carried away.'

'But you have a girlfriend,' I accused.

She smiled. 'Yes, have a girlfriend.'

'And you go potholing. Have seen you with ropes and stuff.'

'Am a man.' Another smile. 'And sometimes I like to do manly things.'

'Oooo-kaaaay.' My mind being opened.

'And sometimes I like to wear beautiful things.'

'Give me example.'

'You like Alexander McQueen?'

'Yes!'

Fell into passionate chat. Discovered I had much, much in common with Chloe – admiration for Alexander McQueen, Thai food, Smythson's passport covers, Nurofen Extra, sycamore trees, Law and Order –

'– Law and Order! I LOVE Law and Order,' I said. 'Is best show on telly.'

'Yes! "These are their stories" –'

'Duh-duh!' we both exclaimed. (Duh-duh is gavel noise at start of each episode. Very pleased that Chloe knew to say it. Not some dilettante Law and Order fan, but the real thing.)

'Only a true believer would know that noise,' I say.

'That's because I AM a true believer.'

'Tell me what is happening in it,' I beseeched. 'Haven't seen it since September.'

'Why not? What is the true situation with your microwave-telly?'

'Only plays DVDs.'

'But you must come to me to watch Law and Order! Is

not right that a true believer should miss a single episode. Thursday nights, ten p.m. It's a date!'

'To you, Chloe – or to you, Rossa Considine?'

Pause. 'To me, Rossa Considine. Am not usually Chloe during the week. Too much work.'

'Hmmm.'

'Problem?'

Might as well admit it. She had alluded to it earlier. 'Perhaps. When you are Rossa, we . . .' What were the right words? 'We seem to rub each other up the wrong way.'

Chloe considered the matter. Didn't deny it. Admired her honesty and maturity. 'Let us consider it an experiment. If it doesn't work, notice can be given on either side.'

'Very well. Thursday ten p.m. it is.'

Other trannies were clamouring for a 'go' of Chloe, wanting to hear her stories so turned her loose onto them.

You know what? Had a fantastic night. Enthusiastic discussions of clothing. Only sad note: Osama didn't seem to enjoy self. He tried hard to hear film – much shushing from him – over racket of the rest of us making whooping noises.

22.13

Musing on events

Trannies gone. Thinking about evening's strange revelations, to wit: Rossa Considine a trannie. You would NEVER think it to look at him. When he's a man, looks like he doesn't even comb his hair.

Further musing on events

Jake. Could you credit it? Isn't it always the way? The minute you decide you no longer care about a man, they show up, cap in hand. Decide to decide that I no longer care about Paddy, just as an experiment.

Imagined self at some time in the future, having conversation with invisible person. 'Oh yes, madly in love with Jake. Yes, Love-God. Of course, will always think fondly of Paddy. But have to admit, could never really love a man with hair that bouffy.'

Enjoyable. Uplifting.

Phone rang, jolting me from reverie.

I looked at it. Recognized number. Stared hard. Wondered if mind had finally cracked.

Through bloodless lips I answered, 'Lola Daly.'

'Lola? It's Paddy.'

Roaring in ears. Hope. Never before felt hope in such quantities.

'I . . .' His voice choked. '. . . really miss you.'

'You're a stupid, useless bitch and this is your own fucking fault.' He was panting from exertion as he stood over her, curled in a ball beneath him. 'Say it. You're a stupid, useless bitch and this is your own fucking fault.'

He was pulling his leg back for another kick. No. She didn't think she could take another one and still live. The toe of his boot slammed her stomach against her spine. She retched, retched, retched, retched, nothing but bile left.

'Say it!'

'I'm a stupid, useless bitch,' she whispered, tears streaming down her face. 'And this is my own fault.'

'Own fucking fault. Can't you get anything right?'

Grace

'Oh here's Paddy,' Dee Rossini said. 'I need a couple of words with him. I told him we'd be having a quick drink in here.'

For a moment I thought she was having me on. With trepidation, I raised my eyes. Christ. There he was, filling the pub doorway, darkening the room.

Panic swelled. I had to get away, but I was trapped; there was only one doorway and he was in it. My head swivelled, as I sought an escape route. The Ladies – there might be a window I could climb out of. At the very least I could hide there until he was gone. 'Dee, I'll have to go now . . .'

But she was waving and calling, 'Paddy, over here,' and didn't hear me.

Paddy looked around the pub with his blue seek-and-destroy gaze, spotted Dee, then me sitting next to her, frozen like a rabbit caught in headlights. For a long neutral moment he watched me, before deciding to unleash his devastating smile.

Another Dee Rossini scandal had just broken, but this one was far, far worse than any of the others: her boyfriend – yes, she'd had a secret boyfriend all along, I should have known, what kind of journalist was I? – had sold his story to the *Sunday Globe*, probably the most scurrilous of the red-tops. And it was chock-full of the most cringe-inducing details about their sex life. According to him (his name was Christopher Holland and he claimed he was selling his story because he was tired of 'living a lie'), Dee was 'mad for it'. Any time, any place, anywhere. (The 'anywhere' bit was because they had once – *once* – done it in her back garden.) She particularly liked it 'doggy-style', he said.

The front-page splash kept referring to her as 'Kinky Dee', but just in case there was any danger that she'd come across as a sexy minx, there was other, even more gruesome, information: she didn't shave her legs more than once a fortnight; her bra and pants rarely matched; the soles of her feet were so hard and yellow, if she rubbed them together for long enough she could start a fire; she had cellulite on her stomach. In other words, she was a normal forty-something woman.

The first I knew of it was the headline screaming, 'KINKY DEE AND ME', in the newsagent's on Sunday morning. Mesmerized I picked up the paper and a quick scan showed that the level of detail was unprecedented. They must have paid this Christopher Holland a fortune to spill his guts in such a treacherous fashion. I pitied Dee as I had never pitied anyone before and it made me itchy with shame that I was a journalist. Even the fact that I knew the journalist – it was Scott Holmes, the Kiwi who'd been my boyfriend while I was trying to not be in love with Damien – made me ashamed.

The thought of having to endure an exposé like this myself sent my intestines into a twisty spasm. Could *anyone* endure having the honest details – and I'm talking honest, down and dirty, not soft-focus pretendy-stuff – of their sex lives published on the front page of a Sunday paper? Christ alive, wouldn't you die?

Still standing in the shop, I opened the front page – and literally recoiled. Filling the full length of page three was a photograph where they'd stuck Dee's head on a picture of a flabby woman with a stubbly bikini area and mis-matched underwear. It made everything a thousand times more terrible. From now on, whenever people thought of the leader of NewIreland, that's the image their mind would send up from the vaults.

It was unquantifiably damaging. Much more so than the 'corruption' stories because even though Dee was a single woman and was entitled to have sex with whoever she liked, how could you watch her on telly shaking hands with famous types and not wonder if her knickers matched her bra?

'This isn't a library,' a voice said.

Quickly I turned around. The flat-eyed man behind the counter was watching me. He indicated the *Sunday Globe*. 'You going to pay for that?'

'Yeah, but . . .' I couldn't let go of it long enough to go to the counter and cough up. The compulsive story had me in a death grip. Still reading, I jingled in my pocket for change and clanked down an uncounted handful beside the till. 'Help yourself,' I said.

'Thank you,' he said snippily, sliding coins into his hand.

He used to be a lot nicer to me when I was a smoker. I'd been such a dependable source of income, but since Damien and I had given up the cigs, no matter how much we spent on withdrawal confectionery – and God knows it was a considerable amount – your man had probably had to kiss goodbye to his retirement villa in Portugal.

On I read, dumbfounded by what was said: the day Dee

415

had been appointed Minister of Education, she'd 'demanded' sex four times; she loved to be dominated; she didn't like oral, apparently she thought it was 'boring'.

She'd have a hard time coming back from this. She'd always seemed strong, independent and in control; now she seemed ordinary and flawed – and a very poor judge of character, to choose a boyfriend so disloyal.

(The very worst thing, in my opinion, was the cellulite on her stomach. I was ashamed to admit it, but it dimmed her lustre slightly for me – and I *loved* her. So what effect must it be having on people who were more ambivalent?)

Since I'd interviewed her, we'd become sort-of friends because we kept bumping into each other in the red-wine part of our local off-licence and a couple of times we'd nipped next door to Kenny's for a quick drink. Only a week ago she'd even had Damien and me over for dinner and treated us to some of her expensive off-ends pasta. (No nicer than the ordinary stuff, if you ask me, but all the same I was touched that she obviously thought highly of us.)

I stood outside the newsagent's in the cold – it was perishing for mid-November – and rang her. 'Dee, I know you're screening your calls, but it's Grace Gildee and I just want you to know –'

She picked up. 'Grace, it's me.'

'Are you okay?'

'A bit wobbly,' she said, her voice shaking. 'But I've got through worse than this.'

'They're bastards,' I said with feeling. 'Did you know it was coming?'

'Hadn't a clue,' she said. 'Totally embargoed. I was with Christopher on Friday night, he didn't say a thing. Naturally,' she added with a bitter laugh.

'I'll support you any way I can.' I meant both personally and professionally.

'Thanks, Grace. You don't mind about the cellulite on my stomach?'

'No,' I said stoutly. (What's the harm in a white lie?) 'I do not. Every woman has cellulite; they'll be relieved to find out that even someone as fabulous as Dee Rossini has it.'

'Yeah, but on my stomach, Grace. It's not like on your thighs, everyone has it on their thighs. Having it on your stomach is nearly as bad as having it on your . . . your . . . eyelids. On your ears, even. Can you get it on your ears?'

'Dee, you are a survivor of domestic violence, you help hundreds of other women, you've set up a political party and you're a force to be reckoned with. Don't let a little bit of cellulite on your stomach become more important than all those achievements.'

'Okay, you're right.' She took a deep breath to settle herself. 'Anyway it's really not much, you can only see it if you squeeze it.'

'Would you like me to come round?' I asked. The implication was clear: I was offering not just as her friend, but as her tame journalist. This was her chance to give her side of the story to a sympathetic ear.

'I'd love to see you,' she said. 'But don't come here. Let's go to Kenny's. I've done nothing wrong.'

'If you're sure.' God, she was great. Tough as old boots. 'I'll meet you there in five.'

I rang Damien.

'What's keeping you?' he asked. 'Where's my stuff?'

'I'm on a story.'

'*What?* You only went to the shop to buy sweets.'

I gave him a quick resumé of the situation. I was surprised he didn't already know. Damien was a compulsive news hound, constantly checking the internet for breaking news. 'The one morning I have a lie-in . . .' he grumbled.

We'd planned an easy day, in bed, reading the papers, keeping safe. We were both a bit fragile. It had been little Maximillian's christening the day before and the weight of the chip on our shoulders as we'd moved among Damien's warm, clever, glamorous, terrifying family meant that this morning we'd woken up exhausted – and actually, I have to admit, haunted by a strange feeling of disquiet, almost dread. Too much contact with Damien's family did that to me.

(Or it might have just been a hangover. We'd had an awful lot of Martinis at the post-church shindig in Christine and Richard's.)

'I'm meeting Dee in Kenny's,' I said. 'Then I'll have to go straight into work.'

Damien groaned. 'That's shit for you! And what about me? What about my fizzy snakes?'

'You'll have to do without them. Sorry.'

Jacinta Kinsella had left a message while I'd been talking to Damien. I rang her back. From the word go, Jacinta had been withering about my friendship with Dee, but today, when it mattered, when every paper in the country would be tripping over themselves to talk to Dee Rossini, I had access all areas.

'Milk her dry,' she said, over the sound of children shrieking and screeching in the background. 'And I'll talk to Big Daddy about the front page.'

A broadsheet, even a mid-market one like the *Spokesman*, wouldn't normally devote a front page to what was essentially a frivolous story about a politician's personal life, but this was too big to ignore.

'Will you be in later, Jacinta?'

'Me?' She sounded shocked. 'Grace, you are Chief Features Writer.' She emphasized the capitals. 'I can't keep holding your hand for ever.'

'Fine, fine.'

Lazy bitch.

Dee's arrival in Kenny's generated a low rhubarby murmur. Not many in at ten past twelve on a Sunday morning, just a few men with drink problems.

'. . . doggy-fashion . . .'

'. . . she did it with a *dog*? . . .'

'. . . no, *like* a dog . . .'

'. . . did she bark? . . .'

'. . . that's right and she chewed slippers and retrieved sticks. What do you think, you cretin . . .'

Dee looked good: dark jeans, crisp white shirt, chic, drapey-collared cardigan and matte red lipstick. And if she heard the comments, she elected not to hear them. She was a trouper.

She ordered coffee. 'I can't be seen to be hitting the hard stuff, much as I'd appreciate it. Okay, here's how it is.'

She laid it out for me: she'd been talking to Sidney Brolly, NewIreland's press officer, who'd decreed that she do just one interview. With me. And yes, I was pleased. I wouldn't

419

have wished Dee's situation on anyone, but it had happened and I could help with damage limitation. There was to be no rebuttal of the charges of cellulite or hard-soled feet and a wall of silence was to surround Christopher Holland. Quiet dignity and a focus on all that was positive about Dee Rossini was to be the order of the day.

'They'll be calling for my resignation in the Dail tomorrow,' she said gloomily.

'For what? For having hairy legs?'

She squeezed her eyes shut. 'For a loss of public confidence. For behaviour unbecoming an elected servant. Basically because I have sex.'

'But you're not married. And I take it this Christopher isn't married? So what have you done wrong?'

'Nothing – in theory. But in practice . . .' She meandered into silence, then exclaimed, 'Oh Grace, I really don't want to go. There are so few female politicians. And you should see our new manifesto – we have brilliant woman-friendly policies, really far-reaching: longer maternity leave, a massive child-care programme . . .'

'What would happen if you were forced to resign?'

'Worst-case scenario: the whole NewIreland party could be so discredited by my sex life that the Nappies would be forced to pull out of coalition with us. But the Nappies don't have enough TDs to stay in power so the government would have to be dissolved and the country would have to go to the polls now instead of next year. The long and the short of it: my cellulitey stomach could bring down the government.'

'But that's crap! Don't resign. Just tough it out. Keep telling yourself that you've done nothing wrong.'

420

Her mobile rang. She checked the number. 'It's Sidney, I'd better take it.'

She listened in silence, her expression growing more thunderous as time passed. 'If that's how it has to be,' she eventually said and snapped her phone closed. 'Sidney wants me to do a photo-shoot,' she said angrily. 'Styling me for the weekend pages. He thinks it's vital to counteract that *fucking* composite on page three.'

'He's right.' I wondered if she'd go mental at me.

More in sorrow than in anger she said, 'I'm not in a girl-band, I'm a politician. It shouldn't matter if I have three heads, all of them cellulitey, so long as I do my job properly.'

'It would never happen to a man.'

That was when she said, 'Oh here's Paddy.'

There he was, suited and wide-shouldered, blocking the doorway, putting me at a panicky disadvantage. I'd fallen out of bed, not expecting to be in the world for more than the five minutes it took to go to the shop – I hadn't even combed my hair.

Normally Damien was the one who went to the shop on Sundays. The only reason I'd gone today was because he'd claimed he couldn't walk properly because he'd hurt his knee playing five-a-side football on Friday night.

I began shrinking into myself as Paddy wove his way through the men with drink problems, cutting the alcoholic air with his sharp cologne. I despised myself for caring what he thought; I didn't need him to find me attractive, but I didn't want him to see me vulnerable.

'Dee,' he said, giving her a quick hug. He was so vibrant, like there was more life force concentrated in him than in normal people, as if he'd got a double dose.

'Thanks for coming,' she said. She indicated me. 'Do you know each other?'

There was a horribly awkward moment. I was waiting for Paddy to come up with some platitude and he was waiting for me. 'What?' Dee asked.

'Of course we know each other,' Paddy said easily. 'Hello, Grace, lovely to see you.'

He bent down to kiss my cheek politely. I held my breath. I didn't want to smell him.

He touched his lips to my cheek, then – did I imagine it? – blew on it softly. Had he actually had the nerve?

His eyes were laughing.

His touch sat on my face, like an unbearable itch. I wanted to wipe it away with a lavish smear.

'Things are not good, Paddy,' Dee said, straight down to business.

He shook his head. 'It's a compliment. They're scared of you. They're taking you seriously.'

'But who is "they"? Christopher wouldn't have had the cop-on to do this off his own bat. Who put him up to it? It's time we dealt with it properly.'

I rested my head on my hand, trying to inch my sleeve up my face and surreptitiously wipe it.

Paddy watched me, moving his eyes from my sleeve to my cheek.

He knew.

*

Dee went to the loo, leaving Paddy and me alone. He looked far too big for the little stool. Neither of us spoke. He flicked a quick glance over his shoulder, checking that Dee was out of earshot, then he said, with low urgency, 'Grace, I –'

'How are your wedding plans going?' I interrupted.

'Grace, can't we –'

'No,' I said, too loudly, causing a couple of drunken heads to jerk up off their chests. I dropped my voice. 'Just answer the question.'

He stared at my mouth. 'You never answer my calls.'

That was typical of him: he hadn't rung me in weeks.

'Why won't you talk to me?' he asked. The way he was staring at my mouth was making me uncomfortable.

Suddenly he said, 'I can smell you, Grace. And you know what you smell of?'

I knew what he was going to say.

'You smell of sex.'

Under my sweats, prickly heat flushed down my body and my nipples shot to attention. 'Shut up,' I said quietly. 'Just shut up.'

'Whatever you want,' he said lightly. 'Your wish is my command.'

'You would have said that no matter what I smelt of – paint-stripper, lamb curry . . .'

He shrugged, his shoulders beautiful in his suit.

Recovering myself, I said, 'So tell me, Paddy. How are your wedding plans going?'

'Fine, all fine. But that's Alicia's area, really.'

'How is the lovely *Alicia*?'

'Wonderful. But that was a strange profile you did of her,

Grace. She was disappointed that you weren't . . . warmer.'

I gave a short bark of laughter. 'Well, *Alicia* insisted on me, so what did *Alicia* expect?'

'She expected you to be a professional. As did I.'

I looked at him with contempt. 'I *was* a professional.'

'We expected you to keep your personal feelings out of it.'

'I did.' I hadn't wanted to interview her, but when I'd been coerced into it I'd decided that the best way to manage it was to pretend to myself that I'd never met her before. But she hadn't bothered to mask her smug triumph and I suppose, as a result, I couldn't help letting my bitterness leak through. Not that I wrote anything terrible, as such. Just not very nice.

Cigarettes punctuated everything; they declared things started and they declared things completed. Whenever I sat down to write an article, my starting ritual was to have a cigarette. Since I'd given up, I hadn't been able to type anything without a nagging feeling that I'd sneaked in ahead of the starter's gun, that I shouldn't have started *yet*. And when I finished the job, I had no sense of completion because a cigarette wasn't there to declare the task done. In the seven long weeks since I'd become a non-smoker, I was perpetually troubled by the weight of unfinishedness, a sense that I was dragging around all of the jobs that weren't properly completed.

But hard as it was, I couldn't give in because even though I wasn't a superstitious person, I couldn't shake the black fear that if I went back on the cigarettes, Bid would die.

After I'd – eventually – filed my stories on Dee, I stopped off at the cinema – they have the biggest range – and bought

Damien a big bag of pick'n'mix, shovelling in a hefty selection of cola bottles, gummy dinosaurs and jelly strawberries, to make up for abandoning him on a Sunday when he had a banjaxed knee, nicotine withdrawal and no sweets.

He was on the couch, looking grumpy and watching the twenty-four-hour World War Two Channel – not its official name but, whatever it was, it seemed to run round-the-clock documentaries on the Nuremberg rallies and the bombing of Dresden – with his knee stretched out on a chair.

He looked up from the grainy images of troops landing in Normandy. 'I tried ringing you!'

'Sorry. I switched my phone off. I needed to focus.'

'Did you bring me anything?'

I dropped the bag into his lap. 'Present for you.'

'For real?' he said, his face creasing into a smile. 'I was only joking, you never bring me anything.'

'No wonder, when you're so ungrateful.'

He rooted through the bag. 'Top class, Grace. Fizzy pigs! A rare delicacy. They're hard to come by.'

'How's the knee?'

'Agony,' he said through a mouthful of pink pigs. 'Have we any ice for it? Hey, catch.' He tossed me a jelly bat from his bag and I lunged and actually managed to catch it between my teeth.

'Christ,' he said, clearly impressed. 'I take it all back.'

He ran his eyes over me and something changed. He was looking at me, the way he perhaps hadn't looked for a while: like he'd like to have sex with me. Feelings moved inside me, relief replacing anxiety.

'Come here,' he said, his eyes full of intent, and instead

of telling him not to order me about, like I usually would, I moved closer.

The air was charged with the promise of sex – then Damien interrupted, 'Hey, Bomber Command, while I think of it, how're we fixed next Friday night?'

Alarm rose in me. 'Why?'

'Dinner with Juno and her husband.'

The sentence hung between us. We could really do without this.

A month ago, he'd actually gone to his school reunion – Damien, the man who'd often said that he 'pitied' those who felt such a need – and apparently had a great old wander down memory lane with Juno, laughing mistily eyed about all the arguments they'd had when he'd insisted on working but she'd wanted to go out and get scuttered.

All fairly harmless and the only thing that made me nervous – and no, it wasn't the fact that they were once in love and married – was that Juno smoked.

A lot, according to Damien, who'd staggered in from the reunion drunk and sentimental, waxing lyrical about Juno's forty-a-day habit, and relating a rambling, incoherent story about how she'd sneaked a cigarette at the dinner table and set off an overhead sprinkler and drenched some poor sap called 'No-balls Nolan' and lied to the hotel manager when he asked if she'd been smoking, and how it was all so funny, he'd thought he was going to be sick . . .

Since we'd had our nicotine supply cut off at the knees, we were both irritable from withdrawal but, in addition, I suspected that Damien resented me: it was my aunt who had lung cancer, it was my mother who'd shamed us into stopping.

Suddenly, like a lifeline, I thought of something. 'Won't you be in Hungary on Friday?' Covering the elections there.

'I'll be just back. Flying in Friday afternoon.'

Ah feck.

'Grace, are you okay?' he asked. 'You look a bit . . .'

'I'm fine.'

He patted the couch. 'Sit down beside me here and have some cola bottles – I can offer you both the fizzy and the non-fizzy variety.'

My mood hovered on a knife edge, it could have gone either way – butter-side up, butter-side down – but I decided to smile. I was being paranoid. Not something I was prone to (except sometimes when I was premenstrual and turned into *The Last Days of Stalin*). I rewound my day seeking the nub of the badness: Paddy de Courcy.

'And when you've eaten your fill of sugar and E numbers,' Damien said, 'might I suggest some light sexual activity?'

He kissed me. He tasted of artificial strawberry flavouring. Then he tasted of him. A spark lit inside me. I was overtaken by a sudden rush of need and I felt an answering hunger in him.

He stopped and looked into my eyes, my dirty desire mirrored in his. 'Wow,' he said. 'What happened there?'

He kissed me again and we were snogging like teenagers. Neck twists and direction changes and clawing at clothing, almost unable to decide what to take off first.

He reached for his belt buckle, and pulled himself out, already erect. I tore off my sweatshirt and unclipped my bra.

He reached for my nipples and said, 'Christ! My knee.'

'Stay still.' What was the best way to do this? Because there was no way we weren't. 'I'll go on top.'

'How do people have sex when they're in plaster?' he gasped.

'Some people actually have a fetish about it.' I got up and pulled off my trackie bottoms and pants. 'About being encased in a full-body plaster cast. They're called "casties". Remember, I did a story on them.'

I didn't know why I was telling him this, I couldn't care less.

He took my hips in his hands, to guide me down onto him. 'Could we get a fetish?'

'Right now?' My knees straddled his thighs. My breath was coming in shallow pants. 'You pick your moments.'

'Not now. Sometime.'

'Sure. Anything in mind?' The tip of him was just touching me.

'Nothing off the top of my head.'

'Well, have a think.' He was pushing up into me, I was pushing down onto him. Just enough resistance to make me feel swollen and tight. He moaned. He was filling me up and out and in. 'Get back to me if you come up with anything good.'

'Where are you going?' Damien asked, as I tiptoed out of the bedroom. 'Why aren't you asleep?'

'Just getting a nicotine patch.'

In the darkened living room, I rummaged in my bag and switched my phone on. I knew he'd ring me. That's why I'd kept my mobile off all day.

There were three voicemails. I put the phone to my ear and listened. Two were from Damien, wondering where I was.

Then I heard his voice. Just three terse words. 'Call me. Please.'

In a way, the green-handbag days were the worst. Although black (unrelenting negativity; a proclivity for despair) was bad, as indeed was red (unfettered rage), at least you knew where you were. Not that beige was exactly pleasant – benign though the colour was, it made her over-breezy and smart-alecy.

But green – green was an unknown quantity. Green warned us to expect dark, cryptic mutterings, abrupt reversals of opinion, continually shifting goalposts. On a green-handbag day she could praise you and mean it. Or she could praise you and then screech, 'And if you believe that, you still believe in the tooth fairy!' Which wasn't so bad when she shouted it at me or TC – we could take it – but it had been uncomfortable to witness when she'd yelled it at Oscar, her five-year-old, on Bring Your Son To Work Day.

Monday morning and my byline was on the front page of the *Spokesman* – admittedly shared with Jonno Fido from news, but that didn't take the lustre off it. Getting your byline on the front page was like having a number-one record. Obviously the hard-news journos were the Westlife of the newspaper world – any old shite would bag them the top spot. But for features writers like me it happened less frequently, which made it all the more satisfying.

In addition, spread over pages two and three, I had an in-depth profile of Dee. *And* for page five I'd written a spirited opinion piece headed, 'It Would Never Happen To A Man'.

TC watched me make my way to my desk. 'The *Spokesman* by Grace Gildee,' he said.

'You're flavour of the day,' Lorraine observed. 'Jacinta will be thrilled for you.'

We all snorted at the unlikeliness of that, but nothing could bring me down. I was in love with my job. I was thrilled by it all – the sound of phones ringing, keys clicking, voices chatting. I was so in the moment I was convinced I actually felt the hum of activity in my veins.

'What colour handbag?' TC asked.

'Are we putting money on this?' Lorraine asked. 'Or is it just for fun?'

'Fun.'

'Green,' Lorraine said.

'Green,' Tara agreed.

'Not yellow?' My little joke. Yellow meant ice-cream, sometimes even Coke floats.

'Black,' Clare said.

'Ah no,' TC said. 'No, no. She's Head of Features. Grace doing so well is good for her empire.'

'But it kills her to have to acknowledge someone else's success, even one of her own,' Clare said. 'I'm not saying she's a bad person . . .'

'Not now you're not,' Tara said. 'But you'd want to hear you in Dinnegans on a Friday night after three vodka and tonics.'

'I'm going for green,' Lorraine said.

'Me too,' said Tara.

'And me,' said TC.

'And me,' I said.

'I'm sticking with black,' Clare said.

'I think you're all being silly,' Joanne said. 'It's only a handbag.'

Everyone seemed to withdraw a little from Joanne. She'd never really fit in.

*

To: Gracegildee@spokesman.ie
From: Pattilavezzo@oraclepr.com
Subject: Interview with Madonna

Please forward detailed readership demographic of the *Spokesman*. Also circulation figures for last eight quarters.

Madonna's PR had already asked for examples of my work. Then she'd asked for a few more. Then I'd had to write an essay on why I loved Madonna. If she'd moved on to checking circulation figures, I must have done okay. This was looking very positive. God! I was seized by a mixture of terror and elation. What if it happened? What if it actually, really happened? I would meet Madonna. I mean, Madonna!

'Here's Jacinta,' TC whispered.

'I can't see the bag, the photocopier is in the way.'

'And she's got her coat over it.'

'I think it's green.'

'No, it's black.'

'No, it's green.'

It was green.

'Very well done on the Dee Rossini coverage,' Jacinta said briskly.

In silence I waited for the stinger.

'Cat got your tongue?' she asked.

'No.'

'So what happened to "thank you"?'

'Thank you.'

I followed her into her office.

'You needn't think you can sit back on your laurels and freewheel today. You're only as good as your next story. What've you got for me?'

'Romance at office Christmas part – '

'It's only the seventeenth of November!'

'The average spend on Christmas pres – '

'No!'

'The homeless at Christmas.'

'Is it uplifting?'

'. . . No. They're homeless.'

'And it's still only the seventeenth of November. No! This is what I mean – ' she muttered. Her eyes slid past me and whatever she saw caused her to freeze as though she'd been turned into a pillar of salt.

I looked behind me. It was Casey Kaplan, in his tight black jeans and tangled hair.

'What the hell are you doing here?' Jacinta quivered with murky emotion.

'I work here.' He smiled a wide, cocksure smile.

'I thought you were allergic to daylight. We've never had the pleasure of your company at this hour of the morning before.'

Casey brought with him an aura of cigarettes and pubs and good times. He'd obviously come straight from a party or club.

His slipstream wafted through the office and when the smell reached Jacinta, she leapt to her feet. 'Get back!' She flapped her arms. 'You're smelly!'

'Someone wound your top too tight this morning, Jacinta.' Casey laughed and lounged away.

'Thanks, Casey,' TC muttered. 'That'll definitely calm her down.'

From the far side of the office, I heard Casey ask, 'Morning, Rose. Coleman in?'

'Yes,' Rose said nervously. She was Big Daddy's PA and guardian of the gateway. 'But he's not to be disturbed.'

'It's okay. He just texted me. He's expecting me.'

My phone rang. It was my parents' number. I didn't know how, but whenever they called, they seemed to be able to make the ringing sound more urgent than normal. They always got my attention.

'It's Bingo,' Dad said.

'For the love of Christ.'

'He's in Wales.'

'Wales? Wales the country? Across the sea? How?'

'He got the ferry.'

'How?'

'We assume he made his way to the terminal and boarded when everyone else did. And got off when everyone else did. A civic-minded Welsh citizen, male, found him on the open road, headed for Caernarvon and rang the number on his collar.'

'Didn't they ask to see his ticket when he got on the boat?'

'We're assuming that he attached himself to a family group, passed himself off as one of their members and slipped in on their group boarding pass.'

I was silent. You had to admire the dog. They should change his name to Marco Polo.

'The fast ferry leaves from Dun Laoghaire at four,' Dad said. 'It takes only ninety-nine minutes to reach Holyhead. Or so they say. I suspect that that is a Stakhanovite ideal, formulated to entice the credulous ferry-goer. I'd put money – if I had any – that, in actuality, human error, inefficiencies, inclement weather conditions, etc., extend that estimate indefinitely.'

'Enjoy the trip.'

'*Who?*'

'You. Ma. Bid. Whoever goes.'

'But won't you . . . ?'

'I. Am. At. Work. You. Are. Retired. He. Is. Your. Dog.'

'You. Are. Our. Daughter. We. Are. Elderly. And. Poor.'

'I. Will. Pay. Your. Ferry. Fare. Good. Bye.'

The phone rang. Dad again.

'What now?' I asked.

'How many?'

'How many what?'

'How many of us will you pay for? Just me or all three of us?'

'Three, of course; three, by all means.'

He fumbled his hand over the mouthpiece and called excitedly, 'We can all go.'

High-pitched happy squeaks from Ma and Bid reached

434

me. Poor fuckers. How easy they were to please. Especially when Bid was so sick.

Then Dad came back on the line. 'You have a good heart, Grace. Like Damien, you can be brutal in your execution – in that regard you two are well matched – but there is kindness underneath it all.'

When the phone rang again, I answered by mistake. I was expecting it to be Dad once more, wondering if they were permitted to have an allowance to buy tea and sandwiches on the ferry.

'Grace Gildee, please.'

No! Fatal error! Never answer your phone if you don't know who it is! Now I'd have to have a long, sticky conversation with a PR person, as they tried to twist my arm into covering whatever book/gadget/charity they represented.

'Who's calling?'

'Susan Singer.'

'What's it in connection with?'

'My mum. Me and my sister, Nicola, our mum, Mrs Singer? You came to the house in September and talked to her about her biopsy? You sent us the photo of the three of us?'

'Yes, of course!'

'She died. Last night.'

'God! That's so sad! I'm really sorry.'

'I just thought you might like . . . to know. You were nice that day you came, and you sent the photo. She framed it. The funeral is tomorrow morning.'

'I'll be there. Thanks for letting me know.'

*

I was going down to Chomps sandwich bar to get my lunch (it was ten past eleven, but I couldn't wait any longer) and just before the lift doors closed Casey Kaplan darted in.

'Tell me,' he said. 'Is Jacinta right? Am I smelly?'

'Yes.'

'What do I smell of?'

I sniffed the air and thought for a second. 'Debauchery.'

He seemed pleased. 'Nice work on Dee Rossini, Grace, that was a rockin' profile.'

The lift doors opened and we stepped out into the lobby. 'But what about Chris? Who saw that one comin'?' He added thoughtfully, 'Always thought he was a sound guy.'

'Chris?'

'Christopher. Holland. Dee's boyfriend.'

'*You know him?*' My voice was high and anguished.

He gave a what's-the-big-deal shrug. 'Yeah.'

'You knew he was her boyfriend?' No one else in the entire world had known there even *was* a boyfriend.

'Yeah. Always thought he was a great guy. But,' he sighed sorrowfully, 'the *Globe* ponied up a shedload and I guess, with his gambling debts, it was too much to resist. As the man said, money talks . . .'

I'd heard enough. I couldn't take any more of his showing off. Abandoning him mid-conversation, I stalked towards the door, watched by Yusuf and Mrs Farrell, who elbowed each other gleefully.

It was all on the evening news.

That morning in the Dail, the leader of the Christian Progressives, Brian 'Bangers' Brady (he had a thriving second-hand-car empire; Irish politicians encouraged nick-names in order to seem like men 'of the people'), stood up and said, 'If I might give my right honourable friend, the leader of NewIreland, some advice . . .' Then he leant down to his chair and produced a pink object. Heads stretched to get a better look, then pockets of laughter rose into the air from those who'd seen what it was.

'This fine object –' he raised it above his head and the laughter got louder – 'is a lady-shave.' He read from the packaging. 'I'm assured it guarantees "silky-smooth legs".'

The crowd roared their amusement. They looked like apes at a rave.

With an unctuous bow of the head Bangers said, 'We offer it to you, Minister Rossini, a gift from the Christian Progressives, in the hope that you may find it useful.'

'It was disgusting.' Damien had actually been there, reporting from the journalists' gallery. 'Playground bullying. And it gets worse.'

The leader of the Labour Party was getting to his feet. 'That was a low blow from the leader of the Christian Progressives,' he said. 'The Labour Party would like to offer our support to Ms Rossini. In the form of this useful item.' He whipped out something from his pocket.

'What is it?' I asked Damien.

'Scholl foot rub.'

Even the Green Party offered Dee a bottle of lavender oil for her cellulite.

'Nothing from the Socialist Workers' Party,' I remarked, touched by their forbearance and wondering if I should vote for them at the next election.

'Probably because they didn't have the funds,' Damien said. 'If they could have raised the price of a tub of foot cream between them, you can be sure they would have.'

Dee's eyes were suspiciously shiny, but she stood there and took it, she even managed to smile and, as a result, the government survived.

'But she's on her last chance,' Damien said. 'One more drama and she's a goner. And if she's gone, so's the Nappies' coalition partner. Which means the government is gone. How many pairs of socks do I need to pack?'

'How many nights are you going for?'

'Tuesday, Wednesday, Thursday – three.'

'So how many pairs do you need?'

'Three.'

'Excellent. Catch.' One after the other, I lobbed three pairs of balled-up socks across the room. Gracefully he caught each of them one-handed, and dropped them into his bag, one, two, three.

'Poor Dee,' Damien said.

'Who's doing that stuff to her?' I asked.

'The Chrisps, obviously. They're the only ones who stand to benefit.'

'But do you know individual names? Like, is it Bangers? Is it coming from the top down or what?'

'I don't know.'

'But even if you did, you wouldn't tell me.'

'I couldn't.' He had to protect his source.

'Why are they picking specifically on Dee?'

'Because they've already tried a direct hit on the Nappies with Teddy's "loans".'

The leader of the Nationalist Party of Ireland had been caught accepting personal 'loans' that ran into tens of thousands, 'loans' that he'd had for over a decade and hadn't made one repayment on. But he had toughed it out and simply refused to go.

'The Nappies and Teddy are Teflon-coated. The only way left for the opposition to attack them is to go for their coalition partner. And unlike the rest of them, Dee is honourable. If she's pushed enough, she *will* resign. How cold will it be in Hungary?'

'What am I? The weather channel?'

He shook his head, almost in pride. 'You're so narky.'

It made us both laugh. 'You've taught me everything I know,' I said. 'It's November. Leave your shorts at home.'

'. . . God, look, Grace.' He was staring at the telly.

A juggernaut carrying cigarettes had been hijacked. The two thieves had shoved the driver out of his high seat into the road and screeched away, heading north, no doubt laughing their heads off.

'That could have been us,' Damien said, his expression aglow with cigarette hunger. 'A whole lorryload. Once we were sure we'd shaken them, we could have pulled into a lay-by and climbed into the cargo bit of the lorry and smoked ourselves sick.'

'We could have opened hundreds of packs – ' I cried.

' – and thrown handfuls of cigarettes up in the air and covered ourselves in them – '

' – and lit dozens and only half-smoked them – '

' – or smoked six at the one time – '

439

'– and had mad nicotiney sex, rolling around on a bed of cigarettes. God . . .' My words trailed away and I sighed.

Then he sighed and, with resignation, returned to the business of packing. It reminded me of *The Little Matchgirl*, when her flame goes out and the beautiful vision disappears.

I put an emergency stash of sweets in his suitcase and, for a moment, considered adding a note saying, 'I love you,' but that was so out of character for me that I thought it might scare him.

'Charity.'

'No!' Jacinta said it automatically now, no matter what I proposed. 'You've gone so . . . *do-goodery*. With your abused women and your homeless people and now your charity.'

'Three or four profiles on the different faces of charity.' I just carried on as if she was fizzing over with enthusiasm. 'The society woman who goes to all the fund-raisers; the administrator who controls funding for developing countries; the compassionate individual who gives up her job for six months to feed the starving.'

She liked it. I had her at 'the society woman'.

'Hey, Declan, who's the hottest charity queen?' she called.

Declan O'Dowd ('He never gets out') squinted at us. 'Rosalind Croft. Wife of Maxwell Croft.'

'I knew that,' Jacinta hissed in triumph. 'I'll spend the day with her, shadowing her every move. I hear she's very generous. She might give me a handbag. Set it up, Grace.'

'And I'll do the dull ones?'

'Yes, yes, you'll have a wonderful time with the bleeding heart who goes to Africa. You can have a good old rant together about globalism – you'll enjoy it! Try to find someone who's not too minging for the photo.'

'And the administrator?'

'Send TC if you want. Or you can do it. But get a looker. Where are you going?'

'Funeral.'

The church was packed and sombre. The two daughters, Susan and Nicola, neat in dark coats and formal shoes, sat in the front row beside a white-faced man whom I assumed was their father. My head ached with unshed tears.

Mr Singer spoke with great tenderness about his wife. Then Susan and Nicola stood on the altar and said formal words of goodbye to their mum, and it was so very sad that I thought my skullbones would burst apart from the pressure. It was a crying shame that the profile on Mrs Singer had never been published. It wouldn't have cured her, it wouldn't have changed the outcome, but it might have made the girls feel a tiny bit better.

'We stand up now,' the old man beside me whispered. He had taken it upon himself to prompt me because I didn't know the sitting/standing/kneeling sequence of Mass.

The sound of shoes scuffing the wooden floor echoed in the church as we all got to our feet, and in the gap briefly opened up by the moving bodies I saw, several rows in front of me, his unmistakable shoulders. But it couldn't be him, what would he be doing here?

441

A wall of backs faced me and I could see nothing else until the old man whispered, 'Now we kneel.'

The congregation dropped to their knees and I stayed standing long enough to see that it was definitely Paddy.

'Kneel, kneel!' the old man said. 'Get down!'

I dropped to my knees before the old man had apoplexy.

What was Paddy doing here with the Singers? How did he know them? Then it dawned on me: this was his constituency. Politicians always showed up for their constituents' funerals, in an effort to make voters think they were human.

Outside the church, I watched him, with his overcoat and his height and his charisma, bending his head down to offer words of sympathy to the girls. I remembered Mrs Singer saying that they were fourteen and fifteen – around the age Paddy had been when his mother died.

You could see that even though their mother was dead, it was nonetheless a thrill that the famous Paddy de Courcy had come to her funeral.

Poor little girl-women, to be deprived of their mum at such a vulnerable age. But at least they seemed to have a loving dad. Not like Paddy.

'Oh my God . . .' Marnie had stopped, like she'd banged up against a force field.

It had been a bright June evening, the night before Marnie's and my Leaving Cert history exam and Ma and Dad were forcing us to walk Dun Laoghaire pier, in the hope that the fresh air would give us a boost in the exam hall the following day.

Business on the pier was brisk; the sunny evenings always

brought out the crowds and lots of other parents had had the same idea as Ma and Dad.

'The Marshall Plan was dressed up as aid but it was a perfidious plot to . . .' Dad was 'helping us revise'. He came to a halt and looked back at Marnie, a few feet behind him. 'Why've you stopped, Marnie? What's wrong?'

'Nothing.' Her face was suddenly bloodless.

'What? You can't just say ''nothing''. Are you going to faint?'

'Don't look,' she muttered. 'Don't say anything, but it's Paddy's dad.'

'Where?' Ma and Dad's eyes sought drunkards on benches, enjoying the last rays of the sun.

'Over there, but please don't look!' Marnie indicated a tall erect man, with tightly cut, bristly grey hair, a creaseless tan-coloured shirt and pair of matching trousers. He could have been an army officer.

'*Him?*' This picture of military-like respectability was not what Ma and Dad had been expecting. They'd known from Paddy's impoverished, hungry demeanour that Mr de Courcy was a mostly absent parent, but as Paddy had never gone into detail they'd drawn the not-outlandish conclusion that drink was the trouble.

Marnie stepped behind me. 'Don't let him see me.'

'He looks pleasant enough,' Ma said.

'You mean clean,' Marnie said.

'I do not!' Ma was wounded. 'When did I ever like clean people?'

'He looks like he's in the army. But is he?' Dad checked. Marnie shook her head.

443

Satisfied that he wouldn't be fraternizing with fascists, Dad took Ma by the elbow. 'We should introduce ourselves.'

'No, don't. Please!' Marnie said. She pulled them back.

'Why not? His son and our daughter have been "going" with each other for the last year. It's only polite.'

'You don't understand. Wait a minute.' She corralled us into a tight circle. 'Don't look! Don't let him see you looking!'

We flicked discreet glances at Mr de Courcy.

'What is it?' Dad asked. 'I see he's carrying a microphone. Does he sing?'

Marnie paused, swallowed, then said, 'Yes, sometimes, I believe.'

'So he's a singer,' Ma said. She liked singers, musicians, people in the arts, basically anyone without a regular income. 'Paddy never said.'

'He's not a singer.'

Marnie had told me about Mr de Courcy but she'd threatened that if I ever breathed a word, she'd tell everyone that I hadn't yet lost my virginity. (Mortifying at almost eighteen.)

I understood why she was so protective of Paddy. Marnie and I were embarrassed by our parents: Dad and his nose and his commie notions; Ma and her bluestocking chic and her do-gooding tendencies. But Paddy's father was in a different league.

Personally, it was electrifying to finally get a look at the man that I'd heard so much about. He had a massive jaw, which he kept working, like he was crushing raw potatoes between his back teeth. His skin had a tender-looking raw-ness to it, as though he'd shaved off three or four extra

444

layers, just to teach his face a lesson. His eyes were the same long-distance blue as Paddy's but his had a staring glassiness to them.

'He takes them out at night and polishes them,' Marnie said, reading my mind. 'Can we go back? We've walked enough.'

'Let's just go and say hello.'

'No, Ma. You wouldn't like him.'

'You can't decide that,' Dad said.

'We like everyone,' Ma insisted. 'Look, he's switching on his microphone. He must be about to start his act.'

'He's not a busker,' Marnie said somewhat desperately.

'Ssh, let's hear the man,' Dad said, turning an expectant face in Mr de Courcy's direction.

What had Dad been expecting? Jokes? Ballads? Sinatra covers?

He got the last thing on earth he'd imagined.

Mr de Courcy clenched his back teeth nine or ten times, held the microphone with white-knuckled fingers before his mouth and barked, 'Now hear this! God so loved the world that he sent his only begotten son to save us. His only son. To save us miserable sinners. Yes, you, that woman right there in the blue anorak, and you, sir, there. And are we grateful? Are *you*?' he asked a startled jogger. 'No, you most certainly are not. How do we repay this great act of sacrifice? By sinning. Sins of the flesh. Lust! Greed, gluttony, anger, envy, but mostly lust!'

Men walking their dogs, young mothers wheeling their babies, family groups enjoying the last hour of daylight – the invective reached them all. They looked variously surprised, alarmed, sometimes offended. Such freelance

God-bothering was highly unusual. Ireland had official channels for this sort of thing – an army of priests who ran a closed shop.

Ma and Dad were rooted to the spot. Their expressions were so radiant with shock, they looked like converts.

'Can we go?' Marnie pleaded, shaking Ma's elbow. 'I'm afraid he'll see me and shout at me about lust.'

'Yes, yes, of course.' Protectively Ma and Dad hurried us towards home and eventually Mr de Courcy's voice faded away. Perhaps it was the curve of the pier or the direction of the wind, but when we were almost at the end, Marnie whispered, 'He's singing now.'

We cocked our ears and heard – very clearly – carried to us on the wind, 'She's just a devil woman, with evil on her mind.' He sang in a lumbering, dirge-like fashion, divesting the song of any jauntiness. 'Beware the devil woman, she's going to get you from behiiiind.'

Dad stared in the direction of the noise. 'It's a downright tragedy,' he said.

'I must admit I'd been expecting a waster who drank,' Ma said. 'If only.'

'But he is a waster,' Marnie said. 'He got sacked from his job and didn't try to get another. He doesn't earn any money. This is all he does now.'

'Poor Paddy. And his mother is dead. No one to take care of him.'

'Poor Paddy.'

'Poor Paddy.'

'Poor Paddy.'

*

'Damien! Damien Stapleton! You great, big, sexy ride, over here!'

'Ah there she is,' Damien said.

A woman at a faraway table was standing up and waving: tall, busty, blonde, loud; the type who yelled greetings from four miles away.

'That's *Juno*?'

'That's her,' he said happily, grasping my hand and hurrying us across the restaurant. 'Don't worry. You're really alike. You're going to get on great.'

She wasn't what I'd expected and this made me very anxious. I hate to have my prejudices overturned. The picture in my head had Juno as a lady-who-lunches type, who wore a lot of white and starved herself into early-onset osteoporosis. I mean, she'd worked in PR, for Browning and Eagle no less, could you blame me? But she was hale and hearty, and dressed in jeans and a rugby shirt worn with the collar flicked up. Many things annoy me – I'd be the first to admit that I'm deeply intolerant – but rugby shirts worn with the collars flicked up make rage boil up inside me like toxic black smoke.

'Still the latest man in Ireland,' she chided, giving him a quick peck – to my alarm – on the lips.

'It was Grace's fault,' Damien said. 'She was stuck at work.'

Thanks, you disloyal fucker.

'Earthquake in Pakistan,' I said. 'Mostly women and children killed. So thoughtless of them to die on a Friday evening when I'm on my way out for dinner. Ahahaha,' I added mirthlessly, in a fruitless attempt to seem good-humoured.

'Work,' Juno exclaimed. 'Give it up, I say! Send the men out to graft and let us women stay home and spend the money!'

She was trying to be friendly – shocked as I was, I could see that – and this was my chance to show good faith by replying in kind: Yes, men, lazy bastards! Good enough for them. That'll teach them to throw their dirty socks on the bedroom floor!

But I couldn't.

I looked at the empty chair beside her. 'So where *is* your husband?'

'God knows,' she said, throwing her head back and hooting.

'. . . What do you mean?'

'On a corporate jolly in the Curragh. Cristal tent. Been down there all afternoon. Just had a call from him.' She held up her mobile. 'Too drunk to drive. He might make it later, but fuck alone knows what state he'll be in. He's in big trouble with me, he lost two grand on the horses. If I don't get some decent diamonds as an apology, guess who'll be sleeping in the spare room for the next month!' She roared with laughter – and so did Damien.

Her husband wasn't coming?

I hadn't wanted to have this dinner. In these nicotine-free days it was a complication I could have done without. However, a group event, including me and Juno's husband, had seemed a benign enough proposition. Now everything had changed and I knew I'd be spending the next four hours sitting like a big plank while Damien and Juno played Do You Remember The Time We . . .

And why had Juno arranged a night out when Miles was on a jolly?

And why hadn't she apologized?

Was that not . . . rude?

I'd suddenly come over all polite.

The waiter appeared. 'An aperitif?'

'A pint of Guinness,' Damien said.

'Make it two,' Juno said.

She drank pints? I'll tell you, it was a novelty to feel girly and prim.

'You and your pints of Guinness,' Damien said happily. 'I'm getting flashbacks to our misspent youth. Remember? When we had no money and had to make drinks last as long as possible.'

'Yes,' I said. 'I remember having to do that too. And the cheapest pint you could buy was –'

'Grace?' Damien indicated the waiter. 'Drink?'

'I'm sorry.' I'd been so desperately trying to fit in that I forgot he was still there. 'Gin and tonic, please.'

'Large?'

'Oh why not?'

'I'm just popping out for a cancer stick. I can't tempt you . . .' Juno slanted a smile at Damien.

He shook his head ruefully.

'How are you two getting on since you stopped smoking?'

'Fine,' I said, at the same time as Damien said, 'We're at each other's throats.'

'No, we're not,' I said.

'We are. We're not getting on at all,' he insisted.

'Aren't we?'

'No. We're not.'

'We are!'

'We're not.'

'We are!'

'We're not!'

Juno flashed us her pack of Marlboro, like it was an FBI badge. 'I hate to interrupt,' she twinkled, 'but I'll be out the front, while you two get your story straight.'

'Why did you say she was like me?' I raged in the taxi home.

'Because she's her own woman. She gives as good as she gets. Like you.'

'Like me! We've nothing in common. She doesn't have a job.'

'She has two kids.'

'She has a nanny! She plays hockey. She goes horse-riding. She says, "Everyone, let's get naked!"' (The punch-line to some pointless anecdote involving an all-day drinking orgy and a swimming pool.) 'She's a female jock.'

'She's fun.'

She wasn't.

'If you don't like her,' he said, 'you don't have to meet her again.'

'But you will, won't you?'

'I might . . .'

'Ah Damien, she's your *ex-wife*.'

'But sure, that's immaterial. That was a thousand years ago.'

'*Don't* start hanging around with her.' Drunkenly and childishly I said, 'Don't be so *mean*.'

'What's the big deal? I love you. I'm with you.'

'Just bloody stubborn,' I muttered into my chest. 'Only doing it to be contrary.'

'No, no.' He was being irritatingly reasonable. 'Juno's a part of my past and I'm glad we're back in touch with each other.'

'But –'

Then I was suddenly reminded of another conversation we'd had, not so long ago, and with the fighting spirit of the drunk person who knows she's beaten but can't bear to lose face, I said, 'Fuck it, then, fine, fine, have it your way. Lez all be friends with lovely Juno.'

It was 6.58 a.m. when the phone rang.

I was already awake. All the same, it must be something big. Another tsunami? When something of that magnitude happened we were all called in to work immediately.

'I'm on my way to the hospital!' It was Jacinta. 'Oscar's burst his appendix!'

'. . . Right.'

'Natural disaster?' Damien asked sleepily.

'Take it easy, Jacinta,' I said.

'Jacinta,' he muttered. 'I might have known.'

'No one dies from a burst appendix nowadays,' I said. 'He'll be fine.'

'No, you don't understand! Today's my day for interviewing Rosalind Croft and I'll be stuck at Oscar's bloody bedside. Of all the fucking days he has to pick! Never have children, Grace, they're the most *profoundly* selfish – '

'We're not running the piece until Friday. Change the interview to tomorrow or Thursday.'

'No, no! Rosalind's schedule is so full, it has to be today. Today! You'll have to go instead of me.'

'Okay.'

'Okay? Is that all you have to say? Aren't you glad?'

'. . . Ah . . .'

'If she gives you anything, like a scarf or . . . or *anything*, you give it straight to me.'

They valet-parked me. A *house* with valet-parking.

A suited PA-type person escorted me to a dressing room that was bigger than my entire house, where Mrs Croft was getting her hair blow-dried. She was already fully made-up. It was hard to put an exact age on her – maybe forty-five?

I'd expected to dislike her. I was more than slightly judgemental about society women who did charity work; I suspected it was just an excuse to buy lots of frocks. But she squeezed my hand and smiled with a warmth that seemed genuine.

'You're going to shadow me today, Grace? I hope you won't be bored to death.'

I sincerely doubted it. Much as I might disapprove of the super-rich, I was shamefully fascinated by their lifestyles.

People were constantly in and out of her room, bringing her phone messages, menus to approve, documents to sign. Being rich was a demanding job. Mrs Croft was chatty and pleasant to everyone. But maybe only because I was there.

A stunningly good-looking Nigerian girl called Nkechi was flitting around, laying out clothes, flicking through hangers and shouting dog's abuse at another Nigerian girl called Abibi. 'MaxMara, MaxMara, I said MaxMara. Why do you give me Ralph Lauren?'

'You said cream trousers.'

'I said cream *MaxMara* trousers, you moron. There is a *world* of difference.'

'I'm chairing a committee meeting this morning,' Mrs Croft said, as Nkechi helped her into a strokeably soft cream cardigan. I didn't know much about wool but whatever this garment was made of, it was clearly very, very expensive. I was saving up phrases to tell Damien later. I decided on, 'A cardigan knitted from the hair of newborn babies.'

'What sort of committee meeting? Charity?'

'Are there any other kinds of committee meeting?' Her eyes twinkled. 'Thank you, Nkechi.' Nkechi zipped up the cream MaxMara pants that had caused all the shouting. 'Sugar Babies. For babies with diabetes. Then a lunch.'

'And what sort of lunch?'

'Take a guess. Charity again.' Leaning on Nkechi, she stepped into a pair of cream and brown patent, low-heeled pumps. 'Thank you, Nkechi.'

'Same charity?'

'No, no, different. The Sweetheart Foundation. For children with heart defects. Thank you, Nkechi.'

Nkechi was fussing at Mrs Croft's neck with a cream scarf decorated with horseshoes and stirrups. 'Okay, it appears we're ready to go.'

It was a right cavalcade. There was me, Mrs Croft, the

PA, the hairdresser, Nkechi, Abibi, two cars, two drivers and a large number of Louis Vuitton suitcases.

Mrs Croft, the PA and I were helped into a Maybach ('the dearest car in Ireland'), while Nkechi, Abibi, the hairdresser and the suitcases 'had to suffer the ignominy' of travelling behind us in an S-class Merc.

The other committee ladies were exactly what I'd expected: freshly blow-dried hair, impractically light-coloured clothing and accents like angle-grinders. It seemed that everyone served on everyone else's committees and they all attended each other's shindigs. ('Every lunch and dinner must be like *Groundhog Day* with tit tape.')

There was lively discussion over the theme for the Sugar Babies ball, or at least to find a theme that hadn't been used in the previous six months at another ball. Suggestions were bigged up and shot down, according to whatever personal animosities were in play. Mrs Croft kept it all under control without having to raise her voice and they finally settled on a Marie Antoinette theme. ('Super!')

Then the agenda moved to the menu.

'Like it matters.' Mrs Croft sighed.

'Excuse me?' one of the angle-grinders said.

'Like anyone eats the food at these things.'

The angle-grinder stared. 'That's hardly the point, Rosalind. We still have to have an innovative menu.'

'Of course, Arlene, you're absolutely right. How about partridge?'

'Done. Only last week.'

'Poussin?'

'Done.'

'Woodcock?'

'Done.'

'Duck?'

'Done.'

'Pheasant?'

'Done.'

'Chicken?'

'Done.'

'Grouse?'

'Done.'

'Why hasn't someone invented a new bird?' one of the angle-grinders whined. 'This bloody country, I tell you.'

In a suite in the hotel, Nkechi helped Rosalind out of her committee clothes and into her luncheon outfit. The hairdresser did a quick change of style, then it was down to the ballroom for the lunch.

Hellish. A hundred and fifty clones of the women who'd been at the committee meeting. It was like a nature programme about a colony of breeding seagulls. The *noise*.

Once the women on either side of me discovered that I was unable to discuss the terrible traffic in Marbella or the drop in standards in private schools, they turned their respective backs on me. I didn't care; I zoned out and fantasized about a warehouse full of uncountable numbers of cigarettes. Shelf after shelf, so many you had to drive along on a mechanical platform thing to view them. A cigarette universe. Cigarettes by the million. Although I'd have been happy with just one.

At 2.30 on the dot, the PA poked Rosalind and Rosalind got to her feet like an automaton and the cavalcade was off again. To be honest, I was shattered and I couldn't understand why. I'd done nothing all morning, except make snide remarks in my head.

Our next stop was a yoga lesson with a man who was often on telly. Another change of clothes, then on to dress fittings in Brown Thomas. Then back out to the house in Killiney for her amatsu practitioner, followed by a quick break for tea and victuals – ricecakes for her and handmade biscuits, spookily similar to the ones you find in posh hotels, for me.

'Have a biscuit,' I said, as I watched her tuck into the styrofoam discs. 'Those things taste of nothing.'

'Thanks, love, but I'm on one thousand two hundred calories a day, have been for the past nine years, since Maxwell made it big – if I can't fit into size ten ballgowns I'm a goner. But you eat up.'

She opened a massive desk diary. 'You'd like to see my calendar for next week? Take a look.'

It was awe-inspiring: acupuncture, committee meetings, hospice visits, cranio-sacral treatment, photocalls, colonics, Pilates, teeth-whitening, Christmas gift-buying for her army of staff, lunches, teas, business breakfasts . . .

'. . . and always, balls, balls, balls,' she said, her tone suddenly and unexpectedly bitter. 'Sorry,' she said quietly.

'That's okay,' I said. 'It can't always be fun.'

As far as I was concerned, it would never be fun. If by some bizarre quirk of the universe – like the plots in *Quantum Leap* – I ended up as a society wife, they'd have to fish me out of the canal.

Then something happened – I didn't know what it was but it made her hands clench and her knuckles flash white. 'Maxwell's home. My husband.' She flicked her wrist to see her watch and said, 'He's early.'

I'd heard nothing.

As if her switch had clicked from medium to extra-fast, she was gathering her sheets of paper and banging them on the desk. 'We'll have to finish for today, Grace.' She was standing up, tugging down her skirt, moving towards the door.

'But . . .' My brief had been to shadow her until bedtime.

'Rosalind, Rosalind!' a man's voice yelled in the hall.

'In here!' She dived to open the door but, before she got there, someone outside thrust it inwards. A narky-looking man. Maxwell Croft.

'What are you doing in here?' he asked Rosalind.

'I didn't expect you for another hour –'

He looked past her and stared, without warmth, at me.

'Grace Gildee,' Rosalind said. 'She's doing a piece for the *Spokesman*, about the charity balls.' She spoke quickly, almost hiccuping over her words.

'Maxwell Croft. Nice to see you.' He gave me a brief glance. 'Rosalind will have your car brought round.'

Any protests I'd been about to make died in my mouth. My will was no match for his.

'What did she give you?'

'Nothing. How's Oscar doing?'

'Fine, fine. She gave you nothing at all?'

'No.'

457

'She probably didn't think there was any point. Why give you an Hermès handbag? It would only make the rest of you look worse.'

'Jacinta, would you mind not being quite so insult –'

'It's not too late. Maybe when the piece comes out, she'll send something. Now, I take it you've seen the contract?'

'. . . Yes.'

Jacinta had promised the Crofts copy approval, which never happens, not even for Tom Cruise. Therefore my profile of Mrs Croft would be an absolute rave.

Good job I'd liked her.

I was the one who introduced them: Paddy and Marnie. It was the July I turned seventeen and I'd got a summer job as a lounge girl in the Boatman, where Paddy was working as a barman.

It was actually the night of my seventeenth birthday – also Marnie's. Marnie dropped by with Leechy when I'd finished work; we were on our way out to celebrate the only way we knew how: drinking heavily.

'Come and meet Paddy,' I said, with a little pride.

Paddy was cool. He'd already finished school, had worked in London for a year on a building site and was starting university at the end of September to study law.

Marnie and Leechy had heard all about him – as had Ma, Dad and Bid – because he was the only barman who was nice to me. From the moment the rest of the staff discovered I lived on Yeoman Road, they had regarded me with hostility. They mistakenly thought I was from a well-off family and set out to torment me, starting on my very first night, when Micko, the manager, said, 'There's a phone call for Mike Hunt, ask around and see if anyone has seen him.' It was only Paddy's intervention that stopped me wandering around the pub calling plaintively, 'My cunt? Anyone seen my cunt?'

'They do it to all the new girls,' he'd said. 'Don't take it personally. There's a bet on to see how long before they make you cry.'

'They won't make me cry,' I'd said, filled with resolve – for about five minutes. Then I decided to leave and get a job somewhere else.

'They're afraid of you,' Dad explained. 'You're educated and different. You're just passing through, but that's their career. Have compassion.'

'Don't leave,' Ma agreed. 'Being despised is character-forming. Think of Gandhi.'

'Fuck them,' Bid said. 'Ignorant knackers. Work in McLibels instead, you can get us a family discount.'

In the end, because the tips were good and the place was only round the corner, I'd decided to stick it out. What would have happened if I hadn't?

'Paddy,' I called. He was loading glasses into a dish-washer. 'This is my friend Leechy. And this is my sister, Marnie. My twin sister.'

He said hello to Leechy, then I waited for him to express the obligatory surprise about Marnie – your *twin*? You're so different!

But he said nothing and for a baffled moment I wondered what was wrong. But when I looked at him, he was staring open-mouthed at Marnie and she was gawking back in the same stupefied fashion. Something was happening – you could actually feel it. Shivery, snaky sensations zigzagged over my scalp. Micko turned from doing something clangy with a metal barrel, his face confused, because he didn't know why he was looking. Even a very drunk man and woman, curled up in a booth, left off their slurred accusatory conversation and stared at us.

Instantly Paddy and Marnie aligned their lives. Within fourteen hours Marnie had handed in her notice in Piece'a Pizza, where she and Leechy had both had jobs, and started working instead in the Boatman where she charmed Micko into synchronizing her shifts with Paddy's.

Despite her living on Yeoman Road, the other barmen treated her with tenderness and affection; that was the effect Marnie had on men. Also she was a protectorate of Paddy's and despite being educated and ambitious, everyone loved Paddy.

Marnie couldn't stop thanking me. 'You found him for me.'

I'd never seen her so joyous, and it was a relief because I couldn't breathe easy if Marnie wasn't happy.

But all of a sudden I was the extra wheel. We'd had other boyfriends in the past, but this was different. Not that I was abandoned and alone. Leechy was almost like another sister, she lived only five doors up and was always in our house. Then there was Sheridan, Paddy's best friend since infant school. It was as if, at the age of four, they'd selected each other because they knew that when they grew up they could go womanizing as a pair: they were about the same height and build (vital for womanizing pairs, you just can't take them seriously if one is six inches shorter than the other) and both very good-looking.

In fairness, though, handsome as Sheridan was, with his clean, Nordic looks, Paddy had something extra. Sheridan was foisted on Leechy and me, accompanied by a little lecture from Paddy that Sheridan was practically his brother and that we were to take good care of him. Together the three of us formed an uncomfortable little gang of leftovers.

The funny thing was that I had as much contact with Paddy as if he'd been *my* boyfriend. I saw him all the time at work and I saw him all the time at home. It felt like you couldn't walk into a room without finding him already in there, crotch-to-crotch with Marnie, his hand up her T-shirt.

Ma and Dad had always encouraged us to bring our boy-friends home, but their famed tolerance ran out within days.

'I go down to the kitchen to cut myself a slice of cake,' Dad raged, 'and there they are . . . at it.'

'*At it?*' Ma asked anxiously. Liberal as she was, this was not welcome news.

'Not that sort of at it. But kissing. Sucking face. Whatever dreadful expression is currently in vogue. He's always damn well here. And when he does bother going home, she spends half the night on the phone to him. What do they talk about? He gives me the creeps.'

'The creeps! Why?'

'He tries too hard to be liked.'

'No he doesn't!' Ma and I were in unison.

'He's only a boy!' Ma said. 'You can't attribute such cynicism to someone who's only a boy.'

'He's nineteen. He's too old for her.'

'It's only two years.'

'Two years is a lot at this age. And they're never apart. It's not healthy.'

But Ma couldn't resist taking Paddy under her wing. She was a sucker for any waifs and strays and Paddy was perfect: his mother was dead; his father was rarely at home; there was never any food in his house. The least she could do was feed the poor creature.

'You think it's bad now,' Bid said to Dad.

'Yes, I do actually, thank you very much,' Dad said.

'You wait till he goes to college in September. That'll be fun and games in earnest. He'll have no time then for the likes of our little Marnie,' Bid predicted.

'Our little Marnie' must have been on the same page as Bid, because when September rolled around, a series of emotional upheavals kicked off and set the tone for the next three years:

Upheaval 1

'It's all ruined!' The sound of Marnie yelling came through the wall. 'This summer has been the most perfect time of my life. Now I have to go back to school and you have to go to college. Don't go!'

Ma winced and muttered, 'She shouldn't have said that.'

Ma, Dad, Bid, Leechy, Sheridan and I were sitting in the kitchen, while the shouting match played out in the next room. It was impossible not to hear them. Initially we'd tried to keep a pretence of a conversation going, but in the end we just gave up and listened.

'But I have to go,' Paddy cried. 'This is my future, my life.'

'I thought I was your life.'

462

'You are! But I have to get qualifications so I can earn a living. How else can I take care of you?'

'But you won't want to. You'll meet all these other . . . *girls*! You'll fancy them and you'll forget about me.'

'She's right,' said Bid. 'I've always thought she was a bit thick, but she's right.'

'I won't!' Paddy shrieked. 'I love you, I only love you and I will never love anyone else.'

'Well, well, if I had a pound for every time a man said that to me . . .' Bid murmured.

Upheaval 2

'Sssh, sssh, I can't hear,' Bid said.

'What's it about this time?' Dad asked.

'Not sure.'

' "Let's fight until six, then let's have tea," ' Dad said. 'Tweedledum to Tweedledee. Page eighty-four, *Alice in Wonderland*.'

'Ssssh!'

'Paddy, what's wrong?' Marnie was pleading.

'If you have to ask,' he accused, 'there's no point telling you!'

He had arrived, cold, imperious and very angry, and a nervous-looking Marnie had quickly closeted him in the living room.

'I tried ringing you last night . . . but the phone was engaged . . . you're meant to keep the line free from eight till midnight . . .'

'But Paddy, other people live in this house, they might have made a call.'

'But it wasn't other people, was it? It was you. Look, I know, Marnie, you can stop lying to me.'

'I'm not lying!'

'I *know* who you were on the phone to.'

'Who was it?' Ma asked.

'Graham Higgins,' Leechy said. 'His mum made him ring her, to get Marnie to explain Yeats's poems to him, because she's afraid he'll fail English.'

'Tall chap? Plays rugby?' Bid said. 'How does Paddy know who she was talking to?'

'Leechy told me!' Paddy yelled. 'I know everything!'

Shocked, Ma, Dad, Bid, Sheridan and I whipped around to look at Leechy.

'I didn't know that he didn't know,' Leechy wailed. 'He rang me. He tricked me into telling.'

'How?'

'Shut up! I can't hear!'

'But Graham is nothing, he's nobody!' Marnie declared.

'He fancies you.'

'He doesn't.'

'And you must fancy him. You spoke to him for at least seventeen minutes, while I stood in the cold, beside a phone box, trying to ring the girl I love, who couldn't even be bothered to – Fuck this! I'm leaving!'

'Oh Paddy, no! Don't go, Paddy, no!'

'God, it's so romantic,' Leechy said quietly.

'You're a sap, child,' Bid said.

'Is Paddy . . . *crying*?' Dad asked.

'Someone is.' Energetic sobs could be heard clearly.

'I think they're both crying,' Ma said. It was how their

fights often ended. Either that, or one of them stormed from the house. Sometimes it was Paddy, sometimes it was Marnie, although she lived there. Whoever it was, they never went far. Within minutes, they'd ring the bell and one of us in the kitchen would have to answer the front door to let them back in to continue their shouting.

The weeping noises eventually ceased. Silence prevailed. That meant they'd moved on to kiss-and-make-up sex.

'That's all, folks,' Dad said, getting to his feet.

'At times it's as good as a soap opera,' Bid said. 'Speaking of which, I hope they're decent because my show is starting and I'm going into that room.'

Upheaval 3

'It's over,' Marnie said. 'Me and Paddy. It's different this time.' It *was* different. She was calm, rather than hair-tearingly distraught.

'But you love each other!' Leechy protested.

Marnie shook her head. 'We love each other too much. We're tearing each other apart. It's got to stop.' Something about her composure made us begin to take her seriously.

'Maybe you're right,' Leechy said. 'He does love you but you bring out the worst in each other. All that jealousy . . . Maybe you need a different type of man and he needs a different type of girl.' We didn't realize at the time that she herself was planning to volunteer for the position.

'Don't.' Marnie doubled over, clutching her stomach. 'The thought of him with someone else . . .'

'But you'll meet someone else too,' Leechy predicted.

Marnie shook her head and produced a large green bottle,

from which she swigged heavily. Dad's absinthe. He'd go *spare*.

'I won't.'

'You will, you will!'

'I don't even want to. That's it for me. Paddy was the one. I'm going to kill myself.'

'Don't be mad.' Leechy was appalled.

'People kill themselves. It happens. And I'm the kind of person who does it.'

'I'm getting Ma.'

'I always knew I'd die young,' Marnie explained, curling up on her bed.

'She's been at the Brontës again,' Dad whispered angrily. 'And is that my absinthe she's drinking?'

'No offence,' Marnie told Ma and Dad, 'but I wish I hadn't been born. I feel too much, all the time, and I hate it. I actually want to die.'

'How would you kill yourself?' Ma asked, following the advice given in the information booklet for parents of suicidal teenagers and calling her bluff.

'Cut my wrists.'

'With what?'

'This.' Marnie fished out a scalpel from her jeans pocket.

'Give me that! Give it to me!'

Sulkily she surrendered it. 'But Ma, there are blades in the bathroom, knives in the kitchen, more scalpels in my art bag. And if you take them all away, I can climb onto the roof and throw myself off or I can go down to the pier and fling myself into the sea.'

Ma and Dad stood, their heads together, trying to formulate a plan.

'Let's just get her through tonight,' Ma said. 'Even if it means staying awake all night with her, then we'll find a good Jungian first thing in the morning.'

'I wish we'd had boys,' Dad said. 'We'd have none of this sort of trouble with boys.'

Despite absinthe's reputation for sending people bonkers, Marnie made a frightening amount of sense. She sat on her bed, quietly explaining how she was unequipped to deal with the feelings that everyone else could process. 'I can't survive the pain of not being with Paddy,' she said.

'But we all have to have our hearts broken at some stage,' Ma said. 'It's part of the human condition. I remember being fifteen and thinking I'd never be happy again.'

'But some people just can't take the pain of being alive. Why do you think people kill themselves?'

'Yes, but –'

'There's a bit missing in me that Grace got. A stop button for the feelings. You got a whole person when you got Grace, but you just got a runt when you got me. I was the one made up of the leftovers.'

'No, Marnie, no!'

'I wish I could have chosen not to be born. Do you think they have a holding pen for unborn souls? Some black place for all of us who are too defective to be born?'

'You're not defective, you're perfect!'

'You don't know what I know. You don't know what it's like to be me.'

Ma, Dad and I did our best but whatever we said, she

countered it with her own certainty that she was better off dead. Eventually we lapsed into a despairing silence and listened to the hiss of the rain on the road and the roof. Dad was starting to nod off, when we heard the wail from outside.

'What was that?' Ma asked.

'I don't know,' I said.

Our muscles froze as we listened intently.

Then we heard it clearly. 'Maarr-nie.'

The four of us lunged at the window. Outside the house, in the middle of the road, in the teeming rain, stood Paddy, wearing his Russian army greatcoat, a white dress shirt missing all of its buttons and his ancient black barman trousers, torn at the knee.

'Maarr-nie.' He flung his arms wide, exposing his bare chest. 'I love you!'

And then Marnie was off and down the stairs and out of the front door, running towards him. He grabbed her up, swung her round, then set her down, fastening his face to hers. Joined at the mouth, they sank to their knees, their tears mingling with the rain.

'I suppose that means we can go to bed now,' Dad said.

'It was the most romantic thing I've ever seen,' Leechy said the following day. 'It was like *Wuthering Heights*.'

'Gothic bollocks,' Dad said scornfully. 'Doesn't anyone remember that Heathcliff was a psychopath. He killed Isabel's dog.'

Marnie and Paddy were curled up in Marnie's bed, both sleeping peacefully, like children recovering from an ordeal. The rest of us were nervy and exhausted, wrung dry from the emotional rollercoaster.

'Forgive me for asking such a bourgeois question,' Ma said. 'But all that, last night? Is that normal?'

'No,' Dad said. 'You don't see Grace behaving that way.'

'Only because I haven't got a boyfriend,' I said, jumping to Marnie's defence.

'Why not?' Bid asked. 'What's wrong with you?'

'Noth –'

'Too choosy, that's your trouble. Have you still not lost your virginity?'

'Bid! Stop it!'

'I'll take that as a no. What about Sheridan? He's a phwoarr, not as ridey as Paddy, but not at all bad,' Bid said. 'Would you not ''go'' with him?'

'No.' Sheridan was witty and dry and yes, good-looking, but I didn't fancy him. And he didn't fancy me either. He fancied Marnie. I was sure of it.

'Even if Grace had a boyfriend, there wouldn't be any shouting,' Bid said. 'Grace has always been dull. If it's drama you want, Marnie's your girl.'

'Did you see the photo in the *Indo* of Kaplan looking very lovey-dovey with Zara Kaletsky?' TC asked me.

'Who? Oh the model?'

'Actress, actress. I used to love her in *Liffey Lives*. Till she left Ireland for bigger and better.'

'Has she moved back here?'

'Just home on holiday.'

'Can't be serious with Kaplan so. What do you mean, ''lovey-dovey''?'

'Hand on her arse, what little there is of it. God, she's

beautiful, so she is.' TC sighed. 'What does she see in that plank?'

*

To: Gracegildee@spokesman.ie

From: Pattilavezzo@oraclepr.com

Subject: Interview with Madonna

Thank you for your interest in Madonna. Regrettably it has been decided to go with another journalist.

Bloody *Irish Times*, I bet. Disappointment slithered down-wards, pulling all of me right into the pit. I rested my forehead on my hands.

It was unbearably frustrating. I'd do a better job than the *Times*: I *loved* Madonna. I'd grown up with her, I *got* her.

I sat and stewed and waited to feel better and waited a little bit longer, and when the disappointment still ached inside me I had a brainwave: I'd ring Patti Lavezzo in a last-ditch attempt to get her to reconsider! At this stage, there was nothing to be lost and if I did it with enough passion, she might change her mind.

'PattiLavezzo.' She always answered the phone like someone was timing her with a stopwatch.

'Hi, Patti, Grace Gildee here, from the *Spokesman* in Ireland. Can you please reconsider your decision?' I talked fast so she couldn't interrupt. 'We'd do a stunning piece on Madonna. We're the highest circulation broadsheet in Ireland. We have integrity and can guarantee an in-depth, intelligent profile, but at the same time we have an excellent commercial sensibility . . .'

'Hey! Hold up! You're calling from where?'

'The *Spokesman*.'

'Yeah, but ... we're giving the interview to the *Spokesman*.'

Hope broke open in me and the sun emerged, warm and dazzling. 'You are? But I just got an email –'

'Yes, one moment please, let me just get you up on screen. Yes, here we are. Ireland. The *Spokesman*. Casey Kaplan. Is that you?'

I went to the Ladies and I actually shed tears. Then I rang Damien and shed more tears.

'I'm trapped in the Dail,' he said. 'But I could get away in an hour.'

'No, no, do your job. I'll see if some lead-swinger here will come to the pub with me. I'm either going to drink or smoke and drinking seems like the safer choice.'

'Look, I'm on my way over to you. It might be even less than an hour –'

'No, don't, Damien.' I was touched by his willingness. 'I'll be grand.'

I didn't have to look far for a drinking buddy. Even though it was only three in the afternoon, Dickie McGuinness was game to down tools and accompany me to Dinnegans.

'Why were you crying?' he asked, putting a gin and tonic in front of me.

'Who said I was crying?'

'Mrs Farrell. She did a ring-round, told everyone.'

Normally I'd deny it, but I was too sad. 'Kaplan shafted me. He stole my Madonna interview. He knew how badly I wanted it.'

471

'Did he, though?'

'Everyone knew! Bad enough to lose to another paper, Dickie, but to one of your own ... It's too much. I hate him.'

'So does everyone. We're after finding out how much they're paying him.'

I paused. I didn't know if I could take it. 'How much?'

'You sure you want to know?'

I sighed. 'Go on.'

'Three times what you're getting.'

I let that sink in. 'How d'you know what I'm paid?'

He tapped his nose. 'You know me, Grace. I know plenty.'

I sighed again. What could I do? Nothing. The world was unfair. Since when was that news?

'Tell me a story, Dickie.'

'What would you like?'

'Your first decapitation.' There was comfort in the familiar.

'Right you are, here we go.' He settled himself into his seat and began his trip down memory lane. 'I was a raw-boned youth, all of nineteen years of age, covering every dog and pony show for the *Limerick Leader*, when the call came in that a body had been found.'

But the crime correspondent was in hospital with a gun-shot wound to the buttock.

'But the crime correspondent was in hospital with a gunshot wound to the buttock and Theo Fitzgibbon, the editor, says to me, "McGuinness, you'll have to go." Said I, flourishing my notebook and pen, puffed up like a peacock, "What can you tell me, Theo?" "It's Mr Fitzgibbon to you," says Theo. Old school, none of this first-name stuff.'

Never saw him without a collar and tie.

'Never saw him without a collar and tie, Grace. "Deceased was discovered in a disused freezer. Young, male, dead as a dodo," says Theo. "And one more thing – he's missing his head." "His head? Where's it gone?" says I, like a gombeen.'

Someone must have cut it off.

' "Someone must have cut it off," says Theo. "Don't let us down, McGuinness," he said. Meaning –'

' – Don't puke in front of the rozzers,' we said together.

'. . . He kept finding her. No matter where she moved to he always tracked her down. Her house was like a fortress. She had all kinds of security. Alarms, panic buttons, even a panic room. But there was a cat-flap in the back door.'

I was in the offices of Women's Aid, talking to their director, Laura Venn. Jacinta had, very reluctantly, agreed that I could write up a piece on domestic violence – not that she was promising to run it, she said we'd keep it in reserve for a slow news day.

'What about the cat-flap?' I asked, feeling anxious on behalf of this unknown woman.

'It had no alarm, it was the one place in the house where you could enter undetected.'

'But surely it would be too small for a man to get through?'

'It was. But she went away for the weekend with her children and while they were gone he brought his toolbox and made the cat-flap bigger. Big enough for himself to crawl through and get into the house but not big enough so that they'd notice it had been altered.'

'And what happened?'

'He got in. He hid in the attic.'

'And then what happened?' I was on the edge of my seat.

'Oh he killed her.'

'What? Completely?'

Laura half smiled.

'Sorry,' I said. 'That was a really stupid thing to say.' But I'd been waiting for some sort of last-minute redemption, as if life was an episode of *Happy Days*.

'When she left him, he'd sworn he'd find her and kill her and so he did. In front of their children.'

'And that was the end of it? She was dead?'

'She was dead.'

I was left with a breathless emptiness. 'And her children had no mother? Or father, I suppose, if he was in prison.'

'He wasn't in prison. The judge felt sorry for him. He walked free on a suspended sentence.'

'No!'

'It happens a lot.'

'But why do women get together with these psychos?' I cried in a burst of frustration. Of course I knew the answer – at least theoretically I did – but the reality maddened me.

'Because the men don't advertise the fact that they're psychos.' Laura laughed sadly. 'Often these men are very charming. And the process is a subtle one. Their initial controlling can seem romantic – you know the sort of thing, "Let's stay in, just the two of us, I love you so much I can't bear to share you." Until one day the woman finds that she's alienated her friends and family, and she's completely isolated.'

'So why doesn't she ring the rozzers?'

Again I knew the answer, but I couldn't not ask the question.

'Because he keeps promising he'll change,' Laura said. 'That he won't do it again. On average a woman is hit thirty-five separate times before she contacts the police.'

'Thirty-five times? No, that can't be right.'

'Yes. Thirty-five times.'

'Grace, baby, I'm sorry. I really am.'

Casey Kaplan, standing in front of my desk. I didn't need to look up. I knew it was him because suddenly the area around my desk smelt like a nightclub. 'About what?' I kept typing.

'About your Madonna interview. I didn't go after it. They offered it to me. I didn't even know you were in the running.'

'No big deal.' I still didn't look up. All I could see of him was the crotch of his jeans and a big, stupid, silver-eagle belt buckle.

'I didn't even know you wanted it.' He shrugged helplessly. I knew this was happening because his hands appeared in my line of vision, then disappeared again after a moment. Just long enough for me to see his rings. Big, stupid, silver rings on many of his fingers. 'Grace, I owe you. If there's any way I can make it up to you, let me know . . . I'm begging you, baby.'

'Fine.' I bit the end off the word. 'One more thing,

475

Kaplan.' I stopped typing for this part and met his eyes. 'Don't call me baby.'

'Curiosity killed the cat,' Dickie McGuinness said out of the side of his mouth. 'And information brought it back.'

'What?'

'Information for you.'

'Oh stop it, Dickie!' I said. 'Talk normally. If you've something to tell me, just tell me.'

'Okay,' he said, pulling a chair up to my desk. 'I know who burnt out your car last September.'

I just looked at him.

'Lemmy O'Malley and Eric Zouche.'

The names meant nothing to me.

'And d'you know why they did it?'

'. . . No . . . ?'

'Because they got paid, Grace. Three hundred euro each.'

'They got *paid*?' I'd thought it was just random, one of those things that happen when you live in a big city.

'Yeah, Grace, they got paid. It was deliberate. You were targeted.'

The way he said 'targeted' tightened a fist around my heart.

'Who paid them?' The words came out as whispers.

'Now that I don't know.'

'Why didn't you ask them?'

'I wasn't dealing with them. It was just some information that emerged in the course of another –' he paused, searching for the right word – '*investigation*. Who has it in for you, Grace?'

476

'Dickie, I don't know.' And I'm really scared.

'Come on, Grace, up there for thinking –' he pointed to his head – 'down there for dancing.' He pointed at his feet.

'Dickie, I swear to you –'

My phone rang. Automatically I checked caller display: it was Marnie. Seized by a new, different anxiety, I said to Dickie, 'I have to take this. But don't go.' I grabbed the receiver. 'Marnie?'

'It's me, Nick.'

'Nick?' No. This was very bad news.

I was only half aware of Dickie tiptoeing away and mouthing an indecipherable message to me, pointing at the door and tapping his watch.

'It's . . . it's happened again?' I asked Nick.

'Yes,' he said.

No. No, no, no. 'I thought after the last time . . . How bad is it?'

'Very bad, Grace. She's in hospital –'

'Christ, *no*.'

' – three broken ribs. Concussion. Internal bleeding.'

'Jesus Christ. And it's only been – how long? – six weeks since the last time.'

I should have gone to London then. I was seized by guilt.

'The gaps are getting shorter and the injuries are getting worse,' Nick said. 'That's what they told me would happen. I told you, Grace.'

'Nick, you've got to *do* something. Get help. Professional help.'

'I have!'

'This can't go on!'

477

'Grace, I know. I've *tried* to get help, I'm *doing* all I can . . .'

We couldn't agree on what to do and eventually I hung up and sat curled in on myself, my hands trapped between my thighs.

Should I tell Ma and Dad?

No. They had enough to worry about, with Bid: the chemo took so much out of her, so much out of them all. I'd go to London and sort this out myself.

He carried her bag from the car and solicitously helped her inside. 'What would you like to do now?' he asked.

'I'd just like to go to bed.'

'Okay.' He grinned. 'Mind if I join you?'

'Um . . .' Perhaps she had misunderstood. 'I'm going to go straight to sleep.'

'Come on, you can stay awake for twenty minutes.' He was steering her towards the bedroom. He was opening his jeans, his intention clear. 'Take your knickers off.'

'But – no! I've just had an abortion.'

'Excuses, excuses.' He pushed her onto the bed, his knee pinioning her in position while he wrenched off her tights and pants.

'Please stop, please. I could get an infection. I can't have sex for three weeks.'

'Shut up.' He was on top of her, he was shoving up into her, into the blood and loss, rubbing her raw with his frenzy. Then he pushed himself up on his hands, as if he was doing a press-up, and slapped her, hard, across the face. 'For fuck's sake, try and look like you're enjoying yourself.'

Marnie

Grace was coming.

'She'll be here tomorrow morning.' Nick stood in the doorway of the bedroom. He delivered the information coldly, then seemed to relent. 'Anything you need?'

She wanted to know how angry Grace was, but she couldn't ask. Without looking at him she shook her head.

Nick left her alone with her unendurable shame. As soon as he shut the door, everything in the room looked like a weapon: she could smash the mirror and slash an artery with a shard, she could drink the bathroom bleach, she could fling herself from the window . . .

But killing herself wasn't an option: she'd already treated everyone – her blameless daughters, poor Nick – so shabbily. Her penance was to stay alive.

I'll never drink again I'll never drink again I'll never drink again.

The horror of coming round had been like being delivered into hell. This time she'd found herself in a hospital, rough hands on her, a foul-tasting charcoal drink being forced down her throat. 'To detox you,' the nurse had said.

'Where am I?'

'The Royal Free. Three cracked ribs, concussion, internal bleeding. Good night out, was it?'

In hospital. Jesus Christ, no. She needed to get out of there before anyone – Nick – discovered where she was.

But Nick had already found out and had been on his way; and now she wished she was still there because being injured enough to be hospitalized, even through her own fault, affected people, Nick, anyway, with a peculiar awe. It – at least temporarily – halted his anger, and perhaps it would have worked the same magic on Grace.

But the hospital trolley had been needed for 'real' sick people, not those who drank so much vodka that they thought it was a good idea to nip across the road after the traffic lights had changed to green and get themselves knocked down by a motorbike. After only six hours she'd been discharged, and as soon as she was at home, in her own bed, the protection of hospital was gone and she was considered well enough for Nick to turn his cold silent fury on her.

The doctor had downgraded his diagnosis. Marnie wasn't even, as he'd originally thought, concussed: the reason she hadn't known what day it was, was simply because she'd been 'stupefied with drink'. That was the phrase she'd heard being given to Nick and it stuck in her head, repeating itself again and again.

Stupefied with drink.

Stupefied with drink.

The strange thing was that she hadn't intended to get drunk. It hadn't been a bad day at work for once, and when Rico had suggested a quick drink in the local, she'd refused. Whenever she went for a 'quick drink' with Rico, things got messy.

'We're bad for each other,' she'd said. It sounded like a come-on line from a B-movie.

'We're just misunderstood.' Rico had held her gaze, like a hammy hero. His puppy-dog eyes had suddenly given her the creeps.

482

'Guy says I should stay away from you.'

'Guy's not here.'

But Guy might find out . . .

'What if he sacks me?' she'd asked. 'Us.'

Rico had shaken his head. 'He's just jealous that you prefer me, but I'm the best broker he's got. And he's not going to sack *you*.'

She'd hesitated. No, she shouldn't even consider this.

'One drink, Marnie. It's nearly Christmas.'

'It's only the first of December.'

'What harm can it do?' he'd wheedled.

What harm can it do?

Indecision had paralysed her. She should be strong, but it would be so easy, so painless to simply . . . *slip* . . .

'Just one,' she'd said.

Maybe two. Definitely no more than three.

By the time they were on their fourth, it hadn't mattered. She'd been happy and garrulous, friends with the whole world and free of all worry. Nick would go mental when he found out she was drinking again – and worse, drinking with Rico – but *it didn't matter*. Guy would also lose the head, but – again – it didn't matter.

She and Rico had got talking to some people at the next table in the pub: a man in a blue tracksuit and three glammed-up women. Or maybe there had been only two, even now she still wasn't entirely sure. She *thought* she had a memory of asking one of the women where her sister had gone and the woman saying, 'No, love, she's only the barmaid. God, you're even more pissed than us.' But she might have dreamt it.

The women had been deeply tanned and weighed down with jewellery, more than a bit chavy but they'd been friendly.

And when one of them had poked Marnie in the shin with a pointy-toed, lizard-skin shoe and said, 'We're going on to a club,' Marnie had decided to go too. Rico had tried to stop her. They'd had a row, but patchy though the details were, she knew it was a little half-hearted, they'd been too drunk for it to be anything more spirited.

'They're CRIMinals,' Rico had kept saying. 'They're CRIMinals. They seem like a laugh but they're CRIMinals.'

That was the last thing she could remember – blank, all blank – until the hospital. She'd lost eight hours of her life. Had she gone to the club? Had she stayed in the pub with Rico? She didn't know. The ambulance had picked her up in Cricklewood, the far side of London – what had she been doing there? She was suddenly light-headed with horror.

Don't think about it.

She looked at her mobile. She could text Rico and try to piece things together, but the thought repulsed her. *He* repulsed her, and contacting him would mean that it had all really happened: the drunkenness, the argument in the pub. As for the stuff she couldn't remember – she would prefer not to know.

And actually, everything was okay. Yes, everything was okay. Regardless of what might have taken place, she was at home and safe now. Home and safe, admittedly injured, but only mildly – anyone could crack a rib, she was sure she'd heard it had happened during a yoga class, when someone got carried away with their deep breathing.

Everything was okay.

Then she remembered that Grace was on her way from Dublin, and Grace would only be getting on a plane and coming to London if things were very serious.

The fear was back, bad enough to choke her. How angry

was Grace? She could ring her to find out but – again – she was better off not knowing. Until Grace's arrival, she would cope by shutting down: hearing nothing, thinking nothing, feeling nothing.

But her head flickered on and off, on and off, incessant phrases echoing.

Stupefied with drink.

Three cracked ribs.

Could have been killed.

A new wave of shock washed over her and suddenly, as if hearing about it for the first time, she was appalled at the extent of her injuries. Broken bones! Not just bumps and bruises, but actual broken bones. That was serious, serious, serious.

At least it made everything crystal clear for her: she could never drink again. She *would* never drink again. It was clear and easy. Her behaviour and its consequences were so far beyond the bounds of what was acceptable or forgivable or even explicable, that she had scared herself into a cast-iron certainty. No drinking, never again.

At supper time the girls tiptoed into the bedroom, proudly carrying a bowl of vanilla ice-cream. Marnie swallowed three mouthfuls before she had to stop abruptly: she couldn't eat, she never could after a bout. And this one – she glancingly acknowledged – was probably the worst yet.

She slept alone that night, Nick refused to share the bed with her, and there was no relief from her flickering head. On and off, on and off, all night.

Stupefied with drink.

Grace was coming.

Three cracked ribs.

Now and then she drifted into a sweaty, confused half-sleep before crashing against the mattress in an explosion so filled with horror that she eventually decided it would be preferable to stay awake.

'Marnie!' Grace rushed into the room, but was brought up short at the sight of the bruises and bandages. Marnie saw tears in her eyes: that meant she wasn't angry.

Thank God thank God thank God.

Fear, which had weighed on her like a heavy stone, rolled away and suddenly Marnie felt lighter, freer – ridiculously, almost cheerful. The clouds of black horror that had wreathed her since she'd woken up in the hospital, began to disperse.

'Can I hug you?' Grace asked her. 'Or does it hurt too much?'

If Grace had been angry, she'd have let her hug her; she'd have given or done anything to win back her love. But she could afford to be honest. 'It hurts too much.'

Grace climbed onto the bed. 'So what *happened*?'

'You know me. Accident-prone.'

'. . . No, I mean . . . you got really drunk again. Why?'

Why?

She didn't know why. She hadn't meant to.

'Didn't you hear? About Nick's bonus? He bought us this huge bloody house and now he can't afford the mortgage repayments.'

Marnie didn't care about the house or the money. But she needed a reason. Grace needed a reason.

'But you've known that for ages.' Grace was puzzled. 'I thought something terrible must have happened. I mean, after the last time you got so drunk . . . when was it, six weeks or so ago? You swore you were never going to drink again,

486

remember? You hurt yourself so badly when you fell down Rico's stairs –'

'Her partner in crime,' Nick said.

'So now I'm a criminal.'

Marnie remembered very little of the episode that Grace and Nick were talking about. She could evoke the run-up to it and the aftermath, but there was a vast chunk of time in the middle that was unaccounted for.

It had been about six weeks ago, that horrendous day with Wen-Yi and the discovery that Mr Lee was in Shanghai, when she'd been caught out in her inefficiency and – worse – dishonesty. The shame had been so painful that when Rico invited her for a drink, she'd been overtaken by a pleasure rush which had swept away all in its path. She'd been power- less against it; she'd had to go where it took her. The need to drink had been building for days and weeks, she'd tried to deny it even while the tension wound tighter and tighter – and her resistance had finally broken. She'd promised Melodie that she'd be home by 6.15 so that she could leave for her next job, but even as she was swearing black was white to Melodie, she knew she wouldn't be back and she felt nothing: no guilt.

She and Rico had gone to a newly opened bar in Fulham, far away from the office, where they drank vodkatinis and complained about Wen-Yi. She remembered being there for a very long time, long enough for reality to become reduced to splinter-like flashes. There was a sliver of memory of them leaving the bar and Rico accidentally dropping a bottle of vodka on the pavement where it smashed in an explosion of silver light. There was a burst of recollection of buildings rushing past them – they must have been in a taxi – and a picture in her head of Larry King interviewing Bill Clinton.

But was that real? Had she been watching telly in Rico's apartment? Or had she simply conjured it up?

Then there was nothing – blank, blank, blank – until she'd woken up in her own bedroom – which she hadn't recognized at first.

She discovered afterwards – courtesy of Nick – that she'd gone missing for a full day and a half. She'd made the phone call to Melodie on Monday evening and it was Wednesday morning when Nick found her.

Nick – having intuitively sensed that this was going to be bad – had driven to Basildon and deposited Daisy and Verity in the care of his mum. Then he'd phoned Guy and got Rico's address.

When Nick told this to Marnie, she wanted to die with shame – he would have hated having to do something so humiliating.

In Rico's apartment block, Nick had found Marnie, spread-eagled, face down and unconscious, in the communal hall.

What was I doing there?

Perhaps she'd been trying to leave?

She was black and blue all along the front of her body because – Nick deduced – she'd toppled down the wooden staircase from Rico's first-floor flat. There was no answer from Rico's door because – as Marnie discovered a week later when she returned to work – he'd also been dead drunk.

Nick had taken her home, dressed her in a cotton nightdress and put her to bed.

When she'd come to that time, she didn't have words to describe her horror. The front of her body was patterned with astonishing bruises. Bumps and cuts had become a feature of her life; emerging into reality after a bout always involved taking an inventory of her injuries. But that had been the worst ever. One of her teeth felt wobbly and for some reason that horrified her utterly.

Worse than her physical damage was the scalding guilt about what she'd put Daisy and Verity and Nick through. It made her want to – quite literally – cut her own throat, and she'd sworn to Nick – and to herself – that she'd never drink again.

But she'd remembered none of what had taken place, and because she couldn't remember, she became able to pretend that it hadn't really happened. She'd sealed it away in a vault in her head where she put things she was far, far too ashamed to think about.

And now it had happened again. The same, only worse because this time she'd been in hospital. With broken bones.

And Grace was here.

'She's out of control. She needs residential help.' Nick was still standing by the bedroom door, neither in nor out of the room.

Marnie stared, plunged into mute terror. It was the first time he'd made such a suggestion. Was he serious? Or was he just trying to frighten her?

'You mean . . . ?' Grace, always so sure, looked uncertain. Scared even.

'Rehab, treatment,' Nick said. 'Whatever you want to call it.'

'Isn't that a bit . . . ?' Grace jumped in.

'A bit what?'

'. . . drastic?'

'Grace, she's an alcoholic!'

Marnie was relieved to see Grace flinch; obviously she wasn't buying any of this.

Nick turned to Marnie. 'Face it, you're an alcoholic.'

'I'm not,' she said anxiously. 'I'll stop, I'll –'

'There's a place in Wiltshire,' he said. 'It looks nice. They let kids visit at weekends, so the girls would get to see you.'

Christ, he was . . . he *was* serious!

'Nick, please, wait.' The words tumbled from her mouth in a scramble. 'Give me another chance –'

'Yes, Nick, calm down,' Grace said. 'Let's not go mad here. She's had two bad experiences –'

'Two!' Nick put his hand to his forehead. 'For crying out loud, Grace. Two hundred, more like! Not all as bad as this one, yes, I admit. But the gaps are getting shorter and the injuries are getting worse. That's what they warned me to expect. I *told* you all of this.'

Confused, Marnie watched the interplay between Grace and Nick. 'Who's "they"?' she asked in creeping fear.

'The alcohol counsellor,' Grace said.

'What alcohol counsellor?' Marnie's lips had gone numb. 'How come you know and I don't?'

Grace sounded surprised. 'Because Nick rings me about you . . .'

Does he?

'He has done, over the past couple of months.'

Marnie was stunned. 'Grace . . . ? You're talking to Nick behind my back?'

Grace stared. She looked shocked. 'I'm not doing anything behind your back! The first thing I did after he rang me was ring *you* and shop him.'

Did she?

'We were on the phone for ages, you and me. Don't you remember?' Grace sounded panicky.

No. And it wasn't the first time she'd found a blank where there should be a memory.

'I *thought* you were drunk. I asked you at the time,' Grace said anxiously. 'You said you weren't.'

'I wasn't! I remember it all.' Then Marnie understood something. 'So that's why you've been calling me so often, all concern?'

'I've been so worried.'

'Why? I've always been a drinker. How many times have I told you that the only time the world seemed normal was when I'd had two drinks?'

She could see Grace struggle. She could see Grace asking herself what right she had to begrudge Marnie those two drinks.

'Look, I can stop,' she said reassuringly. 'I can go for weeks without a drink.'

But Grace turned away from her and looked at Nick. 'Can she? Can she go for weeks without a drink?'

'Maybe.' He sounded reluctant. 'Although there have been times when she says she hasn't had a drink and I can smell it on her breath. I've found bottles of vodka in her handbag –'

Grace looked shocked. 'Have you?' she demanded of Marnie. 'You never said –'

'Once! One time! Because they'd run out of carriers in the off-licence.' She stared into Grace's eyes. 'I *can* stop for weeks at a time. I *do* stop.'

'And then you disappear!' Nick said. 'You don't come home for days –'

'Not "days"!' Marnie cried. 'Nick, you make it sound like . . . Grace, don't listen to him. It hasn't ever been even two days! Twenty-four hours at the most.'

'Twenty-four hours is a long time,' Nick said. 'Especially when you're a little girl.'

'Oh go on, make me feel guilty! As if I'm not feeling awful already!'

Suddenly Marnie's eyes were spilling tears. Nick clicked his tongue impatiently and announced that he was going to work but, to Marnie's relief, Grace crumbled into sympathy.

'Marnie, please, this is way too serious. You fall. You hurt yourself. You could get raped. You're lucky you haven't been done for drunk-driving. You're lucky you haven't killed someone.'

'I know, I know, I know.' Tears poured down her face, their salt stinging her cuts. 'But you don't know what it's like to be me.'

She saw pity flare in Grace's eyes and that made her feel worse.

'I'm sorry. I'm sorry, but I'm always sad,' she wept, all of a sudden feeling the full weight of her constant burden. 'When I drink it takes the sadness away. It's the only thing that does.'

'But it only makes things worse,' Grace said helplessly. 'Surely you're sadder now than before you drank?'

'Yes, I'll stop. It'll be hard but I'll stop.'

'You don't have to stop completely. Just don't go mental on it. Are you still on anti-depressants?'

'They don't help.'

'Could you get a higher dose?'

'I'll ask. I think I'm on the highest, but I'll ask. I'm begging you, Grace, don't let him send me to rehab.'

'Okay.' Grace moved a little closer and in a quiet voice asked, 'What about this Rico bloke?'

'Rico?' She wiped her face with her hand. 'He's just a friend.'

'Is there something going on with the two of you?'

A flash of bodies, naked limbs, Rico on top of her, his rough breathing in her ear.

It didn't happen.

'No, no, he's just very kind to me.'

'But you drink with him?'

'You make it sound . . . like tramps drinking meths. We *go* for a drink sometimes.'

Grace got into bed beside her. To forestall any further interrogation, Marnie put on the television. *Trisha* was on; today's theme was 'I Hate my Daughter's Boyfriend'.

'Will I change to something else?'

She didn't expect Grace and her right-on sensibilities to go for *Trisha*, but Grace was transfixed. 'Leave it on, leave it on.'

There was shouting, swearing and accusations of jealousy and infidelity.

'I despise myself for watching this sort of crap,' Grace said. 'But I can't help it. It's too big to fight.'

Now you know how I feel.

When it ended, Grace suddenly asked, 'Marnie, have you ever heard of a man called Lemmy O'Malley?'

'No.'

'Or Eric Zouche?'

'No. Why?'

'Nothing.' Grace jumped from the bed, full of vigour. 'Right, you've to start getting back to normal. Get dressed, just for a couple of hours. Which one's your wardrobe?'

'That one.'

Grace opened it. 'You have so many clothes. And shoes!' The wardrobe floor was covered in boots and shoes. 'Those riding boots!' Grace bent down to take a closer look.

No, wait. Stay away from them.

'Funny, aren't they?' Grace was half inside the wardrobe

493

and her voice was muffled. 'So stiff, the leather almost looks plastic.'

'Because I never broke them in –'

'God, you're a right swot, with boot guards still in them to keep them standing straight –'

Don't touch them. Leave them alone.

'Grace, don't –'

But Grace was sticking her hand down into the boot and her face was changing and her hand was emerging with something and she was looking at Marnie with an expression she had never seen before, and in a calm little voice, sounding so unlike Grace, she asked, 'Now why would you keep a bottle of vodka in a riding boot?'

'Grace, I . . . don't!'

Grace had thrust her hand into the matching boot and drew out a second bottle of vodka, this one empty. She turned that same strange face to Marnie, a radiance of shock and understanding, then whipped back to the wardrobe, launching into a frenzy of excavation.

'Grace, no!'

'Fuck off!'

Half in, half out of bed, Marnie could only watch the horror unfold. Grace was scrabbling with her hands, snatching wildly at shoe boxes, boots and handbags, flinging them out onto the bedroom carpet, upending them so that bottles clinked and scattered as they tumbled from their hiding places.

This isn't happening this isn't happening this isn't happening.

When Grace was finished, she lined them up boldly on the dressing table, banging each one down hard. Nine in all – full bottles, half bottles, quarter bottles. Marnie found it hard to believe there were so many, she'd known there were one or two in there, stashed temporarily until she got an opportunity to dispose of them – but *nine*? All were vodka bottles and all were empty except for the first one.

Grace was breathing heavily and gazing at Marnie, as if she'd never seen her before in her life.

'Have you been drinking since you got home from hospital?'

'No, I swear it!'

She was telling the truth. She had wanted to drink – especially after she'd discovered that Grace was coming – but she wouldn't have been able to keep it down. She knew her body well enough to expect that any alcohol would kick-start an orgy of vomiting that could go on for days.

Then Marnie saw new knowledge being visited upon Grace – she actually saw the change in Grace's eyes as it happened – and Grace lurched from the bedroom, full of dread and purpose.

Marnie realized where she was headed for. 'No, Grace, please!' She hurried from her bed, ignoring the electric blue pain that crackled through her ribs – this time she had to stop her – and followed Grace into Daisy's pink bedroom.

But Grace had already found one. She brandished the empty bottle at her. 'In your daughter's wardrobe. Nice, Marnie!'

'She wouldn't have found it.'

'It didn't take me very long.'

Then Grace went into Verity's room and found three empties under the bed.

'Don't tell Nick,' Marnie begged. 'Please.'

'How can you ask me that?' Grace said. 'How can you be so selfish?'

The sound of retching echoed through the house. Again and again and again. Marnie rattled the knob. 'Please, Grace, let me in.' But Grace kept the bathroom door locked and didn't reply.

'I don't understand it,' Grace said weakly. She seemed devastated. Marnie had never before seen her so reduced. 'You were able to stop the last time you came to Dublin. When you were on antibiotics.'

She hadn't been on antibiotics, but now really wasn't the time.

'You didn't have anything to drink the whole weekend,' Grace said. Then she lunged at Marnie because it had obviously just dawned on her that Marnie could have been drinking in secret all that time. 'Or *did* you?'

'No, I didn't. I swear to you!'

'You swear to me?' Grace's laugh sounded bitter. 'Yes, now I'm really reassured.'

'I'm not lying, Grace. It's the truth. I can stop whenever I want.'

'"I can stop whenever I want,"' Grace parroted angrily. 'You know what you sound like?'

'What?'

'An alcoholic.'

'But . . .'

The truth was that she hadn't had anything to drink in Dublin – because, inexplicable as it was, it was easier to have no drinks than to have two. It was why she'd pretended to be on antibiotics. Over the previous year – maybe longer – she'd come to know that once she had even one drink, she was overtaken by a raging need to drink to incapacity, to drink enough so she could leave her body, so she could leave her life, so she could abandon everything with glorious freedom and roar towards oblivion. She couldn't predict what would

496

happen if she started drinking, she could end up anywhere, doing anything, and she couldn't take that risk while she was away from home.

'I'm sorry I didn't tell you everything,' Marnie said. She couldn't bear this – Grace was angry with her. Worse, Grace was disappointed. 'I'm sorry I've kept you in the dark.'

'This isn't about me! It's about you being ... an ... alcoholic.' Grace swallowed hard on the word.

'Not an alcoholic, just a –'

'Marnie!' Grace opened and closed her mouth like a fish and pointed towards the bottles on the dressing table. 'Look at them, please look at them.'

'It's not as bad as it seems. Please let me explain. They've been in there for ages. Please, Grace, listen to me –'

Suddenly Grace said, 'Right, that's it! You're going to AA.'

... What? Alcoholics Anonymous? No, she wasn't.

'I'm going to ring them. Right now. Where's your phone book?'

'We haven't got one.'

In a very soft voice, Grace said, 'Do not fuck with me any more than you already have.'

'In the cupboard in the hall.'

Grace left the bedroom and when she came back, she said, 'There's a meeting at one o'clock in a community centre in Wimbledon. Get dressed.'

'Grace, this is mad,' Marnie begged. 'I'll stop, I swear to you I'll stop, don't make me go to AA, things aren't that bad, I just have to make the decision to stop, look, I'm making it, I've made it, it's done!'

She could see that Grace was wavering.

'And I can't go like this.' She indicated her cuts and bandages.

Grace's face was a picture of hesitancy – then she said with distressing certainty, 'They won't care. They're probably used to it.'

'What if someone from work sees me?'

'Maybe they already know what's wrong with you. In fact, I bet they do. They'd probably be glad you're doing something about your drinking problem.'

Drinking problem.

While Grace watched, she got dressed. With every movement, she winced with exaggerated pain – but she wasn't faking her shaking hands. She couldn't button her jeans. This was new.

She cast an involuntary glance at the wardrobe, repository of at least one bottle that Grace hadn't found. A mouthful, maybe two, might settle her. But even if Grace left her alone for three seconds, she couldn't chance it today. Apart from the likelihood of vomiting, if she got found out, she'd be packed off to rehab by dinner time.

Grace drove. Marnie let her get snarled up in the one-way system in the hope that they'd waste so much time driving around in circles, they'd miss the meeting. But she'd forgotten – how could she have, considering she'd lived with it her entire life? – how capable Grace was.

'This is the street,' Grace said, driving slowly, peering at a low building. 'And . . . *that's* the place.'

Marnie wasn't concerned: they'd never get parking.

'Are they coming out?' Grace asked. She rolled down the window and mouthed at the occupants of a car: Leaving? Nods and smiles and thumbs up, and Grace was sliding into the space.

How could it have happened?

Don't think about it don't think about it don't think about it.

'Out,' Grace ordered.

Marnie unclicked her seat belt and slid to the ground. Her legs felt like they belonged to someone else; this was the first time she'd walked since she'd woken up in hospital and it felt like an entirely new activity. Actually . . . 'Grace, I think I might faint.'

'Breathe,' Grace urged. 'And lean on me if you need to.'

'No, really . . . I feel really –'

'Marnie, you're going to this AA meeting. I don't care if you keel over and die.'

Marnie didn't think her heart could get any heavier, but when she realized that this was the same place as the last time, she could hardly move because of the weight of dread dragging her down.

In the room, there were eighteen, maybe twenty chairs in a circle. People were chatting and laughing and tea and biscuits were set out on a table.

As Grace led her to the top table, Marnie could see she was unsure, almost nervous.

'This is Marnie.' Grace presented her to some woman who looked like she was in charge. 'It's her first meeting.'

Actually it wasn't her first meeting, it was her second, but she wasn't telling Grace that because then she really *would* think she was an alcoholic. She cast a furtive glance around, hoping that the Jules woman wasn't there, the one she'd seen that time at the cinema. If she showed up and said hello, her cover was blown.

The people – the *alcoholics* – were very friendly; she remembered that from the other time. They didn't embarrass her by mentioning her injuries and they kept giving her warm, welcoming smiles. *Dying* for her to be in the gang with them.

'Cup of tea?'

Marnie accepted. The heat would be nice; she was so cold. But to her shock – and to Grace's evident horror – her hands couldn't hold the cup. The hot liquid trembled and slopped over, scalding her fingers. The man who'd given her the cup retrieved it without fuss and placed it on the counter.

The loss of control was so unprecedented Marnie decided that it simply hadn't happened.

'We've all been there,' the man said kindly.

Maybe you have, you drunken loser, but I haven't.

'Biscuit?' the man offered.

'Okay.' Her stomach was begging for food, but it felt as if the signals were coming from a hundred miles away. She bit a tiny corner off the biscuit but it was so long since she'd held a morsel of food in her mouth that it felt unnatural. She swallowed, forcing the crumbs down her closed throat and her stomach juices squirted with joy.

'Let's sit down,' Grace suggested.

Flanked by Grace, she sat on a hard chair.

This isn't happening this isn't happening this isn't happening.

She broke small pieces off the biscuit, letting them dissolve in her mouth, and zoned in and out as the alcoholics whinged on. 'Sharing' they called it, what a cringy word. Surely Grace would hate that? Surely she wouldn't have any time for an organization that used that sort of term?

'. . . drinking was a full-time job for me. Sneaking alcohol into the house, hiding bottles, pretending to walk the dog so that I could dispose of the empties in my neighbours' bins.

Then they started charging for rubbish collection and I got caught . . .'

'. . . when I had dinner parties, I always kept an extra bottle in the kitchen cupboard, so that when I brought the plates back in or whatever, I could help myself . . .'

'. . . I was self-medicating. I thought I was drinking because I liked drinking but I was drinking to kill the pain of my feelings . . .'

'I had bottles stashed everywhere. Even in my wardrobe.'

Dispiritingly, this confession moved Grace to elbow Marnie. *See*, the gesture suggested, *you're just like them, you're meant to be here.*

'I kept bottles hidden in the pockets of my winter coats,' the woman continued and Marnie felt Grace tense with sudden suspicion.

Fuck fuck fuck.

'. . . I could stop, that wasn't the problem. I could manage a week, maybe ten days without a drink. The tough thing was staying stopped. I couldn't do that . . .'

'. . . I lost everything to drinking, my job, my family, my home, my self-respect, and I didn't care, I just wanted to drink . . .'

'. . . Marnie . . .' Grace murmured.

'Hmm?' Emerging from torpor, Marnie found a buzz of attention around her. The focus of the entire room seemed to be on her and the leader woman was smiling kindly.

'Marnie, would you like to say something?'

'What? Who, me?' She looked down at her feet. 'Oh no.'

'Go on,' Grace whispered at her.

'. . . My name is Marnie.'

'Hi, Marnie,' the room chorused.

God, she felt so *stupid*.

'And . . . well, here I am.'

'Say you're an alcoholic,' Grace whispered.

But she wouldn't. She didn't. Because she wasn't.

'Just so you know,' Grace said, her mouth a grim line, as she drove them home, 'you don't have to drink every day to be an alcoholic. The woman said lots of people stop drinking for long periods of time, just like you do.'

Ignore her ignore her ignore her.

'So what did you think of the people?' Grace asked, after a period of silence.

'They're nice.' They're freaky.

'You'll go again?'

'Mmm, next week.'

'How about tomorrow?'

'*Tomorrow*? Isn't that a bit . . . extreme?'

Grace didn't reply, and when they got home she went straight up the stairs and into Marnie's bedroom, where she flung open the wardrobe doors and rummaged in the furthest reaches. Within moments, she emerged with a half bottle of vodka and demonstrated it with a silent flourish, like a magician whisking a white rabbit from a hat. Back in she went again, like someone diving for pearls, feeling about in the deep pockets of winter coats and emerging with another bottle.

When the number of bottles had reached four, she said, 'Extreme? No, it's not fucking extreme.' She sank to her knees and dropped her face into her hands, then she clambered to her feet.

'Grace . . . where are you going?'

'To the bathroom. To throw up again.' She stopped at the doorway and whirled around and demanded, 'Funny, isn't it?'

Marnie recoiled from the aggression.

'You're the one who drank yourself into a coma,' Grace cried. 'But I'm the one who's puking!'

Grace returned from the bathroom and curled on the bed beside Marnie. They lay in silence.

'What were you doing in Cricklewood?' Grace suddenly asked.

'What?'

'Cricklewood. Nick says that's where the ambulance picked you up.'

'. . . Yes, I know.' *But I don't know what I was doing there.*

'What happened that night?'

'Nothing. I just went to the pub after work with Rico.'

'Not in Cricklewood?'

'No. Wimbledon. Near work.'

'I'm afraid I don't know London very well.' *Was Grace being sarcastic?* 'Is Wimbledon near Cricklewood?'

Not even remotely. It was the other side of the city. 'No.'

'So you and Rico . . . ?'

'We had a few drinks.'

'And then?'

'I met some people, they were going to a club, I went with them.' *I think.*

'Where was the club? In Cricklewood?'

Please shut up about Cricklewood. 'In Peckham.' *Peckham? What had she been thinking? Peckham was a ghetto.*

'Is that near Cricklewood?'

'No.'

'Do you know anyone who lives in Cricklewood?'

'No.'

'So why do you think you were found in Cricklewood?'

'Grace, if you say Cricklewood again, I'm going to the off-licence.'

'Cricklewood, Cricklewood, Cricklewood. Which off-licence? The one in your wardrobe?' Grace slung her leg across Marnie's to stop her from moving. 'Don't even think about it.'

'I was joking.'

'I know. Look at me, I'm in hysterics.'

They spiralled down into gloomy silence, then Grace said, 'Don't you think it's kind of . . . ?'

'What?'

'You were lying alone on a roadside, injured, poisoned with alcohol, in a part of London you didn't know, with no memory of how you'd got there or what you'd been doing there.'

Before Grace had got more than five words in, Marnie had stopped listening and was preparing her response. When she saw that Grace had finished she said, 'It won't happen again.'

'But –'

'I agree with you, it looks pretty bad when you put it like that. But it was an accident, a one-off and it won't happen again.'

'It's three o'clock.' Grace swung herself off the bed. 'I'm going to collect the girls from school. I'll be back in twenty minutes.'

'Thanks, Grace.' Melodie had finally walked; they were currently without a nanny. If Grace wasn't here, Marnie didn't know how the girls would get home. Perhaps one of the other mums . . .

She heard the front door slam shut and the sound of the car

start up, and she settled herself into her pillows. She was sleepy now. But as she hovered on the brink, Grace's words replayed themselves. 'You were lying alone on a roadside, injured, poisoned with alcohol, in a part of London you didn't know, with no memory of how you'd got there or what you'd been doing there.'

Oh.

A tiny chink opened, giving a glimpse of the vast cavern of horror beyond. Seized with terror, Marnie scrambled to sit up, gasping for breath, her heart pounding. She was more frightened than she'd ever been in her life.

Lying alone on a roadside, with three broken ribs, at five in the morning.

She was that person.

She had always liked a drink – she never made any bones about that – but the truth was that she was a moderate drinker. When she'd been a full-time mum, she never drank during the day. She didn't approve of it. The rule was, no alcohol until 6 p.m. She'd spend the day taking care of the two babies, but once the hands of the kitchen clock aligned themselves into a straight black line, she poured herself a vodka and tonic. She looked forward to it, she wasn't going to deny it, but since when was that a crime?

Perhaps she could have started earlier – there were probably other mothers who did – but rules were rules. No drinks until 6 p.m.

Except for the day two Octobers ago – or was it three? – after the clocks had gone back and five o'clock felt like six o'clock. It was dark outside and the day had gone on for long enough and it seemed unnecessary to wait, particularly because Nick hadn't changed the clock. The hands actually pointed to six and if it had still been yesterday, it would already *be* six. So on that particular day, she was comfortable with five o'clock. And – perhaps because the world didn't end when she broke the 6 p.m. rule – a few days later 4.30 seemed fine. Later that month, so did 2.15. Then 1 p.m. The first time she had a drink in the morning, she felt giddy with freedom; astonished that she'd spent so many years hidebound by artificial barricades. Time was only a concept – what did it matter when she had a drink, as long as she did her job as a mother properly?

And she did do her job properly. The girls were her life and it was her purpose to feed, clothe, entertain, cosset and comfort them. They came first, before all else. That was the bargain she'd made with herself.

The 6 p.m. rule was broken only in extremis: she had to feel particularly black or bleak or bored or lonely in order to justify flouting it.

But then again, who was she hurting by drinking before six? Nobody. In fact, everyone benefited, because when a few drinks took her away from her life and into a happier place inside her head, she got great relief. She was doing exactly what she wanted, the only time she was being true to herself. Being personally fulfilled made her a better mother; it must do.

Nevertheless, she had a suspicion that Nick wouldn't see daytime drinking as the life-enhancing asset that she did. After he began wondering out loud why their vodka was disappearing so quickly, she began to buy her own special bottles and keep them in her own special secret places. She had never intended to have a stash of alcohol in her wardrobe but she needed to be able to drink without restraints.

She took care never to slip into slurred incapability around

Daisy and Verity. But sometimes the effort became too much and she began giving them their dinner at 4.30 and putting them to bed while it was still daylight, turning a deaf ear to their startled complaints.

By the time Nick got home from work, it had become her usual practice to have a bottle of wine opened and to be sipping demurely at the first glass. It had a two-fold benefit: it explained any smell of alcohol on her breath; and she could relax into her drunkenness because, after all, she was drinking.

At times he was surprised at how drunk she seemed to get, and how quickly. 'You've only had two glasses,' he used to say. 'Your tolerance has gone.'

'Cheap date,' she'd quip, pleased that her subterfuge was working.

But what she longed for, lived for, were the evenings when the girls were in bed and Nick was out late at work parties. Only then could she really surrender, pounding the drinks, one after the other, in glorious abandon, until her bed tilted and the room swirled around her, whirling her away to oblivion.

Sometimes – usually in the dead of night, when everyone was sleeping – she saw the full, fractured kaleidoscope of her secret life, saw it as others might see it, and it froze her with fear.

What does it mean? What will I have to do?

But I am a good mother.

I am a good wife.

I am a good person.

Everyone finds it hard to cope, we all do what we have to.

Good mother, good wife, good person: these are the important things.

Good mother, good wife, good person: I have the basics in place.

She kept worrying at the information, twisting and turning her badness into goodness, until the broken pictures rearranged themselves into something less ugly and she was able to fall into a light, anxious sleep.

Then she got caught, drunk and messy. She couldn't understand how she'd let it happen. Nick was due home from work at 6.30, it wasn't one of the nights where she could let her guard down, and although she'd had her first drink at one minute past eleven, she'd kept an eye on things all day. She'd certainly been sober enough at 4 p.m. to drive to playgroup to collect the girls. Then they'd settled down on the squashy couch, all three of them, to watch a DVD. She'd been sipping from a glass, pacing herself, with plenty of time to clear away all evidence long before Nick got in.

But she must have fallen asleep and when she jerked awake, her heart pounding hard enough to jump out of her cottonwool mouth, Nick was leaning over her, his features blurred. Chaos; a bad smell; a horrible screeching noise; black smoke billowing from the kitchen. Even in her confusion, she knew she'd better start thinking fast.

'What's wrong? Are you ill?'

She nodded.

'What is it?'

She tried to speak but her words came thick and slow.

His face changed. 'Marnie, you're pissed!'

'No, I'm –'

'You are, you're drunk.' He was obviously alarmed and confused. 'Were you out for lunch?'

But she knew that he knew she hadn't been; he'd spoken to her at home in the middle of the day. And when did she ever get to go out for lunch anyway?

He disappeared into the hall and after a few moments the screeching noise ceased abruptly. The smoke alarm; he must have taken the batteries out.

Then he was back. With a finger, he pointed in outrage towards the kitchen. 'They were standing on chairs at the stove, making spaghetti hoops in a frying pan.'

So that accounted for the smoke.

'How did they turn the gas on?' he demanded. 'What's going on, Marnie? You've been drinking?'

There seemed little point in denying it.

'On your own! Why?'

Why? Because she liked it. That was all she could think of but she knew that that wouldn't do.

'I . . . I was upset.'

She watched him soften. 'About what, Sweets?'

'I was thinking about your dad.' He'd been diagnosed with prostate cancer some months earlier. A slow-metastasizing strain. He was expected to live for years.

Nick gaped. 'But we've known for ages.'

'I think it's just hit me now.' Tears came from nowhere and suddenly she was sobbing, 'Your poor dad. The poor man, it's just so sad.'

'But he's fine about it now, Mum's fine, we're all fine.'

Nick stroked her hair and treated her gently for the rest of the evening. But she knew her excuse hadn't worked. She'd woken something in Nick, a suspicion, an alertness.

Only days later came the 'Fiona Fife incident'.

Daisy and Verity were on a playdate with Alannah Fife and Marnie had the afternoon to herself. The price was that at some stage in the not too distant, she'd get lumbered with four-year-old Alannah for several hours. But she wasn't thinking about that. She was having a nice time, thinking dreamy thoughts in her own head; and when the phone rang she decided to let the machine pick up.

'Marnie?' It was Fiona, mother of Alannah, leaving a message. 'Are you there?'

She grabbed the phone. 'Sorry, I'm here.'

'Bad news. My car won't start.'

'That's a bummer.'

'So . . .'

'So . . . ?'

'. . . I can't drive Daisy and Verity home. Can you come and fetch them? It's too far for them to walk.'

'Oh God, yes, sorry! Just being a bit thick. I'll be there in ten minutes.'

Marnie scrambled around in her handbag for her car keys and had a moment when she wondered if she shouldn't be driving. She hadn't had much and her judgement wasn't in any way impaired, but she was probably over the limit.

She would drive extra carefully.

But outside the Fifes' house, she somehow overshot the parking space she'd been aiming for. She hit the brakes and, in protest, they gave a tight, bat-like screech. Two seconds later, Fiona's white, wooden-spoon face popped up at the window, then disappeared almost immediately – but it was still long enough for Marnie to register Fiona's anxiety.

Almost immediately the front door opened and Fiona stood on the step, watching as Marnie slid out of the car and walked towards the door. Fiona's manifest shock told Marnie that she wasn't as sober as she'd thought.

'Marnie, are you okay?'

'Fine!' No, too loud. 'Fine.' Better this time.

'Are you . . . ?' Fiona asked. 'Have you been drinking?'

'ME? Joking? I never drink before six o'clock.' She hadn't

intended to sound so belligerent – and she shouldn't have lied; she realized that afterwards. She should have pretended she'd been out for lunch, she should have giggled and used words like 'tiddly' and 'squiffy' and it would have been fine.

Fiona left the step and walked with purpose at Marnie, straight into her space, almost colliding with her, and even though vodka wasn't supposed to smell, Fiona began fanning her hand in front of her nose like she was being attacked by fumes. She said accusingly, 'I thought you sounded strange on the phone.'

'Hi, Mum.' Daisy and Verity tumbled out of the house, pulling on coats and trailing backpacks.

'This isn't the first time I've noticed,' Fiona said quietly.

Marnie turned away. 'Come on, girls.' Her voice was shaking. 'Got all your stuff?'

'Should I be letting you drive?' Fiona asked.

Marnie couldn't find the words. Should she be defensive? Apologetic?

'Say goodbye to Alannah.' She pulled Daisy and Verity towards the car.

That night she woke in the early hours, cold and sober and terrified, reliving the episode. Hearing her own voice, thick and drunk, insisting, 'I never drink before six o'clock.'

I never drink before six o'clock.

What a stupid thing to say when it was obvious Fiona knew she was drunk.

And the guilt about the girls! They were so precious and she had endangered their safety by driving them around while she was . . . not drunk . . . it wasn't that bad, but not sober either. If anything had happened . . .

Although it wasn't as if she'd planned it. If she'd known she was going to be driving, she wouldn't have had anything to drink – not much anyway. Guilt slid into self-pity: why did it have to be that particular day that Fiona's car had refused to start? Normally she'd be sober mid-afternoon.

It's been weeks since I've waited until 6 p.m.

Weeks and weeks.

For a moment her heart felt as if it had given up beating, and that was the first time she thought, I've got to stop.

'Why would Fiona Fife ask me if everything was okay with you?' Nick asked.

Fuck.

She stared him dead in the eye. 'I have no idea.'

'What happened?'

'I haven't a clue what you're talking about.'

Not for a moment had she expected that Fiona would rat on her.

'Marnie, please tell me,' Nick said. 'Trust me, we can try to fix things . . .'

'Nothing to fix,' she said sincerely.

She'd got good at lying. But this time she didn't pull it off. Nick was obviously beginning to make connections, to join up the dots. She watched as he took an overview of their recent past and saw how the landscape undulated and shimmeyed for him, rearranging and repositioning itself into the truth.

He knew.

She knew that he knew.

And he knew that she knew.

He said nothing.

But he began to watch her all the time.

'What about your job?' Grace asked.

'Exactly. How could I go to rehab? I've got a job. Income that we need.'

'I mean, don't they mind you missing all this time?'

'It's not "all this time" –'

'Oh shut up, it is. Why haven't you been sacked?'

'My boss –'

'Guy?'

'Yes, Guy, I think he . . . likes me.'

'What do you mean, likes you? You mean fancies you?'

'No. More like a . . . brother.'

'Brother,' Grace snorted.

This time last year, she'd been so excited at returning to work. Nick hadn't got his bonus and it should have been regarded as a disaster but, at the time, she saw it as the saving of her. Suddenly she had a purpose; she would no longer feel the need to drink – at least not in the way she used to, lonely and alone. Her job was highly sociable, she was out and about meeting potential clients, having boozy business lunches and post-work debriefs in the pub with the lads. For the first time in a long time she was having fun.

But the days passed without her bringing in any new business. The days became weeks and the sparkle of her new life began to dim. Then there was a lunch, with a potential client, and she thought they'd been getting on great; there were gin and tonics and wine, then port, then grappa, and they'd been matching each other drink for drink and she didn't understand how she was so drunk and helpless, while he remained capable enough to laugh at her. The maître d' was sharp-eyed enough to ring for a taxi for her and the following day she was grateful for the incessant vomiting that prevented her from going to work and facing her shame. She got Nick to ring and tell Guy she had a gastric bug; Guy replied that the maître d' had phoned to remind her that she hadn't been able to remember her pin number yesterday and she still owed for the lunch.

After two days she returned to work and endured the good-natured jibes about her drunken state; Guy was the only one who didn't join in. She apologized and promised him it wouldn't happen again. But that very evening she went to the pub with the lads and drowned her shame in vodka, enough to make her happy and numb. Rico was the one who helped her walk to the cab.

Another week passed without her making a sale and she began to wake with dread. When each fruitless day came to an end, she sought someone to go for a drink with; there was so much fear to wash away. Sometimes Craig or Henry popped into the pub, but after one or two drinks they peeled away; lightweights. The only person she could rely on to be consistently available was Rico.

The number of nights when she lurched home, late and incoherently drunk, stacked up.

Initially Nick reacted with fury, then one Sunday afternoon he sat her at the dining-room table and said, with heavy portent, 'We need to talk.' When he told her he was 'desperately worried' about how much she was drinking, she already had her response prepared: most of her business was done socially; she wasn't out enjoying herself, she was *working*.

In that case, Nick pleaded, could she please do so in moderation.

A reasonable request, she decided: from now on three drinks would be her limit. But despite her sincere intentions, her after-work drinking continued to be shambolic and excessive. She couldn't understand it – after a couple of drinks, the whole thing seemed to take on some life of its own.

She started to miss days at work; she'd only been back twelve weeks and she'd taken five sick days. And she had yet to do one deal.

Her life began to feel full of sharp edges, there was no comfort to be found: she hated being at home because of Nick's watchful anger; she hated being at work because of her failure as a broker; the only place she wanted to be was the pub, and the only person she was comfortable with was Rico. He was the one person whom she felt wasn't passing some sort of judgement on her. Also, he made no secret of the fact that he found her attractive, and she was flattered. He was young – younger than her, in any case – and very good-looking: dark-haired and dark-eyed.

After less than two weeks, Nick sat her down for another serious conversation. Once again Marnie promised a fresh start, and she meant it. Really meant it. She thought she had already been making an effort but she swore to Nick that she'd try much much harder.

A week later he had to ask again; confused by how she had continued to fail, she made yet another promise.

'This isn't working,' Guy said.

It had taken so long for him to acknowledge this manifest truth that she'd managed to half convince herself it might never happen.

'You've been back at work for four months now,' he said. 'And you haven't done a single deal.'

'Sorry,' she whispered.

'Do you think that if you weren't under such pressure you wouldn't need to drink so much?'

She flinched. It couldn't have hurt more if he'd punched her.

'Bea is leaving. We have a vacancy for office manager. Do you want it?'

Anything to win back his approval. 'If you want me to,' she mumbled. 'I'll give it a go.'

'You should be able to do it in your sleep. One other thing. I want you to go to an AA meeting. Alcoholics Anonymous.'

She lifted her head, her voice suddenly restored. 'Oh my God, Guy, I'm not that bad.'

'That's the deal. If you want to keep your job, you'll go to the meeting.'

'No, Guy . . .'

'Yes, Marnie.'

So she went to a meeting – it wasn't as if Guy had left her with much choice. As she expected, it was strange and awful. The people were all over her, smothering her with niceness. A woman called Jules was almost creepily friendly, giving her her phone number and begging Marnie to ring the next time she felt like drinking.

It was imperative that Nick never knew that she'd been. She couldn't risk ideas being planted in his head.

Guy was full of questions about how she'd got on at the meeting.

'It was . . . Sorry, Guy, I don't even know what to say because it was so . . .' She located the exact word. '*Inappropriate*, me being there. They're alcoholics. It was wrong that I was there *spying* on them.'

'You should go to a few more,' Guy said. 'Just to get a feel for them.'

Marnie found this utterly astonishing. 'Admittedly, Guy,' she said, 'perhaps I *had* been going through a *brief patch* of heavy drinking but now that I have a new *less stressful* job, everything will improve.'

'One more meeting,' he said. 'Just try one more.'

He was stubbornly insistent – but she was even more so. Right down at her very core she knew she was blessed with superior knowledge: she was right, he was wrong.

For over half an hour they tussled back and forth. Finally Guy conceded defeat with a murmured, 'Let's see how it plays out over the next few months.' He looked quite exhausted.

Then she brought the news of her new lowly administrative job to Nick – and he put his face in his hands and rocked back and forth. 'Thank God, thank God, thank God,' he moaned.

Marnie stared at him in mute surprise. She'd expected him to be disappointed about her low salary – not that she had yet earned any broker's commission, but there had been the expectation that when she eventually did, it would be fat and satisfying.

'I've been so worried,' Nick said. 'About your drinking. But now you can stop.'

Marnie felt like she'd had a blow to the chest: Nick was right. Her new working hours were nine to six, with no requirement to socialize. She would clock off at six on the dot and there was no reason why she shouldn't be home twenty minutes later.

Guy would be watching her at work, Nick would be watching her at home: she was trapped.

It was exhausting: planning when she could buy it, when she could drink it, how she could hide the smell, how she could hide the effects and how she could dispose of the empties.

Her life became even more boxed in when Nick let their full-time nanny go and hired a part-timer, who needed Marnie to be home each evening by seven; the expense of a full-time nanny couldn't be justified on Marnie's new salary.

The problem was Rico. Almost daily he tried to tempt her

for an after-work drink and sometimes she gave in – maybe once every three weeks, or once every two weeks, or once a week, and although she never intended to have more than a couple, again and again she found that she didn't return home until she was fall-down drunk.

She hated herself. She loved Nick. She loved the girls. Why did she do this to them?

Nick raged and begged, and she promised she wouldn't do it again, but Rico continued to issue his invitations and she wasn't always able to hold out.

Inevitably the night came when Rico lunged at her. Aghast, she sidestepped him. 'Rico, I'm married.'

Undeterred he tried again. And again. And eventually – why? She was never really sure – she let him. It was a scuffly, inexpert sort of snog, their tongues darting and clashing, both of them too drunk for it to be any better.

The following morning, in the cold light of day, she was sick to her stomach. A kiss counted as cheating and even though she and Nick were having a rough time, she loved him. He deserved her loyalty.

But the next time Rico invited her for a drink, she found herself accepting. It was peculiar, because, handsome as he was, he sometimes – often – gave her the creeps.

But she had to like him. You couldn't go to the pub with someone you didn't even like; what kind of person would that make you?

Their nanny left, after one too many evenings of having to stay late. Nick found a new one, another cut-pricer who needed Marnie to be home by six-thirty. Marnie swore she'd give this nanny no reason to leave.

The morning came when she woke – to her unprecedented horror – naked, in Rico's bed. She didn't know what, if anything, had happened. And she was too appalled by her memory lapse to be able to ask him.

All she could think of was Nick. She'd gone way too far. This time she really might lose him. And in the midst of that paralysing fear she knew how much she loved him. In the horrors, she raced home, her whole body trembling.

When she walked in through the front door, Nick went berserk – he'd been up all night waiting for her – but she lied, lied, lied; a dry-mouthed, tight-headed, elaborate story involving a night out with Lindka (she barely knew Lindka, but nonetheless managed later that morning to extract a promise from her that she'd swear to Nick – if asked – that Marnie had spent the night in her place), disconnected phones, mobiles out of batteries, no taxis available.

She *had* to make Nick believe her. She *couldn't* lose him.

As it happened, she didn't think he did believe her but he couldn't break her down. For every hole he found in her story, she plugged it with something even more implausible; in the end she so exhausted him that he simply surrendered.

Later that day, she looked across the office at Rico and something inside her curdled.

I was drunk and you took advantage of me.

Then another voice said, *No one forced me to drink those drinks . . .*

One thing was for sure, though, she thought: staying the night with Rico had been the biggest mistake of her life. She'd risked her marriage just because she'd had too much to drink. It would *never* happen again.

Three weeks later it happened again, almost to the exact detail.

Then again.

The new nanny left and Marnie's guilt felt like hot knives

in her chest. She loathed herself and the unerring ability to destroy everything she touched.

Her life felt as if it was folding ever more inwards on itself, and some mornings she felt so wretched that a mouthful of something made it easier to leave the house. And sometimes the terror of actually being out in the world was so huge that she started to take the precaution of carrying a bottle in her bag. Until Nick found it.

He began to smell her breath; he pretended he was just doing something else, like helping her off with her coat, but she knew what he was doing. If she was ten minutes late home, he panicked, convinced she'd embarked on a bender.

Another nanny left.

Nick's vigilance increased. In response, so did her subterfuge, then his watchfulness and her lies.

But even while she was being wound tighter and tighter around alcohol, she was struggling to escape. Praying to a god she didn't believe in for the strength to stop drinking for ever, she regularly went on raids around the house, retrieving bottles from their hiding places and pouring the contents down the sink, her head averted because it made her too sad to watch the silvery beauty gulp away from her.

Please make me stop please make me stop please make me stop.

At Nick's urging, she tried acupuncture to stop the craving; she tried meditation to calm down; she dosed herself with tryptophan and chromium; she harassed her doctor for better anti-depressants; she tried generating a natural high by running.

But if her guilt didn't get her, the sadness she carried was too much to bear. She could manage perhaps a week without a drink, but the depression during that time was like walking on knives. Stop, start, stop, start. Start, always start again.

She loved alcohol, a love that was fierce and hungry. Alcohol – vodka – was all she craved and there was nothing to compare to that first swallow. The taste so clean; icy cold and fiery warm, coursing down her throat, spreading heat through her chest, burning off all fear and anxiety in her stomach. It was as if stardust had been sprinkled from her head to her toes, and she was suddenly alert, yet calm, hopeful but accepting. Then giddy, giddy and free, soaring with relief.

'I've to go back to Dublin,' Grace said. 'I've got to work the weekend shift to make up for missing days earlier this week.'

'I know, I understand. You're good to come, very good.'

'Now listen, pep talk before I go. I'm not trying to scare you, but Nick won't put up with this for much longer. He's a really good man.'

'I know,' Marnie muttered.

'I always liked him but . . . I suppose I thought he was a bit of a lightweight. I think I judged him on his clothes. Anyway I don't any more. He's fantastic. Oh, and you didn't tell me that the reason he didn't get this year's bonus is because he had to miss so much time at work because of you.'

Marnie buried her face in her pillow, the shame too much.

'He had to keep leaving work early so your nanny could go to her next job, right? Because you were hardly ever home in time? And he had to stay late in the mornings to take the girls to school when you were too hung-over to do it? And yes, Marnie, I know that parenting should be a shared responsibility, but in all fairness, Nick earns fifteen times as much as you do.'

Marnie knew. She agreed.

'Listen to me, Marnie, this is important. If it came to it, Nick would get custody of the kids.'

Nick will leave you.

You will lose custody of your children.

I want a drink.

'The way you're drinking, no court in the country – what? Is that the doorbell?' Grace pounded down the stairs and pounded back up a few moments later. 'It's your boss.'

'Guy?'

'Lanky posh bloke? Yeah.'

'What? *Here?*'

'In the sitting room. Put on your dressing gown. Brush your hair.'

'I've got a proposition for you,' Guy said.

Marnie's heartbeat accelerated and suddenly the room was far too hot.

'I care about you, Marnie.'

Mutely she watched him. Was this really happening? What would be the price for keeping her job? Just a one-off? Or a regular three-bonk-a-week arrangement?

Whatever, he could so forget it.

'Even though you are at times – frankly – a nightmare,' he said.

She nodded. She knew. It still didn't mean she was going to sleep with him.

'I've never told anyone at work this,' he said. 'But . . . my mother was like you.'

'. . . What do you mean?' Oedipus with floppy hair. Christ, that was all she needed.

'A drunk.'

A *drunk*. The word conjured up a vision of half-human types warming themselves around a brazier and fighting over a bottle.

'What?' Guy asked. 'You don't like that word?'

'It sounds . . . rough.'

'Rough?' Guy looked pointedly at her broken ribs. 'Okay, like you, my mother was an alcoholic. That any better?'

'Please.' She was so weary from it all. 'I'm sorry, Guy. I'm so terribly terribly ashamed and sorry and I promise you it'll never happen again.'

'Can I tell you some things? Some truths?'

She took a deep, deep breath – why did everything have to be so hard and painful and brutal? – and sighed, 'Go on, Guy, if it makes you feel better.' He deserved to have his say.

He watched her; she could see that he was deciding whether or not to let her have it.

'You don't wash enough,' he said.

She felt nothing. Nothing, nothing. Thousands of miles away, a different Marnie was on fire with shame, but this one felt nothing.

'You're wrong,' she said.

But he was right, she didn't shower daily, not any more. Some days, getting out of bed and putting on clothes burnt up so much of her will to live that there was no endurance left over for the nails of water on her cold, cold body.

He said, sounding almost kind, 'But that's part of alcoholism.'

She winced.

'I've seen it with my mother,' he said. 'The depressions, the lying, the self-pity –'

'Self-pity?'

'You're riddled with it. Something else, Marnie – whoever

told you that vodka doesn't smell, misled you. One final thing: stay away from Rico. Or you'll both be out of a job.'

'Hey, now, Guy, just one moment! I'm a grown woman. What goes on with Rico is none of your business.'

He shook his head. 'I'm your employer. It is my business.'

'It's not –'

Guy sighed. 'You do understand that Rico is an alcoholic too?'

Marnie didn't know why, but that frightened her to her core. Rico wasn't an alcoholic, he just liked to drink. Like her, exactly like her.

Indignantly she asked, 'Assuming that's true, which it's not, why do you keep employing alcoholics?'

'I don't know,' he admitted. 'It's not something I ever intend to do. The experts would say that I'm drawn to help you, in the same way I had to help my mother.'

God, she thought, everyone's a bloody psychoanalyst these days. Even posh blokes.

'The same dynamic,' he said, 'that ensures alcoholics like you and Rico find each other. I suppose you scare away normal drinkers and the only people you are left to drink with, are each other.'

No. It was because Rico fancied her and wanted to get her drunk so she would . . .

'Nevertheless, Rico won't bother you any longer. I've spoken to him. And you should have no problem with the other guys. They won't even go to the pub with you any more, because you embarrass them so badly.'

Her face flamed. She'd noticed that they didn't stick around.

'Which brings me to my proposition. You still have a job on condition that you go to AA meetings and you don't drink.'

*

'Marnie, you're on your last chance,' Nick said. 'If you refuse to go to rehab –'

'Nick, there's really no need for that.'

' – then you have to find some other way of stopping. I'll do whatever you want to help you. Anything, Marnie, anything. But if you drink again, I have to leave and I have to take the girls with me.'

'Mum?' Daisy slunk into the bedroom, looking unusually shifty.

'Yes, sweetheart?'

'Mum.' Daisy climbed onto the bed and whispered, 'Something terrible has happened.'

'What is it?'

Daisy rested her forehead on her knees and began to cry. Marnie straightened up in alarm. Daisy prided herself on never crying.

'It's okay, sweetheart, whatever it is, it's okay.'

'Mum, I . . .' She was so choked with sobs, her words were incomprehensible. Then she hiccuped out a complete sentence. 'I wet my bed!'

The guilt was so violent that Marnie's stomach folded over on itself.

'I'm nearly seven.' Daisy gulped, her petal-like face distorted with tears. 'And I wet my bed!'

Marnie gazed at Daisy, as though she'd been hit with a thunderbolt. The moment was here. It had finally arrived. The moment she would remember, when she understood, with mystical certainty, that she had to stop.

She had fraternized with criminals, she had broken her own bones, she'd been forced to attend AA, but this was what she needed to bring her to her senses.

She loved her daughters with a passion that was painful. Her drinking was damaging them and she couldn't do it – the guilt was crucifying.

I love them more than I love to drink. It was as simple as that.

She realized that it had probably taken years to bring her to this point but the decision seemed to happen in an instant. She was calm, clear, resolved.

I will never drink again.

Monday. She walked into the office, her head high. She didn't feel as raw as she usually felt, returning after a drink-related absence. This time she was a new person with a new life plan and she felt good. She was clean and decent, a devoted mother, a loving wife, a hard-working employee.

Craig said hello, Wen-Yi nodded at her, Lindka called out, 'Morning.' No one remarked on her bruises or her almost week-long absence, which meant that everyone knew exactly what had happened. Guy must have told them to pretend that everything was normal. It felt uncomfortable but at least it was the last time she would have to live through a morning like this.

Rico was in. He gave her a sheepish smile and her stomach flipped in revulsion. He'd texted her countless times while she'd been recovering, but she'd replied only once: a few brusque words, to let him know that she was alive.

I've probably had sex with him.

Did it count as infidelity if you couldn't remember it?

At 12.45, Guy appeared at her side. 'Time for your meeting.'

The AA meeting. Throughout the morning she'd wondered if he'd stick to his threat that she had to go.

'The thing is, Guy,' she said quietly, 'there's no need. I've decided – and I really mean it – that I will never drink again. Because of my daughters. I saw how I was damaging them –'

'Excellent. The meetings will help you stick to your resolution.'

'But if I've given up, I'm not an alcoholic, so why do I need –'

'Off you go.' He wasn't yielding. 'No need to hurry back. Stay for the whole hour.'

'Well?' Guy's face was lambent with hope when she returned at 2.15. 'How did it go?'

'Good, thanks.'

'Helpful?'

'Oh yes.'

Very helpful. An hour in Topshop had certainly lifted her spirits.

Thursday. She was flicking through the hangers looking for a size 8 when she felt someone staring at her. She looked up. Lindka, her eyes hostile. Shit.

'Aren't you supposed to be at an AA meeting?'

'Excuse me?' Did the whole world know her business?

'All week Guy has been giving you an extra half-hour for lunch so you can go to a meeting.'

'Look, Lindka –' She was ill at ease around her, ever since the time she'd begged Lindka to lie to Nick about staying the night in her place. 'I'm just about to go to it now.'

'It's twenty past one. The meeting starts at one.'

How did Lindka know? Did the entire office know everything?

'Have you gone to any of them?' Lindka asked accusingly.

No, as it happened. Every lunchtime had been spent killing time in the shops. Why would she need to go to a meeting with alcoholics when she knew she'd never drink again? She'd been having a good week, a great week. The atmosphere was happy at home, she'd actually had fun with Nick and the girls, she'd cooked dinner for the first time in ages and she hadn't wanted a drink, not once. She was passionately grateful for her family, for Nick's patience, for her two beautiful children.

'Come on,' Lindka said. 'I'll walk there with you now.'

For God's sake. But she was too scared of Lindka to take her on.

They walked along the cold street in tense silence and when they reached the community centre, Marnie said, 'This is the place.'

'Which room?' Lindka actually walked into the hallway.

Marnie refused to answer. Lindka was treating her like a child.

'Which room?' Lindka hardened her voice.

'That one.' Marnie pointed at a shut door, which Lindka opened. She stuck her head in and took a good look round and seemed satisfied with what she saw. 'In you go, Marnie, and when you get back to work you tell Guy where I found you.'

'Please, Lindka –'

'You tell him or I will.'

Marnie slid into the room and took a chair. Lots of people smiled and mouthed hello at her. The whinging was in full flow.

'. . . I tried to stop drinking on my own, but I couldn't. The only thing that did it was coming to these meetings . . .'

'. . . I couldn't bear my feelings. I was always angry or jealous or depressed or afraid, so I drank . . .'

'. . . I had a beautiful girlfriend. I loved her. She begged me to stop. I tried for her but I couldn't. She left me and the grief nearly killed me, but it wasn't enough to stop me drinking. The truth was I loved alcohol more than I loved her . . .'

'. . . I blamed everyone else for my drinking: my wife for nagging me, my boss for working me too hard, my parents for not loving me enough. But the only reason I drank was because I was an alcoholic, which was my responsibility . . .'

'. . . I was always different, even as a teenager, even as a child, in fact . . .'

Now that she was here, she wouldn't mind a cup of tea and a biscuit; it might make the time go faster. She looked around to see where they kept them and, by accident, she locked eyes with the man at the top table. 'Great to see you again,' he said. 'Would you like to say something?'

She shook her head.

'What's your name?'

For God's sake! 'Marnie.'

'Hello, Marnie.'

There was an expectant pause. She was supposed to say, 'And I'm an alcoholic.'

But she wasn't, so she didn't.

At five to two, she slipped out. The whinging was still going on, but she'd had enough. She actually ran down the corridor towards the doors to the outside world, she was so desperate to escape.

'Marnie?'

What? She turned around. A graceful woman had followed her out. Pink hoodie, swingy ponytail, big smile. 'I don't know if you remember me. I'm Jules. I met you once before.'

'. . . Oh yes.'

'How's it all going?'

'Great, yes, great.' Daylight was visible through the slit windows in the wooden doors. She'd been so close . . .

'Here's my number.' Jules gave her a card. 'If you're thinking of drinking, call me any time, really, day or night. I mean it.' She smiled warmly. 'And would you like me to take yours?'

Marnie didn't know how to refuse without appearing rude; reluctantly she spelled it out while Jules put it in her phone.

Can I go now?

'Guy, I have a confession.'

Dread swept over his face. 'You've been drinking?'

'No!'

'You didn't go to the meeting?'

'I did, but I didn't go for all of it. I went shopping first.'

'But that's okay.' Relief made him generous. Then he noticed Lindka watching them across the office. 'What's Lindka got to do with this?'

'. . . She found me shopping.'

It took a moment for him to understand. 'You mean you wouldn't have gone if she hadn't caught you?'

'I would have.'

He clearly didn't believe her and, in frustration, she burst out, 'It just seemed silly when I know I'll never drink ever again. It's different this time, I don't even want to drink.'

He seemed to sag. 'You didn't go to any of the meetings, did you?'

She contemplated lying. But this had to stop. She couldn't spend every lunchtime for the rest of her working life lurking in Topshop. 'No, Guy.' Her tone was reasonable. 'There wasn't any need.'

He exhaled. 'Okay.'

'You mean . . . ?'

'Okay. Don't go any longer. I mean, don't pretend to go any longer.'

She should have felt better. But as she went to her desk, she felt sick. He'd meant well and although it had been infuriating that he hadn't understood, she was sorry she had hurt him. All of a sudden she was angry with him for making her feel guilty. And she was angry with Lindka for dropping her in it. And she was angry with Nick. And she was angry with Rico. Fuck them. Fuck them all. Who the fuck did they think they were, trying to run her life? Treating her like a child. Humiliating her.

She was a grown woman. She could – *would* – drink if she wanted.

Yes, drink.

She hadn't wanted one since Daisy had made her shameful confession. She'd been free. Proud of her decision and not a little scornful that everyone made such a big deal of it.

Drink.

Now.

Now now now now now now.

Her body was possessed with craving – where had it come from? Every cell was lit up by an irresistible compulsion. She was slick with sweat, her blood was racing and her head was clicking calculations: Go to the off-licence buy a bottle drink it in the Ladies fill me comfort me heal me.

I need it I need it I need it now.

Daisy and Verity? What about Daisy and Verity?

But her mind slid over them. She barely knew them.

'I'm just popping out.' Her voice was wrong. She'd striven for casual but she sounded afraid.

'Where?' Guy was alert, he knew something was up.

'The chemist.'

'For what?'

'Tampons.' She stared him dead in the eye.

'You're busy. Those documents need to go in tonight's post.'

'I'll only be five minutes.'

'I've got tampons,' Lindka said. 'Save you nipping out.'

'I'd prefer my own brand.'

'You don't know what my brand is.'

By now the whole office was watching. Panic made her dizzy.

'. . . I don't feel well. I think I'd better go home.' She was going, she was leaving, it didn't matter what any of them thought. Sack me, I don't care.

'It's three-thirty,' Guy said. 'Try to last two more hours.'

They watched each other, locked in a silent stand-off, and the tightness in her chest unwound a little.

'Okay,' she whispered, and returned to her seat.

She bowed her head and tried to bring her mind back to her work but she couldn't read. She couldn't see what was in front of her.

The need was back, more compelling than before. Building, expanding, swelling, burgeoning, she couldn't bear it.

She jumped to her feet and grabbed her bag. 'The loo,' she called, as heads snapped up to watch her.

She was out on the street, no coat, running, a vague impression of shops and offices blurring past, the cold wind skinning her face. The off-licence was at the far end of the street. Her legs were heavy, children tangled her path, she bumped her hip against a buggy, tinny Christmas music spilled from shops, people were staring and swearing after her.

Then, a pub. Right before her, as if it had dropped straight down from heaven. Through the doors, to the counter.

'Vodka and tonic.' Her tongue thick. 'Large one.'

Drenched in sweat. Trembling. Ice cubes, fat and glassy, in a sweating metal container. Watching them slip from the pincers. Fall, pick up, fall, pick up. The world reduced to ice cubes. One tinkled against the glass; success. The pincers poised to pick up another cube.

'No! Duss mata.' She sounded drunk already.

'What?'

'Ice. Duss mata.'

'You don't want any?' The barman poised the glass to tip the one cube away.

''Sokay! Whassintheresokay!'

The vodka, the vodka, the vodka, just do the fucking vodka.

As if to deliberately thwart her, he approached a plate of lemon slices.

'Nolemon!'

'No lemon?'

'Nono.' Christ. 'Justthe . . .'

She jerked her head towards the vodka. Optic. Finally. Pushing up into the bottle and releasing the flow of liquid crystal. She watched without breathing.

'Did you say you wanted a large?'

Her heart stopped. Should she take the single measure now? Or wait an extra two seconds for the large?

'Single'sokay.'

'You said large.'

'Allrightthenlarge!'

In slow motion, the optic pushed up again. Then the barman bent down, the glass placed out of her reach. What now?

'Slimline or normal?' The tonic. She swallowed a moan.

'Norm'.'

'Looks like we're out of normal. I'll have to go downstairs.'

She was afraid she might scream. 'Dussmata,' she said desperately. 'I'lltaketheslimline.'

'It's no trouble. I have to go downstairs anyway.'

'No please! Just the . . .' She reached for the glass.

Then it was in her hand and it was roaring down her throat and the heat was in her stomach and the stardust was stealing through her, thrilling her with its magic, drawing back a curtain to reveal a better, cleaner, sparklier version of everything.

The glass hit the wood of the counter. ''Nother.'

She drank the second standing at the counter, then took a seat for the third and, able to breathe again, considered her options.

She could go back to work, no bridges burnt there, she'd only been gone a few minutes, but on balance, she decided she wouldn't. The boiling hunger had abated, in fact she was feeling good, great even, but she liked it here, she'd prefer to keep drinking. And why not? It would be Christmas in two weeks.

She swallowed another mouthful of liquid glitter and cushioned herself further into the glow.

She'd never before walked out of work in the middle of the afternoon.

First time for everything.

A stab of conscience. The documents that needed to go in today's post? If they were that important, someone else would do them.

And Daisy and Verity? They'd be fine. Everything was fine, fine, lovely and fine.

'Another one.' She waved her glass at the poker-faced barman.

Everything felt gorgeous, except she'd like someone to talk to. And who better than Rico? Just as Guy had promised, he had kept well clear of her all week, but actually, *actually* she was very fond of Rico, *extremely* fond, and suddenly she wanted to see him.

She fumbled for her mobile. 'What's the name of this pub?' she called.

'The Wellington.'

In the Wellington. U&T?

She held her phone, waiting for a reply. Go on, she urged. Go on.

B wit u in 5!

Five minutes! Fantastic! She ordered him a drink and watched the door, thinking about how fine everything was, and then there was Rico! Hurrying towards her, a big grin on his face.

'I'm not supposed to talk to you.'

She couldn't help laughing. 'I'm not supposed to talk to you either. Here's your drink.'

He downed it in one and they both dissolved into manic laughter.

'Did he make you go to AA meetings too?' she asked.

'Yeah, but they had to be in the evening, they had to be different to your ones. Mad, isn't it? The whole thing? Guy's a headcase.' He nodded at the barman. 'Two more.'

She'd forgotten how good-looking Rico was. She nuzzled his neck. 'I've missed you, you know.'

'Missed you too.' He put his lips to hers and thrust his tongue into her mouth. Nice. Sexy. Sort of.

The pub was filling up now; people in antlers and draped in tinsel.

'Time's it, Rico?'

'Ten past five. You're not going to skip out on me?'

She should go home, everyone was expecting her. But she had a husband and a nanny to take care of her children.

'Me? No, going nowhere.'

Another unwelcome stab of conscience. She should ring them, it wasn't right to worry them, but they'd only give her a hard time and she was feeling so happy and she so rarely felt happy . . .

'Hey, hey, hey, I have to tell you about –' She took a long swallow from her glass, ice cubes banging against her teeth, and when she put it down again, Guy had materialized in front of her. Cushioned though she was, it was a shock.

'. . . Guy, I . . .' She sought an explanation but couldn't fashion one.

He loomed over them, tall and haughty, while she and Rico looked up like guilty schoolchildren.

'Marnie.' He handed her a white envelope. 'One for you too,' he said to Rico.

Then he left.

She and Rico turned wide-eyed to each other. 'How did he find us?'

'God.' She snorted with laughter. 'We're sacked. He's sacked us!'

She tore open her envelope and they pored over it together. Words jumped off the white page. '. . . drunk . . .' '. . . patience . . .' '. . . warnings . . .' '. . . dismissed with immediate effect . . .'

'It's true, he's done it, he's sacked me.' She couldn't stop giggling.

Grim-faced, Rico ripped his envelope open and scanned the page. 'I don't fucking believe it. He's sacked me too.'

'I told you.'

'I didn't think . . .'

'Why would he sack me and not sack you?'

'Because I'm a fucking genius.'

'And I'm not?'

He rolled his eyes. 'Well, no.'

'Well, fuck you.'

'And fuck you. You've just lost me my job.'

'Me?'

'If he didn't have a thing for you, he wouldn't care what I did.'

'Look, he doesn't mean it.' She ran her hand up Rico's thigh, stopping just short of his crotch. 'We're not sacked, he's just trying to scare us.'

'How do you know?'

'It's obvious!' Wasn't it?

'You sure?'

'I'm sure. Look, am I wasting my time here?' She drummed her fingers on the top of his leg.

'Oh.'

Now she had his attention. Discreetly she began stroking the fabric, finding and encouraging his erection with her fingers. He kissed her again, deep and searching, and slid his hand down the back of her skirt, under her tights and knickers, cupping her buttock.

They drank and kissed and drank and touched and when the barman bent over their table, she thought he was collecting the empties. Then he spoke. Quietly he said, 'We'd like you to leave.'

What?

We'd like you to leave.

Her face flamed with mortification.

547

'Finish up your drinks and leave.'

'Now, look –' Rico started threateningly.

'Don't,' she said. 'Come on, let's just go.'

'Fuck them, we'll go back to mine.'

Their faces averted with embarrassment, they swallowed the remains of their drinks and gathered up their stuff.

At the door, Rico suddenly stopped and called back over his shoulder, 'Fuck you. You couldn't pay me to drink in this shit-hole.'

'We *were* actually drinking in that shit-hole.' Marnie couldn't stop laughing and she knew she was getting on Rico's nerves. The more irritable he got, the more she laughed.

'Fuck you.' She imitated his voice. 'You couldn't PAY me to drink in this shit-hole.'

'Shut up.'

They fell in the door of Rico's apartment and she tumbled onto the floor, pulling him down on top of her, causing him to bang his elbow hard.

'Christ! For God's sake, Marnie, that really fucking hurt!'

'Shut up, you milk-sop, I've got THREE CRACKED RIBS. I know ALL about pain.'

'Stop laughing! Get up and get your clothes off.' He pushed her towards the bedroom, tugging at her skirt.

'I want a drink.' She lay on his bed and yelled with mirth, 'I WANT A DRINK.'

'There isn't anything.' His eyes were half shut and his mouth was slack. Being drunk didn't suit him, it made him blurry and soft around the edges. 'I'll have to go out and get some.'

'What do you mean?' she cried. 'Really? Nothing? Why not?'

'I drank it all.'

'Hah! You *drunkard*.'

'Marnie, if you don't stop laughing, I swear I'm going to smack you one.' He loomed over her and pressed himself against her, his erection digging painfully into her pubic bone. She made herself focus on him: his face looked like it was melting.

He ground himself against her and thrust his tongue into the back of her throat. She wasn't enjoying this and she didn't know why.

She wasn't drunk enough. That was what the trouble was. They'd been ousted from the pub too soon.

'Stop.' She was pushing his face away and trying to clamber out from under him.

'What? Why?'

Why?

'I'm married.'

He pulled back in amazement. 'It's never stopped you before.'

So she *had* slept with him. Oh no, no, no. She couldn't behave as if this was news.

'It should have stopped me.' She wanted to leave. She was revolted by him. 'I love my husband.'

'What?' He was shocked.

I love Nick and I love my children and I don't know what I'm doing here. 'Rico, I want to go.'

'Go on, then, go.'

Out in the street, a taxi driver with a yellow light slowed down, then speeded up again when he got close enough to take a proper look at her. She shivered on the street corner, scanning the cars. Without a coat, the cold took bites out of her. Lots of taxis were around but they were jam-packed with office-party types, leaving a suggestion of discordant bugles and cheap red-satin dresses in their wake as they whizzed past. By the time the yellow light of an empty taxi finally hoved into view, her feet were numb – but this driver also refused to take her!

'I'm freezing,' she pleaded.

'You're pissed,' he said, and accelerated away.

She stared after him; she had no choice but to walk back to the office and get her own car. It wasn't so far, perhaps a mile, but it took a long time; people were everywhere, spilling out of pubs, singing, shoving and shouting.

When she reached the car park, she had a moment when she wondered if she was sober enough to drive – and decided she was. That walk would have sobered up George Best. And although she grazed the car slightly on a pillar as she pulled out of the parking space, it was a good thing because it reminded her to drive extra carefully.

The roads were full of pre-Christmas traffic. People driving like nutters, and pedestrians falling out into the street, almost under her wheels. It was like an obstacle course. Then she got stuck in front of a police car, racing off to some crime scene, blue lights flashing, sirens wailing. Right up behind her it drove, destroying her concentration.

She slowed down. 'Go on,' she called in frustration. '*Over*take me.'

Unable to take the wailing, she nipped into a bus stop so they could zip past her.

But when they pulled in behind her, filling her car with blue light, the truth was like a punch in the stomach. They were for her. For *her*.

There were two of them, men. She rolled down the window.

'Step out of the car, madam.' A look passed between the two coppers. 'Have you been drinking?'

A police car brought her home. She'd gone through a red light. She'd been arrested for drunk-driving. It was eleven o'clock at night. Nick would go berserk.

The lights were off, thank God. They were all in bed. She might have got away with this. Quietly she let herself in and went straight for the cupboard under the kitchen sink; some months ago she'd decanted a bottle of Smirnoff into an empty bleach container, as an emergency stash. There was some upstairs in her wardrobe, a bottle that Grace hadn't found, but she'd wake Nick if she tiptoed in and rummaged for it.

She'd noticed the envelope propped up against the pepper grinder, as she located a glass and a bottle of tonic, but it was only when she sat at the table with her drink that she picked it up. No address, just her name in black type.

Another letter from Guy, perhaps? Reinstating her?

The memory of getting caught by him in the pub felt like a cloud passing over the sun. And then being asked to leave . . .

God.

She opened the envelope. The letter was typed on heavy cream paper and it wasn't from Guy. It was from a company: Dewey, Screed and Hathaway, Attorneys at Law.

What was this?

It wasn't about her job.

It was something to do with Nick.

She forced her eyes to focus and to stop sliding into double vision long enough to make sense of the words.

Nick had left her. He had taken the children. The house was on the market.

She'd thought there had been a strange feeling in the house, now she knew what it was – there was no one here.

She sprinted up the stairs and into Verity's room. Empty. She wrenched open the wardrobe door; bare hangers rattled. Then she raced to Daisy's room; bed neatly made and empty. Into her own room, up on a chair, opening the highest cupboard: this would be the proof. What she saw made her actually gasp: all the Santa presents for the girls were gone. Impossible though it was, the emptiness seemed to pulse.

He'd left her, the bastard. And he'd taken the girls with him.

She sat on the top step of the stairs, swallowing and swallowing, trying to wet her dry mouth.

They would come back, they were just trying to scare her. But it was a bad, bad thing to do.

She heard her own shriek and was on her feet, tugging her hand from his, without knowing why.

A cigarette. He'd put his cigarette out on the palm of her hand. He'd gripped the hand so hard the bones had squeaked, and ground his cigarette into the centre of it.

Red mist floated before her eyes. She couldn't see.

He stared at her palm, at the round red burn, the grains of ash still scattered across it. There was a strange smell and a plume of smoke rose from the wound.

'Why . . . did you do that?' Her teeth were chattering.

'It was an accident.' He sounded stunned. 'I thought it was an ashtray.'

'How?'

The pain was too bad, she couldn't stay still. 'The cold tap.' She stood up and all the blood left her head.

'I've proper bandages,' he said. 'And antiseptic. Don't let it get infected.'

He dressed her wound, he gave her codeine, he brought her dinner in bed and fed it to her bite by bite.

He'd never been more tender.

Lola

Thursday, 11 December 21.55
I quietly opened front door and tiptoed out of house into dark night. Cast furtive look around. No sign of Jake the Love-God, thanks be to cripes. Although he could be out there somewhere, lurking in the shadows, ready to ambush me with his surfy love.

21.56
Limbo'd under wire fence and knocked on Rossa Considine's front door.

'Right on time,' he said. 'Come in.'

Awkward conversation ensued as we sipped beer and waited for *Law and Order* to start.

I cleared throat. Asked, with attempt at cheeriness, 'All set for trannie night tomorrow night?'

Was only trying to fill silence but my chance remark triggered a revelation – a trannie is not the same thing as a cross-dresser!

'Trannies are gay,' Rossa said. 'Cross-dressers are straight.'

Now I understood why Noel from Dole continued to eschew the word 'trannie' and would only answer to 'cross-dresser'!

'To be honest, Rossa Considine,' I admitted, 'just thought they were different ways to describe same thing.'

'Like Snickers and Marathon?'

'Correct. Like Ulay and Olay.'

'Like porridge and oatmeal?'

Pause. 'Please do not say "oatmeal", Rossa Considine, is irritating word.'

'Why?'

'Cannot explain. Just is.'

Sudden strained atmosphere. Rossa Considine focused with hard stare on the telly. Lengthy ad break before *Law and Order*. Taking long time to start.

When Rossa Considine had so unexpectedly shown up as 'Chloe' almost four weeks ago, I had been shocked, bewitched, stunned – many emotions. Astonished at my poor powers of observation – had been living next door to trannie (beg your pardon, I mean *cross-dresser*) for some weeks and hadn't had a clue. Even more astonishing, that taciturn – at times, yes, even surly – man could be transformed into radiant woman, all smiles and chat and perfumed kisses.

Had been quite dazzled by her and readily accepted invitation to view *Law and Order* with, of course, that caveat that if we got on each other's nerves, we need not repeat the experience. She insisted we exchange mobile numbers so, if required, we could end the arrangement by text. Nicest way, she said.

But! Oh yes, but! The following Thursday night, as I furtively exited the house (by then, Jake's nocturnal lurking was well under way), and slipped under the wire fence that separated me from Chloe's/Rossa's, I realized I felt shy. *Immensely* strange situation, entirely without precedent. Had been invited by adorable Chloe – but unkempt Rossa answered the door and relieved me of bag of tortilla chips and cans of beer. Odd. Like going on a date set up by absent, matchmaker-style third party. Very, very strange, if I thought about it too much. So decided not to. Had other things on mind (which will get to — yes, yes, will get to).

Despite acknowledged tensions between us, the first Thursday had gone well. *Law and Order* watched and savoured and conversation light and pleasant.

Second Thursday could also be deemed a success. Also third Thursday. However, here we were on fourth Thursday — perhaps no longer on our best behaviour? — and it seemed, as a result of my oatmeal comment, we might be running into difficulties.

I asked, 'You going to sulk now, Rossa Considine?'

'Why would I sulk, Lola Daly?'

'You are quite sulky, as a rule.' Had a thought. 'At least as a man, you are. But as a woman, you are charm itself. Perhaps you should be a woman all the time.'

'Couldn't go potholing in high heels.'

'That is defeatist attitude. May I ask you further questions about this trannie/cross-dresser dichotomy?'

'Please do not say "dichotomy", Lola Daly, is irritating word.'

'Wh —? Oh is joke. Careful, you almost smiled there.'

His lips were definitely turning upwards.

'Come on,' I coaxed reluctant smile, 'show us your teeth.'

'Am not a baby,' he said gruffly.

'Very well. Now. Will employ frankness, Rossa Considine. All my "girls" are straight, i.e. cross-dressers. But I like the word "trannie". What am I to do?'

'Sue is gay.'

'Really?'

(Sue was new. Noel/Natasha had located her on chat-site and invited her along the previous week — much to my dismay. 'No more, Natasha,' I had begged, when they showed up together. 'No more.' But Noel regards our Friday nights as cross-dressing homeland. Everyone welcome, by dint of their cross-dressingness, regardless of how much — little, actually — room there is.)

'Okay,' I began again. 'All my girls *except Sue* are straight, i.e. cross-dressers. But I like the word "trannie". What am I to do?'

'Learn to live with it.'

'No. Don't think I will.'

'No matter what I said, you would have done the opposite.'

Pause while I considered his comment. About to deny it then realized would be proving him right. 'So it would seem, Rossa Considine, and I am at a loss as to why. So yes, even though it is wrong description, I will continue to call them all trannies.'

'They won't like it.'

'No one is forcing them to visit me on a Friday night.' I was flexing power muscles. Like Mrs Butterly barring those people she doesn't like the look of.

'Power corrupts,' Rossa Considine said.

'So they say. And absolute power corrupts absolutely.' Quote from someone. 'Who said that?'

'Confucius?'

'John le Carré?'

'Duran Duran?'

'Someone,' we were agreed upon. 'Definitely someone.'

23.01
End of Law and Order

Excellent episode, we both agreed. Dark, gritty, compelling.

I got to my feet. Brushed away tortilla crumbs from my dress, watched them sprinkle onto the rug. Flicked glance at Rossa Considine. He was also watching tortilla crumbs sprinkling onto rug.

'I will have to clean that up,' he said.

Knew it, knew it, just *knew* he'd be sulky! 'Apologies, apologies, please give me sweeping brush. I will do it myself right now.'

'No need, no need, guest in my home.'

'Only you seem riled.'

'Not riled.'

'Sulky, perhaps?'

'Shut up, Lola Daly.'

'Thank you for sharing your television with me,' I said. 'Sorry about your rug. See you tomorrow night when you will be a trannie?'

'Cross-dresser. No need to rush off immediately, Lola Daly.'

'Oh yes, need, I think,' I said. 'Let's not push our luck.'

23.04
Safely back in own house, without confrontation from Jake the Love-God

Wiping toner over face when phone rang and every nerve in body leapt. At this stage, poor bastards ragged and exhausted from all the leaping.

Checked caller display. Not Paddy. That was all I needed to know.

Since the night of his unexpected phone call, almost four weeks ago, had been bag of nerves, almost as bad as when news first broke that he was getting married.

When had answered phone to discover was him on the line, swearing how much he missed me, I simply *could not believe* it.

'I'm sorry, I'm sorry, I'm sorry,' he'd said, into my flabber-gasted ears. 'Little Lola, I treated you so badly. The way you found out about Alicia . . . I'm so sorry. The press got hold of rumour and whole thing blew up before I had chance to talk to you.'

Every word I had ever fantasized about him saying was issuing from his mouth.

'Even Alicia didn't know she was getting married until she heard it on the news.'

Wasn't so interested in hearing about Alicia.

'I miss you so much,' he said. 'In all these months, haven't been able to stop thinking about you.'

Is this happening? Is this actually, really happening?

'Can I see you?' he asked. 'Please, Lola. Will I send Spanish John for you?'

'You still getting married?' I asked, not quite the malleable fool I used to be.

'Oh Lola.' Heavy sigh. 'You know I am. Have to. She is right woman for my job.' He sounded so bleak that for moment genuinely felt his dilemma. 'But you are woman I really want, Lola. Is impossible situation. Am torn in two. Will be quite honest, this is the best I can offer you.'

I let this information settle. At least he was being straight with me.

'Will I send Spanish John?' he asked.

'Am not in Dublin.'

'Oh?' Change in tone. 'Where are you?'

'County Clare.'

'Clare. Right. But you could drive to Dublin. How long it take?'

'Three hours. Maybe three and half.'

'That long? Even with Kildare bypass?'

They speak about Kildare bypass as though it was magic hole in hyper-space. Funny the things you think about when in shock. Was also thinking something else. Was thinking that it was 10.30 at night. Earliest time I would get to Dublin, even if drove like the clappers and got speeding tickets and points on licence and appearance before magistrate and name printed in local paper, would be 1 in morning. Too late. Not right.

'Paddy.' Reaching deep into self, rummaging around in drawer containing rarely used emotions and locating and dusting off self-respect. 'Is already ten-thirty. Ring me again in the morning and we'll make arrangement for better time.'

'Oh . . . right . . . I see.' Sounded startled.

Pleased with myself.

'Grace Gildee still bothering you?' he asked.

'. . . Um . . .' Abrupt change in conversation. 'No. She stopped long time ago.'

'Good. Tell me, Lola, do you hate me?'

Sometimes I did. Flashes of bad, burny hatred. But now that he had rung, with such anguish in his voice, all bad, burny feelings were gone. 'Don't hate you, Paddy.'

'Good. Great. Better let you go now.'

Wanted to stay talking to him, wanted to hold on to this precious, precious chance for ever. But knew that best way to hold on was to let go. (Paradox.) 'Yes. Talk to you in morning, Paddy.'

'Yes, talk to you in morning.'

Straight away, incandescent with triumph, I rang Bridie. Who made me repeat entire conversation word for word. She listened without interruption and when I finished I said, 'What you think?'

'What I think?' Bridie said. 'What I think is he won't ring in the morning. Or ever again,' she added.

'Unnecessary brutality, Bridie!' I exclaimed.

'Cruel to be kind.'

'You may stick your kindness!'

'You will thank me for this.'

'Words of comfort, please, Bridie, I insist on words of comfort!'

'Only words of comfort I have for you, Lola, are "Heavy doses of vitamin B." Especially B6 and B12. Also maybe B5. And B2. Your central nervous system will be worked to the bone every time phone rings for next two weeks, setting up false – yes, entirely false – expectation that it is Paddy de Courcy on the line. Vitamins may prevent you from having breakdown.'

'He will ring me tomorrow.'

'Lola! It was BOOTY CALL. It is OBVIOUS.'

'He said he misses me.'

'He misses having someone to handcuff to his bedpost, to act out his rape fantasies. You don't think horse-face lets him do that, do you?'

'Horse-face repressed. I am sexually evolved.'

'One way of putting it.'

'Am sorry now I rang you to share my good news. Goodbye, Bridie.'

I hung up, and lay on couch, eating savoury snacks and thinking about strangeness of things – life, trajectories of romance, shape of Monster Munch. One minute had been rejected by two men – Jake, Paddy – and the next, both were prostrating themselves and requesting forgiveness. What's it all about? Universe is contrary diva.

Mid-reverie, my phone rang again and I almost levitated above couch, every nerve ajangle.

It was only Bridie. She said, 'Did I say B5?'

'Yes, yes, yes. Get off line, please, you are blocking Paddy de Courcy from ringing.'

'Strongest dose in the chemist, remember.'

The following morning, I awoke at 6 a.m., waiting for Paddy to ring. Knew he would. I had held out, had refused him. He liked what he couldn't have.

When phone rang at 9.16 a.m., although hair stood briefly on end, smiled to self. Last night's sacrifice had been worth it.

But no! Last night's sacrifice had not been worth it! Was only Bridie.

'Hello,' she said. 'Let me guess. Your heart is pounding, your blood is racing, your mouth is dry. If you *knew* what all that was doing to your poor central nervous system. Is your synapse endings I feel for.'

'What you want, Bridie?' Attitude of coldness.

'Checking you okay.'

'Not checking on me. Gloating.'

'Not gloating. Caring, yes, caring, Lola, caring. So he hasn't rung yet?'

'How could he ring when you are constantly cluttering up bloody line?'

Sudden noisy rapping on front door.

'Bridie, someone is at door! Is probably Paddy!'

'How he know where you are?'

'He is powerful man. Can find out these things. Goodbye, Bridie, goodbye.'

Ran to door and swung it wide, having convinced myself

that Paddy would be leaning against jamb. But not Paddy. Jake. Tangle-haired, tanned, silvery-eyed, large-lipped.

Disappointment crushing. Stared and stared, unable to believe it was wrong man.

'I come in?' he asked in croaky voice.

He sat on couch, hands hanging between his knees, looking abject as can be. 'Have you had chance to think about us getting back together?'

Looked at him and thought, Oh cripes.

Had gone off him anyway, with his request for 'space' and his indignation that I hadn't stalked him, but now that feelings for Paddy had revived, all residue of lust for Jake had dissolved like footprints in sand.

Horrors – no longer thought he was most good-looking man on planet earth. Actually thought he looked – terrible thing to say about another human being – slightly deformed. That mouth. Not sexy. No. Instead looked like lip augmentation procedure had gone wrong. Too much puffing and pouting, as though stung by wasp on bottom lip.

Simultaneously discovered had gone off his odour. Previous to this had enjoyed his natural unwashed smell, it had seemed authentic, unapologetic and, yes, manly. But now faint studenty miasma of unwashed socks hung around him like cloud.

He pulled me to him and said, 'Please, Lola,' at same time as slipping his hand beneath the waistband of my pyjamas. Recoiled! Bum skin goosebumped with desire to be not man-handled by him, and prospect of multi-positioned sex no longer seemed remotely inviting.

Jake pressed his erect boyo at me, through thin fabric of my pyjamas, and whispered, 'See how much I want you.'

Gak! Yes, gak! Even I was surprised it was that bad. He took my hand to rub against his mickey, but I stepped away from him, freeing my bottom from shuddery revoltingness of his handfeel. His expression was one of great surprise. I looked into his silvery eyes and thought, What peculiar colour for eyes. What is wrong with brown or hazel?

'You not want me to touch you, Lola?' he asked.

Saw the confused boy in the body of a man and had moment of cold realization. Knew had to be brutally honest with him. Otherwise would end up sleeping with him, out of kindness, and my skin and soul were curdling at such a scenario.

'Jake,' I said. 'Am very sorry, but it's a no go, you and me. Was fun but let's just leave it at that.'

'Admit have been stupid fucker,' he said. 'But have apologized and am willing to change.'

'No need,' I said. 'Is pointless. There is someone else. Another man.'

'You have met someone else already?'

'No, no. Someone else all along.'

'Thanks for telling me!'

'But it was only bit of fun, you and me! That's what you thought too!'

'Yes, but didn't realize was going to fall for you.'

Exasperated. 'Is hardly my fault.'

'Very mature, Lola!' He had turned sneery. 'Very responsible.'

'But if had fallen for you and you hadn't fallen for me, you would tell me, It was just bit of fun, sorry you have fallen in love with me, now sling your hook.' Was true. Had happened to me often enough with other men.

Tired now. 'Jake, look! Tide is in! You must go surfing.'

He looked out window. Easily distractable, thank God. Like jingling a lead at a dog and shouting, Walkies, walkies!

'Okay, am going,' he said. 'But you will change your mind.'

'Won't.' Tried to sound kindly. 'Swear to you I won't.'

Once got rid of Jake, returned to phone vigil. At 10 a.m. on the button, phone rang. But still not Paddy! This time Treese, sounding grim.

'Heard about your late-night phone call from de Courcy. Listen to me, Lola.' Tone low and angry. 'You make sure you get back with that surf boy.'

'Too late, Treese, have just shown him the door.' Chirpy.

She moaned with – it sounded like – despair. 'Paddy de Courcy ruins everything for you.'

'What he ruin?' Was actually curious.

'Apart from your career and your sanity? He almost ruined your friendship with me, Bridie and Jem.'

'... What? ... How?' Frightened. Where did this come from?

Treese sighed. 'We never saw you. You stopped coming out with us. You were always with him. Or – worse – waiting for him.'

Oh yes, this was familiar. Had heard it before. 'Yes, but, Treese –'

'I know, Lola, yes, know he worked long, unpredictable hours. If I had latrine for every time you told me that, every home in Malawi would have full sanitation. But he didn't see you every night, did he?'

'... Not every single one.'

'But you made yourself available every night for him?'

Uncomfortably I said, 'You know what it's like when you're in love.'

556

'Yes. Do.' She meant Vincent (gak). 'And I still see my friends.'

'But Treese, Paddy is *politician*. Session in Dail can go on very late. No idea when will end.'

'All more reason for you to make own arrangements for nights when he can't commit.'

'No, all more reason to be ready to see him at end of his long, stressful day.'

'You've been brainwashed.'

Stunned by her harshness. Frankly stunned. Said as much.

'Lola, we've been so worried about you. Getting free of him is the best thing that's ever happened to you.'

Shaken after hostile call from Treese. Returned to gazing at phone, urging it to ring.

Morning elapsed without call from Paddy. Of course Jem rang.

'Bringing up the rear,' he said. 'Urging you, at Bridie's behest, to have sense.'

At 1.17, wondered if had misunderstood arrangement with Paddy. Perhaps we had agreed that I was to ring him, not him ring me. (Of course, knew the truth. Am not stupid. Merely delusional.) Tried his mobile, landline, office line.

Voicemail, voicemail, voicemail.

And all feeling horribly familiar.

Paddy didn't call that day. Or the next day. Or the next day. Or the next day. I gave up trying to contact him.

Admitted unpalatable truth to self. Bridie had been right. It had been a booty call. Tried but couldn't reachieve that magic state which had facilitated call in first place – Paddy would ring me *only if I didn't care about him*. But as long as

I wanted him to ring, it meant I cared about him, therefore he would not call. Universe can be perplexing.

Yes, eventually did succumb to strong doses of vitamin B – dispatched Boss to Ennistymon with detailed list. Not that said vitamins did any good. Still leapt like scalded cat each and every time the phone chirruped.

Other interesting behaviour from universe – as though seeking to demonstrate how unattractive unrequited love was, Jake became obsessed with winning me back. He kept showing up at the house, urging that we should 'try again'.

'But Jake, this is crazy,' I kept saying. 'You weren't even that into me.'

'I *know*.'

'Am not even your type.'

'I *know*.'

'Am not as good-looking as your other girlfriends.'

'I *know*.'

'Or as good in bed.' (Had taken guess on this.)

'I *know*.'

'So why you want me?'

'Because I do.'

He made charming picture of good-looking anguish, but my heart was cold as stone in my chest. Jake was spoilt, immature, had always had life too easy and wanted me only because couldn't have me.

Good for him, bit of disappointment. Character-forming. I mean, look at me, character very formed.

I pitied him. But was 100 per cent certain that if I suddenly exclaimed, 'Right you are, Jake, you've persuaded me! Let's be boyfriend and girlfriend again and be mad about each other and have sex all night long and buy a nice lamp and feed each other with our fingers,' we would have three

558

happy days before he would turn moody on me and let himself be coaxed into admitting, 'It's just not right, Lola.'

Do not relish causing him pain. But if it's a choice between him and me, am afraid that the surf boy gets it.

Thursday, 11 December 23.04
Return from trip down memory lane
Phone still ringing.

SarahJane Hutchinson. Why she calling so late?

'Great news, Lola! Have scored major coup. Zara Kaletsky will be keynote speaker at my charity. Know what you're thinking, Lola, you're thinking, Zara Kaletsky is nobody.'

Correct. Zara extremely nice girl but, in celebrity terms, could not get arrested.

'Have inside-track knowledge. Zara Kaletsky just been cast in new Spielberg blockbuster. Starring role. Jermond' – SarahJane's new beau – 'involved in the financing. I have Zara on board before movie press release even been issued. Just been speaking with her in LA. She is hot, hot, hot and she is mine, mine, mine. All those other bitches will have to bow down before me!'

Was glad. Glad for SarahJane. Also very glad for Zara.

'She live in LA now? Thought she moved to South Africa?'

'Oh God, no! Bel Air, Bel Air! Need you to fabulize us both for the lunch. Need something extra special. Only ten weeks away. Put your thinking cap on!'

Friday, 12 December 7.04
Awoken by frenzied banging on front door. Incorporated it into my dream for as long as possible, then gave in and got up. Who was calling at this early hour?

Probably Jake to tell me how much he loves me. Usually

is. Is bloody *ridiculous*. Is 7 a.m. Pounded down stairs and wrenched door open.

Yes, Jake standing there, exuding wild defiance. Time was when I would have been stunned by his beauty. Now all could think was, I wish he would

  a) put bag of frozen peas on his lips to stop the
     swelling
  b) wash himself
  c) piss off

'Had sex with Jaz last night,' he declared, flecks of spittle around his mouth. 'What you make of that?'

'Good, marvellous, excellent.'

'You are glad?'

'Thrilled. Nice to see you are moving on.'

He turned away, the picture of misery.

I almost had door closed, when he turned back and yelled, 'You are shallow bitch.'

Oh abuse, now, was it?

A sign that he was healing. Like when a cut starts to itch.

12.19
The Oak

'Morning, Lola,' Osama said. 'Keeping well?'

'Good, yes, and you?'

'Terrific, thanks!'

'Excellent, yes, excellent!'

We smiled brightly at each other.

Quite honestly, relations with Ol' Prune Eyes have been a little awkward since he joined us for trannie night. He came only once and couldn't be persuaded to return, claiming it

560

was due to calibre of movies. Has resumed his solo trips to the pictures in Ennis on Friday nights. In meantime, continues to be perfectly delightful barman and still laughs when I enquire, 'Is it lumpy?' about soup of the day — but perhaps not quite as heartily as he used to.

I looked around for a seat. Only other customers in pub were Considine and the ferret. Unusual to see them — Considine usually at work on a Friday. He and the ferret embroiled in intense-looking chat.

Considine spotted me. 'Lola,' he called. 'Join us.'

Reluctant to. Quite shy around Considine and had never been introduced to Gillian the ferret.

But obliged to sit down and shake hand of Gillian, who looked exactly like cartoon ferret. How talented cartoonists are. They can take any creature — dingos, bulls, ferrets — and while retaining distinctive features, can render them cute. Gillian really very pretty. But, yes, undeniably like a ferret.

'How are you, Lola?' Considine asked.

'Top-notch.' Do not know what it is but have uncontrollable impulse for sarcasm every time meet him. 'Yourself?'

'Top-notch also.' Yes, him sarcastic too.

Gillian spoke up. 'Lola, Rossa would like to ask favour.'

And I'm thinking, Oh Mother of sweet suffering Jesus, what now? Is it not enough that I give my home over to trannies one night out of every seven? What more do they want?

'Go on,' Gillian urged Rossa.

'Can I borrow your plunger?'

'You mean coffee plunger?' I asked.

'No,' Gillian said. 'Other one. Am having problem with plumbing.'

'Euphemism for girly innards?'

'God, no. House plumbing.'

(She tried to explain. Something to do with 'drains'. Cannot supply further info. Whenever hear the word 'drains', momentarily black out.)

'Plunger under your sink,' Rossa said. 'Borrowed it once before from Tom Twoomey.'

Handed him key to the house. 'Go. Take the wretched appliance. Do what you need to do. Return it to where you found it. But please do not involve me because will faint.'

Off he went, leaving Gillian and me alone.

'He should be at work,' she said. 'He took day off to help me.'

'Kindly of him.'

More silence. Then she said, 'Is wonderful thing you are doing.'

Not entirely sure what she was referring to. The plunger? The Friday nights?

'Is great outlet for Rossa. Or should I say Chloe?'

'Er, yes. And you don't mind . . . ?'

'Worse things he could be doing.'

Impressive girl. Riddled with sangfroid. 'The pity is,' she said, 'that I'm no use to him. I live in jeans and don't wear scrap of make-up.'

Yes, her ferrety little fizzog free of all artificial unguents.

'Is funny,' I remarked. 'He makes far better-looking woman than he does man.'

'Oh yes?' Smile fading. Expression faintly huffy. 'You not think Rossa is good-looking man?'

Cripes! Had just insulted her boyfriend!

'Of course is good-looking man. Simply meant is more

groomed as a woman. Must go. Have urgent appointment in Galway.'

Luckily actually had urgent appointment in Galway, as would have driven the seventy miles to Eyre Square (centre of Galway) simply to extricate self from awkward situation.

14.30
Big, shiny American bank, Galway
Getting little bits and pieces of styling work. This job had come from unexpected source — Nkechi. She didn't want to drive from Dublin and I was in locality. Suited us both.

Female CEO was getting head-and-shoulders taken for company prospectus. Brief was to make her look warm, efficient, steely, feminine, approachable, hardworking, humorous and deadly.

Easy.

(All about the accessories.)

18.39
Terrible bloody traffic. Friday-night exodus from Galway.
Afraid I'd be late for trannies
Finally reached home and jumped from car only to discover had no house key! Limbo-danced under wire fence to Rossa Considine.

'Key.' He jingled it at me. 'Replaced plunger under your sink. Much obliged.'

'Cease and desist from further details. That sort of thing gives me the heebie-jeebies.'

'Hey, Considine!' Some sort of ruckus out by front gate! Someone shouting from darkness beyond the house. 'Listen, dude, don't bother, right? She's just a tease, yeah?'

Startled, Rossa and I strained our eyes at the blackness where the voice had come from.

Jake walked into pool of light spread from the front door, like denouement in bad thriller. He looked at me and sneered. 'You didn't hang around. Won't be long now before you've slept with every man in Knockavoy.'

'Let her alone,' Rossa said, low and quiet. 'Only borrowed her plunger.'

'Yeah.' Jake laughed nastily. 'She let me borrow her plunger for a while too.'

'Now just a –' Rossa said.

'Stop,' I said. 'Don't bother.'

Fascinating, that's what it was – a masterclass in how not to win someone back. If there had been tiniest pocket of Jake-love remaining in my heart, would have been erased for ever by this lunacy.

'Will I walk back over with you?' Rossa asked me.

'No, no, is only few yards. And you've to get ready for tonight.'

'But your man seems a bit . . . unhinged.'

'He's harmless.'

'Would prefer to accompany you if it's all the same.'

'But he will shout at us.'

'Sticks and stones.'

'Okay, I will wave the sticks –'

'– and I will throw the stones.'

19.27

Had noticed interesting phenomenon over last few weeks – evenings didn't really get going until Chloe arrived.

Natasha, Blanche and Sue the new girl were getting

changed in kitchen, but I felt as if were hanging around, killing time.

Sue was bachelor smallholder from 'out the road'. (Seemed to function as actual postal address.) His real name was Spuds Conlon. Presumed his *real* real name was not actually 'Spuds' but refrained from asking why called 'Spuds'. Presumed it was because he

a) ate spuds
b) grew spuds
c) . . . erm . . .

He was scrawny, bow-legged man, missing many, many teeth. Took lot of persuasion to get him to remove his flat cap. Reminded me of chicken from third world (sorry, developing world) country, the sort you would see pecking on dirt road, as you whizz past in your air-conditioned jeep. Nothing like plump Irish chickens, all top-heavy with breast, but bird where you would have to do much poking with your fork in order to find any bit of meat at all.

'Where's Chloe?' Noel yelled from kitchen. 'Need her to do my nails.'

'Any minute now . . .'

Then in came Chloe with sparkling eyes, smiling mouth, pleasant comments, and readiness to help the other girls. Very, very likeable. If she really was woman, would have wanted to befriend her.

'Love your hair, Chloe.'

Long, dark wig she usually wore, but backcombed slightly and pinned on top.

'Was feeling Jacqueline Susann,' she said.

Now that Chloe mentioned it, Jacqueline Susann was

exactly what I was feeling too. (Unsettling to be stylist, i.e. a person who makes their living from anticipating and enacting fashion trends, to be overtaken by trannie-man.)

Unlike my other trannies who had their look and stuck to it (Natasha, leopard-skin, Blanche, tailored classics, etc.), Chloe arrived in different look every week. This week, black leggings, shiny, pewter-coloured ballet flats and excellent metallic off-one-shoulder sweater-dress, also in pewter colour.

She probably really could pass for a woman. Tall, yes, and not skinny, definitely not skinny — but not like brick shithouse either (unlike, say, poor Blanche).

Shapely legs — perhaps little too muscular around the calves and thighs, if you wanted to be critical, but didn't want to be critical — and really lovely face. Very pretty dark eyes, enhanced by expert make-up and lush dark lashes.

Clamour came from kitchen. 'Chloe's here? Chloe's here! Chloe, come in, need you to help me with my monobrow . . .'

Chloe flitted about helping the other girls. She had much specialist information because had done year of eco-swot training in Seattle, city with 'sizeable' cross-dressing population. She knew about 'male' foundation, a thick, wet-cement-style unguent which filled in gaps and entirely covered evidence of beard on face and set into natural-looking, attractive finish. She advised on waxing of chests, shaving of backs of hands, helping affix false nails, etc.

But despite giving freely of her knowledge, she looked like princess and the best others could manage beside her were Ugly Sisters from panto.

Plan for the evening — we would watch film, *The Devil Wears Prada* (delivery of new stock at Kelly and Brandon's) — then have 'deportment lessons', where we would practise walking like ladies. (Had got book on subject.)

19.57
'Ready for film?' My hand poised over remote.
'Just need to do little tinkle . . .'
'Better refresh my lipstick . . .'
'Must look in handbag for my glasses . . .'
Girlish clamour eventually died down. I hit play, song started – then four slow heavy raps on front door!
Jake? And if not Jake, then who? Not another bloody trannie?
'Girls, anyone got any friends they've invited and not told me about?'
Fearful shaking of heads.
'You sure? Because if I open that door and find trannie outside looking for sanctuary, will be very cross.'
'No. Promise.'
'Then hide,' I urged. 'All of you.'
They scampered away upstairs and I opened front door. Large, intimidating-looking policeman, in navy serge uniform and brass buttons, standing there.
Game was up.
Mixed emotions. Undeniable relief that Friday nights had come to end, the responsibility had been heavy one. But also sadness on behalf of trannies. Feared they'd get into trouble, that their names would be published in the *Clare Champion* and they would be laughing stock throughout county.
'Am Guard Lyons, can I come in?' deep voice boomed from beneath peak of cap.
'Why?'

'Believe you hold cross-dressing events here on Friday nights.' Was almost blinded by shininess of his enormous polished black boots.

'Is not illegal.' My voice wobbling. 'Doing nothing wrong. Tom Twoomey knows and doesn't mind.'

(Had continued to check with Tom every time a new girl joined. His unvarying response was that so long as no one broke the toaster again, he didn't care what we did.)

'No one said it was illegal. Can I come in?'

'No.' Sudden defiance. 'Trannies inside. Nervous dispositions. Need to protect their identities.'

'Look.' Sudden drop in decibel of voice. 'Would like to join in.'

Oh for the love of God! Cannot believe this. Simply cannot believe this. Who knew there were so many trannies in County Clare? In Ireland, for that matter?

'You are trannie, Guard Lyons?'

'Not gay. But, yes, like to dress up in ladies' clothing.'

Heart heavy in chest. 'You'd better come in, then.'

20.03

Ran up the stairs. Trannies clustered in my bedroom, their little fizzogs bruised with anxiety.

'There is policeman here.'

'No!' Noel began moaning. 'No, no, no, no, no, no, no! It's over, am sunk, am ruined, am —'

'Stop it! He is one of us. You. He is cross-dresser.'

Lipsticked mouths fell open. Pancaked jaws swung with surprise.

They clattered downstairs in their high heels and suspiciously circled Guard Lyons, like pack of mascaraed hyenas. I effected introductions.

'How you know about us?' Noel asked with some defiance.

'Happenstance, Natasha, happenstance.'

Guard Lyons had slow, ponderous way of speaking, as if giving evidence in petty larceny case.

'Please explain.' Noel sounded positively bitchy.

Guard Lyons cleared his throat and got to his feet. 'On the morning of Tuesday, December the second, a housewife, to be known from hereon as Mrs X, domiciled in the townland of Kilfenora, North Clare, mistakenly took delivery of a parcel from An Post.'

'Please sit down,' I murmured. 'Is not court of law. Rest of you, also sit down, enjoy your little drinkies. Yes, thank you, Guard Lyons, continue.'

'Mrs X, a busy woman, the mother of three children under the age of four, neglected to notice that said parcel was not addressed to herself but to one Lola Daly of Knockavoy –'

'Nosy bitch,' Noel said.

'– and had it opened "before she knew what she was doing". Direct quote.'

'Nosy bitch.'

'On divesting the box of its packaging, the housewife discovered strange undergarments within, to the sum of four. "Pervy" was the word she used to describe them. In considerable distress she summoned the parish priest, who blessed the garments with holy water and advised bringing in the local constabulary. Who happened to be none other than my good self.'

(Had half noticed that consignment of underwear had failed to reach me. But so many deliveries of clothing arrived on almost-daily basis, had never fully focused on missing order.)

'On account of my specialist interest in the subject,'

Guard Lyons said, 'I recognized the items for what they were – merely reinforced jocks. Nothing at all "pervy" about them. Did not explain this to the woman. Simply removed the items and the box addressed to Miss Daly for safe keeping and swore Mrs X to secrecy –'

'How?' Noel demanded. 'How you know she'll keep her mouth shut?'

'Because I have something on her. Everyone has their secrets, Natasha. Mrs X will keep her mouth shut.'

'Oh. Well, good. Good.'

'I then proceeded to make enquiries about Miss Lola Daly and discovered that gatherings were held at her Knockavoy address at seven o'clock every Friday night. I "put two and two together" and concluded that the Friday-night gatherings and the reinforced jocks were linked. My conclusion was correct.'

'Nothing short of amazing!' Noel had changed his tune considerably. 'That's three of us who have come to you, Lola, by accident. Me. Chloe. And now . . . ?'

'Dolores,' Guard Lyons said. 'My name Dolores.'

'Welcome, Dolores! Yes, welcome, welcome.'

'That's all very well,' I said. 'But what about my delivery of reinforced jocks?'

'Impounded. Write them off. Blame it on An Post.'

20.32

Dolores Lyons very tall. Six three or thereabouts. Large-framed and actually extremely overweight but carried it well. Unbuttoned thick serge jacket, releasing enormous stomach harnessed to super-sized ribcage, and I thought, My biggest challenge yet.

22.07

Everyone gone except Chloe, who was helping with tidying up.

'And then there were five,' Chloe said, clattering wine glasses into sink. 'You seem to have vocation, Lola.'

'I don't want fecking vocation.'

'But that's the trouble with vocations, you don't choose them, they choose you.' Chloe amused at my plight. 'Think of Mother Teresa. When Career Guidance asked her, What you like to do when you grow up, Mother Teresa? Maybe she said, I'd like to be air hostess. Unlikely, don't you think, that she would have said, Would like to befriend lepers. Unlikely, yes, Lola, unlikely?'

'Glad you find this so funny.'

'Maybe Mother Teresa didn't even like lepers. Maybe she had a "thing" about lepers but the lepers didn't care and flocked to her anyway.'

Chloe highly entertained. I lined up empty wine bottles by door for when I go to bottle bank with Rossa Considine.

'. . . As the trannies seem to be flocking to you, Lola.'

. . . go to bottle bank with Rossa Considine . . .

'Saint Lola, patron saint of cross-dressers.'

Chloe is Rossa Considine . . .

Why is life so effing peculiar?

Saturday, 13 December 11.22

Phone call from Bridie.

'Am rough as a badger's arse,' she said hoarsely. 'Christmas party last night. You are lucky being self-employed –'

'– Unemployed.'

'No need to endure Christmas party. Oh God, Lola, rough as a badger's arse.'

'Where you hear that expression?'

'Telly. Good, isn't it?'

'Yes, very.'

'Been thinking. About Paddy de Courcy. A man like him could get booty call off anyone.'

'Your point, badger's-arse woman?'

'He wasn't ringing you for booty call.'

'For what, then?' Was suspicious. Unlikely Bridie was going to say, 'Because he still loves you.'

'Was keeping you sweet. Onside.'

'Why Paddy need to keep me sweet?'

'You have stuff on him. Few weeks ago there was lots in papers about that Dee Rossini and her sex life. She nearly had to resign. You could spill the beans to papers about all that peculiar sex Paddy made you do. Would be explosive sensation.'

'Wasn't peculiar sex.'

Moral high ground was mine because Bridie had recently admitted terrible shameful secret. Since she got married, 'relations' with Barry had taken downward turn. He did end-of-year appraisal (he works in HR) and told her they had had sex only fifteen times in previous calendar year – once a month, plus extra go on his birthday, their anniversary and the day Kildare won All-Ireland football championship. (Strange as neither of them Kildare fans. Perhaps it is bypass related?)

'Oh yes, was peculiar sex, Lola. I admit that, at the time, I felt like sexual dullard compared to you. But looking back . . . Not a lot of love in that sort of sex you had with Paddy de Courcy. And bet you didn't tell me half of what went on.'

Startled. Bridie been taking mind-reading lessons?

'He said he missed me.' Clutching at straws.

'Course he missed you! Alicia the horse unlikely to indulge his need for kinky sex.'

'Not kinky. Erotic.'

'Kinky. Kinky, kinky, kinky.'

Bridie strongest-willed person have ever met.

12.04

Internet café

Popped in to see Cecile. ('Popped in'. Do not like that phrase. Reminiscent of small-minded yummy mummies wearing pristine, pastel-coloured linen trousers. Will cease and desist from using it again.)

Had feared Cecile would take agin me when I rejected Jake, especially considering she had brokered our alliance. But her response was complete opposite. Gleeful, she was, as she reported on Jake's glum state. She informed me it was 'high time' 'that gombeen' got 'what was coming to him'.

'The snivelling little gobhawk didn't know when he was on to a good thing,' she said. ''Tis soft the wool grows on him.'

Fascinating (if baffling) usage of colloquialisms.

15.27

Coming home from town

Rossa Considine outside his house, 'tinkering' with his car.

'Hey,' I called to him.

'Hey, yourself.'

'How come you not down in potholes like peculiar person?'

'Going tomorrow instead.'

'Right. Listen. Been thinking.'

'About . . . ?' He got up from his tinkering and walked out to meet me on road.

'Soon be Christmas. We should have Christmas party. Our Friday-night gang.'

'What's brought this on? Thought you were reluctant participant in cross-dressing – sorry trannie – activities.'

'Am. But was talking to my friend Bridie. She had Christmas party last night. Kept saying she was rough as a badger's arse. Was taken with the phrase.'

'You can get drunk any night of week.'

'Need an excuse. If start getting drunk without needing excuse, am afraid will be drunk all the time.'

'So what you thinking of?'

'Tuesday after next? Is day before Christmas Eve.'

'What you doing for Christmas?'

'Going to Birmingham for four days. My dad lives there. Then going to Edinburgh with friends Bridie and Treese for New Year. Won't be back to Knockavoy until fourth of January, so we better have party Tuesday, twenty-third. Any later is too late. I can organize mince pies, mulled wine, crackers, that sort of thing.'

'But would cause extra work for you. Let me discuss it with the others.'

The trannies had formed some sort of informal network, where they contacted each other by email during the week. I was not party to it. Was glad.

'SHALLOW BITCH!'

It was Jake. Had appeared from nowhere and was going past on a bicycle. Was not sure which was most disconcerting. His sudden appearance. Or the fact that he was on bicycle. (Being on bike did nothing for his sex appeal. He was definitely not bicycle person. Few people are.)

'Yes, shallow, but not a bitch,' I shouted after him.

Realized he couldn't hear me, but needed to defend self so turned to Rossa Considine. 'Am not a bitch,' I said. 'Was on rebound.'

'Why you say you shallow?'

'Because of my job. Everyone says stylists shallow morons. Once heard great phrase: cocaine is God's way of telling you you have too much money. Likewise, when enough styling jobs to keep all stylists with roof over head, a country has perhaps become too prosperous.'

'So you getting plenty work at moment?'

'Oh no, but that is my fault. Have lovely client, SarahJane Hutchinson, she referred new client to me, but I couldn't go to Dublin, so lost new client.'

'Why couldn't you go to Dublin? Apart from it being total kip of a place?'

'Because ex-boyfriend lives there. Last time I went, saw him with his horse-faced fiancée. Almost puked in the street and that was the least bad thing that went wrong.'

'So just operate out of County Clare.'

I shook head. 'West-coast styling never going to be as effective. Most rich women live in Dublin. Most of good shops are in Dublin. Yes, can get things couriered to here, but is lot more expensive than when I physically run around the good Dublin shops, filling up wheelie bags with top-notch stock.'

'I see.'

'Styling is fear-filled job at the best of times. Yes, honestly, Rossa Considine. Can see from your fizzog you are not convinced. Obviously is not as important as eco-swot job you do. But to the people I help, is important.'

'Hey, who you telling? I know value of what you do, Lola.'

Looked hard at him. 'Sarcasm, Rossa Considine?'

He sighed heavily. 'Not sarcasm. Tell me more of fear side of job.'

'Wee ... ll, if I turn up at session and discover have misread client's desires or she has lied about size – always happens, they say size ten, because too ashamed to admit size fourteen – there is no room to manoeuvre. In Dublin could run out and get more clothes, but down here, if mistake is made, no opportunity to remedy it. We are stuck with wrong clothes and the session is disaster.'

'See your point.' Thoughtful, interested look on his face. Unusual response. Well, suppose he is a trannie.

'Cripes, Rossa, better go home, all sensation gone from my feet.'

We had been standing in the cold for ages.

'You like come in for cup of tea or something?'

'Oh no, no.' Suddenly shy.

Monday, 15 December 19.29

Mrs Butterly's

Heart-warming news, courtesy of Mrs Butterly! Osama no longer alone. On Friday nights he will be accompanied to pictures in Ennis by Ferret Kilbert. She has car and will drive him, so he doesn't have to get bus. Also, it will give her something to do while her boyfriend is dressing up in women's clothing. (Although Mrs Butterly didn't say that. That was own private thought.)

Community spirit in action.

Tuesday, 16 December 11.22

Lying in bed, idly having thoughts

If I was a man, would fancy Chloe.

Wednesday, 17 December 12.23
Passing Internet café
Cecile sees me and beckons hand in invitation. I wave cheerily at her, but continue to walk briskly.

Shameful to admit, but have started to avoid Cecile, because her County Clare dialect has become too hard to comprehend. Suspect could discern better if she spoke in French. From pitifully few intelligible bits and pieces she told me, it seems that Jake and Jaz have become item. ('He sez to her, "D'you want to be buried with my people?"') Very pleased. Hopefully it indicates cessation of Jake's cycling abuse.

19.07
Going down town for my dinner
Rossa Considine arriving home from work. He called out to me, 'Operation Badger's Arse coming together nicely!'

'Good, good.'

Friday, 19 December
Rossa Considine had lied to me! Operation Badger's Arse not coming together nicely at all! Operation Badger's Arse been hijacked by Natasha.

'Don't want to spend our Christmas party stuck here watching *It's a Wonderful Life* and eating fruitcake,' she said, with fox-featured defiance. 'We want to go out dancing.'

'A little sanity, Natasha, I beg of you!' I cried. 'We'll be lynched in Baccarat.' (Baccarat the local disco.)

'No.' Natasha shook head. 'I know venue that is "sympathetic" to our needs. In Limerick.'

'And the problem is . . . ?'

'We need minivan. Someone needs to be designated driver.'

577

'I'll do it,' Chloe said. (This week wearing unbelievably stylish halter-neck dress. From Topshop! Ordinary woman's dress, simply size 18.)

'No, you won't drive,' Natasha snapped. 'Is our Christmas party, us ladies, and if Lola won't drive, Lola might find difficulty with local welfare payments.'

'Is blackmail!' Chloe was scandalized. 'Natasha, Lola was the one who suggested Christmas party in the first place!'

But Natasha had filled other trannies' heads with talk of a disco where they could dance freely with their own kind.

'Please, Lola?' Blanche said. 'Would love to go.'

'Yes, would love to go,' Sue said.

'Yes, please, Lola,' Guard Dolores Lyons begged, with piteous puppy-dog eyes.

'Will do it,' said grumpily. These bloody trannies . . .

'No, Lola,' Chloe protested.

'Is okay,' I said to her. 'Is my vocation. Will do it.'

'Was joking when said you had vocation.'

'But it seems to be truth. Saint Lola of the Trannies.'

'Cross-dressers,' Natasha snapped.

'Trannies, trannies, trannies, trannies, trannies.' Was in no mood. 'Shut up or I won't drive the van.'

'Excuse –!'

'Could I suggest solution of sorts?' Chloe trying to restore calm. 'Lola, we could go out another night? Locally, so no need for driver. After Christmas? When you back from Birmingham. Pour drink into you and get you rough as badger's arse. Doesn't have to be with the ladies from here. Could be with other Knockavoy pals of yours.'

'Like who?'

'The surfer? Jake, is that his name?' Twinkle in Chloe's eyes.

'Yes, we could invite Jake.' Laughter bubbling in stomach.
'He could stand on far side of pub –'
'– and shout at us.'
Dissolving into laughter while Natasha looked on coldly.

22.13

Everyone gone except Chloe.

Habit now for Chloe to stay behind, after others had gone, to help me clear up.

'You think Noel's wife really believes he's out with the lads every Friday night?' I asked, tipping uneaten savoury snacks into bin.

'Hard to say. Maybe easier for her to just pretend to believe.'

'You're lucky,' I said. 'Gillian really cool. Not at all bothered.'

'Very lucky,' Chloe acknowledged, following me into kitchen. 'Gillian remarkably easy-going. She says if she had choice, would prefer me to give up potholing. Too dangerous, she says.' Chloe squirted washing-up liquid over dirty glasses, then out of blue, asked, 'You ever have cross-dressing boyfriend?'

Pause. Long pause. Too long because answer was a short one.

'No,' I said. 'But . . .'

'But . . .'

'. . . Had a boyfriend who had other . . . interests.'

Chloe stopped running hot water into sink. 'Interests?'

'You know . . . sexually.'

Careful face on Chloe. No readable reaction. 'That sort of thing is fine,' she said. 'If you enjoy it.'

'Was . . . interesting. Is good to push your boundaries, no?'

'Yes . . . if you are both happy.'

579

Had unexpected flash of memory. The time Paddy took me to Cannes. Private plane. Limo to meet us at bottom of steps. Massive suite in Hotel Martinique. On arrival, bed strewn with stiff carrier bags from expensive shops on the Croissette. Me, running about from room to room, squealing, until came face to face with beautiful, cold-faced Russian woman in Chanel suit, waiting in living room.

What she doing here? For short-lived moment, thought she might be secretary. Paddy might have to do some work over weekend.

Then he said, 'This is Alexia. She is going to be our . . . friend . . . while we're here in Cannes.'

Friend? Friend?

Oh no. And Paddy said, with wolfish grin, 'Oh yes.'

Felt rush of nausea and chill down arms, as I remembered.

'Lola, you okay?' Chloe asked, concern in voice.

'Yes, fine, fine, just . . . that boyfriend I mentioned . . .'

'– Yes . . .'

'. . . He made me have sex with a prostitute. Russian one. Then he had sex with her and I had to watch.'

'. . . Er . . . and you were okay about it?'

'At the time, thought I was.'

'But now?'

'No.' Voice choked and whole body trembling. 'All of sudden, think it's appalling. Shameful. Humiliating. Can't believe I did it. Not pushing boundaries. Not being sexual adventurer. Simply let myself be humiliated.' Voice getting higher and faster. Gasping for air.

'Come and sit down.'

In living room, she took me on her lap, like mother with small child, and held me so tightly that I eventually stopped shaking. I grabbed air with my mouth, forced it down into lungs, until breathing became normal again. Leant against her. Great, great comfort in the way she held my weight, and I thought, How nice and big her hands are.

'Could have refused him.' I gulped. 'Suppose I should have.'

'But you couldn't. Because if you could, you would have.'

'Yes. Yes.' So grateful she understood. 'Was afraid to. Afraid he would . . . mock me. Afraid he would not love me. Afraid . . . just afraid.'

There were other times, other terrible things too. Didn't know why that particular event was so outlandish that it had to rush up from my gut and out of my mouth.

0.44

In bed

Couldn't sleep.

Thinking about admission had made to Chloe. About how having a threesome with a prostitute had seemed almost normal.

But now didn't seem normal. Seemed sick and strange.

In fact, obvious to me now that right from beginning sex with Paddy had been sick and strange. Imagine that I had thought being taken to sex shop on first date was erotic! Saw now that it was a test. He was checking me out, to see how much I'd take. And he decided I'd take anything.

Even though went through with the business in Cannes, I must have known it was wrong because had never told anyone else about it. Time was when I had boasted about sexual shenanigans I got up to with Paddy.

But point came when I had stopped telling Bridie and the others. Had detected change in their attitude. They'd stopped being impressed and jealous and were becoming something else. Concerned, I think.

Saturday, 20 December 8.33

En route to Christmas party styling job in Tipperary
Rossa Considine getting ropes and that sort of stuff out
of car boot.

He came over to dividing fence and asked, 'How you today?'
Very kindly expression on face and for moment I wondered
why. Had forgotten that had told him about Paddy and
Alexia. Because, of course, hadn't told *him*. Had told Chloe.

Felt angry that he knew. As if Chloe had broken confidence
and told him, like Rossa was her twin brother.

'Good. Must go now.'

He could keep his sympathy and kindly eyes and all the
rest of it. If I had wanted kindness off Rossa Considine,
would have told Rossa Considine.

19.17

Passing the Dungeon

'Ho, Lola Daly! A word, if you please!' Boss on the lookout
for me.

Stepped inside, accepted quick drink.

'Is it true,' Boss demanded, 'that Ferret-Face Kilbert is
keeping Osama company on Friday nights while rest of ye
are running around wearing ladies' clothing?'

Aghast! Utterly aghast! 'How you know about ladies'
clothing? Is meant to be secret.'

'No secrets in town like this, Lola Daly. Not for long. Never
really believed your revenge-clothing movie-club story, so
last night spied on ye. The three of us hid outside and looked
through windows. Surprised you didn't hear us laughing, the
scarths and screeches that were coming out of us.'

'Almost slipped another disc,' the Master said. 'Laughed
so much.'

Cripes above!

'Am hurted you didn't trust me, Lola,' Boss said. 'Thought we were friends . . .'

'Are friends, Boss, yes, we are friends.' Shamed. Has been kind to me, bullying me to get dole, buying vitamin B capsules, etc. 'But not my secret to give away.'

'Know exactly who every one of your "ladies" are. Ran check on licence plates.' Tipped his head at Moss. 'Moss is "connected" that way. Found out names and addresses.'

Oh God. If Noel knew that his Friday-night activities were public knowledge, he would have conniption (whatever that is). And one of my 'ladies' was officer of the law . . .

Laid my hand on Boss's arm, not something would usually do, except in time of crisis. 'You mustn't tell anyone,' I beseeched. 'I beg of you . . . These poor men . . . it's only outlet they have.'

'Who would I tell?'

'Everyone, of course!'

'Sure, what harm are ye doing? Not like ye're making snuff movies up there. And haven't you given the rest of us great oul' laugh.'

'Cease and desist. No laughing at the trannies!'

'Actually,' the Master said, in pompous, pompous voice, indicating incoming lecture, 'incorrect to call them trannies as none of them gay.'

'Spuds Conlon is.'

'He is not.'

'He is.'

'Drunken encounter on shore leave in Singapore doesn't count.'

Long dissertation from the Master on sexuality and cross-dressing ensued.

Sunday, 21 December 20.47

The Oak

Although Sunday night, place thronged. Festive season doubtless to blame. Had to wait ages for my non-lumpy soup of the day. Poor Osama run off his Egyptian feet.

Considine in the thick of large cluster of macho men, wearing sizeable muddy boots, sitting with muscular legs wide apart and dwarfing pint glasses in their manly hands. His potholing buddies, I deduced. If only they knew what Considine got up to on Friday nights . . . But perhaps they did. After all, Gillian knew.

Rival cluster of surfy people, including Jake. Braced self for abuse, but he ignored me. Too busy doing elaborate tongue-kissing with Jaz. Jaz was the tattoo girl from party in surf boys' house all those weeks ago. The one who'd said to me, 'Remember my name,' and I had promptly forgotten it.

Jake gave me sneery sneer, then increased snogging intensity and slid his hand under Jaz's waistband, openly groping her left buttock.

I gave kindly smile. Hoped they'd be happy. Was horrified to discover this wish was sincere. How could I be so unaffected by seeing him with another woman? Had he meant nothing to me? Was I numb, strange, damaged oddball who would never have normal relationship again? No. Reminded self: had been mad about Jake until he began displaying signs that he had plans to wreck my head.

Also, let's not forget, had been on rebound.

Monday, 22 December 5.05

Unable to sleep. Waiting for dawn.

Memories of Paddy bothering me. Had actually been woken by them.

Tried to think of happier things – Operation Badger's Arse coming together nicely. Minivan booked from Gregan's of Ennistymon. ('For all your car-hire, pharmaceutical and undertaking needs.' Catchy slogan.) Chloe had organized it.

But couldn't lift mood. In blackness of predawn, felt lonely, lonely, lonely and wished could talk to Chloe. She had understood when had told her about Paddy. No judging. Just kindness.

Incredibly strange situation. Chloe available to me only one night out of every seven, like once-a-week Cinderella. And not as if could ring her in the meantime, or anything.

Closed eyes, trying to fight past bleakness and go back to sleep. But couldn't shift the terribleness.

'Mum?' I asked.

But instead of hearing her, a horrible Paddy memory flashed into head.

'Mum?' I called again. But the awful pictures in head insisted on playing themselves out.

Had been sick with severe flu sort of virus. So unwell that I was staying in Paddy's apartment for few days until was better. In mornings before he left for work, he dosed me with Uniflu and Lucozade, then same again when he got home at night.

One of those nights, heard him come in. He turned on lights and woke me from sweaty, delirium-style sleep in which had been dreaming about walking through enormous house, looking for bathroom. Half awake, realized wees needed to be made and after few moments of desperately wishing had colostomy bag, forced self from roasting-hot sheets and into bathroom.

Was sitting on toilet, my forehead leaning against cool of tiled wall when saw that Paddy had followed me in.

No big deal. From very start, he'd insisted on bathroom open-door policy. Never really got used to it, but considering everything else we got up to, insisting on privacy to make my wees seemed pointless.

'How you feeling?' he asked.

'Sick as dog. How your day?'

'Ah, you know.'

I got up, flushed, ran hands under deliciously cold tap and when tried to return to bedroom, Paddy blocked my way.

'What?' I asked.

'You.' He pressed my back against rim of sink.

He couldn't be . . . In my condition . . . ?

But hardness of his erection through his trousers left me in no doubt — yes, he was looking for sex.

I could hardly stand.

His hands were on my shoulders and he was kissing side of my neck. 'Paddy,' I said, 'not now, don't feel able.'

He slid palms of his hands under my pyjama top and tweaked each nipple into erectness. Had to bite back urge to scream.

In a moment, his lad was out and he was tugging at my pyjama bottoms. My still-erect nipples were rubbing against nubby pyjama fabric and the sensation made me want to tear at my skin.

'No,' I said, louder this time. 'Paddy, I'm sick.'

Tried to twist away from under his grasp but he was so much stronger than me. 'Paddy.' Louder this time. 'I don't want to do this.' But my pyjama bottoms were yanked down to my knees, my thighs goosepimpling at the air, and Paddy was shoving his way up into me despite my dry resistance. It hurt. Short brutal thrusts, each one accompanied by a grunt.

'Please –'

'Shut. Up.' Ground out between clenched teeth.

Instantly I stopped struggling and let him batter his way into me, the rim of the sink digging painfully into my back.

The grunts got louder, the thrusts became more like stabs, then he was shuddering and groaning. He went slack, draping his body over mine, so that my face was buried in his chest. Could barely breathe. But didn't complain. Waited for him to do whatever he needed. After some time had passed, he pulled himself out and smiled tenderly at me. 'Let's get you back to bed,' he said.

I stumbled towards the bedroom, and because hadn't known what to think, decided it was best to think nothing. Day or two later, I decided his behaviour was understandable. Because had always gone along with the kinky stuff, he must have thought my sex drive was as high as his and not even a bout of flu would diminish it.

Tuesday, 23 December 19.30

Chloe arrived. Gave me hug. Since had spilled the beans about Paddy and the Russian prostitute, seemed natural to hug.

'Am early,' she said. 'Hope you don't mind. Just wanted to check you still okay to drive tonight. Confident about route, etc.? Can go away and come back at eight-thirty when others arrive, if you like.'

'No, come in, come in.'

'How you feel?' she asked. 'After the stuff you told me on Friday? Hope you weren't embarrassed? Or sorry you told me?'

'No, Chloe. Actually remembered other stuff.'

Then was telling her, about the time had the flu. Then other memories came spilling out.

587

Chloe kind. Didn't say, 'Why you not just leave him?' Didn't ask anything frightening or unanswerable. Just listened and held me tight and let me cry.

20.30

Lying on bed, eyes covered with two cotton pads soaked in cucumber toner, to bring down crying swelling. Excited shrieks and screeches from downstairs as ladies changed into their glad rags.

21.15

Operation Badger's Arse officially launched. Natasha, Blanche, Chloe, Sue and Guard Dolores Lyons all seated in minivan, Chloe in front beside me. Everyone in their dazzling finery (apart from Dolores who was dressed as female guard, right down to the truncheon). Was feeling considerably cheerier. Cannot beat a good cry.

22.30

Club HQ, Limerick

Parked the minivan. Piled out into car park. Mood high-strung. Combination of anticipation and anxiety.

This would be first public outing as a lady for all of them (except for Chloe who had done it many times in Seattle). What if Natasha had her information wrong and this Club HQ was simply normal, trannie-free disco? We would not walk out alive.

But from calibre of other women in car park making their way towards club entrance – adjusting wigs and private parts, saying, 'Oh shite,' in male-sounding voices as they went over on their ankles because of height of their heels – I deduced we were in right place.

'Come on.' Chloe and I strutted forward, the others falling in behind us, and were graciously granted admission.

Small, dimly lit place. Glitter ball. Bubbles of moving colour on walls. Loud music. Thronged with glamorous-looking women and happy-looking men.

'Hello, sexy,' one of the happy-looking men said to Natasha. 'I love redheads. I bet you've some temper on you. Like to dance?'

'Why not?' Natasha said – and off she went.

We were barely in the door!

There is actual name for men who fancy trannies – 'admirers' – and Club HQ was riddled with them. Dolores was next to be selected to dance. Her bloke said, 'I love a woman in uniform. Care to take a twirl?' Then, no time later, Blanche was swept away.

Sue, Chloe and I found a ledge to balance our sticky pink drinks on. Stared out at dancefloor. Some cross-dressers looked like real women.

'Because they are,' Chloe shouted above the music. 'Wags. Wives and girlfriends of cross-dressers, who come to be supportive.'

Fascinated, I was. Had thought every woman would be revolted by her man dressing up in ladies' clothing. Because I found it repulsive, I suppose. Not repulsive per se. But repulsive in man I was having relationship with. How could I ever find him sexy again, if caught him wearing pink frilly knickers?

'Incoming bloke,' I yelled into Chloe's ear. 'Will ask you to dance.'

But he didn't. He selected Sue instead, and I was astonished. Chloe was the only one of my girls who hadn't yet been asked to dance and she was easily the best-looking and best dressed – in claret wrap-around dress with lustrous sheen (both sexy and stylish), zig-zag patterned tights and ankle boots with stunning heels.

'You're giving off the wrong signals,' I yelled at her. 'Sticking too close to me. You go off and dance.'

'No, am grand – Jesus!' Chloe was staring in drop-jawed amazement at dancefloor. 'Is that Sue?'

Stretched to see better. Jaw dropped just like Chloe's. Couldn't believe what was seeing. Astonishing the talents we all carry inside us! In one life, Sue, a taciturn, flat-cap-wearing, small-time potato farmer. But in this one, she was spectacularly gifted dancer. Moving her body like shimmering mercury. Lithe, lissom, head going one way, shoulders going another. Legs that normally looked scrawny as chickens' were taut and defined in shiny tights. Creating quite a stir out there.

'She really is grooving,' Chloe said with admiration.

'Who knew?'

Despite Chloe's beauty no one approached her and eventually she said, 'Let's have a dance, Lola. Better than standing here like pair of eejits.'

'Okay.'

Fabulous dancer, Chloe. Great fun. Best time had had in ages.

Two admirers cut in on us, then cut out again very quickly when they discovered I really was a woman.

'What about her?' One of them jerked his thumb at Chloe.

'No, she's a man.'

He stared doubtfully at Chloe. 'Ah, lookit, we'll leave yiz to it.'

2.07

Everyone back in minivan. Returning home. Mood high-pitched and excited. Babel of voices as stories exchanged about admirers, the pleasure of being out in public as a woman, the many compliments received. Everyone happy.

Despite it being 2 a.m., many cars on road. Christmas parties and suchlike.

Progress slow.

Progress slower.

Progress stopped altogether.

Queue of cars like evening rush hour. Glow of lights from up ahead.

'What's going on?'

'Garda checkpoint,' Guard Dolores Lyons said. He indicated walkie-talkie. Silly of me, but hadn't thought it was real. 'Operation Sober Christmas.'

Garda checkpoint! Sudden and terrible fear filled vehicle. Not because I was drunk – I wasn't. But was driving carload of trannies, one of them a guard, not only that, but *dressed as guard,* albeit female one. (Could he be done for impersonating an officer?) Knew what they were thinking – we would be hauled out of car, hands on roof of vehicle, frisked in private places. Families would be informed. Names leaked to press. We were sunk.

Turned to Chloe. Our eyes met. We both reached for map on floor.

'I'm doing U-turn,' I said, but she already knew.

'I'll navigate,' she said.

I put foot on pedal and did immediate and neat turn in road, then whizzed back towards Limerick, away from the police. But Dolores had more bad news. 'Other checkpoint up ahead.'

'What you mean?'

'I mean other effing checkpoint up ahead!' Waved walkie-talkie to emphasize point. 'We're driving straight into it.'

We were trapped.

'No, no, no, no, no, no, no,' Natasha moaned.

'Get a hold of yourself!' Dolores cried.

'Have got so much to lose!'

'Need to get off main road,' Chloe said, poring over map.

'You've got so much to lose? I am officer of the shagging law! How you think I feel?'

As they squabbled in the back over who had the most to lose by exposure, glow from the other checkpoint became visible in night sky. Traffic beginning to slow.

'Shit,' I breathed.

'Lola,' Chloe said, 'according to this, should be small road to left coming up . . . it's here! Here!'

No signs to indicate small road, came upon it too suddenly, twisted steering wheel sharply to left and, as made the turn, tyres screeched loud enough to alert Plod who were standing in middle of road, lit by sodium glow, like aliens emerging from spacecraft. Even as I plunged car into dark side road, aware of them tensing and staring at us. Shouts filled the air.

'Fuck! They've seen us.'

'Just keep driving, Lola,' Chloe said in calm voice. 'Right turn will be coming in four hundred yards. Take that.'

'They're following us!' Dolores cried. 'I can hear them on walkie-talkie.'

'You serious?'

'Yes, yes! Two officers in a squad car.'

Shock so bad, actually felt myself lift and float. I was in car chase with police. How had this happened?

'They'll know local roads better than us,' Sue said. 'We're fucked.'

'Just keep driving, Lola,' Chloe kept repeating in calm, calm voice, as I hurtled along narrow, twisty, potholed road in pitch black. 'Now, ladies, listen to me. Shortly we're going to pull in and the four of you are going to get out. Quick as you can. Then hide yourselves. Lola and I will keep driving and they'll keep following us.' *Hopefully*, I could hear her think. 'We'll come back when we can. Turn right here, Lola.'

My responses super-fast. Terror is a marvellous thing. 'Chloe, you get out too –' Why should she stay with me and take the rap?

'No way am I leaving you on your own.'

'Oh my God, is that sirens I hear?'

Yes. Horrors. Even worse, could actually see the Plods' headlamps. Countryside so dark that, depending on twist of road, at times they were lighting my way.

'Okay, Lola,' Chloe said. 'Get ready to pull in. Rest of you, prepare to jump overboard.'

Road too narrow to conceal four trannies. Couldn't see how throwing them from car would save them. But had swerved into scooped-out entrance to something. Trannies tumbled out like skydivers. Doors slammed shut. Pulled away in hail of gravel.

'What was that place?'

'Quarry.'

'How you know about it?'

'On map.'

On map. 'Jesus, most women can't make head nor tail of maps. Squad car still following?' But knew it was, because siren still wailing.

'Village coming up. We'll pull in?'

'Okay.'

'Remember, we have done nothing wrong. Okay, here we are, stop here.'

Parked car beside darkened pub. Nervous. Peelers pulled up behind. Two got out, looking very, very cross. Angriest-looking one ordered me, 'Get out of car.'

Chloe and I both got out. I asked, as innocent-sounding as possible, 'Is there problem, officer?'

'Why you drive away from road check?'

'What road check?'

Gave me knowing stare. Thought he had me on drunk-driving.

'Why you not stop when you hear siren?'

'Did. Stopped at first safe spot.'

Another hard stare.

'Blow into straw,' milder-looking one told me, then they exchanged spiteful smile, promising each other they would push for custodial sentence for me.

To their great – and bitter – surprise, I passed breath-alyser and they couldn't get me on anything else. Licence clean. Car not registered as stolen. No dead bodies in boot. No drugs in car. Just two girls on their way home from night out dancing.

Fifteen minutes later

Policemen very reluctant to leave. Knew something was being hidden from them, but they couldn't nail it.

Slowly they got back into squad car, all the while giving me filthy looks.

'You'd better make sure you never cross my path again, Ms Daly,' angriest one said in farewell.

'And a happy Christmas to you too, officer.'

Beside me, heard Chloe snigger. (Have to admit, actually said it because showing off in front of Chloe. If on my own, would have been far more respectful.)

Engine started, lights on, exhaust pumping smoke, squad car left us. Watched until it vanished from view, then I asked, 'They gone?'

Chloe stared down dark road. Red rear lights had disappeared. Even sound of car had stopped. Pure silence.

'They're gone.'

We'd got away with it.

We'd got away with it!

Suddenly fizzing with adrenaline, with joy, with relief, with pleasure at having pulled a fast one.

'Chloe, you were brilliant! Turn right, pull in –'

'No, you were brilliant.'

'Left turn coming up –'

'And you just kept your cool and did it!'

'Thelma and Louise, that's who we're like!'

Wanted to high-five her, hug her, pick her up in my arms and twirl her around.

In the end, settled for snogging her.

Grace

Casey Kaplan tore a sugar sachet open with his teeth.

'Gobshite,' I murmured, amazed – almost pleased – that Kaplan had found yet another way to irritate me.

'Yeah, gobshite,' TC agreed. 'What's wrong with using your fingers?'

'I know this might sound mad,' I said in an undertone. 'But I almost *enjoy* hating him.'

'Me too.'

Kaplan's desk was set a little way off from the cluster of Features, far away enough for us to be able to bitch about him but close enough that we had to do it quietly. Discreetly we surveyed him tipping the sugar into his coffee then – we were agog – stirring it with a blue biro.

'Gobshite,' TC breathed.

'Yeah, gobshite,' I whispered. 'What's wrong with using a spoon?'

'He could just shout in to Coleman Brien to bring him one and Coleman would jump to it, probably offer to stir his coffee for him –'

'– with his mickey –'

'– yeah, with his mickey –'

Suddenly Jacinta's witchy face appeared between TC and me. 'I hate him too,' she hissed angrily. 'But do some fucking work.'

Office-wide the mood was volatile. Half the paper had given up smoking on the first of January. Eight days in, it was ready to blow sky-high. Because I'd gone through my initial withdrawal in October, I wasn't too bad. It didn't mean that I didn't ache for cigarettes – because I did – but I wasn't locked into a state of near-blind rage, like everyone else.

Mind you, nor did I feel the comfort of marching shoulder to shoulder with fellow sufferers because I knew what was going to happen: tomorrow was Friday, and after work everyone would go to Dinnegans and three-quarters of those who had given up would resume smoking between their third and fourth drink. The other quarter would fall off the wagon over the weekend, and come Monday morning I would be restored to my position of lone non-smoker. (Or rather, non-smoking smoker. There were one or two people dotted among the staff who had never smoked, but I felt no kinship with them.)

'Grace!' Jacinta urged. 'Work!'

Reluctantly I returned to my story, and when my mobile rang, a thrill – small but nevertheless a thrill – lit me up like a power surge. Any kind of diversion would do. I checked the number. Was it safe to answer? Dickie McGuinness.

'McGuinness here.'

The static was so bad I could barely hear him. He sounded like he was ringing from Mars. Which meant he was probably fifty yards down the road in Dinnegans.

'Dickie, we miss you!'

Dickie had been 'out on a story' since the start of the week. It must be great working crime. So long as you came up with an exposé of ne'er-do-wells a couple of times a year, you could spend the rest of your time enjoying a life of leisure.

'Grace, I've something for you.' Static fizzed on the line.

'I dread to think.' Dickie could be very vulgar, especially when he had drink in him.

'Do you want . . .' He dipped out of coverage. '. . . don't you?'

'What is it?'

'Do you want it or don't you?'

'Yes, I said! What is it?'

'The name of the person who paid the two characters to burn out your car.'

My heart seized up in my chest and I pressed my phone so hard against my ear that the cartilage clicked.

Alerted by intuitive nosiness, TC abandoned his typing to look at me.

'Are you listening?' Dickie demanded.

'Yes!'

'Do you want it or don't you?'

'Of course I fecking do!' Half the office jerked their heads around to stare in my direction.

'Am I . . . *ah* . . . *ih* . . . to . . . self here?'

'No, Dickie, I'm here, it's the line. Tell me.'

'John Crown.'

'Say it again.'

'John Crown. C-r-o-w-n. Like crown of thorns. John. J-o-h-n. Like John the Baptist.'

'I've never heard of him.'

'. . . *wah* . . . *nih* . . . Salome.'

'No. John Crown. I've never heard of John Crown.'

'Up there for . . . *geh* . . . *buh* . . . dancing.' A great ball of static roared on the line, then I was suddenly disconnected.

With clumsy hands I rang him right back and got a two-note, high-pitched tone I'd never heard before. Maybe he really was on Mars. I tried again and got the same noise. Then again. I stared at my phone wondering what was going on. Was I calling the wrong code? Was my phone broken? Or was it simply the 'Dickie effect'? He worked hard to create an air of mystery around himself and, to be fair to him, he sometimes pulled it off.

'What's going on?' TC asked.

'Nothing.' I clicked off a quick text to Dickie asking him to call me.

'I will ask again.' TC bit out the words. 'What's going on?'

'Nothing.' I needed him to be quiet. My thoughts were racing. John Crown? John Crown? Who was he? Did I know him? What had I done to him? Had I written something bad about him? I searched in my head, flicking back through all the stories I'd ever covered, but I couldn't get any matches.

My thighs were shaking and I planted my feet firmly on the carpet tiles in an effort to stop them. Knowing the name of an individual who hated me enough to set my car on fire was distressing in a way I couldn't ever remember feeling before. In the five weeks since Dickie had told me that it hadn't been an accident I'd been in such deep shock I wasn't sure I believed it was true. The only time I felt the fullness of my terror was in the early mornings – six mornings out of seven the fear was waking me at 5.30. However, learning this man's name had brought the horror of it right up against me. It was unavoidable – I was petrified.

'It's obviously not nothing,' TC persisted. 'Do I look stupid?'

'Yes. Really stupid. Especially when you're doing a sudoku. You press your tongue against your upper lip and we can see the funny black bits under your tongue and you don't even know you're doing it.' I looked up from examining my phone and made humble eye contact with him. 'Sorry, TC.'

'Who's John Crown?' Tara asked.

'Yeah, who's John Crown?' As well as the narkiness, another feature of a nicotine-starved workplace was a great hunger for entertainment.

'I don't know.'

'You do!'

'Yes, you do!'

'Tell us, you do!'

Lorraine didn't ask me anything: she'd buckled and resumed smoking on 3 January.

Joanne didn't question me either. She'd never smoked in the first place. (As people frequently observed, she'd never really fit in.)

'Your ear's bright red,' TC observed. 'It looks abnormal.'

Actually it was very painful. Could I have broken it? Can you break your ear?

'Work!' Jacinta hissed like a goose. 'All of you, work!'

'Can we get cake?' Tara asked.

'Oh yes! Please, Jacinta, cake!'

'No, no, we can't bloody well get cake!'

601

I couldn't work. The pressure in my head was building. John Crown? Who was he? Why would he pay people to steal my car? Why would some complete stranger do that to me? Perhaps it was a case of mistaken identity? But how could I find out?

Without explaining myself, I slipped out of my seat and made my way to the fire exit.

I needed some peace to think. And perhaps the cold air might calm down my red ear.

The fire escape – strewn with a thick carpet of cigarette butts – was deserted. I sat on a metal step. The air was bone-cold and misty and the quiet roar of the city was all around me, but at least people weren't yelping into my banjaxed ear about cake.

I took a deep breath and acknowledged something: Damien might know who John Crown was. I could ask him. But something – and I didn't know what it was – was stopping me. The same something that had stopped me from telling him what Dickie had originally told me – that my car had been burnt out deliberately. Usually I told Damien everything; well, nearly everything. I mean, he didn't know that every month just before my period I had to pluck three wiry whisker-style hairs from around my mouth. Not that it was exactly a state secret – if he asked me straight out about it, I wouldn't lie, but I wasn't going to unilaterally volunteer the information.

Anyway . . . I didn't know why I hadn't told him that someone had had it in for me.

Maybe I was afraid that if he knew, it would make it real? And it was real.

I started shaking again but at least this time I could blame it on the cold.

God, what a life. All this on top of me going out of my mind about Marnie. Shortly after I'd last seen her, the worst-case scenario came to pass: she'd lost her job, Nick had left her, taking the two girls with him, and he'd put their lovely big house on the market. The only reason it hadn't sold yet was because we were in the depths of winter, but it wouldn't be January for ever.

Christmas had been utterly miserable. Bid's fourth bout of chemo had finished on Christmas Eve but there was no way of telling if it was working. Apparently it didn't bring about gradual healing; in fact, it might have no effect whatsoever until the very last dose on the very last day. Until she had a scan after her final bout in February, no one would have a clue if she was going to live or die.

Poor Ma and Dad were showing the strain and it was sad to see because Christmas usually energized Dad. He had a conspiracy theory which got a great airing every year, kicking off in early December. He would rant and rage at anyone who would listen that the Christian churches were in cahoots with big business, compelling people to spend shedloads of money on novelty socks and cranberry sauce and bottles of Advocaat.

In other homes, you know it's Christmas when the decorations come down from the attic. In ours, Dad's first conspiracy-theory rant declared the season open.

But this year, apart from a half-hearted tirade on the uselessness of pot pourri, he barely bothered.

Marnie came to Ireland – without the kids, of course – and passed through the 'celebrations' like a whey-faced sleepwalker. Up to that point I'd been able to prevent Ma and Dad from knowing about the drinking but if Marnie decided to go on a bout, there would be no way of keeping it from them. The carry-on of her was so bad, she could end up on the six o'clock news.

Perplexingly, though, she didn't drink. Mind you, she didn't eat or sleep or speak either.

But I was tentatively hopeful. Perhaps she had finally come to the end. Perhaps the shock of Nick leaving her had finally done it.

It was Damien who suggested that I ring Nick to apprise him of the progress – but Nick was nothing like as pleased as I was. 'Ten days without a drink? Not good enough. Needs to be a lot longer than that.'

'But Nick, if she had your support –'

'No, Grace, I can't do it to the girls.'

'But –'

'No.'

I didn't like it but I sort of understood it.

I decided that when Marnie returned to London on 30 December, I would go with her to get her over the hump of New Year's Eve. 'In fairness,' I said, 'New Year's Eve is enough to turn even the Dalai Lama into a pisshead.'

Damien offered to come with us and I was tempted. I wanted to be with him – it felt as though I'd barely seen him in weeks, even though I had; after all I lived with him – but having forced him to give up cigarettes because of one member of my family, I thought it was pushing my luck to ask him to babysit another of them. And on New Year's Eve.

'Go out,' I urged. 'Have fun. I'll be back in two days.'

'I've had enough so-called fun to last me the rest of my life,' he said gloomily. 'Certainly enough seasonal cheer.'

His siblings were great ones for Christmas and threw a variety of bashes. Mid-December, Christine and Richard had a glamorous White Russian ball where the invitation ordered you to wear white. 'Or what?' Damien had asked the little rectangle of stiff cardboard. 'Or we'll be sent to Siberia?'

Two days before Christmas itself, there was a three-line whip from Deirdre. 'A family dinner,' she'd said. 'As we'll all be with our own families on the day itself.' She'd created a Christmas grotto in her dining room, the floor strewn with pine needles, sconces flickering, and she served a full-on traditional dinner to twelve adults and ten children, without her smile ever once faltering.

On Christmas Eve, the cousins who were aged around nine to eleven put on a 'Christmas revue' with puppets they'd made themselves. In a way this wasn't the worst of the gatherings because conversation had to be minimal in order to hear the puppets' dialogue. But in another way it was strangely depressing. These weird children. Shouldn't they be out nicking lipglosses from Boots?

There were also any number of 'impromptu' 'get-togethers', from 'pot-luck suppers' to 'We'll be in the Dropping Well from 9.30. Do come.'

Damien and I had to show our faces at a couple of the events because if we didn't – we'd learnt this from previous years – his mum rang us and said everyone was worried about us.

'Christmas is the pits,' Damien mused. 'I know we say it every year, but let's go away next year, Grace. To Syria or someplace Muslim where they don't have it.'

'Grand.' I'd have gone this year if it hadn't been for Bid. And Marnie.

'But bad as Christmas is,' he said, 'New Year's Eve is worse. I *hate* it.'

'Who doesn't? But whatever you get up to, it's got to be better than sitting in Marnie's mausoleum drinking Appletise.'

'Juno's having a party,' he said.

My heart was suddenly heavy. It felt like Juno had us bombarded with invitations. Since the night Damien and I had had dinner with her, she'd tried to lure us along to hundreds of different affairs. (In fact, once I focused on the exact number, it turned out to be only three, which I found amazing, it felt like so many more.)

Damien had persuaded me to go to one of them, on the Friday before Christmas, an afternoon, mulled-wine thing. I'd only gone because I was carrying around a suspicion that Juno and her husband must have split up. Why else would Juno have got in touch with Damien so unexpectedly?

But as we arrived, standing on the front steps, smoking a cigarette, was a stout, red-faced man who squashed my hand with drunken bonhomie and introduced himself as, 'Warner Buchanan. Juno's husband, the bloody husband, for my sins!'

Then he recognized Damien and, I swear to God – I wasn't being paranoid – his expression became wary. 'You're the first one! First husband.'

Damien politely admitted that he was indeed and Warner's face fell – it really did, I wasn't just imagining it. It sank down into jowly discontent, and beside Damien's handsome good looks, Warner looked dishevelled and, actually, a little pitiful – and it occurred to me that if I was comparing Damien and Warner and finding Warner a bit lacking, what was to say that Juno wouldn't also?

Warner slapped an arm around Damien's shoulders and led him into the house. 'You and I should swap war stories,' he roared, but I wasn't convinced by his display of camaraderie. Too little, too late, is what I would have said had anyone asked me. But they didn't – no one was interested in me. Juno – as if alerted by a sixth sense to our arrival – swooped out into the hall and yelled at Warner, 'Get your fat hands off my lovely Damien!'

She kissed Damien – again, on the lips – then me, but not on the lips.

'Grace!' she said. 'Aren't you at work?'

'Yes,' I said. 'But I've mastered the cunning art of bilocation.'

No one laughed. Because no one was listening.

'There're loads of people here that you know from school,' Juno said to Damien. 'Let's get you a drink.'

It was the kind of party where they absolutely pour drink into you, where people end up falling into walls and passing out spreadeagled on the bathroom floor and having to be put to bed in the spare room. Much as I wanted to join in the seasonal good cheer and imbibe enough to end up comatose, I was driving.

I found a seat and nursed a hot Ribena as Juno squired a flush-faced, fluthered Damien around the room. 'My first husband,' I kept hearing her say. 'Isn't he gorgeous? Look at the cut of Warner next to him. Isn't he an absolute bloody fright?'

She must be really drunk to talk about her husband that way, I decided. But she didn't look drunk. In a slinky, beaded, champagne-coloured dress – no foul rugby jersey with the collar turned up today – and her blonde hair twinkling in the light from the chandelier, she was radiant and pretty.

Actually I'll tell you what she was. She was dazzling.

As I drove him home, Damien declared himself delighted that he'd attended and expressed his drunken appreciation that I'd accompanied him. (The next morning, however, was a different story. We were meant to be braving the scrum, shopping for Christmas presents for his enormous bloody family, but he felt so queasy that he refused to get out of bed.)

'So Juno's having a New Year's Eve party,' I said. 'Now why doesn't that surprise me? Does she do anything *other* than throw parties?'

'I won't go if you don't want,' Damien said. 'I hate New Year's Eve. And I hate parties!'

I had to laugh – in order to pretend I wasn't a possessive bunny-boiler. But I couldn't sustain it. I burst out, 'What's Juno up to? Why has she suddenly emerged from nowhere with her fecking DVD? Why is she so mad keen to be friends with you? What's her game?'

'There's no game.'

It was a short, simple sentence, three to four words. So how had Damien infused it with such defiance? Or perhaps he hadn't.

'Well, why do *you* want to see *her*?' I just couldn't see the appeal.

'I'm not that bothered,' Damien said.

'Aren't you?'

'No. Really.'

'In that case, go with my blessing.'

So Marnie and I flew to London and the first thing I did was a trawl of the house, where I found bottles of vodka in all kinds of hidey-holes. 'Pour them away,' Marnie said. 'Get rid of them.'

Like I was going to suggest we drank them.

On New Year's Eve we spent the afternoon with Daisy and Verity. We tried our best, but Christ . . . Daisy's glow had disappeared; from day one she'd been a charming, beautiful child and now she was flat and plain and sullen. As for poor Verity, she was a ball of twitches and tics. They kept asking – *kept* asking – why they didn't live with Marnie any longer and when they'd be coming home. 'Soon,' Marnie kept promising. 'Soon.'

When Nick came for them, they both cried violently and I thought my head would explode.

But their tears were like nothing compared to Marnie's. She convulsed so long and hard that I actually wondered if I should try to get medical help.

'All I ever wanted was to be a mother.' The words were wrenched from her. 'How did I let this happen? My children have been taken away from me and it's all my fault.'

'You just have to stop drinking,' I said. 'Then you'll get them back.'

'I know, I know, Grace, oh God, I know and I just can't understand why I keep . . . I'll tell you the most awful thing, Grace. All I want right now is a drink.'

'Well, you're not getting one,' I said grimly. 'Have a sausage roll and get through it.'

As the clock hit midnight on New Year's Eve, Marnie had finally stopped crying and was two weeks sober.

'New year, new start,' I said, as we clinked our glasses of Appletise. 'Everything's going to be okay.'

'I know.'

The following day as I climbed into the taxi taking me to the airport, she said quietly, 'It really is going to be okay.' She gave me a smile of such sweetness that it shifted me back into a mindset where I wasn't climbing the walls with worry the whole time. I'd forgotten what it felt like to be normal. It was *lovely*. All I had to worry about now was my aunt dying of lung cancer. And someone with a big enough grudge against me to burn out my car. And my boyfriend's ex-wife sniffing around. Glorious!

But an hour later, after I'd checked in, I decided to give Marnie a quick call and she didn't pick up; and I knew, standing in Terminal 1, with crowds of post-festive people pushing and shoving all around me, that she had started drinking again.

I turned around – yes, dramatic as it sounds – and went right back to her.

I was so angry I could hardly see. 'What the fuck are you at? You've thrown it all away!'

'I'm sorry, Grace.' Tears poured down her face in a torrent. 'Being away from the girls . . . the pain is awful . . .'

'Whose fault is that? You're just a selfish bitch and you could stop if you tried hard enough.'

My jaw clenched with purpose, I hit the phones and rang sixteen treatment centres – who would have thought it was such a growth industry? – and to my amazement many of them were booked out. 'Busy time of year,' one bloke laughed ruefully. 'Peak season.' Like we were talking about a holiday in the Maldives.

Maybe it should have been a comfort to know that I wasn't alone, but actually it was a shock to discover there were so many other selfish bitches in the world. Even if there had been availability in any of the rehab places, not one of them would take Marnie unless she admitted she was an alcoholic – and she wouldn't. For someone so seemingly fragile, she could be as adamant as bejaysus.

'Grace, I'm going through a bad patch. I can't stop right now. I need it to get me through this but this will pass –'

'*How* will it pass?'

'Nick and the girls will come back, everything will be okay and then I won't need to drink so much.'

'But Nick and the girls *won't* come back.' I was almost in tears with frustration. 'They left because of your drinking. Why would they come back when you're still drinking?'

'I'll get stronger, and when I'm stronger, I'll stop. The pain won't be so bad. And I'll drink less.'

But I'd learnt a thing or two from my conversations with the treatment centres. 'Things will only get worse. You're an alcoholic, that's what happens.'

She shook her head. 'I'm just unhappy.'

My yawning terror was that she had nothing left to lose; everything was gone; why would she stop?

I got a flight home later that evening. I had to, I was rostered to work the following day.

'But I'll be back at the weekend,' I warned Marnie.

'It's Thursday already.'

So it was. I'd sort of lost track of the days because of the Christmas break. 'Okay,' I said with grim cheeriness, 'in that case I'll be back tomorrow night. And,' I continued, surprising myself because I hadn't planned this, 'I'll be here every weekend for the foreseeable future.'

'Why?' she asked.

'To keep you off the fucking sauce. Why else?'

But the following night – last Friday – when I'd arrived to find her passed out in the kitchen, stinking of urine and as slight as a child in my arms as I moved her upstairs to bed, for the first time – Christ, the *fear* – I understood the real reason I'd decided to visit every weekend: I didn't want to leave her alone for too long because I was afraid that she might die. Anything could happen: she might tumble down the stairs and break her neck; her body might just give up from so much alcohol and so little nourishment – and she'd always been a candidate for suicide.

I tried talking sense to her, but all weekend she held tight to her mantra: she would stop when things were better. It sent me wild with frustration. But as I left her on Monday morning, I saw something different in her: fear. What did she have to be afraid of, I wondered. She was grand, she was the one drinking her head off, having a great time.

But once my bout of sarcastic inner-dialogue passed, I started having creeping thoughts that perhaps Marnie wasn't simply insanely selfish. That perhaps she *couldn't* stop drinking. And that no matter how much she insisted otherwise, she knew it too.

When my bum started to go numb from cold on the fire-escape step, I decided I'd better go back into the office. Funnily enough the freezing air hadn't cured my ear; it actually felt worse, like it was on fire.

When I approached my desk, Tara looked up hopefully. 'Did you get cake?'

'Uh . . . no.'

'We thought you'd gone to get cake.'

'Sorry. No.'

'She didn't get cake?' Clare asked.

'You didn't get cake?' TC stared at me accusingly. 'So where the hell were you?'

'But I never said –'

'For the love and honour of Jesus!' Jacinta slammed a pen down on her desk. 'If it means that any of you will do any work this afternoon, I will buy you a fucking cake!' She grabbed her handbag (black, of course, it being January) and stormed towards the swing doors.

'Don't get an orange one!'

'Or coffee.'

She swivelled around to look back at us, planted her legs wide, like a superhero, and yelled over the heads of countless staff, 'I will get whatever flavour I fucking well like!'

*

613

There was one person who would definitely know who John Crown was. He would know because he was a smart-arse who knew everything. But I would not ask him. I'd go to my grave, still ignorant, rather than ask him.

I didn't mean to look. I actually meant to look at my slice of cake (walnut and coffee, Jacinta had found the worst in the shop) but my eyes were operating independently of the rest of me and they went ahead and stared in the direction of Casey Kaplan. He was on the phone and when my treacherous eyes met his, he smiled and winked.

I tore my eyes back from him and focused on my cake; maybe if I could pick the walnuts out it mightn't be so bad . . .

Then I grabbed my phone and tried Dickie again. Still on Mars.

'Kaplan. Can I have a word?'

He had his feet up on his desk, looking like a sheriff in a cowboy movie. I found this profoundly irritating. He swung his feet onto the floor and sat up straight. 'Grace Gildee, you can have anything you want from me. Is this a private word? Should we repair to Dinnegans?'

'Shut up. You know everyone, right?'

'Well, not everyo –'

'No need to be modest, we all know you're fabulous. I need you to help me.'

His body became still and when he spoke again, the bantering tone had disappeared. 'Just a soupçon of advice, Grace. When you require someone's help, it oils the wheels somewhat if you can manage to be nice.'

614

I stared stonily at him.

'Nic-*er*,' he amended.

'You stole my Madonna story,' I said. 'You owe me.'

He tilted his head in acknowledgement. 'If this is what it takes to balance the books . . .'

'Does the name John Crown mean anything to you?'

'Yeah.'

'Yeah?'

'Yeah.'

'Who is he?'

He stared at me. 'You don't know who he is?'

'I wouldn't be asking you if I did.'

'I'd say you know him.'

'I've never heard of him!'

'Why do you want to know?'

Suddenly distraught, I said, 'That's my business.'

'Grand. Sure. Sorry. John Crown is a driver, a rich-man's fixer.'

I kept looking at him. I needed more than that.

'But you might know him better as Spanish John.'

Spanish John?

Paddy's driver.

'He works for Paddy de Courcy.'

I was going to vomit. The urge happened so quickly: a draining away of my blood, a wash of puke in my throat, a tingling in my feet and fingers. (And ear, for what it's worth.)

Paddy had arranged – *paid* – for my car to be burnt out. It was unbelievable – it was like having wandered into a true-life crime – but I knew it was real because the timing was right. Six days earlier . . .

'Grace, are you all right?'

'Yes, look –' I lurched towards the Ladies and my lunch roared from me. My stomach convulsed and squeezed until all that came up was bitter yellow bile.

Once I knew, it was like I'd always known.

I *should* have known. I wasn't stupid and I knew what Paddy was like. He'd known how much I loved my car. He'd watched me driving it, whizzing around with pride and pleasure.

I got to my feet and on trembly legs made my way to the taps. I looked in the mirror and I asked my waxy reflection, What can I do?

Nothing.

Forget it, I advised myself. It was done, it was over, it was in the past. The most sensible thing I could do was to pretend that it hadn't happened.

We needed a new couch. The frame had cracked on our current one. 'Grace,' Damien said, 'I'd rather saw my own leg off than spend a Saturday in the January sales traipsing around a furniture shop, but we need to buy a couch this weekend.'

'I can't,' I said desperately. 'I've to go to London. I can't stay away from Marnie.'

There was just the tiniest of pauses. 'I know, I know. I understand.'

'I'm sorry, Damien.'

'I'll come with you to London,' he offered. 'Why won't you let me come with you?'

'Because it would be awful for you,' I said. 'I'd feel shitty about your weekend being ruined too.'

'Couldn't be any more shitty than having to go to World of Leather.'

I sighed and shook my head. 'It would.'

'Why won't you let me help you?' He sounded suddenly angry. 'You're so . . . independent.'

'I thought that's what you liked about me.' I tried a smile.

'I've changed my mind.'

'Damien, it's just . . . having to watch Marnie all the time, it's so . . . sordid. It's so soul-destroying.'

And I had a suspicion that Marnie mightn't like it if I arrived with Damien. Not that I was making any progress with her, but I had a feeling that Damien's presence might shame her into drinking even more than she already did.

'Let's see how I get on this weekend with her,' I said. 'Could that be some sort of compromise?'

'Okay.'

On Friday night when I let myself into Marnie's house, I was very glad I'd talked Damien out of coming with me. Marnie was lying in the hall, naked – why? God only knows – and so drunk she was incoherent. I poured water and B vitamins into her (as advised by the helpline), sobered her up and got her through Friday night without her drinking again. Then I slept with one eye open (at least that's what it felt like) and got her to an AA meeting on Saturday morning. On Saturday afternoon I made her go for a walk, then cooked dinner for her on Saturday night and again slept with one eye open. (Different eye this time, just for the variety.)

But somehow, on Sunday morning, she got her hands on some alcohol. One minute we were having a perfectly normal conversation about Sienna Miller's thighs, then the next I noticed her words were slowing and slurring. I was astonished – I thought I'd disposed of every bottle in the house – then a disappointment so bitter swept over me that I wanted to simply lie down and sleep for ever.

'Where did you get it?' I asked.

'Got nothing,' she mumbled. 'Les have some music.'

With astounding speed – whatever she had drunk, she must have imbibed an awful lot of it – she passed out.

Angry and frustrated and oh so *depressed*, I rang Damien.

'How is she?' he asked.

'Comatose.'

'What? I thought things were going well!'

'So did I. But I think she has a bottle salted away in the bathroom and I can't find it. I've done everything bar move the bath into the landing and I still can't find it.'

He sighed. 'Come home, Grace, you're not helping her.'

'Don't say that, Damien.'

Silence fizzed on the line. After a while I asked, 'How was the poker game in Billy's last night?'

'Hugh turned up.'

'Your *brother* Hugh?'

'That's the one. He bumped into Billy at a funeral. Got himself invited along.'

'Ah here.' Hugh was like a radioactive terrier. All teeth and hunger to win. His competitive spirit would have changed a casual beer-and-cards night into something with a nasty edge.

'Did he win?'

'Need you even ask? All fifty-one euro and seventy cents.'

'It's not even like he needs the money.'

'Not like us.'

'You know, Damien, one day it'll all come crashing down.'

'Go on.' Damien liked this game.

'Hugh's kids.' Agrippa, Hector and Ulysses, the poor little bastards. 'They'll join the Moonies.'

'Say the –'

'Hugh –'

'– or Brian –'

'– or preferably both, will get done for having sex with one of their anaesthetized patients on the operating table.'

Damien laughed quietly. 'That's my favourite.'

'They'll be struck off and it'll be a huge scandal. And in the meantime you'll be made editor of the *Press*, the youngest ever.'

'Yeahhhhh . . .' He sighed, a little disconsolately. *Time for me to stop slagging his family.* Personally, I could have gone on for ages longer but too much bitchiness made Damien uncomfortable. Because – credit where it's due – they never meant to make him feel bad. It was never deliberate.

'So what are you doing today?' I asked.

'I'm going out to buy us a new couch.'

'No!' I barked with shocked laughter. 'No. Please, Damien . . . God alone knows what you'll come home with.' *It would probably be black leather and enormous.* 'Get brochures. Get swatches. But Damien Stapleton, I'm warning you, do not buy anything.'

'Don't you trust me?'

'To buy a couch? No! Ring me tonight with a report. And I'm telling you again, you buy something at your peril.'

On Monday morning I woke at 5.30 a.m. in Marnie's bed. I had the quickest shower ever – it was an unnatural time to be washing myself – and as I got dressed I tried to give Marnie a rousing, you-won't-drink, you-can-do-it speech. But it was too early and too cold and I couldn't summon the energy. All I could do was beg. 'Just don't drink, please, Marnie, please. I'll be back on Friday, just try not to drink until then.'

I caught the 7.45 flight to Dublin and got a taxi to work – straight into a black-handbag day. I'd have delighted in any other colour, even red. I was so tired and black was so *wearing*.

'Ideas,' Jacinta commanded, smouldering with a bitter black energy.

'Sibling rivalry?'

'No!'

'The renewed popularity of poker?'

'No!'

'Alcoholism in women in their thirties?'

'No! Back to the drawing board.'

'Grand.' As soon as she'd left my desk, I rang Damien. He hadn't phoned me last night and I was afraid it meant that he'd been persuaded by some slimy sofa salesman to buy a half-price, shop-soiled monstrosity.

'Why didn't you ring me last night?' I asked.

'Because –'

'You didn't buy a couch, did you?'

'No.'

'You sure?'

'Yes.'

'That's all right then.'

'It was terrible, Grace. The places were overrun with couples fighting and it was roasting hot and really crowded. Just like hell. Anyway I got brochures and yokes.'

'Maybe we'll take a look at them tonight. When you get home from your me-time with the boys.'

'I don't have to go.'

'Why wouldn't you go?'

'Because I haven't seen you all weekend.'

'Ah no, go on. It's important to have a routine when everything is a bit fucked. Anyway I'm too knackered to be any fun. I'll see you in bed.'

With the aid of unseemly quantities of coffee and sugar, I dragged myself through the day. Unusually for a Monday night, people were going to Dinnegans, but I decided I'd rather go home because I hadn't been there since Friday morning.

But as soon as I turned my key and let myself into the house, I knew something was wrong, off, call it what you want. I could smell it.

I wandered from room to room, sniffing, concentrating, trying to nail down the elusive, discordant, alien presence.

Something didn't belong. It hadn't been here when I'd left the house on Friday morning; whatever it was, it had moved in some time over the weekend.

I stared at the sofa brochures on the kitchen table. Was it them? But surely it couldn't be?

I climbed the stairs and the sense disappeared. I must have been imagining it. I was just tired, very tired and overwrought. But when I walked into our bedroom, I sensed it again. Or did I? It was hard to trust my own experience.

For a long time I perched on the edge of the bed, sniffing the air and analysing. Smell or no smell? Imaginary or real? And what was it of anyway?

I needed to talk to Damien about it. I'd ask him later.

Or maybe tomorrow when I wasn't so tired.

I fought my way upwards but slabs of exhaustion pushed me back down into sleep. I had to wake up, I had to come to, why was it such a struggle? What day was it? Maybe it was Saturday, a nice day, and I could eddy back down into the depths? But then I knew it was Tuesday. I had to get up and go to work, but I was so so tired.

Also my nose hurt. Last night I'd been reading the new Ian Rankin – one of Damien's siblings, I couldn't remember which, had given me the hardback for Christmas – and I'd fallen asleep and it had landed on my face and the bloody thing weighed a ton.

I opened my eyes and groaned, 'Oh Goooooood.'

Damien emerged from the bathroom, a towel around his waist, his face half-shaved.

'Are you okay?' he asked.

'Very tired.'

'You were comatose when I came in last night.'

'Taking lessons from Marnie.'

'You want anything?'

Plenty. My sister to stop drinking. My aunt to recover from cancer. To have never met Paddy de Courcy.

'Coffee.'

He headed to the bedroom door, to go down to the kitchen. 'Hey, Damien,' I called weakly. 'Was anyone here over the weekend?'

He turned to face me. 'No.'

But there was a little flicker. A tiny little something. I was on it immediately, my heart suddenly pounding. 'What?'

'It's nothing.'

'Obviously it's not nothing.'

'Okay.' He sighed. 'I met Juno.'

I thought I was going to puke. The tiredness, the shock . . .

'But she wasn't here. We just went for a quick Indian on Sunday night. Warner was away.' Then he added – and I couldn't decide if it was defiance I was hearing, 'And so were you.'

'Why didn't you tell me?'

'It was nothing, a last-minute thing. I'm telling you now because I didn't want to tell you over the phone while you were at work yesterday.'

'But if it was important enough that you didn't want to tell me on the phone, then it's obviously not nothing.'

'You're being ridiculous,' he said firmly.

Was I?

If there really was anything going on, he wouldn't tell me he'd met her. Or would he? Was he simply covering his tracks, in case they'd been spotted together? Would he even have told me if I hadn't guessed something had happened?

Or was I just going mad?

I thought I could trust Damien.

But could any human being really trust another?

'I love you,' he said. 'She's nothing to me.'

'Then why see her?'

After a pause he said, 'I won't see her any more.'

'Okay.' I hadn't the energy to be feisty.

'What?'

'Okay, then, don't. Don't see her.'

'Okay.' He nodded his head. 'Done.'

Marnie

Sky News was her only friend. It gave her vital information without passing judgement. Today, it told her, was Thursday, 15 January, 11.40 in the morning. (Also that there had been a coup in Thailand but she wasn't so interested in that.)

The last day she had any memory of was Monday. Grace had left for Dublin at ten past six in the morning and as soon as the taxi taking her away had turned the corner at the bottom of the road, Marnie was overwhelmed with guilt and loneliness and had retrieved the vodka she'd hidden in the bathroom. Since then she'd come in and out of reality only briefly, but now she was sober.

She was shaky, fearful, nauseous – but she didn't want a drink. It happened that way. It seemed to go through a cycle: she'd start drinking and be unable to stop; and then, almost abruptly – although she could never predict exactly when – it would come to an end.

Today all she wanted was her daughters. The smell of Daisy's skin, the feel of Verity's trusting hand in hers . . .

Oh the guilt. God, the guilt, the guilt, the guilt. They were so young, so fragile . . .

How had she ended up in this life? How had they all ended up like this? She living in this huge empty house, her daughters and husband in an apartment two miles away.

It was so strange, so not what she had planned, that it was hard to believe it was real. Perhaps it *wasn't* real. Maybe she'd never been married. Maybe she'd never had children. Maybe she'd imagined her entire life? Maybe she'd never been born . . .

She managed to frighten herself so much with this line of thinking that she had to get up and walk around the house, trying to see reason. She was being silly. Worse than silly. But the thoughts wouldn't stop.

I'm not real.

I was never born.

She needed to talk to someone. But who? They'd just think she was a nutter.

I am real, I am real.

Struggling for breath, she rang Grace at work. 'Am I real, Grace?'

'Oh for the love of Christ! What's up with you?'

Marnie explained, as best she could. 'Am I going mad, Grace?'

In a very quiet voice, Grace said, 'It sounds like you've got the DTs.'

'No, not at all –'

'Delirium? Tremens?'

'I just miss my daughters.'

As soon as Marnie hung up, the panic returned, choking the breath out of her. She was fixated on Daisy and Verity. If they existed, then she existed.

Perhaps she should talk to Nick. Perhaps he could confirm whether or not Daisy and Verity were real.

However, all-consuming as her fear was, she knew she couldn't ring Nick when she was in such a state. He thought badly enough of her as it was. But the fear squeezed tighter and tighter and eventually she found herself grabbing the phone and calling his office and even as she asked to speak to him, she was seized with terror that a voice might say,

'Nick Hunter? No one of that name has ever worked here.'

Someone who sounded like Nick answered and seemed to know who she was. The clouds of horror dispersed – then regrouped. She had a wild moment when she wondered if the part of Nick was being played by an actor.

'Nick, I have to see the girls.' She needed physical evidence.

'They're in school,' Nick said.

School. That must mean they existed. 'Can I go and see them?'

'No, no!' Then, more calmly, he said, 'No, Marnie. It'll upset them.'

'They haven't seen me in weeks.'

'Whose fault is that?'

After he had left her – *left* her – Nick had decreed that Sunday afternoon would be their designated time. But, on the first Sunday, the unprecedented strangeness of getting a mere afternoon of their presence – she, their *mother*, who had given birth to them – had compelled her to have a drink before they arrived. Then another. By the time Nick showed up – alone, doing a recce while the girls remained in the car – Marnie was accepting of the situation. But Nick pronounced, like an autocrat, that she was drunk, that it would upset Daisy and Verity to see her in such a state.

'For shame on you,' he had said.

He changed her allocated time with the girls to Saturday morning. Then to Friday evening.

'Dirty tricks,' Marnie had told Grace. 'Messing with my head. Using the children as pawns.'

'No. Surely he's trying to find the best time so that you'll be sober?'

Dirty tricks.

*

Marnie had a revelation, which instantly dispersed her panic: she'd take the girls to the zoo! She'd go to their school right now and take them out of their classrooms and the three of them would go to the zoo together. They'd *love* it. Well, Daisy would. Verity was afraid of animals. And the weather was very cold – maybe not suitable for the zoo. But that was just defeatist thinking!

Yes, they'd go to the zoo and she'd buy the girls sweets, zoo T-shirts, anything they asked for, anything to let them know how much she loved them, how sorry she was to have broken up their lives. Then she'd go to Nick and persuade him to come back.

Once the decision was made, she was frenzied at the idea of all the different actions she had to execute before she would see them. What could she dispense with? No need to eat. No need to wash. No, perhaps she'd better. It had been a while. She darted under the water and squirted herself with shower gel but another flurry of anxiety propelled her back out of the shower, still covered in suds. No time to rinse off.

Dragging a towel around herself, she looked for something to wear and the first thing that came to hand was a floaty dress, she'd never worn it much and now was as good a time as any. Then she took a bundle of banknotes from a little carved box on the window sill. Nick had cancelled her cards but – way ahead of him – she'd withdrawn thousands from the cashpoint and hidden it all around the house; who knew she could be so clever?

Then she was leaving the house and getting into her car, and as she drove through the gates she had a moment when she wondered what life would be like if she was banned from driving? If that case ever came to court?

But why would they ban someone like her? She was no

criminal. Besides, she had two young children, she needed her car.

As she stopped at the lights, she saw an off-licence. Well, *the* off-licence. There was a time when she had rotated five or six different ones, never visiting the same place more than once a week. Now the one nearest to the house was the one she invariably used.

She surprised herself by pulling in – force of habit, she thought; blame it on the car – and entering the shop.

'Five bottles of Absolut,' she said to Ben. Sheepishly she added, 'Having a party.'

'Aren't you cold in that frock?' Ben asked. 'It's below freezing out there.'

'. . . Um . . . no.' But she was suddenly aflame with embarrassment. This was a floaty summer dress. She had bare arms. And no coat. What had she been thinking of?

She grabbed the carrier bags and anxiously returned to the car. The moment she was back in her seat, she was breaking the safety seal on one of the bottles, tilting her head back and pouring the liquid magic into her. She gulped it down, then wrenched the bottle from her mouth, gasped for breath, then tipped her head back again. Within seconds, the humiliation melted away, her purpose was restored and, fuelled by molten stars, she sped to the school.

With buoyant confidence, she swung through the double doors. Two women appeared in the corridor. She recognized one of them. 'Headmistress! Good afternoon. I'm here for my girls.'

'Mrs Hunter, they're in class.'

'I know. But I'm taking them out for a treat.'

'I'm afraid that won't be possible.'

Aha! She suddenly saw what was going on. 'He told you

I was coming? My husband? But it's okay, I'm their mother.'

'Mrs Hunter –'

'Please let me see them.'

'If you could perhaps speak a little more quietly, please. Come into my office, we'll discuss it.'

'Which rooms are they in? Okay, don't tell me then. I'll find them!'

They physically manhandled her! They actually restrained her as she attempted to run down the corridor, flinging open classroom doors. She tried to twist away from their hold. 'Get your hands off me!'

Alerted by the commotion, heads began to peep out of classrooms. Alarmed teachers, followed by wide-eyed, giggling little girls, spilled into the corridor.

Then she saw Daisy. 'Daisy! It's me, Mum. We're going to the zoo. Get Verity!'

Daisy seemed frozen to the spot.

'Go on! Quick!'

One of the giggling girls asked, 'Daisy, is that your mum?'

'No.'

The next time she woke, Grace was in the bedroom with her. Was it the weekend already? How many days had she lost?

'What time is it?' she croaked.

Grace looked up from her book. 'Ten past nine.'

Morning or evening? Of what day?

'Thursday night, the fifteenth of January,' Grace said. 'Do you need to know the year?'

'What are you doing here?'

'I came over after work. I'll take tomorrow off and stay for the weekend.'

Marnie suddenly knew why Grace was here in London. It

was that phone call she'd made to her earlier that day – hard to believe it was still the same day – when she'd asked Grace if she was real.

Oh God, no. She'd behaved like a mad person and scared Grace into getting on a plane. She was so ashamed she could hardly utter the words. 'Grace, I'm so sorry, I was a bit . . . anxious . . . but I'm okay now.'

That was actually a lie: she needed a drink right now. The want was making her tremble and sweat. It was pointless checking for her bedside bottle – Grace would have emptied it. But there was one hidden in the loftspace above the bathroom. If she balanced on the side of the bath, she was just tall enough to lift the MDF rectangle and retrieve it.

A memory zipped through her, a split-second sequence of colour and noise: shouting and scuffling with the headmistress at the girls' school; yelling at Daisy that they were going to the zoo; the headmistress taking away her car key; being driven home by one of the teachers.

No, it hadn't happened.

She clambered out of bed and went to the window – her car was out there, parked innocuously in the drive! A great wave of giddying relief almost brought her to her knees. She had dreamt it all.

'One of the teachers brought it back here,' Grace said from behind her. 'It all happened, it's all true.'

Lurching and sinking with shame, dragged towards the centre of the earth with its weight, Marnie remembered Daisy's face. The hatred stamped on it.

She couldn't let Grace see how she felt; she'd seize on the weakness and try to crowbar it open. But the need to drink was upon her with renewed intensity. It couldn't be ignored, sidestepped, resisted; it was too big.

'Grace.' Her voice was trembling. 'I've got to go to the bathroom.'

'I'll come with you.'

'Don't. I just need to pee. Trust me.'

'Trust you?' Grace was scornful.

'I'm begging you.' Hot tears were suddenly pouring down Marnie's face. 'Just let me go to the bathroom alone.'

'No. I know you've got drink hidden in there.'

'I'll get on my knees, Grace. I'll beg you. Is that what you want from me?'

She toppled to her knees and Grace seized her elbow and yanked her painfully upwards, back onto her feet. 'Get up, get up, Marnie! For God's sake, get up!' Now Grace was crying too – which Marnie had to admit was a novelty.

'Look at you!' Grace said. 'Marnie! This is breaking my heart.'

'Please, Grace,' Marnie begged. 'Please stop coming here.' They held on to each other, part-scuffle, part-embrace. 'I can't change. Stop trying, don't do it to yourself. You've got your life. What about Damien? Doesn't he mind that you're always here?'

'Never mind,' Grace said wearily. 'Ups and downs, everyone has them.'

It didn't take Grace long before she brought up the subject of rehab. You could set your watch by it.

'If you just gave it a try, Marnie, something might stick.'

But Marnie didn't want anything to stick: it was what she was most afraid of. Alcohol was all that was keeping her going.

Grace eventually gave up and changed the subject. 'Have you heard from that Rico bloke since you left work?'

'No,' Marnie said quickly. That was an episode so shameful

she could never let herself think about it. Ever. If thoughts of Rico appeared in her mind, she immediately drank them away.

'Or Guy?'

Guy.

At the sound of his name, guilt flooded her. He'd been kind and patient, astonishingly so; he'd had no choice but to sack her. 'No.'

'Do you mind?' Grace asked.

Please let's not talk about it.

Grace drove Marnie to an AA meeting at lunchtime on Friday. She made Marnie go to meetings every time she visited London but she no longer sat in on them. Instead she waited outside in the draughty hall because – Marnie knew – Grace was worried that by flanking Marnie at the meetings, she might be inhibiting Marnie's Big Admission. The admission that she was an alcoholic.

But, as far as Marnie was concerned, Grace could have saved herself the hard bench in the cold hall. She might as well be in the warm room drinking tea and eating jammy dodgers with the alcoholics because there would never be a Big Admission.

Good job too, Marnie thought, looking around the room, because if there was ever anything she'd wanted to get off her chest, she'd be hard-pressed to get a word in edgeways. Chatty lot, alcoholics.

'. . . I drank because I hated myself . . .'

'. . . thought I was the most special and different person alive, so complicated no one could understand me. Then someone told me that alcoholism is called the disease of "Terminal Uniqueness" . . .'

'. . . everything was always someone else's fault . . .'

'. . . one day I woke up and just couldn't do it any more. I don't know what was different about that day, maybe I'd just had enough of treating myself and everyone around me like shit . . .'

'. . . I thought I was doing everything I could to stop drinking. But the truth was I tried everything to *stay* drinking. I loved it more than anyone or anything else and it was when I realized I actually couldn't stop, that my power of choice had gone . . .'

'Marnie, would you like to say something?'

All right then, to be fair, Marnie had to admit that they always invited her to 'share', but she invariably shook her head and looked at the floor.

But today she said, 'Yes, actually, I would.'

A frisson of anticipation moved through the room: they thought she was going to admit she was an alcoholic. 'I'd just like to say that my husband left me and took my two little girls and won't let me see them. He's cancelled my cards and he's selling my home.'

When the meeting was over, the Jules woman appeared, her jaunty ponytail swinging.

'Hey, Marnie, like to go for coffee?'

'Yes, yes, she would!' Grace shoved her towards Jules, like a pushy mother. 'Off you go, I'll come back for you in half an hour.'

In the coffee shop across the road, Jules put a smoothie down in front of Marnie and said, 'So how are you?'

'Not so good. I miss my little girls.' She poured out the story.

'My partner left me too because of my drinking,' Jules said. 'Took the kids with him. Well, it was great really. I could drink

634

as much as I liked without anyone on my case. I had such a great excuse. All that self-pity.'

'. . . But it's not self-pity, not in my case.'

'No, I'm just saying it was in mine. Yes,' Jules said thoughtfully, 'I'd drink red wine and cry and phone them when I was drunk and tell them that I loved them and that it was their daddy's fault that they weren't with me. A bit like watching a weepy movie, I suppose, crying for all the wrong reasons, but I enjoyed myself. Terrible thing to do to kids, of course, but I couldn't help myself.'

Marnie listened in fascination: Jules had been far worse than her. At least she didn't ring the girls and slander Nick. Well, not often.

'If you were that bad, Jules, how did you stop drinking?'

'By coming to the meetings.'

'So how come they haven't worked for me?'

'Are you an alcoholic?'

'. . . No, no, the opposite, if anything. I'm just very unhappy and alcohol helps me cope.'

'There you are, then,' Jules said cheerfully. 'Why would they work when you're not an alcoholic?'

'. . . But . . .' Marnie furrowed her forehead. What had just happened there? Jules had foisted some sort of sneaky mindgame on her, yes? But she wasn't able to twist her brain around it.

'Sorry, gotta go,' Jules said. 'I've to pick up my kids. See you tomorrow?'

'. . . Actually, no, Jules.' Marnie had just made a decision. 'I don't think so. I'm going to stop coming to these meetings.'

Grace would kick up a stink, but . . .

'They're not helping me,' Marnie said wearily. 'But why would they? Like you said, I'm not an alcoholic.'

'Actually it was you who said it,' Jules said.

'Whatever. Anyway, I'm not coming to any more meetings. They're just a waste of time.'

Jules nodded sympathetically. 'I'll miss you.'

'I'll miss you too,' Marnie said politely, although she wouldn't. Not that Jules wasn't nice. 'Before you go,' Marnie said, 'can I ask you something? Your kids? Who has custody? You or him?'

'You're not going to like this.' Jules's face burst into a grin. 'My partner and I got back together. After I stopped drinking.'

'No!' Marnie put her hands over her ears. 'I don't want to hear your propaganda. Stop drinking and everything will be perfect!'

But Jules just laughed.

She found herself lying on the hall floor. The house felt cavernous and cold.

A black shadow passed over her, like a bird of prey.

What was that? A fast-moving cloud beyond the front door? A lorry trundling past?

It felt like death.

Lola

Friday, 16 January 10.07

Phone rang — Nkechi. Again! She'd gone to Nigeria for first two weeks of January (only genuinely quiet time of year for stylist) but since her return, was all go. Had me effing tormented, if you want the truth. She was in process of 'hiving off' her clients from mine. *Hiving off?* Where she learn that expression? Certainly not from me.

As she had predicted correctly — what with her being fabulous and everything (not being sarcastic, or perhaps only mildly) — not every client wanted to be 'hived off' with her and Abibi, but preferred remain with me. Quite respectable list actually. Heart-warming. Nice to be thought well of.

But Nkechi — going back on original promise — wouldn't take some of 'my' ladies at their word. Some of mine, i.e. the biggest spenders, she wanted for her own. Kept ringing me. Horse-trading.

I snapped phone open. 'Nkechi?' Tone of voice conveying, 'What the eff is it this time?'

'How about this?' she says.

I listened. What insulting, lopsided bargain she proposing?

'Will give you Adele Hostas, Faye Marmion and Drusilla Gallop if can have Nixie Van Meer.'

Bloody cheek! Adele Hostas wouldn't spend Christmas, Faye Marmion pathologically impossible to please and Drusilla Gallop the worst kind of offender: wore the dresses but pretended she hadn't, then tried to 'return' them, stinking of fags and Coco Chanel and with long-last foundation smeared around collar. Nixie, by contrast, was loaded, extravagant and pleasant.

'Three clients,' Nkechi urged. 'For price of one. Deal or no deal?'

'No deal,' I said. 'Nixie Van Meer not for sale.'

'We'll see about that,' Nkechi muttered darkly and hung up.

Cripes. Put head in hands in attitude of weariness. Was fighting for livelihood here. So – question had been trying level best to duck and dodge – what was I still doing in Knockavoy?

My time in exile was up, my sentence had been endured, I was free to go. Needed to go, if wanted to hold on to any clients. Had responsibilities to them – a society woman without a stylist is as much use as one-legged man at arse-kicking competition. My ladies had been more than patient during my autumn 'sabbatical' (or 'breakdown' if we are to speak freely) and if I didn't appear in Dublin soon, they would think was never coming back and would make alternative arrangements.

Nkechi, sensing my weakness, was circling like shark. Because, honest truth of matter, unwilling – yes, deeply unwilling – to leave Knockavoy.

Institutionalized in culchie-land? No longer able to cut it in the big city? Not that Dublin exactly *big* city. Not talking Sao Paolo (20 million people) or Greater Moscow Area (15 million).

10.19

Phone rang again. Girded loins to withstand Nkechi's pressure. However, not Nkechi but Bridie's Auntie Bunny (did I mention that family specialize in peculiar names? Even Tom isn't Uncle Tom's real name. Real name Coriolanus and Tom only nickname. He insisted on 'Tom' because didn't want people trying diminutives of Coriolanus and calling him 'Anus'. True story) saying she wanted to stay in Uncle Tom's cabin for Easter week. 'Getting my spoke in early,' she said. 'The place gets booked up so fast!'

'Yes, of course, haha. Popular spot, yes, despite no telly.'

Hung up. Swallowed hard. Tremendous shock. Really quite cataclysmic shock. Ears tingling from it.

Writing on the wall. Universe entirely unequivocal. Had to return to Dublin.

Of course had known couldn't stay here for ever. Of course had known that soon would be spring and Bridie's extended family's thoughts would turn to minibreaks, fresh air, ozone. Of course knew was lucky to have stayed so long without interruption. Was not stupid, merely gifted at self-delusion. Over the months had elected to indulge in some light denial. If I pretended would never have to leave, then would never have to leave.

But denial a faithless, flimsy friend and no protection against the truth when it decides to come after you.

Okay, shameful admission. Here we go. Had been toying with embryonic notion of remaining in Knockavoy. Yes! Surprising, I admit. Had entertained fantasy of somehow managing to retain nicest and/or most profitable (overlap very rare) Dublin clients, commuting to take care of their needs, while building up client base down here. Details not fully fleshed out in head but knew it would be hard work. Would involve lots of driving, lots of sweet-talking clients nervy as racehorses who usually insisted on round-the-clock hand-holding, and would never make as much money as if Dublin-based — but worth it if happy, no?

But universe having none of it. Universe was ousting me from lovely little house and ordering me, with long, bony, grim-reaper-style finger, back to big city.

Was plunged into wretched despair, almost as bad as desperation had experienced during cheerless Christmas dinner with Dad and Uncle Francis.

Had come to Knockavoy to escape shambles of life, to hide out until restored to mental health, but unexpectedly had become happy here. Only saw it now that it was nearing end. Effing typical, of course.

11.22

Wandered into kitchen, stood at window, gazed out at Considine's house and wondered if Chloe would come to trannie night tonight.

She hadn't come last week, our first Friday back after the Christmas break. No invitation had been extended to watch *Law and Order*. In fact, hadn't seen her since *Thelma and Louise* night.

Exceedingly worried, if truth be known, that my impromptu kiss may have caused trouble for Considine and Gillian and fatally wounded my friendship with Chloe.

Was not first time had kissed a woman – Paddy had seen to that – but was first time had done so without big hairy man watching and masturbating.

Chloe exceptional kisser. Slow and sweet and sexy. Kissing with whole mouth, not just doing hard, tongue-darty swordplay that many people think is good kissing.

Had felt quite swoony in my head and knees were going weak – then Chloe went rigid as plank and wrenched away from me. Outrageous reality of situation was like bucket of ice cubes tipped over head. 'I forgot . . .' I stuttered. 'Gillian.'

Poor little Ferret-Face. Thinking her boyfriend was having innocent night out dressing up in ladies' clothing and instead was in sexy clinch with me.

'Chloe, sorry, I'm sorry –'

'No, Lola! My fault too –'

'Just got carried away, adrenaline of the escape, will never happen again –'

'Yes, me too, adrenaline!'

We got back into minivan and drove back to get girls in speed-limit-breaking silence.

Early next morning, went to Birmingham for four days of wretchedness of quite spectacular proportions with Dad and Uncle Francis. I tell you, that pair, they could not enjoy themselves if you put gun to their head. Then on to Edinburgh, with Bridie, Barry and Treese, staying with one of Bridie's many, many cousins, for several days of drunken debauchery, singing 'The Flower of Scotland' and doing strange stuff with lumps of coal. (Although – believe I may have mentioned in passing – am not a coal person, this was not problematic.)

Without doubt, had developed schoolgirl crush on Chloe, all the more silly because Chloe not a real woman. But worst aspect of whole business was Gillian. I was deeply ashamed. Karmic no-go area, putting moves on 'attached' individual. Nice and all as kiss had been, wished desperately had never done it.

Tried to confide in Bridie and Treese in distressed attempt to untangle snarled-up feelings, but got no sympathy.

'Your life like soap opera!' Bridie declared, then proceeded to tell all her cousins. Cousins told all their friends and no one stopped telling until whole of Edinburgh Greater

Metropolitan Area knew. Kept stumbling across conversations about myself: '. . . So then she gets a ride off this surf boy and apparently you'd want to see him, he's fucking GORGEOUS, and MAD about her, even though he's far better-looking than her. And is she glad? NO! Instead she gets this thing for her next-door neighbour, a transvestite. Yes, that's right, *Uncle Tom*'s next-door neighbour! The trannie has a long-term girlfriend. But this is best bit – Lola doesn't fancy the trannie when he's in man-clothes, only when he's in ladies' clothes! Yes, I know! And she's not even a lezzer!'

When man in tartan tam-o'-shanter engaged me in chat at a piss-up and told me about 'Bridie's loony friend', the story had mutated so that Jake was now round-the-world yachtsman and Rossa Considine was transsexual who had lopped off his doohickey in bid to woo me.

'Happy now?' I asked Bridie.

'. . . Ah sorry, Lola, it was just too good a story . . .'

Back in Knockavoy on 4 January, all anxious and longing for it to be Friday so could gauge how things were with Chloe.

But Friday came and Chloe didn't. Natasha appeared, and Blanche, then Sue and Dolores. But no Chloe.

'Maybe she didn't know we had started back,' Natasha said, brow furrowed unbecomingly. 'Maybe she thinks next week is first week back.'

As if trannie nights were like evening classes.

'Maybe.' Felt sick.

Of course she hadn't come! Chloe's loyalty was to Gillian.

But was hungry to promise Chloe that Thelma and Louise kiss would *never* happen again, that it was one-off reaction to unusual, highly fraught situation. Had to take bull by horns (rural phrase which now understand – bulls terrifying), but could not summon required nerve to propel self across the grass to Considine's front door and request audience.

Too scared – yes – that he would tell me baldly to fuck off and that would be end of that.

Hoped that could just leave it to fate, that might bump into him over weekend. Kept nervy eye out but no sign. Short relief from hideous anxiety when jumpy thoughts alighted on notion that he might be away on minibreak, down some foreign pothole. But early Monday morning, was woken by him slamming front door. Hopped out of bed and spied on him striding to eco-car, leaving for work as normal. He didn't look up and then knew for sure something was awry. Hated self. In despair.

Spied on him Tuesday, Wednesday, Thursday and today and he never once looked up. Obvious was blanking me. But I still hoped that Chloe would show up tonight, as usual.

16.01
Popped over to graveyard before it got dark.

'Mum, I don't want to go back to Dublin.'

'All have to do things we don't want. You think I wanted to die and leave you?'

'No, but –'

'Only ever intended to be temporary thing, you living in Knockavoy.'

'. . . Okay.' After all, was probably not really in communication with Mum. Was just listening to voice in my own head, and in fact could do exactly what wanted to . . .

'Why you ask my opinion, if you just going to disregard it?' Mum's voice exclaimed.

. . . Although, of course, might be wrong on that score.

'Am sorry. While am here, what will happen with Chloe? Will she come tonight?'

No answer.

'Mum? Mum?'

'You will have to wait and see.'

18.29

Phone rang. Bridie.

'Come in, Lola Daly, your time is up! Believe you're being turfed out of house.'

'Yes.'

'So question is, are you well enough to come home or are you still nuts? Ask me, I think you're worse. You went down to Knockavoy nice heterosexual girl, now you coming back part-lezzer.'

'Is there purpose to this phone call, Bridie?' Attitude of coldness. 'Or are you doing it simply to taunt me?'

'Only joking. You seemed sane enough in Edinburgh. So how you feel about de Courcy?'

'Don't know.'

'You wish him well? You feel you could throw confetti at his wedding? Only truly over a man when you can throw confetti at his wedding.'

'Certainly don't feel like that.'

But no longer thought about Paddy every waking second and no longer dreamt about him every night. The days were gone when was hair-rendingly crazy because couldn't be with him. In fact — narrowing feelings down here — didn't want to see him. Actually didn't want to. Ever again. Now that was new.

Also something else new, but couldn't identify it. Sadness? No. Longing? No. Grief? No. Anger? Getting warmer. Hate? . . .

644

Mmm, maybe, but not quite . . . not exactly . . . something . . .
what was it? Fear? Could it be fear? Yes, might be fear.

19.01
Natasha and Blanche arrived.

19.15
Dolores arrived.

19.27
Sue arrived.

As I granted her admission, was frantic with anxiety.

'Where's Chloe?' Sue asked.

'Not coming tonight,' Natasha said. 'Yes, Lola, sorry,
forgot to tell you. Chloe texted me. Can't make it tonight.'

'Why not?' My voice shrill. And why she not text me? She
had my number.

'Didn't say why. Now, does my penis look big in this?'

19.56
Sat girls down and broke news that current arrangement
was nearing an end.

'Tom Twoomey's family want the house for minibreaks.
And time I went back to Dublin for work.'

'Oh,' Natasha said. 'When you going?'

When indeed? 'Sometime in next two weeks.'

Nothing to stop me from going right now – wouldn't take
ten minutes to fling clothes back into suitcases – but
needed time to come to terms with departure.

The girls exchanged glances and shrugged and one of
them said, 'Always knew it couldn't last for ever.'

Baffling response. Had expected wailing and gnashing of

teeth and pleas to stay. Instead atmosphere of mature acceptance. Why? The disco before Christmas, that was why. Had shown the trannies that there was great big trannie world out there. They didn't need me any more.

'You've outgrown me,' I said, then broke down into choking sobs. 'You came to me as little fledgling chicks and now . . . now . . . YOU'REALLGROWNUP!'

'Thought you'd be glad,' Natasha said sourly. 'You've done nothing but complain.'

Saturday, 17 January 10.15

Got up, got dressed and left house. After sleepless night was finally doing right thing. Was going to talk to Rossa Considine.

Eco-swot car in drive, hopefully he at home and not down a pothole. Also hopefully not in bed with Gillian. Although they didn't seem to do that — spend the day in bed. They were Up And At 'Em outdoorsy types.

Considine opened door as if he'd been expecting me. Followed me into sitting room, where we perched on edge of couch, ill at ease and sad. Strange atmosphere prevailed as if we'd once been in love, but it was all over now.

'You didn't come last night?' I said.

'No. Told Noel to tell you.'

'He did. Rossa, my behaviour that night we escaped from the guards, I assure you it won't happen again —'

'Is okay —'

'I apologize, Rossa, I sincerely do. And to Gillian. From bottom of my heart. Am so ashamed. But will never happen again. Was just insane, adrenaline, mad moment. Please come back, we miss Chloe.'

'Sorry, Lola,' he said with regret. 'Chloe's gone for a while.'

'I promise won't lay finger on her –'

'Nothing to do with you, Lola. Not your fault. Just one of those things . . . for the best . . .'

'But –' Tears in my eyes! For mythical character!

'Sorry, Lola,' Considine said with infinite kindness. 'Know how much you liked her. Oh please don't cry, Lola, come here.' Took me on his lap the way Chloe used to and I sobbed against his shirt.

'Will she be back?'

'Probably, yes, at some stage, just . . . you know . . .'

Didn't. Must be something to do with Gillian. Maybe she'd finally started kicking up at her boyfriend wearing ladies' clothing.

'But by time Chloe comes back, I'll be gone.'

'What?' Barked word out. He sat up straight, nearly sending me toppling onto floor. His body rigid and no longer comfortable to lean against.

'Yes, Considine. Have to go back to Dublin. Twoomey family want the house and I need to go back to job.' At thought of leaving, cried all the harder. Remarkably sad.

'When you going?'

'Don't know. Haven't decided yet. Can't bear to. Soon, though. Next two weeks.'

'Right.'

His body sagged and although once again comfortable to lean on, it was different, not as pleasant, like a couch that has lost its oomph. Felt the weight of his head, leaning against mine. Mood a peculiar grieving one. Like we were both mourning loss of Chloe. Know it sounds stupid, but simply telling it like it was.

Considine patted hand on my back and my sobbing slowed, then stopped. I closed eyes. Feeling a bit calmer. Warm. Nice

647

smell from Considine's throat. Big, big sigh came all the way up from pit of my belly. Exhaled in long, loose breath of acceptance. Pushed self away from him. 'I'd better get up, Rossa Considine. If stay any longer, will fall asleep.'

'Lola, sorry I've upset you –'

'S'okay, s'okay.' Had done my best. And was leaving Knockavoy anyway. Leaving all of this trannie-malarkey behind.

'You want come over on Wednesday for *Law and Order*?' he asked. 'One final time?'

'Thought it was on on Thursday night.'

'New year. New schedule. On on Wednesday nights now. You come over?'

'. . . okay . . .' Hadn't got what had come for, but okay . . .

12.12

Knockavoy main street

Saw Jake and his mouth sauntering along in Love-God fashion on other side of street. Braced self for insults. But he gave cheery wave, devoid of bitterness, obsession, insanity. So it is true! According to usual sources (Cecile) he is fully restored to old cocksure self. He has reduced Jaz to shell of a girl, made casual, cruel attempt over Christmas/ New Year wasteland of time to come between Kelly and Brandon and is now embroiled with engaged woman from 'out Liscannor way'. I am blip on his otherwise impeccable record.

12.16

Supermarket

New *Vogue* in! Kelly had it on special order for self. Obliged to tell her to cease and desist as would be returning to

Dublin. She expressed sadness at my imminent departure then turned attention to shockingly high cost of *Vogue*.

'Nearly a tenner!' she cried, clinking change out into my upturned hand. 'And nothing in it but ads! Hey!' All excited. 'How you get that mark?'

'What mark?'

'That.' She indicated small, baldy-looking circle of shiny pink skin in middle of my palm. 'Is it burn? You self-harmer?' she asked eagerly. Kelly fascinated by lifestyles of starlet types she reads about in cheap magazines – little girls with big handbags, bulimia and spells in rehab under their belt before eighteenth birthday. 'Would love to meet real self-harmer.'

'Birthmark,' I said apologetically. 'Born with it.' Then added, because she looked so disappointed, 'Sorry.'

13.15

Passing the Dungeon

'Ho, Lola Daly! A word, if you please.'

I stepped in.

'Item of gossip for you,' Boss said.

'Hot,' Moss said.

'Red-hot,' the Master confirmed.

Shameful thrill ran through me. This trio know everything. Whatever they told me would be true.

'Are you ready?' Boss asked.

I nodded.

'Gillian Kilbert . . .'

'. . . also known as Ferret-Face . . .'

'. . . and Osama the barman . . .'

'. . . are an item.'

Extreme shock.

Gillian and Osama? Was seized with terror. This my fault?

Had I driven wedge between Gillian and Considine, propelling Gillian on 'revenge fling'?

'Does Rossa know?' I asked.

'No.'

'So how do you know?'

'Expected it. Have watched situation with interest since they first began going to them Danish films together on a Friday night.'

'Thought they were both ripe for it,' the Master said. 'Little bird tells me Considine and Ferret-Face haven't done the needful for many weeks. In fact, not since the night they got back together.'

'How the hell you know that?' Bad, burny feeling at invasion of Considine's privacy.

'Small town. Anyway, sure enough, instead of coming straight home from Ennis, Gillian and Osama have taken to parking the car half a mile out the road there, and snogging the heads off each other.'

'They didn't go to film at all last night,' Boss said. 'Just parked the car in their favourite spot . . . and . . . well, you know yourself.'

Bad, burny feeling intensified. 'Have you nothing better to do than spy on people?'

Startled hiatus. 'What's up, Lola?' Boss upset. 'Thought you'd enjoy the bit of news.'

'Not right that I know and that Rossa doesn't.'

'Someone will tell him soon enough.' Moss seemed to think that this was good thing.

But not!

Sudden and extreme compassion for Considine. Proud man. And although sometimes cranky, a decent man. I too have been the rejected sap in my time.

I should tell him.

But could I? Despised all that nosy-parker, fake-sympathy, 'Thought you should know . . .'

Although my sympathy not fake.

And if did break news to Considine, he would hate me for evermore. Messengers always got the blame. Did not want him to hate me for evermore. Discovered unexpected fondness for him.

'You leaving?' Alco's Corner cried, as I got to my feet.

'Yes.' Needed to think about this.

Left pub, to sounds of Boss muttering, 'Don't know what's up with her.'

Jesus Christ! As stepped out into daylight, first person I encountered was Gillian. I was rooted to spot with guilt, shock, then more guilt.

'Hello, Lola, happy new year.' She stopped for chat. Seemed in blithe good form.

'. . . Erm . . .'

'. . . You okay . . . ?'

Cripes alive. Was trying to decide what right thing was. She was right in my path – what were chances of that happening? Was she there for reason? But this was hard. A) I was fine one to bloody well talk, having made pass at her boyfriend, even though not him was interested in, but his lady alter ego. B) Interfering in other people's affairs anathema to city person like myself.

'Gillian.' Cleared throat. 'Is none of my business and am not passing judgement, really not at all, but heard . . . heard that you and Osama, I mean Ibrahim, have been . . .'

What would I say? All sounded sordid. Fumbling in lay-bys?

'. . . You know what am getting at?' I said, mortified.

She was staring, ferret-face immobile, eyes full of fear.

'People talking about it,' I said. 'Rossa will find out. Would probably be better if he heard it from you.'

'Where you hear? Not in there?' She tipped her head at the Dungeon, her little face white as milk.

I inclined chin in reluctant assent. Would not wish this fate on worst enemy – Boss, Moss and the Master being privy to their intimate business.

'Fuck,' she whispered. 'Okay.' She nodded, nodded, nodded, then scampered up the street and dived into the Oak, no doubt to consult Ol' Prune Eyes.

15.37

Not spying. No. Simply happened to be cleaning windows in preparation for my departure when saw Ferret-Face and Ol' Prune Eyes approach up the road, reeking of determination. Like gunfight at the OK Corral. At Considine's they turned right into his boreen. Rapped on door and short while later were granted admission. Door shut firmly behind them.

I listened hard, anticipating perhaps shouting and crashing of breaking crockery, but heard nothing.

16.19

Ferret-Face and Ol' Prune Eyes emerged, heads bowed in what assumed was shame. Could discern nothing further.

18.24

Cleaning oven, although had barely used it during Knockavoy sojourn, when heard knock on the door.

Rossa Considine leaning against door jamb, looking mildly dishevelled.

'Badger's arse,' he said.

'Have you?'

'Your badger's arse night. You were promised one and you never got it. How you feel about doing it tonight? Right now?'

'What wonderful idea! Let me just take off apron.'

Of course, was simply being kindly person. Considine needed excuse to go out and get mouldy drunk to drown pain of ferret betrayal, and was dressing it up as gift to me. However was – yes, proud – he had picked me over his potholing buddies. Mind you, knowing those macho types, I expect they would mock him something ferocious. 'Ha ha, you hear about Considine? So crap in bed his girl ran off with suicide bomber. HAHAHAHA!'

18.37

Standing in Knockavoy main street

'Which pub?' I asked.

'The Oak.'

The Oak? You blame me for expecting boycott of the Oak?

Fair play to him. Man of forgiveness. Unless he planning to deck Osama?

No. No decking. Purchased drinks from Osama. Aspect civil. Impressive. Rossa Considine like Gandhi! Osama, on other hand, was creeping about, eyes lowered with remorse. No sparkling, pruney-eyed smiles this evening.

Couple of drinks in, Considine cracked and told me about Gillian and Osama. I behaved as if was first had heard of it.

'Is tragedy,' I said. Meant it. Other people's break-ups give me pain, almost like it's happening to me. 'How you feel?'

'Is end of an era,' he said. 'But had run its course. We should never have got back together after first time we broke up. Reasons we broke up were all still there – I had no interest in her depressing films and she had no interest in my, what you call it? Trannie-ism. Or potholing. And they're happy, the pair of them.'

'Not pleasant to be rejected,' I prompted. Just little bit sick of men denying their feelings.

'No. Stings. You're right. But will survive.'

'No need to put on brave face. Being cuckolded' (Margery Allingham) 'is *humiliating*.'

He twisted round to look at me. In amazement he said, 'You *want* me to be depressed?'

'No. Want you to be honest.'

'Am being honest.'

'No, you not.'

'Am, Lola, am. Me and Gillian, gone bad ages ago and me too . . . too . . . whatever . . . to do something about it. Hoped it would get better. Or hoped . . . just hoped wouldn't have to do hard thing.'

'Don't tell me you relieved!'

'Not relieved. Not so simple. But decision was pending. Now decision made. Actually, yes, now that you mention it, am relieved.'

'God's sake.' Tutted to self. 'Another drink?'

20.49

Still in the Oak

'How you feeling now, Considine?'

'Rough as badger's arse.'

'Wrong usage of phrase. We are not meant to feel rough as badger's arse now! We are meant to feel rough as badger's arse tomorrow morning.'

'I know, I know.' Surprisingly attractive smile. For moment he looked so like Chloe! 'But will not see each other tomorrow morning.' Little stumble in mutual eye contact. 'So let's say it now.'

'. . . Er . . .' Took me moment to recover from the eye awkwardness, then cried gaily, 'Okay. Rough as badger's arse it is!'

21.17
Still in the Oak
Brandon and Kelly came in for post-work libation. Expressions wary when they saw me and Considine – news of the cuckolding had obviously reached them.

'Lola, Rossa. How are you?'

'Rough as badger's arse!'

21.21
Still in the Oak
Cecile popped over to say 'ello. 'God bless all 'ere,' she chirruped. ''Ow's she cuttin'?'

'Rough as badger's arse!'

We told everyone we met we were 'rough as badger's arse'. Was crying with laughter. Really very funny and, of course, was quite drunk.

'We are the badger's arse gang!' Considine declared.

'The *notorious* badger's arse gang. Let's go and see Mrs Butterly before she goes to bed.'

21.40
Mrs Butterly's
'Oh hello, Lola, Rossa, how are ye both?'

'Rough as badger's arse, Mrs Butterly!'

'No need for language. Or shouting.' She looked almost

alarmed as Considine and I clambered onto breakfast bar stools, gripped by weeping-style hilarity. 'Or unbridled mirth without letting me in on the joke.'

Tried explaining to her. But laughing too much. Also, what is funny about saying 'rough as badger's arse' eight hundred times? She tried hard to understand but much shaking of head and saying, 'No, still not funny to me. Now, Eddie Murphy, *he* is funny. You see him in *Big Momma's House*?'

Considine's mobile rang. 'Is Gillian,' he whispered conspiratorially, even though had not yet answered phone so Gillian could hear nothing. 'Wanting to know how I am. You ready?'

'Yes!'

He opened phone. 'Gillian?' Listened for moment. 'Will tell you how I am.'

Gleefully gave me the nod and we both yelled into mouth-piece, 'ROUGH AS BADGER'S ARSE!'

'Go home, the pair of ye,' Mrs Butterly said. Irritable. Had had enough. 'Am going to bed.'

'To watch Eddie Murphy in *Dr Doolittle*!' Considine snorted. 'Or *Beverly Hills Cop*!'

Considine and I almost incapable with merriment, as she ushered us down from our breakfast bar stools and towards door.

22.01

Knockavoy main street
We staggered up road. Staggering not from drunkenness but from howling with laughter. Progress slow, as had to stop every four seconds to double over.

'Ho, Lola Daly, Rossa Considine! Heard ye were on the rampage!'

A summons from sulphurous interior of the Dungeon.

In we went. Were bought many, many, oh many drinks. Bloody great night.

Sunday, 18 January 10.03

Only one way to describe how I felt – as rough as a badger's arse. Worst hangover had had for long time.

Concerned for Considine. Good chance last night's badger's arse glee had worn off and he was in the horrors – part hangover, part cuckoldage. Nothing worse than waking up morning after the day before when you were dumped. Especially if you had got mouldy drunk to drown sorrows.

Texted him. Seemed silly urban thing to do, to text someone living next door, when could just get out of bed and communicate in person, but didn't want to barge in on his sorrow.

Also feared might vomit if I stood upright.

Morning. Am ruff as badgers arse. U?

Reply came quickly.

Ruff as badgers arse 2.

Sent another.

U down a pothole?

Speedy reply.

U mean real pothole or emotional 1?

Had meant real one, but this was leading question.

Emotional 1?

Immediate reply.

No, think is just hangover.

Fecking men! Just when you think they're opening up to you!
Decided to go back to sleep.

15.10
BEE-BEEP BEE-BEEP. Text noise woke me. Groped for phone. Message from Considine.

Walk on beach? Kill or cure?

Novel notion – painkillers, flat Coke, expensive crisps, couch and duvet the normal person's response to hangover. Nevertheless, replied:

Y de hell not? C u 20 mins ure gate.

15.30
There he was, in serious-looking fleece and stampy-style boots. Hair uncombed, as if he'd just tumbled out of bed, and pale, oh yes, really quite pale. As soon as saw him and his pale-green fizzog, I was seized by paralysing mirth. Forward propulsion halted by it.

He too was in grip of spasm of hilarity so powerful he was clutching his sides. When – eventually – able to speak, he called, 'How you feel, Lola Daly?'

'Rough as badger's arse, Rossa Considine. You?'

'Rough as badger's arse.'

One of those hangovers where everything seems funny.

16.27
Walk over, thanks be to cripes.

'Feeling miles better,' Considine said happily. 'You?'

'No. Have pain in ear from wind and nothing will fix hangover except glass of Fanta and plate of chips.'

'The Oak?'

'Why we not try somewhere different?' Wanted to save him from own macho posturing, insisting by his very presence in the Oak that he didn't mind at all, *at all*, that his girlfriend had left him for Osama. 'The Hole in One?'

'Would rather set my face on fire.'

17.03
The Oak
On second Fanta. Plate of chips in front of me. Planned to have cheesecake of day (strawberry) next.

Considine's phone beeped.

'Text from Gillian,' he said. 'Checking I haven't topped myself.'

I guilt-flinched. Will it happen every time Gillian Kilbert is mentioned, till the end of my days?

Considine noticed. 'What's up?'

Had to ask. Needed to know. Made self ask question, like squeezing icing out of cone-shaped force bag. '. . . Did you . . . and Gillian . . . split up because of . . . that business with Chloe and me just before Christmas?'

'No. Keep telling you. Has been dead on its feet for the last Christ knows how long.'

'Did Gillian ever . . . say anything about me?'

'No,' he said, but hesitation was there.

'She did!' I cried. 'She did! Tell me.'

'What? So you can feel even more guilty?'

'Just tell me, Considine.'

'She said, you know that day of the plunger? That there was . . . tension, like sexual tension, between us.'

What? Gillian Kilbert, cheeky bitch! 'Thinking she can deflect attention from her own adulterous liaison by accusing you and me of tension of a sexual nature!' I said. 'Don't mean to kick a man when he's down, Considine, but don't fancy you.'

'She didn't mean that,' Considine said patiently. 'Obviously she was talking about buzz between you and Chloe.'

'But what Gillian base her statement on? Cripes alive, you didn't *tell* her about the snog, did you?' Hid my eyes with my hands.

'No. Especially considering it hadn't even happened on plunger day.' He was laughing. 'She said we were sarcastic to each other.'

'What you say to that?'

'That we were sarcastic to each other because didn't really like each other. Most obvious solution is usually the correct one.'

Grace

'I need to talk to you,' Damien said.

I went cold all over.

'I've something to tell you,' he said.

Christ alive. This was supposed to have been a lovely, romantic evening. I'd flown back from London this morning – I'd been there for ages, since Thursday, since Marnie made an alarmingly mad-in-the-head phone call – and Damien had insisted on cancelling his Monday-night poker game, so we could have some rare time together.

But even though I'd lit my precious Jasmine candle and we'd knocked back a bottle of red, the romance hadn't really kicked in. I was too tired and, as the couch was broken, I was in the only armchair and Damien was bolt upright on a hard kitchen chair.

By mutual unacknowledged consent, we'd eventually given up on conversation and turned on the telly. There was a documentary on about incredibly violent gangs in Brazilian prisons – the sort of thing we usually relished – but neither of us was paying attention to it.

I was thinking about Marnie, how she seemed to be getting worse, how she had started being a bit peculiar even when she was sober. I couldn't shake this awful feeling that things were coming to a head.

Damien too was locked in his thoughts, obviously going

through stuff, analysing, sorting and – it must have been because I was so knackered – instead of peppering him with questions like I usually would, I let him do it in peace.

'Grace, I've to tell you something,' he repeated. It sounded like he'd arrived at some sort of a decision and suddenly I was so frightened.

Was this really happening?

I realized I'd been waiting for this, without even knowing consciously that I had.

When I'd let myself into the house this evening, I'd thought I felt that strange presence again. It was hard to know for certain, because I'd been flat-out looking for it. I'd wandered from room to room, flip-flopping between thinking, Maybe yes, Maybe no. Unable to decide if something, someone, had been here over the weekend. Someone who shouldn't have been.

Now Damien was going to tell me and the *fear*, I can't tell you. I was suddenly drenched in sweat.

'Is it . . .' My voice was croaky and I cleared my throat. 'It's Juno?'

'*What?*' Damien frowned. '*Juno?* No.'

It wasn't Juno?

But then what was it? Who was it?

I wouldn't have thought it was possible to feel any more afraid than I had twenty seconds previously, but there we are. I did.

'I found out by accident . . .' Damien said.

Found out what?

'But now that I know . . .'

Know what?

662

'It's about Dee.'

I was so surprised I couldn't speak for a few moments. 'Dee *Rossini*?'

'Yeah. They're putting a story together at work. Apparently she's been harbouring illegals.'

'Oh –' I knew it was true. I'd seen it myself. But I couldn't find the words. I was still in the fear.

'They're going massive on it,' Damien said. 'If it comes off, she'll never come back from it.'

I stared into his eyes searching for . . . what? A second layer of truths? The stuff he hadn't said?

'That's it?' I said. 'That's all you wanted to tell me?'

'I've taken the risk of my career telling you th – Why? What did you think I was going to say?'

'. . . Nothing . . .'

'Not Juno?' he said in exasperation. 'Not still? Didn't I say that I wouldn't see her?'

'Yes, yes, yes.'

'I don't know why you think I would *ever* get involved with her.'

'I know you love me –'

'Yes, I love you, of course I love you. But even if I didn't, after what Juno did to me?' His voice was high with frustration. 'You know I'd never trust her again.'

He glared at me and I glared at him, then we both began to laugh.

'Do you want to hear this or don't you?' he asked.

'Yes.'

He set it all out for me. His paper, the *Press*, had a source who'd come with a story that Dee Rossini was part of a small, clandestine circle who were helping young women, mostly Moldovans, who had entered Ireland illegally. The women were living as slaves, were beaten, starved and pimped by the men who'd brought them into the country, but obviously they couldn't look for help from the legal system because legally they didn't exist.

'So Dee and her merry band of do-gooders are helping them. The women get access to a doctor, they get new documents, they stay with one of the do-gooders until it's safe.'

'Then they go home?'

That wouldn't be so bad: if Dee was helping illegals to *leave* Ireland.

Damien shook his head. 'They don't send them home because apparently it's just as bad there as it is here. They try to fix them up with live-in employment, as a nanny, that sort of thing. Some of the women they send to the UK. Which will do wonders for Irish–British relations,' he said wearily. 'An Irish government minister facilitating the entry of illegals into Britain. I'm fond of Dee, very fond. She's a true idealist. But sometimes . . .'

'Who's putting the story together?'

'Current affairs. Angus Sprott and Charlie Haslett. It's Code Black.'

'You have codes? You're all so macho in there in the *Press*. So how did you find out?'

'Charlie hacked into my files. I wondered why he couldn't have just asked me for whatever he needed. The obvious conclusion was that he was working on something dodgy.' He shrugged. 'How could I resist?'

'It can't be *that* Code Black, then, if you were able to just hack into the file.'

'His new baby is teething. He isn't getting much sleep. I guess he forgot to secure it.'

'How far advanced are they? When are they planning to run the story?'

'As soon as they've got pictures.'

'And when will that be?'

'The next time one of the women is spirited into Dee's house. Photographers are watching the place twenty-four-seven.'

I was shocked. Dee under constant surveillance? Like a terrorist?

The question that always cropped up whenever Dee was in trouble, cropped up again. 'Who's doing this? Like, any idea who the source is?'

'The source?'

'Right. I know.' The identity of sources was never revealed because then – duh! – they wouldn't be sources any more. 'Keep your knickers on.'

'Yeah, sorry. Anyway, the Chrisps have to be behind it because it'll knock out not just Dee but the entire NewIreland party. There are rumours that a general election will be called soon. Probably in March. Like last time, the Nappies won't win enough seats to form a government on their own. But if NewIreland is in disarray, they won't have a coalition partner – leaving the way clear for the Chrisps.'

'Damien, I've got to tell Dee.'

'Why do you think I told you?'

'But if anyone finds out it came from you . . .'

He'd lose his job.

He paused. 'I've thought about it. Let's take that chance.'

'Damien, you're . . . you're very good.'

'Dee, who knows about it?'

I'd managed to get her early in the morning, before work, in her office in Leinster House, and I made her sit down then I told her what Damien had told me. The blood receded from her beautiful face and she became waxy and immobile. 'How . . . ?'

'That's what I'm asking you. Who knows about it?'

She undid her topknot and ran her fingers through her loose corkscrew hair, then she rounded it all up again, bringing stray springy strands into the fold, and twisted it back onto her head, even tighter than before.

Finally she spoke. 'Only the girls themselves. And a handful of other people. But there're so few of us and we all want the same thing . . .' She suddenly focused on me. 'And *you* know, Grace, but as you're here warning me, I presume it's not you.'

'What about the other people? Damien said there's a doctor? And a person who does documents? Could it be one of them?'

'They've got as much to lose as me.'

'Who could have accidentally found out? Who comes to your house? Have you a boyfriend?'

She shook her head sharply.

'You said that to me before and you did have one.'

'I'm sorry about that but I really don't have one now.'

'Your daughter?'

'She lives in Milan.'

'A cleaner?'

'You've been to my house. Does it look like I've a cleaner?'

'Friends? You have friends over for strange-looking pasta. You had Damien and me.'

She placed her palms flat on her desk. (Again, very attractive nail polish. A type of dull heather shade. As was the case with all Dee's nail varnishes, it was nicer than it sounds.) 'Look, Grace, this is how it works. It's planned. Helping a girl get away isn't easy and the window of opportunity is quite specific. I always have advance notice, usually a few days, when a girl is coming. So I clear the decks. Make sure no one else will be in the house at the same time.'

'But Elena –'

'Elena was an emergency. They don't happen often.'

'The fact is, Dee, that someone knows and someone has told.'

'They're only children, you know,' she said sadly. 'Young girls. You wouldn't believe the appalling things that are done to them. They're raped, starved, beaten, their bones are broken, cigarettes are stubbed out in their vaginas –'

'Stop.'

'I couldn't not help them.'

'Dee, I'm on your side, but you're breaking the law! I'm not saying it's not a cruel law but you're a government minister. If you don't want to lose your job and your career and your political party – and you will if this comes out – you'd better find out who's behind this. And find out quickly because the *Press* are keen to run the story.'

'It's got to be Bangers Brady and his Christian Progressives.'

'That's the obvious conclusion. But *who* in the Christian Progressives?'

'They're a big party. It could be any number of them.'

'No, Dee, you have to focus. Some*one* has it in for you.'

She rolled her eyes. 'Every day of my life I know that lots of someones have it in for me.'

'What I mean is, Dee, you're so used to being pilloried from all quarters that you've forgotten that terrible things don't happen simply because of random forces of evil swilling around in the ether, but that terrible things happen because individual human beings make them happen.'

I thought it was a very good speech actually. I wondered if she was impressed.

She looked like she was fighting back a smile. And this was no smiling matter! Briefly I had a spy-film, betrayal-all-around, no-one-can-be-trusted moment when I wondered if Dee herself was the source. It was like seeing double, but in your brain.

'Dee?'

'Grace, I'm not laughing. I'm very grateful. I'll go through everything I have, I'll talk to the others, I'll find out who's done this.'

'Dee, you need to find out *fast* and get them to stop the story. And in the meantime you can't have anyone – any of the girls – showing up at your house. Once the *Press* have photos, they're running the story.'

*

668

'Morning, morning, morning, morning, morning,' I greeted TC, Lorraine, Clare, Tara and – yes – even Joanne.

'Still freezing out there?' TC was keen to moan about life in general and usually he would find a willing accomplice in me.

'Still freezing,' I replied briskly, scanning the deluge of press releases in my mailbox. Without wasting time wondering if they were good or bad, I picked out five possible stories to pitch to Jacinta whenever she came in, then, watched with extreme suspicion by TC, I began to write names in a random fashion on my jotter: Dee Rossini; Toria Rossini; Bangers Brady; Toria Rossini's husband, whatever his name was; Christopher Holland; Me; Damien; Paddy de Courcy; Sidney Brolly; Angus Sprott; Scott Holmes, the journalist who'd done the horrible piece with Christopher Holland.

Anyone I could think of who had been connected with Dee over the past six months, I scattered their names around the page.

'What are you up to?' TC asked.

'Nothing.' I shielded the page with my arm.

I was doing something that I'd read of detectives in Val McDermid novels doing: they write down everything they know about a case, including all the confusing loose ends, and they look for a pattern or a connection. But maybe it doesn't happen in real life. Maybe real detectives can't break into houses with a credit card either. Maybe real detectives in Hawaii never say, 'Book him, Danno.'

But I didn't know any other way. I bounced my pen off my page. Who else? Dee's ex-husband, of course. As I sightlessly scanned the office, seeking inspiration, David Thornberry unfolded himself from his desk and grabbed his cigarettes. There's another one, I thought, and scribbled his name down. He'd had an exclusive on 'Dee's daughter's unpaid wedding scandal', which Big Daddy hadn't let him go with. While I was about it, I wrote down Coleman Brien's name too.

Then I scribbled a series of questions, scattering them around the page, trying not to overthink them. 'Who painted Dee's house?' 'Where was her daughter's wedding held?' 'Who recommended the hotel?' 'Where did Dee meet Christopher Holland?' 'Who was his previous girlfriend?' 'Who was Dee's previous boyfriend?' 'Who told Dee about the Moldovan girls?' 'Who did the documents for them?' 'Did they know someone in the Chrisps?' 'Did they know Christopher Holland?'

The page was pretty full. Maybe I was going to have to go to the stationery cupboard for a bundle of index cards and write stuff on them, then fling them around the floor to see what story unfolded in the formation they landed in. But maybe real detectives don't do that either.

I stared at the page, dense with writing. Assuming I'd included everything that was relevant – and Christ alone knew whether I had or hadn't – somewhere in there was a connection which should hint at the person or persons who were gunning for Dee.

I drew arrows, connecting names to statements, trying to stay open-minded, trying to let a different energy guide me.

But I don't believe in energy. I don't believe in intuition. I don't believe in hunches.

I'm not that kind of journalist. My skill is in wearing people down, in chipping away at the poor bastards, keeping on and on at them until they eventually crack and give me a quote or a story just to get rid of me.

I studied the results: not encouraging. According to my arrows, Bangers Brady had painted Dee's house, Christopher Holland was his own previous girlfriend and Dee's daughter had married me.

'There's one,' TC said, leaning over and pointing, as if he was helping me to do a sudoku. 'Look, that one there. "Paddy de Courcy" linked to "Who recommended the painters?" That could make sense. It could have been him.'

'Here she is!' Lorraine had spotted Jacinta arriving. 'God, no, it's red today!'

'Red!' Three weeks of black had been very wearing but red would be worse. It presaged rage, raised voices and definitely, definitely no cake.

I folded my page into my pocket and readied myself for Jacinta's fury.

The tail-end of the January sales was what she wanted covered. How low did they go? What happened to the unsold clothing? Destroyed? Returned to the manufacturers? Off-loaded onto TK Maxx? 'Find out about Missoni,' she ordered. 'There's loads left in the Brown Thomas sale, but they're sticking hard at 40 per cent off.'

I couldn't help suspecting that Jacinta had a personal interest in this story.

Traipsing in and out of clothes shops which offered the ragged dregs of Christmas party frocks, I kept thinking about Dee and I kept coming back to her runaway boyfriend,

Christopher Holland. He had, to quote Hercule Poirot, means, motive and opportunity. As he had already shafted Dee way beyond the point where he could ever be forgiven, there was nothing to stop him from shopping her on harbouring illegals. Casey Kaplan had mentioned him having gambling debts and, much as I'd prefer to think that Kaplan was full of shit, maybe Christopher had needed more money.

He'd been in Dee's house a lot; whatever she said about compartmentalizing her life, he could easily have coincided with one of the girls. No life was entirely airtight. I mean, *I* knew about Dee sheltering women, therefore her life was evidently *not* airtight. I was just some stray journalist who happened to turn up on the same day that a badly beaten woman had taken up residence in Dee's bedroom. Luckily I liked Dee. But she might have done another interview that day, some other journalist might have come along and sat in her kitchen and eaten home-made macaroons and then gone upstairs and . . . and . . . what? *What was it?* Something in my head had caused an adrenaline surge. Suddenly alert and thinking with crystal clarity, I stopped dead in the street and a man slammed into the back of me. 'Sorry, sorry,' I exclaimed while he muttered about fecking eejits who have no respect for other people . . .

I stepped out of the pedestrian traffic and backtracked through my recent thoughts, examining each one.

'Some other journalist'? No, it wasn't that.

'Sat in her kitchen'? Not that either.

'Eaten home-made macaroons'? That was the one!

The home-made macaroons. I hadn't eaten any but Dee

had told me that that was okay because Paddy was coming over for a working dinner and he'd eat them.

Assuming that Dee hadn't cancelled on him and assuming that Elena hadn't been moved on before he arrived, Paddy was in Dee's house at the same time as Elena.

If Paddy had known about Elena, what else might he know?

I reached for my phone.

'Dee, remember the day I interviewed you. Paddy de Courcy was coming for dinner that evening. Paddy could have seen Elena. He could have done what I did. You know, opened the bedroom door and seen her. So did he?'

'Why?'

'Will you just tell me?'

After a long silence, she said, 'Maybe. I'm not exactly sure, but maybe.'

The tips of my fingers tingled.

'Dee, you know your painting and decorating scandal?'

She sighed her assent.

'Let me just check some facts.' (I knew all the facts, I was just spelling them out for her.) 'You got your house painted, the company never sent you a bill and when, off your own bat, you eventually sent a cheque it wasn't cashed, so basically you'd had your house painted for free. So who-ever wanted to shaft you must have got to the decorating firm after you'd decided to use them. Or someone was already in cahoots with them and persuaded you to use them. You told me that the painting and decorating firm came recommended. Yes? Well, who recommended them?'

Another long silence.

'Was it Paddy? Paddy de Courcy?'

A sigh. 'Yes.'

'It's him, Dee.'

'It's not him,' Dee said. 'Don't be an idiot. When I'm damaged, the party is damaged and when the party is damaged, so is he.'

'Look, I'm not saying it's a perfect plan.' I noticed that in my excitement I was talking too loud and half of Kenny's were listening in. It would have been better to have had this discussion somewhere private but I didn't want to go to Dee's house in case the hidden photographers mistook me for a Moldovan woman and I didn't want Dee to come to mine in case it would draw attention to Damien.

'Precision bombing,' I whispered. 'To take you out but to keep the integrity of the party intact. That's what he's trying.'

'Precision bombing,' she repeated and shook her head with some derision.

I realized how melodramatic I sounded. 'I'm sorry . . . this isn't *Black Hawk Down*, but I don't know what other way to say it.'

'It's too risky for him,' she said.

'He's a risk-taker.'

'How do you know?'

I shook my head. 'That's a story for another day.' I took a deep breath. 'Dee, I'm sorry, but Paddy de Courcy is not the lovely man you think he is.'

She looked at me in amazement and I regretted having to destroy her illusions, but it was necessary if – as I was kind of convinced – he was the person who was shafting her.

'I never thought Paddy de Courcy was a lovely man,' she said.

'Is that right? Well, good, because –'

'Paddy de Courcy is a ruthless, treacherous, greedy, graspingly ambitious, profoundly unpleasant man. He'd sell his own granny at a car-boot sale if he thought it might buy him a couple of votes and, by hook or by crook, he'll be Ireland's leader one day.'

I was stunned into silence. *Stunned.* Her opinion of him was almost worse than mine. And she had never said. Had never given any indication. Politicians, I tell you!

'So why do you work with him?'

'We all work with people we don't like. It's handy for the party – people who distrust me because I'm a mouthy feminist are reassured by my having a good-looking, charismatic man as my deputy.'

'You admit he wants to be taoiseach?'

'God, yes, he's always had his eye on the prize, but I've never thought he planned to do it via leadership of NewIreland. He's using us because we're small but we punch above our weight. He's a big fish in NewIreland and it's got him noticed, but we're only a stepping stone. His next big move will be to defect to the Nappies and he'll take it from there.'

'Say it again, Dee. ''A ruthless, treacherous . . .'''

' ''A ruthless, treacherous, greedy, graspingly ambitious, profoundly unpleasant man.'''

'And say the part about selling his granny.'

' ''He'd sell his own granny at a car-boot sale if he thought . . .'''

' ". . . it might buy him a couple of votes," ' I prompted.

' ". . . it might buy him a couple of votes," ' she repeated.

Once again astonishment washed over me. 'I thought you were thick as thieves with him.'

'Now you know.'

'And I think you're wrong. I think he does want to be leader of NewIreland. At the very least it would get him a ministerial post.'

'What's Paddy done to you?' she asked suddenly.

'. . . Erm . . .'

'Something, right? Something bad? But Grace, don't try to make the facts fit just to find him guilty.'

Was I doing that?

Was my personal stuff getting in the way of reality? Was I trying to blame Paddy de Courcy for everything? Global warming? The destruction of the rain forests? The attacks on Dee Rossini?

Maybe. I was prepared to admit it was a slight, tiny possibility.

But as soon as I tried to let go of him and slot another person – Christopher Holland, for example – into the box marked 'Guilty' my brain refused to cooperate.

I just needed one more event to link Paddy to the persecution of Dee and we were in business. Who could I ask? There wasn't any point ringing Angus Sprott at the *Press* and asking him if de Courcy was his source. For one thing he'd never tell me and for another I'd be fingering Damien and for yet another there was no way it would be Paddy in person. He'd have gotten Spanish John to pay someone else to pay someone else to do it: a long enough chain of command that it would never come back to him.

'Your daughter's wedding, when so many things went wrong, do you think someone in the hotel could have been paid to cock it all up? To "lose" the wedding cake? To cause chaos in the kitchen so that there weren't enough meals?'

'It's a theory. But there's no way of proving it.'

It mightn't be that hard. I'd need to talk to everyone who worked in the hotel on the day of the wedding. Mind you, it was five months ago, staff turnover in hotels was notoriously high. But worth considering.

'It's not Paddy,' Dee said. 'But it could be Christopher. Really it could be.'

'Okay.' I decided to go with this different tack. (In the Val McDermid novels, the detectives say you must stay open-minded.) 'Why did he sell his story about his relationship with you?'

'The *Globe* paid him lots of money, I presume.'

'You presume? Haven't you asked him?'

She looked at me like I was insane. 'I haven't spoken to him since the story came out. Two days previously actually.'

'Nothing at all? You never got the urge to ring him and shout abuse?'

'No.'

'Or to get answers to some questions?'

'No.'

'Not even some night when you were drunk?'

'I don't get drunk.'

'Don't you?'

'Well, all right then, I do. But why would I bother wasting my good drunkenness on him? He let me down. I knew he would. Men always do.'

'So why did you bother with him at all?'

'Because he had a big dick and could do it three times a night.'

'. . . Er . . . really?'

'Yes, sometimes four.'

Christ alive, but she was fabulous.

'No one – almost no one – knew that you had a boyfriend. How did the *Globe* know that there was even a person to approach and offer money to? Somebody had to have told them. Did Paddy know about Christopher?'

She hesitated. 'Perhaps. There was one time Christopher showed up at my office. I got rid of him sharpish but Paddy asked about him. I said he was a friend of Toria's. I've never been sure he believed me,' she admitted. 'Paddy misses nothing. But I thought we'd moved on from Paddy.'

'So did I.'

There was something that naked curiosity compelled me to ask. 'Casey Kaplan said he knew Christopher. Is that true? Or is he entirely full of shit?'

'It's true.' She laughed at my sour face. 'Christopher and Casey are very close friends, they were at school together. He really does know everybody. He's just one of those people.'

'It could have been Casey Kaplan.'

'It wasn't him.' Dee was scornful. 'He wouldn't have given the story to Scott Holmes, he'd have done it himself. Anyway, it wasn't him because he's a sweetheart.'

'Surely you mean a gobshite?'

'Okay, those ridiculous clothes, the swagger, the rock-star jargon . . . But he's a pet. It's the main reason he's so connected – everyone likes him.'

'I don't.'

'Except you, then.'

'I'm ringing Scott Holmes,' I said. 'He might tell me something.'

'He won't,' Dee said.

'Let's see,' I said, locating my phone and hoping I still had Scott's number.

'Scott? Grace Gildee here.'

'Gracie!' I endured the 'How's tricks' conversation for as long as I could, then I said, 'Scott, I need your help.' (Good thing to say. Act helpless. Gets results quicker. A truly depressing indictment of the state of male/female relations but I'm only telling it like it is.)

'Aw, Gracie, you only call me when you want something.'

'Back in November, you did a big piece with Christopher Holland, Dee Rossini's boyfriend. Remember?'

'Course.'

'The initial contact? Was it Christopher Holland himself? Or was it agented?'

'Aw come on, Grace, that's confidential.'

'Scott, we're not discussing the Good Friday Agreement. Was it Paddy de Courcy?'

'Wha –? Are you crazy?'

'John Crown?'

'De Courcy's driver? No.'

Silence hissed on the line.

'Grace, I'll tell you this much, it was agented, but I never got the name. I never even met them.'

Shite. 'So how were you contacted? Did someone appear to you in a dream?'

He laughed. 'Mobile.'

'Any chance you've still got the number?'

'It's probably been disconnected by now. Usually the account is opened just long enough to set up the deal, then shut down again.'

'Thank you, Scott, I too am a journalist, I understand your nefarious ways. But give it to me anyway.'

'The usual caveats. You didn't get it from me etc., etc. Let me find it.' After a few moments of clicking and rustling, he called out a string of digits.

'Thank you, Scott, you're a decent man.'

'Let's get together some evening,' he said.

'Let's,' I said and quickly disconnected.

It wasn't that I didn't like him but he was into all that hearty New Zealand stuff. The main reason I'd broken it off with him – apart from being in love with Damien – was that he was always making me trek up the side of a mountain in the snow.

'Have you any change?' I asked Dee. 'I need to make a phone call.'

She held her mobile towards me.

'No, I need to use a public phone. We can't leave an electronic trail.'

'*The Bourne Identity* now, is it?'

She produced a fifty-cent piece and I made my way to the

grim alcove that housed Kenny's phone. I punched in the numbers Scott had given me and held my breath as I waited.

I'd expected all kinds of noises – but not a ringing tone. It rang! It rang three times, then it was answered. A man's voice said, 'Ted Sheridan's phone.'

I disconnected immediately.

My hands were shaking.

Ted Sheridan.

Sheridan.

All the proof I needed.

I returned to Dee.

'Was it Paddy?' she asked.

'No.'

'Told you.'

'Come on. We're going for a drive.'

'*The Godfather*? *Goodfellas*?'

While I drove I called Ma. 'I need you to find a photo. From long ago, when Marnie was going out with Paddy de Courcy.'

Dee, sitting next to me in the passenger seat, gave me a sharp look.

'Not of the two of them,' I told Ma. 'I need one of Sheridan. I know there's one knocking around.'

It wouldn't take Ma long to locate it. They thought it pitifully bourgeois to record every family occasion with a fat pile of photos. They didn't even own a camera and the few photos they had of Marnie and me as teenagers had been taken and donated by Leechy.

'What are we doing?' Dee asked.

'Picking up a photo of de Courcy's old friend Ted Sheridan, then we're going to show it to Christopher Holland and ask him if this is the man who persuaded him to do the kiss'n'tell on you.'

'I'm not . . . There's no way I'm talking to Chris –'

'You don't have to talk to him, but you do have to be there. How else will you have proof that de Courcy is behind all this?'

Because it was late the roads were empty and we reached Yeoman Road in ten minutes. I ran into the house and Bingo threw back his head and howled with joy to see me. Ma had found the photo; it was of Marnie, Paddy, Leechy, Sheridan and me, clustered together and laughing.

'Thanks, Ma, you're a superstar. But I can't stay.' I tried to shake Bingo off my leg. 'Get off me, for the love of God!'

'Come on, Bingo,' Ma cajoled.

Finally I broke free of Bingo's passionate hold. Back in the car I handed the photo to Dee. 'Hold this. Now, where does Christopher Holland live?'

She looked like she was going to refuse to tell me, then caved. 'Inchicore.'

She was transfixed by the photograph. 'Paddy looks so young, better now than he did then. And look at you, you're exactly the same! Who are the other people?' She was studying Leechy. 'Is that . . . surely it's not –'

'Who? Show. Oh yeah.'

'I didn't know you knew her.'

'I don't any more. Listen, ring Christopher Holland. Make sure he's at home. Tell him you want to see him.'

'I don't want to see him.'

'Well, *pretend*. We're trying to save your career here, in case you hadn't noticed.'

'What if he won't see me?'

'Say, "You owe me that at least." Shame him into it.'

She produced her phone from her bag, but sat with it resting in her hand, her head bowed.

'Ring him!'

With a marked lack of enthusiasm, she made the call. He must have answered because she said, 'It's Dee.' Then a few more sentences. 'I need to see you.' 'Now.' 'Ten minutes.'

Then she hung up and shuddered.

'Come on,' I coaxed. 'You'll be in his flat. You can break something belonging to him. Something precious.'

Christopher Holland's door opened immediately and he was already knee-deep into his apology. 'Dee, I'm sorry, I –'

Then he noticed me and he stepped back, suddenly wary.

He was *immensely* sexy and knowing what I knew about his large member and his stamina, I *so* would. (Only in theory and if I wasn't with Damien, etc., etc.)

'Grace Gildee, Christopher Holland.' Dee's introductions were terse. We stepped into the hall and I followed Dee into a living room.

'Dee, I shouldn't have done it –' Christopher's prostration was back on track.

With a wave of her hand, Dee dismissed him. 'I'm not here for an apology. I just need to know if you shafted me off your own bat, or if someone persuaded you?'

'Persuasion,' he said, sounding eager to absolve himself of blame. 'As if I'd come up with something like that by myself. Dee, the money was so big. I said no, they came back with more, I said no again, they hiked it again. It was the toughest call of my life – '

'You're breaking my heart,' Dee said. 'Grace, show him the photo.'

I thrust it at him. 'It's old, I know, but do you see your – ' I coughed sarcastically – ' "persuader"?'

It was donkey's years since I'd seen Sheridan. I had to hope he hadn't aged dramatically or had transformative plastic surgery.

Christopher stared. 'Is that Paddy de *Cour*cy?' He laughed. 'No way, man. The state of him! He had a mullet.'

'Never mind him.'

'And is that you?' He looked me up and down. 'You haven't changed much.'

'Would you . . .' I redirected him to the job.

He gazed at the photo sitting in the palm of his hand for so long that I began to sweat.

'Yes?' I encouraged.

'No.' He shook his head. 'Sorry.' He looked genuinely regretful.

'I know it's old but try to imagine seventeen years on.' I was beginning to sound desperate. 'Think different hair, maybe less of it now, more jowly perhaps . . .'

He pulled the photo closer to his face, and tried it with one eye shut, then the other. 'Wow! Yeah, right, I see it now! You've gotta admit she looks *totally* different now, much classier – '

She?

She?

'Who?'

'Her.' He pointed at Leechy. 'Alicia Thornton? Paddy's lady? When she showed up here she had a mad scarf on, trying to change her look, but I knew who she was. Like, from the papers. Isn't that who you're talking about?'

I turned to Dee. The shock on my face was mirrored on hers.

'You mean –' Dee hissed in a most terrifying way at Christopher Holland – 'not only did you tell the entire nation every detail of our sex life, but you neglected to let me know that my closest colleague is out to get me?'

'I –'

'Please don't tell me you thought Alicia Thornton was doing this off her own bat? Please don't let me discover that you're that stupid.'

'I kinda felt . . .' Christopher stammered. 'I'd hurt you so much with the story. I didn't think anything could hurt you more.'

'I see. Stupid, treacherous *and* arrogant. FYI, Christopher, my career means far more to me than you ever did. Come on, Grace.' She swept out.

I whipped the photo out of Christopher's hand, then hurried after Dee, back to the car. We got in but I didn't switch the engine on, I was so overwhelmed I couldn't trust myself to drive safely.

'It's Paddy,' Dee said.

I nodded.

'It's definitely Paddy,' she repeated. She twisted her neck to look at me. 'Isn't it, Grace?'

'. . . Looks like it.'

'Are you okay, Grace?'

'Mmm, yeah.'

But I wasn't. Abruptly I found I was having a major rethink on the wisdom of this entire enterprise. Up until now it had been – almost – like a game; playing girl investigator during a slow week at work. Because of what Paddy had done to me it had been gratifying to pursue further evidence of his badness. But now I had the proof – he was involved in high-risk political games, he really was – and all of a sudden I'd come to my senses. What had I been thinking with my idiotic bravado? I should have stayed well clear. This was real life and I knew what Paddy was capable of.

Sitting in the stationary car, I made a decision: this was where I bowed out. Dee could take it from here. She was the politician, she'd be good at all that Machiavellian stuff. I was just an ordinary Joe Soap. A scared one.

'I'll have to call him on it.' Dee's eyes were narrowed as she visualized the scenario. 'But I need something to bargain with. What have you got on him, Grace? What skeletons are rattling in his cupboard?'

'None. Nothing.'

'What?' She turned in surprise. 'But I thought –? Oh no, Grace. You can't!'

'Dee, I'm not that type of person, journalist . . . whatever. I thought I was but it turns out I'm not. Sorry,' I added.

'You mean you're scared of Paddy?'

'. . . I suppose.'

'But that's good! It means you know something about him. Something that can help me.'

'Yes, but –'

'Whatever he's done to you, don't you want to have your say?'

'No.'

'That's not the Grace I know.'

'It's not the Grace I know either,' I said gloomily. 'It just goes to show.'

'Grace, you're my only hope. My political career depends on you. Without you, I'm sunk.'

I laid my forehead on the steering wheel. 'Don't.'

'And if I'm sunk,' Dee said gently, 'so are thousands of Irish women. Women who live in fear. Women who have no one to speak up for them. Women who have no one to give them a voice, no one to articulate the deepest hopes of their hearts.'

Marnie

Sky News was still her only friend. Even if it did have a tendency to repeat itself, every fifteen minutes or so. Today it was telling her that it was Wednesday, 21 January. (Also some tedium about football transfers, which she tuned out.)

When the phone rang, Marnie regarded it fearfully. Just out of habit. Somewhere along the line, the phone had become a bringer of only bad news and she'd stopped answering it.

The machine kicked in, then she heard Grace.

'Marnie, it's me, Grace, are you there?'

Marnie picked up. 'I'm here.'

'Are you sober?'

'Yes.' But only because she was waiting for the off-licence to open; there wasn't a single drop of vodka left in the house. She didn't know how she'd let that happen.

'Are you really?' Grace sounded anxious. 'This is important.'

'Honestly I am.' Marnie's heart twisted with sorrow; she couldn't blame Grace for being suspicious.

'Okay – right, I've got a favour to ask. Blast from the past. Brace yourself. Paddy de Courcy.' Marnie flinched. She just had to hear his name. Even now.

Grace continued. 'Don't feel any pressure to do this. Don't do anything you don't want. I'm only doing this to help someone else, so you won't be letting me down.'

Marnie was confused. 'You want me to help Paddy?'

'Christ, no! The total opposite.'

'. . . Okay.' So Paddy didn't want her to help him. She felt oddly disappointed.

'He's up to all kinds of political dirty tricks,' Grace said. 'I said I'd try to help the person he's shafting.'

Marnie was startled. This was all very dramatic. Alarmingly so.

'You were what I came up with,' Grace said.

'*Me?*'

'The way he used to . . . hit you and stuff. I think he might have done it to other women too. If I can find some, would you be interested in coming with them? To put pressure on him?'

'*Pressure?*' Marnie heard herself ask. How very, very strange this was. Paddy de Courcy, after all this time. Putting 'pressure' on him?

'If he doesn't back off, you and the others will go to the papers with your stories.'

'The papers!'

'It probably won't come to that. The threat will be enough.'

'Oh. Okay.' She couldn't have her story in the press. '. . . But Grace, what on earth makes you think there are others?'

'One or two things. Not fully checked out yet. I wanted to see if you'd do it, before I did anything else.' After a pause, Grace said, 'You don't have to do this, Marnie. I'm only asking because I promised this person, Dee, that I would. But life hasn't been easy for you lately and maybe this is the last thing –'

'Don't you want me to come?'

'In a way, no, to be quite honest. I'm only asking because I said I would –'

'So you keep saying.' Marnie almost laughed. 'But I'll come.' She was quite definite. The draw to Paddy was still there, even

690

after all these years. God, she was pathetic. But she already knew that.

'You don't think it'll make . . .' Grace hesitated. '. . . *things* worse for you?'

She meant the drinking, Marnie understood.

'You know what, Grace, it might actually help.'

'It might,' Grace agreed, sounding doubtful.

'Putting the past to rest.'

'. . . Mmm, it might . . .' Then Grace's tone changed. Delicately she said, 'The thing is, Marnie, if this happens, you'd have to come to Dublin. You'd have to get a plane.'

Marnie understood the implication: Marnie mightn't be sober enough to manage the journey. Who could blame her for thinking such a thing, Marnie acknowledged sorrowfully.

'It's okay, Grace, I'll be fine, I promise. So when do you want me?'

'If it happens, it'll be soon. The next day or so. And you're sure you want to come?'

'Yes.'

Paddy de Courcy. She hadn't thought about him in a long time. Occasionally, every year or two, his name was mentioned by Ma or Dad or even Bid, but she never indulged herself in bittersweet memories. She only had to hear his name for a barrier to come slicing down, like a guillotine, cutting off all thoughts of the past.

But this morning there was no defence against unwanted memories. They were there, sharp and fresh, and she was plunged back into remembering the dizzying relief she'd felt, when she first met Paddy, that she'd finally found the lost part of herself.

Up to that point she'd lived her life incomplete and skewed

and it was a joyous revelation to discover that he was as hungry and empty as she was. His beloved mother had died and his father was too strange to provide him with love. Paddy was alone and lonely and the tenderness Marnie felt for him was so exquisite, she could hardly endure it.

It was as if they existed on a frequency which only the two of them could hear. Terrible fears and unbearable griefs had always controlled her; she couldn't remember a time when she wasn't at the mercy of powerful tides of emotion. No one else – certainly not Grace with whom she was inevitably compared – endured life with the painful intensity that she did. Even Ma and Dad at times watched her with confusion, as if they didn't know where they'd got her.

It shamed her, her difference. Other people, the lucky ones, seemed to have an internal stop button; a buffer, beyond which their feelings didn't extend.

But Paddy was like her. He experienced life with the same transcendent loves and bottomless despairs. She was no longer a one-off freak.

Their connection was instant and intense and time apart was unendurable. Even if they had spent the entire day together, the first thing they did when they got home was ring each other.

'I just want to crawl inside your skin,' he said. 'I want to pull you into mine and zip us up.'

The first time he took her to his home it was so cold and loveless it broke her heart. It felt like the *Marie Celeste*, a place abandoned; there was nothing to eat and the heat wasn't on. The kitchen was chilly, the table-top sticky, the bins unemptied. It was clearly a place where meals were never cooked, where milk was drunk straight from the carton and jam sandwiches were assembled without plates and eaten standing up, leaning over the sink.

This absence of a loving heart to his home visited Marnie with a terrifying insight – and her insights, particularly the painful ones, were always spot-on – that if his mother hadn't died, Paddy would not have fallen in love with her. He'd been different before the death of his mother, he had told her this, and she knew – even if he didn't – that it had changed him into a person vulnerable enough to need her.

It made her suspect not only that she was taking advantage of him but that she wasn't good enough to have a relationship with a healthy man. Only a broken one would be interested in her because she was broken also, and – most paralysing terror of all – Paddy's brokenness might heal whereas hers was permanent.

She tried to tell Grace, who rolled her eyes and exclaimed, 'You couldn't be happy if your life depended on it, could you? Who cares why he loves you? He just does, okay? Can't you see how lucky you are?'

Humbled, Marnie worked hard to achieve glimpses of her good fortune: Grace was right, the connection Marnie and Paddy had was rare.

They lay in fields and painted the clouds or looked at the stars and planned their future. 'We'll always be together,' Paddy promised. 'Nothing else matters.'

The dark flipside of his love was his jealousy. Even though she swore that she would never stop loving him, he treated every other man in the world as a threat. Not a week went by without him accusing her of flirting with Sheridan, or 'looking' at some other man at a party or not spending enough time with him.

One time, when she made the mistake of saying she thought Nick Cave was sexy, he went mildly berserk, ripping to shreds the magazine pictures that had triggered her remark. For months afterwards he would get up and stalk from the room if the Bad Seeds were playing. His paranoia infected her and – almost to please him – she became as suspicious as he was. Passionate disagreements were routine, practically mandatory. It was like a game, this ritual of dramatic accusations, followed by tearful reunions; their way of demonstrating how much they loved each other.

There were times when she accused him of wanting Grace. Even, at times, Leechy. Leechy wasn't exactly a looker – there was more than a hint of the equine about her features. (Indeed her own father used to say to her, 'Why the long face?' Which Marnie and Grace were horrified by. They used to ask each other, 'Can you believe he said that? Her own *dad*?') But Leechy was sweet and kind, one of life's carers, and began to show up in the aftermath of Paddy's and Marnie's frequent wrangles, to counsel and comfort Paddy. Marnie was actually surprised by Leechy's boldness but when she objected, Leechy urged compassion. 'He was upset. He loves you so much and he has no one else to talk to.'

'He has Sheridan.'

Leechy made a dismissive face. 'Sheridan's a boy.'

From time to time the emotional game-playing spilled over into the physical: a shove here, a slap there, on one over-wrought night, a punch in her face.

When Grace expressed her urgent alarm, Marnie said, 'It's not as bad as it looks. His feelings are so overwhelming that sometimes that's the only way he can express them.'

Even the cigarette burn on her hand was explicable. 'He's putting a permanent mark on me. Like a tattoo. But don't tell Ma,' she added.

He outgrew her, it was that simple. This became obvious only with the benefit of long hindsight. The rot in their three-year relationship could be narrowed down to the last five months, which coincided with his final five months in college, January to May. Viewed objectively it made sense: real life was looming for him; he was no longer the bereaved half-feral boy but a man with his eye on a career as a barrister.

Time to put away his childish things, as Dad might have said.

During that spring, perhaps they had more fights than their already very high average. Perhaps, as Marnie subconsciously felt him slipping away, she became more clingy. And as he desired to be free, his disdain became more overt.

He told her he no longer loved her. But every time they'd had a minor dispute he'd told her he hated her.

This time I mean it, he said. But he'd always said that too.

During his finals in May, she clamped her paranoia down. She couldn't jeopardize his degree. Even though she'd discovered from Sheridan that Leechy had been visiting Paddy at his home, she kept her mouth shut.

But the night after he sat his last exam, she allowed herself to let the pent-up accusations fly. 'What have you and Leechy been doing during her home visits? Having sex?'

It was simply a tried and tested method to extract a declaration of love – one he had introduced her to – and at her core she knew there was no truth to it.

'That's right,' he said.

'No, really, what have you been doing?'

'I just told you.'

She thought he was joking. Any other interpretation was unimaginable.

'It's real, Marnie. I've fucked her every day since I started my exams. It's over, you and me. When will you listen?'

When she understood that it was true, she doubled over

695

and howled like an animal – but still she didn't understand that this was the end. Years later, when she was able to get some sort of perspective, she realized that that wasn't her fault. His sleeping with Leechy was agonizing, but it was part of their pattern to hurt each other because they loved each other so much.

'You said you'd love me for ever.' She was wild-eyed.

'I lied. Look, we were just a college thing.'

No, they weren't. He was the love of her life, the type of love you could wait a hundred lifetimes for.

Thrashing around like an animal caught in a trap, she wondered what she had to do. She was so distraught she thought that sleeping with Paddy's best friend was the next logical step.

Persuading Sheridan wasn't as difficult as she'd expected. But when it was over, he was stricken with instant remorse. 'Don't tell Paddy,' he said.

She looked at him almost with pity. Don't tell Paddy? Why did he think she had slept with him?

'Paddy, ask me where I was last night.'

'I couldn't give a shit.'

'Just ask me.'

'Okay, Marnie.' In a monotone, 'Where were you last night?'

'In bed. With Sheridan.'

She was confident that his jealousy would send him hurtling back to her, more devoted than ever.

'Sheridan?' he asked sharply.

'Yes, I've slept with another man.'

But it transpired that he didn't care that she had slept with someone else; he cared that it was with Sheridan.

'Sheridan?' Paddy's face was contorted with wild emotion.

'He's the only person in the world I trust, and you've . . . *corrupted* him.'

She wasn't surprised when he hit her. She stumbled against the wall, and he punched her again, this time sending her staggering to the floor. But when he kicked her in the stomach, she knew she'd gone too far.

In a frenzy he kicked her in the ribs, in the chest, in the face. She tried to protect her head with her arms but he peeled them off and stamped on her right hand.

'You're a stupid, useless bitch and this is your own fucking fault.' He was panting from exertion as he stood over her, curled in a ball beneath him. 'Say it. You're a stupid, useless bitch and this is your own fucking fault.'

He was pulling his leg back for another kick. No. She didn't think she could take another one and still live. The toe of his boot slammed her stomach against her spine. She retched, retched, retched, retched, nothing but bile left.

'Say it!'

'I'm a stupid, useless bitch,' she whispered, tears streaming down her face. 'And this is my own fault.'

'Own *fucking* fault. Can't you get anything right?'

When she came round in hospital, wired up to instruments, she'd expected Paddy to be sitting by her bed, his head bowed in penance.

But only Grace was present. 'Where's Paddy?' she rasped.

'I don't know.'

Marnie assumed he'd just popped out for a cigarette or to get a drink.

Foreboding lay heavy upon her. It was going to be hard for them to come back from this. He'd have to do something, go for counselling, get professional help, to ensure nothing like this happened ever again.

Then she discovered that Paddy hadn't just popped out for a cigarette. He wasn't at the hospital. He hadn't been there at all.

'Does he know I'm here?' she asked Grace.

'I'm sure he knows you're in hospital,' Grace said. 'That's the only place you could be. Assuming you were still alive.'

Marnie didn't understand. 'Hasn't he phoned?'

'No.'

'*No?*'

He was too ashamed of what he'd done, Marnie realized. She'd have to go to him, but she was physically incapable. The list of her injuries went on for two pages. Grace insisted she read it: a cracked knuckle (from when he'd stamped on her hand); contusions to the liver; bleeding from the spleen; severe bruising to the ribs and clavicle.

A terrible thought occurred to her. 'Grace, do Ma and Dad know?'

'No. I couldn't get hold of them.'

Thank you, God.

Ma and Dad were on holiday in France with Bid.

'Grace, please don't tell them.'

'Are you mad? Of course I'm going to tell them.'

'You can't, you can't! They'd try to stop me being with him.' An even more frightening scenario unfurled. 'You haven't . . . you haven't told the police?'

'. . . No . . . but . . .'

'Grace, no, no, no you can't!' Tears of panic and frustration rushed from her eyes. 'Please, that would be the worst thing ever –'

'But the nurse says he might do it again.'

'He *won't* do it again. Grace, you don't understand. That's just him and me, how we are with each other.'

'But look at you! You're in hospital. He did this.'

'Grace, you couldn't. It would be like turning in a member of the family. Paddy's one of the family!'

'But look at what he's done to you.'

'Grace, I'm begging you, swear to me that you won't tell them. Or Ma and Dad. It'll be okay, it'll be okay, it'll never happen again, I swear to you.'

Eventually she extracted a reluctant commitment but Grace drew the line at helping Marnie from her bed and down the corridor to the phones.

'You have internal bleeding,' she said. 'You're not well enough to stand.'

Marnie waited until Grace had left and, wheeling her drip along the lino, inched painfully to the public phones, but when she got no reply from Paddy's number she was overtaken by a kind of vertigo, like she was about to topple off a high building and just tumble, tumble, tumble, feet then head then feet then head, air whistling past her.

The following day she said, 'Grace, he's not answering the phone. Please will you go to his house?'

'No.'

'Please, Grace, I have to see him.'

'No. I won't tell Ma what he's done, but I'm not going to his house.'

Marnie lasted another twenty-nine hours before the compulsion became irresistible. She pulled the drip from her arm and left the hospital without telling anyone and caught a taxi to Paddy's house. The peculiar father answered the door, seemed shocked by Marnie's bruises and bandages and said in answer to her desperate questions, 'He's gone. Since last Wednesday.'

'Last Wednesday?' Four days!

699

'Packed a bag and off he went.'

'Packed a bag? You saw him? Why didn't you stop him?'

'He's a grown man.'

'Where did he go?'

'I haven't an iota.'

'But you must know!'

'He tells me nothing.'

'I need to look in his room.' She limped up the stairs. It still smelt of him but his clothes and books were gone.

'Grace, should we go to the police?'

'Good idea. He should be arrested.'

'No, I meant a missing persons thing.'

'He's not a missing person. He left. His dad saw him.'

'But where is he?'

'Wherever it is, it can't be far away enough.'

'He could be in London.' Already she was thinking of going there.

'No,' Grace said. 'You can't go after him. He could have killed you. He hasn't even bothered to find out that you're still alive –'

'Because he's scared, that's why he left –'

'No, because he doesn't care.'

'I have to see Sheridan. He'll know.'

But Sheridan either didn't know or wouldn't tell. Marnie was never sure.

Inconceivable though it was that Leechy would know and she wouldn't, she swallowed her pride enough to ask, but Leechy didn't know either. In fact, Leechy had the cheek to look almost as wretched and nervy as Marnie.

Paddy didn't reappear. Days, then weeks passed. All through the summer months Marnie remained on high alert, every cell trembling with tension, desperate for his return.

October was her focus; he'd have to come back then, to start his training at the Bar.

Until then, the agony of summer had to be endured. The sunny weather and long evenings of July and August took an eternity to elapse. Every morning she woke to dazzling mocking brightness; it laid her bare and raw. But she knew that the chill of autumn would eventually arrive. The air would change, the seasons would slip down a gear and Paddy would come back.

He tried to blank her in the street. 'Don't come near me. You disgust me.'

He kept striding while she did her best to keep up with him. 'Paddy, it's okay, I forgive you.'

'For what?'

'For . . . beating me up.'

'That?' He was incredulous. 'That was your fault.'

Was it? But she didn't have time to decide because he was moving so fast and she was so hungry for information. 'Where have you been all summer?'

'New York.'

'Doing what?'

'Having fun.' The way he said it let her know that the fun he'd had had been of a sexual nature.

'Why didn't you tell me where you'd gone?'

He stopped and looked down on her from his great height. 'Because I didn't, and don't, ever want to see you again.'

She had that toppling sensation again, like she'd fallen and was tumbling over and over.

'You'll have to get over him,' Grace said, as if it was as simple as just deciding to change the sheets on a bed.

'If I could, I would.' She'd have happily cut off her arm if she thought it might stop the pain. But she was tiny and powerless against its terrible might.

During the summer months she'd had the expectation that her suffering was finite. Now she understood that her agony could last for all of eternity and nothing would happen to interrupt it.

'Have some self-respect,' Grace urged.

'I'd love some,' she said quietly. 'If I knew where to get it I'd be there like a shot.'

'You just need to decide you have it.'

She shook her head. 'Grace, there is nothing so frightening . . . or humiliating as loving a man who no longer loves you.'

'It happens to everyone.' Grace was defiantly practical.

'I'm not everyone. I'm not normal.'

She was an emotional haemophiliac. She couldn't heal. Every bad thing that had ever been done to her – going right back to her first day at school when she'd been separated from Grace – she carried, each wound as fresh and painful as if it had happened yesterday. She never got over anything.

'And let's face it, Grace, even if I wasn't a fuck-up –' she actually managed to laugh – 'even if I was the most well-balanced, sunny-natured person alive, Paddy de Courcy would take some getting over.'

She passed through the following nine months – her final year in college – like a ghost. She graduated and barely noticed. Time passed. A year. Two years. Three years on and the torment of his absence remained the most important fact of her life. It was as if she was paused, waiting for his return to click her life back on and for forward propulsion to begin again.

Years later, when she looked back at that time she wondered

why she hadn't simply killed herself. But she had been too stunned with pain to have had even that volition.

News reached her that Paddy and Sheridan were sharing a house and it was like a knife in her gut: why had he forgiven Sheridan but not her?

Only one thing mitigated her pain in the smallest way: Paddy wasn't with Leechy.

Through the worst of the post-Paddy times Ma and Dad had been quietly, sensitively supportive. They never pressed for details on the end of the romance, they never asked why Leechy no longer called around. It was Dad who suggested she tried out living in a different city for a while, and Marnie was surprised by how the idea infused her with fresh energy. Her life was so wretched in Dublin that starting again in some other place might clean it up, render it usable. She considered San Francisco then Melbourne, then, beaten back by visa requirements, ran out of steam and thought herself lucky to have got as far as London. Where she also surprised herself by getting a half-decent job as a mortgage broker. But, still reeling from the loss of Paddy, she embarked on one doomed romance after another, lurching from man to man, trying to right herself.

She read self-help books and saw counsellors and listened to subliminal tapes and – trying not to cringe – repeated validations in front of the mirror, in a ragged quest for healing and self-respect. Her wounds were impediments she tried to ignore but, despite her valiant efforts, they thwarted her by revealing themselves to the very people – usually men – she was trying to conceal them from.

After a time Ma and Dad began dropping an occasional mention of Paddy, relating – almost with pride – his political ascent. Clearly they had no idea of the agony it caused her to even hear Paddy's name; they would never have done so if they'd known. They thought – perfectly reasonably – that her relationship with Paddy had happened so long ago that surely she must be over it by now.

At some stage she accepted that she'd be spending her life without Paddy but – she caught a glimpse of it from time to time – a small despicable part of her continued to wait. She visualized it as a room which had been shut up and preserved exactly as it was when he went away and was waiting for the right circumstances for the door to be flung open, the dust-sheets to be snapped off the furniture and the light to flood in.

Grace

I rang Damien. 'Marnie says she'll do it if there are other women.'

I must have sounded as dismal as I felt because he said very gently, 'Grace, you don't have to do this.'

'I gave Dee my word.' She'd guilted me into saying I'd try to put something together; and when I said I'd do something, I did it, even when I didn't want to.

'I shouldn't have told you about the story.' Damien was grim. 'I thought you could just tell Dee. I'd no idea you'd get embroiled in . . . all this. This de Courcy business.'

'Maybe I won't be able to find Lola Daly.'

'Maybe you won't.'

Then I could walk away with a clear conscience.

'Keep me posted,' he said.

'I will.' I hung up, then got to my feet and, with great reluctance, approached Casey Kaplan's desk.

'Casey, you know how you told me who John Crown was and I was so grateful to you?'

'You weren't that grateful.'

'You stole my Madonna story. I was as grateful as I could be. Can you help me again?'

'Try me.'

'I need to find someone. Her name is Lola Daly, she's a stylist.'

'Yep, know her.'

'You know where she is?'

'No.'

Fool.

'Last sighted in Dublin in September,' I said. 'But she's fallen off the edge of the earth. She doesn't answer her mobile, but the number hasn't been disconnected. That's all I have. I know it's not much but could you put the word out among, you know, models and those types, socialites, It girls, see if anyone has been using her?'

Only his eyes moved. He was scanning them over my face in a searching way that I was meant to find disconcertingly sexy. He nodded slowly. 'Okay.'

'For real?' Could he actually find her? Or was he full of shit? I was depending on the full-of-shit option.

'Might take time.' He lounged back into his chair. 'The difficult we can manage. The impossible could take a bit longer.'

I returned to my desk and picked up the phone, then put it down again when I saw Casey approaching.

'What?' I said impatiently. 'I can't give you any more information. I've told you everything I know.'

He dropped a piece of paper on my desk. 'She's in County Clare. A backwater called Knockavoy.'

Ten full horror-struck seconds elapsed before I could speak. '*You know already?*'

'Got it in one. First call I made. Some days you get lucky,' he added modestly. 'I met SarahJane Hutchinson last night. She was looking hot. Mentioned she was being styled from

County Clare these days. Seemed sorta likely it was by our girl.'

I couldn't speak.

'Happy?' Kaplan prompted.

'Thrilled,' I said faintly.

I'd thought Lola Daly would be impossible to locate. In my worst imaginings I hadn't thought that she'd be found with just one phone call.

I was seized with desperate frustration. Bloody Casey Knows-Everybody Kaplan. *Why* had Big Daddy decided we needed to be sexed up? *Why* had he hired Casey Kaplan? *Why* had my path ever crossed his? Look at the disaster he had wrought on me! I'd have to drive to County Clare. And Christ alone knew what other terrible shite was poised to rain down on me.

I laid my forehead on my desk for a brief soothing moment then, pushing against my palms as leverage, lifted it again. My skull was very heavy.

'What's up?' Kaplan asked.

'How long – ?' My voice was faint and croaky, so I started again. 'How long would it take me to drive to, what's the name of the place? Knockavoy?'

'Dunno,' Kaplan said. 'Only time I went to Clare was by helicopter.'

I mentioned a vague memory of driving there some bank holiday weekend; it had taken seven hours.

'Oh God, no,' Lorraine piped up. 'It won't take anything like that. Not since they've opened the Kildare bypass.'

'The Kildare bypass is great,' Tara said.

'A godsend,' Clare agreed.

'I don't know if it makes that much difference,' Joanne remarked.

'TC?' I asked. It was odd that TC – i.e. a man – hadn't weighed in with his opinion of how long a journey would take, boring us all to death with detailed discussions of possible routes, roads, etc.

He wasn't listening. He was humming to himself as he aligned handfuls of printouts, knocking them against his desk and punching them with neat holes. He was full of industry, focused on some task that was absorbing all his focus.

'Leave him,' Lorraine said. 'He's getting ready for his big profile on Friday. You'll get no sense out of him.'

'Nothing new there,' I said, but he didn't rise to even that.

TC began putting his pages into a beautiful red binder.

'Where d'you get that lovely folder?' I asked, seizing on the diversion. 'I've never seen one like that in the stationery press.'

'Correct,' he said brightly. 'You wouldn't have. Bought it myself. With my own money.'

He smoothed his hand lovingly over the soft red cover and I asked him, 'Who're you interviewing? That you're going to all this trouble for?'

'The most beautiful girl in the world.' He smiled dreamily.

'And she is?'

'Zara Kaletsky.'

He continued to hum and stroke his red folder. Lorraine was right: I'd get no sense out of him today. I stared in his direction for a few more seconds, unwilling to accept that I hadn't been able to annoy him, but he was impermeable.

Deflated, I turned away from him and was plunged back into torment. I stared blindly at my screen. I had a full day's work to do. Even if I could summon the requisite will, how was I going to find time to go to the west of Ireland? I could leave after work but, despite this much-praised Kildare bypass, the journey would take four hours. An eight-hour round trip, and once I got there, God alone knew how long it would take to persuade Lola Daly to spill the beans. Assuming there were beans to be spilled. Assuming she was even there.

I needed biscuits. Something to fortify me against the forthcoming ordeal. I made my way to the tiny office kitchen, but there was nothing to be had in the whole bloody place. 'Vultures,' I muttered to myself. 'Pigs. Gluttons.' I pulled open a drawer and spoons rattled indignantly, like I'd woken them from a sleep. Another drawer contained nothing but digestive dust, proof that biscuits had once lived there but were long gone. In the entire kitchen there wasn't even one meek little marietta. I'd have to go to the shop. I turned and Casey was behind me.

'I don't mean to brag,' he said.

'So it's more like a twitch, then, is it? Or Tourette's?'

'What?'

'You've no control over it?'

He closed his eyes, took a broken breath and said, staring at the wall behind me, 'I don't know why I fucking bother.'

'Fucking bother what?'

'I was going to say, I have a friend . . . with a chopper . . . says I can use it whenever I want . . .'

A chopper? For a moment I thought he meant a bike, the ones with the handlebars. 'Do you mean a *heli*copter?'

'Yeah.'

'Yes,' I said. 'Yes, that would be a big help.' Then I remembered to add, 'Thank you.'

Lola

Wednesday, 21 January 12.15

Getting organized. Everything coming together. Final Nkechi shakedown had left me with thirteen clients. Not many, but they were good ones. Even though needed many more ladies, had actually jettisoned some of the more unpleasant and insane ones, sending them Nkechi's way. Just didn't have the patience any more.

Would be returning to simpler, cleaner life in Dublin than one had left behind. Yes, would also be poorer. But would eventually get more work.

Biggest worry about returning to Dublin was reason had left in first place – Paddy de Courcy. How would I behave when ran into him? And was bound to, Dublin being Dublin. Would there be repeat of the almost-public puking incident? Would I accidentally destroy clothing on shoots?

No way of knowing.

12.33

Helicopter wack-wack-wacked past window, on its way to golf course. No big deal. Choppers always landing on golf course, delivering fat, visor-wearing, rawl-rawl-rawl men for their eighteen holes. Like Vietnam round here.

But seven to ten minutes later, sudden fearful instinct – cannot describe it as anything other than that – made me leap up, rush to front door, wrench it open and glance out. Horrors! Striding up road, unmistakable figure of Grace

711

Gildee. Purposeful. On unbroken trajectory for Uncle Tom's cabin. She had me in her sights.

Why she arriving at Knockavoy in a helicopter?

The day darkened, like sky had filled up with purple-grey thunderclouds. All light was snuffed out and I was filled with dread.

Then she saw me, frozen with sick anxiety in the doorway, and gave big cheery wave, as if we were best of friends.

Not loving her look. Careless hair. Nice honey colour but messy. Could have been from rotors of chopper, but suspected not. Suspected it always that way. Wearing jeans, flat boots, satchel and khaki anorak (perhaps in keeping with Vietnam theme). I could do a lot with her.

Now she was striding up the boreen, great big smile across her fizzog.

'Lola,' she said, extending hand. 'Grace Gildee. Pleasure to see you again.'

'What you want?' Words emerged hoarse and broken.

'To talk.'

'About Paddy?'

'Can I come in?'

Powerless, I let her.

12.47

'I know you're afraid of Paddy.'

'Not. Just because don't want to do a kiss and tell.' Pitiful attempt at defiance.

'How often did he hit you?'

'Hit me?'

'I know he hit you because he hits all his girlfriends.'

'Please go away.'

'He beat my sister Marnie to a pulp.'

'Please go away.'

'Alicia Thornton is no doubt black and blue under those Armani suits.'

'Louise Kennedy. Please go away.'

'You think you're special because he hit you, that he cared so much about you, but you're wrong.'

She was wrong. Didn't think was special. Not any more. Maybe once upon a time had been stupid enough to think that because he hurt me, it indicated strong passion for me.

'Did he do the cigarette thing to you?' she asked. 'Stub one out on your hand?'

Couldn't hide shock. Was – well – amazed that she knew.

Opened mouth to deny it but could only manage, '– Ah –'

She grabbed my right hand. There it was, right in the middle of my palm, a small, pink circle, skin shiny and peculiar.

She gazed at it, her face so radiant and amazed that I wondered about her earlier confidence, when she informed me with such conviction that she knew Paddy hit me. Suspected she'd only been guessing. But it had paid off. Audacious.

'Seems to be his trademark,' she said. 'A form of branding.'

'You're lying.' (Stupid thing to say when so obviously wasn't true, but was desperate for none of this to be real.)

'Not lying! How would I know about it?'

Was silent for long time. Head awhirl. Had thought I was the only one. In the whole world.

'You swear it's happened to others?'

'Swear.'

'Not committing to anything, Grace Gildee, but what you want from me?'

'Come with some of the other women and have it out with him.'

'Why?'

'Because he's stitching up Dee Rossini and he needs to be stopped. Dee Rossini leader of NewIreland.'

'Know who she is.' Irritable. She take me for a total know-nothing?

'Will threaten to take story to press if he doesn't back off.'

'But what's Dee Rossini to me?'

'Nothing, I guess, except good decent woman who wants best for people. But might make you feel better to have it out with Paddy.'

'How many women are there?'

'Three, at least.'

Thought about coming face to face with him – actual, real, live Paddy de Courcy – and was gripped by fear so dark and paralysing, made me want to whimper. Once read about a man who'd been locked in a van with three hungry pit-bulls. Possibility of being in a room with Paddy filled me with same kind of terror.

Ashamed to admit it. 'I'm scared of him.'

'All the more reason to have it out with him.'

Easy for her to say. She didn't even wear lipgloss. She was obviously fearless.

'No, you don't understand,' I whispered. 'Am so so scared of him it makes me want to ... to ... Am shaking even thinking about it. Good luck with it. But you must go now.' Needed to get her out of my house before I imploded.

'In order for evil to succeed,' she said, 'all that is necessary is for good people to do nothing.'

'Yes, of course, quite so, good luck.' Standing up, moving to door, hoping she'd follow.

She stared into my eyes. 'There is nothing to fear but fear itself.'

714

I stared back into hers. 'But fear very frightening. Goodbye.'

Trip down memory lane

Night of appalling, interminable dinner party at Treese and Vincent's was first time. After we finally managed to make our escape, we drove away from house in tense silence. Spanish John on night off and often wondered if it would have happened if he'd been there. Conclusion – maybe it would have. He had to know what Paddy was like.

Quiet road. Paddy pulled the car over. I – idiotically – thought he was stopping for snog. He turned to me, held my shoulder with one hand, then punched me in the face with the other. Quick and efficient. 'Don't ever do that to me again,' he said.

Pain was bad. Shock was worse. Almost vomited. But, in way, didn't blame him. Was horrible night, horrible. Wouldn't have subjected worst enemy to it.

Then, almost straight away, he was lovely. 'Let's get you home and cleaned up.' Gave me hanky to soak up stream of blood from nose. In his flat, he located well-stocked First Aid box, tenderly wiped away my blood, applied antiseptic to burst lip. 'This is going to hurt.'

'You should have said that before you punched me,' I said.

He was stricken. 'I'm sorry, Lola. I'm so sorry. Don't know what came over me. Just stress, such stressy job, night out, wanted to relax, that wanker Vincent goading me, I just snapped.' Put palms of his hands on his cheeks and pulled face downwards. Groaned. 'God Almighty. I can't believe I hit you, my lovely Lola, my little flower. God, how could I? I'm an animal, a fucking animal.' Getting progressively more worked up. Looked at me with desperate eyes. 'Please forgive

715

me, Lola, I'm begging you. I swear to you it'll never happen again. On my mother's memory, it'll never happen again. Can you forgive me?'

Of course I forgave him. Everyone entitled to make one mistake. He was so distraught I thought, God, he really loves me.

No kinky sex that night. Fell asleep in each other's arms. Well, he fell asleep. I was awake most of night because every snuffly breath I took through my punched nose felt like inhaling razors.

Next day, he sent two hundred white roses to my flat. Didn't have enough vases to house them all. Had to use saucepans, wastepaper bin, empty wine bottles. Like the evacuation of Dunkirk.

The next time was different. He opened his front door to let me into his flat and suddenly I was tumbling against the walls, crashing into the cupboard in the hall and cracking my skull against the hardwood floor. Actually saw stars, a big burst inside my head, like fireworks.

Lay on floor for a time, stunned and incapable, Paddy standing above me, breathing like a bull. The cupboard had toppled over and everything – books, keys, all kinds of stuff – had spilled out of it.

Paddy helped me up – my head was ringing like church bells on a wedding day – and led me through cupboard debris into living room. Began shouting, 'Lola, don't fucking interfere with my SkyPlus settings.'

'What?' Hardly knew where I was. 'Didn't.'

'You did. Had it set to record me on *PrimeTime* and you cancelled it.'

'Paddy, didn't touch it.' Something was dripping down the side of my face. Blood. Must have cut myself. 'Why would I?'

'Jealousy. You resent time I have to devote to work.'

Was true, as it happened, but hadn't touched his SkyPlus. Held my sleeve against my cheek to soak up blood. Bones hurting. Especially shoulder. 'Maybe you forgot to set it, Paddy.'

'Forgot! Is important! How would I forget?' Very, very angry.

'You pushed me!' I said, sort of just realizing what had happened.

'I what? You fell! Christ, this is all I need. You fuck up my recording, then start accusing me of stuff! You fell! Okay? You fell!'

Unexpectedly the downstairs doorbell rang. 'Who the fuck's that?' Paddy demanded. Out into the hall, quick conversation on the intercom, then he was back in the room, more enraged than I had ever before seen him. 'It's the police.'

The police!

'You fucking stay in here,' he hissed.

Next thing he was out in the hall, opening the door. 'Hello, officers, what can I do for you?' Nice as pie.

Deep pompous-bogger voice said, 'Neighbours reported a disturbance.'

'What neighbours?'

'Anonymous call. May we come in?'

Thought Paddy would get rid of them. Charming, persuasive, good at that sort of thing. So couldn't believe it when two peelers sidled into the room. A man and a woman. Uniforms, fluorescence, terrible, terrible shoes.

They looked at me. 'You like to tell us what's going on?'

The woman was kindly. 'What's your name? Lola? What happened to your face, Lola?'

717

Paddy loomed behind them and said, 'Officers, can my friend and I have a moment alone?'

The two peelers gave each other a look.

'Please,' Paddy said, with air of great authority.

The two peelers gave each other another look. Female peeler shook her head softly but male peeler said, 'Okay, one minute only.' Female peeler glared at male peeler, then she sighed and they backed out from room.

Through rigid jaw and with eyes alight with fury, Paddy said, 'Now look at what you've done.'

'I didn't do anything.'

'You have any idea how serious this is? You say a single word to either of them and I'll be arrested.'

Arrested!

'I'll be up in court. It'll be all over the papers. I'll be sent to prison.'

Prison! *Prison!* I couldn't send him to prison. This was the man I loved.

But he had pushed me . . .

If it hadn't happened to me, if it had happened to some woman and I'd heard her on the radio or whatever, I would have thought, Why didn't she tell the peelers? Why did she just let her boyfriend hit her a clatter whenever he felt like it?

But when you're in the middle of it, there's a world of difference. I loved Paddy.

Sometimes – often, yes, often, in fact nearly always – he was lovely to me and the idea of me getting him arrested was . . . actually . . . inconceivable. Like him being abducted by aliens. People like me did not get our boyfriends arrested. It was so far outside what was normal in my life that I simply couldn't imagine it.

Up to me to convince him to stop. Not to involve *the police*.

Paddy stepped forward, picked up my hand and kissed it. Laid his forehead on it and whispered, 'I'm so sorry.'

'I won't say anything,' I said. 'But you must promise you will never do this to me again.'

Kissed my hand again. 'I promise,' he said hoarsely. 'I promise, I promise. I'm so, so sorry. This job so stressful. Little Lola, you don't deserve this. Will never, ever do it again, I swear on all I hold dear, if you'll only forgive me. I couldn't bear to lose you.'

'On your last chance, Paddy,' I said. 'Touch me again and I'm gone.'

The peelers were permitted to re-enter the room and Paddy gave them a smooth story about me up on a chair, trying to reach something on top shelf of hall cupboard, when I slipped, fell off and landed on my face, bringing cupboard down with me.

They knew we were lying. Male peeler cheery enough. 'We'll leave yiz to it, so.' But woman peeler concerned. Kindly eyes. Reluctant to go.

Next day several hundred more flowers arrived at my flat. Neighbours complaining of smell.

Was adamant in own head that would break it off with Paddy if he did another violent thing to me, but next time was when was sick with flu and he'd insisted on having sex. Because I was always game for kinkiness, decided wasn't his fault for thinking not even a bout of flu would put me off.

The time after that – the cigarette incident – was even more confusing. Of all the things that happened while I was with Paddy, that was the one that made me most doubt my sanity. How could anyone mistake a human hand for an ashtray? How likely was it? But he was so insistent that it was an accident that I half believed him.

Next time, however, there was no doubt. I was waiting in his apartment for him to finish session in Dail. When heard his key in door, I just knew I was for it. 'Where are you?' he shouted, striding through flat. Found me in the bedroom, pulled me out of bed and threw me against the wall. I slid to the ground and he kicked me in my stomach. I vomited from force of it.

Discovered later that a bill proposed by NewIreland had been defeated in Dail. Hadn't been aware that they were putting it forward. Should have known. My duty to know. This time no flowers. Next time no flowers either.

Worried and worried and worried about situation. Contemplated talking to someone, Bridie, perhaps. But – mad, I know – felt disloyal telling someone else about Paddy. Needed to protect him. He was complex man with abnormally stressful job.

Bridie would insist I broke up with him and I wasn't ready for that. Everything simple in Bridie World – man hits you, you walk. But situation was complicated. I loved him and he loved me. Surely we could address the issues, try to fix them?

I had to take some responsibility for what was happening – takes two to tango. Needed to be more supportive of his work. Yes, it bored me, but was my duty to help him.

Also was ashamed, so deeply ashamed of being hit and of staying with him, that the words wouldn't let themselves be said.

Then everything was lovely again. Relief, relief, oh merciful relief. Paddy adoring, tender, smiling. Sex, dinners, presents, weekend in Cannes, shopping, more presents, all of them kinky, champagne, sex. With Russian prostitute, admittedly. Threesome. Back home to Ireland. All well. NewIreland lost by-election. No one got hit. Everything back on track. We'd lost our way briefly, but was all in the past. Moving on, no need to tell anyone anything. Was elated.

One night we were having sex. Paddy was groaning, moving me up and down on him. Suddenly he stopped. He was looking at the point of contact. 'You have your period?'

Hadn't known. It had come early. And so what?

'Dirty bitch.' He punched me in my throat. Couldn't breathe for so long, I blacked out and it hurt to swallow for a full two weeks afterwards.

He was right, though – it was gross.

That incident was first in new phase when he began hurting me again, more frequently than in past. No longer considered leaving him or confiding in Bridie or Treese. I had changed. My indignation had died and the time when I was strong enough to leave him had passed.

Was desperate to return to early days when he was besotted with me, when I could do no wrong. The occasions when he'd been loving and tender had greatly outnumbered the bad ones – but I couldn't find the way back.

Worked harder to be sexier, to anticipate his moods, his needs, to be more informed about politics, to be constantly available for him, day or night.

Was so anxious about keeping him happy that had no emotion left over to love anyone else. I forgot about Bridie, Treese and Jem, they were just drains on my time.

Tried to control everything in the whole world so that nothing would annoy him. But anything could spark his fury – a red traffic light, a fishbone in his dinner, me forgetting to remind him to do something that I'd known nothing about.

Then it all came to an abrupt end – the news broke that Paddy was getting married to another woman and would have no further use for me. Should have been happy to be free of him. But wasn't. With him I felt worthless. But without him, felt so shamed, thought would never recover.

18.11
Text from Considine.

> **U come for dinner b4 Law & Order?**
> **My place 8.30?**

20.39
Considine's kitchen eating wholesome-style stew
Final Considine mystery laid to rest. The goggles and shower cap? For when he is cooking. Goggles to protect eyes from tearing up when he is chopping onions. Shower cap to stop strong cooking smells pervading his hair. (Thought, but didn't say, If you are so concerned about your hair, Considine, why you not comb it once in a while? But, like said, didn't articulate it, as he had done kindly act of cooking me dinner.)

'Delicious stew, Considine.'

'Good.' Man of few words.

'I had visitor today,' I said.

He looked up. I realized something in my delivery had sounded like coy way of saying had got my period. Very quickly said, 'A journalist came to see me.'

'About what?'

'She wanted . . . She said . . . You know the boyfriend I told you, I mean Chloe, about? Well, she says I was not only one he . . . you know . . . hurt. She wanted me to go to Dublin with other women to . . . talk . . . to him.'

'That is excellent!'

'No, that is terrible!'

'Why?'

'Because am afraid of him.'

'But you won't be alone with him, will you? There will be other women there.'

Long pause. 'You think I should go?'

'Think you should definitely go!'

'But what if it's awful?'

'What is worst thing that could happen?'

Sifted through feelings. Very worst thing? That he would hit me? No. That he would make me love him again? No. That he would leave me convulsed with longing? No. 'That he would mock me.'

'Is that so bad?'

Yes. Really was. 'He made me feel so . . . worthless. I was . . . nothing. Useless, without any importance . . . I don't feel like that now. Not saying am swaggering around thinking am fantastic but . . . don't want to revert to clueless, helpless, worthless person I was when going out with him and when he dumped me.'

'Would it help if you had company? If I drove you?'

Kindly, kindly offer. Who would have thought it, of cranky-arse Considine?

'You know what I wish?' I said. 'Wish Chloe could come with me.'

Thoughtful silence, then he said, 'If that is what it takes to make you go, Chloe will come with you.'

'No,' I said. 'Am being silly. Forget I said it. But will you tell me why Chloe is out of commission at moment? Had thought Gillian had put her foot down, but not that, is it?'

'No, nothing to do with Gillian. Just doesn't feel right.

Has happened in past. At times, very comfortable with Chloe. Other times . . . can't believe am grown man dressing up in ladies' clothing. Fair enough sentiment, no?'

'Nothing wrong with grown man dressing up in ladies' clothing.' Stout defence. 'But think I understand. Your offer very kindly.'

'Because think you should go to Dublin. Is good opportunity. Other women there. Nothing to be scared of. If you don't take this chance, you will be creeping around, afraid of bumping into him. Not good to be always looking over shoulder. Better to just deal with stuff.'

Men. So practical!

Found I was reconsidering bald refusal to go to Dublin. Considine's generosity had surprised me into reopening negotiations in head. If he was prepared to dress up in ladies' clothing even though had knocked it off, then he must really believe I needed to see Paddy.

'Okay,' I said slowly. 'Hear what you're saying. No offence, but I need second opinion.'

Who could I ask? Bridie? Treese? Jem?

No. None of them knew how bad things had got with Paddy. Would involve too much explaining. Would take too long. Would have to spend too much time agreeing that Paddy de Courcy was mad bastard. Would lose sight of objective.

'My mum,' I said. 'She is dead.' Even after all these years it choked me to say it. 'Would normally go to graveyard to ask her opinion, but would take too much time.'

'I see.' Considine handling news of consultation with dead mother with aplomb. 'So you need to get a sign from her, yes?'

'Yes.' Impressive deductive powers, Considine.

724

'How about . . . ? Let's see. Toss a coin?' he suggested. He produced euro from his pocket. 'Heads your mum says yes? Tails your mum says no?'

Marvellous idea. 'But give me a moment.' I walked towards darkened window at back of house, stared out towards foamy sea and asked, *Mum, tell me what I should do.*

I turned around to face the room. Considine had moved away, close to the front door, giving impression of maintaining respectful distance. 'Go,' I said.

'Go?'

'Yes. Do it.'

He flicked euro coin upwards, where it winked and twinkled in the air, then came back down again, to land on back of Considine's hand. He slapped his palm over it.

I was holding my breath.

'Well?' I asked.

He removed hand. 'Heads,' he said.

Heads. I exhaled.

'Okay, looks like I'm going to Dublin. Thanks for your offer but will go alone. Must leave right now, though, before courage deserts. No *Law and Order* for me tonight.'

20.59

Considine walked me to my car, wishing me Godspeed.

He had made me coffee in non-tartan flask. Kindly. Also tasteful.

'Good luck,' he said. 'Kick your man's arse, he deserves it. Drive carefully.'

I stood by car, the door open, but not getting in. Our goodbye felt incomplete.

'Text me,' he said.

'Okay. Bye, Considine. Go home, it's freezing.'

He walked away, then stopped and turned back. 'Hold on a minute.' He approached like he had spotted something about me – lint on my collar, perhaps, or ball of fluff in my eyebrow – and wanted to help remove it.

I waited and he stepped into my space. He put his hand on my neck.

'Is it piece of thread?' I asked.

'What?' He frowned. His forehead very close, so could see it all, where skin stopped and dark hairline abruptly began.

'Dead leaf in hair?'

'What? No.' Perhaps further frowning but couldn't bloody see because he was so close, had double vision. 'Want to show you something.'

Without further ado – really in quite brisk business-like manner – he bent his head and put his mouth on mine. So warm in the cold night.

So that's what had been waiting for! Revelation – Rossa Considine exceptional kisser. Slow and sweet and sexy. Kissing with whole mouth, not just doing hard, tongue-darty sword-play that many people think is good kissing. Felt quite swoony in my head and knees went weak and – wait a minute! Déjà vu! Had been kissed like this before. Only the last time it had stopped just as had really been getting going and this time it went on and on, becoming more gorgeous, more beautiful, my body tingling and alive and . . .

Finally broke apart, Considine almost staggering. 'Go,' he said, in thick, growly voice. Sexy. 'For Christ's sake, go.'

'You kiss just like Chloe!'

He laughed, backed across the grass towards his house (showing exceptional balance on uneven ground). 'Hurry back, Lola. But drive carefully.'

22.12

Just past Matt the Thrashers

Rang Grace Gildee from car. (Yes, know it's illegal.)

'Is Lola Daly here. Will go with you to Paddy on one condition.'

'Which is?'

'You let me style you.'

'Style me?'

'Not for always! Just once.' What she think I am? Charity worker?

'You mean gussy me up in heels and stuff?'

'Correct.'

'. . . And frock . . . ?'

'And frock.'

'. . . But . . . why?'

Because it was a shocking waste, potentially attractive woman like her. 'Hope you don't mind me saying,' I said, 'but you don't make most of yourself.'

She gave little laugh. Couldn't care less that she didn't make most of self. Simply *couldn't care less!* Takes all sorts, as Mum used to say.

'Okay. When you come to Dublin?'

'Am on my way.'

Grace

'Is that her?' Marnie had spotted the woman waiting on the pavement.

'That's her.' I pulled the car over to the kerb. 'Lola, it's me, Grace. Hop in.'

Lola climbed into the back seat. Nervously she said, 'You said there would be at least three women.'

'There will be,' I said. 'Marnie, Lola, Lola, Marnie.'

'Hi,' Lola said quietly.

'Hi.' Marnie twisted right round to face Lola and suddenly I started to worry.

Well, I say that. As it happened, all day I'd been climbing the walls with a variety of worries, not least the fear that Marnie would turn up scuttered. However, she was sober – but was it my imagination or was she just a little *too* interested in Lola?

Jesus. What Pandora's box might I have opened?

I said, 'We've just got to swing by and pick up Dee.'

'Did he hit Dee too?' Lola sounded horrified.

'No, no, she's coming along to get us into his apartment. But she won't be coming in with us.' Dee and I had had an exhaustive discussion about which would be the best tactic and – reluctantly – she'd agreed that it would be better if she stayed out. Things had the potential to get messy, and if she was there it could exacerbate the situation.

'Grace.' Lola's little voice came from the back. 'There will be at least three women, yes? Because I don't want to do it if it's just me and Marnie. I'm too scared.'

'Lola, I need you to trust me.' I made my voice sound reassuring, even slightly amused. I couldn't have her losing her bloody nerve now!

I drew up outside Dee's office and texted her, letting her know that we were waiting. A few moments later she appeared and climbed into the back seat beside Lola. She was nothing like her usual breezy, positive self. She had been devastated when, sitting in my car outside Christopher Holland's house, I'd told her what I'd known about Paddy. She'd been so appalled that she hadn't been able to catch her breath.

'Oh my God,' she'd gasped, rocking backwards and forwards. It had been as if she was crying, but without tears. 'Oh my God. I knew Paddy was a . . . a, like I *knew* he had no loyalty to anyone but himself and I knew he was off his head with ambition . . . but I thought I could just about stomach it because he's so popular with the voters.' She'd heaved in a ragged breath. 'The price you have to pay. But . . . I mean, Grace, *I* was a battered wife. And I had no clue about Paddy.'

She'd bowed her head again and heaved air through her hands. 'My deputy leader is a woman-batterer. Me, and all I stand for. How on earth did I end up in bed with one of them?'

She'd looked up at me, her face red, her eyes bulging. 'I have no time for pop-psychology,' she'd said fiercely, 'no time at all.'

'Me either.'

'But they say we replicate patterns. Am I replicating a pattern? Am I drawn to violent men? Do I recognize something in them?'

'Christ, Dee, I wouldn't have a clue . . .'

She'd fallen silent. Eventually she'd said, 'What am I going to do? There's a saying that a tragedy isn't a choice between right and wrong, it's a choice between two rights.' Yes, I knew it. Ma produced it fairly regularly. Usually when she was trying to decide what to make for dinner. 'But,' Dee had gone on, 'this is a choice between two wrongs.'

'How so?'

'If I do nothing, Angus Sprott will publish his story, my career will be over – then I can't help anyone. But if I shop Paddy to the press, I'll be taken down with him – then I can't help anyone. But if I sack him without making the reasons public, the voters will lose confidence and won't vote for us in the general election – then I can't help anyone. Or if I can persuade him to stop sabotaging me and we carry on working together, it means I'm knowingly sharing power with a woman-batterer.'

'That's four wrongs actually,' I'd pointed out.

'Well, there you are. That's how big a tragedy it is.'

She'd leant back against her head rest and closed her eyes. I could nearly hear her brain clicking, as she did various calibrations, weighing up one unpalatable scenario against another.

'Politics is a filthy business,' she'd murmured. 'I only ever wanted to help people. But even if you think you're incorruptible, even if you think your motives are entirely pure, you end up . . . sullied.'

She'd opened her eyes and sat up straight, seemingly infused with new energy. 'I'm not a do-nothing sort of person, Grace.'

I had begun to feel uneasy. I was going to come out of this badly, I just *knew*.

'What is the least-bad choice here?' She'd looked at me. I'd looked back at her. There had been fresh purpose in her eyes. She had started to scare me then. 'The least-bad choice is that I put my personal qualms to one side and do a deal with Paddy.'

'And that deal is . . . ?'

'If he lays off the smear campaign, the women won't go public with their stories.'

'But you'll have to persuade the women to be in on this.'

She'd looked at me, surprised. 'Not me. You. You'll persuade them.'

Bollocks. Oh bollocks, bollocks . . .

'But you know them, Grace! Your sister. That stylist . . .'

'I'll try. But I *can't* promise, Dee.'

'But you'll try your very best? You swear to me?'

Oh for fuck's sake. '. . . Yes.'

Once she'd extracted a solemn vow from me, she'd sunk back into her torpor. 'God, but I'm depressed.'

She hadn't been the only fecking one.

Funnily enough, three of the four of us knew the code to Paddy's gate: Dee from working with him, Lola from when she was riding him and me from the time I had interviewed Alicia.

Once we were in, I parked three buildings away from

Paddy's, on the opposite side of the road. Paddy and Alicia were out at some function. Dee, who knew their schedule, predicted they'd arrive home at around 10.45 p.m.

It was now 10.38.

'I think we're too near his flat,' Lola said anxiously. 'He might see us.'

I drove forward ten yards. 'Is that okay?'

'No,' Marnie said. 'Now we can't see.'

I forced back a sigh and reversed to my original spot.

'Here's someone!' Marnie declared.

A car had parked outside Paddy's block and the silhouette of a man emerged from the driver's side.

'Is it him?' Lola's voice was shaking. 'Is it Paddy?'

'No,' Dee said. 'That's Sidney Brolly, dropping off tomorrow's papers.'

We watched as the silhouette dumped a bundle of stuff by the front door and hightailed it back to his car, did a screechy U-turn and drove back the way he'd come.

We all looked at the pile of papers.

'It is safe to just leave them there?' Lola asked.

'She's right,' Marnie said. 'Anyone could come along and steal them.'

'Would you steal Paddy de Courcy's newspapers?' Dee asked.

'No.'

'Well, there you are . . . Jesus! Here they are!'

It was 10.47.

Instinctively we all slid down in our seats, like in a seventies' cop show, and watched as Paddy's Saab, driven by Spanish John, glided to a stop.

733

We listened, sweaty with tension (at least I was, I suppose I can't speak for the others) as car doors opened and clapped shut and goodnights were called to Spanish John, who drove towards us and past us without displaying any interest.

Covertly we peeped at Paddy and Alicia disappearing into the building.

'We'll wait ten minutes,' I said. 'Then we'll go in.'

'Ten is too obvious,' Marnie said. 'I say nine.'

'Or eleven,' Dee suggested.

'Okay, eleven,' Marnie said.

Lola said nothing. I was worried that she might puke. She kept swallowing and taking deep breaths. Every time I looked at her I was seized with guilt for making her do this.

'Why does he do it?' Lola suddenly asked. 'Why is he so cruel?'

'His mother died when he was fifteen. Maybe he needs to punish all women for his mother's desertion,' Marnie said to Lola. 'I've done lots of therapy,' she added.

'Lots of people's mothers die when they're teenagers,' Dee scoffed. 'And they don't turn into power-mad women-beaters.'

'Mine died when I was fifteen,' Lola said. 'And I've never beaten anyone.'

God love her, she didn't look like she could beat an egg.

'And his father was emotionally repressed,' Marnie said. 'Maybe he inherited that. Like I said . . .'

'Lots of therapy?' Dee asked.

'Yes.'

When the democratically elected eleven minutes had elapsed, I said, 'Okay, let's go.'

734

We all climbed out and crossed the road. Dee shoved her face into the intercom camera and rang Paddy's bell. 'Paddy, it's Dee. I was just passing and wondered if I could have a quick word about tomorrow.'

(Some bill or other was taking place the following day in the Dail.)

'Sure, come on up.'

The communal door clicked opened, the four of us filed in, Dee wished us luck and Marnie, Lola and I ascended the stairs to Paddy's flat.

We arrayed ourselves before Paddy's door, me front and centre, Marnie slightly behind me and to my left, and Lola slightly behind me and to my right.

'Like *Charlie's Angels*,' Lola whispered.

But Charlie's Eejits would be closer to the truth.

I wasn't scared. I was worse than scared. I'd entirely lost faith in the enterprise: the three of us – Lola, Marnie and I – wouldn't alarm a mangy dog.

'Paddy mightn't let us in when he sees who we are,' I said, although I suspected that was unlikely.

Then the door opened and there was Paddy. There was a moment, just a moment, when his eyes went funny; they flickered over us, recognizing all three of us at once and his pupils did something, went either big or small, depending on what's meant to happen when human beings discern danger, then the next thing he was doing his Paddy-on-parade smile. 'Grace Gildee,' he said. 'As I live and breathe.'

He took my hand and leant forward to kiss me, pulling me into the warmth of his home. 'And you brought Marnie.

Marnie, it's been years and years. Too long.' A kiss on the cheek for Marnie, a kiss on the cheek for Lola and he was welcoming us in. He looked, actually, genuinely delighted.

It would have been better if he'd tried to slam the door shut on us and we'd had to run at it and shoulder our way in; at least then we'd have had a little bit of adrenaline behind us.

'Come in and sit down,' he said. 'Let me call Alicia before she takes her make-up off. She'd be cross with me if she missed you.'

He disappeared down a corridor and the three of us waited in the living room, Marnie in an armchair and Lola and I on the edge of the couch. 'He's trying to unsettle us by being nice,' I reminded them. 'Remember what he's done to you. Don't lose sight of it.'

Lola's knees were knocking. I took her hand. 'You're doing great.'

'Sorry,' she whispered. 'I should have worn jeans. I didn't know I'd be so scared –'

'And remember: leave the talking to me.' I'd practised my speech with Dee. Practised and practised. She'd acted the part of me and I'd played Paddy, then she'd played Paddy and I'd been me and I was afraid that Lola was so overwrought that she might hijack the carefully scripted situation by flinging herself at Paddy's feet and begging him to take her back.

'Alicia will be here in a minute.' Paddy had reappeared. 'Now, what can I get you to drink?'

'Nothing, thanks, Paddy,' I said, trying to make my voice sound deeper than it was. 'It's late, we don't want to take up too much of your time. I guess you're wondering what the three of us are doing here.'

'Always delighted to have three beautiful women in my home,' he said easily.

Slowly and deliberately and with a tiny hint of menace I said, 'Paddy, the story you've planted with the *Press* about Dee Rossini harbouring illegals, we want you to drop it.'

In an ideal world, he would say, 'Why would I drop it?' Which would be my cue to say, 'If you drop your story, we'll drop ours.'

But he laughed and said, 'I haven't a clue what you're talking about.'

'Drop it, Paddy,' I said, trying to get the script back on track. 'And we'll drop ours.'

He was meant to ask what our story was but he simply stretched one leg out and settled back in his armchair and smiled at me from under his eyelids; smiled and ran a lazy gaze over my body, lingering on my nipples, wandering down to my crotch.

Silence endured.

Out of the corner of my eye I could see Lola's knees chattering against each other with renewed energy.

The door pushed open and Alicia walked into the silent room and her gracious smile froze. Anxiously she asked, 'What's going on?'

'I was just explaining to Paddy that if he drops his story implicating Dee Rossini in harbouring illegals, we'll drop our story about Paddy.'

'What story is that?' Alicia asked. Thanks be to Christ that someone around here knew their lines.

'Paddy hurts women. He punches them, kicks them and burns them. But you don't need me to tell you that, Alicia.'

She blanched – she'd thought she was the only one – and I knew then that this was going to work.

'What women?' Alicia asked quickly.

I indicated Lola and Marnie.

Paddy gave a little chuckle. 'Who's going to believe that fashion flake with the purple hair?'

Shocked, Lola sucked in her breath. 'Why are you so cruel?' Her voice was shaking.

'Lola, you couldn't seriously . . . I'm a *politician* . . .' Almost kindly, he said, 'We had fun, didn't we?'

'Fun? I'm a human being, Paddy, not a toy.'

'So why behave like a toy?'

I'd lost Lola. Right on target and shot down in flames.

Paddy turned his attention to Marnie.

'Marnie Gildee? Still crazy after all these years?'

'. . . I . . .'

'You hit Marnie,' I said.

He sighed. 'Anyone would hit Marnie.'

'No –'

'She had me driven mad. The crying, the fighting, calling round to my house day and night –'

'– But you made her like that, and you did it too –'

'Then she slept with my best friend; he was like a brother to me.'

'No long-term damage, though. Seeing as he's brokering dirty deals with the *Globe* on your behalf.'

I was saying that at the same time that Marnie was exclaiming at Paddy, 'But you slept with Leechy. You did it first.'

Paddy rolled his eyes at her and turned to me, as if we were the only two responsible adults in the room. 'It was all a long, long time ago, Grace. We were kids, messed-up kids. It's not going to fly. Is that the best you can do? This pair?'

'No, actually, not just this pair,' I said. It was time for my secret weapon.

Everyone – even Paddy, I have to say, which was gratifying – looked startled.

I leapt from my seat and grabbed Alicia's hands. I opened them both palm upwards, rock-solid certain that one of them would have a small circular scar. But there was nothing there. Both her palms were unmarked. I shoved up her sleeves. No bruises. Fuck. Fuck. Fuck.

Immediately, I moved away from Alicia, trying to pretend that I hadn't approached her at all, that the exercise of gazing at her palms had been a spontaneous but quickly abandoned attempt to tell her future.

Centre floor, all eyes on me, my heart was pounding so hard my ribs, my actual ribs, hurt. I'd been sure about Alicia. Now all my lifelines were gone – I had nothing, and my vision was misty from fear. It was like being in a nightmare where you're in the shop buying a scratch card and you suddenly look down and find that you're naked.

I twisted about, seeking salvation. The only secret I had left would do as much harm as good if I revealed it. The ensuing fallout would be devastating; I couldn't do it. Who was Dee to me, anyway? Much as I admired her, she wasn't worth blowing my life up in my face for.

Everyone was still looking at me expectantly, like this

was a whodunnit. Gripped by another wave of panic, I considered grabbing Lola and Marnie and hustling them out of the door and back down the stairs and across the road to the car. They'd be angry and confused, of course. But I'd take them for a pizza. Over the years I'd noticed that pizzas seem to take the sting out of things for most people. Wine, too. They're a good double act. Then I'd explain everything. Well, not everything. But part of everything. Without giving anything away. And if they began to complain again and they'd finished their pizza, I'd get them tiramisu. And more wine. And perhaps a Baileys coffee . . .

But the right thing needed to be done.

And even if it didn't, pride wouldn't let me give in.

I sighed – at the sound everyone seemed to perk up with renewed keenness – and resigned myself to whatever was going to happen. 'There's someone else,' I said, the words like stones on my tongue. 'A third woman. Who's prepared to tell her story.'

'Who?' Marnie asked.

'Yes, who?' Lola asked.

Poor Lola and Marnie, they were expecting me to pull something truly magical out of the hat, some woman to walk through the door and declare silkily, 'Surely you haven't forgotten about the time you beat the shit out of me, Paddy!'

'Yes, who?' Alicia asked.

Paddy said nothing. He watched, a small smile on his mouth.

'Me,' I said.

*

'You?'

'Why would he hit *you*?' Marnie asked.

'Because . . .' There was no way out. I had to say it. 'I wouldn't sleep with him.'

My words fell into stunned silence. Paddy closed his eyes and smiled to himself.

'Did Paddy want to sleep with you?' Marnie asked slowly, as if she was listening to herself speak.

Paddy opened his eyes and said lasciviously, 'Oh yeah.'

Marnie went the colour of death. 'Did you always fancy her?' she whispered. 'Even when you were going out with me?'

'Yeah.' Paddy stretched lazily. 'Always. When I was fucking you I was thinking of her.'

'No, he wasn't! Don't mind him, he's just trying to turn us against each other.' For God's sake, it was nearly fifteen years since Marnie had gone out with Paddy. When was she going to stop behaving like it had just finished?

'Paddy and I were working together on his biography and he put the moves on me because he does it to everyone. And when I didn't go for it, he gave me a slap, put a cigarette out on my hand and told Spanish John to burn out my car.'

'You were working on his biography?' Marnie said faintly.

'Come on now, Grace,' Paddy said. 'You were hardly fighting me off.'

'When was this?' Marnie asked, her voice thick.

'Last summer. Until September.'

'September,' Lola spoke up. 'But he got engaged to Alicia in August.'

Marnie rounded on Alicia. 'How do you feel about that, Leechy?'

'Fine,' Alicia said, 'because none of it is true. And don't call me Leechy, I always hated it.'

'But he's just *told* you he wanted to sleep with Grace –' Lola exclaimed, at the same time as Marnie said to Alicia, 'Well, *I* didn't name you Leechy. Someone – who was it? Some baby couldn't pronounce Alicia –'

'My sister.'

'So don't act like *we* decided to change your name. *Everyone* called you Leechy. For as long as we knew you.'

'I'm Alicia now.'

'Actually,' Marnie said with uncharacteristic spite, 'Leechy suits you better. Because you were a leech, leeching around after Paddy –'

We were in danger of losing sight of our common purpose here . . . 'Marnie,' I said. 'Please.'

'You were *never* my friends,' Leechy said. 'I was always left out. It was always you and Grace, then me tacked onto the edge –'

You know, that really wasn't true, but before I got sucked into it, Paddy got to his feet. 'I'm off to bed.'

'Wait, Paddy.' I intercepted him at the door. 'We're not finished here yet.' I tried to locate my slightly menacing voice once more. 'Like I said, you drop your story and we'll drop ours.'

He laughed softly and shook his head. Not in refusal but at what a shambles the situation had descended into. I couldn't blame him.

We'd failed. Quite spectacularly.

In disarray, we departed the flat and thumped down the stairs, none of us speaking to each other, to break the bad news to Dee.

Marnie wouldn't get in the car. Her face was closed and tight with humiliation.

Dee and Lola, acknowledging the fracture between Marnie and me, had peeled away with talk of taxis, and left us to it.

'Please get in the car, Marnie,' I said.

'It was such an important relationship to me,' she said. 'Can you imagine how I feel finding out he wanted to be with you?'

'He didn't want to be with me when he was with you. He *loved* you.' Slowly I drove alongside her. 'Please, Marnie, please, get in. It's late. You can't just walk around.'

'I won't stay in your house.'

'Then let me drop you out to Ma's. Please, Marnie, it's not safe.'

Eventually she got in and sat in rigid-backed silence. After ten minutes she asked coldly, 'Does Damien know about you and Paddy?'

'I didn't sleep with him,' I said. 'There's nothing for Damien to know.'

'But something went on?'

Yes, something had gone on.

'You *wanted* to sleep with him? You considered it? You were emotionally involved?'

I said nothing and she had her answer.

'I bet Damien doesn't know about that,' she said.

'Please don't tell him.' My voice was choked.

She didn't reply and I knew then that she might. I wouldn't have believed that this situation was possible. Marnie and I, our loyalty had always been to each other, before everyone – anyone – else. But everything was fucked-up. Marnie was wounded and, with the drink and everything, she was a loose cannon. And Paddy de Courcy was in the mix and he twisted and destroyed everything he came into contact with. When we reached Yeoman Road, Marnie got out of the car and ran up the steps without saying goodbye to me.

'Where's Marnie?' Damien, tense and expectant, was waiting up for me. 'What happened with de Courcy?'

'Oh God, Damien . . .' I didn't know where to start because I didn't know where I could end. I couldn't tell him everything, so I was afraid to tell him anything.

I pressed myself against him and wound my arms around his neck. The terror of losing him was so huge that I had to physically cling to him.

He pulled me into a tight hold and rested his head on mine.

'Tighter,' I said.

Obediently his arms formed a harder band around my back. 'Was it a disaster?' he asked into my hair.

I nodded against his shoulder. 'A disaster. But I don't know if he'll link the leak to you, I think it might be okay.' I genuinely thought it would be. 'Can we go to bed?' I asked.

'Come on.' He helped me up the stairs like I was someone recovering from pneumonia. In the bedroom I stepped out of my clothes, leaving them where they'd landed on the floor, and climbed between the sheets. Then Damien got in and I curled myself around him, against his hard, warm body, like it might be the last chance I'd ever get. I closed my eyes and became very still, wishing I could stay in that moment for ever.

Then Damien shifted and pulled back far enough to look into my face. 'So are you going to tell me what happened?'

'Would you mind . . . ? Could we leave it for tonight? I'm just so . . .'

He looked disappointed, hurt, something . . .

'Sorry.' I backtracked. I *couldn't* not tell him. Not after all he'd done to help. 'What am I thinking? Of course I'll tell you.' But I couldn't tell him everything and that made me so unbearably sad. Then unbearably frightened.

'No, leave it,' he said. 'You're wrecked. Go to sleep. Tell me in the morning.'

'The funny thing is there's nothing really to tell. He totally belittled Marnie and Lola, they just fell apart, they'd be no good in any interview, and he obviously hasn't laid a hand on Alicia. It was a fiasco. He's unscareable.'

'De Courcy.' Damien turned out the light and sighed into the darkness. 'It's a mistake to tangle with him.'

'Yes.' I knew.

When I picture it in my head – and I don't do it often – there's a soundtrack: an orchestra of lush strings swelling, building to a climax which bursts into the fullness of its rich beauty as I turn and see Paddy for the first time.

I was almost seventeen years old and Mick the manager was introducing me to the barmen the night I started work at the Boatman.

745

'That's Jonzer,' Mick said. 'Jonzer, say hello to Grace.'

Jonzer stared like I was the first human being he'd ever seen. His arms hung loosely by his sides but his fists were clenched and one malevolent eye was set lower in his face than the other. Deliverance banjos plucked a few chords in my head.

'And that's Whacker,' Mick said. 'Whacker, Grace, new bargirl. Lives in Yeoman Road.'

Whacker opened his mouth and bared his teeth in a snarl.

'And over there,' Mick said. 'That's Paddy.'

My breathing, which had been going about its rhythmic business year in, year out, causing me no worry whatsoever, suddenly seized up and broke down and I was paralysed by the devastating combination of Paddy's beauty, his life force and his dazzling smile.

I was so overawed that I thought Paddy should be the Boatman's manager. It seemed contrary to the natural order of things that he was just a barman. He was obviously so far superior in every way to runty unpleasant Mick that I had a little conversation in my head where I agreed with myself that if I was the Boatman's owner I'd sack Mick and replace him with Paddy.

Thanks to Ma's indoctrination, I didn't believe in love at first sight. However, one look from Paddy had been enough to turn me into Queen Sap, even worse than Leechy, officially the most (self-confessed) sappy girl Marnie or I had ever met. I wanted him more than I had ever wanted anything and I was terrified that I wouldn't get him.

The normal thing would be to talk about it but I was trying to make sense myself of the cataclysmic effect he had on me before I told anyone else. I couldn't contemplate hours of girly analysis with Marnie and Leechy, lying on the bed, thinking up ways to make Paddy fancy me. My urge for him was immeasurably more visceral and adult than any of the other crushes I'd had and there was one thing I was certain of: sparkly mascara was not the answer.

Another reason I kept my mouth shut was that Ma, Dad and Bid – especially Bid – would have laughed at me. Everyone assumed that I was as tough as old boots – and if I was ever foolish enough to reveal any weakness, the reaction was mild hilarity. Over the years, I'd learnt to never bother with tears, because all I got was chuckles and 'Look at you crying there, like a great big eejit.'

However, my Paddy-obsession came dangerously close to being unmasked when I asked Ma and Bid, 'How do you get a man to notice you?'

Ma's advice was, 'Be yourself.'

Bid's advice was, 'Don't wear a bra.'

Be myself. So who was I?

I was the uncomplicated robust one, so I decided to play to my strengths. No feminine wiles for me. When Paddy loaded up a tray with ten pints of lager and asked, 'Need a hand with that, Grace?' I said stoutly, 'Not at all,' and hoisted it off the counter, my arms trembling with the strain.

(I was subsequently to see Marnie refuse to carry any tray with more than four glasses on it and have barmen tripping over themselves in their desire to help.)

I did every shift I was asked to do, in the hope of coinciding with Paddy's. I was almost afraid to consider it, but I thought he liked me. The night he slipped an ice cube down

747

my back and we had a minor wrestling match, which left me breathless and elated, I was nearly sure of it.

The most important thing I needed to establish was whether or not he had a girlfriend. I lay on my bed plotting and planning. Ask Jonzer? Ask Whacker? Ask any of the other equally horrible barmen?

I realized I could just ask Paddy.

'So, Paddy –' I flipped the lid off a bottle of tonic, caught it and tossed it over my shoulder into the bin – 'you have a girlfriend?'

'Good shot,' he said. 'No. Why? You offering?'

'You wish.' I picked up my tray and swung past him.

'I do actually,' he said to my retreating back.

I laughed over my shoulder. 'Dream on.'

'You're breaking my heart!'

Later at home in my bedroom, I unwrapped those words like they were precious jewels, and listened to them again and again.

I do actually.

You're breaking my heart.

I was building a connection with him, like constructing a house of cards, trembling with terror every time I added a new one, in case it sent the whole edifice collapsing into disarray.

We had lots in common: he was interested in politics; I was interested in politics. Well, I wasn't really, but I knew about them. And we were an obvious physical match – not many girls were five foot nine. (When I was subsequently discarded in favour of a five-foot-nothing, I felt like a shamefully massive, lumbering lunk who couldn't fit through doorways and who broke chairs when she sat on them.)

The night of my birthday, Marnie's and my seventeenth, I added another card to the house by proposing to introduce him to the most important person in my life.

'My twin sister will be in later. It's our birthday.'

'Your *twin*? There are *two* of you? One Grace Gildee is bad enough!'

I flicked water from the running tap at his face and he recoiled, laughing. 'Are you going out later to celebrate? Am I invited?'

'Why would we invite an eejit like you?'

'Ah go on, Grace.'

'No.'

'Ah please.'

'What part of the word "no" don't you understand?' (I was almost pitifully pleased with that particular line, thinking it the height of sophisticated flirting.)

Then in came Marnie and with one look she swept away all that I had built up so carefully and doggedly, and grabbed the prize.

There was a moment when I felt I had a choice, that if I put up a fight I was in with a chance. Then I copped on to myself. Paddy wanted Marnie. But even if he hadn't, Marnie wanted him and I could never deny her anything.

It was hard, though. I saw them at work and I saw them at home: there was no escape. I had to witness him kissing her and holding her hand and giggling with her. I had to listen to her graphic accounts of their fabulous sex. '. . . And then he pulled my legs up around his waist and, Grace, I swear to God . . .'

But I got used to thinking of him as Marnie's. Now and then I had unexpected moments when I remembered the connection I'd felt with him but I realized I must have been delusional.

They were together for nearly three years and I knew Paddy had stopped loving Marnie before she did. It was the spring before our twentieth birthdays, Paddy was in his final year in college, he was due to begin training as a barrister in October and it was obvious – to me, at any rate – that he was ready to move on to the next part of his life.

I tried to warn Marnie, but she was unreachable. In a way it was as bad as if he'd fallen out of love with me. Her pain was mine.

Then Sheridan told me that there was more going on with Paddy and Leechy than their platonic comforting sessions. I couldn't believe it – Leechy was like a sister to Marnie and me. But Sheridan insisted it was true, insisted with such force, that – even though it was none of my business – I went to Leechy and asked her to stay away from Paddy.

Leechy was always eager to please. But instead of acceding, she said surprisingly firmly, 'No, Grace. I'm Paddy's new girlfriend.'

New girlfriend? I was stunned. 'But he already has a –' I gazed at her and the full truth dawned on me. 'Are you – are you . . . *sleeping* with him?'

'No.' She coloured.

'You are! Oh God. God. Oh God, God, God,' I groaned, overwhelmed with fear. What would Marnie say? What would Marnie do? 'Leechy, please stop. You've got to. Where's your loyalty?'

'Normally I would be loyal,' she said. 'Normally I'd never take another girl's man.'

I felt like saying, Normally you wouldn't get the fucking choice! You're not exactly Cindy Crawford.

'What about Marnie?' I begged. 'She's been your friend since you were five!'

'Marnie and Paddy are over,' she said with quiet confidence. 'I'm his type. I'm sensible and steady and I like the Carpenters. Marnie was just a teenage thing.'

'Leechy, you're imagining it –' I wanted to tell her how I'd once thought his type was robust and mouthy. How I was certain that he was simply using the consequences of sleeping with her to somersault himself out of Marnie's life.

'I love him, Grace,' she said with continued confidence and that was that.

I blamed Paddy but I blamed Leechy more. If she hadn't slept with Paddy, Marnie wouldn't have been unhinged enough to sleep with Sheridan, and if she hadn't slept with Sheridan, Paddy wouldn't have pummelled her into unconsciousness, an event that I think altered her for ever.

It was over four years before I saw him again. It was at a work thing, an early evening launch of something, in a crowded hotel function room. Suddenly he was there, taller than everyone else. He didn't look poor and wild any more, his clothes radiated newness and money, but it was definitely him. I stared for half a second too long, enough time for him to see me. Shock stamped itself on his face. He went white and his expression froze. I turned my back to him.

'Gotta go,' I said to the cluster of people I was with.

'Why . . . ?'

I abandoned my glass on a passing tray and zigzagged through the throng, making for the door. By the time I reached it, Paddy was blocking my path.

'Grace –'

I dipped my head and moved sideways but with one lithe move, he was in front of me there also.

'Grace, it is you, isn't it?'

I swivelled in another direction, but once again he was ahead of me. 'Grace. Please . . . Is this how you treat an old friend?'

'What?' I jerked my head up. 'You're no friend of mine.'

It was a mistake to look at him. He was a picture of anguish. 'Grace, please.' Beseechingly he said, 'You and I have always been friends.'

'Friends?' I was disgusted. 'After what you did to Marnie!'

My loud outrage attracted a couple of startled looks.

Paddy noted them. 'Can we talk?' he asked quietly.

'Work away.' I folded my arms. 'I'm all ears.'

'Not here. Somewhere a bit more . . . private. Where I can explain?'

There couldn't be an explanation. But curiosity was always my downfall. Maybe there really *was* something that would make sense of it all.

'There's a private bar here in the hotel,' he said. 'Will you give me ten minutes of your time?'

He made it so easy – if I'd had to go any distance in his company, I wouldn't have done it. And what was ten minutes?

In the hushed wood-panelled comfort of the snug bar, Paddy placed a drink in front of me.

'You've six minutes left,' I said.

'In that case I'd better make it quick. Okay . . . I was young and . . . and . . . off my head and very angry. My mother had died, my father was such a nutjob –'

'It's no excuse.'

'I'm not trying to excuse myself, I'm just trying to explain.' He hung his head. 'I had no home, that's the only way I can put it.' A long pause ensued before he spoke again. 'When I met Marnie she became my home. All of you, really, you and Bid and your mum and dad.' Another period of silence. 'But when I stopped, when it happened that I didn't love Marnie any more, I blamed her. I thought I'd stopped loving her because she was weak. If she'd been a different person, I'd still be in love with her, but she wasn't and I wasn't and once again my home was gone . . .'

I was surprised to feel a little bud of sorrow for him. Then I remembered Marnie's swollen, battered face and it vanished.

'I've been haunted by shame,' he said.

'Good enough for you. And why are you telling me? You should be telling Marnie.'

He hesitated. 'I've thought about it. I still think about it. But, knowing what I know, *knew*, of Marnie, if I got in touch, I think it would . . . open old wounds. I reckon I'd make things worse, not better.'

763

The very annoying part was that he was right. If Marnie was to hear from him now, it would set her back years.

'But I'm never entirely sure, it's something I think about and I wonder . . .'

'And on that fascinating note – ' I swallowed the remains of my drink and got to my feet. 'Your ten minutes are up.'

'How is she?' he asked.

'Marnie? Fine,' I said. 'Far better without you. You were . . . shit to her.'

'I had to be. It was the only way of ending it. She would never have accepted it otherwise.'

Once again he was right.

'She's a very special girl,' he said wistfully. 'Will you stay for one more drink and tell me how she is?'

'No.'

'Please.'

'No. Oh all right.'

I had nothing else to do. Well, that was how I justified it to myself.

Paddy bought more drinks and went on to talk with such kindness about Marnie, such sadness about how sensitive she was, how hard she found it to be happy that – to my eternal shame – I half agreed with him.

The clang of a metal barrel interrupted Paddy's flow of words. 'God, that takes me back,' he said. We watched as the barman changed the barrel. 'Remember we used to do that in the Boatman?'

I nodded, abashed by the memory of me lugging heavy stuff around the pub in an attempt to impress him. What a gobshite I'd been . . .

'You were the only girl who could change a barrel,' he said. 'You were like this . . . amazing Amazon. Spectacular. Nothing daunted you.'

I was stunned. I had always thought that hoicking things around like a stevedore was what had put Paddy off.

'I'd never before met a woman like you,' he mused.

I couldn't look at him. I swallowed, so loud we both heard it and my Adam's apple leapt up and down like a piston.

'I've never met one since.'

Christ! I attempted a sideways glance at him and when our eyes met, emotion surged between us. Resistant though I was – and I was, all I had to do was think of Marnie's swollen, battered face – I felt we were intimates, like he and I truly understood each other. The way we had been before he'd met Marnie.

'Another drink?' he said.

'No. I'm going.'

'Sure? Go on, just one more?'

I hesitated, then gave in. 'Oh okay, just one.'

When he returned from the counter, he placed our drinks on the table, then turned to me and said, 'I've got something to say and if I don't say it now, I'll never say it.'

I had a fair idea of where this was going.

'I made a mistake,' he said. 'I picked the wrong sister.'

I closed my eyes. 'Don't.'

Even if he hadn't done the terrible things he'd done to Marnie, it was taboo to get involved with your sister's – or friends' – old boyfriends. He would always be hers.

'Come home with me,' he said.

I was convulsed by longing. I would have given my all

for just one night with him. One night of his naked body, one night of dirty, tender, heart-aching sex in every conceivable position, one night of him thrusting into me, his face contorted with lust for me, me, me . . .

'No,' I said.

'No?'

'No.' The picture of Marnie in the hospital wouldn't go away. I grabbed my bag and got up to leave.

'You'll change your mind,' he said. 'I'll persuade you.'

'Not me,' I said, wondering what he'd do to convince me.

But nothing happened. I didn't hear from him again, not a word for another eleven years. Plenty of time for me to reflect on my refusal.

Then, last summer, I got a phone call from Annette Babcock, the commissioning editor of Palladian, a publishing house that specialized in celebrity autobiographies. I'd ghostwritten a couple of books for them in the recent past. (A sportswoman's life story and the trials and tribulations of a woman who was once Miss Ireland and who'd had twenty-eight cosmetic surgery operations to keep her modelling career on track.)

It was the sort of work hacks often do on the side, what with most sportspeople or models – or indeed politicians – being borderline illiterate. The work was intensive, also soul-destroying, as you tried to transmute someone's dull life and tedious anecdotes into readable prose, but the money could be good.

'Can you come in?' Annette said. 'I've a job for you.'

When I was sitting in front of her, she said, 'We're doing Paddy de Courcy's book.'

Jesus, I thought, Paddy de Courcy . . .

'We think you'd be the right writer to do it. It'll mean spending a lot of time with Paddy over the next month, but that's no hardship, is it? Is it?' she repeated, when I didn't reply.

'What! Sorry. Just thinking there . . .' I cleared my throat. I had plenty of questions. First and foremost, why me?

'Don't let it go to your head,' Annette said snippily. Clearly she fancied him. 'It's not like he requested you. We've a panel of writers we use. We put a few names to him. He said he'd read *The Human Race.*' (The sportswoman's story.) 'He said he liked your work.'

'Did he . . . ?'

The thing was that I'd sort of forgotten about Paddy de Courcy. I mean, not entirely. It'd be bloody hard to, the way he was always on the news or had his handsome mug grinning out from the social pages. At times when I saw him I got a surprise little twist of something in my gut but most times I felt nothing at all.

'Well?' Annette asked. 'You in?'

'I don't know . . .'

'*What?*'

I was confused. Was this not risky for Paddy? I knew stuff about him that probably no other journalist knew. But maybe that was why he'd decided on me – because he wouldn't have to fess up about putting Marnie in hospital and shock the bejaysus out of me. Maybe he knew he'd have to include it in the book but thought he could get me to do a nice sanitized version?

Or maybe I was overthinking this. Maybe Marnie was so far back in his distant past that he'd totally forgotten what

757

he'd done? Maybe he really *had* liked my work on *The Human Race*? Maybe this really was just a job?

'The money's good,' Annette said anxiously. She threw a figure at me and, in fairness, she was right. 'I can try to get you another couple of grand.'

'Yes, but . . .'

I was all mixed up. Why would I help Paddy? The thought of working with him, of letting him benefit from my writing skills made me feel disloyal and uncomfortable. Then my crusading spirit took over – maybe I could get justice for Marnie fifteen years after the event. I thought about it a bit longer and the conviction that something good could come of this got stronger.

'Okay,' I said to Annette. 'I'll do it.'

'A little bit more enthusiasm, if you don't mind,' she said. 'Personally I'd be creaming myself at the thought of all that time with Paddy.'

I closed my eyes. Christ, did she *have* to?

'Now listen to me, Grace. This is a highly confidential project, because of the danger of pre-publication injunctions from other politicians. Tell no one.'

'My lips are sealed.'

The minute I got home I told Damien.

'His *autobiography*?' Damien was deeply suspicious. 'Why? He's done nothing except shag models. He's not the leader of a party. He hasn't even been a minister.'

'The world of celebrity autobiographies has changed.' I shrugged. 'You don't need to have done anything, all you have to be is good-looking.'

Damien was watching me, his face still, his eyes bleak.

'Why did you say you'd do it, Grace? After what he did to Marnie?'

'That's precisely why. I'm wondering if I can get . . . I don't know . . . something for Marnie. Even an apology . . .'

'It was a long time ago,' Damien said quietly. 'Marnie's married now, the mother of two children. She mightn't want any of this made public. She mightn't want anything to do with him.'

'And then again she might.'

'Perhaps you should talk to her before you go any further.'

'I've already said I'll do it.'

He shrugged. 'You can change your mind. You haven't signed anything?'

'No. I know. But I just feel I have to do this . . . It was such a big thing to happen to Marnie and me,' I said. 'I know you can't understand because you weren't there, but this feels like a chance, I don't know, to . . . Oh I don't know, Damien!' I sighed heavily. 'To undo something bad.'

My words fell into silence. How could I make him understand? The hook was in my flesh. Despite my suspicions and my fears of disloyalty, I had to do this.

'Don't look so sad,' I pleaded.

Damien gave a rueful little laugh – he knew all about my teenage thing for Paddy.

'Okay,' I said. 'Okay, okay. If you really don't want me to do it, just say it and I won't.'

'Grace . . .'

Then I felt ashamed. Damien would never make that sort of request, he wasn't that kind of man. Shaking his head, he began to walk away.

'The money's good,' I called after him.

'Great.' His voice floated back to me. 'We'll buy lots of things.'

Our first session, to discuss the structure of the book, was held at Paddy's office. I'd forgotten what it was like to be within breathing distance of him. His size. Those eyes. That presence . . . charisma, whatever you want to call it. Such a perfect powerful physical presence. There was so much of him, concentrated into just one human being – like really strong coffee or dark dark chocolate – it was almost unbearable. He shook my hand and kissed me lightly on the cheek. 'I'm delighted we'll be working together.'

'God, you're such a politician,' I complained. 'Where am I sitting?'

'Wherever you like. On the couch, if you want.'

'Your casting couch?'

'My *couch*.'

I took a hard-backed chair, muttering under my breath that it was probably safest. Paddy sat behind his desk and I opened my yellow pad. Defiantly I said, 'First things first. Will we be including the episode where you hospitalized my sister?'

'Still the same Grace,' Paddy said, but without rancour. 'Always championing a cause. But I think it's best if we draw a veil over that youthful episode.'

'Oh I see. *That*'s why you asked for me?' As I had suspected. 'If you think I'm going to protect you, you can so forget it.' I stood up to leave.

'Not to protect me – sit down, Grace, would you? – to

protect Marnie. You think she'd want that printed in a book?'

That's what Damien had said . . .

'Would she?' he asked again.

I didn't know. I hadn't asked her.

Slowly I sat back down. But if I wasn't doing this project as Marnie's champion, why was I here?

'The money's good,' Paddy said, reading my thoughts. 'Come on, Grace, we've both got a job to do. Let's do it.'

The money *was* good. I'd recently bought a new car and the repayments were high.

I picked up my pen again and, to my surprise, we worked for three hours and made good steady progress. This was just a job, I realized, and it was going to be fine.

Our second session was five days later and once again the work was productive. We'd covered his childhood and had got as far as the death of his mother – when all of a sudden Paddy stopped talking and bowed his head. When he looked up again, his eyes were swimming with tears. Normally I would think, A man crying, how *funny*. But, perhaps because I'd known him back then, in the aftermath of his mother's death, how lost and wild he'd been, I felt unexpectedly sad for him.

I passed him a Burger King napkin from my bag and roughly he wiped his eyes. Within moments he was himself again.

'Well, that was embarrassing.' He laughed. He looked at the napkin. 'Hold the front page. Grace Gildee was kind.'

'I *am* kind.' I was defensive. 'To those who deserve it.'

'I know you are. You know, Grace' – he gave me the full benefit of his blue gaze – 'I came to Palladian because of you.'

What? Talk about an abrupt change of subject.

'I've always followed your progress, I've always known which paper you were working for, I've always read your stuff.'

'Why are you telling me this?'

'Because in all these years I've never stopped thinking about you.'

An involuntary thrill flamed from my toes to the roots of my hair.

'I've thought about you every single day. You're the only woman who could ever match me.'

I didn't want to be, but I was flattered. I was excited. Just like that, I was right back in it.

The teenage me had been reactivated and I was dreamy and distracted and half blind with lust for Paddy.

But that night I couldn't sleep. There was no way round the truth: my attraction to Paddy was a bad, bad thing; dangerous and dirty.

It was a long time ago, maybe he's changed.

What about Damien?

What Damien and I had was rare and good.

Instinctively I knew what had to be done: I would end my involvement in the project.

But when I met Paddy to tell him to find another writer, it was as if he'd been anticipating it. Before I got to open my mouth he closed his office door and said, 'Don't, Grace. Don't abandon me.'

'But –'

'Please. You're the only one I trust to tell the truth. I need you.'

I couldn't help it – he made me feel too important to him to resign.

That day's work and our next session, two days later, were conducted in such a state of sexual tension that I couldn't think straight. Our early progress had slowed to almost nothing, but I didn't care. I was locked inside myself, in a process of constant negotiation. I just wanted one night. One night I had been owed from eleven years earlier. Or eighteen years earlier. It wouldn't mean I didn't love Damien.

At home Damien watched me and said nothing and I managed to convince myself that he hadn't noticed anything. Until one evening at home after work when a new-age catalogue had come in the post and we were picking out the courses we'd most hate to do.

'Tribal Drumming would be horrific,' I said, laughing with cringy glee. 'Imagine the types you'd get.'

'For me,' he said, 'my very, very worst one would be . . . let's see . . . Here we are! Release Your Locked Emotions Through Song. An entire weekend of it. Jesus!'

'Now I know what to get you for your birthday.'

'Grace, I'll just say one thing.'

Alerted by his sudden change of tone, I looked at him. 'What's up with you?'

'If one of us cheated – Christ, I hate that word,' he said. 'We might survive it, but things would always be different. The trust would be gone. The innocence.'

'I –' The obvious reply would be to ask what had prompted his statement. But I couldn't go down that road. He hadn't accused me of anything, that was what was important, and in fairness I hadn't done anything. 'Okay, Damien. I know that.'

'Good, good . . . because I'd hate to think . . .' He seemed about to say something else and I willed him not to. 'Because I love you, you know?'

My usual response when he told me he loved me was to ask him if he was coming down with something. But this time I just said, 'I know you do.' Then swept along by a sudden deep rush of love and gratitude, I said, 'I love you too.'

'Careful,' he said. 'We don't want to turn into *Hart to Hart*.'

We both laughed, a little nervously.

The following day I had another meeting with Paddy. The sun was bursting from the sky and he was waiting outside for me, watching me whizz into the allocated parking space. I got it first time, one smooth confident swerve, my car landing exactly equidistant from the four white lines, a perfect bit of parking in my perfect car on this perfect day.

'Nice work,' Paddy said, not even pretending to hide his appreciation.

'All down to the car.' I laughed.

'You love your car?' he asked.

'I *love* my car.'

In his office I sat at the desk to start work and Paddy said, 'So what about you and Damien?'

'What about us?' I couldn't help sounding defensive.

'Still in love?'

'Yes.'

'You wouldn't think of breaking it off with him?'

'Why would I do that?'

'So you could be my girl. We'd be fabulous together. Look.' He scribbled a number on a piece of paper. 'This is my private mobile number. My private private number. Only my personal trainer has it. Have a think about what I said.' He shrugged. 'If you make any decisions, ring me any time, day or night.'

I was unable to speak. The nerve of him! And yet I was shamefully flattered. Unless he was just playing games . . . ?

'I'm completely serious,' he said. 'I know you don't believe me, but I'm going to keep on saying it until you do – you're the only woman I've ever met who can match me.'

I nearly puked. With longing and shame and shame and longing.

Three days later the news broke that Paddy was getting married and – I admit it – I felt like I'd been jolted with a stun gun. He owed me nothing, no promises had been made, but he'd behaved as if . . .

The dislocating shock was compounded by the discovery that his bride would be Leechy.

It was my ego, I told myself. That's what it was. Wounded because I'd thought I was special to him.

He rang me.

'Is it true?' I asked.

'Grace –'

'Is it true?'

'Yes, but –'

I disconnected.

He rang again. I switched my phone off.

Then I found out about Lola. While interviewing 'Captain of Industry', Marcia Fitzgibbon, for 'My Favourite Insult', she complained that her stylist was on drugs, screwing up work left, right and centre and insisting that Paddy de Courcy was her boyfriend. 'If you could see this woman,' Marcia told me. 'I mean, her hair is *purple!*'

It was easy to track Lola down. She wouldn't confirm that she'd been seeing Paddy and – paradoxically – that was proof that she had.

Feeling more and more stupid, I rang Palladian and told them I was out of the project. They kicked up but there was nothing they could do because the contract hadn't yet been signed.

For the next two or three weeks Paddy continued to ring me and I never answered his calls – until one day, on some whim I didn't understand, I did.

'Just hear me out,' he said, and although I hadn't a clue how he was going to talk his way out of things, my curiosity – as always – was what did for me.

'My office?' he suggested.

'Okay.'

'I'll send Spanish John.'

'I'll walk.'

Paddy's assistant showed me into an empty room. He wasn't even there waiting for me; I shouldn't have come. I lit a cigarette, the flame of my lighter trembling, and decided to count to sixteen. (Why sixteen? No idea.) If he hadn't appeared by then I was off. One, two –

There he was. Firmly he shut his office door behind him and his presence filled the room.

'Congratulations.' I stood up. 'On your forthcoming marriage.'

'Look, I know.' He looked abject. 'But it doesn't have to change anything, Grace. I don't even love her,' he said.

Much as I despised Leechy, I wondered how anyone could be so callous.

'I'm a politician, Grace. I need a suitable wife. I'm sorry for not telling you personally. What happened was, I asked to see some rings, the jeweller leaked the story, it was out there before even I knew it. We can carry on as before.' He had stolen closer to me, close enough to take the cigarette from my hand and put it in an ashtray. Softly he said, 'Better than before. When are you going to put me out of my misery? I want you so much it's killing me. Sleep with me, Grace, sleep with me.'

He put his hands on my hips and, bending his knees slightly, pressed his erection against my pubic bone and murmured into my ear, 'That's how you make me feel. Always, all the time.' He whispered, 'Think of us in bed together, Grace.'

Like I thought of anything else these days.

It was as if I was hypnotized and I was suddenly certain that I was going to sleep with Paddy. The moment I had fantasized about for years was upon me. But why now? Now that he was getting married to someone else? That, strangely, was the reason. The shock news had showed me how much I wanted him.

We moved closer. The heat of Paddy's breath was on my mouth. He was going to kiss me . . . *But Damien* . . . My body was opening in response to the look of intent in Paddy's eyes. Almost swooning from his nearness, I closed my eyes, then his tongue was in my mouth and mine was in his and we kissed . . . *What about Damien . . . ?* Paddy's hand was on my breast, his fingers seeking my nipple, his body hard and warm against mine . . . *Damien* . . . My knees were buckling with desire – then in my head I saw Marnie, her face purple and swollen.

I opened my eyes and wrenched myself away. 'No, Paddy, I'm not doing this.'

It came from nowhere. A slap with his open hand across my face, catching my eye socket with his ring. The force of it sent me staggering to the floor. I felt wetness beneath my left eye and for one humiliated moment I thought I was crying. It was actually a relief to wipe my hand across my cheek and find it covered in blood.

'You probably won't need stitches,' he said, almost like an apology.

'How do you know?' I said thickly. 'You do this often?'

I'd intended to be sarcastic, but from the way he was considering me, as if weighing up how much of a liability I was, I realized that actually, yes, he *did* do this often. Marnie might have been the first but there had been others since her. I gaped, then dropped my gaze because I thought it might be safer not to look at him.

'If you ever tell anyone,' he said, 'I'll kill you. Okay? Okay?' he said, louder this time.

I was mopping the blood off my face, astonished at its quantity and redness. 'Okay.'

He knelt beside me; I thought he was about to help me to get up and I was preparing to shrug him away. With one hand he took my cigarette from the ashtray and with his other, clasped my wrist.

Our eyes met and after a freeze-frame of disbelief, I knew what he wanted to do.

'No!' Frenziedly I tried to scoot backwards across the floor.

'Yes.' He pinned me down, kneeling on my forearm, bringing the burning red tip onto the centre of the palm of my hand.

It was quick and terrible, immeasurably worse than I could have imagined. But more horrific than the physical pain, was that I'd been marked by him for ever.

I barely remember leaving his office. Out on the street I lurched on leaden legs through the crowds of Kildare Street and, without having consciously decided to, I gravitated towards the peace of Stephen's Green where, incapable of anything else, I sat on a bench.

Everything had slowed down. All my thoughts were dragging.

I'm in shock, I realized. I'm in shock.

My face was still bleeding. Not pumping blood like it had initially, but there was a steady stream that kept using up tissues. I'd hold one against my cheek and a little while later I'd look at it and see that it was red and falling apart, then I'd get a fresh one.

How strange that I had a packet of tissues in my bag, I thought, feeling very faraway. I'm so not a packet-of-tissues person. But when I'd looked for them in my bag, there they'd been, like . . . like . . . little helping things . . .

My hand pulsed with pain, a shocking, somehow menacing pain, so severe that I thought I might vomit.

And then my rage came into focus, red and hot and thick, gathering might and viscosity. Fucking Paddy de Courcy.

I was . . . sickened, quite literally *sickened*, by what he'd done to me. It was unbearably humiliating. He had used his superior strength on me and I hadn't been able to do a thing about it. I'd simply had to take it.

But he was fucked now. As soon as I was able, I was going to hail a taxi and tell them to take me to the nearest cop shop – there was one in Pearse Street – and I was going to get him arrested for assault. He would regret having fucked with me, I promised myself, with bitter resolve. He'd be sorry he'd ever thought he could get the better of me. I wasn't just some stupid girl who was so mad about him that she'd keep shtum.

I've never forgotten you, I've always known where you were working, I've always read your articles. All that stuff he'd said when we were first working on the book, which had soft-soaped me into giddiness even while I wondered if he was just telling me what I wanted to hear, I was now certain was true. But instead of being flattered, I thought it was sinister.

Maybe he hadn't cared about me when I was a teenager, but I was sure now that that time, eleven years ago, when I wouldn't go home with him, had left a barb. Paddy de Courcy probably didn't get turned down very often. Since then he'd probably regarded me as unfinished business. Not a priority – I wasn't that important – but something on his back burner, a grudge to be avenged, if the chance ever presented itself . . .

Then I was on my last tissue. I couldn't stay on the bench any longer. It was time to get up and make my way to Pearse Street.

I got to my feet and maybe it was because I was finally in motion, putting my thoughts into action, that I suddenly understood that I couldn't shop Paddy to the police. All the threats I'd made in my head were just bravado, because I knew the exact conversation I'd have with the desk sergeant.

'Why did Mr de Courcy assault you?'

'Because he was angry with me.'

'And why was he angry with you?'

'Because I wouldn't sleep with him.'

'And had you given Mr de Courcy reason to think you might sleep with him?'

'Probably. Yes.'

I couldn't do it. Not because I thought Paddy was in the right – far bloody from it – but because Damien would find out what had been going on. I'd lose him. And with that, I knew I was fucked. I had to suck it up. I had to take it. I had to keep my mouth shut.

I sat down again, feeling like I was going to rip open with helplessness and frustration and fuckedness. This is what it means to implode, I thought. This feeling of bursting but no relief. I clapped my left hand – the one he hadn't burnt – over my mouth and shrieked into it. I screamed until tears burst from my eyes and my head began to clear and I saw what I had to do.

I had to go back to work.

No grand gestures. No taxi-hailing. No commands to be taken to the nearest police station. No ringing declarations that I wanted to report a crime.

I just had to do the do and act normally and go back to work.

But how am I going to explain my face? My hand?

What am I going to tell people?

What am I going to tell Damien?

I tried to piece a story together. Someone bumped into me? Someone was running and came flying at me and knocked me over? But then I'd have fallen backwards, no? And hit the back of my head? Not the side of my face?

Okay, how about, someone ran into me from behind? Yes. Better. I'd have fallen on my face.

But how would that explain the burn on my hand?

I searched and searched in my head and eventually thought, Okay, how about this? I'd tripped on a loose paving stone, I'd tumbled and banged my face, I'd dropped my cigarette and my hand landed on it?

It was crap but it would have to do.

I tried it out on the motherly woman working in the chemist in Dawson Street.

'Those footpaths are a disgrace,' she said. 'You certainly took a nasty tumble. The wound in your face might need a butterfly stitch. You should go to out-patients.'

No. It wasn't that bad. I wouldn't let it be that bad.

'Could you just put a plaster on it?' I asked. 'Some Savlon and a plaster? Just to stop the bleeding.'

'It's up to yourself. I'm only saying it because I wouldn't want it to scar, a lovely-looking girl like you.'

I would have wept at her kindness, if I'd been that sort of person.

She wiped some antiseptic along my cheek. 'You're a brave one,' she said. 'I thought that would sting.'

It had, but I didn't want to show it because – yes, I knew

it was stupid – I felt Paddy would be winning yet another round.

'Your cheekbone,' the woman said. 'It obviously took a hard crack there. It'll bruise up in a day or so. Black and blue for the next week. Just so as you know. Cancel any photo-shoots!'

Back at work, TC, Jacinta and the rest of them weren't exactly compassionate – they just found it too funny – but they blithely accepted the loose-paving-stone explanation. So by the time I saw Damien at home that evening, my story was smooth, well-rehearsed and obviously convincing because he was concern itself. He cooked dinner, he went out and got a DVD, he opened a bottle of wine and, after a couple of glasses, I became giddy with unexpected elation.

Damien and I were okay.

Damien and I had been saved.

I'd been so stupid. I'd been infected with de-Courcy-itis, I'd run the most idiotic, incredible risk, but it was over now, it had passed, and Damien and I were safe.

I wouldn't think about what Paddy had done to me. I wouldn't even let myself be angry. I would simply be grateful that I still had Damien.

The alarm clock rang and I woke with a jolt, plunged right into the horror of the previous night – the spectacular failure of the confrontation with Paddy, Marnie's cold rage, Damien's questions . . .

My entire body, even the soles of my feet, felt like it had been beaten up. The adrenaline of the past few days had taken its toll. I stretched out a weary arm. Damien's side of the bed was empty. It wasn't even warm. He'd obviously reset the clock and left ages ago.

It felt like an omen.

In the cold light of day, I knew, full and terrible and certain, that Damien was going to find out about Paddy and me. I'd known it last night, but it seemed worse, truer, today.

Marnie was so angry, she'd probably tell Damien.

Christ, maybe she'd already told him? Maybe she'd called him at work? Maybe, even now, he knew? My heart almost seized up in my chest at the thought.

And if Marnie didn't tell, de Courcy would. Again, maybe he'd already done it? After last night there was bound to be some sort of comeback from him. He would find some way to hurt me – to punish me – and the easiest thing would be to take away the person I treasured the most.

The whole appalling scenario played in my head like a horror film – Damien's pain, his grief, his bitterness at having been betrayed by me. He wouldn't be able to forgive me, I was certain of it. It was such a stretch for him to trust people and once that fragile trust was broken it couldn't be repaired. I was panting, actually panting, with fear. This couldn't happen. But I had no way of stopping it.

One thing I was sure of – I couldn't let Damien find out from someone else. I'd have to tell him myself.

Maybe tonight?

But, oh my God, the thought of it . . .

I was trapped in a nightmare. And the thing was, this entire situation, it was no one's fault but mine.

I'd made it happen, hadn't I? Quite apart from my carry-on with Paddy, I hadn't had to get involved when Damien told

me about the *Press* and their story about Dee, had I? I didn't
have to appoint myself as Dee's unofficial investigator.
I didn't have to start poking my nose into secret newspaper deals. I didn't have to start rounding up Paddy's old
girlfriends.

But I had.

I liked Dee, I admired her, and any sort of injustice fired
me up. But, when the chips were down, what was Dee
to me?

A connection to Paddy, that's what she was. Probably the
reason I'd asked to interview her all those months ago; why
I'd been so pleased when she invited Damien and me over
for off-ends pasta. And definitely why I'd got embroiled in
this political skulduggery.

But what the hell was wrong with me? I'd had the audacity
to get irritated with poor Marnie's long-lived attachment to
Paddy, but was I any better? I *knew* what he was capable of,
and I still thought I could take him on. And now – big
surprise – my life had blown up in my face.

Last night, Dee had tried to be 'Art of War' about the
disastrous showdown.

'We can learn from our mistakes,' she said.

But I didn't believe in that sort of thing. I preferred not
to make mistakes in the first place. And if I did make them
I'd rather cover them up and pretend they'd never happened.

God, I'd been so wrong about Leechy; I was *certain* she'd
have a cigarette scar on her hand. Because she'd been the
person who'd persuaded Christopher Holland to sell his
story about Dee I'd made the mistake of thinking she was just
another of Paddy's lackeys. Herself and Sheridan running

around, ordering the world to Paddy's vision, no better than Spanish John.

But maybe Paddy treated Leechy like an equal, maybe they'd come up with the idea together, as a team. Maybe Paddy had found the one woman he didn't need to abuse. Maybe he really did love her.

I was almost an hour late for work and I was wondering what excuse I'd give Jacinta. As I crossed the office to my desk, she was embroiled in some sort of tussle with TC.

Good. Maybe I could just slip in and pretend I'd been there all along . . .

'I can't do it,' TC was saying, in a high panicky voice.

'You have to,' Jacinta said, her voice steely and calm.

TC saw me and his face lit up with hope. 'Grace!'

Well, there was my cover blown.

He darted out from behind Jacinta. 'Will you do it, Grace? Please, Grace.'

'Do what?'

'Interview Zara Kaletsky. I've lost my nerve. I love her too much.'

'I –' Christ, could things get any worse?

'TC, you begged for the job,' Jacinta said with a sort of amused contempt. 'So go and do it.'

'Please, Grace?' TC thrust his beautiful red binder at me. 'I'll cover all your work. I'll stay late. I'll have sex with Damien. I'll do whatever you want.'

'Where the hell have you been?' Jacinta demanded of me. Then she switched back to TC and yelled, 'Why should Grace do it?' She was in her element, having two people to shout at simultaneously – probably as enjoyable as those four-hands massages where two therapists rub you at the same time. (Not that I'd know.) 'For God's sake, TC –' her tone dripped with scorn – 'be a man.'

It was that sentence – the unnecessary disparagement of it – that changed my mind. She was such a bully and right at that moment I'd had a bellyful of bullies.

'Which hotel?' I asked TC. 'Where's this thing going down?'

'The Shelbourne.'

They had nice biscuits there. I hadn't had any breakfast. I'd like some sugar.

'I'll do it.' I scooped up the red folder of loveliness and headed for the door.

'I'll decide who does what around here.' I could hear Jacinta yelling after me, but I was already gone.

A grim hotel corridor; disgruntled journalists lining the walls; the customary impenetrable selection process – business as usual. I parked myself in a plastic seat and prepared to endure. No one spoke. Seconds took hours to pass. Despair circulated instead of oxygen. Hell's waiting room might be a bit like this, I thought.

TC had compiled a volume of research notes weighty enough to rival *War and Peace* but everything seemed so pointless and stupid that I could bring myself only to glean the bare bones about Zara Kaletsky. Her life was such a cliché, it was almost parodic. She'd been a model, who'd crossed over to acting. A few years ago she'd moved to LA and fallen off the radar and the Irish press would have been faster to interview a zinc bucket. Then she'd got a part in a Spielberg film and suddenly all Irish outlets were clamouring like hungry dogs for a piece of her.

The terribleness of last night – the hubris, the failure, Marnie's anger, Paddy's easy victory – had imbued me with wretched hopelessness, with a sense that life on earth was a miserable business, that goodness was always trumped by bad, that those with power would never cede any of it, that the little person would never win even the tiniest of victories. It felt immoral to celebrate a woman who earned a shockingly large amount of money from the frivolous business of pretending to be other people.

'Grace Gildee? The *Spokesman*?'

I got to my feet. I'd only been waiting two hours and seventeen minutes. That must surely count as a record.

'Thirty minutes,' the clipboard maven hissed malevolently as I passed her to enter the sanctum. 'Not a second more.'

'Grand,' I hissed back. I took a moment to gather more spittle on my tongue – proper hissing requires a good deal of it – then, like air leaving a burst tyre, said, 'Cssssertainly, missssss. Not a sssssssecond exsssstra. Thankssssssssss for your assssssssssissssssssstancsssssse.'

I was pleased with the way I'd managed to think of so many words with sibilant sounds. No notice. Just off the top of my head. With a perky – but, I hoped, unsettling – smile at her, I closed the door. Then – I just couldn't stop myself – I opened it again, thrust my chin at her, gave a quick, snaky, 'Sssssss!' and closed the door once more.

She'd think she'd imagined it.

Zara was alabaster pale, with a cap of short shiny hair and eyes so dark and soulful they were almost black. She rose and smiled. Six foot tall and thin as a whip.

I waved her back into her seat, 'Don't get up, no need,' whipped open my notebook and clattered my tape recorder onto the table.

'I didn't catch your name,' she said.

'– Oh? Grace. But it doesn't matter. We'll never meet again. And you don't need to end every sentence with my name to convince me of your sincerity. I'm already convinced!'

She looked a little alarmed.

'So no publicist sitting in and monitoring our every word?' I asked.

'. . . No. I thought – think – it makes everyone uncomfortable.'

'Grand.' It just meant she wasn't proper really-weird-with-many-perversions A-list. 'Okay, Zara, let's do us both a favour. You must be sick of doing interviews and I'm not really in the mood either. We'll make this quick. Wheat allergy?'

'– What?'

'Wheat allergy?' I repeated, louder this time. 'Yes or no?'

'. . . No.'

'Really? Lactose intolerant, then, yes?' I scribbled on my pad. 'No? Sure? Okay. You might want to sort that out, if you don't mind me saying. Yoga? Saved your life?'

'Meditation, actually.'

'Same difference,' I muttered. I'd done neither but why let the facts get in the way?

779

I scanned TC's notes. 'Middle child,' I said. 'Let me guess. Parents more interested in your siblings, blah, you started singing and dancing, blah, to get their attention? Yes? Yays? Good girl. Let's see. Six foot tall at the age of twelve, ugly duckling, blah, swan, beauty queen, Miss Donegal, so far so blah. Anorexia?'

'. . . Um.'

'Bout of anorexia?' I said. 'As a teenager? Yes?' I nodded along with her. 'But you're grand now, great appetite, always stuffing your face, just a very high metabolism.'

My glance leapfrogged further down the page. 'Lalala, let's see, Irish soap. Big success. Mmmmmm, had gone as far as you could go in Ireland, yes? Yes? Yays. Good. Went to LA, hoping to make the blah-time? Struggled initially, then got lucky when Spielblah saw you in something or other.'

Tell me, why did these people bother having lives at all? When they're not capable of one original action? When everything has already been pre-scripted in the pages of *Hello!*

'No, wait, whoops, nearly missed that. You went to South Africa first, *then* you went to LA. Why'd you go to South Africa? Since when did they have a film industry?'

'Fancied a change of scene,' she said, in a strained voice.

'Grand,' I said breezily. 'Don't tell me, I don't care. Whatever it was, bankruptcy, plastic surgery spree, your secret's safe with me. So what else can we discuss? Men? Let me guess. No one special, you're having fun at the moment, but you hope to settle down at the ancient age of thirty. Yays?'

'I'm already thirty-three.'

Was she? Looking good on it. That'd be all the poison she injected into her forehead, I presumed. 'You'd like two children, a boy and a girl. You're based in LA now but Ireland will always be home? Yes? Yays. Excellent! Let's call that done!'

I got to my feet and stuck out my hand. 'Pleasure, Ms Kaletsky.'

She wouldn't take my hand. Uppity diva.

'Come on,' I cajoled. 'No hard feelings.' I thrust my hand at her again.

She looked at it but wouldn't hold it, trying to shame me into letting it drop.

'Have it your way,' I said. 'Nice meeting –'

'How did you get that mark?'

'. . . What mark?'

It was then that I realized she wasn't refusing to shake my hand, but that her attention had been caught by some-thing. She took my right hand between both of hers and uncurled my fingers. 'That mark,' she said.

We both looked at the circle of pink shiny skin in the middle of my palm. '. . . I –'

Then we looked at each other. Something passed between us, information that was fully articulated without having to even say his name. My fingers tingled.

'Snap.' In one lithe movement she splayed the fingers on her right hand, flashing her scar like an ID.

I couldn't speak. I was literally struck dumb.

'Let's see.' Zara surveyed me. 'Always considered your-self a bit of a firebrand. Yes? Edited the school magazine.

Got up a couple of small petitions. Nothing too controversial. Decided not to go to college but to learn at the university of life. Yes? Worked hard news until you found you didn't have the stomach for it. At some stage crossed paths with Paddy de Courcy, thought you'd be the girl to change him, but ended up with a faceful of bruises and a burnt hand for your presumption. Yes?'

I opened my mouth. Sentences floated and danced in my head but none of them emerged as sounds.

Finally I said, 'He's the reason you left Ireland?'

'I made the mistake of going to the police. He was so angry I thought he was going to kill me.'

She went to the police?

'And was he, like, *charged*?' How had he kept that out of the press?

'Not at all.' She rolled her eyes. 'These two fat eejits showed up in their yellow jackets and as soon as they'd established it was "only" a domestic, they told us to kiss and make up, then were off down the road to buy chips and batterburgers. All I could do was apply for a barring order – which would take twelve weeks. By then I was long gone.'

'Why South Africa?'

'It was the furthest place I could think of.'

Why hadn't I thought of Zara? I didn't know. Perhaps I'd assumed that Paddy wouldn't hurt glamorous women, those who might be listened to.

Excitement began to build. An idea was taking shape –

'It's not just you and me,' Zara said.

'I know –'

'There's Selma Teeley.'

'The mountaineer?'

'Retired. He broke a bone in her hand that never healed properly.'

'What? Really?'

'She rang me when I started going out with him, trying to warn me. By the time I discovered she wasn't some mad stalkery ex-girlfriend, he'd made me come off the pill, got me pregnant, made me have an abortion, then raped me the same day.' She paused, then added, 'Among other stuff, of course. But that's the one that stands out most.'

'Christ,' I breathed.

'Did *you* go to the police?' Zara asked.

Ashamed, I shook my head.

'Like they'd have believed you anyway.' Zara flicked her eyes heavenwards. 'It's hard enough if you're getting lamped by a bloke, but if you're being hit by delicious Paddy de Courcy, the housewives' choice, you haven't a hope. I don't know why I bothered. Who would ever have taken my word over Paddy's? Me, an ex-model in a crappy soap?'

'But you're not an ex-model in a crappy soap any longer,' I said. 'You're now a Hollywood star.'

'God, yeah, when you put it like that, I suppose I am.'

'You're powerful now, Zara. More powerful than him.'

'God, yeah, when you put it like that, I suppose I am.'

Marnie

She was lying in bed in what had been her teenage bedroom, playing the Leonard Cohen record she used to listen to when she was fifteen. The original vinyl record. Some people would probably get excited about that – idiotic boys in black T-shirts.

A person was at the front door – her bedroom was right over it, she heard everything that happened down there.

'Grace!' Ma's voice declared. 'What a lovely surprise. And in the middle of the working day!'

Grace. Marnie had been expecting a conciliatory visit from her. In fact, she'd been starting to wonder what was taking her so long.

'Where's Marnie?' Grace's voice was terse.

'Upstairs, in her old room. Playing that wretched Cohen man's record. I should have snapped it over my knee the day she left home.'

A moment later there was a light tap on the bedroom door and Grace's voice called, 'Marnie, can I come in?'

Marnie contemplated refusing: she could simply send Grace away without seeing her. But she'd spent a sleepless night at the mercy of her imagination: the pictures in her head had been excruciating. What exactly had gone on with Grace and Paddy? She needed to know. 'Door's open,' she said.

Grace sidled in. She looked abashed but there was something about her she was trying to contain: an energy, an excitement. 'Marnie, we need to talk. I – I've so much explaining to do to you. And I will. But something has happened and it won't wait.'

'I don't care,' Marnie said. 'Whatever is happening will *have* to wait. I want to know all about you and Paddy. Now. And,' she added with as much hostility as she could muster, 'don't do a PG version to save my feelings so that I won't drink.'

Grace actually squirmed – then rallied with, 'Are you sober? Not much point me telling the story if you're not going to remember any of it.'

'I'm. Sober.' Marnie bit the words out, with icy dignity.

She stared at Grace, hoping the bitterness she felt showed on her face. Grace stared back at her. They flat-eyed each other for several long seconds, then Grace dropped her look.

'How come you didn't drink . . .' she asked.

The truth was that Marnie had no idea why she hadn't got drunk. The rejection she'd experienced last night, the humiliation, the self-hatred, the sense that she was an idiot and had always been an idiot – these were the exact feelings she usually sought to obliterate with alcohol. Add anger into the mix – anger with Grace and Paddy – and extreme drunkenness could be considered a dead cert. Instead she'd sat in the kitchen, chatting with Ma, drinking cocoa and eating poppy-seed cake and complaining about how the seeds stick between your teeth.

'Perhaps I grew up a little last night,' Marnie said with acrimony. 'Perhaps my youthful ideals about people were stripped away . . .' *Or maybe I just couldn't stomach Dad's nettle wine.* 'So, Grace. Tell me about you and Paddy, your big love affair. And remember, I'll know when you're lying.'

One of Marnie's dubious 'gifts': the ability to recognize an attempt to humour her.

'Okay.' Grace sat down heavily, opened her mouth and told the story beginning with her first night working at the Boatman. At times she paused, choosing words with great care, perhaps

– Marnie wondered – words that softened the most brutal parts? But when she eventually finished, Marnie knew instinctively that nothing had been left out.

Grace was as white as milk from the ordeal. 'I'm bitterly ashamed, Marnie, and that's putting it mildly. From day one, I wanted to protect you and I'm the one to cause you so much pain –'

'Stop, Grace, stop. Enough for now.' This wasn't over but Marnie couldn't take any more.

'So can I tell you what's happened?' Grace asked.

Marnie nodded, her eyes closed.

'There are two other women of Paddy's, there might be even more. We're going back again tonight.'

'To Paddy's?'

'Yes. Will you come?'

Would she?

Why would she help Grace? Why would she return to the scene of her humiliation? But the truth, Marnie realized, was that she was glad of the chance. *Why?* Was she a sucker for punishment? But there had been too much confusion and shouting last night. This was an opportunity to do it again, but better.

'We're all swearing affidavits,' Grace said. 'We detail under oath what he did to us. Dee has given us a lawyer. You on?'

Marnie nodded.

'I'll set it up. Can I tell you how we're planning to play it tonight?'

'No.' She wanted Grace to go now. She was exhausted.

After Grace had left, Ma came into Marnie's room and sat on the bed. 'Turn off that dirge,' she urged gently. 'He'd make Coco the Clown feel suicidal.'

'Okay.' Marnie lifted the needle and, mid-sentence, Leonard Cohen ceased.

'That's better,' Ma said. 'Would you like to tell me what's going on?'

Marnie was overwhelmed by the size of the situation. Helplessly she said, 'Paddy de Courcy . . .'

'What about him?'

'It's . . . I . . . Grace . . . It's really complicated.'

'He was your teenage boyfriend. A long time ago. You're married now, you have two children.'

'Yes, but –'

' "If a person continues to see only giants, it means he is still looking at the world through the eyes of a child," ' Ma said. 'Anaïs Nin.'

Marnie nodded.

' "Things do not change," ' Ma said. ' "We change." Thoreau.'

'Good point.'

' "If at first you don't succeed, you're running about average," ' Ma said. 'MH Alderson.'

Marnie stopped looking at Ma.

' "Never grow a wishbone where your backbone ought to be," ' Ma said. 'Clementine Paddleford.'

Marnie stared at her lap.

' "When life throws us lemons –" '

'Thank you, Ma, that's enough!' Marnie said.

It was like a rerun of the previous evening, except that there were two cars this time. Marnie waited in one with Zara and Selma. Grace was in the other with Dee and Lola.

It was ten to eleven and Paddy and Alicia were expected shortly.

788

Selma looked from Marnie to Zara and laughed. 'Paddy definitely doesn't have a type, does he?'

True. Marnie was fascinated by the other two. Zara had a face of transcendent beauty and was so lanky she was like a normal person who had been stretched to twice their length. Selma, by contrast, had a lean bony look, crinkly blonde hair and a short, wiry sportswoman's body. Her calves were far too muscular for the spindly heels she was wearing. Marnie thought she looked like a sideboard.

Even their personalities were poles apart: Zara was languid and sarcastic whereas Selma was confident and mouthy.

As they waited for Paddy and Alicia to come home, they exchanged war stories.

Zara had been his girlfriend for two and a half years. Selma had been with him for *five* – and actually living with him for three of those years. Zara had been pregnant – and raped – by him. Selma – when he'd broken a bone in her hand which had never healed properly – had had her career as a sportswoman effectively ended by him.

'That's horrific, Selma,' Marnie breathed. 'Why didn't you go to the police?' The words were out of her mouth before she'd thought them through.

Selma gave her a hard look. 'Why didn't *you* go to the police?'

'. . . Sorry, I . . .' It was a ludicrous question, considering what Marnie herself had been through with Paddy. But when you heard that someone had been hurt by someone else, the automatic response was to suggest that they went to the police.

'Because you loved him, right?' Selma pressed. 'You didn't want him to get into trouble?'

'Selma, I'm sorry, I just wasn't thinking . . .' God, she was scary.

'Well, I loved him too,' Selma said. 'Or at least I thought I did, but we won't get into that now. Obviously I was out of my fucking mind. *Any*way, I *did* go to the cops. Four separate times.'

'My God!' Zara said. 'I'm surprised you're still alive. So how'd he wriggle out of any charges?'

'You know what he's like,' Selma said scornfully. 'He always talked me out of it, swore to me on his mother's memory that he'd never touch me again, blamed it on his job being stressful. The *usual*. And thicko here bought it every time. Kept thinking things would be different. Hope sprang eternal.' She gave a little laugh, and added, 'Then it stopped springing. And when he dumped me, I suppose *then* I could have gone to the cops, nothing stopping me, but well . . . I wasn't myself, put it that way.'

'Confidence destroyed?' Zara said sympathetically. Marnie listened agog.

'I was a fucking *wreck*,' Selma said. 'It took me a full year before I could eat peas.'

'*Peas?*' Marnie said. 'Why peas?'

'Because my hands shook so much they wouldn't stay on my fork.'

'How come there's never anything in the papers about him?' Marnie wanted to know.

'Until someone actually brings charges there's nothing to report.'

'But what about, "Police were called to a disturbance at Paddy de Courcy's house." That sort of thing?'

Zara and Selma both furrowed their foreheads and looked at Marnie with a sort of concerned pity.

'Unsubstantiated innuendo?' Zara raised her thin black eyebrows.

'Are you mad?' Selma cut in. 'He'd slap a writ on them so fast their heads would spin.'

'And he has the press in his pocket,' Zara said. 'Great relationships with editors and journalists. They love him.'

'Duh!' Selma added.

'I live in London!' Marnie felt she had to defend herself. 'How would I know?' She caught her breath. 'Oh my God. Here's his car.'

All three of them slid down in their seats although they were parked too far away from his flat to be spotted.

Selma couldn't resist sticking her head up for a look. 'Look at him, the fucker,' she breathed, her eyes glittering.

They'd decided upon a three-minute wait this time; Dee had deduced that last night's eleven minutes had been far too long. 'Go in fast and hard,' she'd recommended. 'Ideally before he has time to do a piss. Don't let him get comfortable.'

As they emerged from the cars, two groups of three, and joined forces, Marnie watched Selma walk like a sideboard up to Grace and ask, 'After last night's balls-up, will he even let you in?'

'Yeah.' Grace sighed. 'He's not a bit scared of us.'

Dee got them through the downstairs entrance. '*Courage, mes braves*,' she urged after them, as they climbed the stairs. 'I'll be with you in spirit.'

Grace went first, then Lola, Selma, Zara and right at the back, Marnie. Her legs were buzzing with anxiety as they filed down the hall and gathered outside Paddy's flat.

'Do the knocker,' Selma told Grace.

'But he's expecting Dee, he'll open the door in a minute anyway.'

'Bang the knocker,' Selma urged. 'Be proactive.'

But it was too late. Paddy was swinging the door open, and when he saw the cluster of them waiting to see him, he exploded with laughter. Real laughter, Marnie thought, not the fake kind that people sometimes do in an attempt to undermine.

We left it too late, she realized. He's had his piss.

'For God's sake!' he declared. 'What now?'

'Can we come in?' Grace asked.

He flicked his eyes heavenward. 'Not for long. And I don't want you making a habit of this.'

'This will be the last time,' Grace said.

As they filed through the door he lavished compliments. 'Lola, beautiful as ever! Selma, you look great.'

It was only when he focused on Zara that Marnie noticed the tiniest loss of aplomb in him.

'. . . Spielberg's muse! What an honour! And Marnie, of course.'

In the sitting room, the same venue as last night, everyone sat except for Grace and Paddy. Marnie had somehow ended up in the same seat as last night, which she feared augured badly. She watched as Grace thrust a large, fat, white envelope at Paddy and he ignored it.

'Should I get Alicia for you?' he solicitously asked Grace. 'Will we be having a repeat of that strange little scene from last night, with you shoving her sleeves up?'

Grace's face flamed and she shook her head abruptly. 'No need for Alicia.'

Once again, she thrust the envelope at him and this time – to Marnie's relief – he took it. 'Present for you,' Grace said. 'Copies of affidavits made by the five of us, detailing what you did to us. The originals are in a safe.'

Paddy took a seat, slit the envelope and flicked briefly

through the pages before casting them aside as if they were nothing.

'A lone woman making accusations,' Grace said, standing in the middle of the room. 'You could dismiss her as a nutter. Two even. But three, you're getting into different territory. And when there're five, it's looking very bad for you. Especially when one of them is Hollywood's hottest new star.'

Paddy laughed.

'And it's only a matter of time before we talk to more of your exes,' Grace said.

An amused little grin sat on Paddy's face. 'Grace Gildee, you're gas, so you are. The bees you get in your bonnet.'

Then he turned to Zara and said, 'Zara Kaletsky! Well, I must say I'm honoured to have you in my humble home. Tell me all about Los Angeles. Is it true what they say? That no one ever eats?'

'I'm not here to discuss Los Angeles with you,' Zara said coldly.

'Because if they don't eat, that would suit you down to the ground.' Paddy winked at her. 'You and your ... ahem ... old trouble.'

Marnie had a vague memory of having read somewhere that Zara had had anorexia when she was a teenager. God, Paddy went straight for the jugular with everyone. This was going to be like last night all over again. He'd undermine them all individually and they'd just fall apart.

'And Selma.' He turned the warmth of his smile on her. 'How's the sports consultation going? Oh I forgot. It went belly-up for you. That must have been tough. No money coming in, life can't be easy ... Well, now!' He gave a great big smile around the room. 'It's been a pleasure talking to you girls, but I've had a long day, so if you'll excuse me ...'

'Paddy, the affidavits,' Grace said. 'We're serious.'

He stretched his arms above his head and gave a long, yowly yawn. 'Serious about what?'

'We *will* go to the press.'

'Will you now?'

'Unless . . .'

'Unless what?'

'Unless –' Grace inhaled and the entire room became frozen and focused. Marnie noticed that even Paddy, who was doing a great impression of someone who simply couldn't be less interested, was listening.

'Unless you resign from NewIreland.' Grace counted on her fingers. 'Announce that you're opting out of Irish political life. Accept a lecturing post in a US university for at least the next five years –' As the list went on, Paddy barked with laughter.

'– Apologize individually to each of us here. Withdraw the story about the Moldovan women from the *Press*. Call a halt to all other plans to undermine Dee.'

Grace finished.

'That's it?' Paddy asked, wreathed in smiles.

'Yes.' Marnie heard Grace's voice betray the tiniest little tremor. Perhaps no one else heard it but she knew her so well . . .

'You're not asking for much, are you?' he said sarcastically.

'That's the choice,' Grace said. 'It's either that or we all go to the media with our stories and you're sunk anyway.'

'My word against yours,' he said.

'There are five of us. At *least*. So what's it to be?'

Paddy sat back in his seat and, watched avidly by everyone in the room, he closed his eyes.

Marnie stopped breathing.

Eventually Paddy straightened up and opened his eyes. He looked around the room, at each of them in turn.

The tension in Marnie intensified; she thought her chest might burst.

Then Paddy took a breath to speak. 'No,' he said.

No? Marnie dug her nails into her palms. This was another disaster, worse than last night.

'Resign?' Paddy asked scornfully. 'Give up politics? Leave the country? Lecture in a foreign university? Are you fucking mad? No way.'

'Is there anything at all you'll do for us?' Grace asked.

The tremor in Grace's voice was really audible now, Marnie realized. Everyone – including Paddy – must be able to hear it. Marnie wished she'd shut up, she was humiliating them all.

Paddy laughed. 'No. There is nothing I will do for you.'

'Not even call off the Moldovan story? You call off that story, we'll call off ours. Surely that's fair?'

'Oh all right, all right!' Still grinning Paddy said, 'I don't know where you get the idea that I've any influence with the Irish media. Sure, I'm only a humble TD. But I could have a word, see if, as a favour to me, some of the journos who have it in for her will back off.' With a chuckle he added, 'And – without prejudice – you can have your apologies.' *For what they're worth*, hung unspoken in the air. 'But that's it,' he said. 'That's all you're getting.'

'You'll leave Dee alone and you'll apologize to us?' Grace said in a flat voice. 'That's *it*?'

'That's it. Take the offer right now or it's off the table.'

'Take it, Grace,' Selma urged in a low voice.

'Don't,' Zara said.

'Clock is ticking,' Paddy said.

'Take it, Grace,' Selma repeated.

795

'Don't!' Zara said. 'We can get more.'

'But he says he won't – ' Grace protested.

'This is all we'll get,' Selma said.

'No.' Zara was clearly very angry. 'Wait. We've got the power here.'

Marnie watched Paddy watching the tripartite tussle. His face gleamed: he obviously loved this stuff.

'Time's running out, girls,' he said.

'What do you think, Lola?' Selma asked.

'Hold out for more,' Lola said. 'The resignation at least.'

'Marnie?' Selma asked.

Marnie was surprised to be asked. 'Take it.' She'd like the apology.

'Three . . .' Paddy said. '. . . Two . . .'

'Take it!'

'No!' Zara made one last-ditch attempt to change their course. 'Hold out for more.'

'. . . One!'

With a heavy sigh Grace said, 'Majority vote.' She turned to Paddy, 'Okay, Paddy. We'll take it.'

'Wise choice, very wise choice.'

Marnie was fascinated by how he found this so very amusing. Clearly he thrived on it. 'And I'll have the originals of those affidavits, thanks. Get them round to me tomorrow.'

'Okay,' Grace said, looking very subdued.

If Marnie didn't know for a fact that Grace never cried, she wouldn't have been at all surprised if a tear or two had trickled down Grace's face.

'Go on, then,' Grace sighed at Paddy.

'Go on, then, what . . . ?'

'Apologize.'

'What? When?'

'Now.'

'You mean . . . right now?'

'When were you thinking of?'

'. . . Well . . .' He shifted back in his seat.

'When else?' Grace asked. 'The gang's all here.'

Paddy pushed himself further into his chair. Marnie watched in fascination: he really didn't want to do this. 'It doesn't have to be now,' he said.

'Probably best if it is,' Grace said. 'It might be a long time before we're all together again. Go on,' Grace urged. 'Start with Lola.'

Paddy looked at Lola. He seemed lost for words. '. . . Lola, I'm . . .'

Way out of your comfort zone, Marnie thought.

'– Sorry –' Grace prompted.

'– sorry if I hurt you.'

'And for saying my hair was purple,' Lola said in her little voice. 'It's Molichino.'

'Molichino,' he echoed.

Next along was Zara. 'Zara, I'm sorry if I hurt you.'

Zara gave a sardonic smirk and Paddy moved to Selma. 'Selma, I'm sorry if I hurt you.'

'Marnie, I'm sorry if I hurt you.'

It had happened too fast; Marnie had expected special words which pertained exclusively to her, but already he was on to Grace.

'Grace, I'm sorry if I hurt you.'

Last apology done, Paddy exhaled with evident relief – and after a split second the room exploded into laughter. All of them – except for Marnie – were howling.

What was going on, she wondered.

'What are you laughing at?' Paddy seemed confused.

797

'You,' Zara said. 'We're laughing at you.'

'Why?' Paddy frowned suspiciously at her.

' "I'm sorry if I hurt you!" ' Selma mimicked. 'How do you think a broken wrist feels?'

'Or a ruptured spleen!' Zara said.

'Or a dislocated shoulder!'

'Did you really think we expected you'd resign and go to America?' Grace asked cheerfully.

'But why did you say –?' Paddy asked.

Marnie suddenly understood.

So, from the shut-down expression on his face, did Paddy.

'Oldest negotiating trick in the book,' Grace said. 'Ask for more than you want. And you fell for it because you thought we were just a bunch of stupid women. All we wanted was a commitment from you to stop sabotaging Dee.'

'Did you like the way we did it?' Selma asked giddily. ' "Take it, Grace!" "No, don't take it, Grace!" '

It had all been rehearsed, Marnie realized. Right down to the tremor in Grace's voice. She remembered now how, earlier in the day, Grace had invited her to be in on the whole thing, but she'd been too angry.

'But the apologies . . . ?' Paddy asked faintly.

'That was just for the laugh!'

'Like your apology would count for anything!' Zara declared with terrible scorn. 'Like we'd ever forgive you!'

'We knew you'd hate having to do it,' Grace said. 'After all, being a power-mad mentaller means never having to say you're sorry.'

Paddy rose to his feet; his fists were clenched.

'Whoahhhhh!' All five of them exclaimed in mock fear, as if they'd choreographed it.

'Careful, Paddy,' Grace said. 'You don't know your own strength. You might hurt someone there!'

'Keep him away from any lit cigarettes!' Lola said, and the laughter broke forth again with renewed intensity.

Paddy lowered himself slowly back into his seat and his eyes moved from one woman to the next, as all of them laughed at him. He hadn't expected this, Marnie knew. To her eyes, he actually looked frightened.

'We only made you apologize, in order to humiliate you!'

'And look at you,' Grace declared, breaking into a fresh round of hilarity. 'You're mortified!'

In high spirits, they skipped and tripped back down the stairs to Dee.

'It was a triumph!' Grace told her.

Everyone was talking over each other – everyone except Marnie – telling Dee what had happened.

'. . . and Grace was pretending to be nervous . . .'

'. . . and then Selma said, "Take it!" and Zara said, "Don't!" . . .'

'. . . and Paddy was smirking away, thinking we were falling apart . . .'

'. . . and Paddy was so humiliated . . .'

'Everyone back to mine for drinks!' Dee said. 'Grace, ring that man of yours, he deserves to be in on this. If it wasn't for him, none of it would have happened.'

Grace looked anxiously at Marnie and said, 'Ah no, Dee, it's late, he might be in bed.'

'So get him out of bed!' Dee ordered. 'We're celebrating here!'

'No, let's leave it –'

Marnie understood. Grace was afraid that Marnie would tell Damien about Grace and Paddy.

'Ring him,' Marnie said quietly. 'I'm not going to say anything.'

She'd already caused so much destruction, especially to Daisy and Verity. The world was too full of pain, she couldn't add any more. Yet she was angry with Grace. She hadn't forgiven her. *Maybe I never will*. The thought was surprising. Interesting.

Despite Marnie's assurance, Grace claimed she couldn't get hold of Damien. 'No answer,' she said, snapping her mobile shut.

'Try the house phone,' Dee ordered.

'I've tried it.'

'Try his mobile.'

'I've tried it.'

'Try his office.'

'I've tried it.'

'Leave a message telling him what's going on. Maybe he'll come along later,' Dee said. 'Okay! Everyone, let's go.'

Marnie got into Selma's car but asked to be dropped off at a taxi rank.

'Aren't you coming to Dee's to celebrate?' Selma and Zara seemed quite shocked.

Marnie shook her head. She just wanted to escape. She wished she could go back to London immediately, but the last flight of the night had left.

'If you're sure . . .' Selma said.

'Quite sure.' Marnie jumped out and caught a cab back to Ma and Dad's.

The full import of the night's events was settling on her. There was no getting around it, no avoiding the truth, that she'd been *nothing* to Paddy – nobody; a teenage thing that he'd totally forgotten. So many other women had come after her, including her own sister. Women who overshadowed her, who'd been with Paddy for longer, who'd lived with him . . .

Marnie's face smarted with heat as she acknowledged that she had hoped that he'd behave as though they shared a special bond which transcended the passage of time; that although their love had been too incendiary to survive, they had carried each other in their hearts as they forged their different paths.

But theirs hadn't been a grand passion. The simple truth was that she'd been a neurotic, insecure fuck-up and he'd joined in for a while before changing his mind and deciding that, actually, he wanted to be normal after all.

She felt humiliated and angry, but who was she angry with? Grace? Paddy? Herself?

She didn't know. All she knew was that she was returning to London in the morning and that she was not alone.

Alcohol was there for her.

It would never let her down.

Grace

The phone rang, jolting me from a deep drunken sleep and my heart nearly exploded from the shock of the noise. I'd been up half the night, celebrating with Dee, Selma and Zara. It had been after five when I'd staggered in, rowdy and raucous, and woken Damien up. 'Where were you?' I pulled at him. 'I was ringing and ringing you to come and join the party.'

'I was on a story,' he'd said. 'And I've to get up in two hours.'

'But I want to tell you how we laughed at Paddy.'

'Tell me another time.'

Now, according to the alarm clock, it was ten past nine. I was alone in the bed. Damien must have gone to work.

I picked up the phone just to stop the horrible frenzied shrieking. My nerves were all ajangle. Last night's adrenaline and alcohol had worn off and I was once again enmeshed in the all-consuming fear of Damien finding out about Paddy.

Tentatively I said, 'Hello.'

It was Marnie. 'I'm in Dublin airport, I'm just about to get on a flight.'

So early?

'I meant what I said last night: I won't tell Damien about you and Paddy.'

'. . . Thank you.' I should have been thrilled but her tone was dispiritingly hostile.

'And stop coming to London every weekend. I don't want to see you.'

I was stricken. I *needed* to keep visiting her. So many dangerous, possibly even fatal, things could happen while she was drunk and there really was no one else to check on her.

And God only knew how she felt in the wake of this de Courcy business. Last night some of the other girls blossomed visibly as Paddy became reduced in their eyes. Lola the stylist, in particular. It was as if she'd shrugged off her fear of de Courcy and she was suddenly standing fully upright.

But there were no high spirits and group bonding from Marnie. In the triumphant al fresco debriefing for Dee she'd stayed on the edge of the group, then she didn't come for a drink – cunningly she'd *pretended* she was, she'd got into the car with Zara and Selma but by the time they arrived at Dee's house, Marnie had jumped ship.

I didn't know what Marnie thought of Paddy now – I just couldn't call it, but I suspected it was one of two extremes. Either she'd realized that she and Paddy had been nothing but a teenage thing. Or else she was still holding on to the Love of Her Life theory. Either way, I suspected her way of dealing with it would be to drink a lot.

'Stay away from me,' she said, then she hung up.

I had to confess to Damien. The thought of it was so frightening I whimpered into my pillow, but it was the right thing to do.

But a cowardly little voice whispered, *What if there's no need to tell him?* What if de Courcy had no plans to drop me in it? What if I went ahead and told all to Damien when it wasn't necessary?

So maybe I *shouldn't* tell him.

But could I live with the guilt? Its cumbersome presence had kept us knocked off balance since last summer.

Maybe I should just square my shoulders and bite the bullet and tell him.

Christ . . .

Lola

Saturday, 24 January 10.06
Driving to Knockavoy. Planned to pack up and return to Dublin. Suddenly keen to just get it done.

Much to think about as I drove.

Discovered was glad had made trip to Dublin. Not glad after first night of Paddy confrontation, of course. When he had said, 'Who's going to believe that fashion flake with the purple hair?' I was aghast.

Had seen the light — I had just been little doll to have kinky sex with. Like I was less than a person. Bad, burny feeling. How had I let self be treated so badly?

Had always thought because he loved his dead mother that he was sensitive man. But, as drove along, realized he was sensitive man. But also unpleasant man. People can have many aspects.

Handy thing to know.

But second night, with Zara and Selma and much mockery of Paddy, was liberation. He no longer seemed so scary. Or — interesting this — so good-looking. Bouffiness of hair a bad business.

Also, knowing he had hurt other women was helpful. Wouldn't wish it on worst enemy (technically Sybil O'Sullivan even if couldn't remember why we had fallen out) but no longer felt like it was my fault. He was first — and would be last — man who hit me. He, however, had *form*. So whose fault was it? Yes, his.

He had got me at vulnerable time in life: best friends all

807

coupled-up; mother deceased; no father figure. I'd been bit like Paddy, actually – but at least I didn't go round punching people in fizzog.

12.29
Arrived Knockavoy
Two seconds after parked car, Considine's door opened. I legged it across grass and into his house.

'Tea?' he asked.

'Yes, yes. Okay, you ready to hear everything?'

Had texted him bare outline, but had given no details.

He said, 'Ready? Am so keen to hear didn't even go potholing today.'

Sacrifice.

'Have been listening for your car for last three hours.'

'Like lonely rural person?'

'*Just* like lonely rural person!'

Same wavelength.

'In fairness, must warn you, Considine, I did not cover self in glory. At no point did I swagger in front of Paddy and say, "Hah! Once upon time was mad about you but now see you as bouffy-haired brute that you really are!"'

'That is shame,' he said sympathetically. 'Missed opportunity. But surely you said, "I have moved on with my life"? No? No.' He nodded understandingly. '*Too Hollyoaks?*'

'Exactly, Considine! *Too Hollyoaks* is exactly what it is!'

'Even though you *have* moved on.'

'Yes, but no one should say it.'

'Saying it makes you sound like you *not* moved on,' he said. 'Paradox.'

'Yes, indeed, Considine, paradox. Okay, from start to finish, here is whole story.'

Related it all. Even the unpalatable details. 'First night I said almost nothing to him and my knees wouldn't stop shaking. However, second night, different story.' Bragging slightly. 'Made him eat own words about purple hair! "Molichino," I said. Made him repeat it!'

'Best thing you could have done, taking him on,' Considine concluded. 'Will stand to you, no doubt about it. You not terrified of bumping into him when back in Dublin?'

'No.' On other hand was not relishing thought of it either, but why dwell on negative?

Sunday, 25 January
Packed everything. Tidied house. Said my farewells to everyone in town. Must admit, very choked. Had arrived five months earlier, a wreck. Now returning to old life, not exactly as good as new, because would never be the same as was before I met Paddy, but in reasonable enough nick.

Considine came to help carry bags into car. Didn't take long.

'Everything in?' He smacked the boot.

'Yep!' I slapped the back window. 'Everything in.'

Both of us being over-jovial and manly, our hands hanging conspicuously by our sides as if they had suddenly swollen to ten times their normal size.

'Will you be back?' he asked.

'Yes, probably, some weekend, for hen night maybe.'

He nodded awkwardly. We both swung our abnormally noticeable hands.

After silence, I said, 'Thank you, you have been kindly to me in my time here. Sharing your telly. Advising me on de Courcy.'

He nodded again. 'You have been kindly to me also. Trannie evenings. Loan of plunger. Badger's arse night.'

More silence, then I asked, 'You ever come to Dublin for your eco-swot job?'

'No.'

'Oh. You ever come to Dublin to visit friends?'

'No.'

'Oh?'

'Have no friends in Dublin.'

'Surely I am your friend?' said stoutly. 'And I live in Dublin.'

'In that case might visit you.'

'Good. We will get rough as badger's arse.'

'Will look forward to it. Goodbye, Lola.'

Looked at him. Dark eyes. Messy hair. And God, you know something . . .

Took step towards him, he took step towards me, I tilted my face up to him, he grasped me with hand around lower back and held his mouth against mine, lips touching lips. For few seconds stayed like that, without moving, like movie kiss. Quivered — both of us — actually quivered with want — felt it in him, felt it in me — before melting into each other. Slow, sensual, knee-weakening. Rossa Considine extremely sexy kisser.

18.44

My flat in Dublin

Welcomed home by Bridie, Barry, Treese and Jem.

'Said goodbye to all your Knockavoy pals?' Bridie asked.

'Yes.'

'Sad?'

'Yes.'

'We will go back one day for visit,' she promised. 'Uncle Tom's cabin should be free for bank holiday weekend in about seven years' time.'

Grace

Saturday had passed without me getting up the nerve to confess to Damien. It also passed without de Courcy shopping me to Damien. Sunday too passed without incident. Then it was Monday and Damien rang me from work.

'Charlie and Angus have killed the story about Dee.' His voice was trembling with excitement.

So Paddy had stuck to his word and got his source to withdraw the story. Probably the only decent thing he'd ever done in his life. It was only now that he'd actually done it that I believed it. Even over the weekend, I'd half expected to see the story about Dee pop up in one of the papers.

'You've saved Dee's career,' Damien said.

'So have you.'

'Seriously. A general election is going to be called soon. If Paddy had got his way, he'd be going into the campaign as leader of NewIreland.'

'You were the one who risked his job.' Anxiously I added, 'You haven't been sacked?'

He laughed. 'No. No talk of a leak. No one's making a big deal of it.' Stories were killed all the time, it was a routine occurrence. 'There won't be any fallout,' he promised me. 'It's all going to be okay.'

I wanted to believe him.

One way and another it had been a rough six months.

Since the summer I'd been desperate to make things up to Damien and for us to be back to normal.

Maybe now we could be. Maybe the whole horrible de Courcy episode had finally been put to bed.

Daring to be hopeful, but still holding my breath, Monday passed without Paddy de Courcy ruining my life.

Ditto Tuesday.

Ditto Wednesday.

On Thursday the Taoiseach Teddy Taft called a general election.

This was very good news. Paddy would be up to his tonsils with campaigning. *And* he was getting married in five weeks. He'd have no time to be bothered with someone like me.

I decided it was safe to breathe again.

Lola

Monday, 2 February

Recommenced work. Had expected slow start. But no! Funny thing had happened. SarahJane Hutchinson had suddenly been elevated to queen of society. Combination of her new, wealthy boyfriend and her 'connection' with Zara Kaletsky had thrust her to summit of pile. Despite bloodhound knees, everyone wanted to be her friend. Everyone wanted to serve on her committee. Everyone wanted to use her stylist . . .

Yes! I had stuck with her through the bad times, for once in life backed the right horse and looked set to reap rewards, assuming could hold it together and not burn any expensive dresses at shoots.

Phone began ringing.

First week of February

Snowed under with work.

Changed mind about styling Grace Gildee. People are the way they are. No point trying to change them.

Also cannot spare time.

Monday, 9 February 21.13

Siam Nights

Jem had called emergency summit meeting in Thai restaurant. Despite me being snowed under with work, he insisted that I attend.

Was forty-three minutes late. Rushed in. 'Apologies, apologies, but am –'

' – yes, snowed under with work.'

Sat down. Looked around at Treese, Bridie and Jem. 'What did I miss?'

'He wouldn't tell us until you got here.' Bridie sour.

'Apologies, apologies, but am –'

'Don't say it.'

'Now that everyone is finally here,' Jem said, with ominous formality, 'have something to tell you all.'

Heart sank. He was getting married to stinky Claudia and we would be stuck with her for ever. Worse, would have to go to her hen night, maybe even organize it. Am not a hen-party person. Too dangerous.

'Tell us, then,' Bridie demanded.

Jem suddenly shifty. Making patterns with his glass on the table. 'I've . . . ah . . . met someone.'

Moment to digest his words.

'Met someone? You mean . . . a woman?'

He nodded, still shifting glass about like receiving messages on Ouija board.

'But you already have woman! Claudia!'

'Yes! Claudia!' Treese confirmed.

With his hand, Jem made short, brutal, Mafia-style chop across his neck. 'Gone.'

Claudia was gone!

'Who "goned" her?' I asked. Indignant. 'You?'

He assented. 'Tonight she sleeps with the newsreaders.'

'What? All of them?' Bridie asked.

He shrugged. 'Wouldn't surprise me.'

'So you just cast her aside like out-of-date Muller Fruit Corner?' I demanded.

'Why you annoyed?' Jem surprised. 'You hated her. You all hated her.'

Clamour of disagreement. 'Didn't hate her. No, didn't hate her. Really quite fond of her.'

'Oh all right,' Bridie admitted. 'Did hate her. But she hated me too.'

'Treese?' Jem asked.

'Yes, hated her,' Treese said.

'Lola?' Jem asked.

'Yes, hated her. Of course. Sorry, was just having moment of identification with dumped woman there. Has passed now. Am bloody delighted. Who is this new one? I hope she's a bit nicer than Claudia.'

I would settle for her liking Jem, which Claudia had never seemed to manage.

Jem's face lit up with sappy glow. 'Gwen. You will meet her. You will love her.'

Yes, but he had said that about Claudia too.

Grace

When Ma notified me about Bid's final diagnosis, I could have rung Damien at work, but I decided to wait to tell him in person. Because of the forthcoming election, he was working an average of fourteen hours a day, stuck on tour buses, covering God-awful campaign trails.

It was ten to twelve when he got home from work that night.

'In here,' I called from the living room. 'In here.'

He pushed open the door and cheerily I said, 'Guess what?'

His face went grey. Slowly he sat down on the floor. (Still no new couch, it hadn't even been ordered.) 'Just tell me, Grace.'

Clearly he was expecting some type of bad news. But I'd been so upbeat . . . ?

I looked at his anxious expression and was seized by a blinding flash of terror that he and I would never be right again.

The night with Zara and Selma should have fixed things, but here we were, Damien and I, still mismatching each other's moods.

'Bid's scan,' I said. 'She got the all-clear.'

It wasn't what he'd expected. I could almost see the cloud of angst lift from him. 'Serious?' He began to smile and smile. 'My God, she's unbelievable, isn't she? Unstoppable.'

'The old boot will probably outlive us all.'

'I thought she wouldn't come through it,' Damien admitted.

'I don't know what I thought,' I said. I suppose I simply hadn't let myself think at all.

'It's bloody fantastic news,' Damien said.

'Even more fantastic,' I said, 'we can start smoking again. Six months without a cigarette, I couldn't have done it without you.' Pompously I said, 'Our sacrifice kept her alive, of course, you do know that?'

But instead of laughing, his cheer seemed to drain from him and the mood once again went into a nosedive. What the hell was happening now?

'I've something to tell you,' Damien said with terrible weariness. Instantly I was plunged into the horrors. The hideous fear intensified when he said, 'A confession.'

Don't let this be happening . . .

'I didn't want to worry you while the jury was still out on Bid,' he said. 'But I've . . . betrayed you.'

Such a horrible word that: *betrayed*.

'I tried my damnedest, Grace.' Damien was a picture of remorse. 'But I just didn't have it in me to resist.'

'With Juno?' Why did I ask? Hadn't I smelt her in my house? In my own bed?

I'd known she'd been there. I'd known it in some deep hidden part of me. But I'd wanted so much to be wrong that I'd believed Damien when he told me there was nothing going on.

'Yes, sometimes with Juno.'

'*Some*times?' I was tangled up in shock and confusion. '. . . There have been others?' Was this worse or better? It was hard to know because it was all so horrific.

'Grace, wait,' Damien said urgently. 'What are we talking about here?'

'You tell me.'

'I've been smoking. Cigarettes. While you've been in London with Marnie.'

It took several seconds for me to understand. 'You've been *smoking*?'

He nodded.

'That's all?'

It was what I'd smelt: the faintest trace of cigarette smoke. I'd confused it with infidelity.

'We had a pact,' he said. 'And I didn't honour my side of it.'

'But it's okay!'

'I lied to you.'

'But who cares about a few sneaky fags? You haven't cheated on me?'

'Grace, that fecking *word*. No, I haven't.'

'Oh God, Damien, I thought . . . I'm so relieved, I'm –' I should have been skipping around with relief, but suddenly something else was there.

Where had it come from?

Why now?

And then I understood that it had been there all along. Just waiting for its moment.

'What?' I said defensively. Guilt jumped from my eyes and there was an answer waiting in his. Neither of us spoke and something – anything – was needed to break the strange atmosphere. I pressed my feet against the floor to stand up, but then he spoke and I froze.

'Grace. I know.'

I couldn't speak.

'About you and de Courcy.'

The fear I'd felt when I'd thought Damien had slept with

Juno was as nothing compared to this. This was infinitely, immeasurably worse.

'How?' The word was tiny.

'When you were working on his autobiography. You couldn't . . . miss it.'

My life was draining from me. My entire existence was disappearing, dissolving into nothing. I actually stopped being able to feel my feet.

'Please . . .' I wanted to tell him that nothing had happened with Paddy and me. But that was only true in the strictest interpretation of the words and I had too much respect for Damien to fob him off with that shite.

'Then your bruised face, the cigarette burn on your hand. That story about you tripping on the paving stone.' Damien laughed softly and shook his head.

I was horrified. I'd thought he'd believed me. How could I have been so thick?

'But why didn't you say anything?' My voice was croaky.

'If you were going to lie to me,' he said, 'what good would it do to tell you that I knew?'

That was the very worst moment of my life. Even as it was happening, I recognized it.

Shame engulfed me – pure shame, not that hot, blustery, shouty stuff where you go on the defensive, trying to pretend you're not in the wrong.

I *knew* I was in the wrong. Damien didn't give his trust easily, it was a rare and precious thing and I'd treated it like a pair of old jocks that you use for cleaning the windows.

'It was six months ago. How have you lived with it?' This is what baffled me. 'Without saying anything to me?'

'Because I loved you. I wanted to stay with you. I wanted to fix it if we could.'

Oh Christ . . . Successive waves of shame hit me as I remembered how Damien had tried to patch up the damage I'd caused.

He'd got a bank loan to replace the car that Paddy had burnt out.

He'd instigated date night in an effort to rekindle a connection between us.

He'd given up cigarettes to keep my aunt alive.

I wanted to vomit.

'But why weren't you angry with me?'

He looked at me. He seemed surprised – then almost contemptuous.

'I have been angry. I am angry.' He bit the words out and suddenly I knew the full extent of his rage. He wasn't trying to hide it any more and it was a cruel and terrifying thing.

'Don't blame yourself for not being able to hide your fondness for de Courcy,' he said coldly. 'Even if I hadn't guessed, de Courcy took the precaution of telling me.'

I was shocked into open-jawed silence.

'The night with Zara and Selma?' he said. 'As soon as you'd left, he phoned me.'

So that was why Damien hadn't answered my calls that night.

'Damien . . .' Tears began to pour down my face.

I wanted to tell him that I'd been temporarily mad and that I was better now. I wanted to beg for his forgiveness, but I knew he wouldn't – couldn't – grant it.

The worst thing, the most unbearable part, was that Damien had warned me this would happen. Last summer, when I'd been in the thick of my de-Courcy-itis, he'd said that if either of us cheated, we might get over it but that things would never be the same again. The innocence and trust would be gone.

'I've ruined it, haven't I?'

He wasn't being gratuitously harsh – but there was only one answer he could give. 'Yes.'

Ma opened her front door. 'Grace? What are you doing here?'

'I need sixteen euro to pay the taxi.' I nodded at the car idling by the kerb.

'Why have you come in a taxi? And why can't you pay for it?'

'I can't find my car key. Or my wallet.'

'Where are we going to find sixteen euro? We'll have to go through your father's glass things.' Dad collected one-cent coins in old jam jars.

'I'll go and tell your man we'll be a while.' I dropped my rucksack by the door and started back down the steps.

'Grace, are you all right? You look a bit –'

'You know the way you said there was always a bed for me here?'

Ma gazed at me, her face changing and becoming luminous with shock, as understanding dawned.

'I've come to take you up on it,' I said.

'What happened?' she whispered.

'Paddy de Courcy.'

'Paddy de Courcy?'

He'd won.

Lola

The Horseshow House
Bridie, Barry, Treese and I awaiting the unveiling of Gwen, Jem's new girlfriend.

'Why we in this bloody pub?' Bridie asked. 'Is miles out of the way and full of rugby-type oddballs.'

'Jem wanted neutral venue for "the meet",' Treese explained. 'No reminders of Claudia.'

'He actually call it "the meet"?' I asked.

'Yes.'

'Cripes . . . What you think she'll be like?' I asked. 'This so-called Gwen.'

'Well, she needn't think she can take Jem for a ride, the way Claudia did,' Bridie said grimly.

'Yeah!' Barry agreed. 'Too right. We'll be watching her.'

'Shush! Here they are.'

Jem approached, grinning, grinning, grinning. Also sweating. Also rubbing his hands around and around each other, as if washing them.

Clearly under considerable stress.

He ushered forward tall, dark-haired girl. 'This is Gwen.'

At first glance, her knockers not fake.

'Yes, hello, Gwen,' we all cried. 'Lovely to meet you, yes, lovely.' We were smiling, smiling, smiling with our mouths but our eyes like flint.

'Lovely to meet you too.' Gwen was sweating around her

823

hairline. 'Yes, gin and tonic,' she said to Jem. In quieter tone, she added, 'Make it large one.'

Stab of pity for this so-called Gwen. Few experiences in life more daunting than 'beauty contest' with new boyfriend's old friends. Wondering if you'll be accepted into gang or cast into outer darkness.

However, could not permit heart to soften too much. She could be fake-knockered hustler, like Claudia. Mind you, she didn't seem like hustler. She seemed nice.

Drinks, chat, anecdotes. Under guise of fake friendliness, Bridie, Barry, Treese and I assessed this so-called Gwen's every move. Much shrill anxious laughter on Gwen's part. Perched on edge of banquette, her legs crossed three times around themselves.

Jem watching us, his eyes pleading, Please like her, please like her.

Jem went to the bar — again — to pour more alcohol into us and while he was gone, Gwen slumped.

'Mother of fuck.' She wiped her forehead. 'This is worse than job interview.'

Chestburst of compassion for her.

'You were friends with Jem's previous girlfriend for long time,' she said. 'It'll be hard to accept me. But give me time.'

Bridie, Barry and Treese also riddled with compassion.

'Actually we hated her,' Bridie confided.

'Hated her,' Treese confirmed.

'Hated her,' I said.

Suddenly all of us roaring laughing and firm friends. Yes, Gwen the right one for Jem. In a way, their names almost rhymed.

Everyone truly settled now. Except me, of course. Not bitter. No. Simply observing.

Marnie

She rose inexorably towards the surface.

. . . I'm still here . . . I'm still alive . . .

Desperate for oblivion, she tried to push herself back down into the nothingness, but she resurfaced again, popping up like a plastic bottle on the waves. It was over, she had returned, she was conscious, she was – dispiritingly – still alive. What would it take?

Automatically she looked around for a bottle. The one beside her bed had toppled over and emptied itself onto the carpet, she'd have to go on a search.

She stood up. Her legs felt as if they were being operated by someone else, there was a loud humming in her ears and her tongue tasted thick and numb, as if it was coated in paraffin wax.

Down the stairs, someone else's legs carrying her, and into the hall, where a light flashed on the answering machine. She didn't know when she'd developed a fear of hearing messages, but she had. (The same with the post: she could barely look at it, much less open it and make neat piles.)

She had better listen to the messages, she'd been out of it for nearly four days, something might have happened. When she heard Ma's voice, she bit her thumb to tamp down her dread. But it was good news: Bid was better.

She was too numb, still too stunned from her hangover, to feel glad. But she knew she was relieved, she was simply too anaesthetized to feel it.

There was a second message. Again from Ma. Damien and Grace had split up. Grace had moved out of their house and was back living in her old bedroom.

'Something to do with Paddy de Courcy,' Ma said. 'She's not so good.'

This was such astonishing news that Marnie sank to the cold parquet floor and listened to the message again just to make sure that she'd got it right.

It was hard to believe. Grace and Damien had seemed so . . . together. So unbreakable.

Clearly Paddy de Courcy was even more powerful, more destructive, than she'd realized.

She should be glad. Glad that Grace had paid the price for messing with someone she shouldn't have. And glad that she herself wasn't the only one Paddy de Courcy had ruined – after all, if it could happen to strong, scary Grace, then it could happen to anyone.

But she was surprised to feel something winkle its way through the numb, buzzing force field that surrounded her feelings. Poor Grace, she thought, a shard of compassion warming her deadened heart. Poor, poor Grace.

Grace

I opened my bedroom door and met Bid on the landing.

'You look like shit,' she said.

'Good morning to you too,' I said wearily.

'Would you not wear a bit of make-up?' she asked. 'You'll scare the public, going out like that. It's not fair on people.'

I didn't look like myself, she was right about that. Three nights ago, the night Damien and I had split up, I'd undergone some sort of transformation while I'd been asleep. I'd looked thirty-five when I went to bed but when I woke up the following morning the hollows around my eyes had sunk down into my skull and suddenly I looked like I'd been roaming the earth for four thousand years.

'Even some concealer for those black circles?' Bid suggested.

'I haven't got any with me.' Most of my stuff was still in the house.

'You could go back and get some.'

'Not today.'

'You could ask Damien to pack up some of your stuff.'

'Not today.'

I couldn't cope with any of that organizey-type stuff. All I could manage was the bare minimum required to get through the day.

I'd left our house – my *home* – on Tuesday night and

when I woke up on Wednesday morning, shivering in Ma's spare room, I thought, I have to survive today. The same thing happened on Thursday. Now it was Friday and, like a mantra, going through my head, were the words, Just get through today.

There was an awful tightness in my chest and I still couldn't feel my feet, and my face and head felt like they were going to burst apart and splinters of my skull were going to go flying everywhere, like in a video nasty.

Down in the kitchen, Ma and Dad leapt up, all concern, when they saw me. 'Are you going to work, Grace?'

What else would I do?

'You know you're free to smoke again?' Ma said.

Indeed, thanks to Bid's cancer-free status, everyone was free to smoke again. However Ma, Dad and Bid had decided to stay nicotine-free – they didn't want a recurrence of Bid's cancer. Also I think they liked the extra cash. But they kept encouraging me to start back on the cigs.

I couldn't. When I'd first given them up last September, a peculiar part of me had been glad I was denying myself something I loved. The order to stop smoking had been handed down about a week after Paddy had hit me; bizarrely it had felt appropriate to do some sort of penance. Now it felt even more so.

'I don't want to smoke. Well, I do, but I'm not going to. I have to atone for what I did to Damien.'

Ma flinched. 'You weren't even brought up as a Catholic.'

'Ach!' Dad said. 'If you live in Ireland there's no escaping the guilt. I think they pump it into the water system, like fluoride.'

'I'm going to work,' I said wearily.

'Will you be here tonight?' Ma asked.

'I'll be here for the rest of my life.'

I got through Friday, then I got through the weekend by sleeping for large patches of it. Marnie rang to offer stiff condolences and if I hadn't felt so dismal, the fact that she was talking to me would have cheered me. But I was uncheerable.

Then it was Monday morning and as I was promising myself that all I had to do was get through today, my bedroom door opened and Bid tossed a small beige tube across the room at me.

'What's this?'

'Foundation. We bought it for you. We clubbed together. Put some on.'

I rubbed a handful of gunk over my face and it warmed up my death pallor. But within moments my greyness had risen once more to the surface, cancelling out the Tawny Beige.

I got through Monday and I got through Tuesday and on Tuesday night, when Ma came to wish me sweet dreams, I said, 'It's a week now. It's a whole week.'

'You've heard nothing from him?' She knew I hadn't. I suppose she was just making conversation. 'No word?'

'No. And I won't. There will be no reunion. This is over.'

I knew he wouldn't forgive me – but I accepted it.

That was the one good thing. I didn't daydream about him arriving to claim me. I didn't ring him and call round to the house, pleading with him to forgive me.

I knew Damien. The qualities I'd fallen in love with –

his independence, his conviction in his own rightness, his essential unwillingness to trust another human being – had become the stumbling blocks. He'd trusted me, I'd broken the trust. It couldn't be fixed.

I lay on the bed and thought back to those days last summer and wished fiercely – scrunching up my face and clenching my hands with the force of my longing – that I could go back and change things.

'What are you doing?' Ma asked. 'With your face?'

'Wishing I could go back and change things. I really miss him,' I said. 'I miss talking to him. Right from the start I was pathetically in love with him. Even at parties – on the few occasions I could drag him along to one – he was the only person I really wanted to talk to.'

'Did you tell him?'

'Ah no. We're not like that. But he knows. Knew.'

'So why the hell did you get involved with de Courcy?' Ma asked, almost in exasperation.

'I don't know.' I really couldn't understand it.

Boredom? Curiosity? A sense of entitlement? All shameful reasons.

'People, human beings,' I said helplessly, 'we're fucked-up. Why do we do the things we do?' I sounded like Marnie. For the first time I really understood the despair that ran through her like a black seam.

' "To err is human," ' Ma quoted.

' "To forgive divine," ' I said. 'And I couldn't care less if the divine forgives me or not. I want Damien to forgive me, but he won't.'

Ma acknowledged that by keeping her mouth shut.

'I know you all think he's grumpy –'

She maintained a diplomatic silence.

'– but he's my favourite person.'

Eventually she asked, 'What are you going to do?'

'With what? The rest of my life?'

'. . . Yes, I suppose. Or until you get over this?'

'I don't know. What does anyone do? Live through it.'

Easier said than done, though.

Lola

Monday, 23 February 19.11

Bridie's flat

'Dance, lil' sister, dance!' Bridie urged me.

VIP had done a special 'de Courcy pre-wedding pull-out'. Bridie had removed all the pictures of Paddy and spread them across the floor like carpet tiles.

'C'mon, lil' sister, dance!'

'Lil' sister?' Treese and I exchanged a glance. Perhaps words from a song? No knowing where Bridie gets her phrases from.

She played Billy Idol – no knowing where Bridie gets her CDs from either – and we all danced, and must admit, I gleaned pleasure from stamping foot on Paddy's smiling fizzog.

'Cripes, look at this!' Had kicked up legs so energetically that had overturned one of the pages and on the back was picture of Claudia, at launch of new Athlete's Foot powder. Her 3-D knockers almost jumped out of the page and hit me in the eye. She was posing cheek by jowl with TV3 weatherman. Her new boyfriend apparently. Quote said, 'Claudia and Felix. Very much in love.'

'We can stop worrying about her now,' Treese said. Treese very dry.

Back to dancing on Paddy de Courcy's face.

'What is danger of you having relapse on the wedding day itself?' Bridie asked.

'Time will tell, I suppose,' I said.

Bridie displeased. 'Course you won't have relapse!'

'Well, why you ask —'

'— Rhetorical, rhetorical. You are over him. In fact, let's gatecrash K Club and you can throw confetti.'

'Let's not.'

'You not feel better enough to throw confetti at his wedding?' Bridie's eyes narrowed.

'Not exactly, but don't feel like throwing rotten tomatoes either.'

'So what was bloody point of that lovely showdown with him?'

'Facing fears and all that. And am much better than was. Work going well.'

Modest understatement! Was riddled with work. Had been wobbly when first returned but now was in the zone and at top of my game. Everything I did was a triumph — not boasting, no, not boasting, simply saying how it was. Could 'cherry pick' jobs, keeping best-paid, most interesting ones for me and passing on overflow to — yes — Nkechi. Why not? She was excellent stylist.

Also she had suffered a loss. In stunning, shocking move, Rosalind Croft had left her husband, the horrible Maxwell Croft. Unprecedented. Society wives *never* leave society husbands, always other way round. Rosalind Croft no requirement for stylist because no jingle to pay for one. Nkechi down one very lucrative client.

'Remember the night of the soup?' Bridie chortled. 'When you camped outside Paddy's front door and asked me to bring you soup. God, you were certifiable!'

'Haha, yes, indeed.'

'Was a few months there,' Bridie said, 'when I thought you would never be normal again!'

'I thought would never be normal again either,' I said, remembering just how wretched had felt.

'But,' said Treese firmly, 'your life definitely back on track.'

'Never thought it would happen, never thought it could happen, but damage done by de Courcy seems to have healed,' I said. 'Look at me now.' Swished hand around self to indicate sleek hair, calm demeanour, phone which never stopped ringing.

No need to go into it with Bridie but I knew would never again be the person I was before I met Paddy. Was less naive now, less trusting – but maybe that not a bad thing? Less scared, also. Not afraid of being back in Dublin. In fact, nice to be reinstated in own flat, with fully connected telly, right in the thick of things with grunty men wrestling outside my window at four in morning.

Transition, naturally enough, not entirely smooth. Missed things about Knockavoy: the peace, the cleanness, the sea air – despite ruinous effect on hair – and of course my many, many friends.

Thought of them often, with great fondness. Frequent memories of Boss, Moss and the Master, accompanied with slight dread in case they made good on their promise to visit me in Dublin.

Thought of Mrs Butterly every day, especially when heard *Coronation Street* music.

Also thought of some of others every day. Sometimes twice a day. Or even more if, for example, heard 'Achy Breaky Heart' on radio (mercifully rare occurrence) or saw programme about badgers or passed by eco-swot Prius in street.

Or noticed man with unkempt hair or heard the word 'pothole' or used shower cap or ate tortilla chips and brushed crumbs onto floor.

Or drank Fanta or saw someone tossing a coin or noticed *Law and Order* in TV listings.

Or bought new bulb for bedside lamp or wondered if should do home cholesterol-test or tried new flavour smoothie. (Not Knockavoy memories so cannot account for this phenomenon.)

Considine texted often, with caring questions about my progress.

Always replied:

Am riddled with work, Considine.

Initially slightly exaggerated quantity of work I was receiving. Important for him to think I was doing well. Had been instrumental in my rehabilitation and he deserved to feel warm glow of satisfaction.

However, he did not mention visiting Dublin and – unlike Boss, Moss and the Master – would have actually liked him to come. But that is men for you. All liars.

Not bitterness, no. Simply the way things are.

Grace

'Make sure you put on that foundation.' Bid walked into my bedroom, like she did every morning. There was no privacy in this house. No privacy and no heat and no biscuits. 'We didn't spend our hard-earned pensions . . . What in the name of *God* is wrong with your chin?' The entire lower part of my face was weeping, blistered and crusty.

'It's a cold sore,' I said wearily.

'That's no cold sore.' Bid was appalled. 'That's some sort of disease. Trenchfoot. You look like you're rotting.'

'It's a cold sore,' I repeated. I used to get them when I was a teenager. 'It's just a very bad one.'

Bid yelled from the landing, 'Is that alleged cold sore any better?' She was pretending that she couldn't bear to enter the room because of my disfigurement.

'No. It lasts for ten days, I keep telling you, and I've only had it for four.'

She came in anyway. 'Is that another cold sore on your eyebrow?'

I got out of bed and looked in the mirror. 'I don't know. It might be just a spot.'

'A boil, you mean. Mother of the divine! You've more on your legs.'

I looked down. Christ alive. A selection of medieval-style boils had erupted around both ankle bones.

I was almost afraid to investigate further but I had to. I whipped down my pyjama bottoms to confirm the presence of several eruptions on my thighs.

'Sweet Jesus,' Bid moaned, raising her cardigan to cover her eyes. 'You could have warned me you were going to flash your growler. And why haven't you had a Brazilian? Is it any wonder he got sick of you?'

The following morning, when I woke, I heard Bid poking about on the landing.

'Bid!' I called. 'Bid!'

'What is it today?'

'Bid! I'm blind.'

My right eye had swollen shut because of a stye.

Ma was summoned. 'I've had enough of this,' she said. 'I'm taking you to Dr Zwartkop. You might be anaemic or something.'

'I'm not.' I knew what was wrong with me. 'Ma, I'm not going to the doctor. I've to go to work.'

But she rang Jacinta and said I'd be late – I was thirty-five and I was getting a sick-note from my mum – and I went along with it because I didn't know how to resist. I'd forgotten how to do that; it was a skill I'd had once, but didn't have any longer.

'Interesting thing,' Ma mused, as we sat in traffic, on the way to the doctor. 'Some people, Marnie to take one, become really quite beautiful when they're heartbroken. Strangely luminous.' Then she clapped a hand over her mouth. 'Grace, sorry. I wasn't thinking!'

Dr Zwartkop was a woman – Ma wouldn't countenance anything else. Ma knew her well enough to call her Priscilla. She also knew her well enough to insist on accompanying me into the consulting room, as if I was six.

'Cold sore,' Priscilla said to me. 'Boils. Stye. Anything else?'

'An ache in my chest,' I said. 'And an ache in my face and head.'

She gave me a sharp look. 'Have you had some sort of loss recently?'

'My partner . . . ten years. We split up two weeks ago.'

'No chance he'll come back to you?'

'No chance, Priscilla,' Ma answered quickly.

'I could send you for blood tests –'

'But they'll come back normal,' I said.

Priscilla nodded. 'I suspect they will.'

'Anything else you can suggest?' Ma asked.

'Anti-depressants?'

'Anti-depressants?' Ma coaxed me.

I shook my head.

'Something to help you sleep?' Priscilla said.

'Some nice sleeping pills?' Ma suggested kindly.

Once again I shook my head. I'd no trouble sleeping.

'You could get your hair cut. Or . . .' Priscilla cast around for another suggestion. 'Or have an inappropriate fling. Or go on holiday.' She shrugged. 'Or, indeed, you could do all three.'

'Thanks,' I said. Maybe a holiday . . . 'C'mon, Ma. I've got a job to go to.'

*

I ran out of petrol on the way to work. I'd known my car had needed petrol but over the preceding few days there had been so many choices at the station – premium and super-premium, diesel and non-diesel – that I'd had to drive away, convincing myself that I had enough left for one more journey.

When the engine spluttered and died, I didn't even care. I just abandoned the car on the Blackrock bypass and got the bus the rest of the way to work, then I rang Dad and asked him to get a canister of petrol and go down and retrieve it.

When I finally got to work it was midday. I walked into the office and they howled with laughter when they saw the stye on my eye.

'We've a present for you,' TC said.

'What?' For some reason I thought it might be cake. Between my disfigurements and my petrol-free car, I'd thought they might have got me a nice cake.

It was a paper bag. Big enough to fit over my head.

'We've cut out eye-holes,' TC said.

I tried to laugh but – to everyone's horror – tears came to my eyes.

'It was only a joke,' Lorraine said anxiously.

'Maybe you should take some time off,' TC urged. 'How much holiday time have you left?'

'A couple of weeks.'

'Go someplace. Maybe get a bit of sun.'

I went to Jacinta, who wasn't unsympathetic. 'One of the Canaries?' she suggested. 'Lanza-grotty? Costs nothing at this time of year.'

But I'd no one to go with.

So I'd go on my own, I decided. It would be good practice for the rest of my life.

That evening Marnie rang Ma. They spoke for ages, then Ma handed me the phone. 'She wants to talk to you.'

'I hear you're going on holiday,' Marnie said.

'That's right.'

'I could come with you.'

It was an olive branch.

'I won't drink,' she promised.

Of course she'd drink, but it was better than going on my own.

Lola

Saturday, 7 March

Paddy got married. All over the news. Not exactly skipping around my flat, throwing hat up in the air, as if had just won 8 million euro, but didn't have relapse. No demands for non-lumpy soup, no driving around the city without due care and attention. Day passed 'peacefully'.

Sunday, 8 March 17.05

Phone rings. Bridie.

'You want to go Knockavoy next weekend?' she asks. 'Patrick's Day holiday?'

'Thought Cousin Fonchy had house booked.' (Another peculiarly named relation. Is there no end to them?)

'He had but fell off ladder. Temporarily blind. Can't drive. Will we go?'

17.08

Texted many Knockavoy pals to notify them of my forth-coming arrival.

Grace

We went to Tenerife. We got a little apartment in a resort that was faked-up to look like a fishing village. The place was about a quarter full and Marnie and I were the only people under ninety. Every day we each lay on a lounger beneath the weak March sun and I read thriller after thriller and Marnie read biographies of people who'd killed themselves. Every evening we had our dinner in the same restaurant and every night we both slept for twelve hours.

We took care of each other, finding lost books and sunglasses, rubbing on each other's suncream, warning each other about overdoing it in the sun. There was no mention of Paddy or the bitter falling-out we'd had. We were like two frail, elderly convalescents, doing for each other what we weren't able to do for ourselves.

I'd decided I didn't care if Marnie drank – but, true to her word, she didn't. Maybe that was all she'd needed, I thought wryly. A fortnight in the Canaries, to cure her of alcoholism.

We talked a lot while we lay on our backs facing up through sunglasses at the sky.

'Funny how our lives have paralleled each other's,' I said.

'You mean, both of us being left by our men?'

'Yes, I suppose.'

'Was it my fault that you and Damien split up?' she asked. 'Because of all that time you spent with me?'

'No, of course not.'

But I understood that perhaps I'd welcomed the chance to spend weekends in London with Marnie, because it took me away from the stilted terribleness of Damien and me.

By the time we'd passed the halfway point on the holiday, I was certain that Marnie wouldn't drink. Then, on the eighth day, she had a tearful phone call from Daisy – and just like that, she was off, drinking round the clock.

For three days I spoke to no one. I just read my books and lay on the lounger and let the sun warm my eyelids. Now and again I'd go back into the apartment to check that Marnie was still alive.

Every five hours or six hours, she'd come to, get up, go out, buy more vodka, come back, drink it and pass out again. Dutifully I'd pour away whatever was left in the bottle, but when she emerged from her coma, I didn't try to stop her from going to the mini-market to buy more.

After three days she stopped, like she'd run out of the necessary self-hatred to fuel the binge.

'Sorry,' she whispered at me.

'It's okay. Don't worry. Do you feel well enough to go out for dinner tonight?'

'Maybe. I don't know.'

'I could cook. You haven't eaten in days. You should have something.'

She was confused. Through her haze, she asked, 'Why are you being so nice to me?'

'Because I love you.' The words were out of my mouth before I'd thought them through. 'You're still my sister. I've always loved you. I'll never stop.'

'Why aren't you angry with me for drinking?' Marnie asked.

Again the words came without my volition. 'Because there's nothing I can do about it.' It didn't mean that it wasn't breaking my heart, because it was, but I knew now that there wasn't a thing I could do to change things.

'And Marnie, there's nothing you can do either. You've no choice. I used to think you had but you haven't. You're powerless, as powerless as I am.'

It was the strangest feeling – I'd forgiven her. She wasn't going to stop drinking, I knew that now. Nothing could make her stop. She would keep drinking and keep drinking and – sooner or later – it might kill her. But even for that I'd already forgiven her.

Lola

Saturday, 14 March 18.59
Bridie, Barry, Treese, Jem, Gwen and I arrive Uncle Tom's cabin. All together in Treese's new SUV. (Present from Vincent.) (Vincent not present.)

19.03
Open bottle of wine.

20.08
Knock on door.

'That'll be Considine.' But when opened door, who was standing there? Only Chloe! Yes, Chloe! Eyes sparkling, hair glossy, clothing as on-trend as ever.

Delighted hugs. Proud introductions. Over-interested gawking from Bridie, Barry, Jem and Gwen. Less overt staring from Treese.

Strong drinks. High spirits. Out on the town. Knockavoy crammed with visitors. People everywhere. No one sussed Chloe was trannie, simply thought she was – perhaps slightly tall, slightly bulky – girl from Dublin.

Chloe huge hit with friends.

'Full of life and laughter,' Bridie kept saying about her. (Do not know where she got that phrase. Bridie has propensity for peculiar phrases.) 'Do not fancy her as, unlike you, Lola, am not lezzer-inclined, but full of life and laughter.'

Bridie tremendously drunk.

All of us tremendously drunk.

Great, great night.

Sunday, 15 March 12.09

Quite unwell. Jem and Gwen carried sofa round to back of house for me – too hung-over to do it myself – then lay on it, huddled beneath duvet. Kept Considine's house in my sights, hoping to see him and give little wave, but he never appeared. Down pothole, no doubt.

14.14

Treese got up.

14.22

Treese went back to bed.

17.01

Aided by Barry, Bridie crept downstairs. Had been vomiting since sun-up.

'Toast,' she whispered.

20.27

Jem and Gwen cooked dinner. Bottle of wine opened. Tentative sips. Suddenly everyone talking and colour back in our cheeks.

21.19

Knock on door.

'That'll be Considine.' But when opened door, who was standing there? Only Chloe! Yes, Chloe! Again! Different clothing this time, but just as dazzling. Thrilled, yes, thrilled to see her once more. Could not understand why felt so disappointed.

Strong drinks. High spirits. Out on the town. Knockavoy crammed with visitors. People everywhere. Again, no one sussed Chloe was trannie, simply thought she was – perhaps slightly tall, slightly bulky – girl from Dublin.

Again, Chloe huge hit with friends.

'Full of life and laughter,' Bridie kept saying about her.

Decided to count how many times Bridie said, 'Full of life and laughter,' but lost count after forty-eight.

Bridie tremendously drunk.

All of us tremendously drunk.

Great, great night.

Did not really enjoy it.

Monday, 16 March 6.14

Had been asleep for only two hours but was awake again. Thinking of Considine. Keen to see him. Very keen. Needed to get to him before he started applying false nails and chicken fillets and became Chloe again. Now as good a time as any. Slipped from bed and, still in pyjamas, crossed grass to his house.

Knocked on door.

No answer.

Knocked again, much louder.

No answer.

Knocked again, this time so loud almost missed him protesting, 'Is middle of bloody night!'

'Let me in, Cranky-Arse! Is Lola.'

He opened door and I scooted past him. His hair mussed and face sleepy. Wearing blue sweats and raggedy grey T-shirt. (All traces of Chloe removed, was relieved to see.)

'Badger's arse?' I asked with sympathy.

'Badger's arse.' He nodded dolefully. 'You?'

'Yes.'

'Tea?'

'No.'

'Anything?'

'No.'

'Sit beside me?'

I moved. Emboldened. 'I put head on your shoulder?'

'Yes. I put arm around you?'

'Yes.'

Sat side by side in hung-over silence. Remarkably pleasant.

'Considine.' Cleared throat. 'Never thought would hear self say these words, but am happy to see you. Was starting to think wouldn't see you at all this weekend.'

'Thought you liked Chloe. Got Chloe out of retirement specially for you.'

'Do like Chloe. Kindly of you to go to trouble. But like you too.'

He rubbed hand over stubbly jaw. Raspy noise. Sexy, if truth be told. 'Like you too, Lola,' he said. Silence. 'Like you very, very much.' More silence. But not normal silence. Silence where a lot of emotion happening. 'Very much. Missed you since you left.'

Pause where weighed up what should say. 'Missed you too.'

'Think about you all the time.'

Another pause. 'Think about you all the time too.'

'Think about you every day.'

Another pause. 'Think about you every day too.'

He yawned. I yawned. He said, 'Better go back to bed.' Seemed to be struck by notion. Twisted head to look at me. 'You like to come?'

Gazed into his eyes. '. . . Er . . . yes.'

'Good!' Sudden, most unConsidine-like grin and he swung me up into his arms – carrying me! Was mortified.

'Put me down. You will hurt your back. I have large bottom.'

'Perfect bottom.' He was climbing the stairs. Not even puffing.

'How you so strong?'

'Potholing.'

He kicked bedroom door open, it vibrated with force, then placed me in centre of bed. Still warm from him.

All happening too fast. Lost my nerve. 'We have had no sleep, Considine. Let's have little snooze.'

'Whatever you like.'

Got under duvet but kept my pyjamas on. He kept clothes on also.

Gathered me to him, pulled duvet tightly around us. I began drifting off to sleep, but felt would combust spontaneously. 'Am too hot, Considine.'

'Me too.'

'Am taking off my top.'

'Me too.'

I unbuttoned my pyjama top. He pulled T-shirt over his head. Warm smooth skin against mine. Hard muscles. Taut stomach. Oh delicious.

Shut my eyes and resumed sleeping position. 'Am still too hot, Considine.'

'Me too.'

But once all clothes off, felt hotter still. Freedom of unfettered limbs, legs tangled with his. I shifted and his erection banged against my thigh.

'Sorry,' he said. 'Ignore it.'

'Would prefer not to. If that's okay with you.'

'That's okay with me all right.' Amused.

Was bloody fabulous.

No porn. No prostitutes. Only one position.

Focused. Intense. Holding himself effortlessly on tensed arms, like doing push-ups, he moved slowly in and out of me, while staring into my eyes. Thought would *die*.

15.01

Woken by double beep of Considine's phone.

He read text. Passed me phone. 'It's for you.'

Lola, u getin de ride off Considine?

From Bridie. I replied in the affirmative. Text came back.

Finish up now. Time 2 go home. Treese wants 2 'beat de traffic'.

'Considine, I have to go.'

'Stay,' he said.

'Cannot,' I said. 'Big job tomorrow.'

'. . . Tomorrow. But I . . .' He didn't say whatever had been going to say. 'You still very busy?'

'Oh *very* busy.' Yes, had plenty of work, but making self sound even busier than was.

'No sign of it slowing down?'

'No sign.'

'And you're feeling good?'.

'Excellent.'

'Glad to be back in Dublin?'

'Overjoyed.'

'. . . Okay. Well, for what it's worth, Lola, I want to tell you something. It's important.'

'What is it?'

'Chloe here for you any time you like.'

Chloe? Not what had been expecting to hear.

'Kindly of you,' I said stiffly. 'Will let self out.'

15.38

In the car

'So!' Bridie said. 'You and trannie-man!'

'Is nothing,' I said irritably. 'Holiday romance.'

'Maybe he visit you in Dublin?'

I kept mouth closed. Considine hadn't mentioned any possible visits and so neither had I.

'What's up with you?' Bridie asked.

'Nothing.'

But not nothing. Had been stung by Considine's offer of Chloe's friendship. He hadn't said, '*I* here for you any time you like.' Prepared to offer his trannie alter ego but not himself.

Grace

I arrived home on 19 March, the day of the general election.

'Dee Rossini's party is expected to do very well,' Ma informed me.

'Good, good.' I couldn't care less. I didn't want to hear about Dee or NewIreland or anything to do with them.

'Damien was looking for you,' Ma said.

My heart hopped, then immediately slumped to an even lower position. He must want to talk about what we were to do with our house.

'He rang while you were away but I didn't want to disturb your holiday. He says to give him a ring when you're back.'

I'd give it a couple of days, I decided. It was going to be a painful discussion and I wanted to put it off for as long as possible. He was bound to be working all hours on the election; that could be my excuse. I'd wait until after it was done and dusted.

The following morning I was woken at seven-thirty by voices bellowing from the radio in the kitchen.

'Turn it down,' I yelled. 'Turn the fucking thing down.'

But no one heard me so I stomped downstairs.

'It's a bloodbath,' Dad crowed, sitting at the kitchen table. 'Your friend Dee Rossini is after making shite of the main parties. Everyone has lost seats to NewIreland – even the mighty Nappies. She looks likely to double her number of Dail seats. The Nappies will be gagging to stay in coalition with her.'

'Very good.'

I gave the dial such a swivel I hurt my wrist, then I made toast and went back to bed. I ate my toast and drifted back into a funny, dream-filled half sleep and was woken by a tap on the bedroom door. It was Ma. 'Someone to see you,' she said.

My heart leapt with hope and I sat up eagerly.

'No, it's not Damien,' she said.

'Oh. Okay.' Slowly I lay down on the bed again.

'Get up,' Ma hissed. 'It's Dee Rossini.'

Oh no. I'd have to be enthusiastic. 'Ma, tell her I can't – '

But Ma had disappeared out onto the landing, then, practically bowing, she was leading Dee into the room.

'NewIreland are forming a coalition government with the Nappies. Ms Rossini's just been made Minister for Finance *and* Deputy Prime Minister,' Ma said, bursting with pride. 'She just got a call *this minute* from An Taoiseach. *On her mobile.*'

An Taoiseach? Ma loathed Teddy Taft. She *hated* him, she always referred to him as the Thug and she said his nose looked like a penis. But she'd even said An Taoiseach with its proper Irish pronunciation – On Thway-shaaaaaaackkkhhhh, as if she was dry-retching.

'Dee hasn't been to bed yet,' Ma said with admiration.

'Grace.' Dee came towards me. Then she got a proper look. 'Oh my God! Grace! You look sick.'

'Thanks a million!' I said. 'I'm just back from holiday! I

should look good. You'd want to have seen me before I went.'

'Are you sure you're not sick?'

'Completely sure. I went to the doctor. She made me.' I indicated Ma, who was still in the room.

Ma put her hand to her chest and gave a little gasp, as if she too had just discovered that she was still in the room. 'I should really . . .' She sounded disappointed. 'You must have private things to discuss. I'll leave you to it.' Reluctantly she left.

'Anyway, Dee, congratulations.' I remembered my manners. 'You've done amazingly well, Dad says.'

'If it wasn't for you, Grace, I wouldn't even be leader of NewIreland,' Dee said. 'I'm sorry you had to lose so much . . .'

I didn't know what to say.

'We're having a celebration tonight,' Dee said. 'We're inviting every party member in the country. It's all being put together in a bit of a hurry. It's only right that you're there.'

'Dee, no . . . I'm sorry.'

'I've a surprise for you.'

A surprise? I didn't want a surprise.

'It's about Paddy.'

'Aargh!' I held up my hand, like I was warding off evil spirits. I didn't even want to hear his name.

'Come. Really. You'll be glad you did.'

Marnie

Marnie woke, in her own bed, in her own bedroom, feeling extraordinarily well. She'd slept through the night without once jerking awake from a terrifying nightmare, the sheets weren't tangled around her, drenched with sweat, and she felt full of hope rather than her more customary dread.

She'd got back from Tenerife the previous night. It was four days since she'd had a drink – since the lapse on holiday – and she'd made a little decision. No need to announce it to the world, but she was – very quietly – going to knock the drink on the head.

It was Grace's pity that had done it. After Marnie had emerged from 'the lapse', which had happened a week into their holiday, she'd braced herself for Grace's fury. But Grace had responded with an astonishing lack of anger. There was a new look in her eyes – like sympathy, but not as nice. Pity, Marnie had eventually recognized it as – and it had stung.

The interesting thing was that during the weekends when Grace used to visit, in an effort to police Marnie's drinking, her anger had had no effect at all on Marnie, except perhaps to make her retreat further into the cocoon of alcohol. It was as if Marnie had been able to see Grace mouthing the furious words, but couldn't hear them.

However, Grace's pity, that was a different story. Pity wasn't the same as compassion: a nasty vein of disrespect ran through pity.

Suddenly she had seen herself as Grace – and others – saw

her: not as the intelligent, oversensitive creature she had always been treated as, but simply as a burden. Someone to worry about.

It had been a bit of an eye-opener. That's what people think I'm like, she realized. Perhaps even my own daughters . . .

For the remaining three days of the holiday, words had kept swimming at her: pathetic; pitiful; piteous; tragic; sad.

It made Marnie feel – what? Misunderstood.

She didn't want to be an object of pity. She wasn't the helpless, craven person Grace seemed to think she was.

Especially when it came to alcohol.

She drank because she chose to drink. For no other reason. *And now I choose not to.*

She jumped out of bed and, with great energy, launched herself into unpacking her suitcase. Sandals were flung into the back of the wardrobe, unfinished sun products were dumped into drawers, awaiting another holiday, and the washing machine was loaded up with bikinis and sarongs.

With vigour, she shoved her suitcase under the bed, then got out the hoover. The house was dusty and smelt a bit peculiar after being empty for two weeks, and because the girls were coming after school – it was nearly three weeks since she'd seen them – everything needed to be perfect.

As she scooted along the hall with the hoover, she saw that the answering-machine light was flashing: messages. She switched off the hoover and, taking a deep breath, hit play. There were only four messages: not so bad. Actually a surprisingly – embarrassingly? – small number for two weeks. I've been out of circulation, she reminded herself, flinching slightly.

The first message was from her dentist: she'd missed her yearly check-up and she needed to reschedule; the second was a cold-call from some poor creature trying to sell car insurance;

the third was from Jules, Jules from AA. 'Just saying hi,' Jules said. 'Wondering how you're doing. Call any time.'

And the fourth was also from Jules from AA. Marnie deleted it before she'd listened to it fully, then went back and deleted the other message. She felt uncomfortable – almost sullied – that someone from Alcoholics Anonymous was ringing her.

Right, food. Apart from an almost empty box of Frosties, there was nothing in the house. She needed everything – milk, bread, all the basics, treats for the girls, something for tonight. She'd cook a proper dinner. Maybe Nick would stay.

I miss Nick . . .

Well, who knew, she thought, quite pleased. That's a normal feeling. Everything is becoming normal again. Everything will be okay.

She made a short shopping list, pleased with how efficient and housewifey she felt, got dressed, jumped into the car and drove towards Tesco. A few minutes later, she was surprised to find herself parked outside the off-licence.

What am I doing here?

She had turned the car engine off.

Turn it on, turn it on and drive away.

But she didn't.

I don't want to drink today. I didn't want to come here.

She stared at the key, hanging from the ignition.

Drive away.

She was opening the car door.

I can get chocolate for the girls in here.

She was climbing down onto the pavement.

I can go to the supermarket after this.

She pushed open the door of the off-licence and heard it ping.

'Been away?' Ben asked.

'Mmm.' She picked up two bottles of vodka – 'Only two today?' Ben asked cheerily, just making conversation – and twelve bars of chocolate.

Then she was back in the car, the chocolate bars and the two bottles strewn across the passenger seat.

She looked at the bottles and thought, I don't want this. Especially not today. I want to see Daisy and Verity. I don't want to be drunk when they come. I love them. I want things to be lovely for them. I don't want them to see me incapable. I love Nick. I don't want to disappoint him again. I don't want to wake up cold and wet, trying to remember what happened, wondering what day it is.

But she knew what was going to happen. In a moment she would pick up a bottle and she would drink from it. She would drink and drink and drink until she was lost.

There was no choice.

'I don't want to,' she said out loud. 'Please, something, somebody, I don't want to.'

She was crying now, frightened and helpless, hot tears pouring down her face.

Why am I doing this?

There was no one to blame. She'd stopped blaming Paddy.

So why am I doing this? I don't want to.

Alicia

'Ladies and gentlemen of NewIreland, I give you Dee Rossini!'

In a burst of light, Dee strode onto the stage and all three thousand people present got to their feet and applauded wildly. The crowd was at capacity – party workers, sponsors, well-wishers, and journalists and television crews from both local and foreign news outlets.

Dee took her place at the spotlit podium and Paddy and four other key NewIreland players arrayed themselves behind her on throne-like chairs.

'I want to thank everyone,' Dee was saying. 'But most importantly, the party workers on the ground. Your dedicated and relentless work has given NewIreland these unprecedented returns.' A smile lit up her face. 'NewIreland have agreed to form a coalition government with the Nationalist Party of Ireland. It might interest you to know that I've been offered and accepted the position of Minister for Finance.'

Everyone knew that, it had been on the news, but they roared anyway like they'd just found out.

'And . . .' Dee was bubbling over with pleasure, 'the position of Deputy Prime Minister.'

Everyone knew that too, but again they clapped with rowdy joy.

'Our success has given us a great platform to ensure that the policies and plans that we put to the electorate will form part of the programme for government. I promise to fulfil . . .'

Blah. Alicia wanted to tune out, but she had to listen. She

had to watch Dee and watch how people reacted to her and be ready to report to Paddy if he needed it. This was her job now.

'As you know, our deputy leader Paddy de Courcy recently got married.'

Cheering and whistling and foot-stamping broke out and Paddy got off his chair and acknowledged it with a little bow.

From her position in the front row, Alicia was rapt. God, he was beautiful, she thought: the height, the shoulders, the ready smile, the twinkling eyes, the tie with the fat knot.

And he was all hers. After those terrible days, so long ago, when she'd had to harden her heart against Marnie; the excruciating wait when he disappeared; the solitariness of her life when Marnie and Grace closed ranks against her; the bizarre compromises she'd made during her marriage to Jeremy – it had all been worth it. She'd got him in the end.

Mind you, no honeymoon. She'd really been hoping for a proper one this time, one where she didn't have to go to gay bars; but with the general election being held two weeks after their wedding, the honeymoon had been postponed indefinitely.

'But Alicia's gain is NewIreland's loss,' Dee continued. There was an echo on the mic, her words repeating themselves a split second after she'd uttered them. A tiny sliver of time for Alicia to wonder, What did Dee mean by *that*?

'Paddy,' Dee said, 'has decided to take time out from political life.'

What? *What?* Alicia thought she must have misheard, that it must be something to do with the echo.

But there was a muttering from the assembly that told her that others had heard what she'd heard.

What was Dee talking about? Alicia didn't understand. Was she talking about Paddy going on honeymoon? Was there a honeymoon planned that she didn't know about?

'This evening,' Dee continued, 'in fact, just before we came out onto this very stage, I had the sad duty of accepting Paddy de Courcy's resignation from NewIreland.'

The sad duty . . . ? Resignation . . . ? Alicia jerked her head to stare at Paddy. What was going on? Had this been planned? Why hadn't he told her?

Paddy was slumped in his chair, his mouth fixed in an idiotic beam. Suddenly his face appeared, ten foot high, on the monitors. Blister-like drops of sweat – *sweat*, Paddy de Courcy *sweating*! – sat on his temples and his eyes were flickering beadily, like a trapped animal wondering how best to save himself.

He hadn't had a clue, Alicia realized.

Dee Rossini was sacking him. Publicly. In front of the world's media. And he hadn't had a clue. Paddy, who always knew everything.

Alicia was trying to think, but she was stunned with shock. How *dare* Dee Rossini? The audacity. How could she be so cold-blooded? So *ruthless*?

Admittedly Dee knew how Paddy had tried to sabotage her. But Alicia had thought it was all sorted out, in the past, and that Dee and Paddy were once again moving forward with a shared vision. She hadn't expected that Dee would hold on to the grudge, like a dark, brooding Mafia member. Half-Italian, Alicia remembered – Dee was half-Italian. Mind you, Irish people were champion grudge-holders. Probably far better than Italians.

Dee reappeared on the massive screens and Alicia was glad. Perhaps no one else had noticed Paddy's confusion, perhaps it was only because she knew him so well that she'd seen it, but it was better not to take any chances.

'You've been a good friend and colleague over the years,' Dee was giving the usual platitude-ridden farewell speech.

What are we going to do?

Panic seized Alicia and she tried to connect with Paddy, to make him look at her, but his entire being was still frozen in that moronic smile.

Then she noticed that the mood of the crowd had changed from euphoria to something far more subdued and, in a rush of hope, she thought, The party faithful won't stand for this. They *love* Paddy.

But they loved Dee too. And she'd just won an unprecedented number of seats. She was Deputy Prime Minister. She was Minister for Finance. She was more powerful than she'd ever been before.

'. . . you've made real and lasting changes to Ireland . . .'

What are we going to do?

Alicia forced herself to think. What did this mean for Paddy? If the party faithful didn't rise up in revolt, what could be salvaged? Maybe it wasn't the disaster it seemed. The long-term plan had always been that Paddy would eventually defect to the Nappies.

But now wasn't the right time, she acknowledged woefully. It could hardly be worse. Paddy had wanted to go to the Nappies from a position of power, from a ministerial post. Now he'd have to come cap-in-hand, a sacked backbencher, with no leverage.

And to think that if things had worked out, if he'd managed to oust Dee with that Moldovan story, he'd be leader of NewIreland right now. He'd already be a minister. In fact, he'd be deputy leader of the *country*.

He'd gone off his head with fury when that had fallen apart . . . God alone knew what he'd be like now.

'Paddy,' Dee was winding up, 'you leave NewIreland with your integrity intact.'

Why *wouldn't* he leave with his integrity intact? Alicia thought. How dare Dee Rossini imply that Paddy was anything less than squeaky-clean? And how strange that if you want to imply that someone is treacherous, you thank them for not being so.

That one sentence was enough to do for Paddy. Alicia felt the mood of the crowd change, like a fast wind blowing across a field of ripe wheat. Out of the corner of her eye, she could see people raising their eyebrows and turning to their neighbours. *No integrity? Funny you should say . . . Never really trusted him . . . Too good-looking . . . Too charming . . .*

No one could prove anything, Alicia thought. And no one could prove he'd been sacked. Rumours would circulate, but he'd come back from it. Paddy could come back from anything.

'We wish you and Alicia much happiness together.'

Automatically Alicia slapped a bright smile on her face but inside her head she was thinking, We should have seen this coming. We should have planned for it.

But they'd sincerely thought that Dee needed Paddy too much.

A horrible thought struck Alicia – he wouldn't *blame* her for this, would he? For the fact that they'd got married, which had given Dee a convenient reason to get rid of him?

'I'm sure we haven't heard the last of you,' Dee twinkled over her shoulder at Paddy, still slumped in his chair, like a stuck pig. 'Ladies and gentlemen,' she faced the crowd again, 'will you join me in thanking Paddy de Courcy and wishing him well in his life outside politics?'

Alicia began clapping. They'd all the time in the world to go on honeymoon now, she realized. But she didn't want to go. It would be like walking on eggshells, Paddy would be as angry as a caged lion and they'd have nothing to plan. Plot. No, 'plan' was a better word. 'Plot' sounded a little sinister.

On the monitors, she saw clusters of people in the audience getting to their feet. They were giving him a standing ovation! Thank God for that! But as the seconds passed, most people remained seated and the people who had originally stood up, sat down again, looking a little red-faced.

Shit.

But Alicia wouldn't show her disappointment. She smiled and smiled – because you never knew when the camera might land on you – and clapped even harder, slapping her palms together with force. Her hand was almost better now. It barely hurt at all.

Grace

I gazed up at the stage, my jaw slack. I was gobsmacked. Dee Rossini had just sacked Paddy de Courcy in front of the world's media. Not only that but she'd managed to imply that he'd been up to no good. It was so surprising and amazing, I could almost have laughed.

Why hadn't I seen this coming? Dee was a survivor of domestic violence; she'd set up her own political party and made an unprecedented success of it – she was steel to the core. It was suddenly obvious that there was no way she'd share power with someone who'd tried to shaft her as Paddy had done. Or someone who treated women like Paddy did.

Still, though, I was stunned by her brutality. Stunned in an admiring kind of way.

She was a politician, that was the long and the short of it – as ruthless as the rest of them.

I was glad now I'd come. I so nearly hadn't but Ma had chipped away at me until I had left the house just to escape her.

The clapping began to die down – they hadn't even given Paddy a standing ovation! Christ, it was funny.

I couldn't begin to imagine how angry he must be and I wondered what form his reprisals would take. But I felt safe. Paddy's wings had been clipped and he'd been stripped of most of his power. And even if he'd been at the height of his influence, there was nothing he could do to hurt me.

Well, in theory, of course there was. He could burn out my car again. He probably still wielded enough influence to get me sacked. But the worst had already happened to me. Compared to losing Damien, nothing else could cause me pain.

The glee, which had bubbled up in me from Paddy being brought so low, abruptly drained away. No matter what happened to Paddy, I was still without Damien.

All of a sudden, the sparkle had vanished and I was back in my body, back in the heaviness. The ache in my chest started up again.

People were getting up to leave and I decided to go too. I wanted to go home. Luckily, because I'd arrived late, I was right at the back.

I turned towards the exit – and standing directly behind me, waiting for my attention, was Damien. It was so unexpected that I stumbled.

It was inevitable that our paths would cross sooner or later. I thought I'd prepared myself but, judging from the way vomit hopped up my oesophagus, I hadn't. (It made me think of those fairground things, where you hit a platform with a hammer and something zips up a scale.)

'Mr Brolly told me where I could find you –' Damien, having the advantage, was wearing a smile, which froze when he got a proper look at me. 'Christ, Grace. You look awful.'

'You always were a charmer,' I managed, then ran out of words.

After a few moments had elapsed he said, 'That's it? That's all you're going to say?'

What did he want from me? 'You don't look so hot yourself?' I chanced.

'Yes! You had me worried there for a minute. So have you been sick?'

'No, just . . . destroyed. You know yourself?'

'Yeah.' His look spoke volumes. 'I do.'

In fairness, he *didn't* look so hot himself, like someone who hadn't slept for a couple of years.

'I rang you,' he said.

'Ma said. I thought I'd wait until after the election. I knew you'd be busy.'

'Grace, don't cry.'

Was I crying? I put my hand to my face, it was wet. How was that happening?

'Will we go outside for a cigarette?' he offered.

'I'm still off them.'

'Serious?' Damien furrowed his forehead. 'I've been on eighty a day since you left. How come you're coping so well and I'm a fucking wreck?'

'But I'm not.' I choked. My tears were flowing faster, people were looking and I didn't care. 'I'm a shambles. I'm so bad that sometimes even Bid's nice to me.' I dropped my head and swept my hand across my drenched face. I had to get it together. 'Damien, I'd better go.' It was too painful to be in his presence.

'Come back to me, Grace.'

An eternity of seconds passed. 'You don't mean that.'

'When have I ever said anything that I didn't mean?'

'The time you said my arse didn't look big in those jeans.'

'A man tells one white lie . . .' Softly he said, 'I'm sorry, Grace.'

'Why are you sorry? I'm the one who fucked everything up.'

'I shouldn't have let you leave.'

'I couldn't stay. I didn't deserve to.'

'You're scaring me now. Please, Grace, come back, let's try to work it out. We could go to therapy or something.'

'Therapy?' I managed a smile.

'Well, maybe not.'

'You'd never be able to forgive me,' I said. 'Even if we tried again, it would always be there. I ruined something beautiful.'

'I *have* forgiven you.'

'How?' How did forgiveness happen?

'I don't know, to be honest.'

But forgiveness did happen. I knew it did. I'd forgiven poor Marnie. I'd seen how anger could exist, hot and dangerous, and then dissolve away into nothing. Could that have happened to Damien?

'And I love you a lot,' Damien said. 'That helped.'

I searched his face for the truth. Were these just words that couldn't be backed up by actions? It would be too painful to try again, only to fail. Better not to try at all.

'And I'm not saying I'd like to ride him or anything like that,' Damien said. 'But in a way I can understand you falling for de Courcy. He has charisma, whatever the word is, that's almost inhuman.' He sighed. 'Of course they said the same thing about Hitler.'

I laughed out loud. It was such a surprise. I'd spent thirty-eight days thinking I'd never laugh again.

'So, Dazzler . . . will you come back to me?'

I hesitated.

'Best offer you'll ever get,' he said, and that was such a Damien thing to say that suddenly I knew it was all going to be all right.

'I suppose I'd better,' I said. 'I mean, who else would put up with you?'

Marnie

The whinging was in full spate as Marnie, shepherded by Jules, came into the room.

'. . . so grateful for the clean, decent life I have today . . .'

'. . . thought I was a free spirit, a rebel, drinking, kicking off, no job, no ties, but I was a prisoner to drink, might as well have had the house in the suburbs and the two-point-four kids . . .'

Skinhead Steve pointed out two empty chairs and people whispered their hellos to Marnie as she passed by.

Ulla quietly brought her tea. 'Three sugars, right?'

Marnie nodded her thanks. She took a sip and looked around. There was Australian Des, smiling at her. And Respectable Maureen. Sexy Charlotte pointed at Marnie's feet. 'Nice shoes,' she mouthed, with such pained anguish it made Marnie laugh.

Marnie settled back in her chair and listened and held her tea, comforted by the heat in her hands.

'. . . I still have the extreme feelings I always had, maybe not as bad, but instead of drinking on them, I get to a meeting . . .'

'. . . when I started coming here, you people told me I need never drink again, and I haven't . . .'

As usual, after a respectable interval, they alighted on her. 'Marnie, would you like to say anything?'

Everyone shifted in their chairs towards her. Already they were smiling. She was always treated to the full force of their warmth even though she resolutely maintained her distance.

*

'Look, Sweets, look. Sit up,' Nick said urgently.

She shifted on her towel and groaned. 'I was nearly asleep there.'

'It's good, you'll like it. Look at Verity.'

Marnie sat up on the river bank and shaded her eyes against the sun, and there was Verity, in her mermaid bikini, pushing earnestly through the water.

'Mum, Dad!' Verity called. 'Look! I'm swimming!'

'Go, girl!' Nick called, his voice swollen with pride.

'Look at you!' Marnie waved at Verity, who stopping swimming just long enough to wave back, and almost went under.

'Ow.' She laughed and spluttered. 'I swallowed some river.'

She was different back then, so much more robust than the nervy little creature she was now.

'Quick, Mum, dry me!' Daisy came racing towards her, water dripping from her long, skinny body. 'Did you see Verity? She's not scared any more.'

'I saw. Come here.' She unfurled a huge Minnie Mouse bath towel, got Daisy to hold one end, then wrapped it round and round her, so she was like an upright roll of carpet.

'Dry me!' Daisy stamped her feet and shivered dramatically. 'I'm freezing!'

'Drama queen,' Marnie said.

'Wonder where she gets that from.' Nick threw her a cheeky look.

She widened her eyes. 'Certainly not from me, mister!'

Briskly she rubbed Daisy dry, along the wings of her shoulder blades, her narrow little back and the legs so long and skinny they were cute almost to the point of comedy.

'God, Daisy, you're beautiful.'

'So are you, Mum.'

'Yeah, so are you, Mum.' Nick snapped her bikini strap and

they held a look for so long that Daisy exclaimed, 'That's gross!'

Suddenly Marnie was back in the AA meeting but the soft pink glow of the memory remained.

She turned and smiled at Jules beside her. Jules, who had been so kind, who had come as soon as Marnie had phoned her this morning from outside the off-licence. 'Wait there,' Jules had ordered. 'And don't move a muscle. I'll be with you in ten.'

Marnie closed her eyes. The remnants of the mood of the day by the river had wrapped themselves around her. It had been wonderful. Full of love, in every single word and action and thought. All she had ever wanted had been right there.

But where was it? As the memory receded, Marnie realized she didn't recognize that river bank. In fact, she was sure she'd never been to that place. And the girls looked older then than they did now: Daisy had been missing two of her milk teeth; Verity's squint was gone. Even she and Nick were different. She'd put on some weight, her hair was longer; Nick's hair was greyer. How could that be?

But it had happened, she was certain of it. It wasn't a dream, or a fantasy, it was a memory.

Then she understood it all. It was a memory, of course it was a memory. It had really happened. It just hadn't happened *yet*.

She opened her eyes. Every person in the room was still smiling at her.

'My name is Marnie.'

Their smiles widened. 'Hi, Marnie.'

'And I'm an alcoholic.'

Lola

Saturday, 21 March 7.01

Buzzer ringing. *Excessively* early. Local skanger kids always at that lark. Youthful high jinks, Let's wake up silly purple-haired girl! I usually manage wry twist of lips at their skangy high spirits, but not this morning. In no mood. Very tired. Have not slept well *for entire week* – since last weekend's jaunt to Knockavoy. The entire Considine/Chloe business confusing, upsetting, distressing. Had done much brooding.

Buzzer rang again. Pulled duvet over head.

Rang again. God's sake! Flung duvet aside with narky flourish, stomped to entry-phone in my pyjamas and said firmly, 'Fuck off, local skanger kids, and let me have my sleep.' (They respect use of 'language'.)

'Sorry to wake you,' voice said. *Not* voice of local skanger kids! Instead sexy bogger voice, the voice of Considine!

'. . . What on earth you doing here? You think Dublin is total kip of a place.'

'*Is* total kip of a place,' he said.

'So why you here?'

'Don't make me say it, Lola,' said in low sexy mutter. 'Not out here on street. Gang of young fellas in hoodies already laughing at my car.'

'Make you say what?' Mystified.

Pause. Heavy sigh. Further low sexy muttering. 'I love you, Lola Daly.'

This short – frankly stunning – admission accompanied

881

by explosion of raucous laughter and catcalls from – can only conclude – local skangers. Disembodied skangful voice shrieked, 'The mulchie with the crap car thinks he's in with a shout with Lola.'

'Is that *true*?' I asked. Very early in the morning, all very unexpected, lack of sleep distorting reality. This might be lovely news, but afraid to trust . . .

'Yeh! The mulchie's car IS crap!'

(Mulchie is hybrid word. Conflation of 'culchie' and 'mucker'.)

Enough of this three-way conversation! Local skangers cruel. Needed to save Considine. Humble culchie man.

'Considine,' I said firmly, 'you are coming in. When you hear buzzing noise, push door. Not pull, push –'

'Is okay, Lola. Know how it works.' Sarcastic addendum. 'Read about it in a book.'

Aha! Our old friend Cranky-Arse not entirely dead and buried!

Pressed button, opened my front door. Considine appeared. Unkempt, stridey, sexy. Into my flat. Maleness, muscles, general delicious manliness. Pulled me to him.

Looked up into his face. His mouth very near mine.

'That thing you just said,' I said. 'You say it again, please?'

'Dublin total kip of a place?' But he was laughing. Very, very handsome when laughs. Oh very handsome. 'You mean part when I said I love you?'

'Yes, that bit.'

'I love you, Lola Daly.'

'This news has come as surprise,' I admitted. 'Chloe –'

'Yes, misunderstanding,' he said. 'Wanted to lure you back to Knockavoy with Chloe. Thought you loved Chloe.'

'Do love Chloe. But – and cannot understand this, Considine – love you more.'

882

Both of us somewhat startled. Stared at each other in shock. Eventually he said, 'Don't mean to alarm you, but you used word "love" just there.'

Replayed sentence in head. 'Yes, I did.'

'You mean it?'

Thought about it, about how much had missed him since had left Knockavoy in January, how every tiny thing had reminded me of him. 'Yes, Considine, would appear that I do.'

His hold on me tightened. 'Lola, Lola.' He sighed, as if mightily relieved. 'Christ, you've no idea . . .' Shook his head. 'Couldn't stop thinking about you after you left on Monday; nothing new there, though, think about you all the time, day and . . . night.' Liked the way he said 'night'. Sexy-sounding word.

'Knew had done something wrong,' he said. 'Had misread what you wanted. Going out of my mind. Bad week. Couldn't sleep. Last night, decided, That's it! Had to get in car and find you. I drove all night.' Sexy-sounding sentence.

'If you drove all night,' I said, 'you must have gone via Morocco. Only three-and-a-half-hour journey.'

He laughed. Again! Like comedy festival round here!

'You serious about this?' I asked.

'More serious than . . . trying to think of something very serious.'

'Bowel cancer? Anna Wintour? Rise in ocean levels?'

'All of them.'

Impressive. Anna Wintour very serious, I believe.

'Come on.' I got my car keys.

'Where are we going?'

'To see my mum.'

'Should I wear a tie?'

Considered him. Jeans, black fleece, stampy-style boots. 'No, you have your look, working it well.'

At the cemetery three kids noisily playing football around a grave. Disrespectful. Until realized it was their little brother who had died and they had made him goalie.

Life so very, very precious.

Picked our way through the graves, until got to Mum.

'Mum, this is Considine.'

'Nice to meet you, Mrs Daly,' Considine said to her headstone.

Think Mum said, 'Nice to meet you too,' but hard to hear her because football children shouting, 'Yessss!' and 'Nooooo!' and other football words.

'She says nice to meet you too,' I said (because she probably did, she is tremendously polite). 'Now, Considine, I need to have little private chat with her.'

'I go away?'

'No, is silent chat. You may stay.'

We both sat on little kerb and in my head I said, 'Take good look at him, Mum. Now, not your fault you had to die and leave me but really need your advice. Afraid to trust own judgement after de Courcy. What you think about this cranky trannie who lives on other side of country?'

Voice in head answered, 'He is not cranky.'

'Yes, but –'

'He is not trannie either.'

'True –'

'Admittedly he does live on other side of country, but is very small country.'

'Please do not mention Kildare bypass.'

'Do you love him?'

'Yes, Mum.'

884

'Then you have to go for it.'

Moment of doubt. Was I only telling self what wanted to hear?

'Mum, are you really there?'

'Yes!' one of the kids yelled. My anxiety dispersed – had not imagined that voice – and at same time sun shook itself free of cloud and beamed sudden yellow light down on us all.

'Mum, tell me honestly, will it be okay?'

'Yes!' the kid yelled again.

'You quite sure?'

'Yes, yes, yes!'

He just wanted a decent book to read ...

Not too much to ask, is it? It was in 1935 when Allen Lane, Managing Director of Bodley Head Publishers, stood on a platform at Exeter railway station looking for something good to read on his journey back to London. His choice was limited to popular magazines and poor-quality paperbacks – the same choice faced every day by the vast majority of readers, few of whom could afford hardbacks. Lane's disappointment and subsequent anger at the range of books generally available led him to found a company – and change the world.

'We believed in the existence in this country of a vast reading public for intelligent books at a low price, and staked everything on it'
Sir Allen Lane, 1902–1970, founder of Penguin Books

The quality paperback had arrived – and not just in bookshops. Lane was adamant that his Penguins should appear in chain stores and tobacconists, and should cost no more than a packet of cigarettes.

Reading habits (and cigarette prices) have changed since 1935, but Penguin still believes in publishing the best books for everybody to enjoy. We still believe that good design costs no more than bad design, and we still believe that quality books published passionately and responsibly make the world a better place.

So wherever you see the little bird – whether it's on a piece of prize-winning literary fiction or a celebrity autobiography, political tour de force or historical masterpiece, a serial-killer thriller, reference book, world classic or a piece of pure escapism – you can bet that it represents the very best that the genre has to offer.

Whatever you like to read – trust Penguin.